RONALD FRAME

Penelope's Hat

SIMON & SCHUSTER
New York London Toronto Sydney Tokyo Singapore

SIMON & SCHUSTER
Simon & Schuster Building
Rockefeller Center
1230 Avenue of the Americas
New York, New York 10020

Copyright © 1989 by Ronald Frame
All rights reserved including the right of reproduction in whole or in part in any form.
Originally published in Great Britain by Hodder and Stoughton in 1989.
SIMON & SCHUSTER and colophon are registered trademarks of
Simon & Schuster Inc.
Manufactured in the United States of America

3   5   7   9   10   8   6   4   2

Library of Congress Cataloging in Publication data

Frame, Ronald.
Penelope's hat/Ronald Frame.
p.   cm.
"Originally published in Great Britain by
Hodder & Stoughton in 1989"—T.p. verso.
I. Title.
PR6056.R262P46   1988
823'.914—dc20
91-23183
CIP

ISBN: 0-671-72616-1

For my mother and father

And for Hilary and Paul

Acknowledgments

The invaluable and entertaining *In Vogue* by Georgina Howell, Allen Lane and Condé Nast Publications, 1975.

A very informative article on the wartime assassination and sabotage training centre at Camusdarrach, Inverness-shire, by Iain Fraser Grigor, *Glasgow Herald*, 9 March 1985.

The translation of Stendhal's 'Love' by Gilbert and Suzanne Sale, Penguin Books, 1975.

The Weil quotations on p.434 appear in an essay contained in Susan Sontag's *Against Interpretation* (Deutsch, 1987).

'Strictly speaking time does not exist (except within the limit of the present), yet we have to submit to it. Such is our condition. *We are subject to that which does not exist.* Whether it is a question of passively borne duration – physical pain, waiting, regret, remorse, fear – or of organised time – order, method, necessity – in both cases that to which we are subject does not exist. But our submission exists. We are really bound by unreal chains. Time which is unreal casts over all things including ourselves a veil of unreality.'

Simone Weil, *Gravity and Grace*

'Thus do the days go by. At night, I murder.'

Gregor von Rezzori, *The Death of My Brother Abel*

'Try to talk in a hat, it makes you look like someone . . .'

Estée Lauder, quoted in *The New Yorker*, September 1986

Part One

Switzerland, 1982

Electric gates draw back, and a silver-blue Mercedes – a 300SEL roadster model – enters an underground car park in Geneva. The building above is an office tower of white marble and copper-tinted glass.

The driver parks, gets out – the doors lock – and he walks off towards the lifts.

He's gone for just over an hour. In that interval of time he collects his mail, consults the teleprinter, and telexes a number of coded messages to destinations as far distant from Switzerland as Caracas and São Paolo. He makes several telephone calls; twice he has to speak a message into an answering machine. He dictates three brief letters, and leaves instructions for accommodation to be booked for himself in Amsterdam on a certain day.

He leaves the office and makes a speedy, silent descent in the lift to the car park beneath ground level. In the sodium lights he walks smartly, for a man in his early sixties, across the concourse to where the Mercedes is parked. He takes the keys out of his trouser pocket, unlocks the door, and manoeuvres himself into the driver's seat. He pushes the key into the ignition lock.

The car is instantly torn apart. The explosion has the effect of a massive airlock (so the garage staff will remember afterwards): the air is being sucked out of the present moment. One of the concrete pillars buckles with the pressure. The fire doesn't start for several seconds. In the immediate impact the car is reduced to infinitesimal pieces. Shrapnel pierces the concrete roof and floor of the garage. The sodium lights blow out. A layer of glass in the thick window panel sunk into an overhead courtyard dissolves; it turns to hot powder. Then the petrol flares up, puffballs of fire, writhing orange and yellow flames. Black smoke rolls from under the fire: the sour, poisonous aftertaste of disaster.

And somewhere – or everywhere, as freely dispersed as fall-out – a body burns. Flesh and bone and gut, muscle and jelly and evaporating blood.

Australia, 1985

A woman queues at a checkout counter in the Happy Jack hypermarket in Brighton-le-Sands, Sydney. She has a wire trolley filled with groceries. The tannoy voice reminds her that there's an order-and-delivery service, at a very reasonable ten-per-cent surcharge. But she knows about the facility very well, and has made use of it dozens of times before. Today, though, she has felt the need to involve herself, so she is a personal shopper rather than one of the store's more profitable 'convenience customers'. Even the contact with the girl at the checkout computer is something that she is aware has been missing from the scenario of her domestic life. She spots the name 'Nolleen' printed on a pin-tab on the girl's dress. Below it is another tab with the instructions 'Have a nice day! Have a great life!'

There are at least twenty checkout counters, but half of them are roped off. The others are intended for either Cash or Credit/Account, and again subdivided: 'Five and Under Buys', 'Twenty and Under', and 'Over Twenty'. The lanes are clogged by housewives counting their purchases.

A woman stands immediately in front of her in the 'Twenty and Under' queue. She is aware that she occasionally turns round and looks at her. She is being careful not to push her trolley into the woman's ankles. The woman's look-alike friend (lesbians?) comes up and joins her. Now the two of them are sneaking looks at her as the customer at the front leafs through an accordion wallet of credit cards.

Their attention is embarrassing, even in a country where people will do much as they like and manners are second to saying what you think. But, not having been born here, she hasn't been brought up for this. She leans forward and picks up her straw hat from the folding toddler's seat in the trolley. She puts it on her head as if it might offer a disguise or at least indicate her non-availability for antipodean dykes, her preference for privacy. But this isn't the country on earth to have come to if privacy was what she'd wanted.

She is conscious that the hat doesn't contain the curiosity of the two women. It seems to make them more interested, not less. She hears a few words exchanged between them in whispers and seriously debates with herself the wisdom of moving into another queue. But she glances forward over the women's heads and sees that ahead of them the necessary credit card has been located out of all the others and the business is now being conducted with hi-tech efficiency and speed.

2

'We think we – '

'We think – '

Penelope realises the women are talking to her. To *her*.

' – we know you.'

Ignore them ignore them. Or pretend that you're deaf –

'Meg thinks she recognises you – '

She hears the Englishness submerged in the ugly accent and now she fears the worst. This is what for six years she has dreaded happening to her.

'It's some time ago now, of course,' one voice says.

She clutches the handle of the trolley tighter and wraps her fingers round it. She stares at the girl stooped over the computer-till.

'But Janet is sure.'

'I was just saying to Meg – '

She shifts her focus from the girl to the women. It can't be helped. They're both smiling. She smiles. She sees something possessive in their eyes. She realises too late that she shouldn't have put on the hat, that that was the give-away. She has betrayed herself.

'You wrote books. Novels. The libraries had them – '

She keeps the smile in place.

'In the sixties and seventies, it must have been. No, longer ago, wasn't it the fifties – ?'

The two pairs of eyes continue to own her, to devour her. She remembers too late her dark glasses, left in the front locker of the car.

'It *was* you, wasn't it?'

Their smiles anticipate the answer they want to their question, to prove Janet's powers of recall.

'I'm afraid not,' she replies to them, in her very passable Sydney accent. 'I really don't know who you mean.'

Their faces fall, although the smiles survive somehow, rather shabbier versions of themselves. The two pairs of eyes turn to each other and consult.

'In hats, you see,' one says. 'You wore hats.'

'In the photographs,' the other says. 'On the backs of the books.'

They both look at her.

'Excuse me – ' she remembers the Woolloomooloo accent ' – I think it's your turn.' She nods forward, to Nolleen sitting at the checkout computer.

The two women attend to their trolley, seeming confused. Penelope stays where she is, counting on that gap between them. She realises they still aren't convinced, but she looks away, to an aisle of fake fruit barrows with candy-striped awnings. She continues to occupy her attention while their bill is rung up and they pay. She feels she is being impolite, but she doesn't know what else she should do, in the circumstances.

Walking across the parking lot to the car afterwards, she spots them where they stand unloading their shopping. They're looking at her. One of them half-raises an arm to wave. From beneath the straw hat she smiles back, the most fleeting and mercurial of smiles she can manage, and passes on. She knows they're telling each other, what a strange woman – which she knows anyway – and how snooty in the old English way.

She pushes the trolley through the grid of parking spaces. She spots the metallic green roof of her Volvo. Next time, she tells herself, there won't be a next time: Customer Convenience Service is worth double what they charge.

England, 1986

It's already dark when she arrives. The lights in the lane are wadded by the trees and she moves in shadows.

Her nose tells her this is Cornwall: creosote, and the smell of close vegetation. She can hear, just, the bay at the end of the lane, pulling under the full moon.

She finds herself standing on the path, with the latch gate closed behind her. The slats of white wood are stuck with snails, and she sees their slime on the path. The house is as it was the first time she and Gregor saw it, she has done as little as possible over the years to change it. The steep roof, and the shrunken dormer windows and the fat, buttressed chimneystack give it the look of a gingerbread house. But it's also, she sees not for the first time, quintessentially English: the windows have small panes, there's a solid oak door, a rain-barrel, Cornish slate along the bottoms and on the corners of the walls, and at certain points trained vines of red Virginia creeper against the white roughcast.

The house offers no offence. What had first attracted them was also their complicity in both liking it and no one else – in particular his wife – suspecting that they did. They had speculated about who lived there, but in an incidental way, having no sure notion and finally not caring so much to know. Its position on the lane was midway between the house *he*'d rented and the one *she*'d taken a short lease on, and it seemed a symbol of something; it was *fated* for them.

Buying herself the house later when it came up for sale didn't undo the spell. She made the purchase primarily to confirm her own seriousness in loving him, it nailed her colours to the front latch gate, even though she knew he would never leave Barbara and the children for her. She didn't want to split a marriage, but she already guessed that he would give himself to her in every other way: and the giving to one another, if they could organise an ideal time-plan, could now take place in the house they had lingered at so often, watched like detectives, said of 'If only . . .' She justified it as a reward to herself for her industry, for the success of her books, and – paradoxically maybe – it was also a way of declaring her independence, which wasn't quite what she had intended: if she'd still been married, if she'd ever found her balance and equilibrium in life, perhaps she wouldn't have found the impetus to write her novels, to invent an alternative condition of reasoning uncertainty for herself, an always hypothetical contentment.

She stands in the kitchen. Moonshine is enough to see by, washing over

5

the slate floor and angling shards of cold white light across the walls. The oak door is shut behind her. She listens for the wall clock in the small hall but hears only silence in its place; Mrs Neevey must have forgotten to wind it, although she forgets so little. A joist creaks overhead in the ceiling. In the summer, in the proper season, the wooden skeleton used to expand and contract with the changes of temperature and then the house sounded like a sailing ship at sea. Now there isn't even the polite, sociable beat of time. She listens to hear her own breath, but that too is stilled. Momentarily a branch scratches against the window at the dining end of the room. Tomorrow she can sit at the table and look out, at the gains and losses in the garden since she was last here.

She steps on to the runner of carpet which crosses the kitchen's breadth and the compact square of hall. The sitting-room is a solid geometry of shadows, but she can see quite clearly, and everything is where it has always been: the sofa, the armchair between the french windows and the fireplace, the sea painting above the mantelpiece, the bureau between the doors and the smaller window. It's the right size for one person or two: for a family, less so, but in the twenty years since she bought it it has been used as a holiday base only once for a family, and *they* were here and gone in a single fortnight.

It's a disturbing thought, that last one, and coming out of it she finds herself upstairs. She's standing at the top of the narrow staircase looking down at its three short flights of five steps each. She has run up and down those stairs in every phase of excitement, from anxious anticipation to joyful fulfilment to the deepest, inconsolable grief. Now she understands the atmosphere which a surfeit of emotions is capable of producing, which a staircase can never forget.

She looks into the first bedroom. The tree outside is hunched as ever in its long mac, loitering or keeping watch, and she thinks that a child would need a very strong will not to be menaced and frightened by it.

The bathroom is glassy, reflective, echoey, as pale as the moon. The moon is directly overhead, filling the skylight, a full cream cheese just as she has always suspected. Next to the bathroom, on the third side of the landing, is as far as she feels like venturing. Past the closed latch door at its other end a few steps lead up to a narrow third bedroom, high in the roof and called by Mrs Neevey 'the crow's nest', but she takes that as 'read'.

From the top of the bed all the ceiling shadows are familiar to her: the angles made by the dormer windows and the fin stack, and angles dissecting other angles. She has watched this ceiling in all conditions, from ecstasy to despair. Now she is beyond the untidy clamour of emotion and she only remembers. She doesn't feel greatly wise after all her experiences, but she was warned to expect no such thing. She is merely glad to be here, for however long she can be. The lives of the house's previous occupants have never mattered to her, and even though she meant it for breaks from London it has come to feel as much her 'home' as the very first one she can recall, in the torrid forested foothills of Borneo. She has always resisted the claims of place, as a kind of principle – a building is only bricks and cement however it's finished on top – and she wouldn't be here now if she hadn't been drawn to return, almost in spite of herself and in the face of sound reason – turned back inside, to what she concludes is the vital part of her being.

Part Two

1

Borneo, 1926

It was her ayah who first, after Penelope, became aware of the interloper.

'You looking, Pini?'

The child's head was turned, she was staring behind her, over her shoulder, in the direction of the eaglewood tree, which grew branches like a ballerina's waving arms.

'Who for?'

Ayah Chan watched the two eyes, big as pennies.

'Pini?'

The child didn't move. She was paler now than the spring virus had made her.

'Who you looking?'

In the spring she might have been ready to die. Her mother had thought so; the servants had never seen Missus so thin with her worry-sickness.

'Pini – '

The woman touched the child's shoulder and tried to turn her away.

'Leave here, miss, you hearing me – '

But the child was stuck to the spot. Ayah couldn't budge her.

'Missy quick – '

The child started to blink, several times. She might have been waking from a slow-water trance, how the low valley people were afflicted when they fell into their deep sluggish sleeps and had to be rescued with fire-sticks and drums.

The child stood blinking, looking up at the woman.

'Tell me, Pini. What you been seeing – '

'What?'

'Tell me, Pini. Tell Ayah Chan.'

She gently shook both the child's shoulders.

'It was a lady.'

'Lady? Lady who?'

'Just – I don't know.'

'Where?'

Penelope pointed to the far end of the verandah, where a magnolia bloomed with white wax flowers.

'Your ma?'

Penelope shook her head. The woman nodded in the direction of the nearest house to them, and the other houses strung along the lane.

'Other lady – ?'

'No.'

'Who? Pini – ?'

'Someone.'

'Someone who?'

'I don't know.'

'No lady – '

Ayah Chan smiled. She clapped her hands. She put her fingers in her mouth and whistled, softly so that Missus wouldn't hear.

Penelope walked away.

'Great British lady?'

'Maybe.'

'How?'

How? was Ayah Chan's favourite word.

'In a hat.'

'Hat?'

Ayah Chan mimed the word, and Penelope nodded.

'How?'

'Not with feathers. Not like Mummy's. Like my sun-hat.'

Another few steps brought Penelope, by way of french windows, into the drawing-room. The woman stood outside on the balcony: the room was officially out-of-bounds to the ayah, except on special occasions when they were required to 'present' Penelope. Ayah Chan hadn't been here in the house long enough to know that it was Mr Milne's wife who decreed when the occasions were and were not.

She followed Penelope, and passed between the open french windows and the Sanderson chintz curtains, which hung as stiffly as if they'd been starched.

'Ghost lady, Pini?'

The child might have panicked at the word, but somehow controlled herself. She reached up and fidgeted with a wiry stem of pink ixia in an arrangement on the Pembroke table. Some petals dropped with a whisper and scattered on the shiny walnut. Maybe it was catching sight of that in the second instant which so incensed Mrs Milne, who was famous in their corner of Borneo for her orderliness and for not being able to take the lunchtime heat.

'Ayah, remove yourself at once.'

Penelope jumped, catching the edge of the table with her elbow and sending another soft shower of petals falling. She spun round and saw her mother standing in the doorway from the hall.

10

'You have absolutely *no* right to be in here. Do you hear me?'

Astonishment fixed the woman, as if she had been wished to stone. Penelope felt queasy inside, the strength had left her legs.

'This is quite *disgraceful* conduct.'

The woman started to prattle away. Penelope watched her mother's face redden as she picked up on the queer pidgin.

'What ghost? What on earth are you talking about?'

Penelope realised that the event was happening round about her, that *she* was its frail centre.

'Where?' her mother asked, but clearly she had no intention of believing the woman's wordy, breathless answer.

'Ghosts,' she announced, 'do *not* appear at midday.'

Ayah Chan said something else.

'My child does *not* imagine such things. How dare you say so! Leave this room *at once*.'

The woman stared between mother and daughter.

'My husband will deal with this tonight. From now on you won't have anything to do with Penelope, do you hear me?'

After the command had been given again, more simply and even more directly, the woman left the room, walking backwards and with tears in her eyes. When they were alone, Penelope heard her mother draw in her breath. But the warning came too late, and Penelope was caught off-balance by the shock of the cuff to the side of her head. Her cheek stung, but her own consternation seemed worse than that. She couldn't breathe; she coughed, and spluttered spittle. She felt her face turning even redder than her mother's.

'How could you *say* something like that to her, you stupid girl? How could you even think it?'

It took several attempts – trying to keep her own eyes dry made it more difficult – until the child was able to interrupt her mother at last.

'But – but I *did*.'

'Did *what*?'

'See.'

'"See"? What do you mean? See what?'

Penelope hesitated. She felt winded, as if all her breath had been punched out of her.

'Someone.'

'Who? Who did you see?'

'Someone. In a hat.'

'Who? Mrs Fotheringham?'

'No.'

'Someone you didn't recognise, then. But why on earth did you tell Ayah Chan it was a ghost?'

'*She* said it.'

'Of course she did. She's a stupid, uneducated peasant woman.'

Penelope didn't reply. Her cheek smarted as if she'd been scalded.

'I'll tell your father. He'll find out who it was. For heaven's sake, Penelope, what a fuss you've caused. On *such* a damned hot day.'

The behaviour wasn't typical of her mother, and she must have known it. As an adult remembering the incident – tentatively writing about it and trying unsurely to balance the first person with the third – Penelope saw a very bothered woman as hot as a pepper and with her head feeling twice its normal size. She'd known quite well that she was overreacting, but she was unable to help herself. So the situation had gone from bad to worse.

Her husband was spoken to when he came in. The servants were asked if anyone had come calling. Penelope heard her mother telling her father that that was only drawing attention to the business and it just put silly ideas into their heads.

That day Penelope started to become less like a child: the sensation of feeling and reacting taking precedence over purely 'being'. She'd just happened to turn round and there had stood a woman in a hat, a white cotton sun-hat, like the one hanging on one of the pegs behind the door in her room. The woman had smiled, in quite a kindly way, but she hadn't smiled back at her, she hadn't felt she could, so she'd called out instead. And then Ayah Chan had come running. The woman had noticed Ayah, lines wrinkled her forehead, and she was immediately older than she had been a few seconds before. Penelope later remembered the woman's grey hair, and the thinness of her tanned arms sticking out of the sleeves of her dress: it had a higher hemline than the sort her mother wore, maybe it wasn't a dress at all. The next moment Ayah Chan was speaking to her, in an urgent way – 'Here Pini – ' – asking her in her between-language why she looked so white and stared so with her eyes.

The incident wasn't referred to again. No stranger had been reported in the vicinity. Some days later a new ayah came into the house, and Ayah Chan was sent to another family on the lane, where she was put to work in the kitchen. 'Penelope shouldn't go about at lunchtime in the heat,' a visiting doctor said socially one evening in her hearing. He must have been filled in by her parents about the little bit of trouble they'd been having with her of late. 'Far too hot. For any of us. And I've been here eighteen years.'

For a while the woman in the sun-hat was, as it were, relegated to the shadows of thought, as she had been presumed just to have disappeared into the trees in the garden, as inexplicably as she had made her appearance.

But it happened again, even with the different ayah in the house.

Her mother appeared in her bedroom that second evening with a paraffin lamp and set it down on top of the chest of drawers.

'What you need,' she said a little wearily, 'is a night-light in here.'

Like Penelope, she was held by the distortions of their shadows on the wall. They looked like two giants huddled inside a doll's house.

Then her mother remembered.

'It was nothing, Penelope. We've had all this out before.'

'But – '

'But you didn't see anything.'

'I heard – '

'You couldn't have done.'

'But – '

'But *no*, Penelope!'

Her father's tread approached; he paused outside, just out of sight, and they both stood waiting.

He walked forward.

'Hello, you two.'

He smiled, as if embarrassed to find them both with their faces turned towards the door. He ventured a step or two into the room.

'I thought I heard you talking.'

Her mother turned to look at the wall. Penelope looked too. There were still only two shadows to be seen.

'Penelope was imagining again.'

'Were you, Penelope? What were you imagining?'

'Don't encourage her.'

'She was here again,' Penelope said.

'Who?'

'I heard her.'

'"Her"?'

'Get back into bed,' her mother told her, voice brisk.

'There's no one here, Penelope.' Her father's voice was gentler, sympathetic, sorrowful. 'Just us.'

He departed with another reassuring but slightly sad smile, and the child and her mother stood listening to his footsteps fade.

The top sheet was pulled back, and Penelope climbed up on to the mattress and slid beneath. She watched her mother glance up at her shadow before turning the lamp down very low. Darkness ran down the wall, to a tiny white halo of light.

Her mother stood in the doorway, a shadow again with the lit corridor behind her.

'For the last time, Penelope, there's just ourselves – '

Three days later her father received the letter he'd been waiting for and a mine might have exploded under the house.

He was being offered a new position with a rival firm, accounting the coffee and cocoa business instead of, as at present, 'High Quality and Rare Timbers'.

13

He intended to accept it. The job wasn't in the field this time, but based in London. Naturally that meant they would be leaving Borneo . . .

Her mother was incredulous; her legs couldn't hold her and she slumped down into an armchair.

'But it's nothing like the job you've got!'

'I feel like a change. New people – '

'In *London*?'

'You'll enjoy being back, won't you?'

'It's got to do with that man who called here, hasn't it?'

'Those skinflints in London sent him. To check up on us. That was the last straw.'

'But we haven't even *discussed* it.'

'It's a feeling in my blood, Eveline. You would have said no. But I've got to work with those miseries. They think they can call the tune – '

'But we'll have to leave all this.'

'Yes.'

'It's *madness*!'

The cook timed her appearance and her rapid-fire knuckle salvo on the door badly, informing her mistress that the iceman was here and that the oysters were about to be delivered at any moment.

'I don't suppose we'll be living like millionaires in London,' her father said, but smiling.

'It'll be *your* ruddy fault – '

'Not my "fault", Eveline – '

'We'll drop right back, d'you realise that?'

'You used to say, you knew why the "Bore" was in "Borneo" – '

'But that was *then*. At the start. If I'd known you were going to – '

At which juncture the native factotum rapped on the door to announce that the Phnom Penh visitors were on their way, they had brought their own car over on the ship with them, a 'Roads-Royce'.

Penelope watched her mother digging her nails into the upholstery of the chair-arms.

'This,' she said, 'this is a nightmare.'

'C'mon, Eveline. I'll put the oysters through the books as storm-damage.'

'They're *your* guests.'

'Well, it'll be back to our old ways now.'

'But *these* are – '

'I thought you *wanted* to go back. You kept saying – '

'*Here* is Penelope's home. Borneo – '

'If that's all – she'll get used to it, London. You'll see, in no time – '

'But this house, the garden – '

'You said, six years here – '

'But it's only five.'

'If we stay here, we'll rot.'

'We'll rot in style, then – '
'It's not our country.'
'If I ask you "why?", you won't tell me – '
'Tell you what?'
' – so what choice do I have?'

The Indochinese were dignitaries where they came from. Penelope watched them being received by her parents as equals, like royalty welcomed (in English) by royalty.

Twenty-four sat down to dinner that evening. The fish course was – as if by magic – lobster *à l'américaine*, followed by – more magic – a roast sirloin of beef. They drank lightly chilled champagne.

Penelope snatched glimpses. In the course of the evening a storm did break loose. The sky turned septic green before sea rain blasted the garden. Hailstones ricocheting off the roof and dislodging the tiles sounded from beneath like a bombardment of golf balls. The Rolls-Royce was dented, but that wasn't discovered until the morning. By then it was too late for her mother or father to care: their life in Borneo was to end – the good years, their best years, in the compound of the British North Borneo Trading Company – and they would never set eyes on these Cambodian bigwigs again, or the flattened bushes, or the lightning-shot trees fallen by the rain-washed mud-slide roads down which they were to sail away, back to the first primal life, to the land called 'home'.

Back in London for the first time since her birth Penelope made herself an island.

She drew it in coloured pencils on the second and third pages of a sketching pad.

She drew it so often, erasing with a bunjee and amending, that she wore away the thick paper to almost nothing at certain problematic points.

The coast was indented where it hadn't been, crags were eliminated, ravines translocated, rivers rerouted; lakes sprang into being, rocks yielded silver and a mine was sunk, an entire forest grew in minutes, no longer than it took a ship to wreck or an aeroplane to crash. Comets flared, volcanoes spouted and spurted, fish flew.

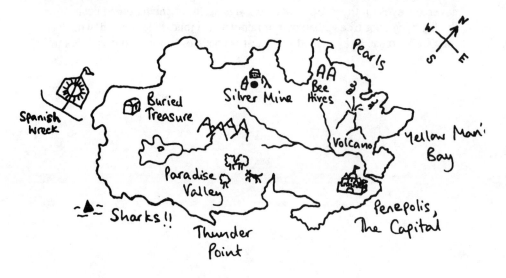

All she needed was a name.

She decided, because she liked the sound, that for ever her island would be called 'Tiktiki'.

'It has to stop now, Penelope, do you hear me? This – ' her mother searched the surfaces of the room ' – this nonsense.'

The girl watched her closely, but said nothing.

'There *is* no woman. How *could* there be?'

Her mother picked up some fallen petals on a tabletop and held them in her hand. English tigerlilies. Then she curled her fingers into a fist.

'We'll just forget you ever mentioned it. We won't speak about it again.'

She opened her fist. She rolled the crushed petals on her palm and still averted her eyes from the corner of the room where her daughter stood.

'We've been thinking, Penelope, your father and I. Until we get settled down again, maybe you'd prefer the countryside, to go to school? A school you could stay at.'

She nipped more faded petals from a potted geranium on a side-table, and the air immediately turned sour.

'It would make more sense, wouldn't it? This is all very – messy. For just now. You'd be living with other girls, English girls, it'd get you back in the swim.'

Penelope offered her no sensible answer. Her mother glared at her.

'Well, think about it,' her mother said, with very forced gentleness. 'For a little while. I'm sure it *is* the best idea.'

She picked up a cushion, to pummel it back into shape. Penelope watched. In Borneo her mother hadn't even had to do that. She'd heard her telling one of her new friends, acquired since their return, that she'd only ever been in the kitchen of the Borneo house three times. *Imagine that*! she'd said, and laughed gaily at such a grand, implausible indulgence. Now so much was different.

Penelope digested the prospectus for her English future during that day and the next, until the subject was raised again as she was picking at her supper in the kitchen.

'Your father says – '

He wasn't here; he had been making a lot of trips away on business recently.

' – until we've settled down – '

But this was their home now. She had supposed that they were settled, for good. Even though her parents had been warned that she wouldn't, she had adjusted quite easily to London's dark afternoons and the drizzly atmosphere and the virtual elimination of colour.

'We'll take you down in the car and you can look around and tell us what . . .'

The last part wasn't finished. Penelope continued pushing her butter beans round the plate. Her mother stood gawkily, uncomfortable to be so close to an Aga stove and pantry cupboards. But this was to be life from now on.

She pointed to a milk spill on top of the table.

'Nancy, that's very *unsightly*.'

The maid hesitated at the word, then dashed to the sink for a dishcloth.

Penelope watched satisfaction return to her mother's face. She was in charge again, the situation was under her control, she had pretty Nancy running, at her beck and call.

17

'So – ' Her shoulders fell, her voice relaxed. ' – I'm sure it's all for the best, you see.'

Without finishing, Penelope placed her fork and knife in the dead centre of the plate, at half-past-six. She didn't speak, because it wasn't good manners. She didn't know what to say anyway. Things would happen, and happen *to* her, that was what she knew best.

'Our station in life, Quintin?' her mother repeated. 'Which is that now? Marylebone? Fenchurch Street?'

'Well, I doubt if *you* would know,' her father said. 'I've made jolly sure that you haven't *had* to know.'

'Maybe it would have done me some good then. I'd have seen how the rest of the world lived. What they put up with and just what they don't – '

Once Rollo was a horse, and his granddaughter was the rider on his back. Another time he was rowing on a river or a lake and Penelope was his passenger. He could pick coals out of the hearth with his bare hands and then place them back in the grate. He painted people's portraits.

The house was in Berkshire, in an acre of garden, surrounded by a high wall that had fallen away in places. The gates were rusting on their hinges and shrieked when they were pushed against. The doors of the house were never locked and invariably stood open: and birds flew through the downstairs rooms and sometimes – the intrepid ones – upstairs too. Many animals had presented themselves in the house over the years of her grandparents' marriage: rabbits, hedgehogs, badgers, foxes, an occasional fallow deer. Vegetative débris blew or wafted, according to the season: pollen, or thistledown, or crisply mobile leaves at the fall-time. In winter the doors were kept closed but nature was given an honorary berth inside: pewter jugs were crammed with branches of holly and ivy, the walls were freshly festooned with dried flowers and mistletoe, every corner smelt of pot-pourri or an orange pricked with cloves, insects crawled off the logs, Christmas fir trees were hung with (a constant danger) small wax candles which made the house as deeply, darkly fragrant as a forest.

In time Penelope was to remember more about the summer, when Hazehill was supposed to be an idyll.

The landlocked watermill – the lawns, the long grass, the old-fashioned flower garden, the box hedges round the herb-beds, the informal rooms, the stencilled linen-presses and the Arts-and-Crafts pewter and brass, the china painted by her grandfather with drooping boughs and stylised doves.

Her grandmother in fine black lace and a rustic straw hat, bought for francs and sous in a Brittany village – her grandfather Rollo in an Augustus John smock and a velvet beret – Topaz typically in a tasselled shawl and a wide gypsy skirt with panels of colour like a golfing umbrella.

18

The doors always standing open, if the weather suited.

The weathervane turning when there was wind.

But it was more wrong than right, certainly in a long retrospect.

'Rollo' was a name for the nineteenth hole, for golf-clubhouses in affable, middle middle-class Middlesex: a good egg in a blazer and cavalry twills, with a fruity voice and an apple-flush face, and a surfeit of white lies against truth in his conversation. The straw hat was a one-off for her grandmother, who bought her town wear from a famous hatter in Savile Row. Topaz, years younger, was far less a stage-gypsy in spirit than she was in dress: the name too was curiously extrovert for someone who volunteered so little of – and about – herself. In clement weather the doors of the house did stand open but the human company had surely been adroitly vetted beforehand: anyway, Hazehill was so hidden and obfuscated that the chances were against any uninvited strangers finding it.

Penelope's grandmother – without a quaint name – flitted about, rather abstractedly, but her eyes missed nothing, and her outfit was invariably smart enough to bring any occasion to heel. Rollo didn't seem sure what his primary rôle should be – Edwardian paterfamilias or a free spirit in flight – and he shifted without warning between the two. On occasions Topaz would allow herself to be intimate – staying Rollo with her hand as they followed his wife across the lawn, supplying some detail of a memory or an ancient conversation when the others couldn't – but for much of the time she seemed to make herself deferential and self-effacing while having a clairvoyant's grasp on potential trouble-spots offstage, in the kitchen or the linen-room, responsibility for which she endlessly debated – as Penelope overheard – with her grandmother.

Rollo lay beneath an oak with a straw hat covering his face.

The child walked several circuits of the tree before stopping and leaning against the trunk.

She said something.

A voice replied, 'Now, who's that you're speaking to?'

She was always to remember the awfulness of the question. She was too astonished at first to answer. She looked all around her.

'Eh?'

'To – to you,' she said.

'Me?'

'Yes.'

'How d'you know it's me?'

'I . . .'

'When I've got a hat over my face, I'm invisible.' She stood staring down at him. '*I* see the world. But *it* doesn't see *me*.'

'Oh,' she said.

19

'I'm dead to the world.' He lay without moving, arms by his sides. 'A dead-and-gonner.'

'Oh.'

'No one can get at me, you see. I'm pretty much my own man. That's how I like to be.'

She nodded.

'It keeps them guessing. Don't let them think they know everything about you, Penelope. So long as *you* know just a bit more – and this is how you do it.'

She nodded again.

'Where do you think it comes from? Nodding your head?'

She stared at the straw hat.

'I – I don't know,' she said.

'Maybe it comes to the same thing.'

'Oh.' She didn't understand the remark.

'It's only between *us*, though,' he told her. His mouth was just visible to her, smiling up into the branches of the tree. 'So you'll keep it under your hat, Penelope, won't you now?'

Topaz was always there.

Penelope decided that the kitchen must really be *her* domain, not her grandmother's; it was she who settled what was eaten and when, even though her grandmother was the one who selected the number and mix of company. Topaz ate with them at the table, but would sit within easy reach of the kitchen; a girl from the village brought the food in to them and took away the used dishes, and Topaz eyed each of her comings and goings. She didn't engage much in the table-talk, but was clearly following the zigzag of the conversation – smiling sometimes, or levelling her eyebrows in disapproval of a remark, or ruminatively clasping her hand to her left cheek, the one with the beauty spot. Her clothes were individual and flamboyant; still in her thirties she favoured bold geometric patterns on blouses and shirts, and wide, full, turquoise or magenta skirts, worn with chunky wooden beads or thick copper bracelets on those slender wrists; out of doors she would don a black Parisian cape that reached almost to her ankles. Penelope thought her grandmother by contrast always a degree more formal than the occasion properly warranted, preferring tailored costumes and afternoon dresses and semi-evening frocks in silk georgette and net, shoes with louis heels and pointed toes for the garden. (Or maybe – in hindsight – it was the occasion which was forever wanting, failing to live up to her expectations of it?)

The child soon noticed that no one appeared to pay Topaz much attention and yet if she wasn't at the table by the time they were ready to start, her grandmother would consult with Rollo – sometimes all that was needed was a hand-hold on his arm, or even just a glance – and things were delayed until she'd arrived. Out of the kitchen and away from the dining-room Topaz was as free to appear and disappear as the flitting finches or the field foxes that sniffed around the house, foraging for titbits. A deck-chair was provided for her on the lawn; she put up a very respectable show whenever she was inveigled upon to be a fourth at badminton or lawn tennis; apparently she went along on picnics, and on the river – Penelope didn't witness the occasions herself – it would be Topaz who rowed the boat to its destination, probably with her customary, rather humourless efficiency.

Penelope once saw her reading a letter her grandfather had written and left on top of a bureau while something distracted him in the garden. On another visit Topaz had taken a cold and was supposedly confined to bed, but Penelope could hear her moving about in another bedroom – her grandfather's – when the others left for the village and she must have thought the house was empty. On a third visit – or it might have been the same one when the letter was read, since there weren't so very many days out in Berkshire, her father finally taking umbrage at something – Penelope caught sight of her opening her grandmother's handbag where it sat on a coffer in the hall and helping herself to some notes out of the purse.

Some years later – after the tragedy in the South of France – she realised that the woman called Topaz with the beauty spot bore an uncanny resemblance to the woman in certain paintings, who – in turn – wasn't far removed in appearance from the woman in earlier portraits whom she knew to be her grandmother. Each had an oval shape of face, high cheek-bones and a forehead of similar breadth, even though one sitter was formal and neatly elegant and uniform, and the other seemingly the opposite – dressing so young, with crinkly Pre-Raphaelite tresses, and – for Penelope grown to a woman – with the mystery of her position in the house adding to the impression of secretiveness.

It was also much later, in memory, that her grandparents looked at their only son with something akin to disbelief, even a sort of helplessness. Topaz, never likely to react as anyone expected her to, seemed to take a quiet, perverse pleasure in their bafflement.

'How – how's business?' the question would be asked by someone.

'Not so bad,' Penelope's father would reply. 'How's yours?' he would turn and ask Rollo.

Topaz had produced photographs once and let her see. They showed her father in his youth, in an exotic garden in the South of France, at the house of an artist. The host was in one of the groups, standing between her grandparents, and Rollo's boy was throwing something out of lens-range, perhaps an apple.

Whoever would have thought it, seemed to be going through everyone's mind, *that this should be the end of it all, Rollo Milne's son toiling for a company of teak importers*.

'How's business?' the same question would be repeated another time, not mischievously but because it seemed the required question to ask a son they didn't understand.

'Fine, not so bad, you know,' he would reply. 'How's yours, Father?'

'Do you remember – ?' Topaz might ask, and she would refer back to such-and-such a visit made to the house, by someone either illustrious or very queer and unconventional. Penelope would see her mother looking discomposed but also interested. This was a kind of history in the retelling, and perhaps in the making too: which must have been why she would whisper little warnings to her daughter on these occasions that she really *should* pay attention, because her grandfather was rather well-known in some quarters and had been friendly with some very notable people. 'He has seen and done so much, Penelope. And talked to so many people who're just names to me.'

Rollo didn't talk so much to *them*, though, about his famous friends of long ago. He may have felt he'd talked it all out, over the years, done it to death. Now he was chiefly interested in himself and his own philosophy and discipline of life. His wife and Topaz were there to serve and enhance the image. Penelope sometimes saw her mother shifting uncomfortably in her chair in the presence of so much blatant masculine authoritarianism. But she was his son's wife, she was daughter-in-law to a man who was modestly famous chiefly by association rather than accomplishment and it wasn't her place to raise an objection.

Penelope realised quite early on that her grandmother was doing all that she could to make the house and its associations special to them, in future memory; that that was her active part in the life and half-legend of Hazehill. Otherwise it wouldn't have been anything like itself, and Penelope was to think back on that as being the finest of tributes to her father's mother's talents as domestic organiser: Hazehill would have been so very much less without her.

Her father never seemed settled there, however: it was no fond homecoming for him on their not very frequent forays down to Berkshire. He grew impatient, creaking the joints of his chair at table and kicking gravel and grass with the scuffed toes of his shoes whenever they were just standing around. He refused to be impressed by anything. It was as if he'd tumbled to the methods by which each visit was intended to be made so memorable for his wife and daughter. For him, the standing about was like waiting for a change of scenery to be cranked into place, and the longer he had to suffer Hazehill the more irritable he became with – in sequence – Rollo, Topaz, then (finally) his mother. It was *she* who made the most effort to appear interested when he could be persuaded to speak of his life but even she was also – simultaneously – looking beyond him and coolly surveying the room or the dining-table to ensure there were no hitches in the house's smooth-running. Her distinctively patrician looks and well-cut clothes a few years behind the fashions must have been a credit to her earlier, at school functions, when her husband could only have been an embarrassment: she wouldn't have been out of place in the staider environs where boys like her son might have been presumed to hail from. But, in their days at Hazehill, it was clear that she had no automatic entitlement to his sympathy. He seemed uneasy with her loyalty, and must not have seen – or just possibly he did? – that she had decided years before that there was no real option for her but to make the best of this marriage (since a fact in law was exactly that), to turn it somehow into the semblance of a success. None of this could account for the fundamental matter of how it had come about that two persons of their separate types – a painter and a judge's daughter – had made such a match, but by that time in her considerations the grown-up Penelope would be starting to lose the thread, family vertigo would be inducing dizziness, and so she would prefer to concentrate on what was simpler and less exacting, her reminiscences of Giverny days in the transformed heart of Berkshire.

Some nights the child would lie in bed trying to remember everything about Borneo that she could. Every detail. In case she should ever let it go. But sleep always came before she was ready.

She also went back to Tiktiki, where the silver-mines were giving their all and gold had been panned from rivers. Villages had become towns and towns had grown to cities.

Here in London – where she had obligations too – she passed among the crowds unrecognised, but her authority was all the greater for being silent and controlled and not requiring the fawning adulation of her minions.

When they had been living in England for two or three years Penelope took her photographs of Borneo to school and showed them to the other girls. Some of them hardly bothered to look; a few were rather sniffy, and topped her images, describing those in their own experience or family history. An older girl called Rosalind Dene, whom she scarcely knew, came to view the photographs; she spent much longer studying them, with her intense brown eyes which could memorise lines of a book-page between blinks. She asked questions about who was who and where each place was and retained all the information, so that Penelope found herself being corrected several times when she was trying to remember the climate or the animals, the stuffy smell of the vegetation. But already Borneo was starting to recede, and Penelope sometimes wondered if she was talking about another person's life, one she must have read about. Once or twice she was tempted to invent where she knew her memory was failing her. But she felt that Rosalind Dene would surely be able to tell her that she was making it up – in other words, that she wasn't being true to the facts. At the time she must have been between nine and ten years old.

'What do you remember?' Rosalind Dene asked her once, after she'd emptied all the memories out of her head.

It wasn't a question she'd been expecting; it didn't seem to make any sense at all.

'I've told you.'

'No. What do you *remember*?'

23

Then somehow she realised – and it shocked her – that what she had been doing had been reciting descriptions of her parents' descriptions, and yielding only a very few of her own jumbled, shaky memories. At the time she had just lived and got on with it; she hadn't thought to remember. But even that wasn't a true memory. Not so long ago, since their return, she had overheard her mother say to her father, 'This is my life. I've no choice, have I? I've just got to get on with it.' She had said it during one of the frosty silences they had had to adjust to in London, along with the weather and gaslight and the smallness and meanness of everything.

Rosalind Dene was looking at her very intently beneath her severe eyebrows.

'How many servants did you have?'

'Six.'

(Was she trying to catch her out?)

'And how many gardeners?'

'Two. A man and a boy.'

'How many fans were there in the drawing-room?'

'Four. Trrp. Trrp. Trrp.'

That was how her mother described the sound to people, a slow succession of mechanical shudders.

'Just like that,' Penelope told Rosalind Dene. 'All day long.'

But she couldn't really remember the sound the fans had made as they turned. Sometimes she thought that she could, but maybe it was only her imagination inventing. Borneo confused her with its distance, its fetid heat, its low clouds and skulking forests of teak, its slashed and bleeding rubber trees, its forked lightning and madcap dancing parties, the cook's *fruits de mer* displays heaped on ice, the slow purring of fans.

'Which do you prefer?' Rosalind Dene asked her.

Penelope stared back.

'What?'

'Which place do you prefer? Here or Borneo?'

She shrugged, and shifted her weight from one foot to the other. She was aware of the shiny brown eyes, of being looked at very closely, very hard. She blushed with the attention or with the length of the silence.

'I . . .'

She remembered so little of the island itself but she had deduced from the talk at home that life there, for all its furnace heat and dripping humidity, had been preferable in many respects to this one in London. Chiefly she had the evidence of her mother's dissatisfaction since their return, her persistent niggles about having to run the house herself, with the very minimum of help from staff: and the further evidence of her father's not seeming to care. They'd come back before her mother could adjust her mind to leaving or adequately make her preparations for the farewell moving-on parties. That was a continuing rankle with her.

'I don't know,' Penelope said.

24

Rosalind Dene kept staring at her. She didn't stop, even though she had forced her to admit that she didn't know the answer to her question.

'Both places,' Penelope heard herself blurting out. 'I mean, it isn't the same here. It couldn't be – '

They were interrupted by the end-of-break bell ringing, and the conversation was hastily concluded, to Penelope's relief. They were summoned to their different classes and she resolved to take care that she wasn't asked that same question again.

Sitting at her desk she thought of the concentration on Rosalind Dene's face. No one else had been so interested in what her photographs showed. She'd peered at the various combinations of people, passing over the harmless panoramas of Samarinda and Balikpapan. The house had prompted as many questions as its inhabitants: how many rooms did they have, where did they do their entertaining, where did they sleep, where were they able – in Rosalind Dene's precocious choice of words – to be themselves?

Penelope was grateful for any show of interest: but its true nature must have been what she later remembered, causing a fresh disturbance to her equilibrium, after the jolts and truces in the way of life in Belsize, which – and not Borneo – was properly her home. Borneo was convenient to her, it was *her* 'subject', but even then she was beginning to think it had been a dream-state. She tried to make it sound as exotic as she could – Sukadana, Palangkaraya, Purukcahu – needing to believe herself that tropical, fecund, colonised but deeply mysterious Borneo was somehow the clue to this personality, life and destiny yclept 'Penelope Milne'.

Then calamity struck, at a remove, incinerating a hotel in Nice.

Rollo had gone south to paint, and the caravan of two had accompanied him. They had visited Cassis, Menton and Beaulieu before reaching Nice. Canvases were sent back home as soon as they were completed, and the three travelled on, as lightly as they were able to – in a car, with the easel roped to the roof and Topaz driving.

The fire raged through the hotel in the darkest hours of the night. Fourteen people all told were killed. 'The three Englishfolk died in their beds,' one newspaper said, and the sentence lodged in Penelope's head when she read the report in after-years.

Their remains (charred twice over) were brought back to Berkshire and the ashes buried in a churchyard, under three gravestones set side-by-side, with Rollo's in the middle. No reference was chiselled in the stones to God or his Mercy: only names and dates were provided, without specifics – there was no 'painter', or 'devoted wife', or 'friend of the family'.

Where they finally came to rest after their tragedy was in the shade of a spreading English cedar tree. No place could have seemed more peaceable, like a little replica of heaven on earth.

3

On her tenth birthday there was a party for Penelope in the house in Belsize.

A dozen girls and boys of her acquaintance were invited and dutifully presented themselves, gift in one hand and a pair of indoor shoes in the other. Her mother had no confidence in her kitchen skills, and they didn't run to a cook, so local suppliers provided vol-au-vent cases with assorted fillings and pastry that flaked and crumbled when you picked one up, tepid sausages, a very chewy hazelnut meringue nest, and thirteen individual mould jellies in lurid, unrecognisable 'fruit' colours. When her mother saw what was delivered she dashed down the street to a superior confectioner's where she bought them all a couple of Lindt chocolate bars apiece.

It was intended to be a day, and a feast, not to be forgotten in a hurry.

Entertainment had been hired: a conjuror called Ali Galigali. He had an ordinary enough face, which you wouldn't have looked at twice if you'd seen him from a car, but he wore a red velvet fez and an outfit of baggy silver jodhpur pants and a matching smock top embellished with gold sickle moons and blue stars, bringing into Penelope's mind the viziers at the pantomime she'd been taken to in the Christmas season, and he then seemed very imposing indeed, if you managed to exclude his face, which – by contrast – was so unexceptional, even framed by the clothes and the headgear. He carried his box of tricks into the house, clearly struggling with the weight of it; Penelope thought that a little odd, when he should have been able to cause it to fly upstairs and spare his back, which she'd heard him explain to her father was giving him some trouble, the weather being what it was, dampish.

They all gathered upstairs in the sitting-room to watch him, her father too, but not her mother who was setting the tea-table with Nancy and attending to the last-minute odds and ends in the kitchen. Her father applauded at certain points and they took their cue from him, repeating the conjuror's name as instructed, 'Ali Galigali Ali Galigali'; otherwise they might have sat watching in silence, puzzled and awed and maybe also a little frightened by what they were seeing.

He juggled with three tennis balls, using two hands then one, and while he kept the other two balls in motion rolled one along his arms and shoulders, then down his bad back. He spirited eggs out of his ears, then his mouth. Objects appeared and disappeared beneath four scarlet cups. A watch left a boy's wrist and came to light when the conjuror opened an absurd tapestry evening bag one of the girls had brought with her. A white kitten materialised from a fluttering handkerchief.

Penelope was to remember his act as very slick, one trick after another after another. The man spoke so quickly that it was very difficult to concentrate on either the words or the movements of his hands. Every few seconds he would wave his wand and several times he opened one fist and threw a scatter of gold dust, which he told them was the special wizard's powder: it sprinkled itself over the carpet and even as he did his magic Penelope was wondering what her mother would say about it when she saw the Axminster glittering.

Years afterwards she could still remember the afternoon and she would feel that she had been in two minds about the performance: impressed and accepting, credulous but at the same time aware subconsciously that it was happening too quickly and that so much magic had already begun to pall a little and she really had nothing on which to latch her belief, to hook her willingness to believe on to. Its very deftness proved in the end a disappointment. Maybe if he'd just made a mistake or two she could have sat willing the rest of the tricks to work as he asked them to chorus his name, 'Ali Galigali Ali Galigali'. But by the midway point she had almost forgotten that they *were* tricks. Her father had gone on clapping, however, and they'd all continued to take their cue from him, and Ali Galigali had finished his act – running a table-tennis ball round the inside of a hoop – with a broad, satisfied smile on his face and a final shimmering shower of the indispensable wizard's dust.

Immediately after the show her mother opened the door to make her announcement that the tea was ready and waiting downstairs. In spite of the circumstances, her face looked rather drawn, and she smiled in a certain way she had, which tensed up her eyes and made wires pull in her neck. When they were all seated in the dining-room, Penelope watched the long faces and straight mouths as her mother and Nancy supervised between them the handing-round of the plates. Her father hovered behind them with bottles of orangeade and lemonade, pretending to be a wine-waiter and either not noticing the adult silence or trying to divert the children's attention on to himself. Gradually the food and drink and their consumption occupied everyone's concentration, and – to Penelope's relief, remembering that the day wasn't to be forgotten in a hurry – her parents and Nancy receded into the background, into the furniture.

Mrs Melchett in a fur tippet arrived for Miriam at six o'clock instead of seven, having failed to comprehend instructions. Penelope's mother dithered at first, not at all her usual self and quite put off her stroke, but then she seemed to perceive some usefulness in the situation and steered the premature arrival upstairs, in the direction of the sitting-room.

'We've never had a proper chance to *talk*,' she told her visitor. 'I don't know why.' She looked over her shoulder, past Penelope, down towards the activity in the hall. 'I think I've earned my rest today.'

They both stepped into the sitting-room, Mrs Melchett first, and the door was closed behind them. It opened again a few seconds later. Her mother lowered her voice. 'The sitting-room is out-of-bounds, Penelope. Mrs Melchett and I are going to have a little chat. You've lots of other rooms, haven't you?' She was too strung up now to even try to smile. Then she hissed, so only Penelope would hear, 'Keep that racket *down*, will you, for heaven's sake!' And with that the door was closed again.

It was turning into a day, Penelope realised at the very moment the noise at the other end of the hall let rip, for this stolen quiet too, for these private, penned-off corners. She stood with her back to the wall and stayed there for several moments until a voice called up to her out of the others.

'It's hide-and-seek, Penelope, come on.'

'You can't go into the sitting-room.' She dropped the warning over the banister rail. 'It's out-of-bounds.'

'No one said.'

'My mother said.'

'I don't believe you.'

'Don't, then.'

'Oh, come *on!*'

Racing into the dining-room behind someone else, she caught sight of a man in a lounge suit helping himself from a decanter on the sideboard and recognised the face of Ali Galigali, but the girl in front of her turned on her heels and squealed that it was the wrong room and after that, in their haste to escape, Penelope forgot all about the conjuror.

They ran up and down the house, from the second floor of bedrooms to the kitchen and the outbuildings behind the basement. Once her mother opened the sitting-room door and looked less angry than queasy with all the noise, greenish, but Penelope streaked past in a posse and didn't stop or even slow, knowing that this was her birthday and that it didn't resemble any other day in the year. Up and down the house, in and out the rooms, and scarcely a moment to stand still and catch her breath. The game had acquired a frantic pace, and they all felt themselves caught up in it. The longer it went on, the greater became the obligation not to drop out, not to be the first to lose stamina. Their shouts and screams forbade them in some way. They were all implicated in a kind of hysteria.

Later, as their feet thundered past and as the floorboards beneath the carpet jumped, her mother opened the sitting-room door with a dire, shrivelled expression of seething frustration on her face. She hissed at her again, but the words were lost and Penelope could only catch that one glimpse of her as she was swept past in the rush of legs and arms. Up and down the house, in and out the rooms, with almost no pauses except those moments of goading and gloating when the discovered stowaway was hauled out screaming from under a bed or from the darkness of a cupboard.

At last, tenth or eleventh in the game, it was Penelope's turn to hide herself.

She planned where as the others counted to a hundred, voices chanting. She crept away from them, up to the first floor – past the sitting-room – and then up to the second, where the bedrooms were. There was a third floor, with attic rooms, which no one had remembered about. The narrow staircase that led up to it was sited behind a closed door next to the big bathroom: usually the door stood open, but probably Nancy – the third floor was effectively all hers – had got wind of their after-tea adventures and decided to shut it.

The voices chanting up the stairwell reached 'sixty'. Penelope turned the handle, and pushed on the door. Nancy could have no cause not to allow *her* to go up.

She closed the door behind her and the voices were immediately silenced. She forgot which number they'd reached but, behind the door, she had gained more time, as much as she would need.

She stepped forward, but cautiously. The quiet felt strange to her after the din that had filled her head since they'd made their getaway from the tea-table. The bare floorboards squeaked beneath her feet and high above her she could hear the dripping of water in the tank under the roof-tiles.

She laid her hand on the banister rail and crept up the treads. Overhead several doors met on a small square landing; each of them was closed. All the doors had locks but only Nancy's occasionally had the key turned in it from inside, when she didn't want to be disturbed.

She was halfway up the staircase when she heard the first detonation of laughter ahead of her. She recognised at once that it was her father's: the sound was unmistakable, hearty and (as her mother was wont to refer to it, complainingly, unless it was encountered in other people) 'structural'.

She stopped where she was. An answering ripple of woman's laughter followed it, and she recognised that too.

What was the joke?

Her father roared again, exploding into his laughter, then Nancy joined in.

Penelope put out her hand to the banister rail and took another few steps, on tiptoe. She was almost at the top of the staircase.

Something prevented her from going any further. Perhaps it was the sight of the closed door: or the sound of pleasure in which she had no part and was excluded from, which had no need of her. More than that, she was struck by the oddness of the circumstances. Her father's life was supposed to be lived downstairs, with her mother. Behind the landing door this was Nancy's nook of the house, cheaply furnished and with the hint of dampness in the air even though there were no wet rings visible on the flocked wallpaper.

One belonged to one: the other to the other.

They laughed again. Penelope remembered her mother telling her, 'A loud laugh denotes a vacant mind'. In which case they were making a great deal of noise about absolutely nothing at all.

The laughter instantaneously stopped, his and hers. She stood waiting for another peal but nothing happened. Of course, they could have decided to hold their own party. But she didn't think a party for two could be much fun.

She heard movements. A chair was pushed back and footsteps crossed the floor. There was a scrabbling sound she couldn't identify, then she thought she picked up a giggle. Some words maybe, spoken very softly, which reached her as shapeless whispers.

She retreated backwards down the stairs. This wasn't playing the game, because no one would find her here, behind the closed door: no one knew that there was a staircase to the third floor. Her extreme honesty appalled her, because she knew she could have held out and beaten them soundly, she could have hidden here for the rest of the evening and nobody would have had a clue where she was. But – she was properly to understand in her teenage years – there was now rather more at stake than winning or losing a round of hide-and-seek.

She got no further than the landing. She was spotted seconds after she'd closed the door. The victorious whoops this time had a hollow ring to them. She wasn't making any attempt to defend herself. She only smiled, and calmly – walking between them, rather baffled by herself – she led the way back downstairs.

Very curiously her mother made no reference to the game of hide-and-seek afterwards; she appeared too concerned with certain thoughts of her own.

Her father by contrast seemed as he had been earlier in the day, good-humoured and smiling pleasantly, pulling at the cuffs of his shirt and still wearing the formal flannel business-suit he had put on for their guests.

Nancy was occupied in the kitchen, with stacks of dishes and tumblers to wash and dry.

Gold wizard's dust sparkled on the Axminster in the sitting-room but it went uncommented upon. Party hats lay where they'd been dropped or where the elastic had perished, streamers were strewn across tables and over chairs. In the stampede of hide-and-seek, globules of food had been trodden into the rugs and pressed flat by buttocks into upholstery.

One end of the dining-table had been cleared and the birthday presents were set out on display. Penelope occupied herself with them for a while. There was a clockwork tin man who lit a gas-lamp with his pole. She sent marbles hurtling round a two-thirds-size bagatelle board. She unfolded a tapestry canvas of Ann Hathaway's cottage and counted all the twenty-six skeins of thread. She blew her nose drily with a white handkerchief edged with lace and embroidered in its corner with alpine wild flowers.

Her mother had already mentioned the hard slog of 'thank you' notes.

She picked up two magnets and watched them attract each other, then repel, then attract, then repel.

One of the bedrooms, the smallest, had been turned into a study for her father. It was furnished with a desk and an armchair and a bookcase holding many fewer books than it might have. Sometimes when she'd stood outside she'd heard him snoring, and it had been tacitly understood in the house that the room was his escape, his bolt-hole, just as her mother had her own, the so-called 'dressing-room'. Both rooms were kept locked.

Her father had a habit of forgetfulness, and he needed to have several keys. She discovered from watching him that one key was kept in the case of the grandfather clock in the hall downstairs. Sometimes he forgot that it belonged there, and it temporarily disappeared: but more often than not that was where it was.

It took her several weeks to screw up her courage for the deed, which she realised would also be a deception, but she managed to at last – and, heart in mouth, she removed the key from the clock case. She wasn't sure why she wanted to see inside the room: except that it was meant as a secret from her, and her father's secrets, his capacity for secretiveness, intrigued her now even more than her mother's.

When at last she did close the study door behind her and she was quite alone, she felt disappointed. She already knew what the room looked like – her father had taken her in twice – and she thought it rather worn and gloomy. Some of the armchair's stuffing was hanging out of the arms, and the side of the desk next to it was very scuffed: as if he must have a habit of kicking the toes of his shoes against it.

She sat down in the armchair. The cushion and back were quite lumpy. She straightened her legs and stretched her toes but she couldn't reach the desk. Through the window there was only a view of the grey-brick backs of the houses in the next street, and windows – and so presumably rooms – much like this one.

She got up and walked behind the desk. She sat on the chair, the eighth from the dining-room set.

The top drawer when she pulled the handle wouldn't budge. She tried another: it wasn't locked. She tried several more, and to her surprise they all slid open.

There was very little in any of them, mainly sheaves of papers. She found a notebook with some addresses and telephone numbers. One drawer contained a few photographs: all but one were of her parents and herself. The other, the exception, showed a different family, her Aunt Louise's: soon after their return from Borneo they had gone to visit a house in the green suburbs, at the end of a long, pot-holed lane they'd gone swinging down in a creaky car; there'd been a spouting hosepipe and a donkey leaning over a fence, but that was as much as she could bring back of the day.

There was one drawer left. All it held was a single buff-coloured envelope. She took it out and felt inside with her fingers. She tipped the contents out on to the desk.

They were pages clipped out of magazines and newspapers, a mixture of advertisements and photographs from the society pages. She leafed through them. Every one showed a beautiful woman: different women, but beautiful in the same way, with a long neck and thin, graceful arms and their mouths only very slightly smiling. Some of the paper was faded, and the magazine pages had crinkled and gone dull with handling. He must have looked at them many times, she decided, even though they'd been put in an envelope and kept in the bottom drawer.

She studied the women more closely. Those in the advertisements were mostly drawings, based on photographs from *The Tatler* and *Vogue* and *Regatta*. They were all elegant and, as her mother said of certain people, willowy, meaning too tall and fine for their own good. She couldn't imagine them running a house, as her own mother did. They wore evening gowns, and gloves, and (some of them) little gossamer veils, and they leaned on the arms of gentlemen. They looked like women who lived for the evenings, even though one of the advertisements was for Driscoll and Bentley's National Furniture Wax and another was for Vanguard Superior Blend Teas. The women didn't seem to be the sort who would know what her mother now did about the shine on tabletops or the best way to extract the full flavour from tea-leaves in the pot. Not really 'women'; rather, *ladies*, like the ones photographed at the Café Royal, and holding binoculars at racecourses or cards at dances, or wearing bridal veils.

She froze when she thought she caught a movement outside the door. But she heard nothing else, and soundlessly she slipped the contents back into the envelope. She replaced the envelope in the bottom drawer and closed it.

She made her escape from the room as surely as a cat-burglar and returned the key to the clock case in the hall downstairs. As she walked away the clock chimed. She didn't jump, and surprised herself by not being surprised. It was her cover, not an alarm. The light from the window caught her double in the glass face, and she and her reflection exchanged nods like accomplices.

Once in Borneo an English jobbing photographer had called at the compound.

In the one extant result her mother and father are standing on the verandah, three or four feet apart. He looks towards the camera, she is posed facing him. Of course it's a pose, because Penelope couldn't remember that that's how it ever was: her father so serious and centre-stage and her mother compliant in that wifely way, willingly side-stepping her husband's limelight, without for once a hand raised to check on the presentableness of her coiffure.

Her father's hair darkened after their return to England: perpetual sunlight had bleached it and given him a boyish look. At that time, when they were in their Borneo prime, his features were clear, untrammelled by care, he smiled a lot, perhaps he made people think of good times. The face was handsome, in a slightly under-developed, boyish way: if he was conscious of his looks, he certainly never *concentrated* on his appearance and so he managed to resist the too easy sin of vanity. Other women had paid him notice – she knew that now –

32

but he probably accepted that it was just a fortuitous means for an introduction to be made.

Longer ago than that it must have been thought that her mother was going to be more deeply attractive than she turned out to be: attractive, that is, in a different, more adult way. Her looks had gelled at some point, however, and the girl's prettiness had locked in place, become stranded on her face, so that sometimes her mother seemed to be simpering and flirty with her Hollywood baby-blonde hair and at other times the prettiness, suddenly redundant against the adult world and its intrigues, was so gravely distorted that she appeared haunted and very nearly manic, with pain shocked into the features. At her worst moments she resembled a woman equipped only for social pleasures who had pushed open the wrong door and seen beyond it a stone lifted on life. When she seemed to have recovered her equipoise, Penelope couldn't forget the other times, and it had introduced an edginess into her relations with her mother: she wasn't able to trust the innocence of some of her smiles and her mother duly became impatient with her when she couldn't feign that life was perfectly pleasant after all. Clearly she didn't want a sceptical daughter, but in that case Penelope would have needed to be someone without memory. And maybe a further strain for her mother was seeing Penelope's heredity every time she looked at her: her own girlish prettiness (which had now, as the expression was, 'filled out' in herself) crossed with her husband's *laissez-faire*, his insouciance, the blandness of a life that appeared to be untroubled.

'Appeared to be'. How little her mother really knew, or had ever known about her and the life building inside.

'He was coming home from business,' she heard her mother telling those who returned to the house from the funeral service at the church. 'Have some sherry, won't you?'

Nancy was in a bad way but had had the riot act read to her; dressed in black she was on hand to serve the vol-au-vent cases and the cod roe canapés. Penelope, also dressed in black, stood against a wall, working out just who were her father's business colleagues: she guessed that they were the rather embarrassed-looking men talking quietly among themselves out of the corners of their mouths, who stopped talking and adopted suitably sympathetic expressions whenever her mother walked past. Her mother smiled at them brightly, not at all with a widow's smile, and they nodded their heads and pulled at their cuffs but there was no other contact between them. Penelope thought that they talked together in quite a secretive way, as if it was important to them that they weren't overheard.

The whole day was shrouded in secrecy. She hadn't been taken to the funeral in the morning, and had been looked after – or, rather, watched over – by a neighbour with a face as improbably oval as a cake of Pears' soap, called Mrs Lambert. When her mother and Nancy returned with company – and feeling no wiser in herself after her morning with Mrs Lambert, which she had spent

33

piecing together a jigsaw of Windsor Castle she had been keeping for a rainy day, so-called (although in fact the sun shone, in a very uncaring way) – she again found that secrecy was like a command in the house, and no one was quite willing to say what it was they meant. Voices were lowered; the words burbled out, but they were counters in private games.

Her mother breezed round the sitting-room, ensuring that everyone was being liberally plied with food and drink.

'He was coming back from business,' she told them. 'Have some sherry, won't you? And a *bouchée*? What about chicken – ?'

But Penelope sensed that her remarks were the spoken equivalents of smiles, and she was already familiar with the power of those, because of what they didn't openly state. Her mother wasn't stating what Penelope understood, that there was something rather shameful about death and about *this* death in particular. There was also rather more to it than anyone was pretending: the recent past had 'depths', of a kind her mother could smotheringly suggest by her tone of voice.

It was therefore a most curious afternoon, or so she was to remember it, with no one properly engaging with the fact of *why* they were present. No one cried, no one's eyes even misted, and there were very few reminiscences. Her mother fussed with her high neckline, chosen to conceal the unflattering rings on her skin. The plates of food were emptied and the glasses disappeared from Nancy's tray.

Penelope found she had no encouragement to cry herself, and she felt guilty. They were all here for her father's sake, she realised, but they were disregarding him. She tried to concentrate her thoughts on him, but the features of his face became teasingly difficult for her to recall exactly, as if he'd been pressing it against frosted glass.

Then she found that *she* had become the object of the other people's attention, which took her mind off her father for a while. No one actually pitied her; instead they complimented her on her dress, on her hair, on her manners. Her mother was careful to overhear, and watched her with wary pride. 'Can I tempt anyone to another savoury? Melon and ham? Something else to drink, Doctor?' Nancy offered everyone the same glazed smile as she dutifully went about her business with the various loaded trays.

After the general smiles in the room there were the first instances of laughter: not belly rumbles, but the sort of polite joy that propels parties on their untroubled way. Penelope didn't associate it with disrespect until the house was empty: or almost empty, since one or two anxious souls were unwilling that mother and daughter should be left quite alone, and offered to tidy up and become bearers – of assorted crockery and suppressed grief – for however long their services might be required. 'I won't hear of it,' Penelope heard her mother tell them, but she knew quite well by her intonation that she wasn't going to resist beyond a certain point – say, if the offer was to be repeated twice. 'Now you're making *me* feel rude if I don't accept your kindness.' So the house wasn't properly theirs again until the mid-evening: as the tidying-up got under way, it occurred to Penelope that laughter might be helping now to make things less staid and awkward, and then she thought back to the afternoon and the houseful of people and wondered if the laughs mightn't have reached her father somehow, in that slightly discreditable white nothingness the word 'heaven' made her think of. She hoped he could distinguish, and that he'd recognise none of the laughs were hers, that she had done nothing at all to the cause of his memory that she need in any wise feel shame for.

'Actually, your father fell on stone steps, Penelope.'
'"Fell"?'
'On stone steps. It was frosty, you see.'
'"Frosty"?' she repeated.
'Yes.'
'Where?'
'A hotel. Actually. A hotel beside the sea.'
'The sea?'
'Yes.'
'Where?'
Her mother stared at her. A tic was pulling in her cheek.
'Where what?'
'The hotel – '
'Well, somewhere we've never been.'
'Never?'
'No. That's what I said.'
She overheard her mother talking to someone on the telephone. He had been there on business, it was explained, there in Eastbourne. He sometimes went there on business. It was there it had happened, he had slipped on steps, stone steps, it was a frosty evening and he had fallen badly, tripped backwards. Just like that. And split his skull.

Penelope listened with horror. She imagined over and over the fall on the frosty steps of the hotel at Eastbourne, but she couldn't bear to hear the eggshell crack of his skull as it made contact with the stone.

But she heard someone say he'd been conscious when he was taken to hospital, and her mother didn't deny it. She heard someone else say he'd broken his neck in the fall, and it was having his neck severed which had caused his death the next day. Her mother didn't deny that either, which meant that there had been a gap of most of twenty-four hours between the accident and his death in hospital.

'He used that hotel,' her mother said, 'as his base.' She spoke without very much conviction. 'It was a favourite of his. When he went on his business to Eastbourne.'

She didn't say what he did when he went to Eastbourne: only that it was

35

his work. His work, his job, had killed him: his devotion to duty, in other words, his meritorious application, as Penelope was always to think of it.

One afternoon in the week following the funeral, the canon who had officiated at the service called at the house. He was shown upstairs and Penelope watched her mother conduct him along the first-floor gallery to the little morning-room.

The door closed behind them and Penelope sat on the bottom tread of the staircase waiting until they would have had their talk and were ready to come out again.

Only a very few minutes passed before she heard her mother's voice, raised to speak over the canon's and pitched high in indignation. A very short time after that the door was thrown open and her mother emerged guns blazing, the scarlet of her face contrasting with the staid, sinister black of her widow's weeds. The canon followed at walking pace; he was breathing heavily and his complexion was bloodless – as if he had received some unlooked-for and particularly nasty shock to his system.

Penelope's mother had never made much of an effort previously with her religious education. Their church-going was irregular and performed with little conviction.

Her education finished – or it started, in a different vein, towards godlessness – while she sat on the bottom step of the second staircase, witnessing for herself the canon's inadequacy because he had thought to offer her mother wordy sympathy which her pride didn't require, because he was only a pithless man after all under his vestments.

She learned very much later that she had misjudged the canon, thinking he had been helpless to offer a reason for the loss of her father. In fact he had guessed that her mother was concealing something in her telling of the sorry, shocking story and he had offended her more than she could abide with his very human understanding and pity. All her mother had been caring for was more proof of the iron rod and implacable will of Almighty God, and what he'd given her was the claptrap of his amateur Teach-Yourself Psychology wisdom of the world instead.

'I have something to tell you, Penelope.'
'Yes – ?'
'About your Aunt Louise.'
Penelope stood waiting. She had seen her aunt and uncle only once since their return from Borneo.
'She's had an accident. Well, not an accident exactly. She went into hospital. For – for an operation. But it was quite a dangerous operation. Unfortunately – '
'What kind?'
'A grown-up operation. For women. Ladies. Of course it's very sad.'
'"Sad"?'

'Your Aunt Louise has – died. She's dead now.'

Penelope's heart juddered; just once though, a single jactitation.

'I'm sorry to have to tell you this – '

In which case, Penelope wondered, why are you not crying, why is your voice so steady?

'We don't need to talk about it again. Your Uncle Robert is going to live far away. With your cousins.'

'Where?'

'Oh, very far away. He hasn't decided. America, maybe, or Canada.'

'Will we see them?'

'We've got on very well without them,' her mother said sharply. 'It's certainly not going to start now.'

'Oh.'

'Anyway, that's the end of your Aunt Louise.'

Penelope opened her mouth to ask a question.

'I'd rather not discuss it, Penelope.'

'Because you're upset – '

'Never mind – '

'But – '

'No more, Penelope.'

The voice was impatient, nervy.

Penelope didn't reply.

'We won't say another word about it.'

All these deaths. She and her mother were like two skittles left standing. Penelope felt almost weary with them, weary more than sad. Although they must be, of course, *sad*: deaths like holes in the world, and some of their happiness drained away, but sadder for the dead every time because for them – unless you believed the Bible, and she had never been encouraged to – their happiness had been stolen and no one ever got it back, even to hope on. Unless you believed in the angels, and those lilac summers of heaven, but she had so many doubts. And somehow being good was still supposed to matter, when – as she had been told – it all ended on an operating-table; or it was like the lights suddenly fusing and you were tumbling into darkness, over and over, for all time.

4

Mr Chapman had known her father. But since then he'd turned into quite a modern man, certainly compared with some of the people her mother knew. He had a moustache and a sapphire-blue Daimler car, and lived – her mother told her – in a smart new block of service maisonettes with a swimming-pool in its basement, where (she also let out) she had swum a few lengths herself. He had business connections in many places, and frequently travelled to Europe by the aeroplane.

The name, Ray Chapman, was just a little colourless, wasn't it, by contrast with his present circumstances. But of course – as she came to appreciate later – that might have been an aspect of his appeal to her mother, and perhaps to herself too in an even less obvious way. She remembered she had been intrigued by what seemed to be his anonymity, or his mystery: a man with an ordinary name but a hidden talent for doing things that made him the money which brought him the luxuries, which only marked him out from all the other people in London with rather ordinary and uninspiring names. Her mother also let slip one day that he didn't appear to know who his neighbours were in the block of flats, and she was unsure of her mother's tone of voice: envy might have been a part of it.

Mr Chapman lived in expensive isolation, and frequently (on his business travels) at speed, and that did give him a romance, of the most modern kind. Moreover he gave Penelope presents, her own modest versions of the ones he gave her mother during the time they knew him: usually gift-wrapped half-pound boxes of Swiss chocolates, or fine quality handkerchiefs from the foreign places he visited, or a wooden box of professional coloured pencils, or a small tin of talcum powder. She sensed that they weren't given to her for the mere sake of giving alone; perhaps they were to draw attention away from her mother's gifts and to make them, too, seem like a not very extraordinary gesture. When she had moved to the school by the sea she took a more critical and sceptical view, and decided that they had been nothing so much as, not consolations, but *bribes* for affection, inducements to win either her favour or her silence. But by then it was too late to redeem the situation; rightly or wrongly the damage had already been done, and Mr Chapman was included in their private, shared but now receding history.

A car had passed up and down the street several times, travelling very slowly. It was being driven by a woman, a rarer occurrence then in her childhood than it was to become in her later life.

Penelope watched from her bedroom window. The car slowed down again every time it passed the house. She couldn't see the details of the woman's face through the reflections on the window glass, although she could tell that it was *this* house she was looking at, most particularly.

It happened another day, a few weeks afterwards, on another weekday afternoon. She recognised the make and model of car from before, and noticed again the woman driving. More shadows blotted the side-window. The woman, she could tell, had pale skin. Again it was this house, *their* house, which was occupying her attention.

She didn't tell her mother, the first time or the second. Her father's death still made a terrible silence in the house, and when they *did* speak words had an offputting density and gravity. She didn't think she had the courage to begin a conversation about a car. '*What* car?' her mother would have asked, sounding as if her voice had been whetted on a stone. '*Which* woman?' She would have told her what she'd seen. 'A car with a woman in it? What's so special about that, might I enquire?'

So the car made its mysterious passage along the street, and Penelope only watched, hoping that the shadows of eaves and clouds were hiding *her* from view too. Out of everything that was happening in London, she thought, something connected them, the woman behind the windscreen and herself: an elusive meaning running beneath all the others in the day.

Quite unexpectedly Mr Chapman drove over one Sunday with a packed picnic hamper in the boot of the car. He paused in the hallway and seemed confused by Penelope's presence. Her mother, brightening, told her to hurry and get ready. Mr Chapman might have been going to say something but he didn't: and it was he and Penelope who stood together in the hall, both waiting for her mother while she slapped on her warpaint and titivated her hair.

Their destination was decided on the way there: a village on the Sussex Downs that Penelope's mother said she remembered from her childhood. After a number of wrong turnings they found their bearings. It seemed that the village wasn't as pretty and ornamental as memory had made it: in fact, as Penelope saw for herself, it was decidedly run down. Her mother smiled nonetheless and pointed out the house she thought must be the one where they'd stayed: unless it had been that other one over there . . .

They picked a field where they could stop the car and enjoy a view with their picnic. Mr Chapman coughed a lot, and swallowed, and pulled at his moustache, and then he began to smoke, which Penelope's mother had never thought best manners in the house (even though it was men and not women who indulged in the habit) because the fumes clung to the curtains for days afterwards. But Mr Chapman was smoking a cigar, and it *was* out of doors, so there wasn't the same menace of the smoke drifting into your eyes.

When they'd had their lunch – Penelope's mother had been very animated while Mr Chapman had been rather ill-at-ease – it was suggested, by her after

39

a word from him, that perhaps Penelope would like to go down to the copse at the foot of the hill and have a good long look and then report back to them what it was like. Penelope was dimly aware as she got to her feet that they were requesting her absence, but she was pleased enough to get the stiffness out of her legs and bottom. She left them and let her legs run away with her down the hill; a couple of times she looked back and saw them talking to each other and forgetting to wave to her.

She was a while in the copse. She found rabbit burrows and watched their occupants from behind trees. But she tired of that at last, and thought it must be time to go back. She didn't catch a sight of them until she was halfway up the hill. They were both sitting on the tartan travelling-rug where she had left them; Mr Chapman had his arm round her mother's shoulders, and her mother had a handkerchief to her eyes.

She stopped and stood still, and stayed there until Mr Chapman spotted her and removed his arm. Her mother lifted her head and, after a final dab at her eyes, returned the handkerchief to her handbag. Penelope started walking again, but very slowly. When she reached them, it took her several moments to find the courage to direct her eyes at them both, and she could only do it covertly. Mr Chapman was picking at daisies and might have been somewhere else entirely. Her mother looked as if she wanted to be anywhere but here: her eyes and nose were red, and she gave Mr Chapman two or three aside glances, and took several mouthfuls of air as if each time she was going to sigh very deeply – but in the end she didn't.

Penelope walked about on the grass for a while, and her mother didn't tell her to keep still, and Mr Chapman didn't try to divert her as he usually did with the intelligent comments he felt a friend of her mother should be saying, encyclopaedic facts about the sky or geology or the wild flowers or the history of the place. She waited until her mother stood up, and then – joints cracking – Mr Chapman too, and then she helped them to put everything back into the hamper. At the start of their picnic her mother had enthused about each item as she'd unpacked it. 'Surprise picnics are the best sort, just like a birthday!' Now no one said anything. Mr Chapman was in a kind of trance. The napkins were approximately folded and the cutlery dropped rattling on top of them.

Her mother shook the crumbs out of the rug but was staring at a point on the grass several feet away. Penelope picked up the few bits and bobs of their rubbish, including the half-smoked cigar, but she didn't know what to do with them and didn't want to ask. She waited until Mr Chapman had his back turned to her, then she squashed them all into the bottom of the hamper.

On the journey back she saw Mr Chapman watching her in the driving-mirror and thought it would be easiest to pretend to be asleep. She'd had her eyes closed for several minutes when the voices started in the front of the car. They spoke very quietly and it was difficult for her to hear. Beneath his moustache Mr Chapman was asking her mother to 'think about it'. Her mother said something or other about *her*, Penelope. 'I have to think what's best for Penelope, you see.' Mr Chapman said it was a perfectly good life out there. Her mother said she had never thought about it, never imagined – Mr Chapman said he was sorry, but really *he* had no choice, it was just business, and he hadn't meant to – her mother said it was all such a shock to her. Mr Chapman said there was a little time left to think about it, think about it very seriously. Her mother repeated two words several times. 'South Africa'. Mr Chapman said that his mind had been made up for him, although the idea had always been there.

'But you never told *me*!'

'I was thinking of *you*, I forgot all about everything else – '

'But there?'

'It's the best place to be.'

'No – '

'In my line.'

'I don't understand.'

'That's just business, Eveline.'

Penelope kept her head motionless against the back of the seat and her eyes tight shut. Then her mother started to sob, quietly at first, so the sound could almost have been mistaken for laughter. Mr Chapman's words were nearly inaudible to her now, he spoke them very gently and – so far as she could tell – with sincere concern. Her mother's sobbing grew louder, then merged into the rumbling from the car's engine.

And somehow, even though she knew she was listening to hear, Penelope lost consciousness of whatever else was happening. When she started awake, with twinges of cramp in her neck and shoulders, the conversation was over. Her mother sat with her compact open, daubing her face with talcum powder and chattering in quite a sprightly way about something, almost as she had been at the beginning of their journey. Mr Chapman was replying, very pleasantly, but Penelope could see his eyes and eyebrows in the driving-mirror and she realised those other thoughts were still in his head, serious and sad.

She saw he was looking at her. She could tell from his eyes that he didn't trust her. A few moments too late he remembered to smile, but she knew that his eyes and his mouth beneath his moustache told different stories. He was pretending they were all good friends: which was an innocent pretence compared to what was to come later, when she revealed herself to be his very worst enemy.

Mr Chapman had said in her hearing that he would phone, and she'd watched her mother nod.

'And we'll talk about it again, Eveline.'

'Yes,' her mother said. 'Yes.'

Penelope had never seen her mother so tearful, not even after her father died. She went about the house puffy-eyed, sniffing into a handkerchief. She would compose herself just long enough to use the telephone. Several times she called a couple of the friends she had known longest, asking them very maundering questions about 'Mr Chapman' in a falsely spry voice and saying that she didn't have anyone else she could discuss him with. Of course, Penelope supposed, if her Aunt Louise had still been alive, then *she* could have been asked: but she wasn't alive, and so that was only wishful thinking.

The answers she received appeared to confuse her mother, although she also seemed to be agreeing with them. She would echo into the mouthpiece their words about his kindness, his thoughtfulness, his gentlemanliness. But each time she replaced the receiver she would begin to sniff into her handkerchief again, then her eyes would take on an ominous shine and in seconds more tears would be flowing. Penelope wished she could help, but her mother seemed unable to take it in, the fact that she was trying to help her make the crying stop. It occurred to her that her mother *might* have stopped, if she'd really wanted to – but maybe she didn't want to, and so meantime there was no stopping and no end to it, she just carried on doing more and more of the same.

Of course it was Mr Chapman's fault, it was *because* of him, even though he wasn't here in the house and even though he was spoken about on the telephone with such praise and respect. She didn't understand how he could cause her mother much more upset than her father's dying on a slippery flight of stone steps had done. She didn't know how Mr Chapman couldn't realise the effect he was having. He had told her mother that he would phone her, he had said it in a low, grave, significant voice and her mother had nodded in the way she did when an event was more important than words could convey. Mr Chapman couldn't have wished her mother to be like this, could he? – not if he'd honestly and truly cared for her, as she'd heard him assure her he did.

Penelope found it very hard to find any forgiveness for him in herself. He was responsible for the tears, which was bad enough; he had also changed the atmosphere of the house, so that she and her mother both seemed permanently uneasy and on edge. He should have been aware of the situation, somehow, and done what he could to save her mother. She didn't believe she could be civil to him ever again. But he was about to leave them very soon, for sunny South Africa where the life was so good, and so it wouldn't continue. Until he did leave, though, her mother would keep on crying; if he came to the house to see her, the situation would become even worse.

He had some last piece of business to attend to apparently, near (Penelope thought he'd said) Manchester. Her mother was waiting for him to call her, all her concentration was focused on the inevitability of his contacting her, of their speaking, of her responding to the question she had told her friends he had put to her, giving her time to finally decide. To Penelope, all it was, was cruelty: Mr Chapman had a job, he was about to have a new job, he had so many different thoughts passing through his mind that he hadn't a chance of being hooked by one and snared by it.

On the fateful evening her mother discovered that there were no matches, and that the gas to the cooker in the kitchen couldn't be lit to give the flame to light the spill to take to the sitting-room fire and the brackets on the wall. 'There's a box of them somewhere, I know there is,' she said, examining the scullery shelves and lifting up and banging down every object that could conceivably be hiding the matches.

'I'd better go out and get some,' she said. 'What on earth has Bridget done with them?'

'I'll go,' Penelope offered.

'It's all right.' Her mother picked up her jacket. 'I could do with some air. I haven't been out all day, I'll just go to Ann's Pantry.'

Penelope watched from a window and listened to the clack of her mother's heels on the pavement. She saw the young man, Mrs Forester's son, come down the steps of the house two away from them and lift his hat. He spoke, and her mother's heels stopped, she turned round to smile at him, then she replied.

That was when the telephone rang. Penelope approached the hall table very slowly. She counted under her breath to twenty before she reached out her arm and picked the receiver up off the stand.

He hurried over the formalities – Hello Penelope, How are you? – and asked her if he could speak to her mother. Please. He had said he would ring, he was sorry he was late but she would be expecting a call from him.

'She's gone out.'

'What's that?'

'She's gone out – '

' "Out"?'

' – of the house.'

'Oh. And left you?'

Penelope didn't respond.

'Did she say when she would be back?'

'No,' she told him, knowing it to be the truth. 'She didn't say when.'

'Was she with anyone?'

Again she kept silent.

'Penelope? Are you there?'

'Yes,' she said.

'Was your mother *with* anyone? Did you happen to see?'

'I saw her with Mr Forester.'

'Who's he?'

'Just someone.'

'Have I met him?'

'No,' she replied very positively. 'No, you haven't.'

'Oh.'

She wondered what they were talking about, her mother and their occasional neighbour.

43

'And what is he like? This Forester chap – '

'. . . quite young.'

'He – he's younger than me, then?'

The laugh in Mr Chapman's voice was rough and unmerry.

'Yes,' she said.

'Your mother's gone out with him?'

'Well,' she said, 'she met him. I saw them.'

'Oh.' There was no laugh in his voice now. 'Oh, I see.'

She stared at a curl of acanthus leaf on the wallpaper.

'But your mother knew I was going to phone?'

'Oh yes.'

'You see, I've so little time. And I have to move about tonight and tomorrow. I'm getting ready to go off, you see. To South Africa.'

'Yes.'

'Maybe later. I could try later – '

But he must have thought better of it because he didn't call again that evening. Penelope told herself her mother didn't deserve to be upset, that she couldn't go another night without sleep. She heard her ring his flat, twice, but there was no reply.

Which was how the past won out over the future. It became the point at which her mother abandoned the dream of Mr Chapman for the new myths of virtue and a good marriage, the one she'd had, to be honoured in her husband's memory.

And all, as it were, for the sake of one single match to light the cooker to light the spill to light the fire.

5

Her mother's mother had died during their spell in Borneo, or so Penelope had believed at the time, because that was the official version she was given.

She survived in photographs: a widow of great conscious regality, always seated. When she smiled in her later years it was done as sainted suffering, and she looked more intimidating then than when she was straight-faced. Penelope grew up imagining that her grandmother hadn't cared for other people to be happier than her. In one photograph she presided at a party, but the jollity seemed tempered in the immediate vicinity of her chair, as if that lace-collared Edwardian formality exhaled a contagious sobriety.

Her husband, a colonel in a fusilier regiment, had been killed at Passchendaele. Penelope's father had joined an officer corps in 1912 after chucking school a year earlier than expected: probably some behind-the-scenes diplomacy secured the commission, but he proved himself adept in training. The Colonel had noted his promise and informed his superiors. The younger man had developed a respect for the older that went beyond considerations of rank and degree; in time he was to tell his future father-in-law that he had worked for his good opinion and approval as he might have hoped for his own father's. (An equivocal manner of putting it, it had occurred to Penelope's mother.)

Penelope was always to feel in some measure deprived that she hadn't been able to witness the life for herself, that she was only an outcome of it. Perhaps that sense of missing out would have mattered to her less if she hadn't been an only child. She didn't relish her singleness, and wished she wasn't so unique but could have seen herself in a sister's or a brother's face. She wondered why there should only have been herself. Had her mother felt it was beyond her strength to bear another child and bring it up, and did that reflect badly on her very early experience with her daughter?

It was Penelope's perception later in her life that she might have been less of a watcher and more of a doer if she hadn't come into the world alone, one of her own kind, an experiment not to be repeated. Watching could show you too much. She felt she had been too ready all along to let things happen, *to* her and *around* her: it had come from habit, from standing back and – earlier than that – from the consciousness of having conversations go on literally above her head, on subjects that were supposed to be well out of her thought range anyway.

Her mother never accounted to her for her grandmother's last days. She wouldn't tell her who had had responsibility for whatever had had to be done, the sort of 'home' it was (which was where Penelope suspected she must have been taken).

She was asleep one night when the telephone rang. The lights were out in the house and she heard her mother blundering her way downstairs from her bedroom. It was a most unusual occurrence, the first time she could remember the telephone bell screeching into the darkness.

She got out of bed and crossed the floor of her bedroom on tiptoe; she opened the door wide enough to let herself out, and crept along the landing to the banister rail, watching the torchlight thin as her mother hurried to pick up the receiver. She was twelve years old, but she had been brought up the hard way, on the fringes of facts, and she had learned – in the fashion of parables – to distinguish the shapes in shadows.

'What do you mean, she's "shown up"? . . . She can't, she can't possibly . . . How did she get there? . . . They told us it wouldn't happen . . . I've no idea. It's you she's come to, so it's up to you, isn't it? . . . I certainly would *not* consider it . . . She's unsociable, a nuisance. That's just how it is now . . . It's not as if it's *cheap* . . . I don't mean that I do. I don't "grudge" it. It's her money, and a bit of mine, and yours . . . Well, *you* can afford it. That's what happens when you marry, for better or worse. You take on these obligations . . . I'm quite aware what *my* obligations are, thank you, if that's what you're going to ask me. I don't feel like a lecture in morality from *you* in the middle of the night . . . You can take it exactly how you like, I've no intention of explaining it. I think you forfeited that right a long time ago . . . Ask your husband, since he seems to have all the bright ideas. And there are two of you . . . She'll go. You can *make* her go back . . . Here? Certainly not . . . Not with Penelope . . . There's nothing she needs to know: about *that* or the other thing . . . *You*'ve made your bed. Several beds, rather . . . I haven't any message for her. What help would that be? She hasn't a clue . . . She came to *you*, didn't she? . . . That's absurd. I can face up to anything . . .'

The receiver was banged down.

Several sighs followed. Then the beam of torchlight raked on to the staircase wall.

Penelope stepped back. A shadow flared on the wall in front of her like a bogy. Then she realised it wasn't hers, but her mother's, in her winter-weight nightgown and with a pigtail swinging like a mandarin's.

Her surprise at the error took several seconds to shake out of her head, still standing on the corner of an alleyway in Old Peking.

Part Three

1

One day in the last term of her second year at boarding school, Myrtle Fellowes stopped her in a corridor, when she must have known there would be people around to overhear.

'My mother saw *your* mother in Rendle's.'

The name didn't mean anything to Penelope.

'The chocolate shop in Wigmore Street,' Myrtle Fellowes told her.

Penelope smiled. It was a guarded response to the remark. She didn't care for Myrtle Fellowes. She had always known it was wise policy to be on the right side of her, however. Her father was a bishop, but she often showed something almost satanic in her expressions: or maybe the most vengeful of the angels had something of Myrtle Fellowes in their make-up.

'My mother was *shocked.*'

Penelope went quite cold. She felt her ribcage was straitjacketed inside one of the farthingales they'd learned about in History. She forgot to breathe.

'She told my father. *He* said it was shocking too.'

Penelope continued to stare. She had no idea what they were talking about. The conversation was confused with another one, and somehow her own mother was muddled up in it.

'How long has she been doing *that?*'

The word was given an unpleasant, disdainful emphasis.

'What – what do you mean?' Penelope heard the feebleness in her voice.

'Just what I said.'

'But – '

'How long has she been doing it, then?'

'Doing – what?'

Myrtle Fellowes, she realised years later, hadn't even had the sensitivity to understand that she didn't have an inkling. Or just possibly she'd thought that she was bluffing her.

'Serving in Rendle's, of course.'

Penelope tried to say the word, to repeat it, but she couldn't.

'I suppose you're going to tell me it was someone else?'

47

She was remembering a plush box of chocolates that had sat on top of the sideboard all last Christmas: and the chocolate Easter eggs in gold foil found by her dinner plate on the evening of Good Friday.

'She knew quite well who my mother was, and my mother told my father it was *definitely* her.'

Penelope couldn't account for the next few moments when she tried to remember them afterwards: they had vanished from her recollection.

The first thing she did recall was walking away, to deprive Myrtle Fellowes of her full victory. She had come to the school on the clifftops imagining she would acquire bravery and the dignity of heroism: she would find the tunnel secreted behind the panelling and disturb the gang of smugglers at their work, and Miss Saxby would grant all the girls of Thurlestone a full day's holiday in recognition of her pluck, just as they'd been given half-a-day's freedom in her first year when Cynthia Dinmont became engaged to Earl Cheveney's heir.

In the corridor between classes, walking away from Myrtle Fellowes, she was wondering – of all things – how the chocolate in Rendle's would be able to stand up to the sun's scrutiny all summer: perhaps the shop had awnings, or that crinkly yellow paper over the glass that wool shops made use of to prevent daylight fading the goods. She might have asked her mother, of course, but she didn't see now how she possibly could. At all costs she must pretend not to know, not to have twigged to her.

In the days afterwards the situation did indeed complicate itself, but that wasn't directly the doing of Myrtle Fellowes, whose eyes she avoided at Assembly and in the corridors. Rather, she understood that her mother had allowed herself to take a job for *her* sake, not to shame her but to help maintain appearances for them both: the school fees had to be paid, and she'd once heard her mother answering the telephone to the bursar, Miss Coote, and making her excuses for forgetting to attend to the business, it had quite slipped her mind.

She thought this must put her under a certain moral obligation to her mother: that at least she must respect her privacy on the subject. She was chiefly worried that Myrtle Fellowes would pass the information about and soon everyone would discover. But before it could happen God mercifully delivered a bolt out of His blue. The bishop's daughter slipped while on an out-of-bounds foray on to the cliffs, and she was only saved from death by Miss Argylle's hearing her cries as she walked her Airedale. A man attached to a rope had to be let down the cliffside but at the last second she slipped further out of his reach and concussed herself on the branch of a tree. She didn't come to until nearly forty-eight hours later, in the nearest hospital. Penelope was drafted into one of the groups that visited her: when she reached the bedside she saw a head swathed in bandages, with spaces left for the eyes and the nostrils and the mouth and jaw. She saw that the mind behind the eyes saw her and was struggling to recognise her, but the mouth didn't move. It seemed to be a moment of the most symbolic kind, and Penelope discerned that the daughter of the reverend bishop had inherited more of her father's awe of God and His justice than she'd given her credit for in the gloomiest moments of her recent, unending mental probings. In its way, it was a little miracle: evidence that nothing, not even the worst contingency, could be depended on. One result was that Penelope, even in these last weeks of the final term, volunteered her services – out of plain gratitude for the patient's silence – to the Chapel Consort Singers and, at the fifty-fifth minute of the eleventh hour, she joined the chaplain's extra-curricular Bible-reading circle. Her comments at the latter weren't profound, but they *were* heartfelt in that interval of weeks while dumbstruck (or amnesiac?) Myrtle Fellowes continued to be intensively cared for.

When school had broken up for the year, God and His mysterious workings evanesced from the spotlit forefront of Penelope's considerations, as did Myrtle Fellowes. Back home, she realised soon enough that her mother no longer served courtesy and chocolates to bishops' wives from behind a shop counter in Wigmore Street. On her return she did find a medium-sized box of Neapolitans embossed with the name of the shop waiting for her on her bedside table. She nibbled at the fluted oblongs of rich chocolate, sharing them with her mother, and the matter was thus – with the minimum of fuss or, even, embarrassment – consumed, as it were.

Through a friend of a friend her mother had been put in touch with the proprietor of a jute retailing business, who acted as the London representative of a Dundee firm of manufacturers. He himself had come to the firm via the Army, and wasn't at all the usual business sort, her mother told her – when she did eventually tell her.

'A gentleman,' she said. 'With a very nice wife, a Maughan-Treve.'

'I see.'

Her mother looked disapprovingly at her. Her confidence deserved better than a curt 'I see'.

'The work has its interesting side. Captain Jackson has explained it to me very well.'

'What – what do you do?'

'Light secretarial duties. They're very necessary, Captain Jackson says, but it's difficult to imagine it's really "employment" – '

'I see.'

'Captain Jackson is very considerate. I hardly think of him as my employer even.'

'Does *he* have employers?'

'Well, not technically "employers". He thinks of himself as his own man. A manufacturer's agent, have you heard of such a thing?'

Penelope nodded, but was almost certain that she hadn't heard of anyone in a situation with that name.

'Well, I suppose that's what he is.'

'I see.'

She saw her mother frown again, more darkly. It's bad enough that I have to tell you this, the scowl meant, without your taking such an uppity attitude. You're my daughter, you're a child of this house, you live as I do, as the times and our needs demand. I wouldn't be working, having to work, if I could have chosen: this is history's doing, in a man's world. As she thought it, Penelope was immediately sorry for her mother, that the job had been compelled on her. If *she* hadn't had to be educated, never to take such work herself . . .

Her sympathy didn't seem to please her mother. Her face grew long and serious. The sigh reached up out of her stomach.

2

For several years they were the best friends in the world, even though Penelope thought she really knew very little about Valerie Hutton and her private thoughts. Later, in their teens, Valerie started to detach herself, while continuing to insist on their friendship. She had her own holiday friends, who were all a year or two older than she was but who accepted her and taught her to sail: Penelope would have been glad if they'd accepted *her* too, but it was as if Valerie wanted to have two types of friend and they shouldn't mix.

Ever since she was eleven Penelope had spent most of the summer with the Huttons. Valerie was a year older than she, but had repeated her last year at prep school after she'd missed three months' work through glandular fever quarantine and her convalescence. Thus they had become academic equals at the boarding-school they were both sent to but not *physical* contemporaries: Penelope always felt the difference in their ages was more than a year, that Valerie was charging into – first – puberty, then adolescence, then adulthood, and each time well ahead of *her*.

The Huttons had a second home on the North Coast of Cornwall, a villa called Tregarrick set among a dozen or so other superior villas and bungalows on Polwynn headland. The sea was on one side of them, and a shallow estuary of sandbanks on the other. The houses were reached by a lane, which forked from another of deep shadows running downhill to a bay with a wide beach of soft sand and famously safe bathing.

Penelope would always remember the tarry smell of creosote from the fence dividing the path from the strip of kitchen garden. In time it was to become the distilled essence of summer holidays, of her youth.

Wet bathing-costumes pegged up on a line between apple trees; seaweed hanging drying from doorhandles; the slate flagstones in the kitchen gritty with sand; along the windowsills, shells and husks and pincers of pink crabs piled up behind curtains, to be forgotten about; buckets and spades thrown down and lost sight of; new holiday-reading passions to be discovered – *The Treasure Seekers, Swallows and Amazons.*

Birds nested in the clematis. They came every year, a different pair, refurbishing the previous year's nest. They stayed for a season, then they were gone.

For some years Valerie's younger brother Oliver had his own room while the two girls preferred to share.

51

At first Penelope felt out of her element. She touched the objects she found in the house just like a thief, lightly with her fingertips, as if she was a trespasser and interloper: as if other people's lives had a desirable density and mass which hers for the while did not.

The summer rituals – the walk up to the post office first thing for milk, collecting the lunchtime pasties from the Tyrolean Bakery with the cowbells on the back of the shop door, the picnic teas every afternoon down in the dunes. In the car, covering the last few miles of the annual journey, Mrs Hutton would call out all the familiar landmarks, 'Look! girls, Oliver!' – the signpost with the three pointing fingers, the standing stone with the carved man on a cross, the house where the famous playwright lived. Penelope always remembered the first year she spied Valerie in the driving-mirror rubbing at condensation on the window and looking quite unastonished by it all.

Any of the years. At the table in the kitchen Valerie is building a house of cards. Floor by floor: she has the patience and the sureness of touch to build her houses taller than anyone else's.

Then, when the inevitable end comes to her towers, the collapse is violent and dramatic in a way that it isn't for the rest of their structures.

Also – as the floors fold in, Penelope can't not notice that Valerie's face has a queer kind of glory shining out of it. She finds that – both the glory and her own looking for it – unsettling.

One particular year the tortoiseshell cat which makes this garden her home is carrying a litter in her belly. She treads carefully through the no-man's-land of jungle between the hoed beds and the clipped hedges. Her bulging flanks swing from side to side like panniers, and maybe somewhere in her mental reckoning there is the thread of a memory, spun out of her innards, of a dark encounter with an unknown tom, in a garden just like this one in another of her lives.

There was an antique coffer in the hall, which was kept locked. Penelope would hear bottles rattling inside, but she couldn't tell what else was there.

How many bottles, anyway? In the kitchen cupboards and in the triangular wall cabinet in the sitting-room there were more glasses and schooners to drink from than she had ever seen in a house before.

She had found discarded bottles in the garage, at the back of the airing-cupboard, in the orchard, dropped in the fuchsia beside the latch gate in the lane.

A neatly folded piece of notepaper falls out of a book.

Deer Mummy and Daddy, I am sory when I lost my tempor. I am sory I broak my cup. I shall pay you out of my poket mony. I doan't know why I lost my tempor.

love from your doter, Valerie.

The evenings took on their own ritual order.

After his afternoon's golf and when supper had been cleared away, Mr Hutton would sit out on the verandah. Inside, Mrs Hutton would take possession of the sitting-room as her own.

Sometimes Penelope and Valerie, with or without Oliver, went for walks, out along the beach in the darkness. Or, letting Mr and Mrs Hutton think that was where they had gone, they would find the blackest shadows in the orchard and from their safety they would just stand watching the two of them.

The foghorn might be hooting from the next bay but one, a low controlled panic wrapped in a muslin bag.

Indoors, Mrs Hutton read, or wrote letters to her old schoolfriends, or sewed, or listened to the wireless with her elbow resting on the arm of the easy chair and her head in her hand. Music seeped out through the closed windows.

Outside, yellow light from the small-paned doors overlaid the pattern of the crazy paving on the terrace like a chessboard. On the table beside Mr Hutton there was always a tumbler of whisky and soda. He would light his pipe and then blue smoke would rise up into the flowering clematis. He would sit for ages and do nothing except sip and breathe smoke, and look up into the tumbling mass of clematis.

The orchard would be damp underfoot. Occasionally an apple thudded into the long grass behind them both. Frogs croaked and snails trailed their silver slime. An owl always hooted from the pines beside the golf course; the pair of wood pigeons in the cedar would wake and stir anxiously. There was a striped cat, not the tortoiseshell, which would pass between the apple trees, halting momentarily as it spotted the girls standing there; Penelope would watch its irises grow in its yellow eyes – and then it would lower its head and the shine would disappear from the eyes as it turned back to its stalking track and its stripes blurred into the grass.

They had noisy, fly-blown teas in the dunes and Mr Hutton would grab the sand in fistfuls and watch it trickling between his fingers. Oliver would sit stalking him through his fringe of hair.

A wasp would sting or drop into a mug of tea or sand would smart in someone's eye and thoughts of mortality were forgotten in the chaos. Mr Hutton attempted to do the proper fatherly thing that's expected to be done on such occasions but it was always Mrs Hutton who had the right word for the moment, who knew how stings were cured and how sand was to be teased out of the corner of a watery eye and how the hurt of spear grass on tender skin was spelled away.

In the quiet evenings Mrs Hutton, reading or sewing, was the stillness at the heart of the house. Beams twitched and the tiles on the roof shifted, but she sat in the lamplight and was constant.

At the back of the old toy cupboard, behind a loose-fitting shelf, Penelope found a crumpled tab-calendar for 1931, with each of the sixty-two days of

July and August most particularly, unforgivingly, X'd off like crossbones by a blunt brown colouring pencil.

For the last three weeks of another summer a child's red tin spade stuck out of the trunk of a silver birch, where it had ferociously sliced through bark, bast and cambium to the innermost core of heartwood, embedded as fast as the sword which only Arthur, with Merlin's magic, could wrest from the stone.

Two rocks, around which invisible currents and eddies pulled and sucked. Always pulling and sucking.

Mr Hutton sat in his Cornish garden before the war, blue cigarette smoke rising into the clematis and whisky tumbler to hand, while Mrs Hutton kept indoors, maybe listening to radio voices, sewing together the day's splits and tears, reading of other lives than her own.

From the gleaming holly hedge at the side of the house Penelope could see the other whitewashed or pebble-dashed, eminently desirable houses on the headland, becoming paler and more spectral as the moon sailed clear of the clouds.

Later she remembered them as ensorcelled houses; beghosted by their occupants' fears of disappointment, by the memories of their lives and other lives they *might* have had.

Much later, in the second half of the 1960s, she went back. Somehow the houses were all still standing, in the teeth of Atlantic storms and the slow destructive wrath of salt and spray, whitening in the moonshine. The walls and paintwork were attended to every two or three years; the rental prices rose annually in the 'Holiday Lets' columns of *The Times*; people – the 'right' people – continued to holiday here. Maybe some of them were the children of children of Edwardian children who came when the railway brought you, when you were driven sleepily the rest of the way in a pony-and-trap, and oil-lamps used to burn in isolated farmhouses up on the high fields in the days before a golf course had been conceived of.

On a rainy day they would pay their annual visit to the museum. Perhaps it was a disturbing collection for children to see, but they didn't think so at the time.

There was an ankle-shackle from the Dark Ages, a neck-brace from Cromwell's time to collar suspected witches, a Jack-o'-nine-tails to flail troublemakers on His Majesty's vessels. In one glass case there was a holy chalice displayed side-by-side with a black-sabbath cup.

As night gathered, apples would drop in the orchard. A cat prowled softly through the long grass like a jungle panther; on the crazy-paving terrace, in the chequered lamplight falling through the french windows, Mr Hutton sat under a ripe clematis where small birds nested. His elbows leaned on the arms of the chair and his head was in his hand. Indoors, Mrs Hutton sat pulling at threads, as if she was drawing the day together.

From years away, with the war and the New Look far behind her and in the age of pea-jackets and suede boots and the country's slow decline, Penelope stood on the headland and remembered. The moon above her was an old mellow moon, polished to marble whiteness with a duster, shining down the lost years.

3

Fifteen months after her mother took up her position with Jackson's Jute Importers, bad went to worse.

'I'm afraid,' her mother said, 'I really have no alternative.'

'No alternative about . . . ?'

'Making some alterations to our way of life.'

'"Alterations"?'

'I'm told that the bottom has slipped out of the jute business.'

'What does that mean?'

'It means, that there really isn't enough work for them at Jackson's. *Captain* Jackson's. It's rather tedious just sitting there twiddling your thumbs, thinking of all the things that need to be done here. So – ' her mother drew herself up ' – so I've decided my services are no longer required there.'

Well, her bravery had to be acknowledged: not in handing in her notice, but pretending that that's how it had been, not that the decision had been taken for her.

Penelope nodded.

'They're not getting the new supplies, evidently. Not as they used to.'

That might have been so. But jute was an unknown quantity to Penelope, and never discussed in the house. Maybe it was only what Captain Jackson had told her mother, and *she* had no way of knowing either.

'So I set my brain to work.'

'Yes.'

'This house is *far* too big, you know. Just for us.' The briskness was her mother performing at her most mannered. 'We could live somewhere smaller, I thought. Or we *could* make the house do some work for *us*.'

Her mother smiled, inviting a smile in return. Penelope awkwardly obliged.

'There are certain people who simply don't want the bother of houses and the upkeep.'

'Who?' Penelope asked.

'Boarders. PGs.'

Her mother's smile looked very shaky.

'I've advertised, you see.'

Penelope stared at her, smile abandoned.

'I ask that they only come if it's for a short time. I think that's most sensible. People have all sorts of reasons. If they're moving home themselves, or looking

56

for somewhere to live, or returning to this country. They'd like somewhere pleasant – '

'*Here?*'

'It seemed the easiest solution. Although it requires a lot of work.'

Penelope didn't reply.

'Haven't you anything to say?'

'What?'

'Thurlestone teaches you better than that, surely?'

Penelope pulled in her mouth.

'Well . . . ?'

'But why do they have to come *here?*'

'I've told you.'

'But it'll all be different.'

'You're away at Thurlestone – '

'Not in the holidays.'

'I might have known you'd be awkward about it, Penelope Milne.'

'You didn't *tell* me – '

'Well, I've decided,' her mother said, her impatience undisguised. 'So that's that.'

Penelope remembered the evening of Mr Chapman's telephone call.

'I've got hold of a part-time help.' Her mother flicked at some dust on the lip of a vase. 'And of course, when you're home in the holidays – '

Penelope stared at her, then looked past her.

'Just some housework. To help.'

'But – can't *they* do it?'

When Penelope looked in the silence that followed, her mother's face was immobile, an omen she was quite familiar with.

'I suppose you think you're just going to *sail* through your life?'

'I – I don't know.'

'*I* thought so once. Now, let me tell you, now I know quite differently.'

'I only – '

'I don't need your excuses, Penelope. There'll always be *some*thing you won't have calculated on.'

Penelope said nothing. She didn't understand what she was being educated for, if it wasn't to rid herself of the obligation of fagging. None of the mistresses at school had ever hinted that their lot should be a subservient one, except – it was taken as a premise – to a husband. Domestic science was on the timetable, but drudgery wasn't.

'One day you'll realise. It had better be before too long, for your own good.'

So, now it was for her 'good', was it?

'Yes,' Penelope said, and squeezed out an intentionally shrivelled smile.

'I'm glad this amuses you so much.'

The smile was tempered.

'This, let me tell you – ' Her mother fixed on her, as if she meant her never to forget what she was telling her. ' – this is getting off lightly, it's like a free pardon.'

From a drawer in the chest in her bedroom Valerie took out ten or a dozen photographs of various sizes. They all showed the same woman: she had a long, tapering, oval face with fine, perhaps nervous features, on top of a slender elongated neck. A man was also included in several of them: Penelope recognised him as a much younger version of Mr Hutton.

'Who is she?'

Valerie laid out the photographs on top of the chest.

'Do you like her?'

'Yes. I think so.'

'I thought you would.'

'But who is she?'

'She's my mother.'

'What?'

'I've collected them. From people. A private collection, of course.'

'But . . .'

Mrs Hutton was downstairs mending the rip in Oliver's blue trousers.

'No, that's not her,' Valerie said.

'Who's not?'

She pointed to the floor and the room beneath them.

'What?'

'She's not my *real* mother.'

'She isn't?'

'She's Oliver's mother. She's my *step*mother.'

'How – '

Valerie reordered the photographs.

'I don't remember anything about her. My real one. I wish I could. I've tried, but I can't. It doesn't seem very much to do, to remember someone. But I was too young.'

'What – when – '

'We don't talk about it. We've never talked about it.'

'Not even with your father?'

'Well, she died. Not *just* "died". That's what I'm meant to think. But I looked it up in a newspaper, you see. In a library. It was made to look like an accident, she left a gas-fire on and she was supposed to have fallen asleep, but the police didn't think so. It was in a hotel, in Ilfracombe. The other guests must have been talking about her, about how strange she was.'

'Was she? Strange?'

'*They* thought so.'

'Maybe they – '

'I found some letters. In London. In a drawer, they were inside an envelope. He's still got them, my father.'

58

'Letters? What kind?'

'They hadn't been opened. Most of them anyway. They were all to the same man. Not my father, though.'

'Who? Who to?'

'Somebody Anderson.'

'Who's that?'

The question was answered by a shrug.

'You don't know what they said?'

Valerie hesitated. 'If you never tell – '

'What?'

'I mean, *never*.'

'No. No, I won't.'

'I steamed some open, over a kettle. It's quite easy, though it crinkles the envelopes a bit. I thought the ink might run, but it was too old.'

'What – what did they say?'

'Actually they were a bit silly.'

Valerie bit her lip.

'How – how were they silly?'

'Sort of lovey-dovey. Sort of. But I mean, they *could* have been written to *any*body. More or less. They weren't really anything about *him*, so I couldn't discover – '

'You don't know?'

'I *think* . . .'

Penelope watched as she rearranged the photographs, like playing cards.

'Well, I've thought about it. Maybe she knew him once. The man. But it was before she married. And maybe he got married too.'

'So she stopped?'

'Oh *no*. The letters were *afterwards* – '

'She wrote the letters even though she was married? To your father?'

'I expect that's *why* she wrote them.'

Penelope stared at her; she didn't understand as she felt she should. She saw Valerie looking back at her inscrutably.

'Well, it doesn't matter.'

'But if she was married . . . d'you mean . . .'

'She just wrote them. She can't have *got* any back. Of *his*. She *sent* them, but he didn't *read* them. He didn't even open them.'

'He kept them, though?'

'I suppose so. They were franked, so they must have gone through the post. But he sent them back.'

'When?'

'I don't know. To her. Or to my father.'

'She really *didn't* fall asleep?'

'What's that?'

Valerie swept up the photographs into a pile.

'She didn't fall asleep? In front of the fire? In Ilfracombe?'

'I don't think so.'

'She left on the gas?'

'Yes.'

'Deliberately?'

'Well, the police guessed that. I don't know. They must have had reasons, mustn't they? To think that.'

Penelope looked at the thin, ballerina's face and neck on the photograph on top of the pile.

'Perhaps she was just bored,' Valerie said. 'Bored out of her mind. Thinking she just had to go on and on and on . . .'

'"*Bored*"?'

'Isn't it pretty boring? If you haven't got what you really want?'

'How do you know that? What it is you want?'

'Well, it's worse if you don't. And all you *do* know is that it's not what you've got.'

The photographs were put back in the drawer and the drawer closed.

'I'm glad you told me, Valerie.'

'Really?'

'Yes.'

Penelope lowered herself on to the bed and perched on the edge of the mattress. She felt quite in the thrall of this surfeit of experience someone of her own age (almost) had revealed to her. But she also sat wondering how things could contrive to be between them as they used to be: she wondered if 'now' and 'then' were the true point, because hadn't they been the most different of people all along, from the very beginning?

'Well, I *have* told you.'

'Yes.'

Penelope ran her hands along her thighs to her knees, several times, and did so without realising, until she looked at Valerie and saw her smiling at her in a newly personal, intimate way.

'You take the sun like Oliver,' she said.

Penelope was surprised to hear it.

'Do I?' she asked.

'You've got quite a lot in common. You and Oliver. One way and another.'

Valerie's smile didn't flag. The earlier scowls for the life downstairs were forgotten. The smile, Penelope was on the verge of understanding, belonged to a woman of the world, and led where she was not versed to follow.

But one of the photographs, accidentally or not, wasn't returned to the drawer in the chest.

Mrs Hutton found it. With the door of the room left open, Penelope heard their exchange on the subject.

'I didn't know you had any photographs, Valerie.'

'I must have dropped it.'

'She – she's very striking, isn't she?'

'Haven't you seen her before?'

'A long time ago.'

'Didn't Father show you?'

'When we first met.'

'But not since then?'

'I don't suppose so. No.'

'Why not?'

'Why not? I've no idea. Because . . .'

'Because what?'

'Because he didn't think – I'd be interested maybe.'

'Aren't you? Interested?'

'Well, I . . . I never knew her . . .'

'My mother?'

'If you want to call her that.'

'She is, though, isn't she?'

'I am too. I've been your mother all your life, more or less.'

'More or less, yes.'

'We've been a family.'

'I'll put it away.'

'Yes.'

Pause.

'I wonder if it's a good likeness, Valerie?'

'You'll have to ask Father about that.'

'Yes.'

'*He'll* know.'

'Yes. If he can remember.'

'Why shouldn't he?'

'Well . . . time moves on. Memories . . .'

'They don't disappear.'

'No. But they change, Valerie.'

'Not if you want to remember.'

'Maybe that's the point then.'

'You always say Father's got a good memory.'

'I've left a pot on in the kitchen, Valerie. I'm glad we've accounted for the photograph.'

'Didn't you know who it was?'

'Well, I think I guessed.'

Pause.

'I don't know how it landed under your bed. It would have got into Mrs Jepps's vacuum-cleaner.'

'I wouldn't have forgiven her.'

'But it didn't.'

'I could put it in a frame.'

'That – that might seem strange to Oliver. And Penelope.'

'I don't see why.'

'But you're younger than I am, Valerie.'

'I'm old enough.'

'Yes. Perhaps. But I'm not sure if a frame is the place for it. If your father would quite agree with you either.'

'You'll ask him, then?'

'*You* can ask him, if you like.'

'Why not you?'

'It was *your* idea, Valerie. So I think it's your job to ask him.'

Even where she was, in her own bedroom, her friend's sigh reached Penelope, clear and proud and sheerly exasperated.

The subject was one which Penelope felt she must return to one more time.

Maybe her friend guessed as much. They were crossing the beach at the end of an afternoon when Valerie made some mention of her mother.

Penelope found the courage not to let the matter slip.

'When – when did your mother . . .'

'When did my mother what – ?'

'Well . . .'

'Die?'

Penelope swallowed. 'Yes.'

'I was just a baby.'

'Oh.'

'A year old or so.'

Penelope considered.

'Then your father married again? After that?'

'Yes. Quite soon.'

Penelope sank her heels into the worm-casts.

'I think he wanted to marry the opposite probably. She's very different. A bit of a china doll, I heard someone say. Pretty-pretty, in a way. Or she was. She's quite dull really.'

'"Dull"?'

'Well, isn't she? My father doesn't seem to mind.'

'She's – ' Penelope thought quickly ' – she doesn't lose her temper – '

'She's good at what she does, I'll say that for her. Or maybe that's not saying so much, because it's all that really interests her.'

'Oliver's your *half*-brother? And you're his *half*-sister?'

'It's more complicated than that. She was a widow, and she already had Oliver. He's my kind of quarter-brother.'

'What?'

'It's not *so* complicated. And not so special really. Everyone just has to shake down. My father said.'

They both fell silent for a while. The bare soles of their feet beat on the hard sand.

'Maybe my father felt sorry for my mother. *This* mother, I mean. And that's why he married her.'

'"Sorry"?'

'She was a widow and she had a baby. Well, toddler. And there was my mother – the other one – I suppose she was preying on his mind.'

'You think so?'

'She's got a haunting face, hasn't she? My real mother?'

Penelope considered again.

'Yes,' she decided. 'Yes, I think she has.'

'Sometimes I dream about her. That's strange, because I don't *remember* her. Then I think she really must be a kind of ghost, and she can come back and haunt us.'

Penelope stared at her.

'Of course you've got to *want* to be haunted. That's very important.'

'I don't know,' Penelope said. Valerie was so calm and collected about it; she seemed to believe that such a thing could be possible. 'It's never happened to me.'

'You'll only see a ghost if you believe in it.'

'"Believe"?' Penelope repeated.

'All but.'

'And *you* do?'

'I do now. But I didn't *not* believe then. So I was like a house just waiting to be haunted, you see.'

But, Penelope came to feel, it really wasn't quite so straightforward as Valerie had convinced herself, this spectral magic, and – on the matter of houses – Tregarrick wasn't such an open one after all.

'Paying guests,' her mother would remind her, 'is what they are.'

But to Penelope they were intruders in the house. They loaded them both with their personalities and their problems. She also realised that they were serving her mother's purpose in a sense other than financial, even if *she* had no awareness of it. They allowed her to be the person she believed it was her right to be.

They weren't *really* guests at all, and – ironically – mother and daughter weren't at polar extremes in their attitudes. Penelope saw how the lodgers were treated with perfect courtesy, and yet they were allowed no privileges; they filled up space in the house and swallowed the air but her mother reduced their personalities to the point where they only served certain aspects of her own. She could instruct the Indian woman medical student in the geography of Rajdasthan and Gujarat because Penelope's great-uncle had been a trader there; with Herr Brugger she could practise her choicely accented German which she'd learned from a Fräulein at school who'd given lessons to the Spanish royal children; she confirmed that the young New Zealand woman who made her own clothes didn't know all the ins-and-outs of the seamstress's art; by dropping names she was able to show the superior Argentinian gentleman that she could more than hold her own in discussing the highfalutin circles he laid such (dubious) claim to.

Their little League of Nations in Lithgow Road lasted less than five years in toto. To Penelope it seemed much longer. The house would be full – with refills – every time she came back from school for the holidays. Her mother told her she kept the door of her bedroom locked in her absence, but she would have the uncomfortable suspicion that it wasn't as airless inside as it ought to have been, that the windows had been opened quite recently for too short a time with the purpose of letting out a presence.

The whole house was haunted by their lodgers and by the spirit of those who had preceded them: the Chinese botanist studying the specimens at Kew Gardens who kept the dirt beneath his long nails; the lofty Cuban widow – more than a match for the Argentinian – who claimed she'd lost a fortune and was apprehended removing the canteen of fish cutlery; the fresh-faced and neurotically hygienic Welsh dental student who left the bathroom awash on his bath nights; the anonymous Irish girl with the thick ankles and delicate anchorite's hands and Egyptian cigarettes who was writing a novel and never wanted to set eyes on Connemara and Ormand Quay and Capel Street again.

In the middle period, when she thought that the 'arrangement' was never going to end, Penelope was only minimally civil to those she was required to share the house with. She knew that her mother expected more and better of her, but she told herself that she ought not to be surprised after her spending term-time in the company that she did. She was being snobbish, even more so than her mother, and it irked her to realise it, but she felt that her nature was something that was already out of her hands.

Worst to Penelope was the ordeal of mealtimes. They were as a trial out of the Bible to her. She endured them only because she taught herself to believe that she must win her reward for her suffering: an earthly one, since the concept of heaven was more or less foreign to her now. There were occasions when her mother appeared to turn a blind eye to manners and table etiquette, at the very times when a salutary cough or the raising of a querying eyebrow might have been called for. The conversation – in fractured English – was painful, talking for the perverse sake of talking. Some people couldn't control themselves, and the words – like the particles of food – fell out of their mouths without their seeming to realise.

Penelope dreaded that anyone at school might discover; her mother seemed to be in sympathy with her thoughts at least, and would suggest instead (paid) trips with her friends for afternoon tea at Derry and Tom's or Gunter's.

Penelope didn't care to have the pound note slipped so obtrusively into her purse; she would have been content that they should do their entertaining in the house, if it had only been their own. However, the Royal Worcester dinner-service stayed in the locked display-cabinet unused, and every so often her mother dunked the best cutlery in silver dip to prevent disuse from tarnishing it: it didn't make any sense to Penelope that they should own things but not be able to use them and still have to earn a living in such a modest, demeaning way.

That was the dark side of her life at that time, and there were dismal days when she was vexed to consider if she was ever going to right herself again.

4

They stayed at the tennis courts until the sun was almost in the sea and their spaghetti shadows reached up the fencing at the sides. One half of each court would be webbed by the shadow of the net.

Penelope would always feel the chill first, even through her woollens. Valerie was never ready to go home. She was one of the last playing on the court, and one of the last lingering in the pavilion, then on the verandah, then on the steps, then at the bushes where anyone who brought a bicycle threw it down.

There was a certain tree she leaned against, with the sole of one foot placed on the trunk under her thigh and the sun falling on her face like a spotlight. While he waited, Oliver paced backwards and forwards on the path; his racquet would be pointing at the red cinders and he would aim the toe of his shoe at the wood on the head. Valerie would laugh and remember jokes, or she would lower her voice for a confidence with her friends. She would discuss any newcomers, rumour-monger about them. She would place her arms behind her, seeming to clasp the tree's trunk, like a martyr in history.

Beneath the trees Penelope felt the day running down. She took her cue to leave from the Easton girls, who perfectly intuited that there was a certain moment to go, and no later, just as the gnats flew out of the bushes, inadvertently thrashed by tennis racquets, and before the air grew heavier as daylight started to seep from it, and before the daisies in the grass closed to pink and dampness rose green through white plimsoles.

Bicycles were retrieved from the undergrowth. Sometimes Oliver walked with her, sometimes he trailed behind. Girls often talked about him, his dark and brooding looks they called 'moody', but he seemed not to be listening; his eyes would look at the ground and he'd aim more of those light kicks at his racquet, staining the wood a redder red from the cinders. The older boys didn't include him, maybe because they were older, or because he made no overtures himself, or because there was too much to discover about the rest of their lives, away from Polwynn and Cornwall. Penelope would see Oliver watching them when he thought no one was looking, and she guessed – in her innocence – that he really did want to belong, just as Valerie did with *her* friends. They were all older than Penelope, and naturally *she* was excluded: she joined in when they let her, though, and she drifted out again when the gossip became their own, about their lives when they returned home at the end of the summer.

*

'Do you like Oliver?' Valerie asked.

Penelope pulled herself up in her corner of the sofa.

'"Like" him?'

'*Like* him,' Valerie repeated.

'Yes.' Penelope nodded. 'Yes.'

'He's good-looking.'

'Yes,' Penelope said. 'Yes, he is.'

'Handsome, people say.'

'Yes.'

'Does *he* like *you*?'

'I – I don't know – '

'Has he told you?'

'No.'

Valerie's lips pursed before she spoke.

'Well, he should do.'

'Not – not if he doesn't want to – should he?'

'If he'd any sense he would. He's older than you.'

'He's a boy, though.'

'That's the point,' Valerie fired back.

'"The point"?'

'He *should* have a girlfriend.'

'Oh.'

'Don't sound so surprised – '

Penelope hesitated.

'But – but not every girl – has a boyfriend – '

'No?'

'Well, I don't know,' Penelope admitted.

'Since when have boyfriends not been allowed?'

'I – I didn't say "allowed",' Penelope ventured. 'There's – '

'Take my word for it, it's what happens. Sooner or later.'

Penelope said nothing.

'Later in Oliver's case,' his sister said.

'He's only fifteen.'

'Nearly sixteen.'

'He's got time – '

'Says who?'

'Well – hasn't he?'

'He's not even *looking*.'

'How d'you know that, though?'

'I'm his sister.'

'But maybe – '

'When my back's turned?' Valerie shook her head. 'I don't think so. I've been watching him.'

'Oh.'

'I just thought – because you were in the same house – '

Penelope made pleading eyes, but Valerie was unstoppable.

'Haven't you thought about it? Honestly?'

'What about?'

'You and Oliver, of course.'

Penelope shook her head.

'Not – not like that.'

Valerie raised her eyebrows quizzically in disbelief.

'It couldn't be better – '

'A *boyfriend*?' Penelope asked, truly surprised.

'Well . . . someone to be thinking about. Until then. You know?'

Penelope supposed the reference must be to *It*. Valerie was the one who had informed her. But that – the business – had always involved other people's lives, because their minds were turned to It.

'Maybe he'll just jump on you,' Valerie said, but she sounded doubtful.

'Maybe,' Penelope agreed, so that they might be rid of the subject.

'Right on top of you. Without a warning.'

After that Penelope was on red-alert. But although she kept looking she saw nothing in Oliver's behaviour to suggest that thoughts of any such sort were even in his mind. She discounted the possibility of an approach until Valerie mentioned it again. She continued to watch, but Oliver betrayed no interest that wasn't compatible with being her friend's brother. And yet Valerie continued to insist.

'He *is* very nice,' she replied when Valerie asked her the question again. 'But – '

'But what?'

'I think he quite likes his own company.'

'That's the trouble,' Valerie rattled back at her.

'Maybe it can't be helped, though.'

'Maybe not. Or maybe it can.'

'But it's up to him,' Penelope said.

'He needs a good push. A shove.'

'I don't know – '

'Well, *he* doesn't know. That's for sure.'

'Maybe we should just – '

'Just what?'

' – let him alone?'

Valerie smiled, quietly enough. In later years Penelope recognised better from experience the absences in that smile, of either humility or repentance, and what its true pulsion was, the conviction that neither of them – Oliver or his sister's friend – were qualified to manage their lives without her.

A girl appeared at the tennis courts one afternoon the next summer, with an American racquet in a cloth case.

Valerie was intrigued – by her appearance, her fine tanned skin and fair, well-cut hair, and by her air of expensive privilege – while feigning not to be. She positioned herself so that the group the girl was with was always in her sights; she watched past other people's heads while the girl seemed to be doing nothing with her time but chattering away.

It took several days for contact to be struck, and it only came about because the girl-with-the-American-racquet's bicycle took a puncture and because one of the party she was with heard that Oliver had a repair outfit in his satchel. Valerie nudged him in the ribs and told him to offer: which he did, but seeming to be embarrassed about it. His face filled with colour when the girl-with-the-American-racquet dropped a cheerful, carefully enunciated 'thank you' behind her shoulder and pedalled off down the track, coasting over dips and bumps. Valerie smiled to see the effect on him; she told her friends that the girl-with-the-American-racquet had made a conquest, and what was Oliver going to do about it?

'*Now* what, Oliver?'

'What – do you mean?'

Valerie kept her smile in place, but it turned grittier: when she smiled like that, Penelope always imagined how a mouthful of red tennis-court shale must taste.

'Well, is that it?'

He repeated her. ' "It"?'

'You've fixed her tyre for her.'

Oliver stashed the repair tin and the pump in his satchel.

'It'll need a new valve.'

'*You* could do it.'

'The garage – '

'*Offer* to do it.'

'She wouldn't – '

'You repaired *mine*.'

'That wasn't a valve.'

'You deserve everything you get, Oliver Hutton.'

She strode off, flailing her honest, British racquet at the yellow privet. Oliver stood watching, his face miserable. That handsome face, Penelope thought, which had no cause to be miserable or defeated, which should have been the stuff of girls' dreams.

'Anyone would think – ' But Valerie didn't tell her later what she was thinking, what it was she'd meant.

Valerie started to wear her brown hair as the fair girl-with-the-American-racquet did, tucked behind her ears and held by a velvet band *à la* Suzanne Lenglen, and abandoned white ankle-socks for the bare-legged look, and wore her pullover (actually in Valerie's case a cardigan, which – like the racquet and the plimsoles – couldn't be got exactly right) over her shoulders and loosely knotted in front, on her chest. She found a way of engineering an introduction and discovered that the girl was even more exotic than she'd thought, with an Italian father and a French mother: her family owned an electronics company, and she had lived in several European cities: currently 'home' was in Switzerland, but she had been sent to England to learn the language for six or seven months. And here, through friends of friends, she was in their midst; Valerie could hardly disguise her curiosity and admiration.

Even armed with an American racquet, the girl's performance wasn't above average for the courts. Her saving grace was that she moved with an antelope's athleticism, even if she was about to miss an easy shot. Very coolly she would recompose herself, as if indeed she had taken the point and was winning a game at Wimbledon; she shook out the pleats in her skirt and pulled any loose threads of hair behind her ear and checked with her fingers that the collar of her blouse was sitting quite flat. Her serve was on the weak side, but somehow her being Continental excused that; her backhand was extremely erratic, but delivering to a backhand was regarded as a bit of a cheat, even by aggressive competitors, and so she could be excused that too.

Valerie talked herself into, first, playing against the girl in mixed doubles, and then partnering her when an all-female quartet was made up one afternoon. Valerie missed a lot of shots she should have got, either because she was demurely leaving them to Milly (as the foreigner quaintly called herself) or – more probably – was concentrating less on the ball than on her partner. Penelope and Oliver joined the cheering whenever a point was won or a second ball being served to them blundered into the net; they tut-tutted and groaned if the opponents questioned the net height, but showed no emotion when a return shot from Valerie or Milly went haywire or they sent a lob skimming over the top of the perimeter fence and crash-landed the ball in the bushes.

'It's only a game, thank goodness,' Valerie said after their first match together, pronouncing the words as c-l-e-a-r-l-y as she would have done in a French oral test. 'They didn't deserve to win, but they'd have been bad losers.' That day and on those following she trailed Milly about, shadowing her as if she had been a twin sister and her other half. The Swiss-girl-with-the-American-racquet hardly noticed maybe, she was polite in an impersonal way, automatically well-mannered but unconcerned. The distance and detachment Milly so courteously observed was possibly another reason for Valerie's intense interest in her: she was someone who switched 'on' or 'off', approached or kept apart just as she chose, just as it suited *her*, and her behaviour couldn't be prejudged. It was her brazen independence which must be the clue to the sort of person she was and the head-turning effect that she had.

Someone told someone, who told Valerie, who didn't tell Penelope but told one of her nearly-friends, who told someone else who let it slip to Penelope, presuming that she knew or was old enough to comprehend.

The girl-with-the-American-racquet had been seen down on the beach at night, jumper knotted over her shoulders and making for the dunes. The person she was with had been swimming in the sea, in his underpants: not anyone Penelope could have guessed at, but a thickset man with a bald head and a deep, rumbling laugh. He took the girl-with-the-American-racquet's hand and ran with her up the beach, towards the empty dunes of blown, warm sand, overgrown with sighing spear grass.

Valerie's mother seemed reconciled to her tasks; Penelope couldn't help comparing her behaviour to that of her own mother, who gave the impression of resenting the time that had to be expended, on PGs or not, whether it was making one of her tried-and-tested mousse moulds or snicking the stems off flowers to fit them into an arrangement. Mrs Hutton was never without a job in hand, and she appeared to apply herself to whatever it was quite willingly. Just sitting with them in the evening she would have created a nest of careful clutter about her – scissors, bobbins and skeins of thread, knitting wool and needles, notepaper and pen, postcards. She was never not in a state of readiness.

Penelope realised that what was being presented to them wasn't the whole story, and that Valerie's mother was more complicated than she wanted them to believe she was. The ploy deserved a little of her admiration. The whetted scissors strode across gingham, the knitting-needles clacked (although the second-cousin's baby for whom the jacket was intended would know nothing about it), the pen scraped over sheets of notepaper (harmonious cursive script, large handwriting, a minimum of four flowing sides to each letter, so that the recipients might imagine they were being done an especial favour with so much attention). But what was she thinking where none of them could see?

She would look up without warning, needles still busy or pen scuttling across the paper, and Penelope would blush, feeling her suspicions must be obvious for her to read from her face. Valerie's mother would just smile, and the next second her eyes would drop to the task and there would seem no more to it than that: a task was being attended to because someone had to, and it was *her* place, *she* was the point at which all their concerns and wants met.

Going away anywhere on an outing, Penelope noticed, induced an alertfulness, as if no situation was to be quite depended on: much as she felt about their evenings all together in the house. But the hazards in the house, whatever those were, were controlled: away from it, even the familiar places might have been colluding in a conspiracy, to judge from Mrs Hutton's watchfulness and a frequent expression of mild dismay when her eyes would open too widely. Mr Hutton and other women, the sort who were as vigilant as she, were her main preoccupation. With her husband, even standing in a shop or walking where there were people about, she was taking an extra-critical view of the situation. It was then that Penelope felt some of her suspiciousness justified, catching Mrs Hutton's eyes as they swivelled into action and swooped on a detail: how her husband was holding his hands as he stood, how his tie was knotted, which particular woman in his immediate vicinity was paying him attention. When they were publicly *en famille*, neither Valerie nor Oliver appeared to pick up their mother's methods, and Penelope felt she was being deceitful and treacherous, given that the family had never stinted in its hospitality to her. At least Mrs Hutton didn't seem aware that she was being so closely observed in her turn, and so the guilt of betraying the other's trust of her remained the girl's own secret, which was a very doubtful solace to her.

5

The worst of the PGs was Mr Jardine. He was a small, hunched Scotsman of sixty or so, with a goatee beard and a lazy eye and a proliferation of couthy burrs in his speech. He smelt of mothballs, and rumour had it that when he was in his room (her father's old study) his tweed suit stayed in the wardrobe while he walked about or sat in his flannel vest and combinations.

Penelope had soon noticed how often he looked at her with his working eye. When he wasn't, or was pretending that he wasn't, his bad pupil would roll about in its socket and follow her notwithstanding. She hated to see it but couldn't stop herself looking.

He tried to make conversation with her at every opportunity. At every opportunity she tried to resist. She invented more and more elaborately pressing excuses why she had to leave the room but he only smiled in response.

She thought she might have counted on her mother's support in the matter, but – very much to her surprise – her mother flinched whenever she yawed and tacked round Mr Jardine, and even started to coax her into staying, into being more polite to him.

'Why should I?'

'Because – because he's our guest. Sort of.'

'We didn't *invite* him.'

'No. But – '

'We're stuck with him.'

'He *pays*, Penelope.'

Her mother spoke the words most decisively. But Penelope was in no mood for pragmatics.

'So?'

'And – and he pays more than he might.'

'What? Why does he do that?'

'Because – because he believes I undercharge.'

'*Do* you?'

'*I* don't believe so.'

'If they're "guests", they shouldn't be thinking of things like what it costs.'

'Don't be impertinent, Penelope,' her mother rebuked her. 'And you've no right to speak ill of Mr – '

'I just know I don't want to talk to him.'

'Talk *some*times – '

'When?'

'When it's polite.'

'What about?'

'It doesn't have to be much.'

'*How* much?'

'Just a little,' her mother pleaded, 'please.'

One evening the sitting-room emptied of the PGs, all except for Mr Jardine. Penelope for once wasn't quick enough to think of a plausible excuse she hadn't used several times before and, at the mercy of circumstances, she decided she *would* allow him to talk to her, but only for a very short while.

He moved closer, using one finger as a marker between the pages of his newspaper, as if to let her know that his intention was only to discuss the affairs of the world with her.

When he was sitting on the next chair but one and he forgot – or seemed to forget – about the newspaper, so that it dropped on to his knees and then to the floor, she saw that his dress needed adjustment.

Immediately a sickness churned in her stomach, as if it had been there all along, only waiting. She had a sour, biley taste in her throat, which trickled into the bottom of her mouth.

It might have been a genuine mistake, because when he followed her eyes with his good one and it looked down at his lap, his face instantly shot scarlet. He grabbed the newspaper, stood up, turned his back on her and walked to the far end of the room. As she swallowed away the taste in her mouth, she watched his goblin's ears burning at their tips. Could he have simulated such discomfiture? But could he have sat with them all for an evening and failed to notice his oversight?

Whatever the explanation, she left the room assured in herself that she wasn't to be blamed any more, that she had given the obnoxious Mr Jardine his first and very last chance.

There could be no doubt that Penelope's calling in life was to be marriage.

Closeted with her in the intimidating study, Miss Saxby scanned the sheaf of reports on her desk.

'Not so good and not so bad,' she said, damning her.

The headmistress continued to consult the paperwork rather than raise her eyes to look directly at Penelope. That was her way.

Whenever she did look up, she would make a business of adjusting her spectacles. But Lydia Bayliss had told Penelope that she'd twice seen Miss Saxby staring after her outside in the courtyard, when she must have supposed she wasn't being watched. 'I think she's got the hots for you,' Lydia had told her, and Penelope had laughed at the ridiculousness of it and in the next minute she'd turned clammy when Lydia repeated the remark and added, 'It's as clear as day. She couldn't take her eyes off you.'

'There must've been a reason. Or she wasn't looking at me at all.'

'You really don't believe it?' Lydia said. She seemed quite bemused.

'Believe what?'

'You're so innocent, Penelope.'

'Why me, though?'

'You don't know?'

'No.' Penelope shook her head for emphasis. 'Truly.'

'*Some* of us are called – '

'How do you mean?'

But, of course, after four years at Thurlestone she already knew.

'You're the gods' favourite now, Penelope.'

'*Why*, though? Why me?'

'Because . . .'

'Because what?'

'. . . they don't know what you're thinking. How you look sometimes – '

'"Look"? What do you mean?'

'Empty. Blank.'

'*Thick*?'

'No. Just – faraway, I suppose. Quiet, still. As if you're somewhere else.'

Lydia Bayliss was the first person to tell her such a thing. After that she often stared at herself in the bathroom mirrors, lined above the row of basins. She waited for the same point in the process, the moment when she achieved the blankness, entered the stillness. It was like an act of self-hypnosis, which she had heard on the wireless the nutbrown Indians could will on themselves walking down a street.

It was uniformly expected at Thurlestone that a suitable class of man would present himself and, when he asked, one would do the only natural and proper thing – that is, gratefully respond, say 'yes' with alacrity, and in the fullness of time wed him. Being set up together, he would provide the wherewithal while one would duly attend to the cutting and trimming of the cloth. The future for any Thurlestone Girl couldn't be more straightforward.

'We aim to provide you with the rudiments of a *practical* education,' the Chairman of the Board of Governors annually pronounced. 'Practicality is all.'

'So-so,' Miss Saxby summed up unsmilingly of her record. Which was only, Penelope realised, as it was supposed to be. Every year a certain sizeable proportion of the girls was required to occupy the middle-ground of potential and achievement. Like the swots, the social high-flyers had already been marked out long ago, those with 'connections'. What was less easy to make calculations about were 'looks', either attained or attainable: in that department of life the mistresses were no experts. Again Penelope considered herself to occupy the middle-ground, spared the unenviable burden of male leering and female jealousy.

'So . . .'

Miss Saxby swept the reports into a little pile. Detritus. She continued to look anywhere but in her direction. The word 'So . . .' made a thin echo in the room: to Penelope, seated on the opposite side of the desk, it was a matter-of-fact but weary-sounding verdict on what might be anticipated in the time ahead, what opportunities the future would bring. Miss Saxby sat pulling at a snag on the sleeve of her tweed jacket beneath her gown; her mouth was prim and censorious. Penelope shifted uneasily in her chair, not knowing if she was free to leave.

'It's thought rather old-fashioned nowadays, I gather,' Miss Saxby said without looking up, 'but *I* was always instructed to sit with my spine flat against the back of a chair.'

Penelope pulled herself up straight.

'That's what *we*'ve always taught. I dare say it's done our girls no harm, quite a lot of good indeed. They appreciate it later.'

Penelope didn't speak.

'It's very useful for dressage,' Miss Saxby said. 'Phoebe Venables told me so herself just the other day.'

If alumna Phoebe Venables had told her so, then there was no gainsaying it: what *she* didn't know about horses wasn't supposed to be worth knowing. The observation, however seasoned, didn't make Penelope feel any better; she wasn't aware that dressage referred to herself in any way.

'It looks to me,' Miss Saxby said, taking care not to lift her eyes, 'that we should just keep a steady course and a clear head.'

It was a favourite Miss Saxby turn-of-phrase: she meant that the circumstances were too dull for her to think originally about, that *this* girl's future didn't deserve it.

Penelope looked back at her stonily. Might it be that with all her experience Miss Saxby was perfectly correct? Which was to say, if she held to a steady course and kept a clear head, then she might have her likely end – a husband and marriage? Rashly, in these moments, Penelope was no longer convinced that that was such a desirable state of being. She didn't know *why* she should suddenly be so sceptical: although, very fleetingly, the memory came back to her of climbing the stairs on tiptoe to Nancy's room and hearing her laughter intertwined with her father's, like party streamers. And later, her mother's voice telling them on the afternoon of the funeral lunch, 'Of course he was away on business when it happened.'

Miss Saxby and the others were deciding for her. Because it had always been so, it continued being so. Penelope was suddenly wary, very dubious. Miss Saxby's unsettled, unfocusing eyes were her give-away: the assurance was just deliberate habit, because it became easier to say things without having to argue them, to prove them. Penelope sensed she was very near to getting the measure of Miss Henrietta Saxby: but when it came to the bit, she felt guilty, she was a little afraid too. If what she said was what she really believed . . . And hadn't she had· all her years of teaching to give her position and reputation and authority? Yet . . . if marriage was so excellent and desirable, why hadn't she pledged *herself* to it? Her directives would surely have had much more effect if she'd had the evidence of her own experience to back them up.

Penelope's conviction was that she had been misunderstood: also under-estimated – except that a Thurlestone Girl wasn't supposed to think proudly of herself. But no one had had the time or inclination to assess her worth properly. They merely deduced from the examples of precedent: she was judged by how she approximated to the greater number of her predecessors, and she must have been thought little different. The school's mission was to make its charges at any one time all resemble each other, as far as that could be done. By now Miss Saxby and Miss Whitstable and Miss Leitch were dab hands at it. They knew from Day One who the exceptions, one or two in every fresh batch, would be. Penelope Milne – however blank or empty – was not among those. It would be all *she* could do to be in the right place when the right man found her; after however long it customarily took, he would make his proposal, and she would accept. *Like*, Miss Saxby always implied without saying as much, *will be drawn to like*: her Thurlestone Girls didn't make mistakes, romance and love came quite far down the list of priorities, you attended to what mattered – a man's social and financial standing – which was only second nature after all. No one was going to marry below their station in life, although there was no rule against rising.

The Thurlestone class of 1936, like decent, well-brought-up young women anywhere in England, would just come in the end to 'know'.

'Penelope is the one in the hat.'

The voices murmured politely in the darkness. Penelope concentrated instead on the mechanical hum of the projector, on the dust dancing in the track of white light beamed at the screen.

Those collected in the room were granted several seconds more in which to admire their hostess's daughter. The whole business was humiliating to Penelope, at sixteen years old. If the voices and watching eyes had belonged to her mother's friends, it would have been different, but the people who shared their house with them were strangers.

She suffered in silence the humiliation of having her past laid out before those to whom it could mean nothing. Sometimes, on other such occasions when the cumbersome projector was unpacked from its wooden box, she wondered what it meant to herself. Her mother recounted it like a succession of stories: 'this was when . . .', 'one day Penelope . . .', 'it happened that . . .'. People must presume a beginning, middle, and end: they must suppose a sequence, and they would forget that the time had been a mystery to her as she'd lived it.

Another slide took the place of the one where she stood with her schoolfriends at seven or eight years old, she wearing her hat while the others went bare-headed. As the voices murmured politely about the view of a maiden great-aunt's pebble-dash house at Broadstairs, Penelope was

77

remembering the episode of the hat, the grassy heat of the paddock where they'd gone to meet the ponies they would be instructed to ride. She had been wearing a sun-hat, the ordinary white cotton sort: it wasn't permitted by St Ronan's strict dress rules, but her mother had insisted, after an incident the previous summer when she'd taken sunstroke on Sports Day. Perhaps when people saw, they assumed she wore it just to be different. She didn't believe now that wearing the hat had wholly been meant to save her from the sun: rather, wearing it had demonstrated her mother's concern and will. For the child, she felt certain, it hadn't served to draw attention but had in fact achieved the opposite: beneath her hat, the little girl retreated and became *less* of a person. Maybe that was only what her mother had truly wanted: to turn her into the sort of person to whom – like the other personae of her years to date – things happen, and happen without respect or justice.

Everyone had called her a fetching child, and her mother had seemed in two minds about the compliment, and would dress her in a way that – perversely – managed to emphasise her natural advantages and at the same time to play them down. So that, wearing that sun-hat, she was really supposed to be saying, *I am to be distinguished from everyone else in this paddock, but I can hold my so-called prettiness in check, in reserve, beneath the shadow of the brim, I'm sacrificing it to be accepted as one of you.* Or perhaps her mother had just been very wary of her 'looks', which had come as much through her father as herself, because it made her think of child stars and pushy stage mothers and vulgarity.

Wearing the sun-hat, her reactions hadn't been so clear to others: they weren't able to decipher the features of her face, and she wasn't obliged to offer back, the way that children do, either loyalty or disagreeableness. In those days, wearing printed white cotton on her head and not comprehending vanity, at such choice and unknowing moments she just 'was': already, at sixteen years old and conscious that her looks had been the too-early-blossoming sort, Penelope felt nostalgia, even though those times had been nothing so special in themselves. Standing about in a field with hay-fever sufferers watching smelly, grumpy ponies being yelled at and lunge-whipped through their paces had meant very little to her. But because she just 'was', it had eddied about her and left her untouched: now, even just 'being', she knew circumstances were working from many angles, so many that she wasn't going to be able to get a final perspective on them. As she grew up, other people had fully grown into their own separate 'was'-ness: years later the other pony-watchers were probably swept up in this talk of a war to come or drifting towards marriages and accepting the situation as such. The more she tried not to think, the more difficult and exacting it became, and yet at sixteen she believed that *not thinking* was somehow the clue to it: that it might even have something to do with that intriguing state of 'grace' the school chaplain was always hinting at without being able to define in so many words.

Another slide appeared on the screen. This one showed the view *from* her maiden great-aunt's house at Broadstairs, a wall of chalk cliffs and the lighthouse on the North Foreland. Penelope listened through the respectful voices to the projector's shudders and grunts. She might have been looking at the screen, but in fact she was watching the dust floating in the rod of white light. In her strongest moments she wished she could be impervious to the past, pulling at her in the way that treacherous currents do to beguile, and she wished the dancing dust might be travelling stars in space she was passing beyond in the infinite wisdom of a life completely in control of itself.

6

They went back to the tennis courts. Valerie wore pleated white shorts and a navy-blue jumper knotted about her shoulders, which someone had told her was the only outfit to be seen in. After a few knockabouts with her Penelope thought she was mysteriously improved in her serves, and she envied her: the serves seemed to come to her with remarkable ease, and weren't at all like the old pat-a-ball sort. Oliver was rather tardy about getting into his shorts; when he did, his legs were unrecognisably hairy, like his forearms, and he might have been in his twenties, not his late teens. His sister fell into a brown study as she watched him, lounging against the wire fence or the pillars of the club-house, in the white blouse which couldn't disguise the fact that, alone of the group, she wasn't wearing a brassiere. Penelope felt her own breasts embarrassingly conspicuous and unruly, even though she was using safety pins to tighten the elastic just as Valerie had advised her to last year.

There was a different feeling in the air this summer, and they each seemed conscious of it, although the change was never referred to. Valerie was less willing to play on the courts, and preferred the shadows of the club-house verandah. Oliver hardly spoke at all, but his eyes missed nothing from under his fringe. He was constantly pulling at his white top-stockings. 'Oh, *do* stop fussing with them,' Valerie would tell him, but he either didn't hear or he pretended that he hadn't. From the courts Penelope studied Valerie's supposed indolence and Oliver's sullenness, and felt peculiar flushes and cramps and emissions as she did her best to keep their joint end up and chased after balls she had no hope of returning. A boy called Matthew Rowley took to tapping her bottom with his racquet, but inexplicably she wasn't aware of it until a pairs partner told her and caused her to feel ashamed, as if somehow *she* was responsible and had only egged him on by not having noticed. Valerie laughed a lot, but in a secret indecipherable way, without allowing her to know what the joke was. Oliver had to be asked anything twice before he cottoned on, and preferred to sit on the tramlines with his back against the fence watching games: the boys' and the men's, because – Penelope supposed – the girls' had no power to it.

A young man started speaking to Valerie.

Penelope had been there to see the first time it happened, on the club-house verandah. He was called Ronnie Hammond and he had a job in London. When he came up to her Valerie's face set hard, as if she didn't want her mouth and eyes to work. Her voice seemed to be wound up very tight, on a spring: the words came out singly, each unconnected to another and pitched unrecognisably high.

Ronnie Hammond persevered, and the incident was repeated the next day, with Penelope watching from a distance. The others on the verandah diplomatically sauntered off, trailing snippets of conversation. Penelope waited for Valerie's helplessness to semaphore itself, so that she could perform a rescue. But as she was stepping back, Valerie called out in a confident tone of voice that she should go on ahead please, she didn't know how long it would be till she was ready. Ronnie Hammond turned the handle of his racquet and smiled, just as Penelope's father had done when he was in one of his 'private' moods and occupying himself with thoughts no one could crack. Penelope sensed that Valerie was capable of these very private moods too and that this was another of them, and that maybe not even Ronnie Hammond had a wrinkle as to what was going on inside her head.

The little church was tucked away behind the dunes. Its steeple was off the straight, like a dunce's cap that had been dealt a cuff.

The building lay so low among the fields that only the bent tip was visible as you followed the sandy tracks, through the long spear grass. Inside the perimeter hedge the graveyard was banked up on all sides; the way down to the church was by steps set in the mown turf.

In the middle of the last century a storm had blown the bay several hundred yards inland and the building had been submerged in sand, to its roof. Once a month the priest had been lowered inside through a narrow window in the tower to deliver the ritual service of worship. Eventually the sand had blown back, but to Penelope the church seemed not to have forgotten, cowering behind the dunes in perpetual afternoon silence.

She sometimes walked to the beach that way. There was usually no one about, but one day when the sun was at its three o'clock zenith she happened to spot Valerie's bicycle and another with a crossbar, ridden into the briar hedge at the back of the churchyard. She pushed open the latch gate and ran down the steep brae of grass, between the headstones, and followed the sand path to the porch.

The door was ajar, so she didn't have to turn the squeaky, rusted handle. She didn't hear anything, not at first, and she crept forward on tiptoe, awed as always by the chill and the stillness. Then, just as she decided there was no one inside, she caught sounds: sighs, and what might have been a moan. A movement registered in the corner of her eye and she pivoted round, quickly enough to see Valerie's arm in the sleeve of her mauve cardigan disappearing beneath the high side-panel of one of the old-fashioned family pews. She heard another sound, like a cry, and wondered if Valerie was quite safe in such a place.

She moved further forward, up on her toes, towards the spot. The wooden gate in the side of the pew was open, and through that she caught a glimpse of what was happening. A boy was stretched flat out on the seat on his back and

Valerie was trying to lie face-down on top of him. She was supporting herself with her left foot on the ground and her left arm pushing against the front of the pew and her right knee seeming to find a space between the body on the seat and the seat-back. At the same time the boy was attempting to pull her cardigan off her left shoulder and she was struggling to help him, while he pecked little kisses at her cheek and her chin. The sound was like scrabbling, just like a scrap.

Fascinated by what she was seeing, Penelope took another step forward – and fell noisily against the front of a pew. The wood made a cracking noise. In the instant before the pain travelled between brain and foot Valerie looked up and saw her. On a reflex the solid gate of the pew was slammed shut.

Ten seconds or so passed before the two heads were visible over the sides of the pew. The boy's was red with embarrassment; Valerie's was white with fury.

There were no apologies, no explanations, no questions and no answers. The boy – it wasn't Ronnie Hammond – walked towards the door, by the quickest route he could, saying nothing and not looking at either of them. Valerie straightened her cardigan, pulled at her cuffs, smoothed her dress, walking small, exact circles in the narrow nave to regain her composure. Her face slowly recovered its colour. Once she turned round and looked at her, a hard and penetrating stare as she tried to calculate what was at stake, how much her friend was capable of understanding. She walked further circles on the floor and seemed to be steadying her breathing, finding a rhythm.

She moved out of the circle and over towards one of the pews. She dropped on to the seat.

Penelope felt obliged to follow her. She stopped in line with the end of the pew.

'Don't tell anyone, Penelope.'

'I only came to – '

'Do you hear?' the voice asked sharply.

'Yes.'

'You won't tell?'

'All right.'

'You'd better not.'

'I wouldn't.'

'I'll find out if you do.'

'I wouldn't, really.'

'Promise?'

'Yes.'

'Say it – '

'I promise – '

Valerie leaned back in the pew. She repositioned a blue velvet hassock with her heel and dumped her feet on top of it. She leaned her back against the wood and took long, protracted breaths. In, out. In, out.

'Well . . .'

Penelope dropped her eyes to the flagstones with their chiselled dedications to long-spent lives. A brass engraving of a coat-of-arms had almost faded into the stone.

Valerie put her hand to her nose.

'What a smell this place has.'

Penelope pointed. 'Is it the flowers?'

'Mouldy Bibles, more like.'

'The candles?'

'I don't know – '

Valerie's face was suddenly downcast, sullen as Oliver's sometimes was, but petulant-looking as his couldn't be. She pushed the hassock forward with her feet: her best friend Penelope forgotten like the flowers, the Bibles, the candles, the odour of stale time.

Twenty-two years later, in 1959, the widowed Mrs Hutton was buried. Penelope was drawn in as a (virtually silent) third party to the debate about Tregarrick.

'We should keep it,' Valerie repeated.

Oliver dropped his shoulders again.

'But it's – '

'It's what?'

' – a bit out of the way. And we don't have children.'

'What's that got to do with it?'

'That's why we remember it. Because we were young there.'

'At least *I'm* married. If I choose not to have children – '

'I didn't mean – '

'And you're *never* going to have them, are we to gather?'

'I don't – '

'I believe you have to find a woman first if you want children. Are they in such short supply in Cambridge?'

Penelope interrupted. 'Why can't you go on letting it?'

'It's a healthy market just now,' Oliver said.

'Do *you* want us to keep it, Penelope?'

'I . . .'

Oliver spoke. 'Does it matter if we *don't* have it?'

'How equivocal,' Valerie said. 'As ever.'

'It's not *just* the financial side – '

'Look on it as bricks and mortar.' Valerie snatched up her bag, black alligator from Asprey's, another present from her silver-haired second husband. 'Look on it as an investment. Money in the bank.'

'You – you don't need income,' Oliver said.

'It's *private* income.'

'But there's the upkeep,' Oliver said. 'Having to attend to that – '

'Oh, I'm tired of all this – '

'I'm not caring about the *money* – '

'Sell the bloody thing, then.'

'Are you – '

' – Sure? Haven't I just said it, for God's sake?'

'It just seems,' Oliver said, 'to make more sense if we – '

'Yes, yes. Don't go on – '

'I just want us – '

'That's that. I told you. End of topic, end of conversation.'

Valerie stubbed out her cigarette in an ashtray.

Penelope opened her mouth to speak.

'It's settled,' Valerie said. 'I'll leave it to you to get rid of it, Oliver. Since you're the man – '

She stared at him. Penelope looked away. It had always been Oliver who'd had to take the brunt of his sister's displeasure, even when it might actually have been with herself.

'I've wasted quite enough time thinking about it,' Valerie said.

'We could – ' Oliver shifted awkwardly ' – go down to Cornwall. Have a last look.'

'Not bloody likely. Anyway, I haven't the time.'

'It – it *is* a long way,' Oliver said. 'Not driving – '

'Haven't some of your chums taught you? Got you behind the wheel?'

Oliver looked at the carpet.

'I haven't the inclination to see,' Valerie said. 'Quite frankly. Not now.'

She picked up her sable coat and threw its weight on to her shoulders.

'Well, that's settled, thank God. Cyril and I are going off for a holiday.'

Penelope smiled.

'Oh, that – that's nice.'

'A cruise. Not my brother's sort of thing at all. Rather beneath his dignity, I should think. Or do you think you *would* enjoy a cruise, Oliver?'

'I – I don't – '

'Just the sea. People like ourselves. And a shipload of greasy Greek sailors.'

'Where – ' Penelope began.

'The Azores. I'll send you a card. I'll send you both a card. In the meantime, can I presume this bloody business will be attended to?'

'I'll try,' Oliver said.

'You'll do better than "try". *You* started it all.'

He corrected himself. 'It'll all be attended to – '

'Are there taxis round about here?'

'I'll go and call you one,' Penelope said.

She walked to the door, opened it, and stepped out into the hall. She pulled on the handle to close the door.

She shut her eyes and leaned on the wall, against the doorjamb. *This is the last time, God help us, the last time. Save me from any more, please.*

Oliver's version in the August of 1937 was that he'd cycled over to Pendizzick in the afternoon, to have a pedal straightened, and that he'd walked about the cliffs and spotted some puffins' nests.

'That's all you did?' Valerie asked him.

'Just because I wasn't sailing – '

'You walked about the cliffs at Pendizzick?'

'Yes.'

'Looking for puffins?'

'Well, not *looking* for them – '

'Then what?'

'Then I came back.'

'What's this, what's this?' Mr Hutton asked them. 'An interrogation?'

'But I saw you at Cove.' Valerie's face split into a smile.'In the *middle* of the afternoon.'

Oliver paled.

'At Cove?' Mrs Hutton said.

Oliver shook his head.

'What?' Valerie dropped her cutlery, in mock-astonishment. 'It *wasn't* you?'

Oliver shook his head: his cheeks and neck were firing.

'It must have been someone else,' Mrs Hutton said, not really concerned.

'Oh no, it *was* him.' Valerie's smile dramatically reduced itself. 'I recognised the bike.'

Mr Hutton swallowed some water from his tumbler.

'But Oliver – '

'I can recognise him by now, you know.'

'I – I cycled about a bit – afterwards – '

'You didn't go to Cove?'

'I forget – '

Mrs Hutton lifted her tumbler of water.

'There are lots of bicycles like – '

'Oh no,' Valerie said. 'That's just where you're wrong.'

She smiled, quite confidently, triumphant.

Oliver had been hanging about on the quayside, Valerie told her. Where the yachting lot gathered.

'Maybe he wants to join you?'

'Celia Frenney told me. She's seen him there before.'

'So?'

'There's a couple of brothers. Called Winternitz. One's at university. They're really quite nice,' she said.

'Are – they're friends of his?'

'Whose friends?'

'Oliver's.'

Valerie sighed. 'You're too young, Penny.'

'Why?'

'Well . . . well, *he's* not *their* friend, Oliver.'

'But maybe he wants to be? On their boat?'

'No. They wouldn't want him.'

'Why not?'

'Oliver would make them uncomfortable.'

'Because he can't sail?'

'Because . . . he just wants to – to look at them.'

'To look at them?'

'Celia Frenney says they've got hairy chests. And could grow beards if they wanted to.'

'But – '

'But you don't understand, Penelope. I'm seventeen, almost. All but. I *do*.'

'Won't you tell me?'

'It's better you don't.'

'Celia knew where you were,' Valerie said, betraying her source to gain her effect. 'Yesterday.'

Oliver picked up a book, opened it at random and stared at the page. His eyes weren't moving.

'She told me.'

'Told you what?'

'That you were down on the quay. Again.'

He riffled through the pages. It was one of his school classics books.

'Really?'

'Yes, really.'

His face was as stiff as board.

'It *was* you, Oliver, wasn't it?'

He got to his feet.

'If *you* say so. There's no law against it.'

'Law against what?'

The book thudded on to the table. That wasn't his usual way at all. Valerie, surprised, smiled.

'Well. I *do* say so. Actually.'

Oliver pushed his hands into his pockets and stood his ground. He kicked at the tassels on the rug with the toe of his sandshoe.

'What were you doing, then? Spying on me?'

'I told you. I was on my bike. With Celia and Muriel.'

'You'll get run over if you don't look where you're going.'

'How kind of you – '

' "Kind"?'

'To be so concerned about me.'

The heel of one sandshoe ground itself into the rug.

'I didn't know I had to tell you everywhere I went.'

'You'd probably just tell me what you tell everyone else.'

Oliver's reply was a long, irritable sigh.

'I do hope you're not becoming *devious*, Oliver.'

He kicked at the tassels.

'When you start lying,' Valerie said, 'it's very difficult to stop. Apparently.'

'I wasn't.'

'You weren't?'

'No.'

'I think you're lying *now*.'

'I don't really care what *you* think.'

Valerie smiled again.

'Pardon me for living!'

Oliver looked across to the window. His lips pulled back at the corners.

'Pardon *me*, I'm sure, Oliver.'

'I can go where I like, can't I?'

Valerie didn't reply at once. As the seconds passed Oliver's eyes moved back into the room, edging closer and closer to Valerie but not settling on her.

From the sofa Penelope saw everything: even Oliver, at thirty or forty years old, grown restless and careworn. The way that single people without outlets become. She was quite aware of herself watching, and felt the significance of these moments with a slight chill running over her skin, along her arms and on to the backs of her hands.

She watched into the future, saw herself looking back and then, years later, every so often and when the chill was upon her, she was to look back and see herself as the girl watching and discovering. She was looking round the room and seeing all its objects occupying their particular space with a weighty, sonorous emphasis she was noticing for the first time: with such a solid *thereness* she could only sit wondering why she hadn't been conscious of it before, like an innocence she'd just broached, as if the things had always been there but she'd never made contact with them until this moment. The effect was also to isolate the separateness of everything, even if they did share a larger communal space: and standing or sitting immobile, she and Oliver and Valerie seemed a part of the thingness of things too: dense and self-contained, individual and apart from the rest. Vaguely she perceived how, in their mutual embarrassment, they feared each other's knowledge – and maybe the knowledge about their own natures, if it would ever be possible to truly know: knowing like the slow chill on her skin –

'Well . . . ?'

'Well what?'

'I *can* go where I like.'

'If you say so, Oliver.'

'But you don't believe what I say. You've just – '

'Was that Joe Jepps there?'

Oliver turned and stared at her. His eyelids didn't blink. His fingers curled up beneath the cuffs of his cardigan.

Penelope spoke.

'Our Mrs Jepps? Her son?'

Neither of them heard her.

Valerie sat savouring these moments of her triumph.

'He *was* there, wasn't he?'

Oliver was trying to contain whatever was inside him.

'It's a big secret, is it?'

Valerie sank back into the sofa cushions, luxuriating in her own assurance, in her skill at bettering someone whose natural inclination was to admit as little of himself as possible.

'*I* don't care,' she said.

'And *I* don't.'

'Joe Jepps?' Penelope asked.

'Thinks he's the bee's knees,' Valerie returned. 'He looks at himself in shop windows, haven't you seen? Muriel says he's . . .'

Oliver still stood with his hands in his pockets. The ramrod position was incommoding him, he looked uncomfortable, but he must have known he couldn't move without letting Valerie see that he was ruffled, irked.

In an instant, though, Valerie appeared to tire of the business, it wearied her beyond endurance. She kicked off her right sandal and, hitching the leg up on to the cushion, tucked it beneath her.

'Pass across that mag, will you, Penelope? Steerage – '

The magazine was sent skimming across the parquet, around the island of rug where Oliver continued to stand, as awkwardly as before. It slithered to a halt against one of the sofa's castors, beneath the tuck of loose cover.

Valerie leaned forward and picked it up.

'You make a better door than a window, Oliver.'

Now she sounded only tetchy, in the way that routine family banter allowed. She dropped her head over the magazine's list of contents.

Oliver stepped forward, off the rug. He looked down at Valerie, not disguising his wonder, and his face seemed lightened of a load. He left his hands in his trouser pockets, but relaxed his arms, pushing them out at the elbows.

It had sometimes happened before, just like this: all in a moment Valerie would lose interest. It was as if what she needed was the pursuit of a point, the chase and the closing-in. She had won herself a moral triumph: the point had been acceded to her. What followed was of no consequence to her, except as it justified her original worrying a matter, the harrying and wearing down.

The glossy paper crinkled as she turned the pages. She sat forward on the cushion with her shoulders hunched. Her eyes hovered inches above the photographs. Some she lingered over longer while, wearing a model's outfit, she moved about a rich man's home, the tasteful, modern rooms of a Syrie Maugham pied-à-terre in Chelsea or Regent's Park . . .

Penelope wished it could be how it used to be in her early teens, those days of never thinking further than tomorrow and time stretched tight like elastic, long afternoons and the slow drift into shapeless evenings with their delicious tiredness and the garden and lane heady with fragrances. It wasn't quite like that any more. Certainly the Tregarrick garden still glowed after supper and yielded its aromas: rubbing against a hedge with your sleeve or grazing a flower-head with the back of your hand immediately conjured up last year and the one before that.

But . . . She could only be conscious of what had changed, that the house had a different spirit now. Each of them seemed to live more privately, even she had dug more deeply into herself. She wondered if they were doing it as the sandflies did, for cover and camouflage.

The days also seemed to adjust themselves differently. She was more aware of their living by the clock, referring to whatever they were doing or planned to do with glances at their watches. She was more alive to the shifts of light, how the afternoon seemed to exhaust itself, then ran down into the time of changeover, the other 'blue hour', when daylight was drained out of the sky. She sensed that it was being syphoned out through the air, because the atmosphere appeared to acquire a dimension she wasn't otherwise conscious of: the flowers in the garden reverberated with the insistence of their particular colours, and when you studied the distance you were looking over and *around* objects. Sometimes she had the impression of swimming through the air, into the massing blueness. And then, always quite suddenly – even though she concentrated on not being fooled again – they were in the evening portion of the day: there was no possibility of confusing it with the afternoon, the blue wasn't any of those blues she might recognise but darker than Quink in a bottle. First would come supper, followed by the individual activities that had taken the place of the shared sort. These lent a final clandestine feel to the day, which hadn't been there before: Valerie announcing various possibilities but not specifying which, Oliver never saying where he was going. Mr Hutton still disappeared into the garden and only his wife was still dependably *there*, settled in a wing chair in the sitting-room, and usually silent and thoughtful. They were almost all adults now (she, Penelope, least of all) and maybe this was only what happened: that they each stopped needing the props of the other characters and were wholly and completely and unmistakably themselves?

Then she was quite ready to believe so, and took it to be the reason why Valerie and Oliver kept to their own ways. She wasn't being excluded, she only had to find the clues to herself. The closeness had gone, but it would have done so anyway even if she had tried to prevent it happening. Valerie's eyes had a tight look that was new, and Oliver was even further from them all some days, and she regretted both changes, but it might only have been that the natures of the people they were had become more stressed: the tight eyes and the distance always having been there, and only waiting to be brought out, bit by bit.

She felt wise in herself as she surveyed them all at the table: Valerie fussing with her food and pursing her mouth, Oliver not meeting anyone's eyes and avoiding Valerie's most (she was his sternest judge), Mr Hutton frowning rather a lot and his brow corrugating with new folds, and Mrs Hutton behaving much as she always had but in a quieter, *paler* way as if she might be gamely keeping up appearances for their guest's sake.

When she asked Valerie, quite discreetly, maybe she'd been a guest a little too long, the force of her reply took her by surprise:

'Jesus Christ, Pen, you're not going to abandon us, are you?'

'But – '

'I couldn't bear it if you weren't here.'

'What? Really?'

In the evenings Valerie would rendezvous with her own friends, and their transport was a motor-car not bicycles.

'Really?' she repeated.

'Well, what do you think? It'd be so deadly dull, it'd drive me mental.'

'But I thought . . .'

'You should stop thinking then. I'll tie you to your bed if you don't shut up – '

After that she tried her best not to associate her own presence with the atmosphere of awkwardness she was quite aware she wasn't imagining. Some years later still she wondered why Valerie should have been so vehement in her response, and why Oliver should have mentioned the matter to her the very next day, unless what she had been witnessing was what neither of them wanted to admit to, the final falling out of innocence and the foundering into not knowledge but *guilt*.

Then Oliver seemed to brighten. He looked less forbidding at the tennis courts and he became quite high-spirited when they all went into the sea. He let Valerie pull him under the waves, and only laughed, and even let her ride him piggyback. Drying off, Valerie tried to knock him off his balance and sometimes they landed on the sand in a heap, the hair on Oliver's thighs and calves matted and Valerie's torso tanned in a complicated grid of stripes defined by straps and neck-lines.

In the evenings Oliver went off on his bike, whistling whatever the wireless had been playing. Valerie continued to give herself to her friends, applying discreet make-up and considering what to wear; she would lie down on her bed crushing whatever she'd just put on and sighing or closing her eyes until a bicycle bell chimed in the lane or she heard the tattoo of a car horn.

Oliver would come back quite late, after ten. Valerie didn't reproach him with any more sightings at Cove; she said very little, and didn't accuse when her mother asked him where he'd been and he told her he'd been cycling the lanes by moonlight.

'Is there *enough* light?'

'Lots.'

'To see by?'

'Yes.'

Valerie didn't laugh, except appreciatively, when he regaled them with passages he'd memorised over the year from his Greek classes at school, Homer and Thucydides and Xenophon. He would recite anywhere. Sometimes he fitted the words to band music on the radio. Perhaps they were the same words he was speaking, but neither of his listeners would have been any the wiser, or even cared. Oliver was being eccentric, and they allowed it and encouraged it because he seemed happier then than he did at other times. And all three of them knew, in their hearts or wherever such matters receive the profoundest thought we can give them, that happiness might not be more than a cheating shadow.

Then the situation changed again, with the speed of those afternoon shadows across the wet sand during that long eleven-week summer of 1937.

At first Penelope thought they had devised another conspiracy of silence against her, Valerie and Oliver. Then she realised that some sort of silence, a different one, bound *them* too. It involved looks exchanged furtively between them, which she had misinterpreted as directed against herself: but she came to the conclusion that they were both almost totally preoccupied with the other's attention and had merely forgotten about her. Valerie had the guile to partially camouflage her distraction: it was Oliver's expression of pain and alarm that gave the game away.

Penelope didn't understand. She didn't understand so much. They were growing apart, she and the two of them – inches and feet every day – and yet neither of them wanted to let her go, there would have been an outcry from Mr and Mrs Hutton too: she was needed as she always had been, and maybe even more so now. The other years she had spent with the family were somehow the burden of proof that she wouldn't do any differently, that she was stitched into the fabric of life here at Tregarrick.

It was with things as they were that Valerie suggested to Penelope one lunchtime that they meet later on the quay at Cove after she had called on friends.

For Penelope it was going to mean a long walk along the dunes or a four-mile cycle ride.

'I'll have my bike,' Valerie told her.

'Yes. All right.'

She wouldn't have any other plans for her day, she knew. And with any luck she might be introduced to some of Valerie's set, who contrived to hold themselves so exclusive.

On the afternoon she was on the quay by three o'clock, waiting, as they'd agreed. Mr and Mrs Hutton had been invited to an adults-only lunch with a business acquaintance and his wife who had taken a house on the other side of the estuary, at Trelissian Bay. That had left only Oliver in the house and he'd been in one of his most extreme wool-gathering moods. She had asked if he wanted to come with her, but he'd told her the chain on his bicycle was in pieces.

'Can't you borrow a bike?'

'Oh, it doesn't matter.'

'Maybe we'll meet Valerie's friends.'

'We'd have met them before now, if Valkyrie had meant us to.'

'Oh well, I only thought – '

'See you, Penelope.'

'Yes.'

She waited on the quay from three o'clock until quarter-to-four. She didn't like to go down on to the shore in case Valerie flew down the ramp from the road and didn't see her, so she stayed beside her bicycle on the road side of the boathouse where she was visible.

'Celia – !'

'What?'

It was one of the Winternitz boys of myth. He held a hand out, not to shake hers but to make a gesture of apology.

'God, sorry! I thought you were Celia – '

'That – that's all right.'

'Because of that,' he said, and pointed to her straw hat.

'This?'

She took it off, blushing.

'It's nothing special,' she said.

'You bought it here?'

'Yes. At the Imperial St – '

'So did Celia, you see.'

She nodded. Of course. That was the only reason why he had stopped. Otherwise he would just have carried on, continued on his way. Celia, they said, was going to turn into a 'killer'. It was very probable. There was a story that she'd been spotted in London drinking at a hotel bar with an American-speaking businessman. But none of her admirers seemed put off by the rumours.

'A case of mistaken identity?' she said.

'Well . . .'

Now it was *his* turn to redden. She watched him, but she took no delight in the sight. Why was her own supply of breath proving so unreliable?

'Anyway – ' she said.

92

'You both have such good taste, that's it. So I – '

'I'm waiting for Valerie,' she interrupted, unpersuaded by the Winternitz charm, hardly believing her own bravery.

He told her he'd been driving over from Pendizzick and had seen her cycling the opposite way, back towards Polwynn.

'Valerie?'

He said he'd sounded his horn and she'd lifted both hands off the handlebars and waved to him.

'When was that?'

'About three.'

'Are you *sure*?' Penelope asked him.

'Oh yes.'

'Why did – '

'Maybe she remembered something. And had to go back.'

'I don't know – '

'But she must have forgotten she was supposed to be meeting *you*.'

'Yes. We agreed.'

'It was *this* afternoon – ?'

'I – I'm sorry?'

' – you were going to meet her?'

'Oh yes,' Penelope said. 'It definitely was.'

'Here?'

She nodded. 'Here,' she told him.

'When?'

She looked at her watch. 'Nearly an hour ago.'

There and then she decided not to wait any longer, although she might have done if a case of mistaken identity hadn't confused her. She could have sat on the beach, practised patience.

Instead she said goodbye to Andrew Winternitz and pushed her bicycle up the ramp. She climbed on to the saddle, trying to contain her disappointment from passing faces. Perhaps they were all too old for this place after all. Neither Valerie nor Oliver seemed to be in the right frame of mind for it any more, attending to so little and forgetting so much.

There were more uphills on the road going back, so she didn't reach Tregarrick until twenty-to-five or so. The car wasn't in front of the house, which meant it had been a long lunch at Trelissian Bay. She saw Valerie's bicycle thrown down under a fuchsia bush.

She went in by the back door. She stopped in the hallway to listen. All she could hear was her own breath heaving in her chest.

They must be in the house, if the door was open. She looked into the sitting-room. There was no one there but she heard a voice from upstairs, then a floorboard creaking.

She found herself tiptoeing up the staircase. Of course she was irritated with Valerie, but her levels of irritation in the Tregarrick season of the year didn't count for much. The afternoon wasn't done yet, they could find another way of filling their time until supper.

She heard more creaking – then a voice, Valerie's. The sounds were coming from Oliver's room. She walked across the landing.

Normally she would have knocked on the door. But she couldn't not help but feel that *some*thing was owed to her this afternoon, and that she had a right to immediate entry.

She lifted the latch and leaned on the handle. The door opened and from where she was standing she saw quite clearly and unmistakably: Oliver and Valerie on top of the bed, and Valerie lying on top of Oliver. She was wearing her brassiere and knickers, and Oliver was in his swimming trunks. Immediately Penelope knew that a sin was taking place: it was like the church all over again, only worse, because –

One of Valerie's knees pushed between Oliver's thighs. He was immobile beneath her with his head turned away, towards the window. Valerie's arms were on his shoulders, and her head almost rested on the pillow beside him but facing the other way. It jerked sideways suddenly, to look over her shoulder. Her eyes swivelled to the door, to the new source of light, and Penelope was held by them, appalled, so that she couldn't think how to make her escape. Valerie's eyes stared from the bed but without shock or horror, with no expression at all: they just stared, as a dead body's were supposed to, and it was only the thought of that – death, the dead – that sent Penelope stumbling backwards out of the room.

She didn't close the door but ran downstairs, through the hall to the front door and out of the house. She picked up her bicycle, jumped on, skidded across the driveway, and lifted her feet off the pedals to freewheel down the pot-holed lane. She hardly had the strength in her arms to support herself but she knew she hadn't ever taken the hill so fast before. She didn't think of falling off, so it didn't happen.

After that she rode the country roads for miles, wanting to lose trace of herself among the high hedges and lush banks of meadowsweet and the shrinking red campion and speedwell. But somehow she didn't quite, never managing to let go her hold on what was familiar to her – fields, farmhouses, copses, barns, the signposts with their long pointing fingers – and too well known to them all.

At supper Mr and Mrs Hutton were both in good spirits. They'd stopped at the Imperial Stores in Cove on the journey back. Mrs Weekes had told them she'd seen Penelope down on the quay, wearing her straw hat.

'Yes,' she told them, with a throat like sandpaper and the tasteless food on her plate barely touched. 'Yes, I went over.'

She realised Valerie was watching her, although she hadn't once caught her looking directly.

94

'She told us it was because you were wearing your sun-hat,' Mrs Hutton said. 'That's why she recognised you.'

Penelope nodded.

'Did you enjoy yourself?' Mrs Hutton asked her.

She willed herself to reply. 'Yes. Yes, thanks.'

'What did you do?' Mr Hutton enquired.

He was only asking for politeness's sake, because they'd had an out-of-the-ordinary day themselves.

'I – watched the boats. And – and talked to Andrew Winternitz. Then . . .'

She stared at the fleur-de-lis pattern worked round the rim of her plate; it had been there every mealtime, except that she had hardly happened to notice before.

'"Then . . ."?' Mrs Hutton asked her gently, but with the same inconsequential regard.

'Then I cycled over to Pendizzick.'

She explained that she'd spent the rest of the afternoon there, on the surf beach and up on the headland, watching for the puffins, until the sun started to drop in the sky. And then – then she'd come back.

'We weren't long before you,' Mr Hutton told her. 'Not long at all.'

Penelope smiled, grimly, and didn't look up.

When she was asked, Valerie said she'd been with the Frobishers. Oliver said he'd been working for next term, cramming for the Uni, and sounded cataleptic, all but, as he forced the words out.

Mrs Hutton laughed lightly, at what didn't deserve it, in a party-ish way that was left over from the afternoon. Mr Hutton was seeing the world in the best possible light this evening and didn't think of sitting alone in the garden when the table had been cleared, but – remembering some remark of their social afternoon – seated himself on the sofa beside his wife, removed a pack of cards from their box, and tried to recall the rudiments of competition bridge.

Part Four

1

Suddenly the PGs were gone, without a proper explanation, and the house in Lithgow Road was their own again.

'I've decided: we're going on holiday, Penelope.'

'On holiday? Are we?'

Her mother smiled as she nodded.

'Since the Huttons are giving Cornwall a miss this year – '

'Yes.'

' – I've had an idea.'

'Where – where to?'

The South Coast, Penelope imagined: or Walberswick, all smocks and easels, which her mother's friends would tell her about.

'To Provence.'

'*What?*'

'Your education must have taught you better than that.'

'*Provence?*'

'We have to broaden your horizons, Penelope.'

'But . . .'

'Isn't it going to be absurdly expensive?' she had to ask.

'If I tell you I've had a windfall, will that do?'

'A windfall?'

'Yes.'

'And we really are going?'

'You do want to go? To see Provence?'

'Oh yes. Yes, of course.'

More than anything.

'Very well then, we'll go. Provence it is.'

Her mother smiled again and poured them both a sherry, from the best decanter. A happy frame of mind subtracted ten or fifteen years from her: Penelope wished she could tell her that. In sun-drenched Provence maybe she would be able to.

Penelope and her mother arrive at a smart-ish hotel on the outskirts of an inland town (a smaller Arles). They settle in.

During dinner on the second evening Penelope was conscious of a young man's attention. Several times when she looked up she caught sight of him watching them both.

Some food fell from her fork and she blushed. She looked across the room and saw him smiling at her mother beside her, dressed in her black crêpe and lace and wearing her good pearls; *she* had also noticed the young man's smile, but then turned to stare at the forkful of food lying on the tablecloth. She didn't correct her for the misdemeanour, however; she looked at her instead, scrutinising her daughter as if she was sizing up someone unknown.

Penelope felt her face turning as bright as a pink spring tulip.

The next day. In an art gallery in the town Penelope and her mother encounter the young man. He introduces himself, he is Henry Kyte. He indicates the intricacies of a painting the two women have been looking at. (Called, say, The Enchanted Castle: *eighteenth century, a girl looks down from the battlements of a medieval tower, at a young man sprawled beneath a tree, either asleep or distracted by grief. The artist's sense of ambiguity, of mystery – or else his mischievous playfulness.) Penelope is wary, but her mother is impressed.*

That evening he spoke to them after dinner.

Penelope was a dumb witness as her mother asked him if he would care to sit down with them. He smiled, dropped a look over his shoulder, then lowered himself into a chair, perching forward on the cushion. He was expecting to meet a colleague, he said, but meanwhile he would be delighted . . .

Penelope stared as her mother thanked him for his help in the morning. She asked him how he knew what he did. He shrugged, saying he had heard his colleague telling someone and he had only stored it away in his memory.

'Have you connections with these parts?'

'My colleague's seeing some people. It's his business. Wine-trade, like mine. We drove south. I'm waiting to meet someone from Marseille. Off the train.'

Penelope's mother nodded. It all sounded very busy.

'It's a sort of crossing-point,' he said, running his right hand through his hair. 'We just happen to be here. Otherwise – '

'This hotel was recommended to us.'

'It's rather good.'

'How did *you* discover it?'

'My colleague suggested it. British people come.'

Penelope and her mother had already spoken to two couples, one English and one Welsh, and to a brace of Gloucestershire spinsters.

'It's well-placed,' he said. 'For getting about. The old towns get so hot and sticky. The views here are A-one.'

The conversation ambled on. Penelope wondered if he might think they were two spiders. But it was he who had looked them out, following them from the dining-room – he had only eaten one course – into the salon.

She was conscious of the attention he was paying her, directing separate smiles to her from those meant for her mother. He brought her into the conversation at several points when she wouldn't otherwise have voiced an opinion. Her mother listened to her and – rather surprisingly – didn't interrupt.

His 'colleague' arrived at last, and stood waiting out in the hall. He looked like a businessman (if one could really tell), very French, swarthy, and perhaps in his late thirties, ten or so years older than their compatriot; he already had a jowl, but wore a neatly cut, sporty suit. Henry Kyte excused himself very properly, wished them separately a pleasant remainder of the evening, and left to join his colleague, who had lit a cigar and must have glanced at his wristwatch at least a dozen times in the short interlude of waiting.

'What a very nice young man,' her mother declared, and proceeded to compliment him.

Penelope didn't reply as his praises were sung.

'What's the matter with *you*?' her mother asked, with some tartness.

'Nothing,' she replied.

'I meant to ask Mr Kyte where he lived. He seems to know London rather well.'

Penelope was still trying to decipher those smiles, the more persistent ones he'd trained on herself. Oliver had been her principal contact with his sex, and she had felt flustered by this man's concentration on her. He'd been looking at her in a way that was quite new to her, but which she was too inexperienced to judge. In the aftermath – when it was too late – she sat in her chair straightening her pleats and smoothing her stockings, tucking back some fallen strands of hair.

Her mother opened a fan and fluttered it in front of her face. *She* had been through the rigmarole before, with her father, and both of them had become versed in such matters to a greater or lesser extent. In that respect her mother was streets ahead of her, travelling at a speed she would never overtake.

Penelope stared down at her hands crossed in her lap. She removed them and dropped her arms by her sides. She felt pure as a nun – or almost as – and wished very hard to know better.

'Like a blow-through?'

It was Henry Kyte. She hadn't heard him approach.

'"A blow-through"?'

He nodded to his car, parked beneath them on the driveway. He stood with his left hand in the back left-hand pocket of his trousers.

'I don't know,' she said. 'I don't know what we're doing, you see.'

'We don't need to be long – '

'I'll have to ask.'

'If you *want* to come – '

'Where to?' she asked him.

'Just tell your mother you want to come.'

'If I say I want to come – ' She realised she was on her guard, that she didn't want to be seen as her mother's servant.

'You *will* come?'

She noticed the monogrammed gold signet ring on his little finger.

'Perhaps – '

Henry Kyte escorts her inside. He goes through the formalities of requesting Mrs Milne's company for an excursion in the car. But she finds an excuse to decline. (It's almost as if Henry Kyte has been able to read her mind, as if she's a type.) Mrs Milne smiles at Penelope to accept. To Penelope it appears a ploy on her mother's part to push them together. Henry Kyte stands charmingly persuading her.

'*I'll have to get changed, wear something else –* '

'*You're fine just as you are. But I'll wait –* '

'*Mr Kyte can talk to me meanwhile,*' *Mrs Milne says, and she clears her sewing from the chair next to her.*

Twenty minutes later Penelope found him sitting waiting in the car, ruffling his hair with his hand.

'How did you know I'd come?' she asked him.

'I just knew.'

She climbed into the front beside him. As he started the engine she looked back and saw her mother watching from the window of her room. On the floor above another face watched, a man's, but it withdrew behind a shutter.

They bowled along, on a road that quickly took them out of the town.

'Is this where you were going?' she asked him, for something to say.

'I don't mind. Anywhere will do.'

'It's all so nice.'

'I don't get to see so much. Being a working chap.'

He said it, smiling, in a silly fol-de-rol voice.

'It must be an enviable job,' she said. She thought she sounded far too serious. 'Coming down here. A treat – to many people.'

'It's just a job to me.'

'Well, yes. I – suppose so – '

'If it wasn't this one, I expect I'd cadge another one.'

'Is it easy? To find one?'

'Chaps I've been to school with – '

She nodded, understanding.

'I keep on the right side of them.'

'Yes.'

'You never know how long it's going to last anyway.'

'"Last"?'

'Until the bubble bursts.'

He'd picked up speed but must have sensed that she was a little uneasy and he slowed again.

'Too much dust today,' he said.

'It *is* dusty.'

'But you're enjoying yourself?'

'Yes,' she said. 'So far.'

He pulled a face at the last two words, then smiled.

She smiled too.

'Yes,' she said, 'I'm enjoying it.'

'Call me Harry, won't you?'

'"Harry"?'

'Or Henry, if you prefer.'

'Yes,' she said.

'You'll settle for Henry?'

'Yes. Certainly.'

'Jolly good.'

She relaxed a little on the seat.

'And I'm Penelope.'

'Great name.'

'What?'

He wasn't laughing. It wasn't a joke to him.

'You really think it is?'

'Splendid,' he said.

'No one's ever told me that before.'

'Obviously you just haven't met the right people, Penelope.'

They stopped at the side of the road, near a melon field, beneath the shade of a tree.

He had brought some cakes and biscuits, with pastry-forks and napkins, packed into a voluminous wicker hamper. There was also a flask, and two bone china cups and saucers.

'Always prepared,' he said. 'Like a Boy Scout.'

'You did this especially?'

'Yes.'

'But how did you know - '

'You'd rather have a melon?'

'No.' She shook her head, smiling. 'Oh no.'

He cleared stones and flints from a patch of dry ground and spread a travelling-rug. They sat down and unpacked the hamper. As they drank tea and ate he asked her questions about herself, and she replied. It was a little disorientating to her to find anyone interested in what she had to say. He asked her about her home, her school, her mother, her father, what she could recall of her life in Borneo.

Afterwards she asked him about himself and he told her about his public school in Suffolk and some friends he kept up with three or four years on. He told her he worked for a firm of wine-importers in Bristol, with premises in – aptly enough – Cork Street.

'My chums call me Corky.'

He laughed again.

'I prefer Henry,' she said.

'Whatever you like – '

He told her he had rooms in Clifton, in the house of one of his mother's friends, at the top of a steep hill. His mother was dead, he told her; his father lived in the North, but he was even less specific about him than about his mother.

Penelope was starting to feel rather sorry for him, having to make a life for himself in Bristol.

'Shall we go?' he said, suddenly jumping up. 'Get back on the road?'

He opened the picnic hamper and began packing away. She helped him, while he whistled and took occasional slaps at the dust on his neatly pressed trousers.

On the journey back she continued to look at him when she felt she could, taking advantage of the views to turn her head and plead an interest. Her mother had called him 'good-looking', and she would have had to agree that he was. His features were regular and maybe a little characterless, but his face carried an open, cheerful expression. His fair hair was neatly brushed, and he had clear skin and neat nails. He hadn't taken much of the sun, and he seemed – she thought – irreproachably *clean*. Her mother had remarked on his 'pleasant speaking-voice', and she supposed that it was, although it denoted nothing about him except that he had been educated at a school where there was a convention of how to speak.

Twice he had let slip some reference to the North of England, other than referring to his father's whereabouts.

'You weren't born in the South?' she asked him.

'Well, I was born south of *some* places. Scotland, for instance.'

'Between Suffolk and Scotland?'

'Somewhere between them, yes.'

She smiled. She thought it might be a subject in general he didn't want to talk about. In that case she wouldn't. It was the least she could do to reciprocate for the double treat of the afternoon, the drive and their picnic.

He has, she thinks on closer inspection, quite a tight face. Somehow his mouth is a little small for the length of his nose; his eyes may be a fraction too near one another. Not in Oliver's class, but good-looking still. He also proves that a favourable light and the proper clothes and a courteous manner can aid and abet,

102

to provide a pleasing and convincing effect. The occasional show of boyishness in his manner reminds her of her father, and she is relieved that like him he doesn't play on his appearance, which has always seemed to her a more heinous fault in a man than a woman. Her mother commented that afternoon in the gallery on his hands, and they are fine and slender; 'an artistic nature' her mother had said, but Penelope supposes they are merely inherited, from his late mother who – she guesses – was not a very strong woman. His hands haven't had to cope with much rough work, but she doesn't think they 'tell' her a great deal more than that, any more than does his wearing a signet ring on his little finger, or his habit of standing with one hand tucked into the back pocket of his trousers, or of running the other hand, his right, repeatedly through his short blond hair.

When they returned to the Eden Hotel in time to change for dinner her mother – eyebrow-plucking over and tweezers still in her hand – wasn't as concerned as Penelope had imagined she would be. What mattered to her was that she should have enjoyed herself with him; she seemed to esteem Henry Kyte's attention as something of a favour done to her.

'Well, he wanted to go out, I expect, and he just happened to ask me.'

'Probably he thought of going for a drive because he guessed you'd like it. *Then* he asked you.'

'I don't know if it could have been – arranged.'

Her mother had no doubts as she applied her lipstick.

'Of course it must have been arranged.'

'The *picnic* was – '

'Why did he speak to us then? It wasn't *me* he wanted to talk to, I'm sure.'

Penelope moved away, to another part of the room. She had supposed that her mother would take the opposite view, that *she* was the reason for a conversation starting, since it was what she chose to believe on her native heath at home, that she was naturally the attention-holder.

'Are you going out again, do you think?'

'I've no idea.'

'Didn't he ask?'

'Yes, he asked.'

'Well, then?'

'I said I didn't know what our plans were.'

'My plans are to do what makes my own daughter happiest.'

Her mother picked up a brush and started on her hair. Disloyally the word 'primping' always came into Penelope's mind when she had to watch it.

'That's what I thought.'

'Well?'

'I'll go wherever *you* want to, it's *your* holiday – '

Her mother glared for a moment; then she softened, as if there were better ways of dealing with such perverse wilfulness.

'I expect he's from a good background.'

'We didn't really talk about that.'

'Later, though. You can talk about it then – '

'I don't know when – '

'You'll get an opportunity.'

'I don't know – '

'He's very presentable. Isn't he? That shows he's been brought up well.'

Penelope didn't reply; she couldn't think how to.

Her mother turned her head several times in front of the mirror. She was quite proud of her hair, and had the fairness regularly topped up with tinting. She was less proud of her spreading chin; she lifted her head a couple of inches.

'It's important to meet the right sort from the opposite gender.'

'There was Valerie's brother – '

'I mean, in the wide world. Adulthood, I suppose. Young men working for a living.'

Penelope closed her mouth.

'He's lucky to have met *you*, of course,' her mother said, placing the stress where she preferred it.

A hand patted down the hair at the back. The lips parted so she could spot lipstick smears, but there weren't any. The teeth were a little yellow with age, and crooked, but they were her own: thus the expense of the gold filling between the top two in front.

'You might find you've got a deal in common, Penelope – '

She meant her daughter to think about it. And as she got ready for dinner, Penelope *did* consider. She found herself putting on her best dress – the grey satin one with the leg-of-mutton sleeves – but not by any clear design, only because her brain was already –

'How lovely you look!' her mother told her, and for the first time lent her her double string of good pearls. They'd been bought from a Dutch jeweller in Borneo, who'd had his own boats; apparently boys would dive down to the coral, without masks and nearly naked, and sometimes one would fail to resurface.

'Mirror, mirror!' her mother said, while her daughter remembered that not all fairy-tales had perfect endings.

2

'Whoever can *that* be?' her mother said.

'Who?'

'The man your friend is chatting to.'

Penelope turned and looked along the terrace to the steps. Henry, right hand pushing through his hair, was talking to a squat, pink-faced man, in his fifties perhaps and wearing an ill-fitting suit.

'What a queer fellow,' her mother said.

The man was shrugging his shoulders inside the jacket and mopping his brow with a handkerchief.

'Brown shoes with a navy suit,' her mother said. 'That's something your Mr Kyte would never do.'

Penelope itched at the pronoun 'your'. A 'possessive' it had been called at school.

'What are they saying? Can you make them out?'

Penelope had better hearing than her mother, but she didn't pick up the words clearly. The word 'telephone' was repeated: the man mentioned something about getting an answer as quickly as he could. Henry Kyte, left hand in his back left-hand trouser pocket, said 'Wild goose'. 'One good turn,' the man replied. It was very confusing altogether.

'He's really rather shabby,' her mother said, sounding disappointed that the young man should be giving the other one his time.

'I expect it's about business,' Penelope said.

One can't be so choosy, she meant, about the company one keeps in *that* line.

'I suppose it must be.'

'A salesman,' Penelope said. 'A representative probably.'

'Is that what representatives look like?'

'I'm guessing.'

'I expect he's trying to sell something to your Mr Kyte.'

Penelope noticed the repetition of the pronoun and was uncomfortable again.

'I'm sure,' her mother said, 'he knows how to deal with *that* type.'

Penelope watched as the older man took the younger one's arm and lowered his voice. Henry shrugged his shoulders, as if the point were immaterial to him. The older man stuffed his handkerchief into his breast pocket, then pulled it out again a few seconds later to remove perspiration from his cheeks and nose.

'He seems very hot.'

Penelope started at her mother's voice.

'I always think doing that's very – very infra dig,' she continued.

According to her mother the world cleanly divided into those with true social grace and those without. Penelope didn't see what a propensity to perspire told you about a person's worth, but there was much she didn't understand about her mother's thinking.

She picked up her guidebook and searched among the paragraphs for where she'd broken off. She finished one page and turned a leaf to the next. After a few lines she looked up and caught the two pairs of eyes moving off them both. She stared at the two men in surprise: she had presumed they were unaware of their presence. They put their heads together and started talking briskly, which she took to be a sign of their embarrassment. Even Henry's face was showing the heat. The man in the blue suit had a foxy look about him, aided by his face's sharper features; she didn't quite trust his appearance. From the little she'd been able to overhear, she thought he must be from the North Midlands or from Yorkshire. Her mother didn't approve of people with localised accents, unless they knew to kowtow to her and she was able to patronise them in turn.

In the afternoon a child walked past them on the terrace, one hand held by each parent. She was wearing a sun-hat, and looked as proud as Punch.

Penelope watched her mother eyeing the trio.

'*You* used to have a sun-hat. Do you remember? A little cotton hat. In fact you had two.'

'I remember *one*. Did I have two?'

'The first one was in Borneo. When you were very small. Of course you would have fried without it.'

'Have you still got it?'

'It was left behind. I was always sorry.'

'Maybe it got lost, en route?'

'I looked on the boat because you needed it there too, of course. I don't know how it was forgotten about. I remember very distinctly, I was in the car: I said to Ayah, for goodness' sake Penelope's hat, and so she got out and ran back.'

She paused in her telling.

'And – ' Penelope prompted her.

' "And"?'

'Did she find it?'

'No. No. I don't think . . .'

'It was already lost maybe?'

'What?'

'She wouldn't have been able to find it?'

Her mother shook her head.

'I don't know.'

Penelope sensed that she was wishing she hadn't begun, that it had been a simple enough story to begin with, but not now. She let her complete it in her own time.

'Your father was in the house. Taking a last look round. He – he must have distracted her attention. In some way. And she forgot about it.'

'I see,' Penelope said, meaning to say the helpful thing, but puzzled.

'So that was that.'

Penelope cleared her throat.

'You – ?'

Her mother sat straightening the pleats of her skirt.

'What's that?'

' – you didn't ask her, though? When she got back to the car?'

'Oh, I forgot. I was waiting for your father too. To finish looking round. It was quite a day in our lives. A big day.'

She leaned back in her chair, following an unravelling thread on her skirt back to its source.

Penelope cleared her throat again. There was a question she had never found the courage or an occasion to put, to the only person who could answer it.

'Why,' she asked, 'why did you leave?'

' "Leave"?'

'Leave Borneo?'

Her mother snapped off the thread.

'Oh, it was such a hot place. Quite a lot of fun, of course. But – well, limited.'

'I wish I could remember more.'

'We were lucky with some things. There was a marvellous little dressmaker not so far away, a Viennese. And the kitchen could do *wonders* with the food.'

'But – ' Penelope craned forward in her chair, in the way of confidence-extracting. The basketwork squeaked, and her mother glanced round. ' – but we left it, though?'

'That was your father's decision,' the reply came back, very briskly.

'Daddy's?'

The face turned away from her.

'That's what I said.'

'And *your* decision too?'

'Not altogether.'

Her mother shaded her eyes against the sun and fixed on a view.

'Oh,' Penelope said.

'He seemed to think – he'd done all that he could there. That there were other prospects at home.'

'Maybe there were?'

'He had a very responsible job there. He was the money man. If he'd stayed with the same firm when he got back, that would have been one thing. But they fell out over something, and the other people he went to never treated him in quite the way he'd been used to: when everything was going well, I mean.'

'Why – why did it change?'

'Why did they fall out? Oh, it was just the age he was, perhaps. Wanting to go back. Some – some silly wanderlust, for England.'

'I always thought – '

'Thought what?' her mother asked her, quite sharply.

'It was something – I don't know, to do with history.'

'"History"?' Her mother's pronunciation of the word sounded nearly incredulous: or sceptical merely. 'How?'

'Something to do with living *there*. In Borneo.'

'No.' Her mother let out a weary sigh. 'No. I don't think it had anything to do with history.'

'Except,' Penelope realised, 'except his own history, of course. Being lived inside him.'

'I thought you said it was Borneo?'

'Trouble,' Penelope suggested. 'Political. A rebellion. Or something.'

Her mother's reply was chilly, even at the afternoon's blood-heat temperature.

'*Nothing* like that.'

'Oh.'

'There might have been no history anywhere for all we knew, and for all the attention we'd probably have paid to it even if we *had* known.'

'I see.'

'Unless your father got wind of something. But we came back at the worst time. We'd have ridden it out out there. But England was the wrong place to be.'

'I see.'

'If we'd waited – '

Penelope mumbled.

'And I think the life was better anyway where we were. Even if things had been normal when we came back. But normal they were not.'

Penelope only nodded.

'I had no choice, though,' her mother continued. 'It didn't matter about those bright young women thinking they were going to have the final say. I was older than them. I was a mother, and I knew what I was good at – keeping a house in order.'

Penelope watched her mother closely and wondered about herself, her own preconceptions. Maybe she'd been too uncritical, too content with that impression of lightness her mother was so ready to give in company. Somehow she hadn't imagined her putting herself in mental competition with those young sparks – sparkesses – dancing the evenings away in London's supper clubs. Anyway, in the end most of them had probably married, and that was the end of one particular adventure and the start of another.

'I had *you*,' her mother said. 'And after the accident, thinking I never wanted to walk down stone steps again – '

Penelope also shaded her eyes against the sun and fixed on a view, looking in the same direction as her mother. Then she noticed what – or whom – she hadn't done in the glare: on the driveway Henry Kyte was standing in animated conversation with the man her mother had considered with such evident disapproval earlier. Doubtless he would have stuck out like a sore thumb in Borneo too.

She turned her eyes away, to the view proper: the hills inland, colouring from ochre to purple against the blue metal sheen sky, and difficult for her now to distinguish from Cézanne's geometric, brutal, wholly individual and maybe maniacal images hanging in the little whitewashed museum like a hermitage.

Penelope and her mother turn a corner and nearly bump into the pair, literally enough. The older man turns and walks off. Henry's eyes quickly, shrewdly calculate. His right hand sweeps through his hair. He makes his admission to them, thrusting his left hand into his back trouser pocket. That the man is no other than his father.

All three look after him as he scuttles along the terrace, towards the cool shade thrown by the hotel's flank. 'Ah,' Mrs Milne says, 'I see.' The words and their delivery speak a small volume. Penelope's eyes turn back to Henry, to his profile, which is actually quite fine, the proportions of his nose to mouth notwithstanding. This, she decides, is probably his best angle.

In the evening there is no sign of either of the Englishmen.

The next day Henry Kyte makes a similar invitation to before, to go for a drive or a walk about the town. Mrs Milne says it's a little too hot for her.

Penelope accepts. She is becoming coy in his presence. She remembers how Valerie expected her to feel with Oliver, which she was unable to do at the time.

'The poor bugger lost his job. Dad, I mean. In 'thirty. He decided *I* was still going to get the best chances, though, so I was kept on at school. Somehow we got by on appearances, just about. He landed another job eventually, but it wasn't very good. A come-down for him.'

He shook his head, steering the car.

'Really – really he's a hero.'

His voice had a catch in it. Penelope gulped.

'It takes guts to do what Dad did. I mean, it pulverised him, all that. Took the spring out of his step, you know? It *shrank* him, really and truly, he must've lost a couple of inches. All that crouching, trying to close in on himself. Jesus, what happens to people!'

'Yes,' she replied, and her own voice had a catch in it.

'And they can't do a bloody thing about it. Pardon my language – '

'Yes. Of course – '

'Part of your life you're responsible for: how you behave and go on, choosing to do certain things. But there's another part you've no control over, it takes over *you*, and you've got no choice. I guess that's history, it snares you, in its net. Somehow you have to live with those two ideas, and try to balance

109

everything out in your head. It's difficult, though, when you don't know what tomorrow's going to bring you, dump on your doorstep.'

She nodded: she intended it as a thoughtful nod, to let him know that she respected his sensitivity and sensibility, that she was also moved by his words.

He walks very close to her, as closely as a man has ever done.

A physical reaction inside her.

She wishes he would touch her arm, move closer still. And –

She waits. 'It' doesn't happen, although she senses that there will never be a better opportunity than this one.

But the moment is let go of: not – she concludes – because he hasn't the courage but because he quite fails to see that it is an opportunity: because he hasn't been looking for one in the first place.

She thinks momentarily of Oliver – a memory flash – then she's puzzling how she is going to extricate herself from the situation: not that he sees it as that, a 'situation', but she knows that when she is back at the hotel what will preoccupy her mind for hours on end is the endless recalling of her own foolishness, her excessive optimism.

Penelope feels obliged to tell her mother about Henry Kyte's father when she returns to the hotel. Her mother says very little by way of reply.

At dinner her mother sat with her back to the room.

'What a splendid view,' she said in a dry voice, unfolding her napkin and looking not out of the window but at the crockery.

'Are you feeling all right?' Penelope asked her.

'Why?' She inspected the black lace décolletage on her dress. 'Don't I look well to you?'

'Yes. Yes, it's just – '

'It's the heat.'

The first few days had been even hotter. She had heard her mother telling the manager so much sunshine was a tonic to her. (The real tonic for her was losing her appetite and knowing her favourite weight of nine-and-a-half stones wasn't in any danger.)

As they waited for their first course she fidgeted, and the joints of her chair squeaked; she reread the menu as if she were really interested. Through the glass doors Penelope noticed the other Mr Kyte out in the hall, pacing up and down.

Between the first course and the second, Henry's car puttered up the drive, sounding not devil-may-care but quite ordinary. Penelope glanced over at a window and saw the two men standing outside talking: Mr Kyte Senior was pointing at his watch.

By the time Henry was dressed and they both walked into the dining-room, the third course was awaited. Penelope watched her mother straighten herself in her chair as Mr Kyte's voice carried; she realised she would have to acknowledge them alone, and looked across and nodded at Henry, quite formally. He responded with a bow, but his father walked behind him staring down at his feet. She wondered why: if he actually disapproved of their afternoon antics: and sufficiently so, it occurred to her, to prefer that neither she nor her mother would receive from him even a curt salutation.

After lunch on the next day Henry Kyte proposes another excursion in the car. Mrs Milne, a little less warmly, claims car-sickness; but she's sufficiently won over by the young man's charm to wish him and Penelope a happy afternoon.

    Penelope is ready, willing.

'You both come abroad a lot?' he asked her as they continued to walk.

She smiled past him, into the distance and a blur of mauve lavender fields.

'You do?' he asked again, slowing and – as ever – not letting the parked car out of his sight.

'No,' she said.

'No?'

She shook her head.

'I'm sorry to disappoint you,' she said.

'You're not.'

'What did you think? That we gadded about?'

'I wasn't sure – '

'Down to the Corniche, up to Switzerland?'

'Well . . .' He pushed his right hand through his hair.

'What else do you think about us?'

'You've come *here*, though,' he persisted.

'It was my mother's idea. It must be costing a king's ransom. Or a prince's one, at least.'

'Your mother must be able to afford it.'

'I'm not sure how.'

'Really?'

He looked mystified.

'But you told me about your school,' he said.

'She scrimped rather.' Penelope knew her mother would not welcome the disclosure. 'A little.'

'I see.'

'She just had this notion.'

'Yes. Yes, like my father.'

'I suppose I should be grateful,' she said.

'Yes.'

'And you?' she asked.

'I suppose I am.'

'So we've got that in common – '

'Yes.'

She felt he was withdrawing. She wondered if he might be a person of moods.

'Just as if we were family, Penelope.'

She stared at him.

'Brother and sister. You at your school,' he said, 'and me at mine.'

'But I've just left it.'

'I'm not *so* much older than you,' he told her.

'No.' Had she offended him? 'I didn't mean that – '

'A chap's got to do something for a living.'

'Yes.' She nodded. 'I'm sure you're – '

'What'll *you* do?' he asked her.

' "Do"?'

'Yes. Haven't you thought about it?'

'When I get back?'

'Dad says it's all pretty black.' He turned the initialled gold signet ring on his little finger. 'In Europe. No time to lose.'

She nodded again.

'I'll drive us back now,' he said.

They climbed into the car. The engine rattled under the bonnet; life sparked, the chassis shook.

Sister and brother. Her heart shrank. If he were to stop the car and ask her now 'May I kiss you, Penelope?' she wasn't so certain what her answer would be. Yesterday she would have been ready to say 'yes' to a man for her mother's sake: now . . .

She breathed in some flying dust, a little, and coughed. She coughed on some more. Suddenly her eyes ran tears, and the terrain turned to Cézanne blocks of rock and tree-streaks.

Henry dropped her at the hotel, telling her he wanted 'to get a bit of speed up'. She didn't understand, for a few moments, that he was going off on a kind of joy ride.

'I don't suppose you want to come?'

'No,' she said, just a little sourly. 'No, I don't think I do.'

'Okey-dokey.'

It was an expression she had overheard his father use. Her mother had heard too, and she'd watched her nose crinkle.

'Be seeing you, then,' he said.

Maybe, she thought: or maybe not.

She didn't wait to watch but ran up the steps to the front doors and the foyer. She looked into the lounge, but there was no sign of her mother. She made her way to the lift and stabbed her finger on the button-bell. As she stood waiting she caught sight of Mr Kyte Senior in the mirror, emerging from the telephone box. He looked rather hot, rather red. The change in his hand dropped on to the floor and she watched him bend down and pick up the coins, counting and checking.

The lift arrived. She opened the gate and stepped inside. She positioned herself so that she could watch for a few seconds longer as Mr Kyte made his hasty, perspiring exit from the foyer. He pushed through the doors and hurried outside, into the broiling heat of the afternoon.

Her mother didn't call out when she knocked on her door the first time. She tapped again. There was a reply from inside, some words, sounding grudging. She had been spared the unpredictable aspect of her mother's behaviour for most of the holiday: she felt she could forgive this lapse, but she wondered what had brought it on, why it should have happened this particular afternoon.

Her mother was sitting in the armchair, with the window closed behind her. The bedspread showed evidence of rumpling; she must have been lying on top of it, always a bad sign.

'Penelope?'

The accent was sharp. Another sign of ill-omen.

'Yes. Yes, it's me.'

'It's been such a hot day.'

'Yes. Yes, it has been.'

'Ridiculously hot.'

Penelope thought of Mr Kyte's face downstairs: and of his son, disrespectful and rather deep, racing round the town in the quest of a breather.

'Too hot for being out in a car,' she said, quite truthfully. 'I'm glad to be back –'

'Are you?' her mother asked, in the most desultory way.

' – indoors.'

'What a very silly climate.'

Well, that just about sums it up, Penelope thought.

'Have you done much?' she asked.

'Oh. I've had enough to occupy me.'

It might have been her mother complaining: or being cryptic. It was *she* who had encouraged the motor trips, and she didn't believe her sympathy was being required on *that* account, because she'd been a gooseberry.

'I'm sorry – '

'Well . . . There's no need to be.'

'While I was gallivanting about – '

'Were you?'

For the first time since she'd come into the room, the eyes betrayed some interest: curiosity, or maybe it was suspicion.

'Dad's got some confidence left.' Henry's right hand combed through his hair. 'That's how he started the business in the first place. Thinks if he can get hold of the ready – some cash – he'll be all right again.'

He put both hands on the wheel to negotiate a bend in the road.

113

'Maybe he will be. He's got high hopes.'

He puckered his lips and whistled, a silly cheerful tune.

'He's got plans. If he can just pull all the threads together. You know?'

No, not about business, she didn't know anything about that. Then she wondered how many schemes the man had in his head; and if he may not have been so deserving of her sympathy after all.

'I think he may be seeing some pal of Blanchard's today. He may be going to put something to him, I wouldn't be surprised.'

'Oh?'

She tried a small smile.

'He said he thought it might be best if I took a little run about for a couple of hours this afternoon.'

Her neat smile suddenly felt redundant. He had told her what he shouldn't. In an instant she was aware why last night, when they'd already taken their very formal leave, Henry's second walk across the lounge had happened: because of an urgent poke in the back from a contriving father. *You can take your young friend out again, go for another spin.*

She listened to him whistling a few more bars of that damned song. How could he have been so stupid as to actually tell her?

Unless . . .

She stuck her tongue into her cheek.

Unless of course he had intended to, because he meant to alert her to what was happening.

She turned her head and looked at him. She watched his face. She couldn't decide: she didn't believe he was being either inadvertently stupid or deliberately mischievous. She didn't believe he was being anything in particular. It may have been that he hadn't planned on being anything from the very beginning, but had only behaved according to his impulses or to a code he'd been instructed in at school: so he had been acting quite unself-critically, without thinking. Using her time to pleasantly and undemandingly while away his own.

She looked away again at a view of ochre rocks and pine and olive trees and low scrub.

In the interim of watching the distance, she failed at first to identify the cause of the blowing dust, a black car that suddenly appeared over the crest in front of them. It was travelling too fast, as they were.

'Slow down, Henry!'

The car sped towards them, and she grabbed with both hands at the dashboard.

It was only by good fortune that both cars didn't collide on the narrow road. In the seconds before they swept past each other, time somehow slowed and she looked over to see who was driving. The face belonged to her father, she saw; he was wearing an open-necked shirt and looking not a day older than she remembered him. His eyes were on the road, and he held the wheel as he always had, with his arms straight out and his shoulders stiff. His face rushed from her, in a blur, and when she could think to turn her head and look back, the car was little more than a speck in the distance, lost in a swirl of dust.

'Are you all right?'

'What?'

'That was a close shave.'

She mumbled.

'You look a bit pale. Shall I stop?'

'No.'

'I *can*.'

'I'm fine, really. Just – '

'The roads are okay if there's nothing else on them.'

'Where did it come from?'

'Don't know.' His right hand riffled through his hair. 'Just appeared.'

The heat, it's this heat, it's too much to cope with, I belong to quite a different latitude, we should never have left London, it was a mistake, quite absurd, and now it's come to this.

'Are you *sure* you're all right?'

'Yes.' She nodded her head. 'Did you see him?'

'Who?'

'The driver.'

'*I* didn't. Did you?'

'Yes. No.'

'Yes, no?' he said, and laughed.

She felt obliged to smile. Rather tiredly though. Back in England, she thought, this will all seem to have been a dream, bizarre and with its own logic. When we get home.

She was conscious of her silence on the drive back. When she wasn't thinking about the silence she was remembering the sight of her father. How exactly did the two parts of her life, the one spent there and the other now being lived here, tie up? Was it possible she would catch a glimpse of him again, several sightings, in other places?

Then without any warning, as he drove the car, Henry Kyte leaned over and kissed her, somewhere between her neck and her cheek. A soft, dry kiss. His mouth moved and he planted another kiss, all warmth, beneath her ear.

After the second she gently twisted herself free. Her heart was banging on her ribs. She didn't know where to look. She turned from him, head angled away.

On their arrival back at the hotel he seemed to be on the lookout for someone.

When he'd opened the car door for her and she'd got out, he coped with the embarrassment by saying he was going to get up a head of steam.

'Does the jalopy good,' he said.

'It's a very nice motor,' she told him.

115

'A bit sluggish. But she *can* go.'

She nodded. She smiled, timorously. She felt the two kisses impressed on her skin: like holy stigmata, she thought blasphemously. She stood reeling a little on her feet, smiling woozily against the sun.

As much had happened as she knew how to deal with. Where did she go from here?

She found her mother counting the sheets of tissue paper in her suitcase, as if she was trying very hard not to think of something else. Her hair was damp on the back of her neck. She had been crying.

'I think we might change our plans, Penelope.'

'What?'

'Yes. I think we've seen all we want to here, don't you?'

Penelope was picturing the car speeding through the town's streets. What of the grand plan concerning her and its driver?

She dropped on to the edge of the bed.

'Has – has something brought this on?'

'Oh, it's just I think we've done everything. Everything we said we'd do. And it's getting so hot, isn't it?'

'Not *quite* so hot as it was.'

'But hot enough,' her mother said quickly, in a voice that wasn't going to brook any arguments to the contrary. 'Which is why I think we might move on now.'

A handkerchief was sticking out of her cardigan sleeve: untidily, which was another give-away to Penelope. Quite clearly 'something' had happened in her absence. Into her head came another picture from a few minutes before: Mr Kyte Senior downstairs in the foyer, with his face boiled by the heat, and looking more than ever like the mere man – not the gentleman – her mother had seen him to be.

'When?' she asked.

'I thought – well, tomorrow seems as good a time as any.'

What about her 'plans', though? – 'to do what makes my own daughter happiest'? Even if the term didn't mean anything, hadn't they pretended that it had? This was how a child stopped playing, suddenly tiring and demolishing the house of cards and not giving it a second thought. Momentarily she remembered Valerie . . .

She tried to argue with her mother, but she realised she wasn't going to be persuaded. The more she said, the more decided her mother became. She wasn't allowed to forget who was footing the bills for their exotic jaunt.

So this really *would* be their last night. Tomorrow they'd be leaving and that must be the end of it.

Penelope sighed, down to her shoes and deeper –

'Have you told them?'

Her mother sniffed. 'Told whom?'

116

'The hotel – '

'What? Oh no, I haven't. Penelope, please – could you be an angel – '

Penelope nodded, and slowly got to her feet. Of course, of course. And now the embarrassment became hers.

Maybe, she thought, maybe all along it *had* been the heat to blame, like a temporary fit of sun-madness.

3

Since it was their last night Penelope walked about the grounds for a while. Her mother thought she was packing, but it was an innocent fraud.

The further she walked from the hotel building the better became her view of the town beneath. As she stopped to watch, something inside her overrode her reason. She felt it was a dangerous force, whatever it was: a will to choose for herself.

What she chose now was to have a last look at the town, but closer to: just to forget for half-an-hour of their final evening the tedious, cloying demands of sense and practicality.

At seventeen and eighteen the sense that all is loss, all is passing from you. Then the slow, receding loss of that sensation of loss, and a terrible, seductively despairing nostalgia like a stomach sickness for feelings always on the point of vanishing.

The streets were busiest naturally in the centre, although the whole town seemed especially alive, in a way that an English town would not have been.

Heads and forearms and bosoms hung out of windows, children played on balconies, stout shapes sat passively on chairs in dark doorways.

The sky was inky blue. She could still tell foreground colours apart without difficulty: flowers in pots, dresses, shirts, jugs on tables.

She was smiled at as she traced the corners and turns of the streets. She didn't feel awkward or conspicuous, nothing threatened her. Her feet walked and she merely followed them.

She came to bars and cafés. People sat at tables set out on the pavement or under trees. They talked and exclaimed and laughed and argued in quite good humour and made simpering love.

She realised she had brought no money with her, so she couldn't join them. She felt that that was exactly what she was wanting to do: but she didn't have the grasp of the language that would allow her to converse with a 'patron', to ask him if she might forward to him afterwards the price of a *p'tit café*.

So she continued walking. She passed through the main square, and turned into the one broad street of the town. It was lined with plane trees on both sides. Locals were parading up and down in pairs, taking the air or showing themselves off.

There was a cinema, and she stopped to look at the publicity stills in the

118

windows. In one crudely tinted photograph a young woman in smart city clothes was walking arm-in-arm with two men: she wore a very stylish wide-brimmed hat that shaded her eyes and she was laughing in a mischievous but contented way while her companions kept straight faces and sheepishly looked away into the white borders like seams at the sides of the photograph. In another still, presumably from the same film, one of the men was standing against a wardrobe looking confused while the woman threw clothes into a suitcase: her hat lay on the bed, she was smiling, and again her look was triumphant. A third photograph showed her carrying her suitcase and jumping on to a train: in the last seconds, as steam rose from the tracks, her hat had blown off and it was being retrieved by a young man in matelot's uniform, who was staring up at the long legs and two-toned shoes climbing the steps to the carriage door.

Penelope turned away. She was conscious of her pleasure – with the balmy air, with the strangeness of the place, its informality, her movements as easy as in a dream. She was thinking of the images in the photographs when she heard laughter and let her eyes cross the street.

Outside a corner café called the Orinoco, seated on chairs, she saw Henry Kyte and his friend Monsieur Blanchard. At the same table sat two young women, joining in the laughter. The men were smoking fat cigars as if they'd won a sweepstake. Henry's other hand was tucked into the back pocket of his trousers, so that she couldn't be confusing him for anyone else. The women, legs crossed, wore over-dressy clothes and too much lipstick on their mouths; each had her hand on the arm of the man next to her.

Penelope stood behind a plane tree watching the merriment. She knew, if not who, *what* the women were – on a woman's instinct, even though she'd never had any dealings with their sort. Her mother had invited Valerie to visit London twice in the past and to stay with them, and it was Valerie who had pointed out the species to her – with a righteous index finger – as the bus they were on pitched along Piccadilly from the Constitution Hill end, by way of Green Park. 'They're tarts,' she'd whispered. '*Are* they?' 'Dirty sluts,' Valerie had confirmed with a hissing ferocity she'd never forgotten.

And now there they were, a stone's throw away from her. No better than they should be, and not even ashamed. It was impossible that their two hosts, filling their glasses with wine from bottles, didn't know.

At some remark they all sat laughing in unison. Penelope turned her back on them and walked away.

It was a tawdry ending. She felt nothing: she wasn't shaking, she wasn't hot or cold or hot *and* cold, sickness wasn't churning at the bottom of her stomach. She was moving easily enough, she wasn't stumbling, she was upright.

Of course it was a slap in the face. But Henry Kyte had never really pretended otherwise, had he? (Except for the two kisses, but that – she guessed – was only the cheap currency in common usage.) It was her mother she thought she must be angry with for having encouraged it – and more angry still with herself for not resisting better. That would be later, though. At this moment, turning another corner into a quieter, narrower street with a curve on it, she felt only modest in her clear-headedness: perceptive at last, and to a fault, but it had come too late.

She waited for her eyes to fill and they did before she reached the turn on the street. The white walls blurred, and all that was left was the echo they held, of her shoes on the hardness of cobbled pavement.

It was a sombre journey back to Paris.

Between the hotel and the station northern-looking clouds had scudded in off the sea and the brightness had gone out of the day. Dust blew up, irritating the eyes and making Penelope's skin itch as she attended to the loading of the suitcases.

As the train steamed inland, the dust soon smeared the carriage windows. Penelope sat in the window-corner of their cabin with a book held open in front of her, but she wasn't reading; nor was she noticing much of what was passing on the other side of the grimy glass. Her mother was keeping silent and immobile, which meant that nothing was as it should be: she was clearing her throat but not to speak, and her bones cracked as she stretched her ankles or turned her wrists but she didn't care to stand up and move about as she had on the journey down.

Their fellow passengers brushed against the glass of the door as they moved along the narrow corridor searching out berths or acquainting themselves with the layout of the services. Some of them looked in but appeared to see only a conventionally English mother and daughter and looked away without interest. Later they would draw down the blinds and set the lock on the door but Penelope wasn't ready yet for that confinement. She wanted daylight and wide panoramic views and the hubbub for as long as she could have them. She wasn't looking forward to evening and dinner and the cramped, formal intimacy of bedding down.

The wheels shuddering on the tracks settled into the rhythm of departure. They didn't talk about the hotel or the past several days, they didn't mention the Kytes, son or father. Penelope sat facing north, and her mother sat on the banquette opposite with no last lingering glances cast through the window for the landscape they were leaving behind them.

With a ceremonial flourish her mother extracted the front-door key from her handbag and pushed it into the lock. She turned it with a wrist-flick, then she leaned on the wood. The door swung back and immediately Penelope smelt the frowsty air come rushing out of the tunnel of hallway; all the pressure of darkness in the house seemed to be behind it, cramming it between the hall's walls and out through the doorjambs, heaving it down the steps where she stood waiting beneath her mother. Waiting, she knew: but she had no sense of what for. The air stank of dead time, all the time before and also to come, which would make her life seem so different from how it had to her in the years of anticipation.

120

Her mother scooped up the mail in both hands and crossed the threshold into the house. Penelope hesitated before she placed one foot, then the other, on the top step. She had no distinct sense of the shape or size of the hall other than she remembered it to be. But it was the sour, lifeless smell of the house that confused her: much worse than that, it *appalled* her.

She heard her mother's voice from one of the unlit rooms. Of course they would have to go through the business of the gas and water being turned on under the floorboards, which – peculiarly – was one messy custom which her mother always reserved for herself.

The rusty gas cock groaned as it was prised down to the 'on' position. The water slopping into the tank in the loft was quite audible to them three floors beneath. The taps were turned on in the scullery and the pipes clattered inside their cases as peat-coloured 'cold' spluttered out: 'hot' would take several hours, and be cloudy when she filled a basin and have a musty taste when she put her sponge to her face.

She did as she invariably did on these homecomings and closed her bedroom door on the din and returned downstairs. She found her mother in their back living-room, the so-called 'morning-room'. She was holding a lit spill to a gas wick. A blue flame appeared inside the gauze, then two shadows slid up the long wall behind: her mother's, and – less clearly – her own, fraying at its edges. She smelt the gas and the sulphur from the match to light the spill; she could hear the flame hissing as it perched on the mantle, holding its balance. All was reverting to its original condition, to how it had been before they'd left on their holiday, and she didn't think she could bear it, being recalled to this life that passed as their version of 'normality'. She felt different now, even though the sulphur smelt the same. The past three weeks had shown her that, for all the disappointments it had kept up its sleeve, the world offered a spread of possibilities like a prodigal feast. *Their* life in the house was as full as . . . – she thought of a comparison, a parallel, then decided – it was the equivalent of a humble, ignominious matchbox left on a shelf with other matchboxes in a great department store packed full along its galleries with all manner of more tempting desirable wares. She already knew this much (and France had only confirmed the knowledge in her), that she didn't want to spend the rest of her life in one or any other matchbox. There was so much to see and to experience, you could choke and suffocate just on the prospect of a tiny part of it, one single storey of that bulging, opulent department store.

Part Five

1

Her mother's nerves snapped during one of the later raids. It was like the whiplash of a cable wound too tight.

They had sat listening to the planes and heard the bombs released, whistling, from the holds. Penelope had watched as her mother put her head into her hands. At first she thought she was doing so for weariness, because they'd had to suffer so many planes of late. Then she saw her shoulders shaking. The first house-quaking sob rose up out of her.

It was the worst night of Penelope's life: trying to calm her mother, which she couldn't do, then escaping to the telephone to ring a neighbour for help, then the pain of letting the neighbour see, then the bother of ringing more numbers through the exchange, trying to find a doctor or a nurse.

Eventually medical help did arrive, and her mother could be sedated.

In the days afterwards she was confined indoors; the doctor expressed solemn concern at her condition.

'This isn't the place for her,' he said. 'She's far too nervy.'

'I don't know how,' Penelope told him. 'How it's happened.'

'Well, it has. And now we have to cope with it.'

Penelope just nodded at the prognosis.

'Would it be possible,' the doctor asked, 'to get her away from here? For a while?'

'How long?'

'Until this spate of raids is over?'

'I suppose – '

'Is there somewhere she could go?'

'I'm not sure. Maybe. If I can think about – '

'I honestly think it would be for the best.'

In the end – after days of trying to extract the details from her mother – she tracked down an elderly cousin to a small market town in Somerset.

'Well, it isn't perfect,' the doctor said. 'Is that the only place?'

'That I know of,' Penelope replied, exhausted by her day and night vigils.

'Bristol's been getting it badly. And the ports.'

'Yes. But it's in the country. It would be better than here.'

'Indeed,' the doctor said. He agreed to provide the local doctor with the information he would need, and so there and then the matter – except the exacting business of the travel arrangements, which were to stretch Penelope's patience to its limits – was settled.

They got there, after a succession of endlessly slow train journeys. Before the war – Penelope calculated, to help to while away the tedium – it would have taken them six or seven hours to reach Yelborne from London, including a taxi trip of eleven miles on the last stage. In the event, it took them more than double that time, almost fifteen hours. The population of central southern and western England seemed to be on the move that day. The compartments were crowded, corridors on the trains that passed them had standing passengers pressed flat against the windows; any hope of comfort or privacy was of course quite out of the question.

They covered the last leg with darkness gathering over the fields like a net. Reflections started to appear in the window glass, but Penelope saw through them; she had the lulling sense that somehow the raids had been for the best in a perverse way (given her mother's condition), because now the two of them were travelling to another, unexperienced England. Villages with lazily smoking chimneys nestled in dells; hills benignly dominated the skyline, like the flanks of macroscopic guardian creatures from myth; here and there a neat copse topped the crest of a hill like seigneurial plumes or a Mohican's shock. She remembered something she had been told at school, how wooded country used to be scoured for the tallest, straightest trees, which would be felled and transported in one piece to supply the king's navy with keels. The land in rolls and troughs seemed to be remembering all its history on this early summer night, with bonfires burning and cows being herded home. Oil-lamps were lit in the windows of cottages, and the windows appeared to be sunk deep into the walls, and the walls sagged under the weight of piled thatch loaded on top of them. Lives continued out of prior generations, in obligatory perpetuity: here, she thought as the train crawled past – looking like a slow glow-worm perhaps to those who were watching them – here is time in its mysterious and private essence, caught on the crossing.

They had a long wait at Malbury station before a taxi came, but her mother already seemed more settled. She told riddles to a boy who was waiting with his mother, until a pony-and-trap came to pick them up and deliver them to wherever they were bound.

After the wait, Penelope let out several sighs of relief when the taxi finally rolled into the yard. Inside, they had to rub at the condensation on the windows with handkerchiefs to see out. It was hard to distinguish more than the outlines of cottages and barns against the theatrical mauve sky. By dim gaslight they had their first glimpse of the small town that would be their home for a while. There was a round, colonnaded butter-market in a square, and an ivy-clad inn, and a walkway of shops above a ford, and a pair of elaborate iron gates between high walls, and it might, Penelope thought, have been the setting for a detective mystery.

West Field, her mother's cousin's home, awaited them at the end of flinty, roller-coaster Badger Lane, a mile or so beyond the town. The thatch had a tousled look, and the state of the plaster on the walls and the paintwork on the windows and drainpipes showed that the house had known better days. But the welcome was warm; elderly Lilian Hollins and her housekeeper were full of concern for them both after the journey. The interior of the house too had a warm charm, Penelope thought, a saggy sort of comfort after their long day's travelling, and she was glad that it wasn't a formal, stiff-back and horsehair place. A grandfather clock ticked (out of time) and chimed (out of key). Already she felt that she was losing her hold on the other existence they'd come from. She was still so tired after the last few days that she couldn't have wished for anything better. She smiled at all that she was shown. Maybe here at last they would be able to snatch an interval of happiness and forgetting.

When she was able to look around it at her leisure, the town reminded her of an invented place, in that detective novel. There was a stately church, richly endowed in its past, with a bona fide lychgate and trimmed yews; houses and cottages lay low behind hedges and walls, yet – she noticed – upstairs windows were invariably so positioned that public goings-on could be observed by the curious. She saw a faded beauty loaded with a garden-trug of vegetables, and a gentleman in legal pinstripes dragged a lame leg; a brassy-haired girl with a knowing eye put a provocative roll into the motion of her hips, like a slattern, and an elderly woman in bottle-green stockings with a tippler's list carried a dog-eared Bible about with her. Murdering birds – crows and jackdaws – were nailed up on a gate as a warning to others, and in one garden she recognised sprigs of poisonous spotted hemlock.

In the shops she introduced herself meekly whenever anyone asked. Eyes, she felt, were taking her in very cannily. Remarks were prefaced, 'A young woman like you . . .' and after a time she started to fancy it was being said almost in an accusing way. The wife of the captain of the local Home Guard unit took a very long look at her and asked what her war had been like, 'so far'; Penelope explained about some ladylike voluntary work in London and the woman seemed to make some rapid mental calculations on openings and suitability before she announced that she would surely be hearing from her. The parson's sister, sharing the same wolfish face as her brother, swooped down a side-lane and assured her she would be in touch later, that there was always so much good to be done in such a place. Again Penelope smiled hesitantly, and felt that smiling might seem to be promising too much. The stooped woman in the post office candidly asked her if she could type, and when Penelope replied 'Yes', she could, the woman merely nodded and seemed to commit the information to her personal retrieval system.

But it was an attractive little town too, she had to concede as she walked around it. She liked the mellow saffron stone and the old ridged roofs invaded by moss. She had never seen a circular butter-market before, and wondered why no one going about their business stopped to look at it. She followed them, finding the cobbles under her feet difficult to adjust to but enjoying the change from the loosened flags of concrete on London's pavements. Creeper covered the front of the hotel, so much of it that the building appeared to be a topiary clipped out of green and russet vegetation. There was another inn, she discovered, called The Stricken Oak: more of a tap, with sawdust blowing from its front door and an unpleasant stench from a gutter in an alley to one side of it. And yet it was from the same low and louche Stricken Oak that she saw emerge – and was seen by in her turn – a young couple of a different sort, he in a Norfolk jacket and she in French-cut trousers. She only glimpsed them for a moment, though, and then that moment was gone: but it caused her to wonder if the town mightn't be more intricately composed than a naïve outsider like herself had too readily presumed it to be.

At least she had the claim of kinship with Miss Hollins, so she wasn't wholly an outsider to the place. Was the relationship an advantage, though?

She sensed quite soon that people were all too ready to presume; they were calculating on her good will without having any evidence of it. She might have been dragooned into any of the church rotas – flowers, hassock repairs, Girl Guides, baby-sitting, garden-weeding for the elderly, gathering jumble – or she might have been shanghai-ed into answering the telephone and opening the door for the harassed doctor with the gammy back whose previous surgery help had gone off to discover her independence in Plymouth, or she might have been coerced into knitting ridiculous patchwork blankets for a major's widow, to send to the Front, to the army's hilarity. She might have been doing these things, that is, if she hadn't persisted in claiming that her mother was too poorly to do without her. She had a presentiment that it was all or nothing, and that if she'd agreed to one request other demands would have been made of her and her situation would have been taken for granted: so, if she felt selfish as a result, that was only the cost of it. She atoned in some measure by anticipating her mother's wants, by doing all that she could tactfully offer to do in the house, from repairing the chimes in the grandfather clock to shelling peapods from the kitchen garden.

It was less than everything, but more than nothing.

At one end of the High Street a wall loomed over a squatter of rooftops. Behind the wall were trees with that uniquely cultivated look possessed by those on private estates.

The wall curved away from the last cottages. A narrow cobbled pavement ran alongside and Penelope followed it.

She had walked a couple of hundred yards when a tennis ball landed on the road in front of her. It had cleared the wall, and bounced high on the tarmacadam. Luckily the road was a quiet one and there was no traffic passing, so no startled driver had to swerve to avoid an accident. The ball came to rest in the far gully where the road sloped away from the camber: a gutter, except that there were no drains on that side of the road where the red tarmacadam became grass and spreading weed.

Penelope crossed over and picked up the ball. Thirty or forty yards further on she saw the gates in the wall she'd noticed on the night she and her mother had arrived in the town. She recrossed the road and made her way towards them.

They were elaborate gates, grandly worked for receiving the world but chained and padlocked. When she reached them, a man and a woman, both young-ish and carrying tennis racquets, were running towards her on gravel. The man called out and waved his racquet above his head.

Penelope offered the ball back, and the two thanked her, as if she had performed some deed of heroism. 'It was nothing,' she said, 'really.'

The couple came as close to the gates as they could. The man was tall, broad-shouldered, with dark thinning hair and a face Penelope immediately felt intriguing her. It might have been an intimidating face – his nose had hawkish prominence, his eyebrows met on the bridge of his nose, the precise contours of his mouth suggested to her a fastidious, determined nature – but she was drawn to it, by the brightness of his grey eyes maybe. She was reassured by the clusters of little lines fanning from the corner of his eyes, and by the concern she recognised in his voice.

'It was nothing really,' she repeated. 'I was just taking a walk.'

The woman called her tennis partner 'Romilly'. She was striking in her own way, because she was so tall and elegant. When another man's voice sounded from the distance, calling the name 'Belle!', she lifted her eyes to the sky.

'I didn't know I was so popular . . .'

They didn't seem eager to get back to their game but were quite happy instead to stand talking with her. In ten minutes Penelope felt she hardly said a worthwhile thing – mostly she chattered on about herself, only from nervousness – but the two of them looked at her as if she had the most interesting and enviable life imaginable.

She wanted to laugh.

'You mustn't do yourself down,' the man told her, holding his racquet behind him.

'I'm sorry – '

'But you shouldn't be.'

She believed him, in spite of everything, in spite of probability. He could persuade her merely by including her in the range of his vision. Whenever he did she felt temporarily mesmerised, until he looked away and she tried to remember what he had just said to her.

She forgot later how exactly they had proposed that she should join them. In practical terms, by way of a side-gate (the only proper means of ingress and

127

egress, the big gates being chained and the garden – really a small park – being surrounded by a high wall). The side-gate directly faced an estate cottage: from which, on most of her subsequent arrivals and departures, she was sure that she was being observed, from behind the lozenges of leaded glass.

The game of tennis was forgotten that first day. Tea in two silver pots was brought out on to the lawn, and she was introduced to the company. She recognised the man she had seen watching her outside The Stricken Oak, wearing the same Norfolk jacket. He winked at her; she found herself blushing, and wondered if Romilly would think it was because of him, as he took her arm later and invited her – if she'd had all the tea she wanted? – to inspect the house.

It was 'a pretty compact sort of place', she was told, although it seemed otherwise to her. Portions reached by half-flights of stairs and dog-leg corridors had been added on by succeeding owners as and when required. 'So it never got above itself, you see.' The oldest parts were sixteenth century, and the floorboards sounded it. The wainscoting covered the full height of the walls, but the ornamental plaster ceilings were low and a number of the windows quite deep, so she didn't feel overpowered by the public rooms. There were twelve bedrooms, here and there and everywhere, not including the attic accommodation for staff. She liked the snug library best, smelling of leather and paper and so quiet that the falling of petals on to a tabletop quite startled her as she and her guide stood together at a window looking out at an immaculate lawn.

'They' were eight.

None of them was older than thirty-five or thirty-six.

There were Romilly, Joss, Harriet, Belle, Hugh, Sonia, Gil and Helen.

Romilly was quiet and the cleverest of the men, and the one of the eight with the most commanding presence.

Joss was Romilly's closest friend, although that didn't prevent them from sparring occasionally. He had a leaner, sharper-featured face; his moods varied, and he sometimes seemed to be protecting Romilly from her.

Harriet was brains to Sonia's beauty, but maybe that was deceptive: Sonia had a very careful memory for what had been said on other days, and Harriet was never able to pass a mirror without examining the evidence in it.

Belle was the youngest daughter of a Scottish lord, flawlessly well-mannered but quite unselfconscious about it. She seemed to have a child's enthusiasm for the world: and an endearing tendency to scattiness.

Hugh was the hearty party of the group. He had read medicine for a couple of years before giving up, and knew as many languages – five – as Romilly.

Gil had a Double-First and two sporting blues and hailed from a Birmingham suburb, although none of it might have been guessed. He never lost his temper, and smiled a good deal.

Helen was the most spirited of the women. A fast, glittery knowledge of the world. No competition for Harriet in intelligence – although alert and vigilant; not in Sonia's league for looks – although careful with her appearance, not admitting what Penelope guessed, that she dyed her hair from light brown to rich auburn.

Penelope understood that Helen and Hugh had had a 'relationship' in London. Sonia told her she and Joss had had a 'whirl', and Penelope puzzled why the most attractive woman and the sallowest man should have paired off together. Gil was making overtures to Belle (who was three inches taller than him), but she seemed unaware that that's what they were. Romilly gave Harriet quite serious attention, yet the looks that sometimes passed between them seemed to lack the indefinable, unquantifiable ingredient of romance Penelope would have expected.

'I get asked about you,' she told Romilly.
'"Asked"? About *me*?'
'About everyone, I mean.'
'Who asks you?'
She pointed towards the town.
'Well, of course they do. And what do you say to them?'
'Nothing.'
'"Nothing"? Really?'
'Really.'
'You get asked what we're doing here?'
'Well . . .'
'So, why *are* we here, do you think?'
'It's your uncle's house.'
'Who told you that?'
'Joss.'
Romilly laughed.
'Why, then?' she asked. 'Why *have* you come?'
'To watch the grass grow. To learn about gardening.'
'No – '
'No, not exactly.'
'Can't you tell me?'
'It's been arranged for us. I *do* have an uncle, fairly high up. They're the best kind to have, Penelope. Let's say he pulled a few strings.'
'But it's *his* house – '
'It was Uncle's *idea*.'
'Why have you come, though?'
'The decision was taken for us.'
'Why, though?'
'It's a boring story.'

'No – '

'While there's a war.'

'You mean you're – '

He looked sideways at her.

'We're what, Penelope?'

' – conshies?'

He might have been going to laugh – but didn't. He waved his hand, as if he wanted to rid them of the tiresome matter. He persisted just a little longer, though.

'But why are they so curious? Have you any idea?'

He was looking sideways at her again.

'It's the war,' she said. 'I suppose.'

'And . . .'

'Well, everyone has to – take care.'

'You can't trust your own shadow, you mean?'

'Why d'you say that?' she asked him.

'It's true, isn't it? Everyone's getting very jittery. You're not really supposed to trust your own wife or your husband, not really.'

'Why's that?'

'So everyone remembers,' he said. 'It makes the enemy even more evil, he could be in the same bed as you.'

Penelope looked away.

'It's healthy,' he told her, 'to have everyone paranoid. So they believe. It takes everyone's mind off the other things – why we're *in* a war for instance, why it's come about – and just whips everyone into a nice frenzy.'

Penelope stared down at the grass.

'I hadn't thought of that.'

'But now – maybe you *should* – ?'

Gil was lying with Belle under a tree when she walked past.

'Penelope!'

She looked round. She watched him pull himself to his feet and come bounding after her.

'I'm glad – that you're settling down. Here. With *us*, I mean.'

She smiled.

'That day when I saw you,' he said, 'do you remember?'

He was smiling as if it was so inconsequential. But why should she have the feeling that it wasn't, not really?

'It must've been Fate,' he said. 'That we saw one another. In the street. Do you believe in Fate, Penelope?'

'Well,' she answered, 'I'm not sure really.'

Her mouth felt leathery.

'Perhaps,' he suggested, as if he had only just thought of it, 'Fate is character? Your character determines what will happen?'

She mumbled 'yes', but wasn't at all sure one way or the other. It seemed a very earnest topic of conversation for such a straightforwardly sunny weekday early afternoon.

'Anyway,' he said, looking back towards the tree and Belle, dressed in cream like a true child of grace, 'it's jolly nice having you. I'm glad Joss invited you that afternoon.'

'Not Joss actually,' she said. 'It was Romilly.'

'Romilly, yes,' he repeated, and nodded, as if it had merely slipped his memory. 'At any rate – the more the merrier! That's what *I* say!'

He *chuckled* rather than laughed. Penelope nodded, and smiled, feeling – she didn't know why – a little stiff about it. The garden droned and trilled and was breathless, for miles, like Eden.

She woke some nights in the narrow spinster's bed at West Field with the raw and brutal memory of those last weeks in London. Her mother so absurdly over-sensitive that if she let out breath like a sigh it would bring an accusation of ingratitude, while five minutes later she was advising her which shades suited her complexion best, mentally dressing her so that no expense would be spared but in the high fashions of twenty and thirty years before. She talked of finding her a husband, one deserving enough, and seeing her settled and nicely set up; or she would tell her, in sour and solemn words, that marriage was nothing but a con man's trick, it turned quite sane people out of their right minds.

Her mother would hear the planes from twenty miles away, she picked them up some nights even before the sirens wailed. She either ran for cover, into the cellar, or she did quite the contrary – which for Penelope was always worse than being confined with her by candlelight beneath the kitchen floor – merely carrying on as normal, except with the blackout curtains pulled, dementedly rubbing the silver and brass to a high polish, balancing on a stepladder to dust furiously along the ledges from which the pictures hung on their hooks, waxing the tabletops until they shone in the fitful light which – alternatively – was as much like half-darkness.

Hugh knew the Duke and Duchess of Windsor and called them 'Teddy' and 'Wallis'. He knew them well enough to be able to compare Teddy's performance on various golf-courses, at Dinard, Paris-Plage, Biarritz. He knew a great many people of wealth and importance, particularly in France. Penelope would have imagined them to be suffering as their country was but his accounts suggested that their lives were continuing much as they must have done before: they still appeared in Deauville, La Baule and Evian-les-Bains, and they moved quite freely about Paris as if it weren't a newly-occupied city at all, eating at restaurants and dancing at private clubs.

Penelope wondered why he chose to spend his time here, with them, when his titled and well-heeled friends – she guessed – would have welcomed him with open arms. But she would have missed listening to his stories of highlife in that case: as it was she could almost forget that their own lives were all topsy-turvy and their ends uncertain. The reality of existence had to do with shortages and ration cards, and yet she started not to remember general circumstances so clearly, being included in the privileged circle of this most dignified house.

At first she supposed that they were treats, the partridge or the venison, and she expressed her appreciation but didn't like to enquire more closely. After several visits she realised that the treats were provided on quite a regular basis. She presumed the foodstuffs came from London, and that they must be bought through contacts; then she picked up, from various remarks that were let slip, that the suppliers were local, and that the sweetbreads or pheasant were acquired as everyone acquired anything, with coupons, but with a plentiful supply of them. 'Local' for them meant thirty miles away or so, and several times she saw a car parked at the side-gate, which would never be there when she remembered to look out of a window later.

At first she ate guiltily, and only sipped at the good wines. No one else appeared to notice that they were indulging, however, and she didn't want to draw any more attention to herself than was necessary. So she tried to put out of her mind the conversations at Badger Lane, about who was wangling what out of the butcher or being slipped an extra measure of butter. She decided she must treat this situation quite differently, the rules of life being in temporary abeyance here at Cheriton Court – or else she simply shouldn't be a part of it. But how could she turn her back on it now without seeming churlish, or opportunist, as if she had accepted their hospitality only in the spirit of selfishness, unbuttoning her cuff – in a metaphorical manner of speaking – only to secretly laugh at them up her sleeve?

Later, in all the years afterwards, she remembered precisely the mood of those afternoons and early evenings, their charged stillness.

She never encountered it again to the same degree because she never again lived so graciously or antiquely behind such high hedges and walls. The spell had much to do with the immaculate good taste and the age of the surroundings and with the air of intense privacy that enclosed them, setting them in a world apart. When the talk did engage with what was outside, it might have been concerning itself with a foreign land in a gazetteer, one she only had the most meagre thumbnail details about. The famous people were names that had appeared in newspaper print, London's geography consisted of certain established points, of drawing-rooms and restaurants and nightclubs, a nebulous *Tatler* cityscape cryptically mapped quite beyond her comprehension by references to rendezvous at flats, in Kensington and Chelsea and in the area of Regent's Park, none of which she liked to ask too much about. She didn't recognise their past, the comparatively little that was disclosed in her hearing; and although she told them something about hers, she wondered how they could possibly affect to be interested in the goings-on at a girls' boarding school she might have memorised from Angela Brazil books, but which seemed to give them much amusement. They remembered the names and nicknames of the mistresses and the private language the girls had used, and sometimes Hugh and Romilly would make up stories using the characters, one of them telling one part and then the other taking over and continuing in the same fashion, with the others laughing even when they were supposed to be enthralled. They pretended to be enthralled: but most things they did, she sometimes felt, were in the nature of pretending. It didn't bother her – she wouldn't let it – that they were using in that way particulars of her school life which she had originally given them in gauche good faith; she supposed it was just how people of their caste behaved.

What exactly their caste was, was never very clear to her. They spoke of the grand and famous but also of (intentionally?) nameless persons met in those flats in Kensington and Chelsea and overlooking Regent's Park. They had moved in the beau monde, but their mode of referring to it suggested to her an age already lost in history. They were thoroughly familiar with the niceties of grouse shoots and débutante presentations and May Balls and yet Sonia and Joss and even Romilly spoke (unlike Belle and Hugh, who perhaps couldn't change theirs) in a colourless accent which occasionally dropped into a suburban twanginess of the sort her mother would have called 'very ordinaire'. They each had about them a 'manner' that knew how to deal firmly but also courteously and respectfully with gardeners and the house staff, yet they sometimes traded stories of rather a cruel kind about the locals, those her mother would have said 'knew no better'. All except scatty Belle and glamorous Sonia had gone to Cambridge or Oxford, but their education appeared to serve no end other than allowing them to drop Latin and Greek tags into the conversation; no one except Joss spoke of work or having a job (he had a position in a stockbroker's office, to the general amusement; Gil had inherited a small hill farm in the fell country, which mysteriously attended to its own welfare); she didn't even hear them discuss money and funds. She learned that Romilly's uncle owned several properties and estates and that their living here was 'no skin off the old boy's nose'. The food appeared, in ample and possibly illegal quantities, and anything else required – replacement croquet mallets, new deck-chairs, a pair of binoculars, even a powerful wireless set – was immediately acquired, and she never did understand how it was effected so easily. (The wireless developed a fault which no one was able to repair, and at the end of its short history inexplicably tumbled from a tabletop on to a stone hearth.) Nor did she ever understand why the war didn't call on their services: they couldn't all be invalids or pacifists, and even an official discharge wasn't a dispensation to do nothing in the common fight: yet the local roster organisers didn't trouble them, and the war news was hardly ever referred to in her hearing.

So it was – with few explanations offered, and questions demanding too much courage to ask – that they lived out their days, at least as Penelope experienced them, in that atmosphere of charged stillness. She was only a guest, but she was made to feel – so oddly – that she was an honoured one. Her mother wasn't well enough to angle for an invitation, but at first Penelope told her what she thought she could: not making too much of the pleasure she took in the plenty of everything, knowing that years of economy had considerably narrowed her mother's moral view in that respect. She was conscious that the Cheriton life sounded nearly idyllic when she recounted her selected highlights, while knowing at the same time that there was often a nervousness in the air which the others may have thought she didn't pick up on. She even found it difficult disentangling for herself what it was she meant, in her own head. Although she was made welcome, she sensed that they weren't as open in her presence as they might have been: but she also suspected that she might be there for an undeclared reason, so that – during the intervals of her presence – they were being just as diplomatically cautious in their speech and evasive in their relations with one another as they were with her. In other words, she saved them all from the onus of full and unremitting honesty.

She put her thoughts into some such order only when the experience was over. It continued to mystify her, but she came to see then a little better her own part in it: that she wasn't involved in the life of Cheriton Court quite as Romilly or Joss or Harriet were, but only to the precise degree that was

134

allowed. All along, from the moment on that first afternoon when she was spotted in the High Street by Gil in his Norfolk jacket, perhaps from the tennis ball's skimming over the wall and bouncing across the road in front of her, it had been meant to happen that she too should have her place in the Cheriton phalanx.

Away from Cheriton Court Penelope spoke less and less about it. Maybe it was as much because of her ignorance as her discretion. But she felt she did owe the group something for their kindness, and not a little: after all, they had taken her in when she might otherwise have been knitting woollen squares for blankets or stooping over a typewriter with a mule-kick. She was aware that she suffered for it – at West Field and about the town she was acquiring a reputation for reserve and stand-offishness – but she understood that was essential if she was to have a legitimate conviction of her obligation.

It struck her one afternoon, they received no telephone calls, and they made none. That was why the house felt – and sounded – so different to her.

She looked for a telephone, but couldn't see one. She asked. Joss explained there wasn't one. She must have looked astonished. She asked if Romilly's uncle didn't approve of modern inventions.

'Romilly's uncle?' he repeated, then he seemed to remember and nodded his head. 'Oh, I expect he's rather set in his ways.'

'Have you met him?'

'Met who?'

'Romilly's uncle.'

'Oh. Not yet.'

'*Will* you?'

'Maybe – one of these days.'

She persisted. 'Don't you miss a telephone – ?'

His smile stuck on top of a tooth.

' – in the house, I mean?'

'It'd be better, yes, if we had one.'

'What do you do?'

'We manage.'

'But isn't it inconvenient?'

'A bit.'

'My aunt has one. My mother's cousin anyway.'

Joss nodded.

'There's a telephone at the post office,' she said.

'Christ, the gossip exchange.'

'What?'

'Isn't it?'

'I – I don't know.'

'Ever-vigilant, what's his name – ?'

'His name? The man in the post office? I forget – '

'Nothing gets past *them*.'

'I didn't know – '

'A place like this is never what it appears to be.'

'I'm from the city,' she said.

'We knew that. The first time we saw you.'

'I don't really know what it's like here, Yelborne – '

'All disadvantages. Pretty much. It's a hole.'

'How do you stand it, then?'

'How can *you*?'

'I have to. Because of my mother. I have to put up with it – '

'And put up with us too?'

Joss smiled. Penelope felt herself colouring.

'Oh *no*,' she said, 'no, not at all – '

'We've saved you?'

'Oh yes.' She nodded. 'You *have* saved me. I just wish – '

' "Wish"?' he said.

' – I could do something for you too. To repay you.'

Joss's eyes tightened.

'Well, you never know,' he said. 'You might be able to. You might just bring something off – '

She pulled at the cuffs of her sleeves, then stopped herself. Romilly would have spotted her embarrassment. Joss looked away across the garden, to the high walls and the front gates held by chains; he was still smiling but his eyes hardened with each second against the beautiful, suffocating inertness.

Everyone in the town knew where she spent her time, and she was aware that they now thought her a selfish, modern, good-for-nothing. Maybe it was half-true. It started to irritate her, though, to be at the mercy of their interpretation, to have passed on her the verdict of strangers who could know nothing.

The consequence was that she gave herself up even more to the life of Cheriton Court. She came to see its high perimeter wall as a protection to her. Some days she hardly gave a single thought to what existed outside it; her mother continued to occupy a certain niche in her brain, of course, but while she sensed that presence it didn't intrude.

She didn't make any vital new discoveries about who Romilly or Joss or Sonia or Harriet actually *were*. As before, she just tinkered with clues and suggestions. They knew people who knew people who knew people . . . She reached the point of wondering if it even *mattered* who they were. If they weren't 'open' with her as she had always imagined that word to mean, they were considerate and treated her, while not quite as one of themselves, certainly as a very welcome guest. Sometimes she wondered if they knew as much about *one another* as she had always supposed friends must know. It struck her on several occasions that what they chiefly had in common was a list of mutual friends. Maybe those friends spoke among themselves in the same way, dropping names and exchanging anecdotes, and talking in the same private language? Friends, and yet . . . Perhaps the term wasn't the most suitable one. There wasn't always consistency. A few names did recur: absolutes of friendship, like 'Diana', 'Katharine', the other 'Diana', 'Stephen', 'Mouse', 'O', those were in a different class altogether. But – to Penelope's ears – all the others came and went, they were in and then out of favour. She didn't know what it was they offered, or *had* offered in the recent past, except minor services; she couldn't even believe that it was such a thing as companionship. They had been encountered, they'd had some small ritual part to play in a tenser pattern of social existence, but that was all. Penelope would watch Romilly watching all of them, and when his face closed with some massive, complex, complete intelligence, she would realise – even from her lowly vantage point, with all her naïvety and stupidity – that he at least saw and defined some method to it all, a form. Occasionally a keenness packed Gil's face too, between the smiles, and Penelope guessed that there might actually be two dominating – and maybe competing – intelligences simultaneously at work in the same room.

She continued to puzzle over their presence here, and why they were still just as they'd been when she'd found them. The house and its park were a perfect location, but they had all travelled widely in the old life, and so she might have expected them to become restive eventually. Yet Joss's words notwithstanding, no one seemed seriously inclined to leave, even for a day, and the place might have held them under a spell. One day passed into another, and there was no presumption that tomorrow would be very much distinguishable from the day that was drawing to an end.

None of their friends – those they mentioned – came to visit. It might have been their intention that nothing should appear liable to the possibility of change: that is, nothing referring to themselves. On hot still days she too was almost seduced by the charm of stasis. Once she'd had to ask the time – she had told her mother she would be back by five o'clock on that afternoon – and the three watches consulted had all told different times, with no less than quarter-of-an-hour between each: no one seemed bothered, however, and gradually she learned not to be either. She settled to days with no precise shape to them, and when she headed back for West Field there was still enough light left in the sky to show her the way up the unlit lane.

She saw that her confusion wasn't lost on Romilly.

'Belle said she fell in love with this place,' he told her. 'So here we are.'

Maybe she didn't look wholly convinced.

'Well,' he added, 'it's out of harm's way. As they say.'

He was watching her closely, as was usually the case, for her reaction.

'I've always imagined,' he started again, 'stumbling on somewhere, and being tempted to just let it take me over. To be taken over by it.'

She understood that feeling.

'And this corner of the world,' he said, 'doesn't mean anything to me. I don't know it. So it seems stranger, and a more *likely* place to think I'm being taken over by. If you see what I mean.'

She nodded.

'Well, I *know* you must understand,' he said. 'Because why else would you come here?'

She couldn't think of a reply to that. He seemed to perceive a situation from all angles. Words came so easily to him and left such a pleasant, hazy after-effect in the air; she couldn't remember them very clearly afterwards, but at the time they seemed to perfectly compose themselves around her own thoughts.

'You appear,' he said, 'from nowhere, Penelope. On our doorstep, so to speak. A veritable mystery.'

'*I* am?'

She wanted to laugh. She could only smile, but she felt that was sufficient as she walked beside him, measuring her steps in time with his.

'Something brings you back, although you keep your reasons to yourself.'

'I don't know if I have reasons. I mean – it's a beautiful house – '

'While *I* supposed it must be its inhabitants!'

'Oh, it *is*,' she said. 'That too. Of course.'

He touched her arm with his hand, placing it on her elbow. The contact produced a brief flutter in her stomach which she knew was quite disproportionate: happiness like a little surge of sickness. It subsided, but she still carried it inside her as they walked on in silence. It was all she was able to think of, that bony point of her anatomy at which his person was temporarily bonding to hers. In the hold of his fingers she felt what she tried to believe was the compelling strength of his will.

As they crossed the lawn she chanced to turn her head and saw that they were being watched. Helen stood above them on the terrace; there was a second or two's delay before she lifted her arm and, with a wrist and forearm movement very like the new Queen's, she waved down to them both.

3

'The barbarians are at the door,' Joss said.

Romilly, writing at the desk, looked up.

'What's that?'

'Nemesis is upon us.'

'I don't get you.'

'Nemesis, my dear chap.'

'Penelope doesn't get you either, I suppose.'

Joss looked between the two of them.

'An ARP warden,' he said. 'Sonia's stuck with him. One of Foster's men, I expect.'

'The policeman?'

'He's a sergeant,' Penelope said. 'Actually.'

They both looked at her. She smiled timidly.

'It's about the lights,' Romilly said. 'Probably.'

'I expect so,' Joss said.

'I told my uncle, Penelope, that we would be careful. About the blackout curtains. It's quite right to check up on us.'

Penelope remembered the candles at dinner in their tall silver sticks and the windows left open to the garden. She hadn't thought at the time.

The half of the heavy front door that was used banged shut. The reverberations carried through the house.

'Nemesis averted,' Romilly said.

Penelope nodded.

Footsteps approached, and they all turned to look with rather long faces. The door of the room opened. Glamorous Sonia walked in, preceded by her laughter. She held her hand across her eyes. Not seeing them, she couldn't control her mirth, the very absurdity of their circumstances.

Blue House, Sugarhill, Roxborough. 4/9/41

Dear Penelope,

I'm now a married woman. The knot was tied a fortnight ago. We didn't want any fuss. Max is the sweetest man in the world. He's older than me, quite a bit, I have to say: but we get on so well. I want someone to look after, and he attends to all *my* wants very generously. We're very, very happy. As you see, we're having our honeymoon on Tobago. From here there might not be a war going on. I'll probably be tarred-and-feathered when I get back, but I'm sending food parcels, so I'm doing something at least for *some* people's spirits. And Max has important friends in America, and he's telling them what's happening in Europe, so we're helping the effort in our own way. Expect some tins and things soon, and some fruit if I can manage.

I don't know if or when our paths will cross but wishing you the best,
affectionately from us both, Valerie X

Every evening Penelope had to pull herself away from the house, to tug herself free of it. Because there was no telephone she couldn't contact West Field to tell them, I'll only be another half-hour. She had borrowed an old, high-wheeled bicycle from a friend of Miss Hollins', and she could cover the distance on that, saving herself some precious time to spend it how she liked best, in the lamplit rooms of Cheriton Court listening to their clever talk and feeling so eminently sophisticated. (No one appeared to expect her to speak, unless she wanted to, and she was happy just to listen. *They* appeared happy merely that she should be there.)

Some evenings there were oysters to eat, and she could let herself be persuaded to stay then, or there were quails' eggs served on moss, or Mrs Crick had made a duck-and-spinach terrine. They would sit at the refectory table, on Charles II chairs with barley-sugar-twist legs and balusters (Edward VII had once leaned back after dinner and snapped his chair in two); white candles continued to burn in tall silver sticks; the windows would be open, the blackout curtains still hadn't gone up, and the garden's fragrances tumbled in over the low sills, with butterflies and bees on their trail. Indoors too the heat and quiet would start to transfix her. The floorboards and the panelling on the walls and ceiling would seem to contain the stillness of lost forests; where they sat, they were lapped by centuries of time. Without the breath of a draught the flames stood straight and tall on their long wicks.

There always had to be 'later', back at the house on Badger Lane.

It was like waking after a dream. It was like being hauled, resisting, back into the world: an involuntary rebirth. The other place on reconsideration became less substantial, she couldn't quite believe that it had been solid, what she remembered were the balancing flames of the candles, and reflections in silver, and fragrances, and words and sentences unravelling like bright ribbons around her.

But substantial or not, it occupied most of her time when she wasn't there. It kept her, she felt, in her right mind as she lay in the lumpy bed at West Field listening to the mice scratching behind the walls and the birds waking and twittering overhead in the attics. She lay speculating on the relationship between Romilly and Harriet, and between Sonia and Joss, and relations among all the pairs, and Gil's part in their lives, or Helen's. Asleep and unconscious, Cheriton Court's rooms and corridors expanded to fill with the charmed friends of their conversations, always walking away from her, with the exception of the Windsors in their Cap Ferrat-wear, whom she recognised immediately; they smiled their approval in her direction and unfailingly gave the impression that they might have spoken to her if they'd only known who she was. Romilly was describing again the lofty proportions of his room at the Palace Hotel in Biarritz, how he had opened the windows and served tennis balls, one after the other, off his racquet, thrashing them into the Atlantic surf the rocks threw up, and the words seemed directed to *her* ear in particular. When she looked to see, he was standing at her shoulder, in very intimate proximity. She would smile, and suddenly a hand would catch her elbow and Helen would sweep past her: her other hand would clasp Romilly's arm and he would be spirited off, with an expression of mock resistance on his face, seeming to plead forgiveness but his purpose betrayed by a smile.

She would twitch out of her sleep and spend the next interlude of the night watching the lozenges of moonlight that shone through the thin curtains glowing eerily on the pitted ceiling. Gradually faces became visible, floating among those capricious arabesques of light, their outlines, and then – like slow magic, taking the ceiling's indentations – the details of the one she always looked at first when she walked into a room of voices and looked at last as she was leaving, meaning her final 'goodbye' to be for him alone.

Latterly Helen was always watching her.

At first Penelope hadn't distinguished her attention from anyone else's, knowing she must be a curio to them all, of a modest sort.

But Helen's looks were even more probing than Romilly's or Joss's. Sometimes she felt she might have been hypnotised by them. She had no instinct to tell her how to respond, and usually she had to look away, which did nothing for her confidence. Was Helen trying to protect her own interests? Was she not as close to Hugh as she had allowed her to believe?

When she was away from Cheriton Court Penelope could convince herself that she only wanted Romilly's friendship, and his respect if she could possibly have that too. When she was at the house she felt much less in control of herself. Romilly's presence made her skin especially sensitive, she blushed a lot, she could turn from cold to hot in seconds if the door opened and he walked into the room. Her eyes couldn't fix on anything, she couldn't think what to do with her extremities – her hands and her feet and ankles – to keep them steady and composed.

She knew that Helen saw it all, which only increased her embarrassment. Even worse to her in those latter days was the ordeal of dissembling whenever she felt the silence obliging her to take the initiative and to engage her in very small, very token conversation. She knew that Helen knew she was humouring her, putting a busy distracting gloss on the situation, and in the process badly underestimating the intelligence of both of them.

Sonia came and sat beside her on a window-seat.

Penelope was a little in awe of her beauty and glamour, although she appeared to wear them lightly.

'Are you a good observer?' Sonia asked her.

'I'm sorry – ?' But she had heard.

'You seem to be seeing so much, Penelope.'

'Do I? I'm sorry – '

'But it's nothing to be sorry about. I wish sometimes *I* saw a little more than I do.'

'You – you're so good at conversation, though.'

'But that isn't seeing.' She smiled. 'Not how I really meant it. Being a conversationalist is only knowing what other people want to hear.'

'But – that *is* a talent, though.'

'Relying on other people. It's not a *singular* talent. Being on your own and observing, that's different.'

'Yes?'

'*I* think so.'

They both looked out the window, between the leads.

'I see a *little*,' Sonia said. 'How you care for Romilly, for instance.'

'"Care"?' Penelope repeated. She felt her embarrassment instantly heating her head, swelling it. She had been expecting Helen to bring up the subject first, if anyone was going to –

'You *like* him, don't you?'

'I . . .'

Sonia touched her arm.

'I'm glad you do. *I* like him too. I want to encourage you, that's all.'

'Encourage me?'

'He thinks you're intelligent.'

'What?'

'And perceptive. And natural.'

'He – he does?'

'But you shouldn't be surprised.'

Penelope looked down at her hands.

'You *do* like him, don't you?'

Penelope closed her eyes momentarily before lifting her head.

'Oh yes,' she said. 'Yes, I do.'

'I'm old, I'm twenty-six, Penelope. I should be warning you against him, shouldn't I? He's thirty-four, you know, our friend Romilly. I should be telling you to be careful, not to be fanciful.'

'He's been very good to me.'

'He likes *you* too. He told me so. In a way I was meant to take note of, if I can put it like that.'

Penelope's mouth was almost too dry to speak.

'How do you mean?'

'I mean – I think he was asking me for my opinion. Although maybe it didn't matter to him really. He was wanting to let someone know how he felt: and he isn't the most open person, I don't think. So it was important for him to tell me. That's all I'm sure of, actually.'

142

'Why – why are you telling me this?'

'Maybe – I'm guessing – maybe you lack a little confidence? Am I right? Your youth . . .'

Sonia's voice was gentle, confidential. It invited a confession.

'Well . . .' But Penelope couldn't think how to reply. Saying nothing, though, that was surely acknowledging the truth of it.

'He has to keep us all in check, you see.' Sonia's voice dropped. 'Romilly is king here. This is his country. As it were. He has a manner to keep up. He's conscious of that. Joss is older, but Romilly's the most – experienced.'

Penelope nodded.

'You're the youngest of us, Penelope. We scarcely know you. But I've seen him watching you. And you watch him.' Penelope held her head steady, staring towards the window. 'Once, you see, Penelope, a few years ago – I felt something very similar.'

' "Similar"?'

'He's so sure, Romilly, he has a manner about him.' Sonia's voice remained intimate, confiding. 'He seemed to me very sophisticated. It's all quite true, of course. But for some reason I didn't want him to see how I was feeling about him. I went out of my way to ensure that he shouldn't see. I think I was afraid of not just me disappointing him but of him not being what I'd always imagined. Well, I needn't have worried about *that*, but I stuck to his friend, Joss – because he was the closest I thought I could ever get – deserved to get – '

Penelope had turned her head to watch her face.

'Then I became more alive, more *alert* to Joss's advantages,' she added. 'I've never trusted my brain very much. The other women they knew, I suspected them of being impossibly clever. I couldn't hope to be any competition for *them* – '

'Harriet – she seems very clever, to me.'

'She is, she is. And *he* seemed too on the ball, Romilly, to be taken in by people. So I thought. I'm sure I was afraid he'd make fun of me. And by that time he presumed – well, I suppose he thought I always made up my mind about things and I wouldn't change it, I was too headstrong, or something. Certainly I had a knack of contradicting him. Only I was doing it – subconsciously – so he would persuade me, of course.'

'I see,' Penelope said in the silence that followed. 'Yes.'

'I don't believe I was very wise. Doing the opposite of what I meant to. I didn't think about it, not well enough anyway, and it ended up with Romilly imagining I was someone quite different. Different to what I knew inside myself. It was very sad, really. But it isn't – '

'Aha! Caught the pair of you!'

They both jerked their heads up. Helen was watching them from the door, hands on her hips.

'Is this a secret confab?'

Sonia stood up.

143

'Not now,' she said. She was smiling, but Penelope saw the gesture was heatless. Until now she hadn't speculated on relations between the two of them.

'A little chat,' Sonia said. 'Woman to woman.'

'Isn't that Harriet's province?' Helen asked.

Sonia's smile acidified.

'Shall I tell her that?'

Helen's hands dropped from her hips and *her* smile turned sweeter. She shook out her mane of hair, like an actress. 'For the sake of harmony,' she said, 'perhaps not. You *have* been telling Penelope about our good life here?'

'I don't think she needs convincing particularly.'

'Well, she can speak for herself, I dare say,' Helen returned: an indication that an answer was expected.

Penelope stood up.

'I've never known anywhere – quite like it before,' she said.

'No,' Helen replied, 'well, neither have any of *us*.'

Sonia pulled her cuffs neat.

'Penelope, I was telling her, is like a breath of fresh air.'

'Metaphorically speaking,' Helen said, smile back on course. 'I don't think I've had so much air in my lungs *ever*!'

'On the journey down, Belle couldn't tell sheep apart from goats,' Sonia told them. 'She got completely muddled up.'

'What?' Helen and Penelope both said at the same instant.

'It's quite true, I assure you. She was right about the four legs, but very confused about the rest.'

And they all laughed, temporarily safe and protected in the community of their mirth.

Nor were there any newspapers.

'Oh, Romilly doesn't like them much,' Sonia had told her. 'He – he's just got this feeling about them. They distort everything. How they're reporting the war.'

It was Harriet who took her aside one day.

'Do you think you could get hold of a newspaper sometimes?'

Her cheek was almost grazing Penelope's.

'A newspaper? Yes. But Romilly – '

'Romilly what?'

' – doesn't like them. Does he?'

'Well, he thinks we'd all get restless.'

'Why "restless"?'

'I suppose he thinks – we'd try to get away, to leave him – '

Penelope couldn't make much sense of the remark.

'You – you could smuggle one in maybe?'

'Yes,' Penelope said, and nodded.

'Under your clothes. Folded up, inside your knickers.'

Harriet's hand settled on Penelope's right buttock.

'So it's a secret, you see.'

'Yes.'

'Could you do that? For me?'

'Oh yes,' Penelope said, very lightly.

'And then we wouldn't have to hurt Romilly's feelings – '

She made her first delivery the next afternoon. To her embarrassment Harriet stood beside her while she undid the buttons on the waistband of her skirt and slipped her hand beneath her knicker elastic. (She'd left off an underskirt on purpose, and had felt half-naked riding down through the town on her bicycle.) To her further embarrassment the newspaper was warm to the touch and had deep creases and folds, but Harriet seemed unbothered by either. Tomorrow, Penelope resolved, she would wrap it round her midriff, like a corset. That, she felt, would be altogether seemlier.

Harriet thanked her with a peck on her cheek. Some of her sweet powder transferred itself to her own skin. Penelope took a step back. Harriet touched her arm, still smiling.

'We don't have to tell anyone,' she said. 'Do we now?'

After that Penelope left her delivery in the cloakroom next to the tack-room, in the gap between the back of the linen-press and the wall-panelling.

Harriet chose not to refer to the business again after they'd settled on the new arrangement, and so neither did Penelope comment upon it: she merely anwered nature's call at the first opportunity she could after arriving and pushed the folded newspaper into the same certain space that she always found empty.

4

'What are you doing, Penelope?'

She started in her deck-chair. Romilly stood smiling down at her.

'Just –' She covered the page with her hand. Romilly nodded at her notebook.

' – just jotting some things down.'

'Can I take a pew?'

'Yes. Please.' She lifted a cushion off the chair next to her.

'Not about *us*, surely?' he asked her.

'What?'

'Your jottings – ?'

'Oh, I do, occasionally. It's nothing really.'

'Why?'

'I like – to remember my impressions. Afterwards.'

'I see,' he said.

She shaped a silent 'yes' with her mouth.

'About the house?' he asked. 'The garden?'

'Yes,' she replied, but can't have sounded quite positive enough.

'*We're* not interesting to you surely?'

'Whyever not?'

'So we *are* – ?'

His eyes were very intense, although he was smiling.

'*I* think so,' she told him.

She closed her teeth on her tongue. She had said too much.

'You can't be convinced any differently?' he asked her.

'"Convinced"?' she repeated.

'Well . . .'

She laid the notebook open on her lap, pages down and covers up, and placed her hands on top of it.

The colour went out of the moment, the tension, and their smiles after that were blameless, as if they might have been accidental neighbours at a vicarage tea-party.

There were stony, concerned looks back at Badger Lane.

Apparently the local police sergeant had let out that the occupants of Cheriton Court were 'under surveillance'. He had instructions to monitor their movements. Various persons in the town and district were co-operating with him. But he wasn't at liberty to say who or how. He had admitted that he hadn't been given a *reason* why he was to watch the party, only that he must.

'And my daughter has taken up with them?'

'Oh,' Penelope replied airily. 'Hardly that.'

'I came here to get better. And now look.'

'You must be confusing them with other people.'

'It was the policeman who said – '

'Sergeant Foster,' Miss Hollins corrected.

'And there's no confusion. There's only one Cheriton Court.'

Penelope nodded. 'I imagine so.'

'And you fraternising with them – '

'They're very friendly, very kind – '

'It must be a mistake,' Miss Hollins said.

'Throwing yourself after *that* lot – '

'*They* found *me*,' Penelope informed her mother.

'They could be criminals,' her mother said.

Penelope laughed.

'We don't know a thing about them.'

'I don't expect anyone else does either.'

'That doesn't mean you should be spending all your time with them – '

'Not "all" of it. And they *asked* me – '

'Please, Penelope, don't be argumentative in front of my cousin.'

'You look a very sensible girl, dear,' Miss Hollins told her. 'I'm sure you'll heed your mother. We thought we should just say, for your own good.'

She came upon Helen and Gil in the glassed-over garage where she left the bicycle when rain threatened. They were smoking and talking; Helen had one foot up on the wall behind her, and Gil was removing a long auburn hair from the shoulder of her jumper.

The moment they were aware of her there, standing watching, they immediately turned their faces towards her and dazzled her with two scintillating smiles.

It took her a few seconds to achieve an appropriate smile in response.

'Penelope!'

Helen's head went back, to shake out the mane of hair.

'I was wondering if we'd see you today – '

'Jolly good – '

'How healthy that bike must keep you – '

They were embarrassed, she could tell: she had surprised them. But the awkwardness was somehow redoubling on *her*: she knew she wasn't going to be able to walk off and carry the moment with her, a little triumph. There was a smiling pretence that she could belong here, but really it couldn't be: she wasn't halfway clever or duplicitous enough, she was a bird confused by shadows and lured into the darkness at the middle of the wood.

(1)   *Romilly draws her aside. He explains that this confinement has actually been forced on him, by his uncle principally and by a couple of doctors. The others here are his friends, but he suspects that at least one of them has instructions to keep tabs on him. He is sure his mail is read: and the reason why there's no telephone is to make him feel more cut off.*

'They think I need a complete rest.'

'Because – of the war?' Penelope asks.

'Yes. Because of that mainly.'

'Like my mother?'

'I suppose so.'

(2)   *It starts with letters. Romilly says, they keep a lookout at the post office and nothing ever reaches London or arrives from there. He asks her, would she be willing to cycle over to Malbury once in a while with some things to post for him? And would she have any strong objection if answers were sent to her, at Badger Lane, and she could bring the envelopes to him? (Better, he says, unopened: so she would know which were for him, the senders could include her middle initial – 'J' – if that would be enough?)*

Penelope agrees, quite willingly. She takes letters from him and cycles several miles to post them. She begins to receive some replies, and delivers them herself to Cheriton Court.

This arrangement continues for several weeks, Penelope to-ing and fro-ing. It seems to draw her closer to Romilly.

(3)   *Gil draws her aside. He explains that he is concerned for Romilly's state of mind. The reason why he has taken his uncle's house is that the war has unsettled him. (Penelope nods.) His friends have come with him, but friends – even for the best reasons – don't always have your best interests at heart. (Penelope steadies her head.) Some of his acquaintances in London aren't of the best kind: more sinners than saints. 'Gamblers, drinkers, etcetera.' It's possible that he's trying to keep in touch with them.*

'Is he?' he asks.

She isn't evasive enough. Gil guesses.

Coincidentally Romilly realises that the ploy with the letters has been seen through. He prises the information from her. He says it's all right, he'll stop writing: but, he asks her, would it be possible for her to use the telephone at Badger Lane? Just occasionally he may have a message to send, or to receive. Penelope is uncertain, but he's persuasive.

The messages are never more than a couple of sentences, going out or coming in, and Penelope doesn't understand their relevance: they refer to the weather, or fruit, or makes of car, or types of cloth, or they're lines from wireless songs. But she passes them on.

(4)   *Romilly always walks as far as the side-gate with her, and meets her there, and that's how the messages are given and received, with no one else to hear.*

(5) *There's a brawl, Romilly slugging it out with Gil. Joss tries to intervene. Gil, punched in the jaw by Romilly, is taken off to a cottage hospital. Tension in the house.*

Penelope deliberates, then goes to visit. Gil asks her if Romilly is giving her messages. She doesn't answer. He tells her that Romilly has a history of instability. He's gambling, ruining his family. If he's giving her messages, she's doing him a grave disservice.

(6) *Penelope can't understand. At Cheriton Court Romilly is suddenly distant, aloof, he tells her she should go and not come back, this isn't the place for her. She watches Sonia watching her; Helen gives her evidence that she (Sonia) knows Romilly intimately.*

Penelope is badly hurt, stunned. She's approached in the town by a stranger, a young woman she half-recognises; she remembers she saw her wearing French trousers, walking out of The Stricken Oak with Gil before she ever heard anything about Cheriton Court. Now she wears a country girl's tub dress; she tells her she works in a lawyer's office, as a secretary. (She points to the building, on the high cobbled pavement, and to the window she works at: it has a full view of the town's activity.) Polite, pleasant, also businesslike authority. She knows how Gil's worry about Romilly is holding back his recovery. He has told her something about Romilly's telephone messages. Penelope tries not to answer. The woman says, it's all right, she doesn't need to know what the messages are. 'You don't even have to tell me "yes" or "no", just let me have a sign . . .'

(7) *Romilly gives Penelope more messages. He sometimes seems to her like his old self. She studies him with Sonia. Sonia is wary with her, appears to be on the point of disclosing something – but doesn't. Penelope – imagining Sonia is becoming suspicious, possessive, excluding – is afraid to stop being a go-between, to lose what attention Romilly still gives her. She's started leaving the house earlier, before dinner, feeling she may have outstayed her welcome.*

(8) *The lawyer's secretary stops her in the street when she's in an especially despondent mood.*

'Pass his messages on for him.'

'"Messages"?' she repeats.

'If you're telephoning for him – keep passing the messages on, don't stop. But if he gives you one – you don't have to tell me, not in so many words – if you've got a message, walk past my window and pause outside. Ring your bike bell, and I'll see you. Ring till I come. I've been thinking – you could wear a hat, and then I'll know, one way or the other. "Message" equals "hat". And if you don't have a message, still pause and ring the bell. But in that case you won't *have a hat on . . .'*

Ridiculous, Penelope thinks, a joke. But she considers the business long and hard, and decides that the woman, like Gil, is only concerned for Romilly's

*state of mind and for his recovery, as she is. Sonia may have won out over her,
but Penelope still wants to do what is best for Romilly, best in the long term.
(Vicar's Sunday sermon in church on the concept of forgiveness . . .) It's not
betraying so much, she feels, to wear or not wear a hat as she's passing along
the cobbled walkway that rises above the ford, outside the front left-hand window
of the lawyer's office. So she does so, in a certain particular manner.*

At the time there were sombreros, Victorian straws, snoods, Flemish
caps, dolls' hats, haloes, shoulderspan Bretons, pancakes, stetson-styles,
shakos, artists' berets, Merry Widows, pillboxes, cartwheels, embroidered
headscarves, turbans . . . It was the age of the hat, there were so many
styles and such excessive ones, trailing feathers and waist-length veils and
topped with cellophane butterflies and fruits, that restaurants banned them
for the evening. But all Penelope had with her was a little poke bonnet her
mother had bought her in Marshall and Snelgrove, which she felt made her
look like one of the 'Little Women'. So instead she used her one headscarf
– silk-and-rayon, the stencilled outlines of camellias on a pale blue ground –
although of course she only wore it for the journey back, when there was
no one like Sonia, who might have been a model or a film actress, or smart
fashionable Helen to spot her. She kept it in her pocket when she had a pocket
or on top of her gas-mask case inside the wicker basket on the front of her
bicycle.

Afterwards, on the last stretch home, she would wear the scarf or not wear
it. If she didn't want to she'd pull it off and throw it into the basket immediately
after she had passed the window and then she would cycle hell-for-leather for
the first of the hills. She couldn't be later in setting out than half-past-six or
twenty-five-to-seven, because supper at Badger Lane was now served on the
dot of seven o'clock: and the dinners at Cheriton Court weren't how they had
been, a solemnity had taken over and the gaiety become a thing of the past.
Even in twilight the fields would be busy with tractors and land-girls as she
leaned against the hill and pedalled with all the might that was in her.

She hoped of course that Romilly could be saved. It didn't occur to her, not
once, that she was betraying him. It was Sonia who seemed treacherous, and
all the more so on account of her beauty. She had said one thing to her and
gone and done another, which Penelope simply couldn't explain to herself.
She wished she could have confided in Joss, but the subject of Sonia and
her defection of heart must be a delicate one with him. At the beginning the
situation had been so clear to her, with Romilly in command. Now it appeared
he was being acted upon, from more and more angles. She knew she didn't
have the experience to judge. All she felt she could do was offer back what
was possible for her, her concern, evinced in a small act that required hardly
any of her time and the minimum of planning and forethought: in the true and
sincere hope that Romilly could be coaxed back to his old self, and that they
all might be returned to the old way of life, where the atmosphere had been

happiest and they'd all sat down at the table of an evening with one accord, in what she now remembered nostalgically as the Cheriton spirit.

(9)   *Then Penelope injures her foot in a fall from her bicycle: a car comes too close and she tumbles into a ditch. Her foot is in plaster, and she's confined to bed at West Field for almost a month. She's called on the telephone but there's nothing she can do: the man's voice sounds concerned, but not – she guesses – on her own account.*

(10)   *She finally returns to Cheriton Court. Gil is there, but not Romilly and Joss. Harriet explains that they 'had no choice'.*
   'They've been called up?' Penelope interrupts.
   'Yes,' she says after a pause. 'They've been – called up.'
   Penelope has been most uneasy about encountering Sonia again, but it's she who seems most aware of Sonia's depression.
   Penelope is also embarrassed by Sonia's care with her, her gentleness. She realises they share a very deep sadness, and that Sonia is trying to resign herself.
   Penelope hears nothing from Romilly. Harriet presents her with a silk square she says he once gave to her; she arranges it on Penelope's neck and shoulders. There's a pattern of the domes and spires of London set against a changing sky, from misty sunrise to the full bright light of noon to the purple silhouettes of twilight.

5

'I feel I should be doing something,' she told Helen and Belle.

'Doing what?' Helen asked her.

'Giving myself. I get looks from people. I know what they're thinking.'

Belle spoke. 'What would you *like* to do?'

'I don't know.'

'Can you drive?' Helen asked her.

'Yes.'

'A van? A truck?'

'I don't know, I haven't tried. Why?'

Miss Hollins called her to the telephone one afternoon when she happened to be at Badger Lane. She heard her name spoken in an imperious tone of voice.

'Yes,' she replied, 'that's right.'

'This is Frances McKillop. I gather you're returning to London, you want something to do?'

The voice continued before she could think of an answer.

'We're looking for ambulance-drivers. We're always short. I'll try to get you fixed up if you need a kipper. We're a bit pushed at present, but leave it with me – '

They left the matter at that: Penelope would make a return call the next afternoon, at a certain time.

In the intervening twenty-three hours she swung round to the idea. She was feeling more uncomfortable than ever in Yelborne.

She stayed away from Cheriton Court the next day and discussed the subject over luncheon. Her mother was agreeable, quite contrary to her expectations: perhaps, like mother like daughter, because her behaviour had been unpredictable for so many months and still was. Miss Hollins offered no objection either, and the housekeeper looked positively relieved to hear she was on the point of returning to London.

When she rang Miss McKillop and was put through, she was ready with her answer.

'Good gel. That's jolly sporting – '

She was going to enquire who had contacted her when another telephone rang in the background.

'Rushed off our feet here. One of our put-up places is sinking into the ground, can you believe, over an inch a week. If you can think of anywhere you'd be able to put your head down – But if it's no-chance, I'll get you somewhere – '

It looked as if accommodation was going to be the main problem. The house in Lithgow Road was too large and inhospitable for one person. They had left the windows with lengths of wood nailed across them and the furniture shrouded in dust-sheets; the doors had been chained, and a set of keys left at a bank.

She announced her news at Cheriton Court. Hugh said, 'Really?' but didn't look surprised. Gil just nodded, Belle dropped her fountain pen (which blotted), and Helen and Sonia considered their responses for several moments before telling her they were very sorry they'd be losing her: but, Sonia added, things weren't quite the same any more, and she envied her London, even in these times . . . Harriet was even more thoughtful, and put her arms round her when she said what a shock it was to her, they simply mustn't lose touch.

She had dinner with them for the last time: really a supper, because there had been less formality since Romilly and Joss left. They toasted her good fortune with ruby port. She asked if they knew when Romilly's uncle was coming back, but no one replied and she had to repeat the question. Hugh said it was all pretty much in the air, and at that second she happened to catch an aside glance exchanged between Helen and Gil. She wondered if it had to do with her defection: did they imagine she was running out on them because Romilly and Joss had gone?

She lost her appetite after that. She thought Gil was watching her with less favour than he ever had with Romilly present, even Belle seemed unsure of what to say – or was unwilling to speak. Hugh and Helen between them kept the conversation in motion. She was conscious that Harriet's eyes were directed on her for most of the meal: when she lifted her own and looked, she was struck by the sadness of the expression on her face. Taking her final leave of them, she happened to be speaking to Sonia last of all when Harriet took her arm and told her she would walk with her to the gates.

They had reached the laurels, out of sight of the house, when Harriet stopped, turned to her, and without any warning clamped her mouth to hers. Their breasts touched.

In her astonishment Penelope dropped the bicycle, it clattered to the ground. She bent down to pick it up, and when she was upright again she saw that the culprit had gone.

Her lips still burned from the contact.

She took a few steps forward, to see round the laurel bush, but she saw nobody and she didn't think she wanted to look further. She had dreamed often of a kiss, in her nights' sleep at West Field, but she couldn't have conceived it would happen anything like this and come from anyone other than Romilly himself.

Part Six

1

Miss Hollins had an elderly cousin with a flat in Weymouth Street, just off Portland Place. When approached, Miss Walfrey said Penelope was very welcome to stay with her and look about for somewhere 'more suitable'.

The flat was mouldering, and must have constituted a health hazard. An infestation of moths stuck to the pileless velvet curtains and pelmets, and the walls were patterned with damp rings; Miss Walfrey's hand shook when she filled the paraffin lamps and the smell of what she spilled competed with the odour of dust and the rancid stink of rat-droppings. The old woman scarcely seemed to notice, however. She talked instead of the days when she'd entertained, when there had always been cars and cabs waiting downstairs at the door. While she could forget that she had turned on the gas or left a tap running, she was able to recount in minuscule detail visits made long ago to Cannes and Capri. She prepared them tea and served it up to her young boarder in the Meissen ware. She laid out pair after pair of shoes from their boxes, all signed by Ferragamo, which might have been a lesson in the history of the woman's fine shoe in the twentieth century.

It was into this mêlée that Valerie stepped: quite literally, picking her way over an unstuffed draught-excluder and an overlooked pair of shoes as she was shown into the drawing-room. Penelope was mortified with shame. Valerie, after the introductions, glared at Miss Walfrey, and Penelope couldn't account for the degree of intensity in that look: she recognised that in part it was shame, perhaps because Miss Walfrey was a spinster and hadn't been able to save herself from this.

'I'm here to take you out,' Valerie informed her in the woman's hearing. Her Caribbean suntan was fading; her skin had an unfortunate tinge of orange to it now, as if she might have been recovering from, not the happiness she had written about in her scribbled notes and big-print postcards, but a debilitating bout of jaundice. Facially she looked not unlike Petula Clark, but without the sweetness.

'Well, well . . .' Valerie pushed her into the back of a taxi. 'I think not, Pee, I think not.'

155

'I've no choice.'

'What're you doing in London anyway?'

'I don't know. Serving. I felt – well, I felt I should.'

'How virtuous.'

'You don't think so?'

'No one asked *me* if I approved of having a war or not.'

'It was awkward at home.'

'You're just like Oliver. He should have stayed at Cambridge.'

'That – ' Penelope ventured, 'that's easy to say – '

'You don't approve of me?'

'Of course that's not it.'

'To each her own,' Valerie said. 'I know how I serve the cause best. I can get stuff sent from America. Just say what you want, Pee.'

'Well, it's very kind – '

'You've got to get out of that pit, though.'

'I suppose so – '

'*Suppose* so? It's an appalling dump!'

'I don't know anywhere else.'

'Well, there's your home, for a start.'

'We've shut it up. My mother's got terribly nervy.'

'Has she? I'm sorry – '

'So I think I'd rather not.'

Valerie paused for thought between the amber of a traffic light and the driver's letting off the handbrake on green.

'Look, Pee, Max knows someone. Cecily Elwin. She runs some pukka chukka services hostel. Our own sort, *compris?*'

Penelope didn't remember this lingo from before. But then they hadn't had to talk about 'sorts' of person and social segregation.

'I'll get him on to it. She's very pleasant, I've met her. It's Winterborne Gardens, Holland Park.'

They refreshed themselves in new tea-rooms on Great Marlborough Street called Pickwick's, an over-the-top bow-window-and-bull's-eye effort to revive the flagging British spirit. They tidied themselves up in the ladies' room, then set out to walk round the shops. In Liberty's Valerie pointed out the new duster hats in millinery and told her, 'She'll make you forget you're young.'

'Who?'

'Old Miss What's-her-name.'

Penelope might have reminded her about Max, that he wasn't in his first – or second, or third – bloom: but Max played golf at least, and could take reasonable aim with a shotgun.

'Here, try one of these on, Pee.'

She was turned by the shoulders to face a mirror and the lilac hat was placed reverentially on her head by an assistant. Two handkerchief-sized scarves in matching rosebud material were attached to the back of a pleated pillbox. The

156

effect was less odd than modern and youthful. The assistant said they were the new craze in Paris.

Valerie bought it for her, on Max's charge-account.

Penelope objected, quite politely.

'You can think of me when you wear it. Please wear it, Pee, and give that old dame the heave-ho and no mistaking. About bloody time – '

'It's only been a short while – '

'Christ Almighty, imagine being left to end your days like her. Maybe she's a psycho, she drinks virgins' blood – ?'

Penelope dropped her eyes. She guessed that her needs – of the physical kind – were rather different from Valerie's. But several times in Pickwick's Valerie had brought up the subject, sex, and heads had cranked round at the other tables.

Valerie linked their arms.

'I'm not sure I was meant to be a London type, you know, Pee.'

'What?' She would have thought quite the opposite. 'But – '

'No, really. In the holidays I never quite believed I *could* be, that I could bring it off. Once a hick, always a hick.'

'Oh no – ' Penelope stared at her. For sophistication Valerie had always been able to knock spots off her.

'So I'm playing a different game entirely. Always make it difficult for other people to judge you, that's my new inspiration.'

'How do – '

'They'll pigeonhole you if they can. Make you fit. I don't *want* to fit.'

'Oh.'

'What have you got planned for yourself, Pee?'

' "Planned"?'

'Yes. *Do* tell – '

'When?'

'For after all this, of course. When the war's done.'

'I really don't know. I haven't thought – '

' – that far ahead? You're hopeless, Pee!'

She felt the strength in Valerie's arm, for holding on to what she didn't intend letting go of, which served her very well for support.

'A wonderful husband?'

'Well, maybe.'

'Maybe wonderful?'

She answered with a nod.

'Max doesn't have any brothers, I'm afraid,' Valerie said, laughing too forcedly. 'Otherwise I could have pushed one in your direction.'

'I really don't know. I haven't decided – '

I'm too young, she meant: and being with you makes me feel younger still, although I know there's only a single year between us. We're so very friendly, but I wonder if that can be: so determinedly together as we are,

157

walking arm-in-arm, mine held in a boa grip. What is it we're *not* saying, the significant point we are taking such intense and deliberate care not to acknowledge?

It had been Henry Kyte who taught her to drive, in no more than a couple of hours, en route for a Roman viaduct they never did reach.

'I've had a brainwave, Penelope.'

'You have?'

'Stroke of genius.'

'Yes?'

'Here, I'll show you how to drive this contraption.'

'What?'

'Well, you said you couldn't.'

'But – right now?'

'Well, there's no time like the present, is there?'

'Shouldn't we . . . ?'

'Shouldn't we what?'

'I don't know – be improving ourselves?'

'Isn't learning to drive improving yourself?'

She shrugged.

'Best afternoon's work ever,' he said. 'I'll make sure you get the hang of it.'

She smiled.

'You really will?'

'Of course.'

'And not lose your patience?'

'Not a jot of it.'

'If you're quite sure – '

'I am.'

' – and you don't mind the risk – '

'One day you'll realise why.'

'Why? Tell me why – '

'I'm giving you a gift, Penelope. Making you mobile. I'm giving you your independence.'

She and Margot had the same hat size.

'Well, *this* has to be fated,' Margot said. 'Friends until death do us part.'

They shared an ambulance, and shared a room at the hostel, which proudly called itself the Winterborne Club, after its address. The appointments of the building were quite adequate, and characterful in a faded way – lime-green paint on the scuffed panelling, horsehair armchairs and sofas with craters impressed in them by an infinite succession of bottoms and backs, wooden standard lamps with puckered time-soiled silk shades that gave a dingy but relaxing light. With Margot's companionship to enjoy, Penelope soon felt quite at home. They pored over the photographs in magazines of models wearing hats, and remarked how odd, that meanwhile a war was going on around them. Loretta Young could get away with a handful of tulips pushed through a Pissot and Pavy turban and look a sensation. Mrs Christopher Sykes had her foot up on a chair at the Ritz, removing her overboot; on her bicycle rides about London on Government business she wore a mustard wool suit with a draped, buttoned skirt run up by her dressmaker, a Pole called Madame Przeworska. Cecil Beaton, photographing a Digby Morton suit in the ruins of the Temple, assured them that 'Fashion is indestructible'. More practically, a Dereta camel winter coat cost only fifteen coupons. While so many women had to stick to the three-inch regulation length for hair, they learned from illustrations how to tie theirs into a net turban, so it could be hidden under their hats.

The photographs, the aloof models, the hats, it served to amuse them and it kept them sane when the world seemed to be losing its head. Going about their work, they had half-a-dozen glimpses of hell some days. It would have been much more difficult to forget if there hadn't been two of them, each trying to keep the other distracted.

'Socials' were organised by some of the Winterborne lodgers, those for whom parties were a hereditary instinct and carried in their blood. Mostly they were with army groups, sometimes the air force, or with the French officers attached to the auxiliaries and voluntary services. They became another matter to discuss, to plan for.

But it had begun with hats. Penelope was surprised to discover that their heads matched for girth. Margot gave the effect of being taller, but in fact it was an illusion; she only seemed taller because she was thinner, with long arms and delicate wrists and hands. She had a fragile beauty, with wonderfully sculpted cheekbones and a sweeping brow and medieval eyelids that might have been indolent or insolent but were neither. From the outset Penelope was politely in her thrall.

It surprised her too that Margot had the stamina for the ambulance work, either driving or seconding, taking turns about with her. 'My mother,' she told her, 'was quite disappointed I wasn't a boy. So she just sort of treated me as one.' She came from Devon but spoke like a débutante, which she had actually been. She didn't have to talk about 'proving herself': Penelope saw how she became a part of everything that she could, without ever holding back. She was unfazed by the injured and bomb-shocked, and eminently practical. Dressed in a hand-me-down Paul Caret georgette gown of her mother's for an early Winterborne exploratory foray to a new Mess, she had resembled on a first impression – to be frank – a pallid, statuesque stay-at-home: but that was then, and as London went up in flames she soon acquired a fine, serene beauty, her eyes took on a very unspinsterish glint, and men fell over themselves trying to get an introduction to her.

Margot noticed the watching eyes. She didn't profess worldliness like the others, but she didn't shy from the contacts which the 'socials' threw up.

She had a habit of pulling at Penelope's arm whenever a move was made, which meant that the interested party had two persons to address. Afterwards Margot would laugh quite unmaliciously at their discomfiture. Penelope asked her why she did it. 'I don't know,' she said, and shrugged, in the bluntly honest but charming way she was able to.

'I'm testing them. They hardly ever try it again – '

'Well, I don't suppose they would – '

For a while Penelope wondered if she might be in the way of sisterly kissing, like Harriet, but she decided that she wasn't. (The kiss still burned on her lips, and filled her with panic.) She decided about something else: that in fact the playfulness was a cover for her intense, avid speculation about men, which still begged all its answers.

A Frenchman called Bosquet was the first to succumb to Margot and suffered a brief delirium of love. Incredibly flowers would arrive at the Winterborne, orchids and irises, and they would have their few days of glory in bloom until they were tipped out with the water. Margot strung him along, and Penelope puzzled not a little about the morality of the situation. But Margot perversely preferred not to believe that there *was* a 'situation' at all.

'That's just Frenchmen for you, isn't it?'

Bosquet eventually disappeared, unrequited to the end. There was a rumour of some substance that he'd gone back to France to help the Resistance in some vital respect; it was said that he'd been playing an important part in the movement's activities from here in London.

'For all I know, it was just a blind,' Margot said. 'Him coming here to the house.'

'How d'you mean?'

'To draw attention from his real purpose.'

'But why would he want to draw attention to himself anyway?'

'Well, search me, ducky. I know you don't believe me but really, I never *did* understand the French – '

After Michel Bosquet there was a War Artist called Sandell, who had gone out with them in the ambulance one day. Margot wasn't much in favour of their being accompanied by non-essentials – nor was *she* particularly – but he had made himself deftly inconspicuous: until, that is, they were back at base, when they thought they weren't going to be able to get rid of him. Penelope realised very quickly that it wasn't herself but Margot who compelled him to stay about them, that first time and the second and the third: it was all too clear from the sketches he produced, which he arranged to show them one evening at the club – almost every one of the dozen or so featured Margot either actively engaged in the foreground or posed as a solitary figure, set against the brutally disfigured landscape.

'Oh God,' Margot said when he'd exited through the front doors after the preview and had clambered on to his bicycle with the unwieldy folder of cardboard and string. 'I don't think I'm ready for this, really.'

'Ready for what?' Penelope asked unnecessarily, but – it seemed to her – as required, to allow Margot to put her thoughts into words.

'An admirer, of the artistic sort. I think this is all going to be far too sensitive for me.'

'What is?'

'Come on, Penelope – you don't think we've seen the last of our Mr Sandell, do you?'

Colin Sandell seemed to extract a masochistic joy from Margot's denial of his infatuation, from her constant refusal to acknowledge his being smitten by her. He wrote to her, he telephoned her, he sent her sketches. At first his messages were respectfully cryptic and impersonal but by the end the pronouns 'you' and 'I' were indisputably at the centre of his thoughts and feelings. He appeared quite unable to think or feel beyond the person who was Margot or who he believed Margot was, since his image of her bore less and less resemblance to what Penelope surmised to be 'fact'.

But there was also an end to that phase of one-way fanciful obsession. Mr Sandell, having displayed his genuine gifts in rendering the work of the women's voluntary services accessible to the public, was despatched on War Office instructions to the dustbowl of Egypt, there to attempt some more of the jingoistic same, namely to render a fine purpose out of war's chaos. To begin with he must have imagined that it was a cruel interdict of Fate to decide so: but apparently – the news filtered back, the world at war having shrunk to a gossiping village – after a sorry, uninspired start when his work seemed as flat and arid as the landscape, his spirits soon rose and his work showed distinct signs of improvement. The reason had two long legs and the chestnut hair and green eyes of Vivien Leigh, but with a gentler, less startling, more inviting presence than the actress's. Her own name was lost en route, as in a game of Chinese whispers, but she was renowned in all that barren land – among the harassed army officers, at any rate – for her consummate secretarial skills. In a magazine Margot and Penelope saw for themselves, the triumphant female form emerging from the back of a jeep, in tropical hatless uniform, eyes searching out an available field-telephone. They both immediately caught the physical resemblance, but neither said so: the longer she looked at the sketch the more convinced Penelope became that Miss 'X' in the desert was a version of Margot and that stalwart Margot in blitzed London had been a prototype of staunchly efficient Miss 'X': or maybe neither was purposely anything except an approximation of the other's form and attractiveness, an ideal rather than personal concept for which Colin Sandell's life was an unresolved quest.

Thereupon, timely into the breach, arrived Anthony Herbert.

His rank was Captain, and his function was to help liaise between army command in the boroughs and police and voluntary services and Home Guard units: in other words, to assist the army's easy co-operation with everyone else engaged in the effective operation of London's civil defence.

He had been present at a sherry party for *distingués* held in Winterborne House, and had first met Margot and Penelope as he returned from using the telephone in the bursar's office. They'd just come off a shift and were in uniform. It had been a quiet night and they were both pretty perky – Margot was especially cheerful – and more robust-looking than their duties usually left them. They were spoken to in the narrow corridor behind the staircase: he confected some lame excuse for talking, saying he'd thought Penelope was someone else, so that when she explained who she was she was obliged to introduce her other half, Margot Parridge. Penelope saw quite well what was afoot, she was learning quickly from her closeness to Margot to read situations in (to her) a newly feminine way. He was responding to Margot, with her he was rarefied, almost decadent – there was no mistaking that – but he was doing it through herself.

They didn't mention him as they walked upstairs, out of his earshot. Even in the room together they didn't discuss him. This, thought Penelope, is suspicious. Margot was preferring to remember something they'd seen on the day's second easy rota-duty: a Mayfair grande dame in evening dress sifting through dustbins on the pavement, seeking desperately – they'd supposed – to come across whatever it was she suddenly found herself without. Penelope pretended too that that was all they were talking about: and that chance just found them both happening to stand in the vicinity of the window as sherry-party voices rose up from the pavement beneath them.

The next time they saw him was at the Red Cross Club.

Penelope saw him first. As he approached, Margot turned to her and launched into some earnest topic of conversation. He had to apologise to both as he interrupted them. Margot, Penelope twigged, was actually relishing his drubbing. Maybe she thought he was good-looking enough to take it on that square chin. (Maybe he was. But Penelope didn't like to look too long, too lingeringly.)

The time after that he was in the American Joint Services Club, as they were. Margot had gone off for purposes of decking up, and so Penelope had to hold the fort alone. He only asked in the fourth sentence if she was by herself this evening. 'Oh no,' she replied, 'I'm with my friend. She's . . .' And at that exact juncture they had both of them cast uneasy, slightly impatient glances round the room.

Penelope felt the picture he must be building of her wasn't quite fair, that she wasn't in essence a party person: and that it wasn't the whole truth about Margot either, who still persisted in her mysteries. But after Margot's return from the powder-room they all three sat down – he consulted his watch with the subtlest movements of wrist and eye – and they hazarded an inoffensive, guileless conversation full (Penelope felt sure) of reverberations. He still included them both, his time was commendably and equally apportioned between the two of them. But Penelope couldn't be fooled.

One afternoon between shifts Penelope tried to remember all that she could of Cheriton Court. She wrote down the details, in a long list, in case she should ever forget.

She did it with a heavy heart, knowing her time at Yelborne hadn't been a success and that the failure had been of her own making. She could only feel furtive with her memories. The experience had eluded her finally: with Romilly, and Joss, with Sonia and Belle, with the house and the town. She would wake from dreams feeling just like this: with the conviction that the dreams had been important to her, but unable to remember the details, only the dreaming of the dreams.

She reorganised the list, to produce a more complete or more consistent version of life at Cheriton Court. She didn't dispute the facts as she'd had them originally, but she arranged them in such a way as to suggest that the appearance might have been the whole truth: from Romilly's absent uncle to the gardener with his stooped back and his countryman's pride in God's work. She showed Romilly in the best light, and credited Harriet with no more than a woman's friendship; Gil had only been concerned for Romilly's welfare, as she had been herself. She hadn't done anything to falsely repay her welcome, she hadn't abused the hospitality she'd received, all she had done was believe in a properly practical and benevolent spirit of unselfishness.

She and Margot both found themselves included on the guest-lists for the 'invites' parties at the Messes, and they reciprocated by serving on the Winterborne Club entertainments committee.

Generally the socials had turned into quite jolly affairs. This jollity increased as the rigours of the war work grew worse. It bothered Penelope that maybe she was becoming hardened, but she also learned in time to see the special, excusing logic in the situation. Tending broken bodies when they were on duty – they'd had to deal with severed limbs and even a decapitation, and hysteria in all its forms – they were only all the more ready to celebrate their fitness in body and mind when they had their time to themselves.

And then on certain other nights there were expeditions up into Town. Those were exceptional, because they required dressing-up: it was a dire enough situation, with coupons killing off courage and inspiration thwarted by there being so little to hand to get to work on. Only two or three dresses worthy of the West End circulated among the eligible Winterburnians, so that those stardust evenings had to be arranged for very small posses each time, preferably with escorts who hadn't been out with any Winterborne girl before and wouldn't recognise the dress from a previous occasion.

When Anthony Herbert proposed an evening out, they both replied 'yes' immediately: especially so since the evening in question was a Tuesday, never very promising in the week's calendar. Between the invitation and the going, however, there was a change of régime in the house: the Honourable Mrs Elwin, with her fond memories of exuberant London before the last war, was replaced by chill Miss Lancaster, invalided in a childhood fall from a pony and – so her reputation went before her – being now in her frustrated mid-forties and with looks approaching the Amazonian, much inclined to frown on fun. Sure enough, true to her reputation, she decided that socialising between the genders had gone too far and that Winterborne women ought to 'set an example'.

Miss Lancaster called the two of them into her room to justify their Tuesday in prospect. Margot confidently informed her that Penelope and the Captain were on the point of announcing their engagement – and this was by way of a premature celebration. Penelope gawped and swallowed noisily; Miss Lancaster's eyebrows arched and she stared very coolly at the 'fiancée'.

'You're a dark one, Penelope Milne, aren't you?' she said. She sounded not at all impressed. 'I wouldn't have thought it of *you*.'

She might have been chastising her for a cardinal sin: certainly not approving a fictional happy event.

'So, you're both going to gad about and kick up your heels? Tell me, do you think that is the Winterborne spirit?'

Margot smiled very charmingly.

'Well, *being* Winterburnians,' she said, '*we* think so.'

Miss Lancaster with her nibbled fingernails rattled her fountain pen on the desk-top.

'I think,' Margot continued, 'it's fairly common to celebrate an engagement. Isn't it, Miss Lancaster?'

'Her Nibs' (as she was known, on account of her handwritten notices pasted all about the building) fixed her eyes on the wall behind them both.

'If the celebration is discreetly done,' she said, 'perhaps there is no actual *harm* in it.'

'I'm glad you think so, Miss Lancaster.'

The remark was greeted by a sniff.

'I'm sure – I'm sure it will be discreet,' Penelope said.

'May I enquire where this "celebration" will be taking place?' Miss Lancaster asked.

Penelope hesitated.

'At his club,' Margot cut in.

'His club?'

Penelope nodded.

'And which one is that?'

'In St James's,' Margot said.

'Can *you* remember?' Miss Lancaster asked, applying her gaze to Penelope.

'The name – escapes me, I'm afraid.'

Miss Lancaster's gaze lingered on her, witheringly.

'Perhaps it will come back to you – '

'His uncle's in India,' Margot said, 'he's a something-or-other to the Commander-in-Chief. Very thick with the Wavells. He stops with the Mountbattens or at the club when he comes over here.'

Penelope stared at them both. Of course it was the winning stroke because Margot realised very well that Miss Lancaster at her stony heart was a snob.

'And this club you can't remember the name of, it admits women?'

'There's a lounge,' Margot said, 'for meeting us in. It's Services, you see. Not Boodles or anything.'

Miss Lancaster nodded, as if she were quite au fait with that world.

'Wherever you may find yourselves,' she told them, 'I trust you will remember that every woman here represents her colleagues.'

'Yes,' they both replied.

'I have my plans for Winterborne House. Ambitions.'

It sounded ominous.

Penelope looked at Margot and she at her.

'Things have got very lax. They need chivvying up. I'm going to remake the Winterborne woman. You'll all be grateful to me afterwards. I want a Winterborne woman to be as good as her word.'

'That – that sounds a terrific idea,' Margot said.

'Not just an *idea*, young lady,' Miss Lancaster riposted. 'We're not going to have any woolly idea-mongering *here*. We'll be Putting into Practice, we shall all become models of the Winterborne Principle.'

'I'm afraid we've got a shift in half-an-hour, Miss Lancaster,' Margot lied.

'Then I'm glad we've had our little chat. I shan't detain you further, ladies.'

'Dear God, she's barmy,' Margot said, running upstairs and stifling her splutters of laughter. 'What a hoot! Loony Lancaster! Well, stuff *her* – '

'But what do we do?'

'Oh Penelope – ' Margot stopped and grasped her hands, 'Oh ye of little faith. Yes, what *can* we do?'

'I – I don't know – '

'Why, *resist*, of course. Challenge her. Frustrate the old battle-axe at every turn – '

How? Penelope was going to ask, but Margot wasn't listening.

'What a ruddy joke. She'll rue the day she first saw this place. Pride gets a fall, and she's in for one bloody long tumble – '

To Penelope she sounded so very positive and assured: how then could she possibly have had any cause to doubt her reading of events future?

The Tuesday was 'on', but Miss Lancaster let them know it was a special and exceptional privilege.

Margot asked the others to collect them a few streets away. Conscious of Miss Lancaster's scrutiny, they left the Winterborne – it was Margot's idea – wearing their uniforms. 'That bloody woman,' Margot had gone around muttering, banging about the building borrowing bits and bobs of make-up.

'We'll put the dresses in Daisy's carrier-bag. Damn Loopy Lancaster.'

A curfew was now in operation.

'*Sod* her. Why shouldn't we get some fun, for God's sake? Sod her,' she said again and swooped on Penelope's claim to fame, her duster-hat. '*Can* I, please?'

Penelope didn't want to deny her.

'But what about the uniform rule?'

Margot showed her what she thought about that by striding out of the front door wearing the prickly green tweed suit *with* the lilac hat. A few steps behind, Penelope looked up and saw Miss Lancaster watching them both from her window; she was bloodlessly white and her hands seemed to be clenched by her sides.

They looked for somewhere to change, but Penelope's watch was slow and they realised they were already late. Two cars stopped on the appointed street corner, six people in one and four in the other. Their destination had already been settled on, a nightclub in Little Saint James's Street called El Maroc.

'Holy smoke!' Margot said.

Penelope repeated the word. 'A nightclub?'

'Here's a challenge for the jolly old Winterborne spirit – '

When they got there they found a couple of alabaster leopards standing guard by the entrance. A dusky doorman wore bulbous turquoise trousers and an embroidered gold waistcoat; he greeted them as they emerged from the two cars with an unintelligible greeting. Jazz music wafted upstairs to pavement level.

Penelope felt clumsy in her uniform, and carrying the dresses in the brown paper-bag added not a whit to her confidence. Car doors continued to bang, there was much hallo-ing and laughter. She watched Margot in the duster-hat, holding their two gas-mask cases and already in conversation with her captain. He had brought one of his Mess chums with him, who was gazing over in her direction. She meant to look away, but he was too practised for her and somehow he was able to hold her attention. She had preferred Anthony Herbert in their previous encounters: he was wry, informed in quite a worldly way, but gentle and sympathetic and utterly in control. His friend at the American Joint Services Club evening had seemed less open, semi-detached (as Margot would say of some people), not quite natural in the way he laughed and constructed a conversation, seeming to lure her (Penelope had felt) by lowering his voice as if he were trading confidences.

Now he was standing beside her, this Bryan (with a 'y') Hawten, whose name made her think he must be haughty by nature and only feigning the sociability of his friend.

'Like one?' he asked, opening a case of cigarettes.

She hadn't tried since Cheriton Court. She hesitated. Then she stretched out her hand.

But as her fingers reached into the case, a voice pitched very loud shattered all the genial bonhomie.

'Penelope Milne!'

The voice that replied was Margot's, however, not her own.

'One shouldn't judge a woman by her hat, Miss Lancaster.'

Penelope froze. Bryan Hawten placed his hand on her arm.

'Fraternising on the common pavement indeed! And this is the "club", I suppose?'

The doorman was attempting to usher them inside, with (if they were) Moroccan inducements. The other voices fell away.

'I suppose you both thought it was a huge joke, didn't you?'

Margot in the borrowed duster-hat spoke. 'I don't think it's a joke, Miss Lancaster. Not at all.'

One of the other women pronounced the word 'pa-a-th-etic'. Miss Lancaster rounded on her.

'I don't believe I asked for *your* opinion, young woman.'

'No?'

'No, I didn't, thank you very much.'

'You can have it,' the voice drawled. 'And welcome, I'm sure – '

Miss Lancaster turned her back on the insolence.

'Well. . .' she said. 'You're just going to stand there, are you? Like two wet dabs?'

A saxophone slithered up a scale and up the staircase, very sinuously, sensually.

'We were going to go inside,' one of the men said. 'Into the club.'

'Oh, you were, were you? All of you?'

'I believe so. Would you care to join us?'

167

'I beg your pardon?'

Anthony Herbert spoke. 'You *are* very welcome – I mean, please feel free.'

'If either of my two women so much as steps into that doorway she's out of the Winterborne. She moves out tonight, bag and baggage. And she'll be out of the Ambulance Corps too, you can be just as sure of – '

'But that isn't fair,' Margot protested.

'Who says what's *fair*? We're in a war – '

'It must be possible we can discuss this reasonably,' one of the men said. 'Maybe inside?'

'I'm getting chittery,' one of the women's voices complained. 'This dress isn't made for standing about in draughts.'

Miss Lancaster stared at the dress with undisguised disapproval, then she closed her eyes against her further tainting.

'This is the last time I intend – '

'Oh buggeration!' Margot said. 'It's ruined now anyway – '

Miss Lancaster looked over at Penelope.

'Fiancée or not,' she announced, 'this is where *your* evening stops.'

She stared at the man beside her, clearly making little of her choice of a lifetime's companion. There was no accounting for taste now, the look declared, and war was wreaking madness in women you might have thought better of.

'I take it – ' Miss Lancaster addressed Bryan Hawten '– you're expecting the presences of Lord Louis and Lady Mountbatten, are you?'

Penelope watched him smile in the helpless way he might have done to a madwoman.

'Morocco,' she continued, 'isn't quite India, though, is it? Lots of darkies, but that's about it.'

Dragging their feet Penelope and Margot walked away from the others, in moribund silence. The intending celebrants said little as they witnessed the departure. The doorman continued to induce, but unheard.

In her car Miss Lancaster was suddenly polite, full of irrelevancies. She commented on the pleasant air this evening, and the state of certain buildings they passed, how they were holding up – just. She wasn't to mention El Maroc even once on the journey, or the reason for the three of them travelling together past mouldering terraces of white stucco, past uprooted lamp standards, past a grand piano standing in its own eerie glory in the middle of a street. She was becoming cheerier the further they got from the West End and the nightclub, back into their own colony of the unbalanced, tottering, haphazard world.

3

Then what might have been an act of God occurred, on a stretch of road in Wiltshire.

A lorry was towing another lorry up a gradient. The drivers worked for the same firm, and – when they were able to – either of them took turns to pull the other. The fuel that was saved by the second lorry was syphoned off and sold, and they split the proceeds between them.

The rope had done so much work already that it was considerably frayed. A cyclist following behind but who hadn't yet reached the gradient heard the sound of it snapping. For a few moments she couldn't think what had happened. Then she saw the lorry moving backwards, rolling from left to right as the driver struggled to steer it. She screamed. Her feet fought to keep control of the pedals. Her legs were like plasticine. She careened at full pelt, right off the road, and so up on to the verge. The wheels hit the grass so fast that the shock knocked all the strength out of her arms and she was sent toppling over the handlebars into the ditch.

It was there that she was found by the lorry drivers, concussed and bruised but without major breakages. 'She', it was ascertained in the ambulance, was a certain Miss Beryl Lancaster, younger sister to Miss Vera Lancaster, who had charge of the Winterborne House Hostel in Holland Park, London. The hostel had to be contacted at once, of course, and the cosmopolitan Miss Lancaster – being the unfortunate woman's nearest kin extant – was informed of what had happened. She immediately agreed to come down from Town for a few days: 'a few days', she was assured, probably being long enough to see the patient get herself back on the road to recovery.

So that, in somewhat unlikely fashion, was how it came about that Miss Lancaster absented herself immediately following the El Maroc débâcle, and also how it happened that the metaphorical coast was left clear in Holland Park.

Glancing behind her, Penelope spotted Anthony Herbert in uniform picking his way through the traffic, only thirty or forty yards away.

She dithered. It was stupid, of course, but she didn't think she had the courage to speak to him without making a fool of herself, especially in her civvies.

She started walking, and when she heard a man's footsteps behind her she quickened her pace. She crossed streets and found herself on the unknown side of Marylebone Road. She couldn't stop, though, and she kept up her speed, midway between walking and running. She made in the direction of other people, single men or women or knots of them, as if they could offer her protection.

She caught sight of him in shop windows, still in pursuit. She pulled at the scarves on her duster-hat. 'Please – ' she heard at last. ' – I give up!' She slowed, but didn't stop, and continued walking. She wasn't sure what to do: if she stopped she would have to pretend that she hadn't known anything about him being there, and if she *didn't* stop it would let him know that she was all too aware and that she was running away from him.

She heard his feet still following her. She turned a corner. The road was broad and she crossed over to the opposite pavement. But she realised just too late that she was walking down a cul-de-sac, with a building facing her at the end and no way out that she could see.

'Have dinner with me, will you?' The voice carried to her quite clearly and now she didn't have an excuse not to hear. 'Margot – ?'

In her confusion she stopped and turned round. He stood in his uniform, looking over. She watched the wide grin on his face shrink. It almost disappeared: then a smile, much more forced and awkward, replaced it.

He did the manful thing and walked towards her.

'Your hat – ' he said.

'What?'

'I saw the hat – '

And he had supposed it was Margot. Of course, of course.

'I knew it was the same one. The hat.'

'I – I lent it to Margot. Last time.'

'Did you know it was me?'

'What? I – '

She looked up and down the road, feeling desperate. All the sooty brick was hopeless. A woman spied from a window opposite, lifting an edge of net curtain.

'Well . . .' she said.

'Pick an evening.'

'What?'

'What's your choice?'

She felt herself reddening.

'I don't – '

'When would you like to have dinner?'

'What?'

'Can you manage – ?'

'But you – ' She could feel cold perspiration trails under her arms. 'I don't – '

'Tuesday? All right? We'll go somewhere there's dancing – if you like – '

Why was he having to be such a gentleman about it? If only he'd just said it was a mistake and left it at that.

'Tuesday?' she repeated.

'Tuesday it is then,' he said, obviously not hearing the question mark in her voice.

'But – '

He lifted his arm as if he was going to tip his cap. She looked down at the pavement and felt nearly distracted with embarrassment. No, no, it's all wrong, you don't even want to take me anywhere, to go dancing with me, so I have to be held, so close . . .

He accompanied her back to the main road. He was telling her about something that had happened on a tour of inspection, but she wasn't listening: or she *couldn't* hear, because the blood was pounding so heavily in her ears.

He hailed a taxi and helped her into it. His smile looked reasonably convincing, but she knew that hers wasn't. The driver was courteously not watching them both in his mirror, as if they were fiancé and fiancée.

His smile transfixed her. She didn't examine the rest of his face, she was afraid of submitting to his charm, knowing she should have been scrutinising beneath that, to the man himself. But a man was also his appearance, and she couldn't separate this man's handsomeness from the effect he had on her, disabling her . . .

The door closed and he continued smiling through the glass at her, also watching her a little curiously, with some concern even. She willed herself to keep smiling back.

The taxi's engine rattled beneath the bonnet. She was going to lift her arm to wave, but then she remembered the dampness underneath. Clutching her gas-mask case with one hand she managed a coy, flirtatious little movement of the other hand, from somewhere about the level of her breasts – and she felt ashamed, that she was stuck in her stupidity like soft, sinking, sucking sand.

When she got back to the club she didn't mention the incident, even when that evening Margot made the remark, Anthony hadn't been in touch with them, wasn't that a bit odd?

A note bearing the instruction 'PERSONAL' on the envelope was delivered on Saturday. 'Greville's, Curzon Street, Tuesday (again!) Half-past-eightish. It's my only night off, I'm afraid. Unfortunately I've just learned I come off rota-duty at half-seven. Would you mind awfully if I meet you there? Looking very forward to it. Sincerely, Anthony.'

On Sunday afternoon Penelope spent an hour and a half scribbling out a story, about a confusion of identity involving two friends. She slipped it into her locker, turned the key, then went in search of Margot and embarked on another fiction.

'Will you help me out, Margot?'

'How?'

'My cousin Lawrence – Larry – have I ever told you about him? – he's over from Australia. He's terribly nice, dashing, but my mother won't allow me to have anything to do with his side of the family. Anyway he's in London and

171

he's asked me to a very posh dinner. At a nightclub. I really do like him, but I don't – I don't want to be tempted. He said he's booked this, and can't unbook it, but I've told him I know exactly the right person to have his dinner with. Please – would *you*, Margot? Go in my place – instead of me?'

To her surprise Margot didn't laugh at the fable. She had obviously been disappointed by Anthony's failure to make contact, and cousin Larry seemed to catch her on the rebound.

'You will?' Penelope said, not quite believing the ease of the conversion.

'But are you sure?'

'Oh yes.'

'He's – all right, Larry, is he?'

'Oh yes. He's splendid. You'll love him. Madly attractive.'

'What does he do? Normally?'

'He – he's a farmer. Hundreds of acres. Thousands, I expect.'

'Is he actually Australian?'

'No. No, he was born here.'

The story was in danger of becoming more elaborate than Penelope wanted it to be. She explained the details again, when, and where, dining and dancing.

'Is he a bachelor?'

'So far as I know.'

'Will I be safe?'

Penelope hesitated before deciding on her mundane but honest answer.

'If – if you want to be.'

Margot no more than batted a medievally top-heavy eyelid in response.

'And you're *sure* you – '

'Yes, Margot, yes.'

'You know, I really wouldn't mind it. An evening of – Will he put up with me, do you think?'

'Oh yes. And I'll pay for your taxi there – '

So Margot got herself ready and went.

Penelope was left a little despondent, but not quite as much so as she had been expecting to feel. She thought she had made a moral choice, a just one: she had done the decent thing. She'd had few occasions in her life to make such a choice. She wasn't quite sure why she'd done it: maybe because if it had been she who had gone to Curzon Street the circumstances would have been quite *false*, her 'self' wouldn't have been the real and deserving one, she'd have been present only because she had been confused for who she wasn't. She knew that people borrow or steal aspects of themselves from other people, they deal in their own reflections, but she hadn't discovered enough yet about Penelope Milne to be confident she could carry off such a major heist. It wasn't properly a sacrifice, because it had begun from a misunderstanding anyway, it didn't involve the surrender of some true and precious thing that was in her gift to bestow.

172

She watched the taxi leave; she waved from the front steps and Margot reciprocated through the oval back window. The weather was milder, and they had settled between them on a little speckled netting lent by a fellow Winterburnian, in preference to a hat, *the* hat. This time there would be no possibility of confusion, there would be no tangled wires.

When the taxi had disappeared from view Penelope walked back inside and went up to their room.

She took out a block of paper, meaning to start a reply to Oliver, who had written to her from his new naval posting in Malta. He'd told her that his job merely entailed desk-work, which suited him: he also confessed to her – she wasn't to repeat it – that sea travel made him ill, but so far he'd fooled everyone: the two interviews had been walkovers, an uncle of a friend had got him in and his cronies had only glanced at his forms, and he'd thought to plead food poisoning on the choppy voyage out from England. He could have been a spy, a Nazi infiltrator, an Eyetie, and he didn't suppose they would have been able to tell. 'These are the days of the Pinheads.' When it was all over he would go back to Cambridge and complete his Tripos, get back to sanity.

She began a letter, in all good faith. But her attention kept returning to Margot, and the evening in Curzon Street. She tore another page out of the block and, calling Margot 'Fleur', she attempted to describe her – her appearance and her effect – in words. She also referred to a character like herself, and then decided the whole would be better delivered in the first person rather than the third. She added some background: the city's rubble sites, creepy nightstreets without lighting and the sinister whiteness of the peeling stucco terraces near Regent's Park seen by moonlight, the air-raid sirens sounding and steering the ambulance down bombed, potholed streets littered by blown bricks, roof-tiles, fallen lampposts and glittering with glass like frost, and everywhere obscured by swirls of dust and billowing smoke from the house-fires. The cries were impossible to describe, and likewise the stupefaction on the faces of the survivors. Fleur would jump down out of the cab and organise the stretcher-bearers, establish contact with any doctors and nurses on site and somehow manage to pacify those who also suffered by merely watching what they could do nothing about.

She took another page of paper and started sketching in a family background for Fleur, a history she hadn't yet heard a great deal about. She sat at the open window in the fading light, with her pen held above the paper, on the point of entering Fleur's own thoughts on being who she was, a person with a private past and, now, a very public present – and unsure, just as Penelope was, how precisely it was that the two conditions connected.

Margot never came back. Nor was Anthony Herbert ever seen again.

Their disappearance would have remained forever a mystery if a woman who had taken the wrong way home hadn't happened to be crossing the rubble flats a couple of hundred yards behind them. She had noticed the couple far off, ambling in a canoodling way towards the bombed shell of St Luke's Church. She heard Margot's screams first, followed by Anthony's shouts. It only took seconds. The ground had just opened beneath them. She'd looked over and seen an arm and hand vanishing, the man's, but that was all. Nothing more.

The woman had run across looking for the spot. She'd yelled for help. The ground was gone over all night, until dawn. Voices called into fissures, but no human sounds came back. They weren't above sewers, so the search couldn't be continued beneath ground. The rubble must have resettled after the fall: every hole was located, but none was judged large enough to have taken one body, let alone two. It wasn't the first such incident, as the authorities confirmed: up to a score of people had already gone to their deaths in the same way, chancing on some spot where victims were dropped, through freak rifts and crevasses, to instant oblivion.

It was wholly incredible, which was why Penelope knew it must be the explanation. First she went into a spasm of shock, and only after that did she cry. She hurried to the place and started hunting herself, scrambling under the police ropes and having to be pulled back by the long, protecting arm of the law.

She had to move out of the room in the Winterborne, because of the locker of Margot's belongings and the memories she very nearly choked and gagged on. In a different room her view of the situation changed. Now she was a hostage to her own envy: she couldn't sleep or eat, thinking of the two of them, Margot and Anthony, only themselves as they would have wanted it to be, eternally together and raptured to infinity. She was the one left behind, solitary and friendless and unclaimed, in a hostile element.

Afterwards she was ashamed of herself. She pitied them instead, which was the very least they deserved of her, who was herself deserving of nothing: and yet at the back of her mind she couldn't lose the blasphemous thought, which was like wishing sacrilege on them, that now they had each other and they always would, and it would be impossible for her to separate the memory of one from the other, so irreducibly bound were they in the oneness of their prodigious deaths.

'You poor betrayed thing,' Miss Lancaster said, alighting on her in a darkened corridor.

'Oh no,' Penelope told her, 'really.'

'Don't think I don't see,' Miss Lancaster confided, meaning her red-eyed condition. 'How it's cut you up.'

'It's poor Margot – '

'Well, she was no better than I supposed, going off with him.' Miss Lancaster shook her head. 'He jilts you and then he never gives you another thought.'

'What's that?'

'If you *had* been engaged, would he still have done it?'

Penelope gawped at her.

'Take my advice, Miss Milne. Just forget the men. They've only one thing on their minds, and I hope you'll excuse my frankness. But I do know what I'm talking about.' The woman's mouth grew very small and merciless. 'Look what happened to your friend. Lest any of us forget. Tempted by false promises, limed by a man's guile.'

'I'm sure you're – '

'He had no compunction. And he had to drag her down with him. But – ' Miss Lancaster straightened her spine ' – that's no excuse. She should have known better. She shamed us, her gender, never mind what she must have done to *you*.'

Penelope, back against the corridor wall, was aghast. But she couldn't deny anything of what Miss Lancaster was saying without letting her know that Margot had set out to lie about the circumstances of El Maroc: and that she herself had been instrumental in their deaths.

'We'll be offering prayers for Miss Parridge's soul on Sunday,' Miss Lancaster said, noticeably excluding mention of the Captain's. Something about the set of her features and a certain prissy tone in her voice persuaded Penelope that she didn't really have much truck with the business of religion.

'Anyway,' Miss Lancaster continued, 'I hope you don't mind me having my little say-so.'

She looked down at her stout, thick-soled shoes, and concluded by smiling, even with the rest of the house in mourning, having seen the brightest of them – the girl most likely – survive a war only to fall in love.

Part Seven

1

Mrs Milne's death was a process drawn out over three years.

Back in Lithgow Road she fell down the steep stairs leading up to Nancy's old room. She never chose to explain what she'd been doing up there. The accident had happened, she would say, and that was the simple fact of it.

She broke one hip and fractured the other. A hip operation was less than successful, the attempted fusing didn't repair the damage, and certain friends claimed it was the doctors' fault. Both hips caused her pain, but it was worse with the one that had been operated on, and she was seldom able to put it from her mind.

She became susceptible to viruses as she hadn't been before. She regularly took colds, flu, stomach upsets, and always had an ache in some part of her anatomy other than her hips. Simple movements involved heroic effort and as her temper and her pain became aggravated, all the strains were further strained.

But more than anything else, perhaps, she lost both the memory of health and of the reason why she should attempt to believe she might get better. She would look most distraught of all whenever someone, trying to be encouraging, would tell her that what it really took was mind over matter, the brain's convincing the body.

'She was very pretty, Nancy. *I* was supposed to be pretty, once at any rate, but I had the sort of looks that "settle". I interviewed several girls. Some of the others had more experience, but she was the prettiest, so that decided the matter for me.'

Penelope nodded, trying to determine the logic.

'I couldn't have been having a plain girl, you see. That wouldn't have done at all. She *had* to be pretty. It was his mother who put the idea into my head. Because of Topaz, you see.'

'Topaz?'

'Do you remember?'

Penelope nodded.

177

'The second or third time I was there I guessed. That it was an "arrange-ment".'

'How? How an "arrangement"?'

'Your grandmother worshipped Rollo. She would have done anything for him, and to keep his affection. Topaz was his model once. I heard that she had infatuated him. It was your grandmother who took her in. They were artists, bohemians, they could do that.'

'"Took her in"?'

'She had household duties, officially: she was also a companion of sorts. But she was really there to keep your grandfather happy, to hold the marriage together. They weren't quite free spirits after all, but they were ready to live so modernly. Although I dare say it's how they lived in the days of the patriarchs. Your father wasn't a bohemian, of course. A reaction, I suppose. But in some ways he *was* like his father: almost innocent.'

'"Innocent"?'

'Well, perhaps. A bit of a fool too. A fool for love. Not "lust". I gave him the benefit of that doubt. Maybe Nancy loved him, in a silly way.'

Penelope put a hand to her brow. She felt the room starting to tilt.

She remembered the shower of gold wizard's dust falling on the Axminster carpet in the sitting-room. Her mother had been proud of the carpet, even though in places it had worn through to the bare cord.

'Yes, Mother. I'll leave you now.'

'What an awful word that is.'

'Which word?'

'"Mother"?'

'"*Mother*"?'

'I wish you'd called me something else.'

'Called you what?'

'There must have been something. It sounds like an accusation.'

Penelope couldn't think how to reply. She was astonished that her mother should have made such a remark, and so directly: and also that she could be so correct about the name sounding like an accusation. But what else *could* she have called her?

'I'll try to sleep now, I think, Penelope.'

Her mother closed her eyes. The day had been too long and too full and now she wanted to drift out of it for a while. Penelope could offer no plausible reason to hold her here.

Still sitting, she stooped forward and kissed the cheek closer to her.

The powdery skin smelt of her mother's favourite lily-of-the-valley toilet water.

So everything was all right, for a while longer at least, just as it always *had* been, and the unthinkable became not more so but less so as time gently adjusted them both to what was only inevitable and, in the simplest sense, true.

*

'Why did we leave Borneo? Do you know?'

'Oh . . . some discrepancies in the books.'

She had known she might catch her mother out, that she hadn't the physical strength for appearances today.

'The accounting books. Which your father kept.'

' "Discrepancies"?'

'Well, they were only discovered later. I'm not sure if it was an accident or not.'

'That it was discovered?'

'That they happened. The "irregularities".'

'They might *not* have been? What you said – "accidents"?'

'It was too hot to think straight,' her mother said, 'out there. For your father or anyone. We had to keep up standards. All of us, I mean. We were British. We had to show we were better than the Dutch.'

Her mother clasped her hands on top of the quilt.

'He was cutting corners perhaps. It's not a proper crime. Perks, let's say. Of the job. Then some miserable penny-pinching fellow came into the office in London. I heard them talking about it. It was having the tennis courts built that finished our lot. We got above ourselves apparently. The London office didn't like it, not one little bit, but then they weren't living as we were. Where did all the timber and other stuff come from, for heaven's sake? They wouldn't have had a job without us. It was all too stupid, too stupid – '

'I've arranged a nurse, Penelope.'

'You have?'

Her mother's hand reached up to her hair. Without tinting it was fading to silver.

'Don't worry about the cost. I can afford it. Quite well.'

'Yes, Mother.'

'She's good at her job.'

'I'm sure she is.'

'I always had a nose for that.'

'Yes, Mother.'

'Even Nancy.'

'Mother – '

' – she knew her job.'

'Please – '

'Knew everything. Everything there was to know, *she* knew – '

By 1946 Penelope had three published short stories to her name. The first contained a schoolgirl not unlike Myrtle Fellowes, the second was a 'mood piece' set in a Cornish village not unlike Polwynn, and the third told a child's

179

memories of an honorary 'uncle', a modern man who lived on the top floor of a block of expensive maisonettes, one with a swimming-pool set in a landscaped indoor garden.

They were long days in the second half of 1946 and she wouldn't have got through them if she hadn't had something else to do. Sitting in her mother's bedroom she scribbled in one of her notebooks, imagining to herself what life must have been like in the time before Borneo. It was also *her* life, by association – since chemically she must have shared an existence with her mother – and she felt she did no harm to anyone in exercising a claim on it. It wasn't a recognisable woman in the short sketches, but she felt something was being given back to her mother: of grace, of independence, of the easy charm of youth, of the perpetual hope of happiness.

As soon as her mother woke in the bed she instinctively closed the notebook. It shouldn't have mattered to her if she had been seen. But it seemed, somehow, not quite 'respectful' in the circumstances to do what she was doing: as if by going back to the origins of the person she was in effect predicting the end – as a sayer of original and final sooths.

'I don't suppose your father had ever seen a house quite like ours. To *him* it must have seemed – romantic, because it was so conventional. After his own, which to him was normal. But it depends on your – your stance, doesn't it?'

Penelope nodded, very slowly.

'She's very respectable now, Nancy. Whoever she is.'

'Mrs Rumbelow. I'm sorry I missed her visit – '

'Mrs Rumbelow, yes.'

'Why did she come to see you, do you – '

' "Why?" – '

'I mean – '

'She talked about your father. Her eyes were shining. At least, I thought, at least he made you happy. It's kept you going.'

Penelope put a hand to her brow again.

'I turned a blind eye,' her mother said.

No, Penelope realised: no, not quite. She remembered the long, long face on her tenth birthday, with the house erupting in noise, like the sound of furies let out of hell.

'I just didn't notice. I looked the other way.'

If that, Penelope thought, is what you want to believe –

'The thing is to be adult about it. I think I was able to be adult then. When I had really just become one. After that you get too fixed. And you can't – can't protect yourself against shocks.'

'I see.'

'Now . . . I'm quite tired out, I think. Knocked up.'

Penelope started, and the joints of the chair creaked. That expression meant something quite different these days but her mother was content not to know. Maybe to her it really *had* been innocence, and for her father the problem was always merely spiritual: it hadn't gone beyond straightforward affection and an amateur aesthete's admiration of beauty.

She remembered the sound of laughter trailing down the staircase, that afternoon the conjuror came to the house and performed his too speedy magic.

'It's been rather a long day, Penelope. A *full* day, I should say.'

She just couldn't get Topaz right, try as she might, the woman failed to 'come' to her. Every time she made the effort to get her on to paper, she just kept on walking, through the room or across the lawn – and right off the page. Even her face eluded her, although she would have recognised her if she had chanced to open the door and walk in at this very moment: everything escaped her except the beauty spot low on her left cheek. But she couldn't devise a picture from such a minor detail.

'I don't know that it was real, the spot,' her mother told her when she asked and she could focus long enough to remember. 'I don't expect it was.'

'Was it a fashion?'

'There was a strange thing . . . Your father pointed it out to me. In the paintings Rollo did of her it was never there.'

'The beauty spot?'

'Never there.'

'Why not?'

But her mother's concentration lapsed at that point, she was side-tracked into another mental cul-de-sac.

Perhaps, Penelope thought, Rollo had merely been discreet, in choosing not to notice it. But if it was an artificial blemish, one wholly of Topaz's volition, why should he have felt any embarrassment? Was it possible that he just hadn't *seen* it? She had never been at all clear anyway whom the portraits were intended to be *of*: her grandmother looked very similar to Topaz rendered in paint on canvas, much more so than in life. It was only the *style* which told them apart, who was her grandmother and who was Topaz. Otherwise, it seemed to her now, they had been essentially interchangeable, the two subjects: as complementary versions of his one enduring, unwavering ideal.

'Are you going to drag all this up again?' her mother asked her. 'What's happening to me – '

Penelope leaned forward in the chair.

'I hope it's not "dragging" anything up,' she said.

'Well . . . you know what I mean. Writing about things – '

Their eyes met.

'You do, don't you?'

'I didn't think I was . . .'

'It came from Rollo,' her mother said, 'it must have done. The short stories.'

181

'Through Daddy?'

'He wasn't here long enough to discover.'

'Poor him – '

'Poor all of us.'

Their eyes met again.

'I wonder what it *is* like – '

'What what's like?' Penelope asked, gently.

'What's coming. Heaven. Or whatever it is.'

'You shouldn't say these – '

'A hotel foyer, I imagine. A very grand, swanky hotel. With porters enough, I trust. And people sitting around you didn't ever expect to see again.'

Penelope watched her mother's hands fidgeting with the top sheet. She was trying to think of how to reply, but wasn't quick enough.

'It'll be grin and bear it, I expect. Much as it always was. Or is that Hell? – things never changing?'

Penelope smoothed the quilt with her palms and fingers stretched flat.

'Or,' her mother continued, 'do you think it's all just the same thing, really, and there isn't any difference at all between them, nothing to choose?'

Penelope anticipated her mother's death two months before it happened, in February of 1947, during the coldest snap.

She suspected her mother had been up and about in the course of one night when she was asleep and hadn't heard. She took a cold with a hacking cough, which slowly developed into pneumonia. She hung on with unexpected vigour, as she was too much of a 'Life-lover' (and had always been so, so she said) to let go. But her mind also seemed uncertain and unpredictable, mixing its tenses. Gradually she retreated from the perfect into the preterite, and from there back into the present. Time past was lived through again; her mother unwittingly provided her with a running commentary on what was happening, then she forgot that there was anyone with her, least of all a daughter, and her remarks were only fragmentary, disjointed expressions of a thought or feeling in speedy motion.

'Your father changed, Penelope. People change. Getting married or making friends is a lottery. You don't know. On the other hand, since you can't know, you just take the risk. And hope for the best.'

Penelope sat on beside the bedside, knowing there could only be one end.

They were living too late in their millennium for marvels.

She listened, trying to relate the words that were spoken to what she knew of her mother's life and the shared history of the country and the world as it intruded on everyone's existence without – except for the exceptional history-makers and -manipulators – their bidding it to.

'About this house, Penelope – '

'Don't talk now, Mother.'

'I must. I want to – '
'No.'
'When I'm not here – '
'Don't talk like that.'
'But I must. I have to, Penelope – '
'Please. Another time – '
'You – you should know something – '
'The house is all right as it is.'
'But you don't – '
'*You* have to stay here and get better.'
'But – '
'*Better*. And that's all there is to it.'

She found flowers in the kitchen. She asked the nurse who they were from.
'They were lying on the top step. They didn't say.'
'There wasn't a note?'
'No.'
'That's strange.'
She thought it would have been better if she hadn't said 'That's strange': she didn't want to create mysteries for the nurse, reasons for speculation. She didn't look the prying type, but she wasn't too strong on types.
'I stood them in water.'
Helps always used to say 'Miss', and she found herself automatically supplying them in the nurse's silences.
'Shall I be taking them up to her?'
A florist's bouquet, unseasonal and not cheap.
'Yes,' Penelope said. 'Yes, I think you could.'

For Penelope the days lost all their definition even as she was passing through them: as they must also have done for her mother, who was ebbing from her, a little further every time she set to a fresh shift, sitting or doing the odds and ends she didn't like to ask the nurse to attend to or preparing herself something, a child's portion, to eat. She seemed to survive on tea, just as her mother was living on spoonfuls of warmed chicken-jelly stock and parings of the abysmal sawdust bread, sawn into pieces small enough for her to swallow. Once, very close to the end, she gathered that what was being spoken of, just a shade louder than a whisper, was the fine white *pain de mie* they used to be served in the dining-room of the Hotel Eden, in a time that hadn't been so paradisial or innocent after all.
If I were married now, Penelope hypothesised to herself, would it be possible for me to do any more than I am doing? On the whole, she thought not. The nurse was costing a small fortune, but that would be forgotten. What a husband would have given her was the opportunity to share this sadness, which he would inevitably have been at a remove from, which she would have had to

bridge at the end of each day (he, solicitous for her own health, would surely have insisted on particular hours for her keeping vigil).

It was because she thought she might lose the memory of these days she was living that she decided she would try to record them on paper, their now-ness, during the stints in the bedroom when her mother was asleep.

She put down everything quite straight, in an unelaborated log of facts, as realistically as a Dutchman of the Golden Age at his easel.

As an experiment she tried to totally eliminate herself.

Sometimes when she woke her mother didn't recognise her at first. Perhaps she was in a time before Borneo, before her marriage even.

Penelope had to sit waiting until she'd leafed through the years, to reach the point where they could begin to talk.

Her mother died without her even noticing. She might have been dead for a couple of minutes when she looked up from the newspaper, a story – she always remembered – about the American atom-bomb tests at Bikini.

It was the middle of a workaday Monday morning, the sun was heating up nicely, the nurse was downstairs attending to the washing and starching, and humouring the roller in the scullery, which had recently become work-shy. The flames licked in the grate, but the room was quite warm enough with sunlight. She stopped reading with the thought of removing her cardigan. The room for once felt optimistic and hopeful.

She noticed through her ears first, that there was no accompaniment of breathing. She leaned forward in the chair and saw that the quilt wasn't moving, that the hands were quite still. The lips weren't pinching and puckering or trying to speak.

She stood up and took several steps forward. The eyes were open and staring straight up at the ceiling: she who had always instructed that staring was the mark of an ill-bred person.

Remembering moistened her own eyes, she blinked, but the tears didn't well up. She realised she had to protect her mother from disgrace.

She called out and a few moments later she heard the nurse running up from the basement, cracking the stairboards. She stood waiting for her with the door open.

'We have to close her eyes,' she told her. 'Please, can we close her eyes.'

It was easily done. After that the nurse hesitated, uncertain whether or not to pull the sheet over the patient's head. 'No, it's all right,' Penelope told her, and the sheet was left where it was, at the level of her neck.

She stepped back on to the newspaper. She sat down on the hard, rush-bottomed chair. The months of waiting were finally over and the end had come without a blast of trumpets. It had come in perfect silence, stealing upon her mother like a back-door interloper.

The nurse respectfully left the room, and it was hers again. Even the coals held steady in the grate; the flames had dwindled to an orange glow. The stillness was total: like the solidity of an inanimate object, like darkness, like an enigma, like the peace of God which she knew now – knew positively, because she had the proof – was only a distillation of enduring nothingness with life flitting, so briefly, round about it.

Several weeks later an envelope reached the house from South Africa, addressed to herself. She opened it with a paperknife of Borneo silver and shook out the sheet of thin paper; she read the signature first, 'Ray Chapman', then her eyes sped over the lines of script.

He expressed his heartfelt condolences, he had read the death notice in the *Telegraph*, he'd been thinking about the past a great deal recently, he was sure her mother would have been very proud of her for all she'd done to help her through . . . And could *she* possibly be the same 'Penelope Milne' whose name he'd spotted on the books pages just a few months back, in a review of an anthology of short stories, how queer if she was. 'About a year-and-a-half ago I was married. I wasn't sure about getting in touch about it: I still don't know if I should have done. It seemed a momentous occasion in my own life and I thought I ought to be sharing it with those I had ever felt close to. At any rate, much water has flowed under the bridge since . . . Connie has been aware of my sadness, and naturally adds *her* sympathies to all my own . . .'

The situation was taken out of Penelope's hands.

The funeral was to be at Yelborne, in the churchyard. Her mother, she discovered, had made all the arrangements herself. Penelope couldn't keep the astonishment off her face when the lawyer told her.

'Are you *sure*?'

'Oh yes. Quite positive.'

She hadn't ever imagined she would be back in Yelborne again.

On the day, the weather kept dry, although a pack of grey clouds hung overhead.

She took the decision to walk to the church; her mother's cousin Lilian supposed it was to be alone with her memories, and looked sorrowful on her behalf.

In fact it was to satisfy her curiosity about Cheriton Court. But the big gates were locked, and when she asked a man pushing a bicycle he told her that the house had been empty for a couple of years, waiting for the owner's return from Africa. Everyone had gone, he said: whoever they'd been.

The service was polite and restrained.

'We give thee hearty thanks, for that it hath pleased thee to deliver this our sister out of the miseries of this sinful world . . .'

The church was airy inside, with whitewashed walls; the brass plaques

185

beneath the windows gleamed, some premature flowers had been rustled up from somewhere. The young vicar, recently appointed, spoke of her mother as if she had been one of the town's own. Through a blue and yellow side-window Penelope thought she could see, just, the top of the great house in its park.

' . . . in sure and certain hope of the Resurrection to eternal life, through our Lord Jesus Christ; who shall change our vile body, that it may be like unto *his* glorious body, according to the mighty working, whereby he is able to subdue all things to himself.'

The lawyer poured her a tumbler of whisky before he explained the will to her. She should have heeded his implied warning about what to expect.

She was the only legatee, certainly. And everything was hers.

'Your mother has left you the contents of your home. And a number of sums of money and stocks and bonds, totalling – let me check – yes, three thousand three hundred pounds.'

The lawyer was overlooking something, of course.

'Yes,' she said, waiting for him to mention the house. 'I see.'

The lawyer removed his pince-nez.

'So,' he said, 'I have done my duty. Your mother was a very pleasant woman. She must be a great loss to you, a very sad loss – '

'And . . .'

She hesitated.

'I beg your pardon?'

'The – the house?'

'The house? Oh.' He looked straight at her. Then his face fell when he realised that she didn't know.

'The house?' he said again.

'Isn't that included – '

'The house was sold.'

' "Sold"?' She giggled.

'Yes,' the lawyer said. 'Six years ago.'

The giggle gurgled down her throat, like water down a drainpipe.

'You – didn't know that?' he asked her.

'*What?*'

She stared at him.

'How . . . I don't . . .'

He wasn't, she guessed, prone to levity. Unless he was confusing her with another of his legatees.

' "*Sold*"?'

'Yes.'

'By my mother?' she asked him.

'Indeed.'

'Are you – you're quite sure?'

'Oh yes. But I supposed – well, that you must know.'

186

'I knew nothing.'

'It changed hands between five and six years ago.'

'Why, though?'

'Oh . . . It was a large house – you know? – difficult to run – times change – '

'Who was it sold to?'

'A Mr Jarvis. No, Jardine, rather. A Scotsman.'

'*What?*'

'Do you know him?'

'Jardine? Yes. Yes, I – '

She saw the little man pacing his room, her father's old study, wearing only his flannel undervest and combinations, to keep the life in his suit.

'Well, then . . .'

'He was a lodger in the house. For a while.'

'He made your mother quite a fair offer, I remember. Market value certainly. Mind you, it was wartime. She agreed, though.'

'But why? We still lived there – '

'There was a tenancy arrangement. Your mother would stay on. The buyer didn't want it for himself. He had other bits of property in the area. Your mother would pay him rent; a very modest rent, sort of peppercorn, and when she died he would have possession – '

'She should have told me. I should have known. I *had* to know, didn't I?'

'Well, she – '

'If I wasn't going to have a roof over my head.'

'She *did* tell me she thought you were going to be engaged once.'

'No. No, I wasn't. Of course I wasn't – '

'She had a lot to dwell on latterly, I dare say.'

'She couldn't have forgotten – '

'Well . . .'

He was wearing his pince-nez again, but not to read: merely as a defence, and dazzling her with those two reflected high-noon suns through the window behind her so that she couldn't continue to look, so that she had to lower her head, in modest, acceding subjugation to the facts.

2

She came back from work to the house in Southampton Place, and ran upstairs to find a man sitting in the shadows at the foot of the second staircase.

She jumped and let out a gasp.

'Penelope – !'

She couldn't identify the voice for several seconds. As the figure rose in the dim blue light from the street-lamp she saw a face as smoothly gilded as a statue's. This is ridiculous, she knew, editorial red pencils go through thoughts like that.

'Penelope, it's Oliver – '

She all but fell into his arms. He took her hands instead. Just as well, or she felt sure she would have stroked those perfectly contoured cheeks, that chin, the jaw-line.

She couldn't understand her own mood. She felt tipsy.

'I've come to take you away,' he said.

'What? Take me where?'

'To Cambridge.'

She laughed. He had written to her months ago to tell her that they had taken him on to the college teaching staff after he'd completed his classics degree.

'Not *now*, though.'

'When?'

'I don't know,' she said. 'The weekend?'

'You will come?'

He sounded so earnest about it.

'Yes,' she told him. 'Very well. I *will* come.'

'I'll treat that as a promise.'

'All right,' she said. 'Yes, do.'

He backed away from her.

'Stay, Oliver – '

'We'll wait,' he said. 'Until the weekend.'

'No, really – '

'I'll ring you. Can I, Penelope? About the train times.'

'Yes. Yes, of course.'

'Fine.'

'But please, won't you – '

Was she trying too hard?

But she couldn't persuade him.

*

Shadow-man, she thought as she lay on top of the bed in the darkness to save on the meter, listening to his footsteps growing fainter on the pavement. Oliver, handsome and improbable.

She reached out for her notepad and a stub of pencil. In case she forgot. She began to write. She called him 'O', 'she' was herself sprinting upstairs at the end of her working day. Some evenings 'she' felt her brain was punch-drunk with too much oxygen, she didn't want to eat or drink for days or weeks. There was a feeling in the air newly purged so clean by war, that she would be sustained by valiant, unsinkable hope alone.

Oliver handled the older dons quite well, on her – as they turned out to be, vestal and celibate – visits to the college. He seemed on less firm ground with some of the younger ones. At first she thought the embarrassment was on her account, for her not being who she might have been. But then Oliver told her, to her complete surprise, that he suspected they were jealous.

She came to feel he was showing her off. She wondered quite how some of them interpreted their chancing to be together. She couldn't help noticing that not everyone viewed her with mild, urbane favour. Two of the younger dons wouldn't let her see them looking at her, although she knew that they did: and whenever she did manage to intercept a glance, she caught coincidental expressions of incredulity or distaste. She wasn't certain that it merely owed to snobbery or to the fact of her unsuitability. Their eyes, in both cases, were wholly excluding: she only entered their orbit of attention by dint of the sorry circumstances, because she had worked on Oliver Hutton so that he would bring her here as his guest. They filled her coffee cup with a dismissive hauteur she had never encountered before, and in the course of several visits they didn't address more than three or four remarks to her between them. They concentrated on Oliver instead, bantering college chitchat, virtually staring him into the panelling as they waited for his replies, eyeing him from head to foot like connoisseurs of the sculptured male form as he poured more coffee or refilled their glasses with port.

She didn't really care to ask him about them, but he told her that he did have some respect for their learning. He could also laugh about them when they were alone together, and that seemed to restore some perspective. They made her feel unworthy, because she worked – now typing and invoicing and telephone-answering in a solicitor's office after her brief stints in an arts materials shop and making tea and mending fuses in the office of a literary magazine – and also because she was a woman. They couldn't know that she already kept a list of their sayings, that she was storing up this time for a later reckoning.

Still nothing 'happened' between them, no more than a customary goodbye peck on the cheek at the station before she climbed into her compartment for the journey back to London.

189

They were early days maybe. She hoped it wasn't herself to blame, but she didn't believe so. She was twenty-six and earnestly trusting it wasn't too long to have waited. No, rather she was saving herself. She would give herself to the man who deserved her.

The next time she always thought: at the last minute, before we leave for the station, it will happen – he'll hold me back, our eyes will lock, his lips will find mine, the moment will have come at last.

Oliver helped her into the sleeves of her coat.

'I'll walk you to the station,' he said.

She told him he didn't need to, but he insisted.

He couldn't find the keys of the doors.

'Never mind,' he said.

'You're very trusting.'

'You think so?'

She couldn't interpret his tone.

'City habits,' she said, 'I expect.'

They walked downstairs and into the quad. They followed the flagstones between the cobbles.

An elderly figure emerging from a doorway saluted Oliver and changed direction to cross tracks with them.

'My hat,' she said, 'I've left it upstairs – '

She turned away.

' – I'll only be a minute.'

She started running. She heard the old man's greeting, and Oliver's response.

She clack-clacked along the paving-stones. She was thinking, she ought to have stayed and given an apology.

She had reached the staircase when he called after her.

'Penelope!'

'It's all right,' she said without turning round, in a voice that wouldn't have travelled.

Upstairs she pushed open the unsnibbed door of the set and passed through the sitting-room. He had taken her outerwear from her and left them in the bedroom. She had never dared go into the room on any of her previous visits, for reasons which she felt were obvious. Even without him there, she crept in.

He had laid the hat on a chair. A black felt Chinese style she'd bought for her mother's funeral.

She took it over to the mantelpiece mirror to put it on. Her eyes dropped from her reflection to a photograph propped up against a candlestick. Oliver stood knee-high in a river with another man. She looked more closely and recognised the student with the sly eyes who preferred to call in with his unfailingly punctual essays rather than leave them with the porter in the lodge. Quite unnecessarily, it had occurred to her. In the photograph they both wore only their underpants, which clung wetly and revealingly so that she looked away: to Oliver's arm resting on the other man's shoulder.

She crammed her hair under the hat anyhow. She fixed herself very hard in the mirror. She heard footsteps outside, on the bare floorboards of the landing, and she prepared herself for Oliver.

It was the student she saw from the bedroom door. He stared at her, across the sitting-room. She glanced back into the bedroom over her shoulder, towards the amply-sized bed, then slipped her fingers into her gloves.

He stood watching, eyes riveted, gaping at her.

'Are you looking for Mr Hutton?' she asked.

'What? Yes. Well, I was passing – '

'"Passing"? I'll tell him,' she said, walking towards him.

He stepped back. Flummoxed. Nonplussed.

She smiled, as wantonly as a Constitution Hill tart. She let her eyes settle on him, momentarily and lasciviously.

'Feel free,' she said, without lowering her voice. 'Make yourself at home. I'm off now.'

She smiled again from the door.

'What shall I tell him?' she asked. 'That you were asking for him?'

'I . . .'

'You *do* want to see him about *something*, I presume?'

She didn't wait for an answer. She took the two steep flights of stairs at a run, clattering down them.

Oliver was standing at the bottom, looking up and seeming out-of-breath. His face was full of warning, maybe he had overheard. She placed her hand on his arm.

'Ready?' she asked him.

He stared at her hand with the same expression of incredulity she had just observed upstairs, almost identical.

'Now I shan't disgrace you,' she said.

'I – I'm sorry?'

'By not wearing a hat.' She wasn't sure of her feelings, what her reactions must be. 'Everyone will see I'm a solid, respectable kind of woman. And your reputation will be quite safe with me, Oliver.'

The visits stopped for several weeks.

She couldn't forget Sly Eyes, his surprise. His face reappeared to her among strangers' in the streets.

Then Oliver phoned her in London, at the house she was rooming in, and proposed another weekend.

He sounded anxious about her reply and she didn't know how to refuse him.

'Yes,' she said. 'Yes, of course.'

'And *I'm* paying.'

'You always pay, Oliver. You mustn't.'

191

'Please. What else do I get paid *for?*'

She couldn't think quickly enough to answer. Her breath rolled down the line to Cambridge.

At ten o'clock on the Sunday morning Oliver collected her at the hotel in Trinity Street. She walked out into temperamental watery sunshine and peals of bells ringing across the city.

He had shown her the complete sights of Cambridge three times in the past months. He had got hold of petrol coupons, so they were to drive out to Ely in a car borrowed from a colleague.

She could tell he was preoccupied on the journey there.

'I'm not holding you back?' she asked him, as politely as she could. 'From doing something else?'

'Holding me back?' he said, first startled and then gravelled. 'Good God, no.'

'I just wondered.'

'This – this is exactly what I want to be doing.'

He still sounded uncertain. But she nodded and looked out the side-window, at the flatness of gouache-green fields and straightness of canals silting with weed.

A little later a shower came on, fine rain slanting like light. The wipers slapped on the windscreen glass and drew her attention to the silence.

In Ely they parked the car in the Close. It was dry, just, and they covered the short distance to the West Door of the cathedral concentrating on avoiding the puddles. A service was in progress and they walked up a side-aisle. Her eyes were fixed by the lantern of window in the roof, at the point where the nave and transept crossed. She was looking up when she felt the pressure of his hand on her arm and found herself being directed by him in a specific direction.

'You should see the Lady Chapel,' he said.

Its ascetic air did impress her when he showed her and explained. Cromwell's men had stripped it of its idols and decoration, and only a few stubborn stone heads survived, in awkward corners. The Protector's demystifiers had put out all the stained glass; the plain glass in the massive tracery windows above the arcades flooded the chapel with the matter-of-fact fen light and flushed out the shadows from their hiding-places. The stone seemed untypically pale for cathedral stone. The spot had been most effectively purged of its medieval arcanum.

He steered her towards a row of rush-bottomed chairs against one of the walls. She sat down where she was being bid, with a single chair left between them.

'I wanted to find somewhere quiet,' he said.

The organ chords and the singing from the nave sounded remote to her and, somehow, ineffectual.

'And somewhere special,' he added.

She raised her eyes to the fan-vaulting.

'Will you marry me, Penelope?'

For several seconds she thought her neck must be in nervous spasm: it was only her neck she was thinking of, how she could unlock it.

'Are – are you all right?'

Feeling his hand on her arm brought her out of her shock.

'Yes,' she said. 'Yes, thank you.'

'Did – did you hear – what I asked?'

'Oh yes,' she said, in a fractured voice that seemed to be flying away from her, up to the roof. 'Quite – distinctly.'

'Do you – would you like to think about it?'

'I'm not sure,' she said. 'That I need to, really.'

'Does that mean . . . ?'

'Oh no,' she said. 'I don't think so.'

'What?'

'I don't – I don't feel it would be such a good idea. Actually.'

'I know it's very soon – '

'It's not that.'

'No?'

'But why? Don't we – '

'I just – don't think – it's suitable – '

'There's someone else?'

'No,' she said. 'No, there isn't.'

She was almost as surprised and ambushed by her own decisiveness. But what else had been the purpose of watching him as she had?

She untied her rain-hood and took it off, smoothing it on the lap of her Burberry. I could even feel resentful, it occurred to her, but I shan't. I know, though: this time I know.

'Is it – what you really mean?' she asked him, and stopped.

He blinked at her.

'What I really mean?'

'Is it because – '

He blinked again.

' – because you're sorry for me?'

Several more blinks followed, until he was ready to speak.

'No, that's not why. Although, yes, I am sorry for you. Because it was such a sad thing to happen, your mother. You want to write, though. Don't you? Seriously? And – I could support you.'

'It'll be all right again, I expect.'

'Yes?'

'I just need time,' she said.

' "Time"?'

'Yes. To think how to . . .'

'To think about your answer?'

She shook her head.

'To get back to normal, I mean. Or get things on an even keel. You know? And write – '

At that moment the door squeaked open and a cleric in a cassock looked in. He saw them both and smiled.

'Perhaps – ' His voice reached them in ringing whispers. ' – I wondered if you'd care to join us in our praises?'

She stared back, her reasoning unable to make the adjustment.

'I thought you might be – embarrassed? Perhaps?'

She gave the man, this softly sibilant stranger, a ghastly sham smile.

'Young couples,' he said in his stage whispers, 'are always most welcome. Whenever – '

'We're historians,' Oliver told him.

'I see. How splendid.'

'That's why we've come.'

'But maybe – there's still a while to go. It's Responses just now – '

She shook her head.

'Time is rather short, I'm afraid,' Oliver said more tersely. 'If you don't mind.'

'No.' The man retreated a couple of steps. 'No, of course not. We're very proud of our cathedral. Any questions you – '

'Thank you,' Penelope said, and smiled again. The door creaked shut.

She couldn't look at Oliver, so very nearly beside her, one chair away, and she dropped her eyes to her hands on the lap of her mackintosh, not seeing that her snood had fallen to the floor, beneath her feet, and was in the process of absenting itself from the scene, to become a silent witness to these moments that were later – decades away – to seem so crucial, so deeply imbued with tragedy and its hidden foretelling.

In the months that followed she told herself she had no cause to regret her decision. It hadn't been a conscious decision even: she hadn't believed she had any real choice in the matter. She liked him; she couldn't be sure that she loved him. Marriage was certainly impossible. She didn't *have* to think about it, it was only what she felt.

'Please, Penelope,' Oliver had tried to persuade her, when they'd driven back from Ely. 'I don't see *why* not.'

'But I don't fit in with all this.' She indicated Cambridge, all about them. 'I couldn't survive here.'

'We wouldn't need to live here. If you don't want to.'

'But *you* do – '

'Not if *you* don't.'

'But that wouldn't be a very good start. We'd both have to be doing what we wanted to do.'

'We could talk about it. Discuss it.'

194

'Yes, maybe. But that's only one thing.'

'What else, then?'

She found a few more reasons to give him – how recent their remeeting was, he hadn't given himself long enough to look around, she didn't know if she was domesticated, she wasn't an academic like him, maybe she was uneducated, she knew hardly anything about herself – yet – so how could *he*, anyway he was still young with his career to concentrate on, also institutions of any sort rather alarmed her – but she knew she wasn't telling him the truest reason, which was that they weren't lovers.

The war had taught a generation to love when they might. She didn't have the experience to initiate, although she had tried: but he had failed to respond. For a while she'd even thought he found her unattractive, that she was reading too much into the situation, which might only be that of an old friendship revived. She had gradually realised that there was more to it than that: what she had hardly liked to acknowledge to herself before. It let her off the hook, but it also left her feeling – not cheated – but vulnerable, and helpless to help him.

'My dear Oliver . . .'

It was a ridiculous thing to say, stagy, as if she was inviting sympathy for herself.

'Penelope, listen to me please . . .'

'I am,' she told him. 'I have. Very carefully.'

'Then why don't – '

'Oh,' she said, 'because . . .'

Because the words he'd spoken were genuine enough but they also lacked the wild ardour, the full unreasoning passion any woman placed just as she was hoped to hear. He hadn't attempted to go beyond these words, to touch her, to stop the words leaving her own mouth by closing it with his own. He might have reached out and taken her hand or laid his on her arm or cradled *his* arm around her waist and held her against him. But he didn't do these things, and there in sum was the sad issue of their relationship, which was fated to remain what it had been – a friendship. However much she hoped for more, she couldn't achieve that by herself.

'You need time,' he said, speaking film lines. 'Time. To think about it.'

'No,' she told him. 'No, I don't think so.'

'But it's so sudden. I just – I thought I *should* ask you.'

She nodded: but she had been anticipating the question for longer than him perhaps.

'I'm glad,' she said, 'but I really don't think I'm going to change my – '

He even interrupted her with an actor's timing. 'Please – '

Unless I've misjudged, she thought, and I've got it appallingly wrong. But her uncertainty didn't last longer than a few moments, and she assured herself that she hadn't misread circumstances, not in their fundamentals. She only wished she might be able to save Oliver from himself, that this – saying 'no' to him – would be the way to do it.

'We could go for a walk,' she said.

He seemed not to hear her.

'Shall we?' she asked again.

'What's that?'

'We could take a turn. Along the Backs. Get some air.'

'Yes.'

He led the way, distractedly, walking several steps in front of her. She followed, no longer surprised or even disappointed. It was only more of the proof she needed, if she did need it. What if she'd told him 'yes', would that have been sufficient to turn him into a different man?

It was only as she matched her tread to his, but a couple of steps behind him, that it struck her, something very significant *had* just happened: she had been proposed to. She had always supposed it to be the apogee of any woman's life. It had come and then gone in the briefest snatch of time. And she had refused to say 'yes'.

She suddenly appreciated the full awesomeness of the transaction, and of her own part in it. A little panic gathered in the pit of her stomach, that she should have been so settled on a final answer, so defiant in rejecting the offer of a new life.

Whom was she really trying to save: him, or herself?

She wouldn't have made him happy to be a husband. And for herself, she didn't know if she was ready yet to recognise all the components of happiness.

Part Eight

1

Penelope Milne's first novel, *Finnegan Begin Again*, was published on 16 August 1948: a chiefly symbolic occasion, since the book had already appeared in certain shops a fortnight before. It would probably be impossible to settle on such-and-such a day as marking her 'rebirth into the world', as she once expressed it. But that official day of publication was surely the most apposite, and it's a date she admits she hasn't ever forgotten.

What did you intend Finnegan Begin Again *to be about?*

'About'? Impossibilities, I suppose.

What are your feelings for the book? Did it achieve what you wanted it to?

I wanted it to have some free life of its own. I saw a film-writer on television recently, he was talking about wanting to surprise an audience all the time by not giving them what they expected. He'd written a script about a hit man: he's just about to go off on some assignment, but before he leaves the house he has to eat, so he opens a tin in the kitchen but as he does so he cuts his hand, his right hand, the one he aims and shoots with, so he has to bandage that, which means that from then on he's dependent on his left hand, which he has never trained. I love that idea. The book's not like that, although I wanted it to be. It's too hesitant, I didn't know enough: I did want the woman to be disappointed, and not in the way that's most ordered and reasoned to her. She takes wrong turnings and comes up against some brick walls, and she retraces her steps and starts again.

You wanted her not to get her man?

I don't think she's very sure that that's what she wants. She's not even terribly thinking about it, about anything. She sort of *feels* the truth of a situation: but never by working it out with any semblance of logic. She's at a point where she has – well, I suppose she's drifted, in quite a pleasant, anaesthetised way, and she's reached a different stage, a little further on, where she's grown up and she's faced with the responsibility of somehow organising her life.

And it's impossible to her?

Certainly it's confusing. She wishes she could tell her story backwards, from the end.

You write a good deal of it in the present tense.

It's the tense she thinks and feels in, which she has to make her judgments in, without anything much to judge from.

Should we sympathise with Helen Finnegan?

I hope so. And feel embarrassed. And relieved.

Did you feel you were close to the book?

About thirteen or fourteen inches, I'd say, from eye-level to the paper on the desk.

When she was flush, she would go and have tea of an afternoon at Gunter's.

If the tea-rooms were busy, she might have to share a table. But since she had recently published a novel, table-sharing was no drawback to an afternoon, whatever happened to her from now on must be 'copy'. It was a very simple, very satisfactory morality, she felt: all abstruse philosophising reduced to so little.

She would listen in to conversations. She once sat next to a separated couple who were having their annual get-together: the strain was exemplary, and the climax occurred when the woman announced fortissimo and very pointedly in her direction, 'I don't see the point of anyone on their own coming somewhere like this, do you?' She once watched a young wife who was sitting with her husband crying into her napkin. She once noticed two women's knees pushing against the other's under the table, where the cover wasn't hanging properly and she mightn't have been expected to see.

One afternoon she found herself being scrutinised from three or four tables away, by a spruce businessman she had observed on another afternoon. Now as then he was sitting by himself, with his back to the wall, and missing hardly anything of what was going on. He was dark-haired, with quite a strong face, a firm chin. Early thirties, he looked a little like James Mason in the films, and – fleetingly – the first time she'd thought that it might actually be him. He had very precise manners, but then as now he struck her as being restive: his dark eyes didn't stop travelling round the room, he inclined his head in ways that made her sure he was tuning into conversations like her, he pulled at his starched cuffs a good deal and made a lot of movements with his feet, which presumably no one else could catch sight of.

She wondered, though, what it could possibly mean to her *how* he behaved, whether he was restless or not. She tended to drift on those afternoons, usually because she had finished a piece of journalism and had handed it in and was waiting to start another: she should have been savouring her freedom but the first time and the second that she saw the man who reminded her of James Mason she felt her attention was being held, in spite of herself.

He was very bespoke in his dress and mannerisms. By comparison, on that second afternoon, she was wearing mid-calf royal blue jeans she'd seen in *Vogue* and bought in Simpson's with her first royalties. In a reckless mood she'd treated herself to one of the new safari hats, with a trailing green scarf. Maybe, she thought, maybe he was looking at her because of what she knew she so patently was *not*?

He did discompose her that second time, her own awkwardness confirmed it. She sensed that he saw through her pretence of confidence, that he knew like her that she only came here to try to believe in herself, in her abilities and her independence. She didn't have sufficient faith yet in her literary capacities to be certain of an alpha and omega that was 'herself'. On her not-so-good days she felt 'self' was no more than cotton-wool sure, wisps of it pulled off everywhere, on to all the surfaces she came into contact with.

Every time she looked up that second afternoon he was watching her.

A woman striding across the room reminded her of Margot, and she finished her Russian tea with a gulp, got up and walked towards the desk to pay. Outside, on Park Lane in daylight, she heard footsteps behind her. She didn't mean to look round, but the voice she heard calling after her exactly matched his face.

She swung round. He stood looking no more than a little sheepish; he was holding out her hat.

One hand instinctively reached out.

'I'm sorry,' he said, 'I believe – this is yours?'

'Yes. Yes, I'm – '

I left my hat behind because I wanted it to be found.

'How stupid of me,' she said.

'It's very easily done.'

He spoke with the clarity of an actor, James Mason in *The Wicked Lady*.

'But I should have remembered – '

'It's quite a hat – '

I wanted him to find it, him and no one else.

' – I haven't seen one like it.'

'It's new. A new style.'

'You like hats?'

'I haven't thought about it. *This* hat. I liked this hat. That's all.'

He looked at her mouth all the time she spoke. Even when she'd stopped he continued to look.

The start.
Romance begins.
Spring in Park Lane.
> *She feels the difference between them, in dress.*
> *But she knows – knows inside, in her being – that neither of them is as they seem to be.*
Romantic overtones, as in a film. Make plausible.
Walks with her. He can't usually, he says, but he's changing jobs. He was in 'brokerage', now taking a month off before going into a bank.
He says he hasn't tried the Hyde Park Hotel for tea, has she?
No, no.
Would she like to try it one day?
> *She delays her answer. She has a choice, she knows. But he's holding the hat: the attention-seeking hat with the trailing green scarf. Choices have already been made, far beneath the surface. Momentarily she thinks of her mother with Mr Chapman, martyring herself.*
'Yes,' she says. 'I think I would. Like to try the Hyde Park Hotel. If . . .'
She remembers James Mason in The Man in Grey. *And* The Odd Man Out.

He didn't care for her working.

He would come and pick her up at the small publisher's where she was the dogsbody in the basement to the chinless, rather too well-bred set-up upstairs.

Guy would sit outside in the car with the window wound down; his elbow would be leaning on the sill of the door and his fingers drumming on the roof. She'd see his face light up as she reached the pavement from the area steps. He always shouted across the new total of days left until she would have served her notice, quite loudly enough to be heard through the raised sashes of the upstairs windows those fresh-air fiends insisted on.

She loved him for his ease and consideration, for his gentleness and also for his passion, for never looking at another woman; she loved him for not being nostalgic and not causing her to be, for making her feel necessary to him, for not making her life feel pinched like her own mother's, for never querying a single purchase she made, for teaching her to *enjoy* the things she'd never much noticed before, food and drink and her body and its health, and for taking her virginity. He taught her not to be shy of sex, and she loved him for that but also for making it their own private business, done in darkness. She loved him for not making her feel inadequate, in bed or in her thinking or in her cooking, and for those admiring looks he watched her with whenever she dressed up for him. She loved him for not reading more books than she did, and for – almost always – seeming to find the same frame of mind for himself that she was in, so that they could either walk in step along a sparkling April pavement and say nothing together or find a quiet beach and relive a boisterous childhood friendship that never was, sprint-racing and swimming and laughing at the tops of their voices and burying one another in sand, and the pleasure of both sorts of day was equal to her. She loved him for the surprises he threw up, discovering he could ice-skate, and could write script backwards which read properly when she held it up to a mirror, and could speak perfect, accentless French just like a native. (His name looked French – Guy Gerrault – but she explained to people that the 'Guy' was as in 'Fawkes', the 'Gerrault' sounded like 'Gerald' with a final 't', and he was as English as anyone could be: but she even loved him for the virtual-confusion.) She loved him for bringing them so close, for each surrendering, but for neither knowing more about the other – for knowing less perhaps. She loved him for allowing her to *be*, and for not requiring her to train herself into self-consciousness, for letting her just forget quite often, for bringing her on certain days to the perfect point of near-amnesia and a slow, rapturous, unthinking fade-out.

Guy, without (as he put it) the complication of a university education, had no intellectual pretensions. He did know something about paintings, however: a good deal, in fact. He was very informed about sale-room prices, and she presumed that might have been on account of his being in the financial line himself. Whenever they visited art galleries, even in a roomful of milling people he was able to concentrate all his attention on the effect of a painting.

200

He could become muddled as to who followed whom in historical sequence, the intellectual subtleties of symbolism escaped him, but he had an instinct for the *impression* a painting made on its beholder, how it worked on him or her: be it of a fleshly nymph, or the Virgin, or a cool bourgeois, or a wrinkled peasant crone, be the background sylvan or photographically Dutch or only hinted at or glaringly orange or blue, as in the tortured Van Goghs that seemed to hold his attention just a fraction longer than any other.

Two photographs, although there were once three. The same house – the boarding-house – and the same garden. There's a sunburst on the front door and the french windows; the sign on the gatepost says 'Stella Maris'.

She sits in a deck-chair in one photograph. In the other she waves from an upstairs window. Ironically, there is no trace of Guy, even though the holiday was his idea. They were still at the stage of planning a marriage, but she offered no resistance when he suggested it. She was too much in love with him to want to refuse him anything.

She liked his crankiness, his alighting on situations at unexpected tangents. She thought their life together would always be fresh and continually interesting if they were to continue to play it just like this.

Six months after the holiday they were married, at Caxton Hall, and she became Mrs Guy Gerrault.

Her editor and a few contacts attended (she couldn't have invited Valerie without Oliver, so she hadn't); a number of his own colleagues and their wives were present, and came on with them to an old-fashioned breakfast at the Berkeley. It was a quiet, expensive, impeccably ordered, slightly impersonal day: a very gentle, very professional launch into the condition of marriage.

Later she couldn't remember how she must have put in all her time. But it had been no problem to her, not then when she was living through those days and never having to think ahead. She had decided she didn't want any help in the house, that that way it might seem more like their own home. Guy told her they could afford it and smiled at her persistence each time she refused, but she saw her responsibility now as being the homemaker: she explained to him, the best she could, and he playfully held up his hands in surrender. Sometimes they had lunch at a restaurant or hotel, and that made the day different: or the wives of his colleagues at the bank invited her to have lunch with them, or morning coffee or afternoon tea. She felt no hankering for wartime conditions, or to be working again: some women's talk of 'independence' used to sound brutal and desperate to her, as if the ammo shifts or the secretary's desk or the shop counter was their last option and all others had been scuppered. She didn't accept that this general shaking down was a negative adjustment: women did certain things better than men and she was only responding to a purpose born in her, which was surely as much biological and femininely instinctive as it was a fact of historical experience and attitude. (After their return from Borneo, her mother had been quite lacking in practical knowledge: Penelope felt that maybe there was a dose-and-a-half of the housewifely genes in herself to compensate, but she had no complaints at all on that count.)

They were happy years, her six happiest, in every respect. She didn't distinguish between this or that, or major or minor in her life; making a comfortable home to be shared with Guy was an expression of her total devotion. She saw how happy it made him, how at peace he was. He liked nothing better than to be there with her; sometimes he told her the world could go to hell and damnation, so long as it left them the house and themselves. He made her feel she had succeeded in something, she had created no little thing – an ambience and an order. No one had made her feel so sure of herself and her capacities as Guy. He noticed small details, which men were supposed not to, which she used to hear her mother accusing her father of never doing: he knew when she replaced the flowers in the vases with fresh ones, when she cooked by a new recipe or using her initiative, when she'd had a cleaning-bee. He didn't stint in providing her with whatever she needed – both financially, and in terms of his encouragement. He accompanied her shopping so that she would feel comfortable about buying herself something to wear. They ate out when they chose to, and would have done so more often if he'd thought it was what she wanted: but it wasn't altogether, nor was it a great fondness of his, so by proper choice they were their own companions at home, or they had guests, and when he was away on business he phoned her on crackly lines and didn't allow her to dwell too much on the separation. In the normal course of things they seldom ventured far from base.

'Don't you wish you were out?' she occasionally asked him.

'"Out"? Doing what?'

'Something exciting.'

'Like what?'

'I don't know.'

'But *this* is what I want to be doing!'

In spite of custom, she couldn't help wondering.

When she wasn't expecting it, suddenly he would revert, turning himself into a schoolboy: he'd hide himself behind tall mirrors when she was trying on clothes in a shop, he'd string chestnuts into conkers and challenge her, he'd actually slide down banisters and walk up down-escalators. Hard to believe that he'd trained soldiers for the war, up in Scotland. In rooms of strangers his eyes would dart everywhere, often with a puckish glint which made her want to laugh out loud. On their social evenings she was jealous of anyone else taking possession of him; afterwards he would joke about the evening but never cruelly, and he would surprise her with the acuteness of his watching eye, remembering the smallest, subtlest particulars. He'd test out snooty waiters by asking them long, involved questions in French or Italian.

Usually he was great company, even – given a loose rein – high-spirited. Every so often, by contrast, he would become quiet and inward, but not for longer than she could bear; she told herself that was only human nature anyway, and that it was everyone's privilege to withdraw now and then, if that was what they needed to do. She didn't ask him questions about it, nothing that went beyond 'Are you sure you're feeling all right, Guy?' or 'Do you want to tell me, dear?' He would come out of it in an hour or two or overnight; there were no histrionics of any sort, and neither of them would be any the worse at the end of it. On his best form he made her feel – she was old enough to believe the truth of clichés – more alive in herself: with Guy she experienced life to a greater degree than she had before she met him and married him. Looking back, the oddest interlude in her history was the melodrama at Cheriton Court, where none of the characters as she could recall them seemed weighted to the ground, in a setting that with time had become incorporeal, ethereal: and yet thinking about it she had to close her eyes against the shame and the hurt she'd caused, which confirmed that what had happened had been actual enough, sorrowfully real. Remembering, she threw herself into the spirit of this marriage with more conviction than ever, resolved that it should be a shining and unforgettable success.

Guy had no family, and neither did she.

He showed her photographs of a country house in Derbyshire called Drewsteignton, which had been his family home: a creeper-clad Victorian version of Jacobean, angled half-timbered gables and fancy brickwork on the chimneystacks. The building had been razed by a fire, and inevitably she was reminded of the tragedy in Nice. His parents had died in a plane crash in Kenya not long after.

She described themselves as two orphans thrown upon the world. He seemed content with the definition, and took it up himself.

'This is the sort of furniture I like anyway,' Guy told her.

'What kind's that?'

'Yours. Your mother's. Your grandmother's.'

'It – it's all right.'

'There are some very nice pieces.'

'But compared with what *you*'re – '

'This is much nicer.'

He was so tactful, always.

'Truly, Penny – '

There *were* some good pieces: a rosewood sofa table, a secretaire-bookcase with glass doors, a Cuban mahogany bureau, a knee-hole dressing-table and a serpentine-front chest in the bedroom, four dining-chairs in the Chinese Chippendale style, a carved oak coffer c. 1650. But she supposed Guy had been used to better, that her own family's tastes and acquisitions would seem all too predictable and middle-class to him.

'It's your *past*, Penny. I want to have that too.'

'But I don't want to inflict it on *you*.'

'You're not, though. We *could* start again, have everything new, but it'd be like – having no photographs.'

His photographs of his home and his parents had intrigued her: he had seemed surprised that she should show so much interest.

'If you're really quite happy about – '

'I am. Of course I am.'

The conversation had ended in smiles, like the best ones, hands touching, an armhold, and a kiss. How could she have wished for anything different? How could she have doubted him, in a hundred years?

Five months after they were married, he gave her twenty-five minutes to get ready and then he took her on a mystery tour in the car. They ended up on the Suffolk coast, in Orford, at an inn in the square at the top of the town.

The proprietor called her 'Mrs Browning' when she asked for the key of the bathroom.

'What name have you used, Guy?'

'Name?'

'In the Visitors' Book.'

'"Browning". An improvement on Brown, I thought.'

'I suppose so.'

'You don't sound too sure about that.'

'Well,' she said, 'I expect I'll need time to get used to my new name.'

'It's just a name!'

'But it matters to you?'

'"Matters"?'

'That you should be Mr Browning?'

'I . . .'

'Not Mr Gerrault?'

His eyes focused on her with that intensity they occasionally had, scalpel-sharp. But only observantly sharp, not critically.

'We could treat it as a game,' he said. 'If you like.'

'A game?' she repeated.

'You'd know if I wasn't telling you the truth?'

'Yes,' she said. 'Yes, I think so.'

'Just *think* so?'

'About the name,' she said. 'If *you*'ve got a reason, I mean, it's all right.'

'So we've become Mr and Mrs Browning?'

She nodded, and felt she'd somehow lost her control of the conversation.

'Just while we're here?' she asked him.

'Oh yes,' he said, in his most agreeable way.

'"Mrs Browning".' She savoured the sound of the name.

'And while we're here,' he said, 'we can make up new lives for ourselves. To tell people.'

'Yes?'

'To go with the names.'

She nodded. There was a plausible logic in the idea.

'What if we tell them different stories?' she said. 'By accident.'

'I expect it happens all the time.'

'It does?'

'If you talk to a couple separately. It's just because they're married – because of the fact – that you *think* they're telling you the same story.'

She smiled. She didn't think she quite believed that. But if he was willing to treat the subject so lightly, then it was all to the good.

'It could be rather amusing,' he said.

'Yes.'

'I think this place could do with some sending-up, don't you?'

'What decided you?' she asked him.

'About the name?'

'No, about – ' she nodded at the window, at the harbour and the sails of the cockle-boats half-a-mile away ' – here.'

'A little holiday, I thought.'

'In Orford?'

'And round about.'

'Is it Mr Browning telling me that?'

'If you want him to be.'

'I – I don't know,' she said.

'He's a perfectly nice chap.'

'I'm sure he is,' she said.

She let him draw her to him. She knew she was sometimes too slow, too set, but not – she hoped – too humourless. Save me from being a stolid person, she wanted to tell him: show me how to become the person who will be worthy of you and this affection like no other I've known.

2

The New Look in clothes, she decided, went with a new life.

She wondered if there was any connection between Oliver's proposal and the position she found herself in now, a young Lancaster Gate wife. But she believed she appreciated Guy for his own sake. Pity did come into it: because like her he had no family. He wasn't very literary, but he remembered the modern names she told him: she saw very little of that Soho company anyway, since she hadn't the learning they did and she might have been looked down upon, being someone who wrote against the odds and only out of her instincts. She was pleased to have an occupation for herself, but preferred to confine it to the mornings and to spend the rest of her time making a home for the two of them.

Guy looked every inch the banker, but she never did quite believe it of him. Her first impressions had stayed with her: he did have restless eyes, and he was hard put to keep his feet still. She guessed that his very rightness in his professional pose had some irony about it, although she wasn't able to guess how much. He explained his life to her, he answered any questions that she might put to him, but she knew too that she wasn't being told everything: neither about his work, nor about his nature. She knew quite enough to live with, and if she hadn't occupied her mornings trying and trying to turn her characters into three-dimensional people perhaps she wouldn't have been conscious of any lack in her knowledge of him. She had told him about herself, most things, but she wasn't able to gauge if he was wary of her morning activities, if he thought she didn't scrutinise *him* too much. She concealed any reservations she had, that he wasn't wholly open with her. And pity – despite their material comfort – remained a key emotion with her, for the little boy lost she thought she sometimes saw.

'We could go and look. Guy?'
  'I'm sorry. Go where?'
  'To your old home. Where it stood. Before the war.'
  'I . . .'
  'Just for a look.'
  'No. I don't think I could.'
  'Really? Would it hurt you?'
  'Hurt me? Yes. Yes, I rather think it would.'

'All right then.'

'Do you see why?'

'Yes.'

'I want you to understand, Penelope. Please.'

'Yes. Yes, I do.'

'It's important to me. That you do.'

'I do, Guy.'

'Truly?'

'*You*'re my life, Penelope. My real life. The one I'm alive in. The rest – nothing matters to me now except that – believe me.'

'I do. I do believe you.'

'I love you, Penelope.'

'I don't deserve you.'

'This is more than I could ever have expected. Hoped for. Ever dreamed possible.'

He bought her a pagoda hat in the Dior style. She wore it everywhere.

The hats became a regular – *quite* a regular – indulgence, on her birthday or sometimes at Christmas. He didn't care what they cost, and he insisted that *she* shouldn't give it a thought either. Only once and quite late in the marriage, when he'd drunk a good deal one evening – itself an unusual occurrence, since she was never to know anyone better able to handle wines and spirits – he told her that his mother had never been without a hat. It was his first memory, of her leaning over his pram shaded by a brim, and also his last, of her climbing into the taxi that took her to the aerodrome and her death, wearing a little fur beret that matched the white fox cub draped head to brush about her shoulders.

1948 The cream pagoda hat
1948 The burgundy velvet side-beret
1949 The white straw and black felt hat, for their going-away
1949 The boater
1950 The black-and-white curé hat
1950 The white plush turban
1951 The ochre cartwheel
1951 The grey coolie hat
1952 The navy-blue Breton straw hat
1952 The black grosgrain beret
1953 The lime-green straw hat
1954 The navy-blue sailor hat

She opened the publishers' parcel and laid the books out on top of the dining-table.

The cover artist had contrived to reproduce the 'Enchanted Castle' of the title, set on a blue Swiss lake. The back inside flap of the jacket carried a photograph of herself sitting on a bench in Regent's Park in sunshine, wearing a humble summer straw hat and not one of her better ones, and smiling – she now felt – rather too obligingly, too transparently.

She walked round the table several times, touching the mint books with her fingertips. She heard a movement and turned round and saw Guy standing at the door. When he saw her looking he smiled: not very comfortably, it occurred to her. But he was smiling, notwithstanding.

He stepped into the room. She picked up one of the books and handed it to him, but said nothing. Still smiling, he nodded at the cover, nodded at the photograph on the jacket flap and raised his eyebrows.

She had given him the manuscript to read. 'Am I in it?' he'd asked her, assuming a jokey manner which she knew was a disguise. She'd told him he wasn't, but he'd sat up until the early hours reading it at one sitting, to confirm as much for himself. At breakfast the next morning he'd said very little after offering her his congratulations and praise. She knew he was viewing her in a different light, although she already had one published novel behind her and half-a-dozen short stories in magazines. She had achieved something, and maybe he imagined it had nothing to do with him: but she couldn't have done it without him there. She had required the routine and tranquillity of their marriage to settle her mind, a stable point from which to look back and fix on the past, to work that personal alchemy on it which restored some surer sense of proportion and order than had been possible to her then when she was living it.

'Is it about your grandfather?' Guy had asked her.

'Well . . . ' she'd replied, not honestly knowing the answer.

'Why – why did you want to?'

'I was intrigued,' she'd told him, 'to know what happened. Or might have happened.'

Now another breakfast. She was trying to reassure him by busying herself with the domestic details, cups, saucers, teaspoons, milk in the jug, knives, tea-strainer, a cosy for the pot. Did he think she was dissatisfied with the marriage and what he offered her? She smiled a lot herself, she tried to suggest her day was empty, stretching ahead, her duties in the house apart.

But of course there was a pile of books in the corner of the room, seven copies of *The Enchanted Castle* as the contract stipulated: she had her back to them, so he was sitting at the table facing them – yet he wasn't looking at them, she noticed, he scrupulously wasn't attending.

She didn't want anything to change after this: although she had hardly gone the right way about it. She smiled more broadly. After all, it was only a book.

She wondered what Miss Saxby would have had to say: if it had anything to do with keeping a clear head and holding to a steady course. Getting into print must pale into insignificance as an achievement beside any of Phoebe Venables', crown-princess of top-hatted British dressage on Fine and Dandy and Buttermilk. Miss Saxby, she guessed, would not have thought very much

208

of it. Thurlestone Girls found Max Factor and Chanel more to the point than the reek of printers' ink.

Was that what Guy believed, despite his appreciative words? Did it bother him to have the evidence of her secret mental life? – in other marriages it wasn't made literal like this, as she had caused it to be.

She told him she thought she would ring the chimneysweep.

'Yes?' she asked him.

'Yes, by all means.'

'If you think we should?'

'Well, I suppose so. I'm sure you know best.'

They'd had so few quarrels. Many less than their quota surely. Ought they to be having more? What was it that seemed more important to them than losing their tempers with each other once in a while? Even the spinster Miss Saxby must have anticipated the intrusions of disharmony on occasions. How could she possibly have foreseen that the marriage of Penelope Milne would have had so few jolts and buffets?

Both Guy and she needed the security, she knew, and also the lenity, the serenity. They were both wanting to believe in the invincibility of their marriage, a union to which they each contributed their part but which was greater than both of them. They both needed to believe in its necessity, to make it the compulsive, overriding *raison d'être* of lives that had been too accidental up until now, seeming to lack connecting form and purpose.

Marriage was the making of them both. If it should become unstuck – so she sensed in her gut that first morning after the finished copies of the book arrived – then it might just prove the undoing of their two lives.

These were her happiest years, also the ones of most mystery: especially the happiest when looked back on afterwards with the shrewd skill of hindsight.

She was presumed to be the homemaker – as Guy was the provider – and had no other ambitions for herself beyond that. Probably she would have a child one day, but Guy appeared to be in no great hurry about that. She continued to feel no hankerings for an outside job, and didn't envy those women who did one, who – she guessed – worked for necessity's sake rather than because they were declaring any pride in their own independence. Their own marriage was a true union, she believed, and she was quite content to work for that from inside: being two, and not a family until they had to be, their marriage seemed as modern a concept to her as any other doing the rounds at that time.

They had rituals, but only because they both wanted to have them. She managed the house, and their domestic life ran smoothly, which gave them the time they needed, to go off at the weekends driving around Norfolk, to swim at the private baths they joined, to improve their tennis, to visit the theatre or cinema when something appealed to them (best was watching a French film and having a replay on the journey home with Guy imitating the Parisian and provincial accents), to sing the idiotic songs from *South Pacific*, for

Guy to play cricket with some of his colleagues from the bank and for her to be (willingly) roped into the teas, to garden, every so often to buy an ingeniously authentic-tasting sachertorte (and damn the rations) from a Viennese baker's in Hampstead, to take fanciful trips with him to car showrooms that once or twice turned out to be not so fanciful after all (even if they *didn't* reach to the Mercedes coupé that was his ambition for them both), to eat at a favourite fish restaurant in Soho, for Guy to go angling while she stayed in the house and wrote a few pages or applied herself to a few more square inches of a tapestry rug, for her to look round the shops while Guy shadowed her, hands in his pockets and change rattling and a sporting smile on his face, or to stay at home in the spacious top half of the house in Rawlinson Road, both of them keeping an intermittently curious eye on their neighbours in the scrupulously decent street and enjoying the speculation about private lives off Sussex Gardens.

They occasionally entertained Guy's colleagues, and received invitations to dinners and Sunday lunches and more unorthodox events: a school sports day once, and an end-of-term play they couldn't get out of, and a noisy christening, and a Highland Ball at a country house in Essex, and a Pre-Raphaelite fancy-dress soirée in (of all places) Harrow-on-the-Hill which they hadn't appreciated was fancy dress and the failing-to-honour which effectively marked their exit from an outer social orbit she wasn't very sorry to be excluded from. She was frequently told that she and Guy made an 'elegant' or 'urbane' or 'mannerly' or 'discreet' or 'tactful' couple: she wasn't sure if that was a half-concealed judgment on their joint conversational performance or not, but it didn't prevent them from being popular and – as these things went – in demand. She and Guy *were* quiet, but also agreeable and affable, and they made no disturbing circles in anyone's pond: she thought an elegant appearance (if she couldn't be a 'looker', or pretty-pretty) must be preferable to making a stir, which some people tried to do and which she thought a retardedly juvenile habit, one she hadn't indulged in even at the true time, when things had been at their worst with the lodgers in her mother's house. She didn't see that that ought to be the point of social intercourse: quite what *was* the point it might have been tempting their luck to think about, like dropping your eyes and looking down when you were scaling a ladder.

Some of Guy's colleagues and wives she cared for better than others. Those she liked best had an easy attitude to life, or so they made it seem: they had hale, unstrained, accessible faces, and smiled and laughed in plenty (without calculating how wide to open their mouths), they appeared interested to hear what you might have to say, you didn't feel they timed you by a stopwatch when nature called and you had to excuse yourself. A couple of wives she didn't much go for, but had to tolerate for their husbands' sakes: she knew they resented her the two books she had to her name by 1953 but, rather more, they spurned her for not having children and because their husbands couldn't camouflage their attention for her. Sometimes when she was sitting at the tables of their friends, the 'best' sort and the others, it would occur to her that notwithstanding their contributions to the conversation, she and Guy didn't seem to 'offer' themselves quite as their companions did. She didn't believe they *meant* to hold themselves back, that it had more to do with the natures they were born with. Maybe their popularity was owing in part to this same (well-mannered) reserve she was conscious of: a blandness even, their two placid and polite exteriors: maybe these flattered their friends (of the two sorts) into thinking they had some sort of influence over them, that they were pliable, even if all they were really doing was reflecting back the indisputable fact of their friendliness and sincerity. She didn't see how anyone would have been offended by them: the wives she didn't really care for were chiefly upset by what they knew to be too true of themselves, that they were shackled by children and had become too inward in the wrong way, that the years were taking away what charms they'd had. All she did by her presence – inadvertently and indirectly – was to confirm this trio of harsh truths.

On their own home ground she had become moderately competent in the hostess's role. She'd taught herself to cook from her mother's recipes, some of which had been gleaned from *her* mother. Rations had thrown everything for six in the early days, but somehow she mastered the substitutes. Now she watched the expressions of the wronged and offended wives whenever they had to be entertained under their roof and she knew that they took malicious pleasure in remembering details to talk over later, snidely and gloatingly, and which – the sniping apart – could only add to the sum of their personal dissatisfaction. Their house was too tidy to ever have babies and children about it: it was more formal and better furnished than those they visited, even though some of her mother's bits and pieces were quite knocked about after tropical journeys and lodgers and even though Guy had none of his own family's furniture. Viewed most negatively, they must seem to be a young couple with ambitions only for themselves; probably they must seem to be lacking a dimension, conceivably of the human. They were to be pitied and envied, both together. Mr and Mrs Guy Gerrault, who may or may not have had everything going for them that they appeared to do.

'Don't you miss having a family? Guy?'

'I suppose I do. But we're in the same boat there, aren't we?'

She agreed.

'But,' she said, approaching a matter she had never quite understood, 'not even having their things about you – '

'But things are just things.'

Which, she knew, wasn't the whole truth of the matter at all: but it was Guy's way of being brave about their lack.

'For sentimental reasons, though?'

'There was the fire. And death duties – debts – '

She nodded her head.

She preferred even that harsh truth to a suspicion she'd lately become prey to, that he might have forfeited his family effects – on the maternal or paternal side there must have been *some*, surviving their deceased owners – because he wanted not to have them.

He was standing looking round the room, at those objects they had collected about themselves.

'At least you've got your memories,' she said.

'Yes.'

'And your name.'

She thought he hesitated before he smiled, a little dejectedly. He had volunteered so little information about his family; she'd presumed that the past must cause him some secret pain and distress. She wasn't irreproachable herself: in the end she had told him rather less than she had intended to about her mother. She had recently started to think, her *own* past might have something of the Pandora's box about it and that, by choice, she was choosing not to lift the lid.

Another time.

'David who?' she asked.

'Hudson,' Guy said. 'David Hudson.'

'Have you told me about him? I know the name – '

'From school. Then in South Africa.'

'How long were you there?'

'In South Africa?' He used the accent.

'Yes.'

'A few months.' He reverted to the voice she knew. 'Seemed like half-a-lifetime.'

'Do you think I'd like it?'

'Some people say it's the most beautiful country on earth.'

'Is it?'

'Maybe.'

'I didn't realise.'

'I can't remember – where I got to – '

'David Hudson,' she said.

His head jerked on his neck.

She laughed.

'Did I surprise you?'

He coloured.

'It's just – hearing the name again – '

'I've ruined your story.'

'What?'

'You were telling me – '

'What about – '

'The Something-or-Other Handicap.'

'Oh, the ostrich race.'

The enthusiasm had gone from his voice. She really *had* ruined the story.

212

'I cut you off,' she said. 'In mid-flow.'

'No. It just sounds stupid, repeating it – '

She shook her head.

'I *want* to hear – '

'Our misspent youth.'

'Racing ostriches?'

'It was us trying to get our revenge on them.'

'Why "revenge"?'

'For being the bloodiest things to farm, to get to do anything. Tempers like camels – '

'But you got them to race?'

'With extreme difficulty.'

'How?'

'David – '

'Hudson?'

'Yes. He was best at it. He held the flame from a cigarette lighter under its rump – '

'Oh, that's *terrible!*' she said, smiling.

'He won every race.'

'Even so – '

He shook his head. He wasn't properly smiling.

She touched his arm.

'That's how a youth *is* misspent,' she told him.

'Did you misspend yours?'

'Not really,' she said. She thought for a few moments. 'Not as much as I should have liked to, anyway.'

'What *would* you have done?'

'I don't know. Something on the spur of the moment. I wouldn't have planned it.'

'That's the best way. The ostrich races got too much of a custom. It was better fun at the beginning. A laugh – you know?'

He still didn't laugh. Asking him about David Hudson had been the turning-point and she wished she had just let the name go.

But he was only occasionally so quiet about the past that wasn't family, and he took care not to seem reluctant about divulging a memory, even if he left it vague. He was diligent that he wouldn't *appear* to be holding anything back from her.

She smiled, so he would see that it didn't matter. Another time if he told her she would know better and not question him, not ask if David Hudson had been lost through a quarrel or a death that came too early.

He was always most loving with her when he came back from his business trips. The upsets and privations of distance seemed to excite and stimulate him. She was ready for him, and they were daring in bed as they didn't normally feel the need to be. It wasn't all high concentration, however: they were light-hearted, and sometimes – strangely, at the most intimate moments – they laughed out loud. On those long nights she felt riotous and reckless, and she didn't know if it came from her or from him, it was communicated so freely between them.

This, she realised, was the love of no restraints, of no impossibilities, of vast distances travelled together. The notion of travel obsessed her after his return, and when she did sleep, lightly, she would be watching blurs from the window of a speeding train or skimming low over trees and rooftops in a hot-air balloon or riding cold spray at the prow of a sea-craft. She would wake for the business of love to begin all over again: until – if it was a Saturday or Sunday, or a holiday – it grew so late on the next morning, eleven o'clock or midday, that a timid but embarrassed concern as to what would be thought in the street about the closed curtains had her reaching her feet at last for the floor. Once the curtains were open and the room was candid with light, she didn't think she could repeat herself, not with the same distraction and abandonment, and she suggested differences they could make to this day, to distinguish it from any other day: an excursion in the car, or a search round shops and stalls where they were known for something luxurious and improbable to eat, some novel foreign fruit.

If they drove off, out of London, they usually ended up walking. The day would then acquire an astonishing innocence for her. Guy would produce two bars of chocolate he'd been able to find – several times it was a Swiss brand, almost black and (she felt) professionally bitter – and that became their hiking fare. It was like slipping back out of adulthood, into virtuous, healthy adolescence as it used to be recommended in high-minded books, written for lads and lassies by elderly bachelors and spinsters who had retired to South Coast resort towns to idolise their lost youth. She stumbled over stiles and closed her eyes crossing narrow plank bridges without handrails and tried her best not to laugh too heartily at their antics, because she sensed that – as well as being shared innocuous fun – it was something he valued seriously enough because it was quite instinctive to him. He led the way and she let him, because he always knew how a hill should be climbed or a wood crossed and she was in generous awe of that knowledge; also it preserved a certain mystery between them – how did he always know? – and because it made a dependence she was only too happy to have. 'I just remember,' he would tell her. 'Men are only schoolboys in long trousers. Having adventures.' For no clear reason – except that she had once gone on holiday with her mother to the Pitlochry Hydro – she would imagine, of all vistas to imagine at the word 'adventure', a Richard Hannay Scottish heather moor spread low among the scree mountains and wraithed with wet mist, and not be able at that most contented juncture of her life to perceive the appalling irony of the picture in her head.

But just occasionally there were questions she wanted to ask him.
Where do you go? Can it always be business?
Why won't you tell me? Why can't I ask?

214

Do you think I shouldn't be concerned? That at the least it shouldn't cross my mind?

Is there someone? 'Someone else', another woman?

Who is she?

Why is she necessary to you?

What does she give you that I don't, cannot?

The questions were too difficult for her to ask, however. She felt the past must be put in jeopardy if she were to open such a crack in their trust for one another. (She had always thought of it as that, as implicit trust.)

So, by doing nothing, she was left for a while with her carnivorous curiosity, her eroding confidence, with the worst that she could construe from the situation.

She had no evidence, though, none at all.

She began to blame herself for daring to speculate, as if they were caffeine brainstorms. She watched him when he was with his colleagues from the bank and realised that he had half a life he lived as one of them – thinking by the same professional telepathy – so why then should he be so comfortable with them if he wasn't wholly in their confidence, and vice versa?

The panic subsided – a long, slow, gradual ebbing back to normality. She still watched how he reacted to other women, she couldn't help that, but he appeared blameless. She caught herself watching him in shop windows, and saw her own stupidity. She thought that, to look at, she might have been turning into the very sort of woman who drives a man to his betrayals.

After that she took herself in hand, by a vast effort of will. She tidily wrapped up her doubts and consigned them to a safe place where they couldn't upset her equilibrium, a cupboard at the back of her mind, and there she shut the door on them and left them, hoping time would do the rest and they would all merely diffuse into the bunker's black.

She asked him, 'What is it?'

'Open it and see.'

She pulled at the ends of red ribbon. The cream and gold paper obligingly unwrapped to reveal a long, narrow, jeweller's box.

She glanced over at him. He nodded at her to continue.

She let the paper fall from the matt black box.

'Go on,' he said. 'Open it.'

She smiled. She smiled even though she felt uneasy. She didn't think that she wanted to see a commercial value placed on the love between them both. But he stood waiting, with his pleasure hardly disguised; the corners of his eyes and his mouth strained, as if he was containing laughter.

'It isn't a present for anyone else!' he said, and she heard the light-hearted lift of the exclamation mark in his voice.

Slowly she lifted the box's lid. Inside, on white satin plush, was spread a coiled bracelet of gold links: the strap of a watch.

'I knew you needed one.'

She laid the box on top of the table and used both hands to remove the watch. The rectangular face contained the full complement of figures, but they were formed of single diamonds in place of numerals; four delicate rubies simulated pins on the surround.

'Guy!'

'D'you like it?'

She shook her head, incredulously.

'What have I done to deserve *this*?'

'Put it on.'

'But – '

'Here, just a moment – '

He took it from her, checked the time by his own watch, then adjusted the hands and turned the winder. He showed her how the catch on the clasp opened and closed.

'It's *far* too good,' she said.

'Do you like it?'

'"*Like* it"?' She continued to smile, in the same disbelieving way. 'It's – it's magnificent.'

He helped her to place it round her wrist. She centred the face between the two knobs of bone, fastidiously using the tips of her fingers. She peered at the glinting figures, and at the hands, and again at the name 'Guibert-Favresse', set very small in those squat bold caps that always seemed to her to be the trademark of good taste and exclusivity.

'Recognise it? The make?'

'Oh yes. I know the name.' She tilted her head. 'But I've never seen them in the shops. Just photographs, in magazines.'

'That's where *I* saw it.'

'But, Guy – it's *wonderful* – '

'I wanted to get you something special. Different. For *you*.'

'It must have cost a fortune.'

'It cost what it had to. It's what you deserve, that's all.'

'It – it's the most splendid present I've ever had.' Then she corrected herself. 'The best present I *shall* ever have.'

'It ought to keep going for ever – '

'Where *did* you buy it?'

'What?'

'If it wasn't Geneva – '

'I – Well, actually – ' He drew in breath, delivering himself the grace of a couple of seconds. 'Actually, I got someone to buy it for me. In Geneva, yes. A good watch, I said. Very good.'

'*Can* you buy it here?'

216

'I don't know. Maybe – '

'I've never seen it in a shop.'

'No?'

'There must be a shop somewhere. In Geneva.'

She looked for the address printed on the white satin lining inside the lid.

' "La Maison du Temps. Rue de Rive, Genève." '

'Since it was Geneva,' he said, 'that this person was going to, I thought it was a good opportunity – '

'Yes.' She nodded. 'Of course.'

'And he bought it.'

'Who did you ask?'

He took breath again, and gained himself another couple of seconds.

'He said you had to imagine that *I*'d bought it.' He smiled. 'I shouldn't have told you, you see.'

'Oh dear, I know now.'

'Well, he said it was best kept a secret.'

'Do I know him?'

'Do you know him? Yes – yes and no. Not very well.'

He smiled again, and she smiled too, turning her wrist to catch daylight on the diamonds and rubies.

But she still didn't know why he had bought it. He hadn't denied the cost when she'd said he must have paid a small fortune. How much *could* he afford to spend on her? She felt that they ought to have discussed such a purchase beforehand: if they had, of course, then she would have told him the idea was ridiculous and he would have been in the position of being obliged not to buy her a gift of such worth. He hadn't told her, precisely because he'd wanted her to have it.

A gift for what reason, though? How *had* she deserved it?

And which friend?

She smiled, and didn't mean the smile to carry any particular significance, just to be a brief cover for her confusion.

Guy stepped back, and folded his arms a little awkwardly in front of himself. She looked down at the watch on her wrist. The chain of links hadn't slipped, it fitted as neatly as if she'd been measured for it. Now she had no excuse: time would always have a claim on her, and she wouldn't be able to say that she'd forgotten, or must be running late.

The watch, she guessed, presaged that her life was about to change in some fundamental way . . .

More than the others and notwithstanding her momentary doubts, he was the great love and passion of her life, because he was the first. Afterwards – after a decent interval of time had lapsed – she didn't even excuse herself for having believed so. She needed very much to have beliefs; her life so far had largely lacked them, her experience was a history too little understood beyond herself. One way and another Guy had filled her head for almost seven years. Everything became 'before' or 'after' that precious and troubled interlude: it was like a gleaming prism that altered her vision by its fragmentations and refractions of what she had imagined was familiar to her.

Since then certainly, in the 'after', there had been dislocations of another sort. But that was the next part of the story, and it hadn't been written to its end yet.

3

She was taken to the scene of the accident, to where it had happened.

The Jaguar rested in a ditch. It was upright, but the front and sides of the bonnet had been crushed by the impact of the drop. The windscreen glass was shattered; both doors hung open. The headlights had smashed; the front bumper was mangled and fused into the twisted metalwork. The radio was still playing; a man's voice announced a performance of Glück's *Orfeo*.

'There's very little to go on,' the police inspector told her. 'We're looking for clues.'

'Yes.'

'We found papers from the car, scattered about.'

'Yes.'

'Even his passport.'

'Ah.'

'This neck of the woods, did it mean anything to him?'

'Not that I know of.'

'You *would* have known?'

'No. Not necessarily.'

She smiled sadly.

'You wouldn't?'

'Well,' she said, 'I don't think I *can* have done.'

'No.'

The police inspector shook his head.

'We're just trying to get hold of any lead – '

'Of course.'

'So, if anything *does* occur to you, Mrs Gerrault – '

The use of the name pulled her back to the present moment.

' "If anything" – ?' she repeated.

'If you can think of anything – '

'Yes. Yes, I will. Tell you.'

She climbed back up on to the road with the inspector's hand assisting. He left her and she stood on the verge looking down. She noticed wheelmarks were gouged on the grass.

'Do – do many accidents happen here?' she asked a policeman who was walking past.

'I don't think so, madam,' he said, touching his helmet. 'It's the first one I've come across. First bad one, that is.'

Penelope nodded at the information. The inspector had already provided her with certain observations. It was becoming difficult for her to see things in quite the same light, in that in which her afternoon had begun, with the telephone call: literally so, because evening was coming on and a couple of arc lamps had appeared, but also in the sense of not knowing what to think and how she ought to be responding. It seemed disrespectful not to suppose that this was what it gave indications of being, the scene of an accident, and that an accident must by definition be a chance, unforeseen event. But *how* had it happened, that the car should have gone off the road at such an angle and covered the particular distance that it had? The inspector had told her that its position in the ditch suggested to him that it must have left the road before it actually entered the corner and before it reached the summit of the gradient: that is, before the driver could have encountered another car on the corner. And that it had taken place in the fullness of broad daylight.

'*Was* there another car involved?' she'd asked him.

'Not that we're aware of.'

'To make him swerve like that.'

'There could have been.'

'But not necessarily?'

'Not necessarily. Probably not.'

No body was ever found.

She told the inspector about her husband's physical fitness, his ingenuity. It was agreed that he could have wandered quite a distance. The terrain round about – as far as Horsham in one direction and Dorking, six miles to the north – was scoured by police beaters looking for evidence. But by the third or fourth day Penelope felt the intensity going out of the search. By the second week their interest was distinctly waning.

She felt lost and abandoned. Guy's colleagues and their wives said and did all the right things, but all she wanted now was the recovery of a body. The longer there was no news, the less she could honestly conceive that he was alive but badly injured. And amnesiac maybe. The longer there was no find, the more despondent she became about the outcome, the more fearful that she would be required to make a formal identification.

A month went by and still no body had been found. Then she began to lose hope more rapidly. She attempted to tidy and organise the house; there was little point in doing it for just one, but – . She accepted (almost) that he must be dead, wherever his body was, awaiting discovery. Already she could think of him like that, as two concepts, an inert body and a freed spirit. She called to mind their best times, so many of them, and after a month she cried liberally, in the privacy of the house where no one could see or hear. She didn't believe that their happiness deserved such an unfair conclusion: why was she being denied what any bereavement entailed, namely a body to mourn? There could be no funeral without one. He might have been lost at sea, of course, but he hadn't been: then she could have thrown a ring of flowers on to the waves and that would have been an official observance of her wind-dried grief. By contrast what was being visited on her was mental cruelty of an appalling sort, and she never knew when she was going to succumb to tears and lamentation, a major dam-burst. (Worse were the nocturnal sobbing fits, when she woke in the middle of the night hearing a wolf's yelp in her dreams, howling on a bare mountain.) She asked herself so many times, what have I done to merit *this*? She wanted to put a notice in the newspaper space where Guy's death should have been announced, but declaring to all instead that there was no heavenly mercy to be had and that it was God who was dead and corpseless, now and for all time, which was no more than her mother before her had conceived the truth to be.

An envelope dropped through her letterbox with others. She spotted Guy's handwriting as she lifted the pile off the mat.

Her hand trembled. Her stomach turned over.

She slid the tip and nail of one thumb under the back flap and pulled out the two pages folded inside.

'Hastings' was written at the top of the outer sheet. The date was the day before the car crashed.

My Dear Penelope,

I've been sitting for ten minutes thinking how to begin. 'My Dear Penelope' seems too little. But we used to laugh at the Whittakers calling each other 'darling', and doesn't 'dearest' sound like Darby and Joan?

I just wanted to say something. That's no easier, though. Please believe me that I love you very much: more than I have ever loved anybody before.

Some things should be said more often than they are. You don't need to be clever with words to say it, you just need to speak what it is you feel. I feel that I owe you so much, that you've made me happier than I ever thought to be or deserved. It was you who put the house together, into a home, and made a life for us both: *our* life.

I'm sure you'll do wonders one day with your writing. You've started – well, more than that. I think I've held you back, but you were too polite to say. I'm not up on these things, I can't pretend to you that I was. I don't even think I wanted to be, because I think it gave you a certain space, your own area, to write in, and I think it was the contribution I was able to make, in a funny sort of way. Do you see what I mean?

I wasn't sure how I would fill one side of this sheet, but that's the bottom of the page turned and I don't suppose I've even begun. I don't think I *can* explain all the rest, though, in the time – and there isn't very much. The important part's in the second paragraph, the short and the sweet of it. I can only hope it's what you remember longest – in spite of everything else.

Take good care of yourself.

Ever,
Guy.

She didn't inform the police about the letter. She gave them no hint.

It wasn't, she believed, any of *their* business. Guy was speaking to her on an intimate matter, the life they had shared together. The police wouldn't have learned any more than her from it about his (possible) state of mind. She didn't want the letter to become public property – maybe, she realised, because what it contained could only be diminished under the unpitying glare of scrutiny, whittled away as the arguments by sceptical police minds reduced its fragile sentiments almost out of existence.

Their lawyer explained the will to her.

She was the only legatee. Everything was hers.

'Everything' comprised the two upper floors of the house, and the effects, and shares to the value of five thousand pounds or thereabouts. A bank account containing just over twelve thousand pounds was in their joint name.

'We didn't really discuss such things,' she said. 'Salary. And so forth.'

'"And so forth"?' the lawyer repeated.

'I – I just meant it as an expression – a turn of phrase – '

'Yes.'

'There was his own family background. Of course.'

The lawyer's eyes fastened on her. She met them. He seemed to be requiring some reaction from her which she felt was beyond her.

She looked down at her black gloves; she picked one up and started fitting her hand into it.

'I have no record of family bequests,' the lawyer said.

'No. I . . . '

'And everything is accounted for. So far as I'm aware.'

'We didn't discuss his family – much – '

At the outset of the marriage Guy had assured her she would have no money problems, that she should only say.

'It's a sizeable house,' the lawyer said. 'Very desirable. In a good area. Property holds its value there. That's yours outright, of course; the top half and your garden. Along with the freehold.'

She had presumed they were still bound to mortgage payments, several years of them.

'"Outright"?' she repeated.

'Yes.'

'Are you sure?'

'I have copies of your deeds.'

Again his eyes met hers and seemed intent on holding them. She shied away, though, and looked across the room, to the window. For years afterwards she was able to recall the view outside, the sooty brick walls, the chimneypots, the marooned city trees: a dull view, and not memorable in itself, but so far as she was concerned etched on copperplate.

'Thank you,' she said.

222

'I'm pleased to do as I'm requested, Mrs Gerrault.'

'May I ask – '

'Yes?'

' – when the will was drawn up?'

'Five years ago.'

She nodded.

'Can I guess that you didn't discuss the arrangements, you and your husband?'

'No,' she said. 'No, we didn't.'

She meant not to appear disappointed in any respect. She didn't accept that she was, not at all.

Guy's not talking about his family must have been for a very good reason. He'd told her about the death duties but she hadn't known if that was the financial full-stop to the family's history. Guy had been brought up to a manner of life now wholly out of historical favour: a house without productive land, as Drewsteignton had been, must have been a hopeless prospect.

Presumably he had used his share of some manner of inheritance to pay for their own half of the house in Rawlinson Road. She was now provided with a home, her own, and the solidity of a base to start from again.

So all was well, in one sense.

For the first time since Guy's death she realised that her life would be obliged to change: Guy had given her a confidence in herself – it was something the lawyer hadn't spoken about but which was of inestimable worth – and she would trust in it to carry her through the next months, until she found some sort of substitute life without Guy which she could settle to.

Valerie, now a Mrs Warne, and Oliver both came to the memorial service. She hadn't invited them, because she didn't think they belonged in that section of her life, but to their own time. They had got wind of the event, however, and she couldn't help smiling when she saw them.

She realised something was amiss, that they weren't talking to one another, but maybe there was nothing so extraordinary about that. She was conscious of Oliver's eyes on her all the way through the service.

'Not *too* religious,' was Valerie's verdict when it was over.

'We're so very sorry,' Oliver told her.

'What a splendid hat!' Valerie enthused. 'Wherever did you get it? Bette Davis, eat your heart out!'

Oliver, out of his sister's hearing, invited her down to Cambridge.

'I really do mean it, Penelope.'

'Thank you.'

'I'd like you to come, very much. Oh, I shouldn't have said that, should I?'

'Well . . . '

Then she remembered.

'Guy was never po-faced you know. Maybe that was one advantage.'

'"Advantage"?'

'Of dying so young. Before he could change. Or feel he *had* to be po-faced about anything.'

'So you *will* come, Penelope?'

'Yes,' she said. 'Yes, I *will* come.'

'Is that a promise?'

'That's a promise.'

Why Hastings?

She went down on the train one grey damp morning.

She walked round the hotels consulting the Visitors' Books, but didn't find his name. Once she thought she recognised his handwriting, but the signature was 'Boxer' and the address was in Norwich.

She stepped into the Fisherman's Church and saw the boat pulpit: she fingered the fossils embedded in the stonework on street corners; she traipsed an obligatory circuit of the castle.

She ate in a cramped tea-room near another church, All Saints' or St Clement's, there seemed to be so many churches that she became quite muddled. It was flavourless tea, a stew, and the two doorstep slices of toast with their crusts attached were each burned on one side. She rubbed at the condensation on the window and stared outside, at nothing and at no one. She hadn't imagined that she could ever feel so lonely, for the aching want of a man whom she had hardly even known.

She collected together everything he had left behind him, which she had recovered from pockets and drawers. She even drew up an inventory.

It was explaining nothing to her, though. From the details alone his life became even more of a mystery, and she was still left guessing. The details refused to add up, they stuck on the ruled lines on the page.

Among the items were:

Six French-franc notes and nine Swiss notes; assorted small French and Swiss change, between twenty and thirty coins.

Three keys on a ring, a miniature saddle-stirrup in hallmarked silver. (The keys fitted none of the locks in the house.)

Receipts, seven all told, for seven long-distance telephone calls.

Two Swiss postage stamps.

A London gazetteer, 'Enlarged', with a street index.

A colour postcard of the Jardin Alpin in Geneva.

A black-and-white postcard reproduction of a Corot painting hanging in the Jeu de Paume.

A box of matches and a facecloth of white towelling, both bearing the name 'Hotel Schleswig-Holstein, Paris'.

Several pebbles, with attractive flaws.

An empty carton of Egyptian cigarettes.

A book, Simenon's *L'Ombre Chinoise*.

A visiting-card, engraved with the name 'Piers Lascelles' and an address in Belgrave Square.

A small folding card, like a miniature menu, with the steps of two tangos printed on it.

An Ordnance Survey map of the area around Deal in Kent.

A yellowing newspaper cutting, a news story about an armed insurrection in Liberia; a newspaper photograph of the Comtesse Guy d'Arcangues; a magazine photograph of Fiona Campbell-Walter wearing a full lemon coat with a triangular cut very like her own.

A two-inch by two-inch photograph, perhaps taken with a box camera and probably no less than twenty years old, showing a seaside bungalow behind palings, and a stretch of sandy lane outside, and not a human in sight.

A small blue feather.

A tiny, perfectly formed pinecone.

A scented cake of soap inside a box, monogrammed 'Hotel Vier Jahreszeiten, München'.

A Waterman fountain pen, finished in red Chinese lacquer.

A ticket stub for the stalls of the Royal Opera House, Drury Lane.

A gilt button.

A postcard of the Pons Perilous, Avalon (viz. Glastonbury, Somerset).

A champagne bottle cork.

A shop receipt for the purchase of a Leica camera and a leather case.

A newspaper photograph of Lady Docker, sitting on the zebra upholstery of her gold-plated Daimler.

A Christie's catalogue, for a sale of Impressionist paintings, the property of the late Mrs Marina Selsden.

A newspaper clipping about the Mau-Mau unrest.

A gent's handkerchief embroidered in one corner with the entwined initials 'LPF'.

A very small, four-inch-long, lethally sharp rapier, unfolding like a penknife and with a steel finger-hold.

A receipt issued by a Bristol post office, acknowledging collection from the counter of a package in the name of 'Mr Miller'.

Several white tablets wrapped inside tissue paper, probably tranquillisers or sleeping-pills.

A common-or-garden woman's hairpin, scratched and seeming to have been opened out and pushed flat again.

A tab carrying the name and telephone number of dry-cleaners' premises in Sloane Street.

A used two-inch Winchester '6' bullet cartridge.

He had given her presents of perfume, but she chose not to finish any of it and to keep what was left in the bottles. She found the books he'd bought for her, and she read them all. To write, she used only a Mont Blanc fountain pen that had been his anniversary present one year: she used that and nothing else. She wore the clothes she'd worn when she was with him, the shoes and hats and bags. She listened to the music he'd liked. She made the dinners he'd enjoyed best, but only half quantities, which was always too much: she could only ever eat half of that. She watched a comedy programme on television, one he'd liked, but she couldn't laugh at the characters and situations any more.

She had never doubted before, but now she had proof certain and positive of it: she had loved Guy from her heart, to the outer limits of herself.

4

She tracked Alex Thornby to a village in Hampshire, to an old mill-house only yards from a rushy, slow-flowing river. The original millstone jutted into the sitting-room. On the walls stuffed fish levitated inside glass cases.

Very briefly she thought of romantic Hazehill.

He knew about the death, and offered his sympathy, but he was also rather distant at first, this Mr Thornby, and she was discouraged. He was a beetle-browed man in his sixties, with a weathered face and veined cheeks; he wore a wedding ring but there was no evidence of a wife, either to be seen or to be construed from the little he told her about himself.

She got to the point soon enough, since he seemed to be waiting for it. She guessed he'd been a man with a position and no great need to be too tactful or too patient. He wasn't offhand with her, but she realised her presence in this secluded house was being tolerated with a will. She explained. About what Guy had told her, and her finding an address and a telephone number jotted down on the back of a scored-out visiting-card she'd found in the breast pocket of a sports jacket.

She couldn't make sense of his replies.

'"*Once*" – ' she repeated what he'd just said ' – you "fished with him"?'

'Yes.'

'But he used to go off with you? You took him fishing?'

'It wasn't me, I'm afraid.'

'He said you – '

'You must have misheard him. It must have been someone else he meant.'

She stared at him, very hard and intently, as if to make him concede. But why should he not be telling her what was true?

'No, I don't think I misheard him,' she said.

'I can't explain it, then.'

'You can't?'

'I hardly even knew him.'

'Where – where did you fish with him?'

'Down in Devon. Torbay way.'

'When, though? How long ago?'

'Five years. Five or six. Bill Holland introduced us.'

She nodded at the name.

'I thought – if you don't mind me saying so, Mrs Gerrault – I *thought* it was a little odd, your looking me out.'

He pulled himself up in the armchair.

' "Odd"?'

'Well, I only met him one other time, or a couple maybe.'

'What?'

'And for all I taught him on the river, I couldn't have landed myself a fortune in his will just for doing that.'

He smiled.

'But he said you fished regularly – '

'Bit of a mix-up, I'm afraid – '

He tried to smile again but stopped when she didn't respond.

'Don't know how,' he said. 'Somewhere down the line someone's got hold of the wrong end of the stick. Or in this case the rod – '

'Was he good?' she asked.

'It's a bit hard to remember – '

'A proper fisherman, I mean?'

'He knew *something* about it, angling. But it was just a hobby, I'd say. Not an obsession, and certainly not a religion, which is what it can become. I'm not sure it was an "interest" even with him. Just what I said: a "hobby", I suppose.'

'Did you hear about him fishing?'

'No. Who from?'

'I don't know. I thought you might have colleagues. Mutual acquaintances.'

'Not that I'm aware of. I went into another brokers. Bill Holland persuaded me.'

'He might have become very good, though, mightn't he?'

' "Good" – ?'

'A good fisherman?'

'He *might*.'

'Even if it wasn't a religion, not exactly?'

'But *you* should know that. Don't you?'

'I – .' She shook her head. 'I'm afraid not.'

He pointed to the whisky and gin bottles on the sideboard. She shook her head again; she smiled, politely and abstractedly.

'No, I mustn't start,' she said.

'There's no harm in – '

'No,' she repeated. 'Thank you.'

'I'm sorry,' he said.

'Yes.'

'I wish I could think how to help you.'

'Oh, you *have* been helpful to me.'

'Can't think how.'

'It'll add up to a picture,' she said. 'One day, I'm sure.'

'He *might* have become very good. If he had lots of practice. It's five years ago, six.'

'Yes, I expect so,' she said, and pulled herself out of the chair. She felt none too steady on her feet. She saw him noticing, and she looked away.

'I'm surprised he remembered, Mrs Gerrault.'

'I'm sorry?'

'Remembered fishing with me.'

'He did,' she said. 'So it seems.'

'So it seems.'

'I really – must be going now.'

He walked her to the door. Unless, she thought, he's lying? What else is to account for it? I'm a woman, a wife, and now a widow: he takes for granted that I'm stupid, too stupid to infer, to catch on.

She stopped still. He was only a little taller than her. She was almost on a level with his eyes. But how did you tell a liar's eyes anyway? What she *thought* she saw was pity, and a confusion more modestly reflecting her own, and maybe too an interest in her, of another kind, that seemed inappropriate in the circumstances, improper.

Did all that leave room for lying as well? And after all, weren't liars able to lie about their lying and to conceal it? If she'd met one, she wouldn't have known it to save her life.

The name was almost too likely to be true. 'Nanny Twisk'. By rights it belonged in a novel.

She lived in the ground-floor flat of a converted house in Blackheath, close to Greenwich Park. There was a pretty garden, presumably shared; it was arranged on a grid of grass and flowerbeds, and stocked with old-fashioned floribunda roses and hollyhocks and nigella.

Miss Twisk was small, with a shrunken neck, rounded shoulders and a stooped back. Her body, excepting her head and disappearing neck, very nearly made a square. She carried her head at an enquiring tilt.

The introductions were made, rather tremulously on the old woman's part. (Eighty if she was a day, Penelope thought.) The front door was closed behind them and Penelope stood back to allow the little woman to lead the way. The flat was dark, shaded by the trees growing against the windows, and made darker by the fading daylight. Penelope watched the woman's hands paddling the air, reaching for but never quite touching the surfaces of walls and doors and the edges of the furniture, steering them both by her command of the familiar.

They arrived at a small sitting-room at the back of the house. A gas-fire cosily lit a private circle, beyond which everything was shrouded in more darkness. Penelope was invited to please sit down, and she lowered herself on to an ample, well-stuffed armchair, a more recent purchase to all appearances.

'May I offer you some sherry, Mrs Gerrault?'

Her voice was soft and a little shaky, but the words were very clearly articulated.

'A *dry* sherry, perhaps?'

'Yes, please. Thank you.'

Penelope watched as she set two glasses on the silver tray and fumbled with the stopper of the decanter. Too much sherry was poured into the first glass and spilled over the top.

'Dear me,' the woman said, 'how clumsy!'

Her hand steadied and she tilted her head as she poured into the second glass, to the correct level.

The glass stopper hovered above the crystal decanter, then it was pushed back into the funnel. It occurred to Penelope that perhaps the sherry decanter had been lifted already in the course of this day.

'Thank you,' she said as the second glass was handed to her.

The woman returned to the sideboard, moving cautiously and placing a supporting hand on the back of the wing chair; her back was to her guest as she lifted the schooner with great care and sipped from it.

'This is a very pleasant surprise for me. Yes, indeed. I told him to bring you along some time. But of course you were busy with all your commitments.'

Penelope lifted an eyebrow, knowing she might not be seen in the late afternoon gloaming.

'Your charities,' the woman said. 'I couldn't have dragged you away from those, just for me.'

Penelope smiled, forgetting that might not be seen either. The old woman must have misunderstood, or else Guy had been trying to spare her the necessity of a visit. She recalled her surprise when she'd learned after his death that there was still a nanny in existence and that he had paid her occasional visits.

'Well,' she told her, 'I'm very pleased to be here.'

'We meet at long last, Mrs Gerrault.'

The woman was about to sit down in the wing chair when she shook her head. 'My goodness, I quite forgot.'

She stretched out her hand and pressed the switch of a standard lamp. The shade spread a modest, shallow pool of yellow light: a rill perhaps rather than a pool, defining with difficulty the objects in its helix. A work-table, a potted begonia with dry pock-marked leaves, a crumpled travelling rug, several shelled pea-pods lying unnoticed on the rug, a pair of blunt scissors that must have dropped off the tabletop.

'That's much better, isn't it?' Miss Twisk said, and seated herself in the wing chair.

They each took a sip from their glass. The woman with the fortuitous-sounding name leaned forward to place her schooner on the work-table and made circles in mid-air above it. Her face was concerned, and irritated. Penelope immediately perceived what she had failed to since the door had been opened to her, that the woman was very nearly blind.

While they exchanged politesse, Penelope observed the clues she had missed

230

earlier: the buttons on her cardigan wrongly done up, a stain like gravy on her dress, a run in one of her stockings, the way her head was constantly in nervous, alert movement, her manner of splaying her hands with the fingers fanned like five sensors apiece. The old woman's eyes, she realised, weren't holding on objects: they would seem to be focused on something, then they would lift fractionally but far enough to be looking into the space between a table and a chair or the empty air above the shade of a table-lamp or, from where she was sitting, to her shins beneath her knees.

The woman must have guessed from the silence following a question just what she was thinking.

'I ought to have helped you with the sherry,' Penelope said, not knowing what else to say.

'Don't think of it, my dear.'

'I'm sorry, I didn't – '

'But you're my guest. That's all you have to be – a good guest.'

'I invited myself, I think.'

'But *I* wanted to talk to *you*. I've imagined you so often, or tried to. Now I can listen to your voice. And I have your outline.'

'I think I've imposed myself.'

'But you had reasons. There are things you wanted to know.'

'I – Yes. Yes, I suppose there were. *Are*.'

'So, maybe I can help you?'

Penelope swallowed.

'I didn't actually *know* he came, Guy. I found it out.'

'He didn't tell you?'

'No,' Penelope said.

The woman's face looked very nearly pained.

'I don't *think* so, anyway. His past, his family – '

'He always had secrets when he was a boy, you know.' The disclosure was accompanied by confirming nods. 'He kept them from his father and mother but he told *me*. Some of them anyway. I didn't let on to anybody, not a soul. He knew that. We got on so well – ' Miss Twisk held up two knobbly fingers pressed tightly together: arthritis would never get the better of *that* pair. 'Even at the difficult time. In his teens. We still talked. And his friend, when he was there. I was closer to Guy than his parents, you see. Much. And that's how it went on. Then we had the war, but that was only to be expected. A few years. That was history's doing.'

The woman, sightless or almost so, crossed her arms against her waist, as if preserving all that lost and gone time to herself.

'When did he last come to see you?'

'It wasn't so long ago. Just before Christmas, I think.'

'What sort of things did you talk about?'

'Private things mostly. They'd be rather dull to other people, I expect.'

'You must have got on well together?'

'He used to be quite high-spirited, quite a handful. I mean, after some of the other charges I had. Compared with them. He certainly wasn't the easiest anyway. Not by a long chalk!'

The old woman smiled at some private memory she had shared with him. Penelope was momentarily jealous; then she remembered why she was here, and lightened her own face with an encouraging, coaxing smile, even though the woman wasn't able to notice it.

'At first, you know,' Miss Twisk said, 'it was very odd, I couldn't think who you meant. Well, the surname told me. But he was always called Kit in the family.'

' "Kit"?'

'To *me*, at any rate. That was from his middle name, "Christopher". His parents used that. The first name, Guy, that was just a sort of stepping-stone to the name *they* liked best.'

'He didn't say.'

'Well, family's family – '

'Yes.'

'He bought me this flat, you know.'

'What? Guy did?'

'Yes. Kit. It was a complete surprise. It came quite out of the blue. He came one day and presented me with the keys and the deeds and told me – well, it doesn't matter – '

'What did he tell you?'

'Oh – just that it was because of all I'd done for him. Now he was doing this for me. He said it was just a little thing.'

Penelope looked about her, at the tidy old-world comforts.

'You're very lucky,' she said. Then she remembered that the woman was almost blind. 'I mean, that someone should think so much of you.'

'Yes, I rather think I *am* lucky.'

But why, why, why hadn't he thought to tell her, his own wife? They could have discussed the matter between them; she would have realised what it must mean to him, such a gesture, to try to make the old woman's final years as easy for her as was possible.

She sat shaking her head.

'Lucky indeed, Mrs Gerrault – '

'And – and not to have regrets,' Penelope continued, because it seemed to follow out of what she'd just said.

'Oh, *some*times,' the woman said. 'You're never quite without those.'

'What sort of things?'

'People I'd like to have kept up with.'

'I see. Yes, of course.'

'Sometimes I remember them.'

Penelope nodded at the information.

'Kit used to have a good friend, I tried to get him to talk about him. He was at his prep school, then they both went on to public school.'

'Who was that?'

'He was called Hudson. David Hudson.'

Penelope nodded again.

'David Hudson. Yes. He and Kit were always very close. His father was abroad, a widower. Kit used to bring him home, to Drewsteignton, at holiday-time. Quite a quiet boy, well-behaved; considerate. He noticed things.'

'And they were good friends?'

'At first I wasn't sure. They seemed rather different. As I told you, Kit could be quite a handful. I suppose David had a spark in him too, otherwise why should they have been such good friends? But I remember him being very polite, David, and attentive, and not making much noise at all. I could usually hear Kit, wherever he was, I'd know.'

Penelope shook her head.

'And later?'

'I'm not sure. I presumed they'd – '

' – drifted apart?'

'Yes. Gone their own ways.'

'Do you know how?'

'One day Kit said he'd rather not talk about him. David. I supposed there'd been a falling-out. There might have been another reason. I can't say. But that's what happens in life – '

Miss Twisk reached out for her sherry glass and Penelope watched. She wasn't as sure-fingered as she would have presumed a blind woman must be with her senses heightened.

'But I have very few regrets. All told. This is the worst. Kit going before me. That's all against God. I don't know what He meant by causing such a thing to happen.'

Coincidentally Penelope caught sight of a large Bible – rather battered from past consultations – leaning against a book-end on a meagrely stocked shelf.

'But I had all his kindness. I have that to remember. He became kinder as he grew older, you know, Kit. Just as he became milder, too. He quietened down so much. The last years were the best ones.'

'Did he – did he mention – ?'

'Oh, he talked about you a great deal, my dear. He was so happy with you, and so proud as well. He described you to me, his dear wife Penelope, all the details. He must have loved you very much. I know you a lot better than you must think I do. Just because you've never met me in your life before. I feel *I*'ve met *you*, though.'

Penelope's eyes blurred with tears.

'How lucky *you* were too, my dear. If only I'd known Kit would grow up how he did and quieten down and find himself a wife like yourself. His parents would have been so glad to know it. It's me who's left, though: that's such an odd thing, it's so hard for me to believe.'

Penelope stooped forward in her chair, preparing to rise and announce her departure.

'How is Sir William?' the woman asked her.

'I'm sorry?'

'Your uncle – '

'My uncle?'

'Kit said – your mother, she was his sister – '

'Oh no.'

'The Reeves' – '

'Yes. That was my mother's name – Reeves. But I didn't have an uncle – a great-uncle – '

'Kit said – '

'No. You must have misheard.'

'Oh.'

'I'm sorry.'

'It – it doesn't matter.'

Standing upright, Penelope wondered if it was on that account she had been tolerated, because of the misunderstanding? Unless Guy had said it as a joke, or a tease, because he knew that that was what the old woman was like? It had never occurred to her that, even jocularly, he was a snob: rather, she used to ask herself if that might not have been a furtive stirring and impulse in *her*.

The old woman seemed confused, but not impolite. Snobbery wasn't the issue anyway: probably she was absorbed in genealogy, having lived as she had, garnering snatches of stories of old scions of Noblesse and scrabbling to piece them together. But Penelope couldn't help feeling that she had disappointed her in some vital respect, by not being *quite* good enough stock for the man who'd grown up from the rather wayward but privileged boy, whom she was supposed to have helped pacify.

Not even breeding stock –

She was leaving her, however, much as she had found her: confined inside her head, trapped there with her recollections of life as they had lived it in the time between the wars. Old Nanny Twisk was deserving her sympathy if anything.

Penelope smiled forgiveness and understanding, even if the woman's blindness was preventing her purpose.

She knew she had no alternative but to get in touch again with Miss Twisk.

When she telephoned, the receiver was picked up jerkily at the other end, nearly dropped, and the old woman's voice enquired with a tremor, who was this speaking to her please?

Penelope explained, and she heard relief change the old woman's manner.

The conversation meandered, quite affably, as if even the loss of fabled Uncle William didn't matter so much. Penelope had decided she needed to put the old dame at her ease if she was going to extract anything at all from her. But at last the harmless talk started to exhaust her patience.

'I'm sorry – ' she said, butting in and knowing that any nanny worth her salt must have a frown on her face, ' – there's something – something I'd like to know – '

'And I can help you?' the woman offered, in a marginally more formal tone.

'I – I *hope* so – hope very much – '

'If it's possible – '

'I was trying to find his friend.'

'His friend?'

'David Hudson.'

'David Hudson?' Miss Twisk repeated.

'I don't know where to start even.'

'I wonder – '

'What did he *look* like? Can you remember?'

'They were quite alike, oddly enough. For size. David was darker.' The woman settled into an answer, and Penelope was surprised. It was more than she had allowed herself to hope for. 'There was something about his face too: Kit was a little – finer. It wasn't so much the details as the cast, if you know what I mean. And their expressions. Kit's was clearer somehow. But some people would muddle the two of them, for a few seconds. In a half-light or something like that: *then* yes, you could have done. Quite easily in fact. If you hadn't known Kit as well as I did – '

'Did other people comment on it?'

' "It"?'

'The resemblance?'

'Kit's mother used to watch them, and maybe she thought it was curious, as I did. Maybe people *are* attracted to those they look like, do you think?'

Penelope nodded, then remembered to say 'yes'.

'But it was rather nice too, that they had something in common with their appearance. It was unusual. It might have been fortune's way – '

'How – how did they think?'

' "Think"?'

'Communicate? With one another?'

'They got on very well. They must have done. I mean, that's how they must have been drawn to one another in the first place. Would you agree with me, Mrs – '

'Yes. Yes, certainly.'

'That's not to say they didn't have – well, "quarrels" is too strong a word. "Tiffs", I suppose that's what they were. "Disagreements". But they never lasted very long. Except one, I think, but that was made up too, and David

235

came to stay, and it was for longer that time. So they must have made it all up between them, mustn't they?'

'Yes,' Penelope said.

'So that's how close they were. Their friendship could survive all that. That was the best proof.'

'Yes.'

Penelope dropped on to the chair beside the telephone table.

'I used to think they were close enough for one to know where the other was. Not telepathic, really, it's just that you know how the other person's mind works.'

'Yes.'

'And Kit didn't have a brother. All the goings-on at school, they had those in common too. Like their own language. But *we* couldn't understand – '

Penelope felt the 'we' included her, in her profound ignorance. The vastness of the mystery appalled her: and still worse was the fact of her never having suspected.

'I just saw one side, of course,' the woman was saying. 'I only ever did. But I'm not complaining, because we always got on so well. He let me ramble on, and that's as much as old folk want, *I* believe.'

'Yes,' Penelope replied, without hearing.

'He didn't mind, not at all. Discussing old times. Drewsteignton, and the fire that burned it to cinders, and his poor parents dying when the plane crashed, in Kenya. But all the little things too, that he said we had to share. I was just to talk, he said, talk about them as well, tell him all over again.'

What had he told *her* he'd been doing when he was actually making his visits? In one sense, it was an innocent deceit: but why should he have concealed his intentions, if it wasn't because he was ashamed in some way? Ashamed of *her*, perhaps, and what she kept him from, his wife? But she hadn't really kept him from anything, she was now discovering: he'd had his two lives, and others as well perhaps.

Only he – the kernel of a person deep inside, if there'd been such a person – only *he* had known where one ended and the next began: in which apparently illegible patterns the shifting dune sand settled.

A phone call produced no result, so she took a taxi to Belgrave Square to see for herself.

The address she had was that of a white mansion house on one corner, so imposing she had to will herself to walk between the gates.

Brass plates beside the double front doors listed a number of occupants. She didn't see the name 'Lascelles' on any of them.

She pulled the bell-stopper, feeling doubtful. A young woman in a maid's uniform opened one of the doors. Behind her, in the background, she caught sight of a butler in tails making his way up the ornate staircase.

236

She said the name 'Lascelles'. The girl looked confused; she glanced over her shoulder but the butler had turned the first corner and was out of view.

'I don't know – '

'Mr Lascelles does live here?'

'It's not my job, you see, madam – '

'I was wondering if I could see him.'

'I – I'm not sure.'

'When I rang, there was something wrong with your phones.'

'The phones?'

'I kept being cut off.'

' "Cut off"?'

'Is Mr Lascelles in?'

' "In", madam?'

'In the building?'

The maid gave another backwards glance.

'I'd like to see him. If it's possible.'

'I don't know – '

'To speak to.'

'He's very private.'

'Could – could you ask him, please?'

'Who, madam?'

'Mr Lascelles.'

The girl rang upstairs on the telephone. She addressed the name 'Mr Lascelles' into the mouthpiece and Penelope, even from the door, heard the voice make a reply. By now it was too late to disguise the man's presence in the building. The girl blurted out her apologies; she explained, in little fits and starts, that he had a caller.

The man seemed to be debating the matter. He must have asked for a description of this woman who'd come calling; and the girl, flustered, said she didn't think she could tell him, because the lady was standing quite close by.

The call ended with more apologies and the girl's face turning a still deeper red.

'He's very busy, madam, but he can speak with you for a few moments.'

Penelope walked upstairs, two floors, four sides of the hall and watching her own progress in the clear, polished glass of the giant lantern hanging from the ceiling.

Flat Number six was at the front of the building.

She hesitated before pushing on the doorbell. She couldn't hear it ringing. She applied the pad of her thumb a second time, a little more positively. She still couldn't hear ringing.

She took a step or two back. She could knock, of course. She looked at the panelled wood painted shiny black, at the gleaming brass fittings. She also noticed a pinpoint of glass inserted in the middle of the top panel, about the level of her own eyes. She was wondering who could require such a device when the door opened.

A large, florid man in a waisted business suit stood watching her. She watched back, staring, now with a professional watcher's interest.

Forty-ish.

Face over-proportioned for his body.

Eyes too prominent in his face. Pupils afloat in the whites, ageing bags underneath.

Bull neck, inside collar of silk shirt.

Overweight but vain. Less disciplined than he wants to be.

These eyes, glassily direct, he lives through them. No charity. Reptilian; a predator's experience of the world?

Not a very pleasant man, she thought, and was pricked by shame to be thinking it. She immediately smiled, to atone for her guilt.

'I suppose you'd better come in,' he said briskly, without a smile.

'Thank you. That's very good of you.'

She walked in and he closed the door. He led the way along a corridor.

The flat was extravagantly, sumptuously furnished. Her eyes stuck, not able to take in its existence properly. Two floors beneath there were cars, buses, passers-by, dog-walkers, housemaids taking exercise, blown newspapers –

'We'll go into the drawing-room,' he said.

It might have been a palazzo in Venice, or Rome, or Palermo. Everything seemed to be there for its grandeur alone, not because anything belonged with anything else. She was shown into a room equipped like a treasure-trove. The objects were too unusual to have been inherited: their distribution and arrangement was too striking to be accidental, gilt against velvet, silver next to silk, Art-Nouveau pewter beside painted wood, blue glass beside old leather, icons next to a cubist portrait.

He walked over to the windows and pulled up cream-coloured linen rollerblinds. She looked all about her. They sat down on stark, angular, not very comfortable Biedermeyer chairs, placed at least six feet apart.

She had to explain her purpose to him for a second time, because he told her he couldn't understand. She thought his face was hardening all the time, but it was in for a penny now, in for a pound.

'I found your card,' she said. 'In my husband's – my late husband's – wallet.'

'I see.'

She perched forward on the cushion. He crossed his legs, tapped his fingers on the arm of the chair.

'He – he didn't mention you to me.'

'No?'

'And I wondered – '

'I don't know who "he" is, I'm afraid to say.'

He had a low, mellow voice: if only you could have closed your eyes and not seen the mass of him.

'Oh.'

'Except what you tell me, that he was your husband.'

She explained what she felt she could, to a stranger, and without betraying her own incomprehension.

'Are you sure?' she asked him.

'About what?'

'That you don't know him. *Didn't*,' she corrected herself. 'Maybe you did meet – '

'*You* seem to think that we met – '

'Your card – '

'*If* we met – does it surprise you that he didn't mention me to you?'

'No,' she said. 'Not really. But . . . '

' "But – "?'

'If it had to do with his business – '

'Which was again – ?'

'Banking.'

'Yes, of course.'

'If it had been his business – a colleague – I shouldn't have . . . But I don't think you are, are you? A business colleague, I mean.'

'I know very little about banking at any rate.'

'I was told – downstairs – you weren't here.'

'Am I not here?'

'Yes. Yes, of course. But when I rang before – '

'A misunderstanding, I expect, Mrs Gerrault.'

Now she even felt in doubt about the name, as if she had no proper claim on it: or it on her.

'Why . . . ?'

'What's that?'

'Do you know why my husband had your card?'

'I can't tell you, Mrs Gerrault.'

'You can't?'

'I mean, I don't know.'

'I see.'

'I leave them around. Here and there. Maybe somebody gave one to him.'

'He might have been using another name.'

'Which name?'

'I don't know.'

'Well, we could start picking our way through the telephone directory – '

The furnishings were fabulous: a giant Arras tapestry, a secretaire inlaid with porcelain plaques, an iron candelabrum set on the floor, a chandelier of opalescent glass, an oriental lacquer cabinet, an astrolabe.

'You'd like to buy something?' she heard him asking her with the same snide smugness.

'Buy?' she said.

He smiled. She thought she recognised a patronising misogynist's smile.
'I'm open to offers.'
'I – I was just looking. Admiring.'
'I'm a dealer, Mrs Gerrault.'
'A dealer?'
'*Un antiquaire. Pour les délicats.*'
'I see.'
'Your husband dabbled perhaps – ?'
'"Dabbled"?'
'In *objets d'art*?'
'No,' she said. 'No, not really.'
'Oh. What a pity. Not even secretly?'
'I think – I think you would have to be very rich. To afford such things.'
'Rich *enough*.'
His little smiles were short-lived: and, she thought, somehow *rancid*.
'So he wasn't a secret collector? He didn't scour the salerooms for you, to make your home a palace? *I* see – '
Which was to imply, she realised, that if she had been someone else then indeed Guy might have thought her worth scouring salerooms for, deserving to have her home furnished like a little palace.
'But you *don't* remember him?' she asked again.
'I do not, I'm afraid.'
'But you must meet so many people – '
'Oh, *I* remember, Mrs Gerrault.'
'Do – do you have a shop?'
'I'm not a tradesman,' he threw back at her, sounding – she thought – just as catty as they come. Then he smiled, another flash-smile.
She didn't trust him; she wouldn't have taken a street direction from him.
'You never met my husband?'
'*Guy* Gerrault, you said?'
'Yes. Yes, "Guy".'
He placed his fingers together, tip on tip, as if he was offering a prayer.
'No. No. I'm afraid not.'
She glanced down at her Geneva watch and then caught his avid eyes moving off it. She picked her bag off the floor and stood up. Suddenly she felt inordinately tired. He was laughing at her, now more than ever, although his face was set very straight.
It was frightening her now to be surrounded by so much splendour. She glimpsed into other rooms as he led her along the corridor to the front door. She saw Chinese vases as tall as herself, a suit of armour, more tapestries, elephant tusks (or were they walrus?), a life-size sculpture of a reclining nude woman, a chair with a towering ladderback, and – everywhere – paintings, paintings and more paintings, up to the ceilings. The walls of one narrow room were covered with maroon velvet plush and hung entirely with mirrors and gilt frames.

When they reached the door he held out his hand.

'I'm so sorry I haven't been able to help you,' he said.

'I'm grateful to you for your time.'

'Your grief will pass, Mrs Gerrault.'

She felt herself reeling a little at the remark: its unexpectedness, and his presumption. Was that what he imagined had driven her here, her not being in her right wifely mind?

'It's not that,' she said, but he smiled at her as if *he* knew better.

In an instant she was jealous of her life with Guy; she didn't want to share even a part of it with anyone ever again. But only seconds later she was wavering in that resolution as she made her way downstairs. She couldn't go on with all these shadows complicating her memories, so many of them that she could hardly get her focus on Guy any longer.

She looked back. The door was shut. She remembered the peephole, invisible to her now in the wood's shiny black paintwork.

She turned round again when she had the sea in her sights and retraced her steps, along the track towards Blairfiddoch and Home Farm. She watched high clouds speeding across the startlingly blue sky, a fast Atlantic sky capable of many changes in an afternoon. She heard a curlew: and then the encircling silence: and then a sough of wind pulling at a bracken brake: and then again the silence of eternity.

A few stones scattered under her feet: lazy London feet that found the track hard-going, even though it was flat. A trickle of water burbled from a tussock of soft, springy moss. Old tyre-tracks were patterned on the hard, dried mud, and pebbles stuck in the impressions like fossils in rock. The curlew called again – 'coorwee! coorwee!' – and she held her breath to listen to it. The bracken stirred, shivered. She turned her head: a flotilla of small clouds had appeared over the sea, high and fleecy and quite harmless. The brilliance of the blue in the sky left her blinking.

I might, she thought, be at the edge of the world.

She saw the abandoned farm buildings two or three hundred yards away. Other than those and the prehistoric tyre-tracks engraved in the hard mud, the human element was wholly missing from the scene. A species might have gone down, and the traces almost blown over – that there had been such a population of tribes to inhabit the earth. Only, in the end, a curlew was left, soaring and dipping over the heather, maybe mistaking those slashes of purple for the under-depths colouring the surface sheen and dazzle of sea.

She found the telephone number neatly noted down with initials, 'C.P.', inside the desk blotter, behind the removable sheet of white blotting-paper.

She rang, and found herself speaking to a pleasant-voiced woman. Of course she was immediately suspicious. She heard a voice in the background, a man's.

'It – it's about my husband,' she said.

'Would you like to speak to Colin?' the woman asked quite cheerfully. 'I'll just get him for you.'

'Thank you – '

'Colin! Col-in!'

When she said her name, it clearly meant nothing to him. Guy's name meant nothing to him. She tried to think quickly.

'He worked in a bank.'

'Which bank is that?'

She told him.

'He must be a friend of Gavin Russell's. Is that it?'

She told him 'yes', feeling ready to panic again.

'This must sound awfully peculiar,' she said, 'but do you think I might speak to you?'

He surprised her by agreeing: a little doubtfully, certainly. But she knew by now how to take full advantage of an opportunity.

She accepted his invitation and went out to the substantial mock-Tudor house in Guildford one Saturday afternoon. As she arrived his wife was getting ready to leave. She looked capable, uncareworn, and pleasantly unpossessive. She said she was off to do her stint at a bring-and-buy sale.

'Tell him to make you some tea. Everything's looked out,' she called behind her and the latch gate in the privet hedge clicked tidily shut behind her.

Her husband was a few years older than Guy, with a neatly bald dome. He was quietly spoken, but not necessarily a meek man: she thought she was catching a faint West Country inflection surviving in the Home Counties RP. She discovered that he worked in a company of underwriters, that he played a lot of golf, that he enjoyed gardening.

'I'm sorry, Mrs Gerrault, I don't know why . . . '

'But the name – ?'

'The name?'

'You recognised that?'

'I'm sorry.' He shook his head. 'I don't, I'm afraid. Recognise the name, I mean.'

She opened her bag.

'My husband – '

She found the photograph and handed it to him.

'Yes. Yes, this is Gavin all right.'

'Who you said? On the phone?'

'Gavin. Gavin Russell. *He* was your husband?'

She stared at the photograph.

'So you're Mrs Russell?'

She shook her head.

'I – don't understand,' he said.

'That – that's the man you know?'

'Oh yes. It's a very good likeness. Excellent. He grew a moustache once, then he shaved it off. I preferred him with it, I think. I haven't seen him for a while. I must – get in touch – '

'Are you sure?'

'I'm sorry – '

'About the name?'

'It's Gavin, yes.'

'That it's him? The man in the photograph?'

'Oh yes. No doubt about it. I've got group shots of us all. It's him all right, always stood with that right leg dead straight.'

She'd never noticed that in all their years together, not once that she could remember. She craned forward to look at the photograph and saw that he stood with his right leg quite straight, rigid, while his left was angled a little, like a buttress.

'No. I'm quite positive about it. That's Gavin – '

She held out her hand for the photograph.

'Is – is everything all right? With Gavin – ?'

'He – he's dead, I'm afraid.'

'Gavin? Jesus Christ – I didn't know.'

'Quite – suddenly.'

'I didn't read about it – Christ, I'm so sorry – '

She nodded and closed the clasp on her bag.

'He must be dead,' she said.

'What? *Must* be?'

'Well, it was his car. It crashed.' She took the liberty of inventing, a little fictional embroidery. 'Burned out. So he must have died. In the heat.'

'Christ Almighty.'

'Yes. Well . . . '

'Gavin, of all – When did I last see him? Nine months ago, was it?'

'You saw him?'

'Gavin. He spoke about you. You're Penelope? You write, don't you?'

'I'm Penelope, yes. I've written, a bit.'

'Gavin, of all people.'

'Why "of all people"?'

'If anyone could have got himself out of a burning car, it should have been Gavin.'

Her lips felt parched.

'He – my husband – he was very fit. With his swimming. And things. Walking, he used to like. But he was trapped – in the car – he must have been. He couldn't have done anything to save himself, I'm quite sure.'

She watched the man, feeling she wanted him to disprove her version of the accident, that Guy's body couldn't have been charred to ashes, and those – somehow – borne off on the wind.

'What did they find?'

'Some clothes. Some papers.'

'And the body?'

'They couldn't tell.'

She knew there had been no body. The car had been consumed in a fireball, she wanted to say. And they'd found the ancient oak trees that surrounded the spot with the bark burned off them.

'I – I don't understand much of it,' she said. 'The police didn't tell me a great deal. It's been a nightmare. Worse than that – '

'I really am so sorry.'

The man touched her arm. She nodded, gratefully.

'If I'd known – ' he said.

'What – how was it you knew him?'

'The war. You know?'

'It was training, wasn't it?'

'He told you?'

'Just that he'd been an instructor. In Scotland.'

'Argyll, yes.'

'Training new soldiers? Recruits?'

'Well, they were hand-picked. And it was all pretty much secret. Then, at least.'

' "Secret"?'

'SOE.'

'What? I don't – '

'Special Operations Executive. Didn't he tell you?'

'Not very much. Not that. I only got to know at the end.'

'Please sit down, won't you, Mrs Russell?'

'Gerrault.'

'Yes. I'm sorry, Mrs Gerrault.'

'Thank you,' she said, and sat down. His eyes looked mystified but she realised he had a story he wanted to tell her.

'He really didn't discuss it with you?'

'Very little. Just – as I said – that he'd trained in Scotland.'

'There's no harm in it I can see. Not now.'

He opened a drawer in the sideboard and took out some photographs.

'I'll show you first. Although it was so different then. There was a war going on. They were the strangest days. And the most fulfilling ones of *my* life, I'm quite certain. Like guns ourselves, bits of a machine, oiled and primed, that was a wonderful feeling, Mrs Gerrault. It was our mission in this life, all we thought about, our work, and we could lose ourselves in it: we might've been born for it.'

She stopped in front of the house and turned to face the way the windows did, towards the Isle of Skye's sleeping warriors.

The rooms were furnished in spare holiday fashion. Once they must have been used to a grander way of life. And in another era yet again it must have been a hive of activity, with uniformed personnel passing in and out of the french windows, women and men.

Round the back she'd spotted some bathing-costumes hanging drying from a line. A couple of bicycles leaned against a wall. Buckets and spades were strewn on the clover lawn. The building had become a second home, and everything was just as it should be.

It had taken her almost as long to reach Mallaig on the train as her informant in Guildford had told her was the case during the war. 'Eighteen hours. It was a different world to us from Galloway on. Wonderful countryside. The foreigners thought it quite a holiday, I suppose. Until they got there.'

She smelt the raininess of the place, the peaty earth yielded it. Burns gurgled where she couldn't see them, beneath the bracken and moss, rippling over stones.

She spotted what she hadn't earlier, on top of an abandoned croft, a thin tree (was it a hazel?) growing out of the accommodating shelter of a chimneystack. She smiled at its ingenuity.

Jokes must become very valuable here, worth their weight. The rocks that showed through the grass on the hillsides reminded her of disapproving frowns, craggy censorious brows.

How much he could have told her about the place if he'd chosen to and if she'd known just enough to be curious and to have asked him. What remained of Blairfiddoch and Sleat and Home Farm were the backdrops left after the last performances, waiting to be painted over, perhaps in order to tell a new story: the names might be retained for very laziness, but the characters would see them differently, coming and going with the ease and confidence of those who bear no history about with them, no swag-bag of remembrance.

'Dirty tricks department, I suppose you could call it.'

'What sort of – "tricks" exactly?'

'It was a sabotage school, Mrs Gerrault.'

Penelope sat back in her chair and tried to assimilate the details as he told them to her. Morse code – of course – and map-reading, but that was the Boy Scout stuff. More to the point, there had been expert training in hand-to-hand combat, and you were taught all you would ever need to know about explosives. The sabotage techniques were directed at destroying methods of communication, especially railways and bridges. Trainees were told how to safely mount and roll free from a train travelling at speed. There were forced marches, living rough and lying low on the wet bracken, target practice with fixed bayonets, ambushes.

That was the more humane and sociable aspect of the course, comparatively. The instructors also taught how to fold a newspaper in such a way that it could be wielded with the force of a hammer, how to release a cork from a bottle so that it could (at the least) maim its victim, how to snap a dog's spine as it made to jump.

245

Tuition was provided in the handling of pencil-bombs, hose-bombs, gammon grenades; among the speciality weapons expressly invented for agents' use was a double-edged assassin's knife and a minute stiletto concealed in the lapel, only three inches long but scalpel-sharp. An officer called Beale had been drilled in his turn by an ex-officer in the Shanghai police, and specialised in the discipline of 'silent killing': techniques included a Chinese method of strangulation which left no evidence behind of how a man had been done to his death.

'It was savage all right. But there was a war going on, and we were fighting it to the death. Only we were doing it through the back door. Infiltration: drops. Maybe it was carrying information – new codes – or it was cash, or bits and pieces for radios, or it might be poison tablets even. You had to be ready to die yourself, an assassin who's been trained as far as he can be knows that. You had to have eyes like the wild cats up there; what it *wasn't* was using a sledgehammer to get at a nut, you couldn't go about your job covering yourself with a sten.'

Penelope sat quite motionless in the chair. The sunlight was warm through the window, swilling into the corners of the room. Outside, Guildford went about its ordinary, unexceptional Saturday afternoon business.

'We caught a lot of big fish. Dead and alive. At the base we had Czechoslovakians and Norwegians especially, dozens went through, then they got sent out again. Also some Spaniards, although they weren't on the same wavelength as the rest of us, real thugs they were.'

'He – he taught them, you said? Guy?'

'Gavin – '

'Yes.'

'He trained them, yes. But it wasn't just theory. He had some missions. To the Balkans, Holland. I was with him once. It was New Year's Day, I remember. Denmark. We had to land in darkness.'

'From the sea?'

'No, air. Airdrop. Can't have been a thousand feet. We had to jump out, into cloud, and it was snowing.'

Penelope closed her eyes. He had recognised Guy from the photograph. But how could she possibly recognise this person being described to her? He was utterly a stranger to her. But as the man continued to talk, almost sentimentally, she was recalling incidents she might have thought she'd forgotten: when she wasn't well, Guy standing in the kitchen skinning a rabbit to tempt her with a surprise stew (which hadn't tempted her, although she'd been very grateful), his hands so gently and persuasively easing away the strains in her neck, catching a daddy-long-legs by one of its long legs and letting it out the window, reaching his hand out in an instant to pull her back as she stepped on to Theobalds Road (or was it Gray's Inn Road?) when she didn't see a car turning out, finding the fault in a wireless when the repair shop she'd taken it to couldn't, infallibly reading and timing rain when the weather forecast said merely grey skies, showing her how to tease open the Chubb when she locked them both out, how never but never to lose the way from either a road-map or a compass, how to whet a picnic vegetable knife on a stone in a stream, letting her see how he could smooth-talk his way into the confidence of old women.

She realised she was staring at the man, without hearing the sense of what he was saying. She smiled with embarrassment and shook her head at her abstraction.

'I've been rambling on,' he said.

'No. No, it's been – very interesting. I've learned a lot. A lot – '

She couldn't retain her smile, but she tried not to look disapproving as it faded. It wasn't his fault that she was left in such a quandary of uncertainty. She shouldn't have attempted to come this far: it was foolish, useless, extreme and meddlesome curiosity, sheer concupiscence imagining a woman had to be involved in it somewhere.

'*Your* name, though?' he asked her. ' "Mrs Gerrault"? I don't understand.'

'It – it's just a name I use. Sort of professional.'

'Oh. I see.'

'To keep everything separate. Apart.'

She leaned forward and picked up her bag. It was time to go. Especially since her host must have the capacity to strangle her and not leave a mark on her body. But Guy too could have done that any time he'd chosen to. He *hadn't* chosen to. And somehow, during his very last moments, he had forgotten so much of what he once knew and so hadn't been able to save himself. It was very, very sad and also – given this man's story – not quite credible to her. But to all intents and purposes she was now a widow. She must agree to be seen like one, marooned in her grief.

'There was nothing he didn't know about guns.'

' "Guns"?' she repeated.

'Sometimes we passed a gunsmith's. Off South Audley Street. After the war, I mean: if we were going for a drink. He liked to go in and spin them some cock-and-bull story, he was going to bring in some other friend who wanted to take up hunting and he would help him to choose one. And Gavin knew so much about them, the guns, that the assistants let him look all he liked, and they'd explain to us which were the best, although Gavin already knew that. But they would also tell him what was new to their stock. It was only the newness he needed to find out about, but he was probably almost as much clued up as they were about that, too. It was bloody marvellous really, watching him. What a performance!'

She found herself staring at him again. Maybe he hadn't looked at the photograph long enough? But she remembered the telephone number, jotted down on the blotter. And this man Gavin had talked about his wife Penelope who wrote –

'My husband didn't keep a diary,' she told him.

'No?'

He looked perplexed.

'It would have been much easier, if I could have referred to one.'

'*I* don't keep one either.'

'It must be habit, then,' she said. 'Your training.'

'Yes. Yes, I've never thought of it like that.'

'It explains *some*thing – '

'I'm really so sorry. I just didn't know.'

'At least I could tell you in person. Give you the news – '

'Yes. I *do* look at the newspapers. I would have recognised the name, you see. "Russell".'

'But you weren't expecting to see it,' she said as brightly as she could, making for the door. 'Your brain had made no preparations for it.'

He still looked baffled. She smiled at him. She knew she was taking too much away with her, too much to think about. Just for that moment she wanted to laugh, in the way that happened when you let yourself go, when you loosened up and forgot about such inconveniences as dignity, and you let the whole damned farrago of circumstances go to brilliant blazes and perdition.

5

Guy's colleagues at the bank invited her to 'At Homes' and sometimes she went and sometimes she didn't.

It was very obvious to her that she was *not* being invited for dinner. Perhaps they were afraid of encountering her grief; or perhaps they simply weren't sure how they could spin out the subject long enough, now that Guy wasn't here to speak up for himself and – more than likely – to confuse them all just as much as he'd had it in his mind to do.

She realised that they all had rather less knowledge of him now than they'd always imagined they had. They resorted to their own particular memories, and she smiled to encourage them, although recognising little and even wondering sometimes if they were just convincing themselves that those were proper memories and not semi-inventions imposed on some happening of a few moments' duration. So she continued to smile, and she drank their decanted spirits, and didn't disgrace herself, and passed – it was her ardent hope – as an unembarrassing woman, deserving some pity for the loss of her husband, but meanwhile coping.

Above all else she was coping.

She went to Fortnum's, to the millinery department, where she confounded good sense by buying herself a scarlet velvet toque, so brilliantly and richly red for a winter's day that it could have been seen at one end of Piccadilly from the other.

She paid a number of visits to Cambridge, just as she had promised.

Oliver entertained her at High Table and told her how she 'enchanted' the rather dry academics she was honour-bound to make conversation with. There was a most meticulous ritual there, of talking to the person on your right or left at certain obligatory points, of being proposed and toasted, of offering back a toast in return. (She discovered at some point – it rather shocked her, and the aspect of miserliness also irritated her – that Oliver was charged on his college bill for these compulsory toasts, that when she was asked if she would care to join the senior company for a first glass of port, it had to be at *his* expense.)

But Oliver persevered, and told her many times what a great charmer she was proving. He booked her the same river-view hotel room, at the Garden House, which he would have paid for every time if she hadn't been quite forceful on the point. He made no advances to her, proper or improper, walking her back along King's Parade and the stretch of Trumpington Street to Peterhouse, then down gaslit Mill Lane. She was always in a state of readiness, and uncertain herself whether *she* should take the first step. But memories of Guy would interrupt her thinking, to fuddle her and also – she felt – to disable her. Occasionally she would recall the last days at Tregarrick, and what had taken place there (she supposed) in Oliver's bedroom, and across the dinner table or watching his profile as they walked the court cobbles she would catch a different kind of 'glamour' about her handsome and gifted companion, a haunted silence once all the social props were removed, an intense inwardness as if every so often, without giving warning, he turned tail on himself and resorted totally to the life within. What was left then – unattended – were his looks, and she knew that he lacked the full pride in his appearance that would have marred them for her. The temporary emptiness lent him a quality of decadence even, not quite like Margot's – *soul-less-ness*, rather – and she was intrigued. She wondered in those interludes if this was why Valerie envied him, why she had attempted to possess him once, because his attractiveness exceeded her own: just as she had taken *her* up at school because physically she exercised quite a different effect from the other girls, even the sports heroines, having that stillness and mystifying air of self-completeness Lydia Bayliss had first told her about.

At the Garden House, guests would watch their departures and returns, staring at them sometimes – at Oliver in his dinner jacket and herself in an evening gown she'd brought down from London with her swathed in tissue paper. She was conscious herself of their formality and the stiffness of their bodies, as if Oliver were reinforced with cardboard and she and her full-skirted gown had been soaked in starch.

Nothing happened, at the hotel or in his set of rooms. On Sundays they sat at the back of King's College Chapel, disbelieving but impressed and somehow chastened, free of guilt. Outside, the Chapel sailed above the street like a glorious ship and she thought she might happily grow old with these same customs to indulge in year after year, she and her companion continuing to make deeper and deeper mysteries of themselves.

In Cambridge she experienced each of the seasons, and all types of weather. She enjoyed late autumn best, November, with windows lit and kettles steaming in little tea-rooms and the blasts of fen air seeming to pep her up and the furtive echoes of running footsteps in foggy courts.

The spring had its virtues too: cold sunshine, greenness, fast clouds, longer afternoons, the Easter festivals, hot cross buns and simnel cakes in the bakers' windows. She felt cautiously optimistic in herself, she wasn't sure why. Guy was more easily included in conversations, she was trying to confine the circumstances of his loss to a certain cordoned-off area in her brain, and she believed – thus far – that she was managing on that score. The journey to Cambridge on the train was easier, she knew one of the taxi-drivers at the station who kept a lookout for her, even though there might be three weeks between her visits. She spotted the same few college dons, the socialites, watching her from the windows of their rooms and timing their constitutionals to coincide with hers and Oliver's. They had slowly worked their way from the seats at the back of King's College Chapel to the first ones behind the rood screen, and had sat through a Byrd mass and a suite of Palestrina motets.

She wasn't excused and apologised for whenever a student knocked at the inner door to deliver an essay or to arrange a tutorial. Oliver's tone would become a little more donnish, but not embarrassed: that was the students' place, to be put out of their stride. She felt far less nonplussed by the situation than those rather earnest young men. Sometimes she was stared at: she caused one or two of them to jump as if they'd set eyes on a ghost who had just materialised out of the panelling. Occasionally they seemed confused, and lost their thread or stuttered; one regular caller she had no great liking for would look daggers at her and tell Oliver that he would prefer to see him 'alone', reminding her of Sly Eyes in the Old Days, the time she had come dashing back upstairs for her hat.

She guessed that Oliver was popular, and she tried not to dwell on possible reasons why essays were handed in in person and why tutorial times had to be double-checked so precisely. Oliver would rarely discuss his students, and they remained a closed book. She didn't suppose that a tutor acted 'in loco parentis', but she wondered – vaguely – if there was an unspoken moral code even behind these high excluding college walls.

At the end of April 1955, Penelope made a trip to Paris. She persuaded herself that she was on holiday. But of course she knew better than that.

On her second morning she took a taxi from her hotel to the Rue Barbezieux in the *huitième*. There were a number of embassies on the street, housed in mellow, dust-coloured mansions behind high spiked walls and formidably secure gates; flags hung limply from poles, she saw solitary figures moving about in sombre rooms.

The Hotel Schleswig-Holstein had a tidy – and, by comparison, modest – exterior. The plaster façade was painted a discerning shade of green, Baltic réséda. She paid the taxi-driver and walked inside, into a lounge of formally arranged directoire furniture, deserted of company. The décor was in good condition, and a French-born would have thought it tasteful.

From behind the desk a svelte red-haired woman dressed in black Parisian chic sat watching her luggageless arrival through narrow cat's eyes. She threw out a chilly routine smile and asked if she could be of help to her.

As Penelope fumbled with her French, she noticed a door opening a few inches behind the woman. She was wishing to discover something, she said: she'd be very grateful if the woman would allow her to ask a few questions. (The woman nodded, but warily.) Penelope explained that she was trying to trace the movements of her husband, that she had reason to believe he had been at the hotel at some point, very probably staying here.

She produced the box of matches and the tariff card and laid them on the desk.

The woman looked at them but didn't pick them up.

Penelope gave her husband's name. The woman's face didn't register any recognition. Penelope repeated the name.

'Or – or "Russell". Just possibly.'

'Not "Gerrault"?'

'Either – '

The woman asked how long ago her husband might have been a visitor. Nine months, Penelope told her, or a year, or maybe it was longer than that. The woman explained in her turn that they had very few English guests, that she would surely have remembered.

'I see,' Penelope said, and gave a dismal nod at the information. She thanked the woman. She opened her bag and returned the matchbox and the tariff card. A thought struck her as she was about to snap the clasp shut. She took out her wallet and skimmed through the contents until she found what she wanted, a small passport-sized photograph of Guy. She placed it on the counter and turned the face towards the woman.

It was the only likeness she had with her, she told her, and not such a good likeness either, but maybe it would . . .

The woman's mouth tightened at the corners and the cat's eyes widened for a couple of seconds. Penelope stared at her, believing she must recognise him after all. But suddenly the photograph was pushed back across the counter-top. The woman's eyes narrowed again, to those wary feline slits, and she ran the tip of her tongue over her lips. 'I don't know who this man is,' she said, and asked her again for the name. Penelope repeated it. The woman shook her head. 'I know no one of that name,' she said.

'I thought maybe – '

'Yes?'

' – maybe you *had* seen him.'

The woman shook her head.

'Or you thought you did?'

'No.'

Penelope stood waiting for several moments, in the hope – against all hope – that the woman might remember, that some occasion would be recalled. The woman's eyes dropped to her hands on the desk-top, to her painted nails.

Looking past her, Penelope saw that the door had opened fully. A man was looking out at her. Her attention seemed to catch him by surprise. He hesitated, then he did the manly thing and stepped forward.

He was tall and sallow, with a cropped blond dome, and wore a dark formal suit. He had a Scandinavian face: flat, rather stodgy, opaque. He didn't smile, but offered her a stiff little bow. He asked, in equally stiff French with a foreign accent, might he be of some assistance?

The woman with the oriental eyes spoke to him very rapidly, in another language, and pointed to the photograph. The man didn't seem to be listening. He walked forward, around the desk, from the back to the front. Out of the corner of her eye Penelope was aware of him considering her from a number of angles as she attended to the woman's face. He picked up the photograph. She shifted her eyes and watched him. If he did know anything he was well prepared and his face gave away nothing.

'I am very sorry,' he said to her in English.

She took the photograph from him. She was putting it back in her bag when she lifted her eyes and caught a look being exchanged between the two of them. She couldn't decipher it. It was too carefully controlled to be alarm: rather, something was being confirmed. It might have been a warning of sorts. To which end she didn't know, except perhaps that neither of them should offer her what she might construe as their curiosity.

She snapped shut the clasp on her bag: as if she was choosing to protect her own secret. Which was hardly the point, since she seemed to have no choice about that. She felt they must know that quite well, the man and the woman.

'If,' she said, 'if you can think of anything . . . '

The man turned to her, but might have been no more interested in what she'd said than if they'd been drifters-past at a party.

She asked if she could leave them her address in London.

'Your address? Yes, most certainly,' the man said, with – she was sure – mockery in his ceremony. The woman handed her a pencil and a sheet of notepaper. She scribbled down the information and could barely read her own handwriting.

She returned the pencil to the woman. She laid the sheet of notepaper on top of the counter. Neither of them looked at it.

At that moment a couple walked in from the street. Respectable, so far as she could tell. They asked for a room key in foreigners' French. They were well-dressed in an understated way, and had Middle-Eastern colouring: they might have been Egyptian, or maybe Armenian. They walked towards the lift in its cage, smiling incognisably, the woman balanced on high, thin heels. As the man opened the lift gate, a few words passed between them, spoken through the same multipurpose smiles.

Penelope felt defeated, by everything that wouldn't explain itself. She said au revoir, in a tired-sounding voice. The man bowed again, with the same ambivalent civility. She would rather he'd been rude to her, and so given her some better justification for doubting him. She couldn't bear this hollow show of gentlemanliness every time, which wasn't really that at all. They imagined she deserved no better. Being 'Mrs Gerrault' made no difference, in fact it seemed to condone her treatment. It was as if she must seem an improbable wife for such a man to have had. While she had always believed the story of their life as he'd convinced her it really was, truth and no myth.

It was in May, almost a year after her tragedy and with her late husband still partitioned inside his privileged enclave of her mind where doubt was specifically warned off, it was in the Gemini month that Oliver made his move.

They were in his sitting-room. She was perched side-saddle on the window-seat, leaning her back against the old sun-warmed wood of the wainscot. Through the flawed glass she was looking out at the crocus bulbs in the window-box.

She heard the question quite distinctly, even though she told him she hadn't.

'I – I'm sorry?'

'Will you marry me, Penelope?'

'I . . .'

'Be my wife.'

She put a hand to her brow. Suddenly her mouth was too dry to speak with, even if she'd known what to say.

'It's not how I *meant* to ask you. I'm sorry.'

'No.' She took her hand away and shook her head. She stared down into the court. 'It doesn't matter.'

'It just seemed – the moment – '

'Yes.'

'I've wanted to know – how to. How to ask you. Again.'

'Well,' she said. The hand she'd put to her brow was now clenched by her side. 'It's happened.'

'Yes.'

They looked at each other, but for no more than a couple of seconds. She bit her lip. The toe of her shoe fussed with the tassels of the rug's fringe. She had stopped considering that the question might re-occur. Now that it had, she was no less certain what her answer must be. Maybe he really did believe the best of himself, that what she had sensed about his mode of life were only misreadings, optical anamorphoses – and anyway, she wouldn't have been able to put an interpretation on them. But very nearly in spite of herself she had. She could have married him for the sake of the past, and to try to make some vital readjustments to it. However, certain images were still too clear and well-defined in her mind for her to begin to take another view of them.

She saw his face was filled with hope. It occurred to her for an interval of four or five seconds that the future might be wrenched into a different shape. But, however malleable it might have proved, a future of that sort would have been distorted out of what Penelope sensed to be true. Nature, she knew, roots out those who offend against its method. She knew what must happen as if it were an instinct of blood and bone with her. A marriage would not be allowed to continue, its doom would be decreed, and they would only be left waiting for the punishment.

With a smile she meant for tenderness, she slowly but most positively shook her head.

She spotted a newspaper advertisement for weekend excursions to Geneva. It was an extravagant indulgence, but she couldn't put the idea out of her head, and finally she seemed to have no choice but phone the company's offices and make her booking.

She found the Guibert-Favresse showroom on the Rue de Rive. She invented a reason for needing proof of purchase – an over-zealous tax inspector – and they consulted their records while she sat on a gilt chair in the little salon, turning the pages of *Paris Match* and *Jours de France*. They told her what she wanted to know, that the watch had been bought on 14 May 1953, by Monsieur Guy Milne; he had left them a local address, the Hotel Beau-Rivage.

She noted the details, thanked the staff for their assistance, and left the shop. She started to walk, back towards the lake.

Why should Guy have chosen to tell her that he hadn't been in Geneva when he had? It needn't have mattered that she wasn't able to go with him. He had spent nights away from home on bank business; why should he have apologised to her for what was only necessary?

He had told her a lie, although she didn't like to admit the word to herself, far less the deed. He had selected an untruth; a trivial one, she supposed, but that's what it had been nonetheless.

And why on earth should he have used *her* surname with his christian name?

She reached the lakeside, and kept walking. A street sign told her she was on the Quai du Mont Blanc. Two or three hundred yards ahead of her she saw the stately demeanour of the Hotel Beau-Rivage. She walked towards it. Blue awnings shaded a terrace bordered with red and white geraniums.

Instead of walking past or turning back she decided to make a proper reconnaissance job of it, since she was here and might not be again. Inside she located a quiet corner in a lounge and sat down. She thought of Guy on his bank business moving in this rarefied company, in the splendour of the surroundings: chandeliers and tapestries and period furniture, everywhere *luxe calme et volupté*. The atmosphere was so seductive, she felt she really wasn't ready to leave just yet.

She decided her departure could be postponed a little longer, and how. She visited the *Mesdames'* cloakroom first, then made her way through the foyer to the restaurant. The maître d' welcomed her and consulted his reservations lists. She looked about her. Geneva was distanced through picture windows; the room shimmered with table silver and glass. The table she was shown to, on a raised platform, had clear views of the lake and the terrace and the room's other patrons.

In the course of the meal she became conscious that she was being studied from one table in particular. Several times she lifted her head and speedily directed her eyes to an older couple seated diagonally opposite her, on the other side of the room. Her own table was in sunlight; although the awnings shaded her face, she felt she was eating under an arc light. She caught her reflection in the gleaming window glass, wearing a Gainsborough-look picture hat; she'd had her hair cut short before leaving London and she'd brought the

255

hat in part as a defence against the cold. The brim was deep, and she hoped sufficiently so to keep her private; she was still a new widow after all, and had her own very good reasons to keep to herself.

But the man continued to watch. The woman he was with had noticed her too, with some awkward, rheumatic-looking turns of her head, and she seemed to be trying none too successfully to distract him, pointing to the far windows and what lay outside. The man wouldn't be distracted. Is this the sort of peril I'm going to be in, she thought: is this what I failed to notice with a husband, that the world is fraught with hazards for a woman on her own?

He appeared to be in his fifties: late fifties probably. He wore a dark business suit: a professional something-or-other, she presumed. She heard some words exchanged with the maître in English: English English, not American.

When she had finished her *sablé aux fraises*, she asked if coffee could be served to her in the lounge. She left the table and was quite aware she was walking very self-consciously towards the doors, with her back held straight and her jaw pulling her neck firm.

She drank coffee in the same seat she had occupied earlier. She read a day-old copy of the London *Telegraph*. Her thoughts went back to Guy; she wondered if he had sat in this lounge reading the London –

'Anything we should know about?'

The voice startled her and the newspaper shook in her hands.

'Did I startle you?'

It was her admirer, of course. She was so surprised that she smiled, as if she knew him, which was quite the wrong thing to have done. But she realised that too late, when he smiled back.

'This is very forward of me,' he said.

She lowered the newspaper a few inches.

'You *do* come from London?' he asked.

'Yes.' There was surely no harm in the reply. 'Yes, I do.'

'Might I be so bold as to enquire . . . you *are* in the arts – ?'

She stared at him.

' – in the writing line?'

For an opening gambit, he'd hit a bull's-eye. She ventured another smile, and his broadened. She thought she discerned something gentle and gentle-manly, and very possibly quite genuine, beneath the anonymous businesslike appearance, the flannel and stiff collar and cuffs.

'You're Penelope Milne, I believe?'

'Yes. Yes, I am.'

'Kaplan. Leopold Kaplan.'

She recognised the name from the roll-call of literary London. He offered her his hand and she took it.

'I enjoyed your novels very much. I've been reading your stories. I'm very impressed by them too.'

'Oh. Thank you,' she said, letting go his hand only at the moment he did hers.

'I thought perhaps you'd stopped working.'

'I was married. I finished one novel. Short stories were easier.'

'Of course.'

She looked past him. Where was the woman with the double chin and the fur wrap?

'I imagine you have your life organised exactly as you want it to be. But . . .'

He slipped his hand into an inside pocket of his jacket and drew out his wallet.

'Would you allow me?'

He handed her a business card. She took it from him and read it. 'Leopold Kaplan and Company Limited. Literary Agents.' The address was Conduit Street.

'That is my business,' he told her. 'I run it in my own way. I'm very concerned for my clients' welfare.'

She nodded. That was only what she knew already, by report.

He looked like a Harley Street consultant. He was decorous and polite in the old-fashioned manner. His eyes were intelligent, sharp. Now she *believed* him at least.

'Thank you,' she said.

'If you ever thought there was any point in my explaining to you how Kaplan's conducts its business – '

She nodded again.

'It would be an honour for *me*,' he said, 'a pleasure – '

She turned the card over in her hand. She was aware that the firm kept a small but distinguished list.

'I shall trouble you no more. I'm very sorry if I've interrupted you.'

'You haven't,' she told him.

'Well, thank you for allowing me, Miss Milne.'

She watched him walk away. He was slightly stooped. Prosperous, she didn't doubt: although *she* was eating here too, and she was a widow let loose on the world. Not of course for much longer at this rate of spending.

She thought about what had just happened as she sat on for ten or fifteen minutes longer. She wondered why she wasn't leaving. She had to find her way back to her hotel, she had to repack and return to London tomorrow and pick up the untied ends of her life. With the last six years tossed up in the air like a pack of cards.

When she went to settle the bill, she was astonished to be told that it had already been paid.

'I'm sorry, there must be a mistake.'

'No, madam, I don't think so.'

She shook her head.

'Can you check the table number, please?'

He showed her the bill.

'Mr Kaplan has attended to the bill, madam.'

'Mr Kaplan?'

'Yes indeed. The gentleman from London. He and his wife are two of our regular guests. I didn't realise you were acquainted, madam.'

She telephoned his suite from reception.

'It was a liberty,' he told her. 'I apologise.'

'You *can't* pay, though – '

'But I have. Whyever shouldn't I?'

'I don't *know* you!'

He laughed. She listened, and found herself almost put off her stroke by his good humour.

The conversation finished with the matter left just as it was: she thought it best not to embroil herself, recognising determination when she encountered it.

'It may be immodest of me to say so,' he told her, 'but Kaplan's agency is held in high repute.'

'Yes,' she replied. 'Yes, I know that.'

'If you would like to know anything further – if I can be of any help to you at all – you *will* telephone me, won't you? And ask to speak to me personally?'

'Yes,' she said. 'Thank you.'

'I do hope you will.'

'It *was* a splendid lunch.'

'I'm only sorry we were on opposite sides of the room.'

'Well . . . '

'I hope it may become a memorable day.'

She mulled over the words as she turned her back on the lake and walked in the approximate direction of her hotel. Earlier – after her visit to the Guibert-Favresse showroom – she had been mulling over quite a different matter, and she was glad now for the diversion.

She was a little ashamed following her internal compass, along the Quai Guisan and the Boulevard Helvétique: a little, but not more so. She had come to Geneva with the specific purpose of bringing herself closer to the spirit of Guy.

But the city was guarding its secrets. At the same time it might also be offering her unexpected, quite unlooked-for openings.

Part Nine

1

'I read Penelope Milne's first books when they came out, when I was reviewing. We were the same age and sometimes you imagine a bond for that simple reason. Afterwards she became more interested in the mysteries that people are to each other, for a while that was "her thing". I'm not sure I could take those later novels "on board" so easily.

'The first books were the ones she struggled at; she wasn't quite sure if she had the makings of a novelist, and if she'd be able to continue. There's nothing automatic about them at all, or programmed, they're pulled out of her but you also feel – I know it sounds a paradox – that they were waiting to be written. Later she became known for her novels about "women coping", surviving, and even some of the early – well, feminists – *they* became fans, although the books probably weren't sufficiently "aware" for them, socially or politically. But they were about women, and their pasts, and the men they encounter and the careers they try to have. So she did fit the times in one sense.

'It was only rarely she was *un*ironical, but her second and third novels seemed to me the most – well, enjoyably mischievous. They least did what you expected, if I can put it like that, although I'm maybe not being very fair to the author's intentions.

'I liked her third novel best – it was published in 1956, I think – *Solférino*. A woman becomes intrigued by what she doesn't know about her recently deceased sister. She sees the body in the police mortuary in Paris – the woman fell in front of a train – and it's a pledge she makes, to discover what she can.

'She traces her sister's movements from a diary. Her search takes her back to France, to a hotel in Paris. She realises her sister was here through the war when she'd thought she spent it all in London. Someone seems to recognise her. That's the first time she passes herself off as her sister. Not quite intending to at the beginning. Then from that point on we're in an adventure story. Thriller-ish. It's very untypical of Penelope Milne. I'm not sure why she didn't continue in that vein. I rather think she felt you can't describe lives with their loose ends finally tied up and knotted like that, it was entertaining but it was false. *Solférino is* an entertaining story. The sister becomes more and more the glamorous woman who had a double-life, working for the Free French movement and who was eventually murdered, having a hand pushed into her back at Solférino métro station. Because she'd discovered that one of their group was a collaborator. Now, after the war, he's a bigwig politician in Paris. And of course the imitating sister, she too finds all this out. It comes to the point where the politician

259

believes the wrong person was killed, under the métro train, so now the dead woman's sister finds events – the parts she hasn't been able to slot into the puzzle – being re-enacted. A hit man follows her. But she eludes him, and at last she exposes the politician.

'Well, I suppose it sounds pretty much humdrum thrills-and-spills. But the best bits for me, which I'm very fond of, are those moments of incredible *closeness* the woman feels for her sister, as if they belong to one another, their characters are truly interchangeable. She has shed her past life and yet she feels this one is no less real to her. It's very convincingly done.

'This is what Penelope Milne has to say about it in a radio recording made recently.'

'My aunt, my mother's sister, died when I was quite young. Very suddenly. I suppose that's what was in my head, what it all started from. A person who seemed more and more – well, alluring, with time. And her life was protected now. Anyway, the idea of sisters appealed to me. Maybe because I was an only child. It got mixed up with the war, the atmosphere of that, feeling you could turn yourself into a different person. People did; I expect there was quite a trade in new identities. And it's about "family" too. The subject has always fascinated me. How they "share" one another, when the members are close – especially when they're first-blood siblings: how they pass in and out of each other. How maybe a person's "character" isn't wholly to be depended on, as total and complete just in itself . . .'

'Before that, in 1953, there was *The Enchanted Castle*. It's got a tragic end, which is a shock, because most of it's done with a very light touch. It's about rather an earnest young man of letters who arranges to visit an illustrious poet at his home and finds nothing quite as he imagines. He shows up with all his serious notions about "high art" and finds a vaguely free-loving atmosphere, but also awful domestic tensions which are really very amusing. The young man can't understand how the work gets written. Then he discovers that the wife and the mistress have a sort of unholy pact; they've stopped competing for the poet, they now share him. As for the poet, the two women are interchangeable entities, or rather they're different aspects of one woman, one ideal.

'The critic-biographer doesn't understand, until the end, anything about the poet's concept of love especially. How it celebrates its unity by including at least two different women. The young man's own life by comparison is fundamentally shallow and mean-spirited. The ménage eventually die in a drowning accident – a Swiss steamer goes down; three gravestones go up, side-by-side, but their bodies are never found.

'It doesn't sound a very promising concept for a novel, but she keeps it short, and it doesn't *read* like a concept. She's demystifying art, rather, and yet at the end of it the poet survives with his reputation more or less intact, while the young man is left with only his sorry muddle of notes, footnotes, etcetera. Also, at the conclusion, the poet has preserved his *mystique*. And it's from this point, I feel – give or take *Solférino* – that Penelope Milne's mind turns more to mystery, and to the opacity of character as we perceive it.'

She spotted him from the opposite side of the room. He had already caught sight of *her*.

They worked their way towards one another.

'So – ' he asked her ' – so, how was Geneva?'

'Well,' she answered him, 'nobody else bought me lunch.'

He grinned at her.

'No?'

'I'm afraid not.'

'Aren't you in the habit of being lunched?'

She shook her head. She was wearing a cocktail hat, a birthday present to herself, and the long black ostrich feathers fluttered in front of her face.

He was looking at her mouth, where the feathers stopped.

'Do you come to many of these?' he asked her.

'I feel I have to put in an appearance occasionally, show myself,' she said. 'I'm out of purdah now.'

'You're going to concentrate on your writing?'

'Yes.' She smiled. 'Yes, that's the plan.'

'I'm very pleased to hear it. I'm delighted.'

She tugged at one of her long black gloves.

'Well, I'll have to see if I've got the sticking power, I suppose – '

'Of course you have.'

'You sound sure – '

'I've got every confidence.'

His eyes passed from her nose to her eyes and back again to her mouth.

She pulled at her other glove.

'I don't know why I came like this,' she said.

' "Like this"?'

'Wearing these things. No one else is.'

'Then I think that's *their* misfortune.'

She smiled into the wall: then hoped to God he wouldn't think she was being coy.

'No,' he said, 'I mean it.'

She shook her head.

'I've overdone it – '

'You're glamorous.'

She shrugged. ' – over-egged the pudding.'

'There's no one here to touch you. With or without it – the hat,' he said, and indicated the feathers. 'Now *I've* overdone it. Over-egged – '

'No,' she told him. 'No. I appreciate your – '

'If you won't give me a black mark – '

She smiled.

'Of course not.'

He emptied his glass of orange juice. His eyes, she saw, were humorous as well as sharp, and kindly although his appearance was also purposeful.

He put down his glass.

'Would dinner be pushing my luck?'

'Dinner?' she said.

261

'If we had something to eat?'

'When did – '

'Like now?'

'I . . . '

'Or maybe you've eaten?'

'No,' she said. 'No, I haven't.'

'Or maybe you feel you should stay?'

'I've been here – ' she looked at her watch, Guy's crazy present from Geneva ' – an hour. Almost exactly.'

'Meeting people?'

'Not really.'

'No?' He showed his surprise.

'I think I've been frightening them off actually.'

'I don't see how.'

'This hat probably.'

'Well, maybe there *is* a reason,' he said.

She didn't speak.

'I expect they're really afraid of *themselves*, their own inadequacies, they don't want to admit to them – '

She didn't pursue the matter further. She only told him – too quickly to allow herself to think – that she had no plans for her evening, that she would be very pleased to accept his offer. But, she added, this time couldn't they divide the cost between them?

If that was a condition, he said, then he feared that he didn't think –

'Then I'll withdraw the remark,' she told him.

The black ostrich feathers fluttered again as she turned for the door. Eyes, she noticed, observed them both while mouths continued with their conversations. His hand rested on the small of her back as he followed behind her. She wondered what appeal literary evenings would have had for Guy: but this was a life to be lived without him, and for the first time in a long while she felt some obscure pattern might be starting to compose itself out of the flux and flow.

It was Leopold Kaplan who masterminded her career.

Really, it was a second career. With her fourth novel she changed publishers. He drew up leak-proof contracts, and for the first time in her writing life she started to earn money. He was a clever promoter of his clients and – when the publisher's publicity department couldn't manage it – he was at pains to arrange lunches with editors and freelance journalists. He knew very well just who 'counted' in the literary funfair and who didn't.

'Your time is precious,' he told her, 'you mustn't waste it, not any.' She nodded. 'And you won't,' he said with his characteristic loyalty, 'so long as I have anything to do with it.' He reminded her several times about Van Gogh, promising himself never to fritter even a single minute.

'People want to steal it from you,' he said, 'all that time. But once it's gone, you can never get it back again.' She would nod at the rich good sense of his instructions, which he meant only in the spirit of kindness and friendship.

For the first time, she found, her books now sold: not in the sort of quantities that might have turned her head, but more than respectably. She was published in the United States for the first time. Leopold fixed up very favourable deals with publishers in Scandinavia and the Low Countries and Germany. One book was translated into French, *L'Heure Bleue*. For the first time she received readers' letters. Leopold advised her which speaking invitations to accept and which not to. She allowed herself the luxury of buying only a particular type of hard-bound notebook and a certain Swedish make of HB pencil, from a specialist shop near the British Museum. Leopold made appointments for her to visit a number of photographers' studios: not 'names' any of them, but much better, and able to put her at her ease, for the first time that she could remember it happening in front of a camera.

He would tell her what he didn't need to, that her career was on the up-and-up: and she would respond with what she knew was a superfluous observation, that it was him and his dedication to 'The Masterplan' she had to thank for it.

'*A Geneva Watch* wasn't just about a marriage. Not really. But I'm not sure how many people saw that. It was about living in the Peace. Having a bright new life. But not knowing where to go. Apart from round and round each other. It's about failing to live up to promises, generally. And how everything became the same again, after the war. It all just fell back into place. But for the husband, of course, the excitement had gone. So he has an affair, which brings some of it back, but *some* excitement only makes you crave more, I think. Wanting and wanting. It's not just about an affair, of course. Everyone was poised on the future's threshold – their lives were going to be better, fulfilled, material. Christopher, the husband, he finds everything different with the other woman: it's an alternative life for him. But then he starts to catch resemblances to the other one. Even in little things, the details of how she makes tea with leaves and serves it, that's exactly how his wife does it. He comes to see his wife differently, though; after a while she acquires a kind of newness for him. That surprises him, very much. He's always driving between the two of them, he gets confused, the car lights dazzle him, he feels a bit like a phantom.'

'This comes from life?'

'From someone's life.'

'Your own?'

'I don't think so. For once I toned it down.'

'There *was* something you worked from though?'

'I suppose so.'

'But this is milder? – what you've written in the book?'

'Something happened, yes – not a trio – but if it hadn't happened I wouldn't have gone on writing – for a job, I mean – and we wouldn't be sitting here talking. I only

263

saw that afterwards. I had to write to find my way out of it. My life got – well, quite highly coloured for a while. If it hadn't happened that way, I wouldn't have been pushed back on myself. I had to understand something about myself.'

'An affair wouldn't have had the same effect?'

'Maybe. But the confusion went deeper. That's all I'll say. Deep into me, into my being. If it had been infidelity, another woman, I'd have bought a madly expensive Paris hat or something, and enjoyed little revenges.'

'Like your wife in the book?'

'If it isn't a contradiction in terms, mystery was confirmed in my life. I knew that what I was going to write would be tamer, it would have to be. The plot, the set-up to chart the effect I wanted to describe. What actually happened to me was like experiencing a little death, and then coming back; I tried to describe the feelings for anyone else to understand, and *myself* too, but making the events a little more muted, a little more – well, believable. Credible, frankly. For me it was the memory of an awful numbing sort of *nothingness*, and I was looking to find the simplest words to tell it.'

Whose idea was the bowler hat you're wearing in the photograph?

Mine. The photograph was really just a joke. We'd finished the 'serious' ones.

It was yours, the hat?

My husband's. I'd hung it up on a peg in the hall. The photographer saw me looking at it and – I don't know – that just made up my mind.

What does it mean?

I don't suppose a husband could put on his wife's hat in a photograph and get away with it. But he might want the same thing: to be nearer to the person, I suppose.

That's what it means on the book cover? – or it was only because you'd spotted the hat hanging up in your own hall?

Oh . . . I'm not sure.

You husband died, I believe?

Yes. Yes, he died.

And the bowler was a way for you to get closer to him, wearing it?

I suppose so. Actually *I* bought him the hat. As a sort of joke: a semi-joke. I'm not sure he wanted it, though – but it became part of his business uniform. In the photograph I was putting on a part of his uniform.

He dressed for a job?

He worked in a bank. A bank.

You repeat it –

What's that?

You said it twice. 'Bank'.

Did I?

I get the feeling – am I right? – he didn't quite fit. Or his heart wasn't wholly in it?

I don't know. You get to feel comfortable in a uniform. Maybe you don't consider its significance so much, after a time. That's one of its properties.

I'm sorry – ?

It's one of its functions, that it should be recognisable to others. That it should be – well, perhaps a disguise.

This is the point of the photo? Or this is what you feel about your husband's bowler hat?

His hat *became* a sort of joke to him too. The photograph was really the woman in the book retracing her husband's steps.

She discovers he was a different man, to the man she thought she knew?

Yes. But she wasn't ever quite sure that she did know him, and perhaps she wasn't ever quite sure that she knew *herself*. He had a licence to be a 'different' man, let's say.

Why a licence?

Because the lines of character are never fixed. You're on very shaky ground with other people sometimes. Maybe if you sacrifice yourself to the person – to the idea of the person – and then you give too much of your own self away, that's when the trouble starts. I think you have to – take it a little easier, hold back a bit.

This is the writer or yourself speaking?

I suppose that's what I mean. The definitions get blurred. I can't really answer you. Maybe if I knew you well enough the two of us would partly overlap, our characters, there'd be giving and taking, bits of us would belong to either of us, we'd understand each other in that way. But I don't think trying to own all the knowledge about another person – or anything like 'all' – I don't think that's feasible, as if you're meaning to possess them. You just have to learn to accept what's possible: give your thanks for some very small mercies.

Then the silly phase began.

No more than a few minutes would pass without her thinking about Leopold. She woke in the mornings, by six o'clock at the latest, and the thought of him would already be there, from dropping off to sleep the night before, and it would stay with her, on and off, throughout the day. At one point, quite early on, she thought a kind of madness was taking over, when her feelings were having a physical effect on her, food went dry in her mouth and stuck in her throat, a boozy pinkness lay on the skin of her upper chest, she had difficulty willing the breath up out of her diaphragm into her lungs and into her throat and mouth.

There were a few days of *extreme* intensity. She didn't know which was mattering more to her: wanting him, or wanting to be wanted by him. Sometimes when she closed her eyes to shut it all out she could hardly remember the features of his face: at other times she could believe she heard his voice at her shoulder and she would jerk her head round.

That intensity subsided – it coincided with his prolonged absence from the office on a business trip abroad – and afterwards she settled from obsession to a level of preoccupation that was more livable with.

She still knew very little about him, and she tried her hardest to discover more. She had heard the gossip about Mrs Kaplan: accounts differed in their sparse details, but the consensus was that she had been a 'looker' in her younger days. Now she was rarely seen: her preference for privacy was put down to shyness or nerves or pride or the loss of her looks and jealousy of the younger women. Her husband *might* have been married before, but unhappily, and there were rumours that he had been unfaithful to *this* Mrs Kaplan, but with the utmost discretion. The couple lived in Highgate, and had a cottage in Sussex. There were no children. There was a lot of money, however, but Penelope had guessed that for herself. Mrs Kaplan was reported to only shop on account, charging all her purchases. Other than *his* few romances, they had no famous failings that were known of, such as gambling or drinking: indeed Leopold Kaplan was TT. His wife was evidently only a few years younger than him; while he had always drawn the attention of the more 'discerning' sort of woman.

Penelope wondered why it was that *she* too should have been 'discerning', and what were the qualities in Leopold Kaplan that drew those certain women to him. He was gentlemanly, considerate, quiet, but there was something else about him that had been overlooked by those who were so ready to trade their observations with her. As *she* observed him, he didn't have the bluff and conceit of some men who are also 'gentlemen'. There was something 'other', and inward, bypassing all the common definitions. He had a sixth sense for how women might feel, which had contributed to his becoming such a success in business. He wasn't feminine in any obvious sense, but his masculinity didn't seem as hard-edged and excluding as it usually was in men. He wasn't especially handsome as that is commonly judged – his nose was rather too long and fleshy, his mouth dropped on one side and upset the balance of the other features – but his looks were nonetheless insistent: his eyes helped to produce that effect, being quite deeply set, and too intensely blue to be ignored. (She had watched him when there were others with him, but they were still as compelling, shining whenever he looked at her: the catch was that she could never know what they were like when she wasn't there, and discovering wasn't a favour she could have asked of anyone else.) Also, so she'd spotted many times, his brow would take two deep vertical furrows, directly above his nose on the bridge, which turned him into the type of man she felt must be beyond such a petty business as gauging the handsomeness of. Maybe the forehead creases, combined with his manner, convinced you that you might even have a part in protecting him from whatever was causing them: if it *was* any one thing at all, and concern wasn't just his natural disposition.

D.P.: You've known such men? Men like Christopher Marrick.
P.M.: Well, of course, characters have to be compounds.
D.P.: So there isn't one person, a mystery-man like him?
P.M.: Christopher Marrick is Christopher Marrick.
D.P.: Some readers have found that book difficult, *A Geneva Watch*, awkward to read. Because you lay the mysteries out, the things that don't add up, which refuse to add up. You don't try to explain them or account for them.
P.M.: No. Well . . . I suppose – I suppose I wanted to suggest – the ways in which circumstances don't always oblige us. The dead-ends. Also, how things, even important events which you think must change everything – they've got a way of fading eventually, burning out, although you think it must be impossible.

Sometimes – well, you feel you can't get your hands on life – it escapes you. That – that's legitimate, isn't it?

D.P.: You sound doubtful.

P.M.: No. Not really. But I have to respect what people say about the books.

D.P.: You haven't ever been quite so enigmatic in your presentation. Your presentation of enigmatic facts.

P.M.: It was something I wanted to do.

D.P.: You knew how? You'd planned that was how it would turn out?

P.M.: Yes, more or less. I knew I had to: that it was a stage in the process.

D.P.: The process to what finally? Can you say?

P.M.: To a state of being baffled: but not defeated. That comes with age.

D.P.: Wisdom?

P.M.: Not exactly, no. Just – resignation maybe. The realisation that you can't know everything. Because everything isn't to be known. There's so much of course, but I mean – certain things won't let themselves be known. And then there are so many viewpoints, on an event or a person: one particular angle determines one specific truth about the event or the person.

D.P.: There aren't always answers –

P.M.: Maybe the interest then is in posing the questions. Who wants to know what.

D.P.: Was Jennifer defeated? By Marrick?

P.M.: When I wrote the book she was, yes. But if I wrote about her again –

D.P.: You haven't though?

P.M.: About women *like* her, maybe. But not Jennifer Henson, as she was then. Not that she's the same now anyway. But I suppose she was too close to it all, too involved. As I was getting with her. I could have left the book, of course –

D.P.: Although it didn't have to do with any person you knew? Any *one* person?

P.M.: I – I just meant – I could have left it until I was a bit better able to – till I was older –

D.P.: But you just have to write it, get on with it, don't you? In the interim?

P.M.: I suppose so, yes.

D.P.: And that was the time when you felt you needed to write about the elusive Marrick?

P.M.: Yes.

D.P.: In that fashion?

P.M.: Yes.

D.P.: A little melodramatically maybe?

P.M.: Well, that seemed apt then. It wasn't Gothic exactly.

D.P.: Christopher Marrick could only have occurred then?

P.M.: The Peace dissatisfied certain people. *Many* people perhaps. He wasn't very – fulfilled.

D.P.: In what respect?

P.M.: Simply, not having the excitement there once was. He wasn't the most complex of men. It's understandable, I think. He was looking for something else. And – and after the war people imagined they could be different, find a new identity, recreate themselves.

D.P.: Wasn't that just fantasy?

P.M.: Not if it could be practically achieved, no.

D.P.: But they retained their memories surely? Of their old life –

267

P.M.: Less than you might think –

D.P.: Star-crossed fools?

P.M.: I wouldn't presume to judge. I didn't know – what the whole story might have been –

D.P.: So the narrator was bested in the end?

P.M.: She wasn't defeated, I don't think.

D.P.: Even married to a stranger?

P.M.: She wasn't unhappy, not at all.

D.P.: Afterwards she was, though, when it was all over.

P.M.: Then happiness became more desirable to her. Wherever it could be found. She wasn't bested, she was humbled maybe. She saw happiness has a vague shape, no recognisable form, and the occasion – however brief – has to be snatched.

D.P.: That's the moral of the book?

P.M.: You don't make it sound very much. A very slight thing.

D.P.: It's a woman's book?

P.M.: The roles could have been reversed. I suppose it is about Jennifer, learning she knows less about herself than she thinks. She's implicated as much as he is. 'Humility' is entering into the life of 'the other'.

D.P.: Even if you're not given a free pass?

P.M.: Then the proper end is forgiveness. Standing on your honour is the surest route to self-pity, and after that bitterness and rancour. It's not nothing, or so little, to know how to save yourself from that.

Since she couldn't discover more about the Kaplans without exposing her naïve wish to find out, she *imagined*, from the information that was available to her: how the couple lived, what they did at weekends, how they filled those holidays on the French Riviera that were the talk and envy of the agency.

One wayward Sunday when she had a whole day to get through and, on the influence of too much caffeine (it must have been), thinking the madness was on her again, she took a bus up to Highgate and traced the street and the house, from the address she'd memorised from the telephone directory.

It was a tree-lined street at the top of a hill, with London spread beneath it. Airy and bracing. Tall Dutch houses, semi-detached, plaster and brick. Leafy front gardens, flights of steps up to solid front doors with surrounding.

She didn't pass directly in front of *the* house and, several times, she stood behind a tree to watch. She must have kept up her vigil for half an hour, but there was no sign of activity. She decided they probably weren't there and had gone to Sussex for the weekend.

She might have ventured closer but in those last seconds she fought shy of a revelation. It occurred to her that the sight of whatever lay on the other side of the window glass might dispirit her too much, it would turn her curiosity to hopeless envy. The woman had her husband, and a fine house, and for all she knew she didn't warrant them.

She turned round and was picking tree bark from her gloves when she looked up and saw him no more than thirty or forty yards from her, walking along the pavement.

Suddenly he changed direction and stepped on to the road, crossing it on a wide diagonal.

He walked briskly, pushing his hands deep into the pockets of his overcoat.

She had stopped in her tracks and was holding on to the trunk of a tree watching him. He had spotted her, she was quite sure: his eyes had been looking towards her, she'd caught them, but then they'd switched away in an instant, just like his feet. Now his eyes were directed at the opposite pavement as he took the kerb, each second shortening the distance left to the house.

Penelope felt her heart jumping in her chest. She also felt desperate, but not in the way she'd been expecting earlier. Her own incaution – no, not that, her *stupidity* – it might have turned him from her for good. For a few moments she considered calling after him to make him turn round, even if it was only to see his anger: anything except that affected accidental ignorance that she was there.

On the journey back however she recovered some of her composure. Then lost it again.

Between Camden Town and Bloomsbury she got on top of her thoughts to the extent that she nearly convinced herself there was some virtue in having been overlooked. He wouldn't have done what he had without very good reason. Namely, to prevent his wife from seeing. But on Tottenham Court Road she realised everything was irredeemably complicated. As the bus rattled down Charing Cross Road she understood that all three of them now found themselves on tenterhooks.

He didn't mention his sighting of her the next time they were together, nor did he ever after that. She understood that that was the proof of *his* discretion. She knew that she was forgiven, otherwise he wouldn't have been so loving with her as he was. The matter faded: except of course that she subsequently felt she had good cause to make less of herself rather than more. By playing herself down, as it were, she gave *him* more reason for trusting her, for pledging himself to her. She never referred to his wife, or to his life at home – and not doing so she couldn't be marked or tainted by it: she was a life apart from that. She was forgiven, but she guessed that her Highgate visit hadn't been wholly forgotten: their silence on the subject was another link between them, bonding them this time and not binding.

2

Valerie rang up and suggested they meet and have tea. The Berkeley, she said, then she changed her mind and told her the Ritz. More people, Penelope thought, to see her in her prime and glory.

She was early for the rendezvous, and Valerie was late. She was seated on a prominent sofa when the doorman held open the door, tipped his cap, and Valerie made her grand entrance in a scalloped mink coat and veil which knocked her own winter tweed coat – figuratively speaking – into her own white fox beret.

Valerie – fairer-haired than before, more ecru than brunette, raised her hand, advanced, pecked her cheek and clasped her arm. Penelope guessed that she wasn't entirely at her ease in these particular surroundings. The head waiter very politely corrected her when she used the wrong name.

'George is the other one?' she asked him.

'The other one, madam,' the man replied, a little stiffly to Penelope's ear.

'And you're – ?'

'Wilson, madam.'

'But your first name?'

He intentionally hesitated. 'I'm Gerald. Madam.'

Valerie ignored, or didn't spot, the hesitation. 'Gerald,' she repeated.

Penelope felt her mother would have disapproved of a head waiter being addressed by his christian name. Valerie just smiled over the little awkward-ness (if she saw it), and voiced no complaint about the table they were shown to in the far corner of the Palm Court. 'Good. We'll be able to hear each other speak,' she said.

Tea was ordered and it arrived as Valerie discussed the new house she and Cyril were buying in Bryanston Square. 'For our visits. I can't stand hotel plumbing. And hot bedrooms.' Penelope nodded knowingly, and asked how her husband was. With her worldlier version of Petula Clark's face, Valerie had all her answers ready and rhymed them off, she was very happy how things had worked out, life was hunky-dory really, there were no problems, even accounting for minor fluctuations in Cyril's health, even with their prolonged stay in Bournemouth because a doctor advised he should clear his lungs for a while.

'I may not be an intellectual like you – '

'That's the last thing I am. Come off it, Valerie.'

'You've turned into a writer, haven't you? Not that I open a book, I should say – '

'It was *in* me. That's all. I didn't have to "become" it.'

'This is all too clever for me.'

'*And* me,' Penelope said, smiling.

'Anyway, I'm really very happy, you know.'

Three times she said it in quite close succession in the conversation, in the same order of words.

'I'm glad, Valerie.'

'I just want you to know.'

'Thank you.'

Valerie was watching her over her teacup. Penelope smiled again, and repositioned herself in her chair.

'I'm sure my brother doesn't approve, though.'

'Oliver?'

'That's the only brother I've got.'

'He doesn't approve?'

'Of the marriage. I shouldn't think he does. He hasn't *told* me so, but his silence is sufficient.'

Penelope didn't say anything.

'In that high-minded way he has. He's really rather puritanical, you know.'

'"Puritanical"?'

'Well, isn't he?'

Valerie was defying her to disbelieve her. Penelope made the effort to meet her eyes. While her manner was blustery and unrepentant, she thought the eyes were wary and unsure.

'That's typical of my brother, of course. He does nothing himself so he expects everyone else to stay in their shells.'

The cup was put down.

'Well, we *think* he does nothing, Pen. But he must have his chances, God knows.'

'I don't really . . .'

Penelope wondered why she was so intrigued. It might be that in very roundabout fashion she was actually wishing him his 'happiness' too, sister to brother, but she rather doubted that. There was something prurient in her curiosity. Which inevitably set her puzzling how content Valerie was with the physical side of the marriage, if it wasn't frustration that might be responsible for her repeatedly speculating on the subject re Oliver.

'I really don't pretend to understand him. He's a dark horse all right.'

'I – ' Penelope didn't know how to reply. 'He – he has his own life.'

It wasn't the safest remark to come out with. She realised her faux pas and caught the sharpness in Valerie's eyes as she raised her cup again.

'Yes, I'm sure he does. But he's not letting *us* in on it. Is he?'

271

Penelope shifted again in her chair. She attempted a chaste, noncommittal smile.

'Well,' Valerie said, 'at any rate *I*'ve heard nothing.'

Penelope reached forward for her cup.

'But I suppose,' Valerie added, 'he thinks I've burnt my boats and no mistake.'

Penelope lifted her eyebrows.

'Still, we can't all just fall into cushy billets like my brother and imagine we're owed a living in perpetuity.'

'I'm sure – '

'What's that?'

'I'm sure he doesn't think that.'

'Well, he'd have invited me down – or is it up to Cambridge? – if he thought I deserved it. But I forfeited my chance, I suppose.'

Penelope continued to look puzzled.

'Has he invited *you*?'

'Invited me?'

'To Cambridge?'

'Yes. Yes, he has.'

'Oh, I see.'

'To – to look around.'

'Are you sure?'

'What about?'

'That's all it was for?'

'It was very pleasant.'

'Maybe it was.'

'Oh yes.' Penelope nodded.

'He's a mystery, my brother.'

'Well . . .'

'I used to wonder – '

Penelope looked away: at the young couple at the next table, who sat holding hands.

'When we were at Tregarrick, I mean. I used to picture what it would be like – if he took a shine to you – '

Penelope shook her head.

'*I* don't know either,' she said. 'About Oliver. We'll just have to wait and see.'

'We *have* waited.'

'With men – it isn't the same. *When*, I mean.'

'Only that they do, for God's sake.'

Penelope couldn't think of a reply to that. She drank from her cup. She glanced at the mass of prime mink thrown on to the back of the chair: at Valerie's crossed legs as she sat back and let her eyes scan the room, among the rich and protected.

*

272

She was surprised by the chasteness of her 'affair' with Leopold – which wasn't really.

It was a delicately old-fashioned, most fastidious arrangement whereby they associated with one another – but not in public, and never cohabiting. He plied her with gestures and tokens of his affection, he said everything she could ever have hoped to hear from him, but he stopped just short – so crucially and frustratingly short – of giving his words a concluding, physical declaration. He chose not to prove himself in the deed, by action. They didn't, in the very simplest language of all, sleep together.

She thought they must eventually, that it was only a temporary hold-up, a little hiccup, but it proved to be not so. She tried to persuade him, even teasing and cajoling, but he was quietly, tenderly adamant. He didn't excuse himself or apologise, which was why she knew it went so deep with him, into his nature and his sense of self, and that she couldn't respect him and care so much for him without also accepting finally his way of thinking.

She was cautious about how she expressed herself, but she also wanted him to be in no doubt.

'It's what I wish most,' she said, 'in the world.'

'But not now, Penelope,' he said, clearly in distress. 'I don't think – '

She thought he meant 'later' by 'not now', but she was to appreciate in time that 'not now' meant, it could have happened once but we've come too far since then, I care far too much for you. There and then, though, she wasn't able to appreciate the situation fully. It even occurred to her that he might be teasing her, to make her admit all her longing to him: she was very willing to admit any such thing, only too willing, and she did so, but it still didn't change his mind. He repeated, simply and persuasively, 'It has to take two, Penelope,' and she felt there was no effective answer she could give him in response.

He told her he was fifty-seven.

'I'm *thirty*-seven.'

'I could be your father – just.'

'Sugar Daddy?'

'God forbid.'

She smiled.

'You don't see me as that?' he asked her. 'Do you?'

'No,' she said. 'Not at thirty-seven.'

He had a small flat in a mansion block on Baker Street. When the windows at the front were open, the sound of traffic was like the swell of the sea. They might have been stranded on an island.

So she didn't think about the difference in their ages, an island offering her no comparisons. She hadn't mentioned Guy more than two or three times, and he hadn't referred to his wife any oftener. She prepared meals for them both, like fancy picnics. The television picture had become foggy, and they decided not to have the set repaired. She found a pack of cards, and he taught her cribbage, whist, bridge, and simple poker. They listened not very hard to the radio.

Staying on and lying alone in bed she might hear signs of life in the building, but rarely. The sea of cars was always there, however, shiny urban tides marooning her, and sleep would drown her painlessly in their muffled roar.

It was his kindness and courtesy she'd fallen for, she decided. She felt wholly safe with him. Even being Guy's wife hadn't convinced her as much as being Leopold Kaplan's companion (and, when it came, his mistress) that she wanted to *care* for a man, to give *him* protection and succour.

It didn't concern her that she wasn't the first, and might not be the last. He didn't talk about that and she didn't ask, and it wasn't an evasion of the subject, it simply didn't matter, not with that surging sea-song in her ears.

Standing at the window one December afternoon, watching the car headlights, she suddenly remembered Guy stopping the car at a street kerb one winter's afternoon of early dark and dipped headlamps and telling her he would only be gone a couple of minutes, he had a message to deliver. He had disappeared into a shop: a furrier's. When he came back she'd asked him, what for? He'd told her the man was going into the shop to collect his wife's fur. Instead of asking who 'the man' was, she had unnecessarily enquired if it was a new coat or being refurbished.

That was all she remembered. They'd driven off after that, to wherever they were going. The memory had been forgotten until now. For a few seconds it shone like a new penny, then it dulled.

She was left at the window in the darkened room looking down on Baker Street, at the first flakes of gritty serious snow floating into the tracks of the headlights.

And so they were loving friends, but not – not ever, as it turned out – 'lovers' in the sense in which the word is understood by the world. The hours they spent in one another's company amounted in toto to several weeks, but none of them occurred after midnight. Of course she suspected that there must be someone else, other than his wife. She quizzed him as subtly as she could, but she never caught him out, and it *then* occurred to her, if there was someone else and there was also herself wouldn't he probably be the man who would take all he could get, double-fun – and so not a man like Leopold Kaplan at all? Afterwards she felt ashamed of having allowed herself to devise such a feeble argument: he had deserved so very much better of her than that, and she began to persuade herself that she wasn't worthy of him.

Then she attempted to reconcile herself to this state of affairs. She continued to believe that it would happen eventually, and that she must be patient: maybe he was only nervous, or timid, or concerned that he might lose her, or there again he might have been a little in awe of her or wary of their professional relationship, or even warier of the simple, indisputable fact that she was twenty years younger than him. But she didn't believe that the discrepancy in years was in her favour. Does he think, she wondered, that I may be looking for a father figure? She couldn't dismiss the idea completely, and for a while she was rather less sure of her own motives. After some gentle mental readjustments, however, she convinced herself she ought to put such considerations out of her head and that she *could*: her father-loss was related to her work only: Camilla Holt's search in her new novel was not the same kind as her own, how could she have confused the two worlds as she must have done . . .?

Maybe, she would think, Guy and Leopold Kaplan are in a kind of balance, an equilibrium. At the beginning of her new life with her mentor she actually tried to calculate for whom she felt more or less love, him or Guy, but it was demeaning to consider, and she soon realised that shame should have no part in her ways of thinking.

She didn't like to imagine beyond their immediate future together, which went no further than tomorrow. She hadn't anticipated Guy's death, although she had started to ponder latterly, just a few times, what the years ahead might have in store for them: if she'd known better, she would have thought less about the might-be to come, and then she would have been able to savour more of the present, to give her more to remember of him. Unhappiness had taught her something valuable, and she respected too much that sad time following the accident to ignore its solid little nut of truth: that the present should be lived in, with all a person's force, until you touched its edges and limits. The nature she had inherited went against that licence more than a little, but now she needed to overcome the resistance of her temperament, which was as much her mother's as her own. Abstinence and self-denial weren't the appropriate discipline any more; during the war even the slowest-thinking washerwoman or kitchen-skivvy had picked up that much.

She settled down to their lunches, and their walks in the park, and their late afternoons and early evenings. Twice he managed a weekend, he booked accommodation and they went away: on arrival they would be shown up to separate rooms, and she could appreciate by now that it was for more than appearance's sake.

She didn't love him any less for his restraint. It wasn't 'old-fashioned' after all, she had to acknowledge: modern hypocrisy was no match for the long-ago sort. This was his own morality deciding, from his own character and experience, and she couldn't overturn that without a superhuman effort. Love needs to be mutual, she knew, but – the small detail of their sleeping arrangements apart –

they were very precisely balanced in their fondness for one another. When she wasn't with him, she was able now not to think about him constantly, but instead at frequent intervals, and of course with great warmth, in the certainty that her life was so much improved. She applied herself to Camilla Holt's story, and she did her best work in years, to impress him. She stopped the reviewing and the jobbing journalism that had briefly supplemented her income and she accepted what he told her, that it needn't take her two or three years to write a novel, not if she had the confidence of her talents. She couldn't *not* have faith once she'd listened to his insistent arguments on the point. For certain hours in the day she retreated into her imagination, and she realised that it was the most and the best that she could offer him in exchange for all that she felt she was never done taking from him.

3

It was the name that drew her eye to the story in the newspaper. *Sonia Pettman*. A woman had been detained by police in connection with undisclosed activities that concerned events in Notting Hill last year. She had been apprehended not in London but in Bristol. A spokesman for the city's police was quoted as saying that forces across the country had been given the names and details of certain persons purported to have directly or indirectly assisted in inciting a riot. Investigations were continuing. In the meantime, according to the newspaper's report, it was expected that Sonia Pettman would face charges, to be brought within the next twenty-four hours.

She kept buying newspapers, several titles, and scanning them assiduously. But the case wasn't referred to in any of them.

Of course it might have been that the charges had been dropped. She had no way of knowing. Finally, itching to learn something, she telephoned a newspaper office in Bristol. A journalist agreed to phone her back, out of his working hours. He told her that an 'embargo', as it was diplomatically called, had been placed on their reporting the matter. She asked why, and he told her that it was a sensitive issue. She asked him 'why' again. Because, he said, it was conceivable that a cell of political activists – anarchists – were involved. Who? Names from the past. Why couldn't the reporters do their job of work, though? Because investigations were being kept under wraps, because the woman's colleagues must have been tipped off by now, but the police wanted them to remain as much in the dark as possible. Anyway . . .

' "Anyway"?'

'There may be other people involved. Who've kept themselves well out of trouble. The police mean to work on them too, weed them out.'

'You said, they were names from the past – '

'From Mosley's time. His followers. Blackshirters.'

'Sonia Pettman was?'

'Yes. It's not the first time she's been arrested. She's changed her name before, gone abroad. But Notting Hill was too good a chance to miss.'

For days afterwards Penelope couldn't put Cheriton Court out of her mind. But she couldn't put *in* any more than was already there, and what she remembered was its sedate charm, its grace and favour ambience, the numbed contentment and inertness of her life then, in that brief interlude of months.

Sonia Pettman had shown her how to varnish her toenails and the tricks she could play with her hair and how walking with a straight spine and erect head could give you a control of any situation you might find yourself in, and she remembered every time she picked her way along the leaf-strewn pavements that autumn how a person's character is gleaned – stolen sometimes – in tiny parts from other people's.

'How did you start? Writing fiction?'
   'I found I was living on my wits' ends, pretty much.'
   'Why was that?'
   'Living in London during the Blitz. Everything was edgy: every*one*. You did what you felt you had to get done, as quickly as you could.'
   'You wanted to write?'
   'I hadn't thought I was capable of it. But things seemed to come to a head then, for so many people. So I began.'
   'And you continued?'
   'After the war I concentrated more. One way and another money was a bit tight. So that spurred me.'
   'Did you do journalism?'
   'Not then. I didn't know the Fitzrovia set. I didn't have contacts. I preferred writing fiction. It was just something I found I wanted to do, arrange things as a story: events, people.'
   'As therapy?'
   'Well . . . perhaps.'
   'It was autobiographical?'
   'It isn't so simple as that. It was and it wasn't. That's all right if you believe in the distinctions – '
   ' "Distinctions"?'
   'Between private and public. Between then and now. What happens and doesn't happen. Actuality and fiction. Doing and dreaming.'
   'You *don't* hold to these "distinctions", as you call them?'
   'Maybe not.'
   'You won't say? Or you don't know how?'
   'Which answer do you want me to give you?'

A car with a woman driver passed up and down the street several times, travelling very slowly.

Penelope watched from the sitting-room window. The car slowed down every time it passed the house. She couldn't see the details of the woman's face through the afternoon's reflections on the window glass, although she could tell it was this house she was looking at.

It happened another day, a few weeks afterwards, on another weekday afternoon. She remembered the make and model of car from before – a Mayflower – and noticed the same woman at the wheel. More shadows blotted the side-window. The woman, she could tell, had pale skin. Again it was *this* house which was occupying her attention.

It hadn't anything to do with *her* necessarily. There were the Morgan-Huwes on the ground floor, and their Norwegian scientist in the garden flat.

278

The car cruised along the street again and she contrived to watch, hoping that the shadows of clouds and a tree's branches were enough to hide her from view.

No, it hadn't anything to do with *her* necessarily. But why then, out of everything that was happening in London, why should the sensation be so strong in her – like a little shock of current to her bodily system – that something connected them, the woman behind the windscreen and herself?

Another day – in the West End, as she was walking down Haymarket – she went hot and cold several times in succession, and could only think that someone had walked over her grave.

She stopped on the pavement and turned round. Ten yards behind her she saw, spinning her head round to look in a shop window, the woman she'd been aware was following her down the staircase in Fortnum's. She wore a headscarf over hair with a steely blue tint and she had pulled up the collar of her raincoat. The coat's full cut didn't hide her hip girth. Her face was as pale as a wartime complexion.

Penelope turned away. There was a break in the traffic and she hurried across the street. She made for the corner, then took a right angle into Pall Mall. She continued walking. It wasn't until somewhere about the Oxford and Cambridge Club that she suddenly wheeled round.

This time she was about twenty yards behind her, hampered by thick ankles, but it was unmistakably her. There was no shop window for her to look into, so the woman had to make use of the traffic for a diversion, also an escape. She raised her hand high and a taxi-driver who was passing stepped on his brakes. The woman got into the back, lowering her head with some difficulty; she slammed the door shut, and the taxi drove off.

Penelope looked about her. But no other taxi appeared and only a few seconds of time were allowing the woman to make her getaway. Cars and vans and buses sped past, and taxis with fares. When she looked along the street towards Trafalgar Square she wasn't able to tell *that* taxi apart from any of the others. Her tracker had vanished with as much cunning as a sorceress in sparks and flames.

She picked up the telephone receiver. Pips warbled out of pitch, then coins – two – dropped into a box. A huge echo shrank to fit a woman's voice enquiring briskly, 'Hello? Miss Smith?'

'No, I'm sorry. You must have the wrong number.'

'That isn't Miss Smith?'

The caller's accent might have pulled itself up in the world.

'No, I'm afraid – '

'I'd like to speak to Miss – '

'You have the wrong number, I'm afraid.'

'I'm sure I – '

'I'm sorry.'

'Who *am* I speaking to, please?'

'This . . .'

Penelope stopped herself. The tone in the woman's voice had changed; it carried too much curiosity, more than the situation merited. She heard a mouthful of breath being held in.

'I'm not who you want.'

'But – '

'I'm not Miss Smith.'

'But if you told me who you are – '

'I'm afraid you have the wrong number.'

'You might know how – '

'I *don't* know, I'm sorry.'

She replaced the receiver, then she sat down on the chair beside the table. Her knees and arms felt weak. Of course it hadn't been a wrong number at all. She had distrusted the voice and its officiousness. A couple of times recently the telephone had rung; she'd picked up the receiver to speak but the line – a house or office line – had gone dead in her ear. Now she believed those calls had been no accident either. Unless the Exchange was to blame, which was unlikely.

She was sitting puzzling on a reason when the ringing started again, making her jump. She stared at the telephone. This wasn't any ordinary fault in the mechanism.

She stretched her arm, reached out her hand, then thought better of it.

She stood up.

The ringing continued for a full minute or so. In the silence of the flat and the building it sounded deadly urgent.

She paced across the hall, from one side to the other, and back again, and back again. Then the ringing stopped.

She stood listening to the blood in her neck, to the quiet in the flat.

She wasn't in a mood for silence and introspection, she decided, and walked through to the sitting-room. She turned on the radio and swung the wand to a channel with music. '*Could you coo, could you care? I never had the least notion, that I could fall with so much emotion . . .*'

She sat down on a chair by the window. The street-lamps were on, turning the blue light pearly. Moment by moment, it seemed, the last of the daylight was draining away. A car – a Mayflower – passed slowly along the street, driving on its side-lights as if it meant to draw no attention to itself. The driver was an indeterminate shape and sex behind the glass. The car slowed when it was almost opposite the house but after a couple of seconds it picked up speed again. She watched the red tail-lights and the two brake-lights blinking on the concealed-crossing. She recalled the phone call and the alertness in the woman's voice: what had been the significance, if any, of the name 'Miss Smith'? She thought for a while, repeating that most common name in the city, in the

280

country, but she could come to no conclusion, it didn't mean anything to her, it surely belonged to no face or voice of her acquaintance.

When she was in Harvey Nichols she always made a point of visiting the millinery department. So, being in the shop one late March morning, she did as had become one of her Knightsbridge rituals and inspected the new French straw boaters set up on their stands. An assistant explained the choice. 'It's the "Gigi" look, madam,' she said, and left her to try one on.

She walked across to a full-length mirror on the wall, adjusting the rake of the brim and thinking she was too old to pass herself off as an ingénue. That guise wasn't at all appropriate to her, given the current state of affairs.

In the glass she suddenly noticed behind her a pair of men's feet, obtruding from beneath a three-panelled full-length mirror on a stand. He might have been with someone, but there were very few other women in the department, in that corner of it, and she'd noticed on past visits that the presence of male staff was not encouraged. (A shop employee in a dark suit and *brown* shoes?) She continued to look but didn't know why she should be concerning herself with what ought to have been quite unimportant to her: two men's shoes turned in the same direction as herself, and motionless.

She tried attending to the hat, but found her eyes returning to the feet in the dark tan shoes. She turned round and walked back to the display-counter. Before she removed the hat she picked up a hand-mirror and positioned it so that she could look behind her. The shoes were still visible beneath the triptych, and angled so that the toes were again pointing in her direction. She could see two trouser turn-ups, but the panels of mirror were too tall for her to catch a glimpse of the man's head.

Again she was stumped. Why on earth should it possibly matter to her who was standing there and for what purpose?

She glanced at her watch. At quarter-to-eleven of a weekday morning, honest men should have had better things to do. And she had seldom seen the department so quiet.

She was taking off the hat when she heard an assistant's voice. It was asking if she could be of some assistance.

Penelope turned round and found it wasn't *she* who was being addressed but whoever was behind the mirror. She heard some words being mumbled, nothing she could make out, then she saw the feet walk away. He emerged from behind the mirror but with his back to her: a man of medium height, strands of hair teased across a balding crown, wearing charcoal flannel trousers and a knee-length belted overcoat in a dull donkey-brown tweed. And those brown shoes, which didn't make a sound – not even a squeak – as he stepped off the runner of carpet on to linoleum and made for the staircase.

She mused as she set the hat back on its stand. She smiled at the assistant, who knew her to be an occasional purchaser, and walked towards the panelled mirror. She stopped when she reached it and looked carefully, and realised that if you were to stand very close you could see through the gaps between the hinges that held the panels together.

She took a little longer to examine the other wares before making her departure. She didn't relish an encounter with the man, whatever the explanation for his voyeuristic antics could possibly be. She delayed two or three minutes and then she purposefully pressed the 'Down' button by the lift doors.

One afternoon in the next week, again when she was up in the West End, she felt dead on her feet and went into Madeleine's on Brook Street for a coffee.

As she was being seated at a table, she happened to look over her shoulder and saw a reluctantly balding man with a sandy moustache and wearing a donkey-brown belted overcoat pass the window.

She immediately changed chairs so that she would be sitting looking out at the street. She couldn't have taken her eyes from the window more than half-a-dozen times in those thirty or forty minutes.

Another afternoon she had tea in Harrods, in the top-floor restaurant. She was looking among the customers for potential 'copy' and not for a belted donkey-brown overcoat. When she saw one hanging from a coat-stand she sat bolt upright and stared at it. Then, as circumspectly as it was possible to do such a thing, she trawled with her eyes among the occupants of the other tables.

Only one person didn't correspond with whom she expected to see: a few tables away, directly facing her, sat a single man in a business suit, with a folded newspaper laid on the cover; he had both elbows on the table, and his hands clasped his forehead. All his attention was for the newspaper, but it was too much attention. A waitress rolled a cake-trolley to his table and he had to half turn round to inspect what was on it: then it was that she spotted the strands of hair damped down on to his balding crown and the sandy moustache. Her eyes passed between the man and the donkey-brown belted overcoat hanging from the hook on the stand.

She didn't know what to do: whether to get up and leave there and then, or to sit it out. In the end she didn't move from her chair, but it was done through cowardice, less a case of sitting it out and defying him than cowering and trying to look like any other housewife up in Town for the day and hoping that his eyes wouldn't at any point engage with hers.

Their eyes did meet at one point however. His settled on her for those few seconds with such deliberateness and accuracy that she knew there was no possibility of doubt.

The telephone rang one evening. Penelope ran through from the study and picked up the receiver, expecting to hear Leopold.

'Miss Milne?'

She recognised it as the voice who had asked to speak to 'Miss Smith'.

'Yes,' she replied.

282

'Would you have a morning free this week? Thursday, perhaps?'

'Could you tell me – ?'

'If we meet at the Savoy, mid-morning, all – as they say – will be revealed.'

'I don't quite see – '

'It's not my wish to waste your time, Miss Milne. I realise you're a busy woman.'

'Can I ask how you found my number?'

'I've taken a liberty, you're right. You're ex-directory. That is Mr Kaplan's doing, I presume?'

'I . . .'

Suddenly she knew, without asking. The inflexible neck in Geneva, the famous enigma of Ethel Kaplan, the former 'looker' now seldom seen.

'Thursday then? The Savoy lounge? At eleven o'clock. I would appreciate it – '

Penelope was curious, more than courageous. She remembered the man in the belted donkey overcoat, and he seemed to be explained: her hired watcher. It must have been important to the woman to discover all that she could. She must have known more about her habits by now than anyone, except herself. That was a very odd, very unsettling thought. It was intimidation she was practising on her, of a professional and expensive kind, and she had precalculated that her quarry would respond in only one possible way.

A wind blew her along the Embankment to their rendezvous. Clouds scudded busily across the blue sky, and the ripples on the river caught the sun. The stone of the buildings sparkled. Daffodils were in bloom in the hotel garden.

While she walked there she didn't feel afraid of what was about to take place. Inside the hotel however her courage deserted her. She spent a long time sitting in front of the mirror in the ladies' room and thought herself obliged to drop half-a-crown into the attendant's saucer on her way out.

Mrs Kaplan's taxi drew up under the canopy on the dot of eleven o'clock. Penelope heard the doorman say the name and watched the arrival from the other side of the foyer. She only remembered a *presence* from the dining-room in Geneva, not an individual.

A long fur coat didn't disguise the woman's stockiness. She had plump ankles, and propelled herself with a hip-roll movement. It was the woman from Fortnum's, who'd followed her down Haymarket and along Pall Mall.

She aged ten years in Penelope's calculations as she watched her walking towards her. A powdered face showed beneath the veil on her hat, and she made out two eyes scrutinising her keenly, already aware of who she was.

An introduction wasn't necessary. The veil was lifted back, over severe, spun blue hair. The eyes were very small, as if they'd collapsed into the puffy cheeks: but they continued to examine her, two piercingly green precision instruments. The agency rumours had it that she'd once been considered attractive, and quite enticingly so, but now she was fifty-five – at least – and the years hadn't chosen to spare her. She looked concerned, worry-worn.

She held out her hand. Penelope took it: the gloved fingers had a nervous person's perverse strength in them.

'I suggest some tea. Not coffee. Yes?'

Penelope nodded.

'This is one place where they know how to make the stuff. Although the Beau-Rivage isn't bad – '

Serving staff hovered about them, and they were led across a pink and blue lounge. They were seated, and Mrs Kaplan was humoured about the weather. When she enquired about who was staying, she was told that Mr Coward had just left and Mr Stokowski had arrived the previous evening. Mrs Bogart was due in the afternoon.

Penelope watched her eyes blink as they received the information, recording and retrieving like camera shutters. The green of the pupils was fiercely green.

'This is the place to be,' she heard her say. The voice was best Home Counties, but voices can be acquired: there was a man in Adelaide Road who could change your accent and the world's response to you in anything from three days to a fortnight. There was some croakiness, not unlike her husband's: which might have been accounted for by the cigarettes that appeared, marshalled inside a gold case.

The head waiter was dismissed with a smile.

'Do you smoke, Mrs Gerrault?'

'I – '

The case was passed across to her. Penelope fumbled with the thin cigarettes beneath the band. She noticed an inscription on the lid, which perhaps she was meant to notice. 'For Ethel, Will you love me in December? Leopold.'

A flame leapt at her from a gold-and-silver lighter and she instantly drew back.

'Perhaps – when I've had some tea – '

Mrs Kaplan's mouth widened to a smile.

'Just as you like – '

The cigarette was taken from between Penelope's fingers and returned to the case. The other cigarette remained unlit, however.

'Well, I'm glad we've been able to meet,' Mrs Kaplan began, not wasting any time.

The adjective was a misnomer, Penelope felt: an Arctic politeness.

'Because I had my back to you in the Beau-Rivage. If I'd been able to read the future, I'd have made sure I took a better look.'

Penelope lowered her eyes.

'Now, Mrs Gerrault, I think we have certain things we need to talk about. Do we not?'

At that moment the bell on a police car sounded from the Embankment. Penelope felt her stomach shrink. She'd been a fool to come, more of a fool than she'd been about all the rest, she should just get up and go.

At the next moment the tea appeared. The table was relaid in seconds. A waiter poured two cups of Lapsang from the pot; on Mrs Kaplan's bidding he added a slice of lemon to one and – when Penelope was asked – some milk to hers. Milk, she guessed, wasn't the correct choice.

'Well now, Mrs Gerrault – '

Mrs Kaplan took one sip, then another, and replaced the cup in the saucer.

'I think we should start with the subject of money.'

Penelope swallowed her mouthful of tea in a gulp. She rattled the cup back into its saucer.

'I dare say it's what's on your mind. You've been looking at me and you've worked out I'm worth something. Enough to be a regular in this place.'

Penelope shook her head.

'I see, you're more tactful, are you? Well, I do think we should get the subject out of the way. I suppose you've got a figure in your head.'

Penelope felt she was on fire, her chair was in flames.

'I don't – I'm afraid – '

'Of course, in films they always come out with lines like "But this is blackmail!" and the other person says how much they dislike that word and that it should all be much more – well, businesslike.'

'I'm not – I really – '

'That's very commendable of you, my dear.'

'I don't understand – "blackmail" – ?'

'Yes, that's another line they use. You *do* know your films, don't you?'

'No. I'm sorry – ' Penelope shook her head. 'What d'you mean?'

'I mean, what is silence going to *cost*?'

'But I can't afford to pay – to pay you, money –

'What's that?' Mrs Kaplan's eyes suddenly shone with amusement; she sat back in her chair and laughed at the joke. 'You can't – for *me*? – oh, that's splendid, my dear.'

There was no malice in the laughter. Penelope couldn't understand, not a thing.

A waiter walked past and smiled at the sound, as if everything were harmless and done just in a spirit of fun.

'But to be *serious*, my dear.' The laughter cleared slowly, the smile took several seconds longer to narrow. 'We must come to *some* arrangement. I can afford it, I admit that to you. *You* ought to be able to have treats too: not *here*, my dear, if you don't mind. Leopold gives me a wide berth: the Savoy is mine, the Ritz is his, although I *do* tell him the Connaught is a mite more discreet, and original. But he imagines he knows best.'

Penelope's slowness must have been undisguisable.

'Do you really *not* understand, Mrs Gerrault?'

'I'm afraid – I'm afraid not.'

'How much, then, *do* you? Understand?'

'Very – very little. I'm sorry.'

Mrs Kaplan tipped her head on one side, as if she couldn't quite believe that such naïvety was possible. Then after some silent deliberation she seemed prepared to allow her guest the benefit of the doubt.

'About Leopold – ' she said, and Penelope felt her face firing hotter. ' – I've been aware of the situation from the start of course.'

Penelope nodded, and looked down at her cup. She reached forward to pick it up, to have the distraction of movement.

'It's only common sense, to be defensive.'

Penelope mumbled, with her lips closed.

'I am – shall we say? – rather anxious to hold on to my husband, my dear.'

'But I don't – it's just – '

'Just what? High jinks?'

'No.'

'A lark? Making merry?'

'No, not – '

'I don't mean you're going to lure him or he'll make off with you.' Mrs Kaplan smiled again, but more pointedly. 'My husband isn't quite so foolhardy as that.'

Penelope fixed her eyes on the disappearing smile.

'He's too practical. There are women with a prior claim, chronologically, from the past. Prior to your own, that is. Or he *could* just leave me: he could set you up – properly, I mean. With a little caravanserai – '

Penelope stared at the tea in her cup.

'He *could* get a flat, say, and – Bob's your uncle – you'd move in. Or someone else would move in, in the future. So I *do* want him to be – well, satisfied, as it were. But I'd like *you* to be sensible: don't *provoke* him to do it. Don't *seduce* him. Please. Let's keep it – well, English and ladylike. *Fascinate* him. And don't give him everything. Keep something back, Mrs Gerrault. I didn't keep enough back, you see.'

Penelope was aghast.

Mrs Kaplan sipped from her cup.

'Did you mean, Mrs Gerrault – you really *haven't* done this before?'

Penelope lifted her eyes.

' "Done this before"?'

'This sort of thing? Been a man's mistress?'

'It – it was an accident.'

'I do rather *like* you, my dear. Of course he's had other women. *Some* have tried to get him. One almost did.'

Penelope stared at the wedding ring, or the glimmer of gold where the band had almost sunk into the flesh of the finger.

'Once he was infatuated with someone. It lasted two years. But we had an arrangement, you see: a private arrangement, she and I: I bought her clothes, so she wasn't pestering him for money. He'd have given it to her, he's so generous: but then maybe he'd have thought, why not go the whole hog, give her the lot? And men at that age are so unpredictable.'

286

Forgetting the cigarette lying on the tablecloth she pulled another from the case, lit it, and drew on it.

'If we had children, it'd be different. But there's only me to hold him. And he was already engaged when we met, you see, so I was the siren myself, in my own way. Now I have to make sure that history doesn't repeat itself.'

She considered the cigarette burning between her squat, pudgy fingers. The stones of other rings glittered fitfully.

'I haven't anything else, you see. No contingency plans. This is it, Mrs Gerrault. This is my life.'

Penelope nodded.

'So – what I'm asking – is that you occupy my husband *enough*. If he asks you – for more – you will tell him that you prefer things just as they are. That you have your pride. There, that's another line from the films – '

She breathed again on the cigarette, but didn't smile this time.

'I'm a commonsense woman, I hope, Mrs Gerrault. A – what's the word? – a pragmi-, pragma-'

'Pragmatist.'

'That's it, yes. You have to know something to survive, Mrs Gerrault. I've survived *this* long at least.'

Penelope crossed her legs: unconsciously, then she saw that the woman was looking at her, at her legs.

'Frankly, I can't compete,' Mrs Kaplan said. 'I'm sixty-three. I tell him fifty-nine, but he knows. I thought I'd hold out, but I didn't. I ended up in Brighton hotels having afternoon teas and listening to the trios and getting very sorry for myself. Let me warn you about that, my dear.'

'I – ' Penelope swallowed. 'Sometimes people – aren't quite what they seem.'

Through the cigarette smoke Mrs Kaplan watched her, with the original keenness back in her eyes.

'This is social chitchat, my dear. I don't know *who* you are. I don't really have a clue. I don't want to. Know about your history, I mean.'

'Why – why did you – ?'

'Suggest we meet? To see what sort of impression I got of you. To guess. What you might be capable of. I don't care for people's histories, but I've become quite a shrewd judge of character. Over the years. It's become a kind of sixth sense almost. Time gives as it takes away, you see.'

The smile reappeared, and the eyes retreated into the puffy, powdered whiteness of her cheeks.

Penelope turned to look at the encounters being conducted at the other tables in the room. Perhaps the two of them appeared to be old friends, with more than just the same man in common.

'It's not quite like that,' Penelope heard herself saying as she continued to look away. 'With your husband.'

'What?'

'I don't *care* for him.' (Help me God, she thought.) 'It – it's just an arrangement.' (Help me just this once, please God.) 'For convenience.'

She closed her eyes: and opened them again on the flowery swirls on the blue carpet.

'I never thought that it was more, my dear.'

Penelope lifted her eyes to Mrs Kaplan's, which were attending only to the gold cigarette case.

'My husband has these – enthusiasms. I believe they mean something special to him. He likes clever women. Talented women. It doesn't matter if they don't like him. In fact – I think he prefers that they don't. It doesn't matter to him that – that he gets nothing back.'

'Why – why are you worried, then?'

'Because I watch him in the house. Sometimes he gets so unsettled, it's like – ' Penelope thought she heard the accent slip ' – like it suffocates him and he just wants out. It's a feeling I get: another instinct, you know? I'm a Jew – half-Jew – and it's never a Jew he goes with.'

'You're still worried, though – '

'He comes back to me, but I'm never sure he's going to. It's a feeling again, I can't explain it. Everything in the house is just-so, it's a beautiful house, I've made it beautiful, a real home. Sometimes he likes that, he's happy, then other times it's as if he can't stand it, it's all on top of him and smothering him, the furniture, the carpets. Every Jew wants to make a good home. I made him a good home – '

The head waiter was standing by their table.

'Is everything to your satisfaction, Mrs Kaplan?'

'Just *lovely*, Norman,' she said, and beamed broadly.

This, Penelope realised, is how she lives her life: it's a precarious high-wire act. Up on the flying trapeze and no net.

The head waiter bowed, smiling, and continued his progress round the room. Mrs Kaplan crossed her hands on her lap: the bright Hatton Garden stones didn't distract from the liver-spots, and Penelope felt uneasy looking.

'I don't want to lose my husband, you see. I'm not sentimental. But as I told you, Mrs Gerrault, I'm a – that word – a Pragmatist. Capital 'P'. It's all I *can* be.'

The memory stayed with Penelope in the months and lives to come: of blue-rinsed Mrs Kaplan sitting in the lounge of the Savoy Hotel with her leopard coat open and a spring morning shining on the just and unjust of the city and her face laden with a sorrow that seemed to belong to the landless, wandering tribes of the Old Testament.

In 1959 someone at a party remembered a story about Borneo in the 1920s.

'There was an English pastor's wife,' the man began. 'It was supposed to have been the heat. Or else the Devil got a hold of her and why shouldn't he in such an improbable place?'

'Yes,' Penelope said, nodding agreement. 'Why not indeed?'

She had never heard the story before and felt inquisitive enough to listen.

'Everything her husband said or did, she started to say or do the opposite. She was the exact reverse. She stayed up at night and slept through the day. She couldn't eat any of the things that he did. He was teetotal, so the only stuff *she* touched now was alcoholic. She was quite comely and found some French dressmaker on Borneo who ran her up some real tarts' outfits. After years of just nodding her head like a good wife, now she didn't agree with him about a single thing. If he said "black", she'd come back with "white", just like that. She never went near the church, of course, and called herself a heathen.'

'A pastor's wife? In Borneo?'

'She cut out all the church business, the flower-arranging and the hassock-repairs. She didn't stay around when any of the church bosses showed up, but she'd take herself off somewhere for a few days and come back without an explanation. Then of course she started flirting, and it went from bad to worse and became more outrageous, and sooner or later it passed beyond that and she was sleeping around. Selectively at first, although maybe it was for revenge. But gradually it was with every Brit Tom, Dick and Harry.'

'What happened?'

'It was a very messy end. The old shooting-party trick.'

'How?'

'Well, an ambush actually. Some of the wives were involved. They hated her, or they were terrified. Anyway, they'd had enough. So they hatched a plan amongst themselves. Something to do with a dummy invitation. She drove herself there, to where she'd been invited (she thought), but the road was treacherous after rains. Undermined, ready to cave in and collapse. They'd guessed, the women. They didn't know positively, but they put their trust in an act of God. And it happened. The road crumbled, subsided, and the car with the pastor's wife in it was sent right over the edge. It was a long drop down and naturally she didn't stand a chance. But it got her out of their lives and maybe they thought they'd be safe from her – or their husbands would be; which was the same thing, because their well-being depended on their husbands and being kept by them.'

When the man had started to tell her, Penelope was sure she had never heard of the pastor's wife. But as the minutes passed and she circulated, finding herself taken up by different people, she felt much less certain of the story's strangeness to her.

Her mother is standing at a window watching the rain tumbling into the garden, cascading off the roof. Her father is somewhere else, not with them, in this house which is their home. Her mother is staring at the rain falling out of a green sky, the same sky which the Sunday hymns call God's. She leans her head on the window glass: it's a slow gesture, done stooping a little forward and inclining her head on her neck, then lowering her brow on to the glass. And all the time the rain drops sheer into their garden. Her father is somewhere else; how simple it might be to have him here, like a lucky wish in Ayah's stories. Rain and more rain, clattering down on the roof; the drainpipes can't cope, the overflow pipes spout. And can she possibly be remembering? Her father's absence, and her mother bending to the windowpane, offering her forehead to the coldness of glass, as if in private prayer.

4

She said she didn't mind where they spent their long weekend he had suggested, so Leopold decided on Torquay. She nodded and told him she approved. It was many years since she had passed through the area, with the Huttons.

They discussed the possibility of their taking the Riviera Express, but in the end he settled on motoring down, in his car not hers, with an overnight stop at a renovated coaching-inn in Salisbury.

It was a pleasant journey, except for an incident on the Saturday morning at a garage in Somerset, when the tank was being filled with petrol.

She saw the youth who was holding the nozzle eyeing Leopold in a hostile way. Then he turned and smiled over his shoulder at his mate behind the garage's grubby window. When Leopold got out to stretch his legs and to pay, the youth in overalls somehow succeeded in simulating an accident – and in doing so knocked the wallet out of Leopold's hand.

Nothing else happened, but the wallet was a very good one, of top-grade ostrich leather, and it was scratched on the side that had landed on the grit. When Leopold climbed back into the car he pretended that it didn't matter, but she took the wallet from him and tried to repair a little of the damage by licking the tip of her finger and smoothing over the marks. She tucked the wallet back into his jacket pocket and he thanked her but said no more about the business.

It was a pleasant journey apart from that, but the recollection of what had taken place took a long time and a good number of miles – most of Somerset – to fade into the background of her thoughts. Every so often she looked across at Leopold and tried to see him as others, strangers, must see him. At school there had been a number of girls from Jewish families (as it happened, most of those related), and she had become used to their creamy complexions and their brown eyes and lightly shadowed upper lips. Leopold's skin wasn't the fine ivory kind like theirs, it was the hue she had always thought 'olive' to be; his eyes weren't brown but a steady blue, a deeper variation on the famous English blue, almost like perse. He had the prominent nose, of course, which wasn't hooked but managed to be long and squat at the same time. The hair on the sides and back of his head was black with a rich sheen which Englishmen's hair tended not to have. He dressed in the bespoke, understated manner a true Englishman is educated to; his voice had a pleasant crack in it, his accent wasn't quite that of a Savile Row gentleman because it carried inside it just the hint of foreignness. He'd told her that he was English-born, so she assumed it was inherited from the generation before, who perhaps had only been able to speak the language patchily.

She still didn't know if she found the difference in his appearance appealing or not. She couldn't be sure how much she was distinguishing between the man who 'represented' her and the man who had told her he always wanted to be more than a friend to her, ever since his first sight of her in the dining-room of the Beau-Rivage. She decided that by not knowing she was being honest to herself, but it also irritated her to be so indecisive, as if really it was her mother and all the ranged phantoms of the past who were preventing her from making up her mind properly. Maybe she was *wishing* to feel she'd had the choice taken from her: but here she was, travelling with him in his Alvis, and she couldn't believe that she would have been doing so without her own private assent.

The hotel in Torquay was, as he had told her and as she might have expected, grand and dignified. If anyone suspected they were not Mr and Mrs Kaplan, which was how they were registered in the Visitors' Book, although occupying separate rooms, there was no letting on. The reception-desk staff and the porters treated them with exemplary deference as did the maître and the waiters in the dining-room (no doubt Jewish money was respected and honoured), and she thought that this must surely have been the very best choice possible.

For dinner he wore a black silk dinner jacket and bow tie and she was glad that she had decided to bring the emerald shantung dress with the wide V-front. She smiled at his attention and his pride in her.

She didn't know why, but for a few moments during the entrée of mousseline of scallops the memory came back to her of the 'Stella Maris' boarding-house, the bare floorboards in the dining-room and the glum silence at the other tables while Guy and she bit their tongues to stop themselves exploding with hysterical laughter; then she was back in the dining-room of the Eden Hotel, with the shutters pulled against a low sun and her future alarmingly transformed from the abstract to the particular and personal. Both memories were compounds of images with feelings; she was spirited out of the present time for several seconds with each, then she found she was chewing the diced scallops in the rich *blanche neige* sauce over and over in her mouth and that she had to make a determined effort to swallow.

'Is it all right?' his concerned voice with the crack in it asked her twice.

'Yes,' she answered him twice. 'Yes, it's lovely.'

It was fine food, as he'd known it would be. She nodded, replenishing her fork. She told herself the past mustn't be allowed to ruin her weekend: *their* weekend.

On the Saturday morning they each slept late in their own bedrooms. She got up at eleven, put on a swimsuit beneath a shift-dress and went down in the lift to the swimming-pool in the basement while he read the newspaper on his balcony. She returned and they had lunch served to them in his small sitting-room.

After that she changed her dress and shoes, made herself up, and they both went downstairs. They inspected the public rooms, read the lunch and dinner menus, and looked at what was for sale in the display-cases; then arm-in-arm they walked outside, into the sunshine.

The hotel was set on a hill, among rhododendrons and feathery palms. Terraced lawns had panoramic views of the sea. There were padded sun-loungers instead of deck-chairs, and tables with raised parasols. The sun was pleasantly warm, hazy behind very high, very thin cloud. The few children they encountered were all well-behaved. The other guests included the new sort, comfortably set up, and also the traditional, staying here because they always had. They all appeared to be responsible citizens; Penelope was reassured, and smiled formally as she passed them.

'How often have you been here?' she asked, inevitably.

'Oh, I come back,' he said. 'Off and on. You know?'

She nodded.

'There's the Manor Gardens. Down there.'

She followed the direction of his index finger, then looked at his hand at the end of his arm, pointing in the way hands used to do on signposts as if they were instructing you in a secret.

'And the harbour.'

'You know it, then?' she asked him.

'A bit.'

She had always felt rather an innocent herself with geography. Maybe that was because she had never been able to get to know particular spots well enough: except one corner of Cornwall, and even then she hadn't been sure where one village lay in relation to another: she had let other people know these things for her, as she had allowed herself to be cushioned against too much in that house.

'Is it how you remember it?' she asked.

'More or less.'

'How far back?'

'Just before the war.'

'Really?'

'The First War.'

She hadn't inquired about his background, thinking – assuming – that perhaps he wouldn't want to have it excavated, that he had travelled a long way in his life to get where he now was.

He asked her if she was warm enough and when she told him 'yes, thank you' he led the way to a couple of the sun-loungers. They sat down and half-reclined. She saw that he was preoccupied; his face seemed to draw in on itself, then his body did the same, so that he appeared to shrink in the chair.

She wasn't expecting to hear what he proceeded to tell her. He spoke quietly, so that they wouldn't be overheard. She sat beside him, quite still and saying nothing.

He explained to her that he'd first come to the town in his childhood. It had been much the same sort of place then: a bit more reserved than it was now perhaps, and it had taken even longer to get to. His family couldn't afford to come, but he was in the position of having what his schoolfriends envied him, a 'rich uncle'. Actually he was a great-uncle. He'd done well from a number of enterprises – stalls in East End markets, a toy workshop in a Bermondsey tenement, a larger toy workshop like a small factory in the next street, a proper factory in Liverpool producing children's clothes, a money-lending business in Manchester and the mill towns. He had retired to Torquay to a gracious house above Babbacombe Bay. Over the years he had made timely gifts of cash and presents to the Stepney branch of the Kaplans; they had politely kept him up-to-date with news about themselves and sent him occasional photographs.

One day Leopold Kaplan Senior, her own Leopold Kaplan's father and nephew of the Torquay Jew, was knocked down in Whitechapel Road by a runaway horse dragging a cartload of potatoes behind it.

'Oh,' she said. 'I'm so sorry.'

'It wasn't quite the end he had in mind for himself.'

'It was a freak accident – I suppose?'

'Maybe.'

'Or was he trying to stop it?'

'If he was, perhaps it was to knock off some of the potatoes.'

'What?'

'Dad had gone off the rails. It wasn't meant to happen in the Jew families. But it got the better of Dad's genes somehow and he went to pot. Bad to worse.'

'I'm sorry.'

'He couldn't keep up with the others. He read books, but they expected him to be good in business, like them. They were always helping out and making me feel guilty. At least Uncle Isak hardly knew us and in Devon he might have been in a foreign country.'

When Penelope's Leopold Kaplan was eleven years old his widowed mother received a letter, a summons from Great-Uncle Isak, who suggested that her youngest son might like to have a look at Torquay. The letter was accompanied by an enclosure: a railway ticket to Torquay and back. The boy's mother had recently sent a photograph of her two sons, taken by their Uncle Solomon. Until he was packed up and ready to go, his mother laughed a lot and told him that his Uncle Solomon was wise like his namesake and was to be blessed for buying that box camera which she had only ever called a fool's toy before: a symbol of the middle-class sin of conspicuous consumption which she had hoped so hard to succumb to herself.

Her son was despatched on the train, all the way to Devon. At Torquay station he was met by a chauffeur; the man in his boots and livery and cap took charge of him and transported him in a long grey motor-car to Denehurst, a sprawling and rather cheerless Victorian edifice set in a tranquil garden of trees which had a look of Palestine about them.

His Great-Uncle Isak was a smaller, sadder man than he'd been expecting to find. He also had exceptionally beady, unreadable eyes, even when he was smiling (in his sad and gentle way) as he showed his great-nephew about the house – like Osborne House in miniature – and its grounds.

There were household staff to look after them both, but Great-Uncle Isak took it upon himself to attend to all the boy's needs personally. He even came upstairs to his bedroom to tuck the sheets tightly beneath the mattress and to turn down the gas in the brackets. Always, even in the darkness before his bedroom door was finally closed, the boy found himself being watched by those vigilant, pin-bright eyes in the doleful face.

One afternoon the two of them went down to Redgate Beach. Running ahead, the boy lost his footing; he fell, and came down on the sharp edge of a rock. He'd cut his shin and it began to bleed. He couldn't stop crying, slow hot tears. When Uncle Isak caught up with him he placed him in a fold in the rock, a tuck like a seat, and undid his top stocking which he himself had had sent up with a pile of clothes from an outfitters in the town. The boy watched as his great-uncle, his dead father's uncle, lowered his head over the injured shin. Then he felt the contact of his tongue, rough and warm, as it lapped at the blood. He was shocked that it was happening, he wasn't sure why, and he went rigid. ('Rigid, I have to stress. But you've been a married woman, Penelope. Rigid, I mean, in a new way – ')

'Something told me it – it wasn't right. A feeling. Even though it was *him*, Uncle Isak, who was a sort of legend. Even though it was Torquay and I was somewhere else and not thinking about London. *How* he did it, on his knees, with his head bowed. As if I was someone to be worshipped.'

The old man stopped licking, but more blood appeared on the wound, and he started again, lapping with his tongue. The second time he stopped, the bleeding also stopped, like a small miracle. The healer helped the patient to his feet; the boy found that he could walk with virtually no pain at all now. Together they made their way back up to the Cove Road (Penelope started when she heard the name again, in such an altered context). Uncle Isak only spoke to ask Leopold could he manage, was his wound hurting him? The boy shook his head, intending to be manful about his injury but truly feeling very little pain.

Back in the grand house, secluded in its sombre garden, no more was said about the matter. But the boy knew from his great-uncle's restlessness that the accident was still in his thoughts. An unease had settled on them, he was aware: the ponderous ritual of meal-times was even more protracted, although he suffered them as best he could, with the same politeness his Uncle Isak had earlier commended him for, as if he had hardly dared to hope to find it in one brought up in Stepney, in such a haphazard, penny-pinching way.

The leg didn't bleed again. Uncle Isak turned his attention to other parts of his great-nephew's anatomy: to his ankle, which pulled and strained, to his thigh, which took a bee-sting; to his elbow when he hit it on a brass doorhandle; to his neck, which acquired a bad crick overnight; to his hand, which swelled with nettle rash in that garden of hidden dangers; to his neck again, when the sun burned it.

Everything that had happened was an accident, Penelope was assured: although psychology might claim he'd *wanted* them to happen. He hadn't, yet it was true that he became used to receiving his Uncle Isak's sympathy and his lapping, curative tongue. Maybe he would have thought no more about the business and accepted it as being another custom of the house if, one day, his dead father's uncle and esteemed relative hadn't lowered his voice to an intimate tone and told him that this method of treatment might best remain their own little secret. As his mouth spoke the words and put a soft chuckle into them, his eyes were very serious and intense. For the first time in his life the boy was conscious of doing deliberate deceit as he allowed the eyes to hold him while he nodded his head and replied 'yes'. Maybe his great-uncle suspected the ruse because his eyes shrank in their sockets: but only momentarily, until the boy could will his most charming smile on to his face. That appeared to placate the old man, and he relaxed a little (in as much as he was ever able to); he took the boy's nod as one of consent or complicity and the most awkward of moments so far in the house called Denehurst was, by a mutual misunderstanding, bypassed.

Over an interval of months – when he was back in London and in a different element – the young Leopold realised that he was in possession of certain 'information' about his revered Great-Uncle Isak which it was in his own gift to either disclose or not disclose. At the same time he came to remember with something very like nostalgia the house enveloped by its garden and the sea-air freedom of Torquay.

He kept his thoughts and reflections to himself, for a whole year, until a letter arrived from Uncle Isak addressed to his mother and suggesting that her youngest son might be allowed to come down to the coast for a second visit – that was to say, if Leopold wanted to and if it were of no inconvenience to anyone. His mother would have rather his sisters had been asked down as well, or instead of their brother – *they* should have had a turn, after all – but she didn't know how to angle for an invitation. So it was that he left London, alone, for a second journey (in the guard's van of the train, at parcel rate), down to the Devon Riviera.

He had developed quite a bit in the twelve months, in the way of Jewish boys, and his great-uncle was quite unable to prevent his eyes resting on him. The boy was fully conscious of the fascination he was exerting. His uncle seemed a couple of inches shorter than he remembered, and a little less imposing, and so a little less unnerving. Mealtimes weren't so daunting as before, because now the boy had the courage to begin – and also end – topics, and to ask for whatever it was he'd seen in the shops that he wanted, which his late grandfather's brother appeared not at all inclined to deny him.

'I can't really explain my behaviour, Penelope.'

'You don't need – '

'I feel quite ashamed of myself.'

'It's all right.'

'I shouldn't be telling you.'

'You don't have to.'

'But – but maybe I *need* to tell you.'

She merely nodded, and was grateful that she inspired that want and compulsion in him.

The rest of the story, she realised, was going to cause pain to them both: an equal pain for *her*, she hoped.

'I became greedy, I don't know why. I really don't. It shouldn't have happened, but it did. I sensed, it was as if Uncle Isak was making a victim of himself. When he gave everyone such a different impression of himself. And I'd also respected him once, just as they all did. I just saw what was weak in him, and weakness like that didn't deserve sympathy. So I thought. And . . .'

She waited until he was ready to tell her.

'Maybe he understood what was happening. He was a shrewd man, except where his failings were concerned. It crossed with the commercial, you see, and there he *was* on sure ground. He gave me pocket-money, and he bought me things. He would put his arm round my shoulders, or push my hair back from my face – that was all. I didn't like it, but I didn't like myself more, for allowing him to do it and saying nothing. Then I got bolder, and I asked him for a bicycle, and I think he had the measure of me then. I knew I was trying to sponge off him, and why: even though it was just a kind of instinct. With me, a bad sixth sense. But I shouldn't be telling you all this – '

'Yes,' she said. 'You *should* tell me – '

He paused for breath, and perhaps for the heart to continue.

'Well,' he began, and the crack in his voice seemed to go deeper, 'I let something out to my mother. Because he wouldn't buy me the bicycle. Or it might've been I was afraid I'd have to pay for the bicycle in some way, by letting him lick another wound with his tongue. I got annoyed with my mother, because I thought she maybe guessed what the situation was – how I was implying – and she'd wanted my sisters to go instead of me because she'd known they'd be safer but still she'd let me go to Torquay. So I had nothing to lose, I thought, even though I had nothing to gain either. So I let something out, and at first my mother didn't pick up on it, or she didn't want to. And then I had to make my point clearer. She couldn't not have understood. And then she became so moral, because I must have made her realise I was really begging – for the bicycle, I mean. And I wanted the anger anyway, because it was as if it was a match for my own, which I wasn't giving an outlet to, letting rip, but which was all bottled up inside me. I didn't want to have to be sorry for anybody, I thought I was above all that. I just wanted to be angry, that was easiest of all. And . . .'

He paused again.

She prompted him, very gently.

'"And"?' she repeated.

'I let it happen. I let her find out. Maybe I was getting bored with it all anyway. Bored – and hating myself.'

'Don't say that.'

'But it's the truth. I did. I despised myself. It ruined everything, feeling like that. And knowing what I did – '

'You just guessed, though. You couldn't have known. Didn't you say that?'

'It was in my nature, sunk down. An instinct – '

'You can't blame yourself for an instinct.'

'The police came to see Uncle Isak. My mother had to tell them, she was forced to: the bloody pride of poverty.'

Penelope didn't speak.

'But it's as if I discovered – how they say – the victim and the oppressor, they're one. One needs the other, each has *willed* the other into their rôle, even the victim. I've never forgotten Uncle Isak. Or *could* forget. There was going to be a police enquiry. But he didn't last longer than the summer. His heart gave out, and everyone said that was the best way.'

'Well . . . well, perhaps it was.'

'What's that?'

'The best way. That he died.'

Her own Svengali looked lost.

'The best way is dying?'

'For your Uncle Isak, I mean.'

'I've always tried to find a reason for it, a pattern. Something that might explain just why I did it. Just to give myself the motive. But . . . I don't think such a thing, that it *can* . . .'

She placed a hand on his wrist.

'Don't, Leopold,' she said. 'Don't fret about it.'

'I don't think I've very much to be proud of, have I?'

'Your job, the agency – '

'No. About Uncle Isak, I mean.'

She was alarmed. She touched his shoulder, then smoothed the hairs on his temple.

'I think – I think this is wrong,' she said. 'To blame yourself.'

He didn't speak.

'It can't do good. And that's what you want, isn't it?'

He lifted his eyes and looked at her, blankly.

'To do good,' she repeated.

'How, though?'

'"How"?' she repeated.

'How is it possible to do something that's good?'

'You *have* done good.'

'No.'

'Yes. I don't know "how" it is, but you have – '

'I don't think we mean the same thing, Penelope.'

'You've done good to *me*. To me, Leopold. And to your wife, I think.'

'Have I?'

'Yes. Yes, you have.'

'It's not much.'

'Doing good to one person, having the good done, that's the most important thing there can be to that person. You saved me at the time I needed to be saved. *That's* not little.'

He touched her cheek with the backs of his fingers, then he kissed her. She felt all the tenderness that was in her welling up, and she tried to conduct it, through her lips, deep into him, into his being, to flush out that age-old sorrow from the space where it had lived for too long.

'Do you mind, Penelope? That I told you?'

They were back upstairs in his sitting-room. They had spent the afternoon in the town, distracting themselves, window-shopping and having tea. She had swum again on their return.

She knew they must come back to the subject.

'I hope you wanted to tell me.'

'Yes,' he said. 'Yes, I think I did.'

'Then I'm pleased. That you felt you could.'

'But it was to be our weekend away together.'

'It *is*,' she said. 'You've helped me to understand you.'

She sat smiling at him with her eyes full of tears. She picked up his hand and held it very tightly between her own. Her breath caught in her throat. She called him 'poor darling'. He seemed so grateful for her simple sympathy, which she felt must be so inadequate. He sat hunched forward on the sofa with his fingers curling round her own. He spoke very quietly; she felt the breath of his words warm on the side of her neck. Two or three times she lifted one of her hands and brushed his hair back over his ears.

In the silence she heard the clock ticking on the mantelpiece, then voices from the garden and barking from somewhere further off, one of those highly-strung, snapping lap dogs that are a peril of hotel corridors. But it was as if she was hearing all the sounds out of context.

She looked at the emptied husk of the man beside her and remembered for an incongruous moment their first long, serious talk about her future, in the imposing, cerebral office of fumed oak in Conduit Street. She pressed his hand between her own. She smiled again, in the same sad way as before, which meant he didn't need to put his thoughts into words for her to comprehend.

'I love you, Penelope,' he said, 'I love you too much to want to sleep with you.'

She was brushing her hair. She stared at him in the dressing-table mirror with her arm and the brush in frozen motion behind her hair.

'Forgive me, Penelope.'

She blinked, several times. Her mouth tried a smile. She shook her head.

'I've been thinking about it all the time nearly. I know – I know it wouldn't be right.'

'Oh please,' she said, 'it doesn't matter. About being right – '

'Being right for *us*.'

'But – nothing's happened, has it? We're just the same – '

'You're too special to me. Too gentle. Too – '

He shrugged.

' – too unselfish,' he said.

She watched him in the mirror. She tried again to smile. This time she couldn't manage.

'Leopold – '

He was staring at the trellis-pattern on the carpet.

'It sounds crazy,' he said, 'I know it does. Crazy, mad. Ungrateful. But I want this to be – unique – '

'But it *is*!'

'I told you that I'd been before,' he said, 'didn't I?'

'Been . . .?'

'To this hotel.'

She replaced the brush on top of the dressing-table.

'With Ethel, of course. Two or three times. But – ' he cleared his throat ' – but another couple of times too.'

She shook her head.

'That doesn't matter,' she said.

'You're too intelligent not to have guessed.'

'Who – ' She didn't know if she should ask.

A pained expression creased his face.

'I liked them, of course. Otherwise I wouldn't have brought them. But I knew – ' he cleared his throat again ' – that it was *just* liking.'

She thought he had aged years since yesterday: he had grown older, more self-contained, more alone even since they'd come upstairs, away from the public gaze.

'I don't care about any of that,' she said.

'But – shouldn't you?'

'No. No, of course not.'

'But it still . . .'

'Still what? Leopold?'

300

' – makes it impossible.'

She sighed, and let her shoulders drop.

'There's a special kind of love,' he said. 'It did happen to me once before. I was – I don't know, twenty-four, twenty-five. The woman was a few years older than me. She was married. Although that wasn't the reason why it went awry, because she had a husband. I worshipped everything about her. We talked and talked: but only talked, though. I thought I idolised her – I thought I was losing my mind to her. Then a chance presented itself. She knew how bad things were with me, I couldn't stop myself telling her.'

He sat down, perching on the edge of the bed.

'It wasn't that she couldn't see other chances ahead for us. Opportunities. There always will be a way. She hadn't any children; her husband wasn't all she'd hoped he would be. But she saw how I was. It wasn't even that she thought I'd be disillusioned if we . . . Just that for both our sakes she felt she had to be – abstracted. Aloof. It was better as a memory. A platonic hope. It was better never to be experienced, the physical part: better to be always anticipated.'

He shrugged.

'I read that about music once,' he said. 'Mozart. How he makes you think you're always on the point of hearing something perfect. And it's always something even better, more perfect, he's leading you towards. Only the most sublime bit never does quite come.'

She turned round on the chair, away from the mirror.

'I – I'm not *afraid* of anything,' she said, as gently as she could.

'But I think *I* am.'

'No – '

'I'm afraid of going back to Ethel afterwards. I can't leave her. We were allies once, the best friends. When I needed that. But people – ' He coughed. ' – they change, of course.'

'You still are, though,' she said. 'Friends. Allies.'

She heard a ghostly question mark in her voice.

'But I know I *might* leave her,' he said. 'Very easily.'

She placed her elbow on the back of the chair and laid her forehead on her hand. She thought she might cry, or scream, or pass out of the room, faint away from what was happening. But her eyes didn't blur, and no cry came out of her, and she didn't keel over.

'I won't ask,' he said, 'if she's been in touch with you. Tried to see you. She – she's clairvoyant, you see. It used to frighten me almost. As if she could *hear* the thoughts in my head as soon as they came to me.'

She didn't reply.

'Not that that has anything to do with it really,' he said. 'I'm not a coward about it. But I have to make up for so much. Even Ethel doesn't know about Uncle Isak. Just that I came here as a boy. No one knows, except you.'

She nodded, but was silent.

301

'I'm just sorry,' he said, 'that I've brought you so far to tell you. So far along the way, I mean. That's unbearable, I know, a man saying, "*I*'ve brought you so far." I only mean – it has to be mutual, giving yourself. And – '

His head hung low between his shoulders, he dropped his eyes to the pattern of diagonals on the carpet.

' – and I don't think – Well, I *know* it can't be – just because . . .'

She crossed to the bed and lowered herself on to the coverlet beside him. She took his hand in hers. She placed her other hand on top.

'You sound so sad,' she said.

'But I'm sure,' he told her. 'That's why.'

'Then we won't,' she said. 'We'll go back tomorrow. Have a beautiful breakfast, and a walk outside, and we'll leave.'

She squeezed his hand. She couldn't quite believe that she'd said what she had.

'You see, Penelope, it's really Uncle Isak's revenge.'

The remark was accompanied by a despondent smile.

'No,' she told him, shaking her head. 'No, it's not that. But I understand. I want you to know I do.'

He pulled himself up and kissed her nose, the middle of her brow, then her mouth. He let go her hand very carefully, and got to his feet.

'I'll go back to my room,' he said. 'We'll have that breakfast tomorrow.'

'A splendid one.'

'Yes.'

From the bed she watched him leave. She had no histrionics, then or afterwards. She returned to the dressing-table and applied herself to brushing her hair. When she finished she stood up and walked over to the bedside table. She turned on the wireless. The wand stood at the Third Programme. Music came up, it sounded – fatefully – like Mozart. She tuned to another programme, the Light. A lush orchestra was playing; she recognised it immediately as Mantovani's. She thought she could cope with 'Moonlight in Vermont', just, but not the Salzburg wunderkind.

There was a rap on the door. She ran towards it, nearly falling against one of the corners of the bed in her haste to reach it. She grabbed the handle, turned it, and threw the door open.

Outside, in the corridor, stood a startled maid, holding fresh white towels folded over her arm.

'Good evening, madam.'

'What?'

The girl looked past her into the room.

'Room service, madam.'

'I – '

'Would you like me to turn down your bed, madam?'

'Yes. Yes, that's fine – '

She stepped back to let her in, then walked through to the bathroom while the bed was attended to. She stood by the basin, turning on the taps full. Through the doorway she saw the girl pulling back the coverlet and the top sheet, making a crisp triangle of them, then laying out her nightdress, letting it ripple over the pillows and the coverlet to the mattress's edge, so that it took the sinuous, sensual shape of a woman posed in submissive abandon.

If only it had been so simple.

They spoke about Great Uncle Isak for the last time on the drive back to London.

He stopped the car in a lay-by.

'It wasn't *your* fault,' she said.

'Wasn't it?'

'No. No, of course not.'

'I wish I could be so sure.'

'But – ' she leaned against the back of the seat, watching him ' – *he*'s the one you should blame. Not yourself.'

'It wouldn't have happened without me.'

'No,' she said. 'No, that's – '

'Yes. Yes, I'm involved all that I can be. Up to my neck.'

'Maybe it would have happened with someone else. Another boy.'

'But it was *me*.'

'You couldn't help that.'

'But I told,' he said. 'I peached, I split, I squealed, I blabbed.'

She shook her head.

'I told on him, blew the gaff. I *knew*. I must have done. So I wasn't an innocent after all.'

'You felt – ' she leaned forward in the seat ' – you felt it was your duty.'

'Why, though?'

'Because – because your uncle had done wrong.'

'Well, if he had, he'd done it. It was over. How did I know, though, that it *was* wrong?'

'You thought – it might happen to someone else?'

'I *wanted* it to be wrong. It wasn't really, though, was it?'

'It was – very odd. It wasn't how a normal person behaves.'

'He wasn't normal. He really let me do what I liked in the house. I could go exploring, whatever I wanted. He let me share his routine. He treated me not as a child, I was an adult.' He closed his eyes. 'And that's what I did to him.'

She sighed, only meaning to sympathise with him. Maybe he misinterpreted the gesture. He opened his eyes again and stared forlornly through the windscreen at the Englishness of poplars and willows, at a prospect of exquisite melancholy.

'I could have done nothing. Maybe it was the suspicion in myself I hated. But *he* had put it there, he caused it. The suspicion. That's how it came out of me – a lie – that he'd taken advantage of me.'

303

'He spared you that.'

'But I realised it could happen.'

'It wasn't just odd then. There was a terrible fault in him.'

'Somehow I forgot all the things that *weren't* terrible.'

'Why have you remembered it for so long?'

'Maybe that's his curse, do you think? Afterwards he wasn't the marvellous uncle who'd done so well, he was sinister, and he'd made his bargain like Doctor Faustus, he'd had his nature perverted. All the time, though, he knew he'd get his way at last; he'd get his own back on me for knocking his house down.'

'*Did* you? Knock his house down?'

'I killed him – '

'No.'

'He didn't last out the year. He died. Oh, comfortably enough, in the middle of the night, in his own bed. A great heart attack, so he didn't have time to know what was happening to him. But he'd been well enough up until then. So I had a kind of murder on my conscience too, you see.'

'He – he murdered your innocence. Your childhood.'

'I don't think you really understand, Penelope.'

'No?'

'No.'

'I – '

'Let's say no more about it. Let's leave it.'

'I wish – I just want to share – '

'You're right, yes. It *was* a long time ago.'

'I just want to – to cheer you up,' she said. 'I don't like to see you so miserable like this.'

He took her hand between his and distractedly made a web of their fingers. She stayed as she was, crouched forwards on the seat, only relieved that she was able to offer him this little capacity in herself, the resource to make some comfort.

5

'Fiedler', she decided, and so she crossed out the *he*'s and *him*'s in the first paragraph. And for herself 'Mona', 'Mona Henderson', not the impersonal *she*'s and *her*'s she'd meant as a modern touch and for discretion's sake.

She was still being discreet, though. It was her theme, that was all: a younger woman meets an older man. Mona Henderson remembers the occasions in her past when men with maturity sitting upon them evoked some response in her. For the first time she considers in full, awful seriousness the loss of her father, and the sudden vulnerability of life at home, as if one wall of the house had fallen whole away and left them open to the general gaze: the specific Generals indeed, who descended on her mother employing expertly co-ordinated ambush tactics. The suburb watched with disapproval; naturally, in the final count, 'the eyes had it'. But she had never recovered from the loss worse than the opprobrium: the echoing lack of a man's tenor in the house to balance her mother's own limited mezzo range.

Mona Henderson has reached here because – She sits at the window watching for her first glimpse of Edward Fiedler's car as it turns into the street. She sits waiting at her window as maidens used to in towers in forests, for the derring to be done that will burst the locks and chains from doors.

She would never publish the book in his lifetime, if ever.

A sheet of notepaper, headed 'Hotel Infante de Sagres, Oporto, Portugal'.

My dearest P,

I was wrong, of course. I should have known not to make the same mistake twice. About being with each other that night, of course. It's only what Ethel thinks, naturally. She *wants* to think so, because it's proof that I came back, that she had the power to hold me, to compel me. So I've done nothing right and my life is so much poorer. I don't mean that selfishly, as it must sound. I don't have enough 'self' left for that, there's so little. Only 'selfishly', because I care to think that there truly was an opportunity, but I proved myself unworthy.

I'm not sure why it should be so important to get this written now. So urgent even. It's after midnight, Ethel is asleep. Why on earth – of all places to be – are we here? It feels like Mars, and I can hardly breathe.

Missing you, missing you, but I have no right.

L.

305

Five days later he was dead.

He expired in the cooking heat of a Portuguese siesta, on a street corner.

She received the news on the telephone from the agency, an hour after his letter landed on the doormat. She was more affected by the contents of the letter, if it was possible to distinguish. She did cry, but calmly, and without letting go of herself. She took down the books he'd had a hand in her producing and leafed through them without reading the sense on any of the pages.

She took three tumblers of scotch before setting out for the funeral at Golders Green. At a set of traffic lights on North End Road she was afraid she was going to have second thoughts and instead furrow-tracked her mind on what would seem to have nothing to do with the day. Her mind selected an afternoon at Tregarrick, any afternoon, with Oliver spouting Ancient Greek at them and Valerie and herself luxuriating in the sense of time never ending.

At the crematorium she stood, a little unsteadily, with some of the agency staff, but was nodded forward to a pew by overseer Miss Carmichael, to join the notables.

In her whisky haze it took her a while before she spotted the widow. Her view was obscured by hats and a spray of white orchids. She was attending meanwhile to the service, which was tactfully Gentile and im-personal. Several times she took a handkerchief from her bag and blew her nose and she was aware of heads turning to look at her: the air was starting to chill round about her and she guessed that *they* had already guessed.

When the final chords of the organ were fading she had a clearer view of Mrs Kaplan as she rose to her feet at the front of the congregation. Penelope drew in her breath, recognising the cut and fit of the black jersey A-line suit she herself had been photographed wearing for a recent magazine interview, instigated – as everything had been – by Leopold. A man was standing holding open her black llama coat and she was slipping her arms in the scalloped cuffs into the sleeves.

A gentle prod on her elbow-bone reminded her that others were want-ing to make their getaway from the pew, and she stepped out into the aisle.

Outside she chatted to Miss Carmichael, as everyone from Leopold down had addressed her. A few other agency authors drifted into the conversation and out again. As she listened she looked over her shoulder and caught the widow's eye. She was standing with several of (Penelope supposed) Leopold's business advisers, but she had pulled her long veil back over her pomander of blue hair and her gaze was trained most particularly on *her*. Penelope felt herself becoming unnerved by the look: it had no recognisable expression to it, all it was was an open-ended questioning stare without any social shame or compunction. 'So, Mrs Gerrault, you think it's also *your* place to be here with us, do you . . .?'

Back at her car Penelope dropped into the leather tub driving-seat. She remembered the river light flooding into the Savoy's lounge; by the end of their second cup of tea, they'd seemed to have arrived at their most unorthodox compact and she'd imagined that things must always be done quite differently in such a charmed place. In the matter-of-fact, non-denominational Golders Green sunlight of a passable English summer's day, Penelope was being given the impression that in some essential respect she was failing to uphold her obligations by the arrangement.

She tapped her fingers on the steering-wheel. 'Oh, Leo, Leo, Leo . . .'

She jumped as a camera flashbulb popped a couple of feet away. The cameraman smiled in at her and walked off with his picture. For those in the know, she was one of Leopold Kaplan's most impressive success stories, principally because it couldn't have been predicted that it would turn out so. He had given her the profile, the cachet, the rewards: but most importantly, she understood, he had given her the confidence in her own abilities as no one else had done before, belief in the belief that she would always have the saving grace of her imagination to deal with the unexpected, the down-turns and the lows – the alchemy of words and the tangential vision to turn pigs' ears into silk purses.

She went away, to forget about him.

She took a mail boat to Dominica, then spent some time on others of the Windward Islands. She found room on a packet boat returning to Venezuela, and from Caracas she travelled south, as the song was to put it later, on trains and boats and planes.

She saw Rio and São Paolo and Buenos Aires.

She put Mona Henderson and Edward Fiedler on the back burner, and flew north and east to Madrid, which wasn't really where she wanted to be, on that high, hot, windy plain, so she made for lower ground, the foothills of Granada, and after a spell there she moved west, ending up in Lisbon.

If Tiktiki had had a city, she decided, it would have resembled this one, with buildings both self-importantly stately and Moorishly eccentric. She enjoyed her confusion, being a stranger there, but also found herself believing occasionally, on turning a corner or looking through an archway, that she knew it already, because it was the city of cities, a proper myth of how such a place should be. It smelt of cigars and perfume, as cities ought to, and she followed the odoriferous trails for blocks along the pavements.

In Lisbon she felt revived after the weariness of her travels and started to write again, most often in the marbled, tapestried public rooms of the

Ritz or the Avenida Palace Hotels where life seemed usefully *un*familiar to her, theatrical, but also contained and self-referring, and so manageable. She realised it was only a subterfuge, to encourage her, and life was very little like this but indeed quite otherwise, disordered and piecemeal and elusive, skulking and secretive and, when the low light of reason dimmed, venturesome, just as the tapestry woodlands became to children in fairy-tales. Sipping lemon tea from a fine bone-china cup, she permitted herself the necessary illusion that she could cope, that she held all the strings looped round her finger-ends.

Part Ten

1

Her Mother's Daughter is chiefly remarkable for the author's depiction of Sarah Wimbush's widowed mother. I feel that Sarah herself is a little flat and grey and also rather shadowy finally, which may or may not be intentional. Mrs Wimbush by comparison is very exactly drawn. We watch a woman who rises above a not very successful past life, so far as the emotions go, to float herself free – as it were – on her own raft of hopes and dreams. Among those saving mental graces is her resolution to extract what she remembers to have been worthwhile in the past, even if it didn't amount to so very much, and to construct from that a personal and believable morality of goodness for herself. Maybe I make the business sound abstruse. But the portrait of the woman is very convincingly done, it reads as 'reality' and touches the reader.

Accordingly we see Mrs Wimbush attempting to make the best of her lot. These days it would have been easy for the writer to have shown us the folly of such an exercise, and while we do understand what the woman's weaknesses and blind spots are, nonetheless Penelope Milne renders these hopes and dreams of Mrs Wimbush as wholly credible to us as they are to her. We too pass with marvellous ease between 'reality', which is all too much in evidence around Mrs Wimbush, and a vicarious imaginative life experienced inside the woman's head.

We might have been left with the picture of a woman merely to be pitied, but Penelope Milne knows much better. Mrs Wimbush may not always be the most *attractive* person, but she is consistently interesting. If she seems to be dealing in untruths, even telling fibs to friends, we appreciate that this is a very crude way of comprehending character and motivation. 'Lies are indicators of what a person is afraid to admit.' None of us escapes scot-free in that respect.

Let me conclude by saying that the book is certainly not without its humorous moments, and moves quickly, propelled by a well-constructed plot.

Cambridge 7.iv.62

Dear Pen,

I loved *The Tennis Club Rules*, it's one of your best. I've never read a novel in galley proofs before! But why oh why should I 'mind'? How could I possibly object? Because of 'Charles'? I couldn't play tennis half as well as he can, and he's far too good-looking. He's much better at English than I ever was! It's a novel, I understand that. Devon/Cornwall, it's wherever you picture it to be. I'd forgotten about that girl, though, the continental one with the fancy tennis racquet – *she*'s pretty real, isn't she? I laughed aloud at the tennis matches. Let me assure you, Rebecca is much too humorous to 'be' Valerie, and Clare's too sophisticated, so – don't worry – no one's going to say 'this is' and 'that is'. Why shouldn't you 'use' the past? – what else *is* there to use?

Up to my eyes in work, which is why it was such a wicked pleasure to actually *enjoy* reading something. TTCR is very far from being 'something', though. You're going to become far too famous (and clever, it goes without saying) to have anything to do with the likes of me for much longer.

You're always v. welcome to come up, remember, any time. Just give me two rings beforehand.

Tutorial in 10 minutes. All power to yr. (tennis) elbow!

Love, Oliver.

In the history of her affections Philip didn't merit a full chapter.

At the beginning she had thought he *would* do: naturally enough, since – at the outset – her affections were always equally stirred. It was only as time went on that the distinctions and qualifications came about.

He was a radio producer with the BBC. Their paths crossed when she was approached to adapt her second last novel, *Her Mother's Daughter*. They had lunch, and – not quite meaning to – she agreed to the proposal over the main course. The adaptation had been his own idea; at the lunch table he praised her books, but he also seemed a little tentative, even diffident, with her company.

Nevertheless . . .

It began by continuing, by their not stopping seeing each other once the play had been discussed, written, rediscussed, condensed by twenty-two pages, rehearsed, recorded, edited, and put in the can. Over the thirteen weeks he gradually lost much of his shyness and coyness.

In a number of respects he was the opposite of Leopold Kaplan: he was younger than she, he was handsome in a rough-about-the-edges way (more like the new Alan Bates than Guy's James Mason), he wasn't very considerate, he sometimes forgot about her, and he wanted her body and wouldn't take 'no' for an answer. Maybe her mistake was in giving herself to him: but she couldn't apportion all the subsequent blame to him, because it had been quite clear to her from the night in the early swinging sixties when he 'jumped' that this was exactly the modern state of affairs she wanted to be a part of, so she would hardly be required to as much as think even . . .

The trouble was, they really had nowhere to go.

He told her very little about himself and didn't even pretend to, as Guy had done; she thought she bored him when she told *him* things, she didn't like to begin another conversation on the subject.

She cared for him chiefly in a bodily way, that he should eat enough and wear

310

clean shirts and wrap up against cold, just as an old-fashioned governess would have fussed with her charge. Like a governess, she wasn't properly a figure of authority but her position depended on her charge's acknowledgment that she was. Sometimes he was willing and acquiescent, sometimes he wasn't. When everything went well, she forgot about when it didn't. She existed somewhere between friendship and passion: friendship that was partly guesswork about him, and passion which was really late-flowering lust. Maybe she gave in so easily precisely because she knew the situation was a lucky shot – or else a long shot – and ordinariness in the shape of reason would intrude as it must when their time was up, when they would hear their number being called.

She went to Amsterdam for the Dutch publication of *A Geneva Watch*. It was winter, the city was in the grip of a viciously cold snap. Fresh snow covered the cobbles. Ice floated in the canals, long icicles hung on house fronts. She walked about in ski-boots, two jumpers, a cashmere muffler, a padded jacket that zipped to the chin, a fur hat pulled down over her ears, and her hands inside leather gloves, with woollen mittens on top.

One frozen afternoon she was making her way down the Keizersgracht, feeling as well-padded and ungainly as the Michelin man on a poster she passed. Lights drew her to the window of an antiques shop. She spotted an Art-Nouveau mirror, considered for several moments, then she pushed on the door and walked inside. The frame of the mirror turned out to be pewter of rather questionable quality, and she shook her head when the shop-owner offered to take it down off the wall for her. The door of the shop opened and more cold air blew in. She nearly knocked something off a tabletop, a box of old postcards, and she took advantage of the almost-accident to stay in the warmth a little longer, picking her way through the cards.

She found several to buy, but one in particular appealed to her. It was a tinted photograph of a pretty, dignified, wide-eyed young woman. She had dark crimped hair with a centre parting and was dressed in sheeny grey silk and a long rope of pearls; she was elegantly seated, ankles crossed, on a sofa against an open window, with calm water and Nordic birches outside. The date printed on the back was 1925: it was followed by the information 'Princess Astrid Sophie Louise Thyra, at the Royal Summer Palace of Solliden, Oeland'.

As she paid, the owner of the shop told her that the princess had married the King of the Belgians, in Stockholm, and the rest was history.

'Ah. I see.'

She smiled, received that postcard and the others in a paper-bag, left the shop, and returned through icy Amsterdam to her hotel.

An idea came to her as she was sitting looking at the cards. Apart from the princess, she had bought half-a-dozen views: they dated from the pre-war years to the early thirties, and showed various spa hotels and hugely dignified palaces. She could send one – or two – to Philip in London and treat them in the required manner.

She turned over the card showing the handsome, demure Queen of the Belgians as she became. *'Our days,'* she wrote in red ballpoint, *'are taken up with weighty deliberations. We are pledged not to think of ourself. Our responsibility is to the good and happiness of others.'*

She wasn't quite sure what the words meant, what it was she had intended to say. Perhaps, that she lived in hope. Philip had recently been telling her she was a career woman, that he could only hold her back: but she'd thought that might only be his excuse. She wasn't ready to give up on it yet. She understood just enough about herself to know that she found the predicament she was in – being seen to be in pursuit of a man – very nearly a humiliation, but a novel experience, and bizarrely exciting to her.

The postcard was signed *'Astrid Regina'* and posted.

Philip was O.B.-ing, on two or three day excursions from London, and she didn't see him for the next six or seven weeks. When she did he made no mention of the card, and she didn't enquire. He proved more tender than she was expecting after their last encounters before Holland, in the garden and ground floors she'd bought in a white house in the Kensington Pelhams: he was clearly making an effort. Things continued in like vein for a couple of weeks, until he told her he had to leave for Dublin. The final days were the least satisfactory. She had received favourable reviews for *The Tennis Club Rules* and she saw that he envied her them. She guessed that he knew he was in the wrong job, that what he really wanted to do was write.

She sent more cards with Astrid's missives, addressed first to Dublin and then to Cork, where he was now working on a six-month exchange. He hadn't said 'yes' when she'd asked if she could go with him to Ireland, he hadn't said anything: she mentioned to him it was getting out of hand, that if she cut and ran she and he would have nothing to be sorry about, but she knew that she wasn't ready to do any such thing. Her work was going well enough, and she wondered – not if the work fed off the relationship – but if the relationship was possible because her sense of *herself*, her professional well-being, wasn't in jeopardy.

The magazines talked of 'relationships' nowadays, but this wasn't a *real* one, of course. Now it had reached the stage of being evenly cerebral and sexual. She felt she had nothing to lose so she continued it: he calculated when he would be indifferent to her, which was like rocket propulsion to him, sending him back into radio studios with a desire to do nothing but work, to immerse himself in it. She didn't like to talk to him about his job in case he thought she was patronising him: he reciprocated in kind – it might have been that he imagined she actually wasn't interested, or that it was 'beneath' her because it was a job involving compromises, whereas hers as he told her several times was one where she pleased only herself.

'Well, I've readers to think about,' she said.

'That's just the public, it's abstract.'

312

'Isn't yours too?'

'I've got time-schedules and sniffy authors and muffed lines and the great and good breathing down my neck to see what I'm up to, and it's always against the clock.'

She was genuinely sympathetic, but she didn't know how she could help. So she sent him the postcards instead. They showed tiered wedding-cake Palast-hotels and formal vistas of gravel walkways and noble fountains. She disguised her handwriting and signed herself 'Astrid R.'.

'We are taking the waters at Carlsbad. Thalassotherapy treats the body royal, but our spirit is undisciplined, unsovereign'd.'

She found the cards in antique shops in Kensington Church Street and on a certain barrow in Portobello Road. She gave them to people to post from abroad.

'We are detained at Schönbrunn for reasons of state business. Absence makes our regal heart grow no less fond of that from which we are separated.'

When the film *Last Year in Marienbad* came out, and they went to see it and couldn't make much of the story at all, she thought it was her Astrid's world to the monumental life, or approximation to life.

'Regards of a right royal nature from our reclusive retreat in the vertiginous Zillertaler Alpen. Our privacy is paramount, our discretion suzerain, our desiderata inscrutable.'

He never told her that he had received them, any of them.

'Our grief is this high solitude of the Noblesse to which circumstances obligate Ourselves.'

She made a last effort, to save what she knew didn't merit it.

They went off on holiday together. They took his car – she suggested it – and she was aware he thought she was condescending to him. But he was too proud to let her see he was thinking such a thing – and, after Calais, they just started driving.

They could have gone north, but when she mentioned Brussels and Amsterdam he seemed to go cold on the idea, so south they went, towards the sun and a lesser latitude.

They ended up in Van Gogh country, in a furnace of heat, among the fields of gnarled trees writhing to find their own shade. They saw the flame and yellow sunflowers, blooms fraying on long stems, and she imagined them nearly demented with thirst. The heat clawed up out of the earth, it knocked distances out of focus so that they wavered, undulated. Everything was either too glaringly present, loaded with that terrible 'thereness', or else it receded from them in pale dust swirls, quivering and somehow irresolute, like sand mirages.

They lay in hotel bedrooms with the shutters closed and the windows open and didn't sleep much. At a filling-station outside one small market-town they were directed to a modest auberge by a foxy-faced youth with a pony-tail and gypsy earring; when they got there they were received by a woman of fifty-plus dressed and made-up like a tarty twenty-year-old. She smelt of drink but she made them coffee, which tasted queer, and Penelope felt strangely queasy in her garden and not herself. The woman told them she was a widow, and Penelope counted three gold rings on her left hand. The cigarette in her mouth never fell below the horizontal, and at certain moments came distressingly halfway to the vertical. She watched Philip as the woman hitched up her dress; she opened her legs wider and wider until her stocking-tops and suspenders were showing. Penelope saw an axe stuck into the bark of a tree and when she could adjust her vision to fix on them, she made out three grass mounds no less than six feet long set in the shade of three trees. The trees were of diminishing age and size, none was full-grown, and the sun glinted slyly off the wealth of gold on the woman's fourth finger. The gravel terrace where they sat formed the greater part of two circles on either side of them; a path ran straight and erect across the lawn, with stupendous obscenity.

Penelope in an instant jumped up, telling Philip she needed to see a doctor and grabbing his arm. She said she had to have the suitcase, she shouted at him to get it please. She ran to the car and waited for him with the doors locked. The woman pleaded with her through the side-window, tapping on the glass with her sharp knuckles but she wouldn't listen to her. Philip came back; she opened the driver's door and pulled on his arm, the woman tugging at his other arm was no match at all for *her*. 'Where's the doctor? Where do we go?' he kept asking, but she'd spotted the furtive, earringed youth with the pony-tail walking in his undervest and tight blue jeans towards the house and she shouted at him again, never mind, never mind, just get the engine going, get us away from this place, for God's sake.

It must have been the heat, but she didn't know then and was never to know. When he'd calmed her down Philip told her her imagination was running away with her. Maybe, she thought: or maybe this is me lapsing into my right mind after too long.

They didn't leave the main roads after that, and she wondered if he really didn't see that their lives – or his life – had been in peril after all.

They chose their stopovers from the Michelin Guide, and they spent their days in museums and old churches and at café tables on the streets. They found excuses for not having to say too much to each other: concentrating on a painting, or a church service in progress, or pleading the din of cars and motor-cycles.

They went down to the coast, lured there by the certainty of crowds. They didn't quarrel, they became more anonymous with each other, and in truth it was best. She started to plot a couple of stories in her head, and it was in Nice that (a) she vainly spent her time looking for a garden where a hotel might have blazed and (b) that Philip happened to spot a girl he'd worked with in Dublin, holidaying with her boyfriend.

In a bric-à-brac shop in Antibes she was riffling through a box of old postcards and came up trumps with a view of the royal palace in Brussels. She happened to look up and there and then caught Philip watching her from the street, his hand shading his eyes against the reflections in the window glass. Even Astrid, a stately queen, was a figure lost far behind him, now shrunk to a mote in the out-travelled purview.

Back in London they 'kept up' for a few months, which was surely a euphemism. But they both claimed their work was now occupying so much of their time, etcetera . . . She felt they were (coincidentally) drawing a line – very straight and very neat – under their past together. It was the first time she had worn out a feeling for someone, but that was only living and learning.

There were no birthday cards the next year. They scribbled brief résumés on their Christmas cards. She toyed with the idea of signing herself 'Astrid, Queen of the Belgians' after 'Season's Greetings', but decided against it: the postcards seemed to her now a desperate semaphoring, although couched in such courtly and undemonstrative terms.

The following year the final test occurred.

She was walking up Regent Street, hurrying to an appointment, when by some fluke of observation her eyes picked him out fifty yards away, coming towards her on the same stretch of the pavement. He was deep in conversation with – she supposed – a colleague.

She slowed. People brushed past her, and the two men continued walking. Forty yards. Thirty yards.

She stood still. He couldn't have been more than twenty yards away from her.

Suddenly she pulled down the skip of her Jackie Coogan cap, turned away and stepped off the pavement. She miscalculated a break in the traffic and a car horn blared, then another, as she ran for the island in the middle of the road. She heard squealing brakes but didn't look back. Eyes were watching her, she was quite sure. She kept her hand raised to the brim of her cap, Joan Crawford style, sort of.

She waited for a gap in the flow of traffic, then set off for the far pavement. Her heels rang beneath her.

She paused in front of a shop window. She scoured the figures passing in the glass, in the furthest distance. It was too difficult to focus, though. The two tides of pedestrians ran against each other, they blurred and individuals were impossible to distinguish.

Love ought to have been like that perfect confusion, she stood thinking, straightening her hat on her head. She'd had intimations, but she lived in eternal hope of a full and final revelation, like a blinding by heavenly light.

2

Oliver rang. Lunch, he said, and it'll be on me, *you* decide where.

The Dorchester, she told him, and we go shares on the bill.

'You're looking well, Penelope.'

'So are you.'

'It's up and down. I suppose things are up at the moment.'

'How's that?' she asked, and realised from the quick flush on his face that it wasn't the question to ask. But, after she'd asked it, she couldn't think how to undo it.

'Maybe because Valerie's wherever she is. The Costa Something-or-Other –'

'Is she? I haven't heard – '

'Valerie's someone to be on the right side of. But I can't remember what it was like to be in her good books.'

There was a moment's pause, a hiatus.

'She liked *you*, though.'

Penelope smiled.

'Perhaps – perhaps she needed me. At first.'

'Needed you?'

She shrugged. Needed someone else in Tregarrick, she meant, to be an ally. But she didn't tell him that.

'She used to talk about you a lot.'

'Yes?'

She shrugged again.

'I sometimes think,' Oliver said, 'she's collecting surnames for herself.'

Penelope laughed.

'Maybe,' he said, 'she'll start choosing the name before she meets the man.'

'Who's this one?'

'Wentworth. Sounds very solid. I'm sure she covets it. Expect news of the nuptials – '

Good for her, she was going to say, but Oliver forestalled her.

'Of course, I know why she does it.'

'You do?'

'For old-fashioned, bloody-minded *revenge*.'

She didn't know if she should laugh.

'Oh no . . .'

316

'Oh yes. I've thought about it long and hard. That's what it comes down to.'

'Why, though?'

'They're really scalps. Conquests.'

'But that's not all she wants?'

'She wants her security, of course. She could never have a family. She's awful with children apparently – '

'But why is that revenge?' she asked, already surmising the answer and knowing that Oliver wouldn't give it to her.

'She makes a mockery of it, of course. Just going through the motions.'

'But *why*?'

'She thinks it's all – well, flawed. A lot of fuss, much ado about more-or-less nothing. A lottery or whatever.'

But 'why' remained the point: why should she have felt so when her life had always seemed to Penelope such a charmed one?

She wondered what else Oliver might divulge: if he was willing to trust her, and was open enough to admit anything of his haunted sibling past, the conclusion denied her in *The Tennis Club Rules*. But lunch passed without a disclosure, very pleasantly, and she knew much better than to force the point.

She didn't doubt that the pleasure was mutual. But at last she saw Oliver sneaking a covert glance at his watch. He smiled in excuse.

'I – I'm supposed to be seeing someone.'

'Oh, I'm sorry,' she said.

'No, this has been really great.'

'Yes. Yes, it *has* been.'

'I wish I could stay longer – '

'But we've met,' she said. 'It's been lovely.'

'You know where I am.'

'Yes. And ditto.'

He pushed his chair back and stood up.

It's unfair, she thought, how the years have only confirmed his good looks. It's unfair on Valerie that he's better-looking than she is, or was. He seems to have everything in his favour. Once he was so dark, living so far inside himself: now he smiles and pulls at his cufflinks in nervous anticipation and looks across the room to the door and might almost be ready to acknowledge the possibility that true happiness exists.

Oliver was first to the desk, and he paid.

She objected. He told her, well the next time it can be *yours*. Did she think there might be a next time?

'I don't see why not.'

'I'll phone you, Pen.'

'Phone me,' she said. 'Yes.'

317

'It's just I have to go now.'
'Excused and forgiven.'

She'd had no intention of trailing him. But her timing was such that she caught sight of him almost two hours later as she was walking out of Burlington Arcade, at the Gardens end.

He was standing on the opposite pavement with his arm held up to hail a taxi. They might have been confused for brothers, the two of them: height, colouring and demeanour matched, there was even a similarity in their facial features and the faces' shapes.

She stood at the Arcade's entrance, on the shallow steps, and watched as a taxi slowed with squeaking brakes, did a U-turn in the middle of the road, and drew up at the far kerb. Oliver was controlling the situation and he bent down to the open window to give the driver information while the other, his double, climbed into the back compartment. Oliver got in after him and pulled the door shut. She was near enough to see a smile exchanged between the two of them.

The taxi rumbled off with its fares. She watched as its indicator winked on the corner and the front wheels turned into Savile Row. She had a last glimpse of Oliver through the side-window: he was leaning his elbow on the back shelf and running a finger beneath his shirt-collar. Then the taxi was gone, carrying the man and his image, and other cars and vans – stuttering on the corner and changing up or down gear – covered the tracks.

She seldom gives an 'objective' description of a character. A person is often seen in a reflecting surface – a wall mirror, a car's driving- or side-mirror, a car window, the plate-glass window of a shop – and frequently we see via the person, as he/she sees him/herself. Two people might see the same one person quite differently, and she ensures that we are aware of this. A person can be 'A' or 'B' with this person or that, i.e., the person subdivides into variant versions as he or she socially engages with the world. In an extreme situation, paranoia takes over. Most of her women characters finally resolve the disparate elements of their character, however, or at least they avoid the hazards of a divided mind and behaviour. Penelope Milne is always looking for the unifying components of a life: a mood or a memory or an object may help to fix a person, to establish a continuity and thus a sense of 'self'.

'You can't go on paying for me, Oliver.'
  'Why not?'
  'It's not fair. And you make me feel like a kept woman.'
  'I *want* to pay.'
  Why? she wondered: so you can pretend it's boy meets girl?
  'I feel guilty – '
  'Oh, we all feel guilty, Penelope.'
  ' – about what it costs.'
  'Everything costs. And we all pay up.'

'I'm not forcing you, Oliver.'

'Am I forcing *you*?'

'Of course not.'

'So what are we talking about?'

They were in Regent's Park, walking, and in an oddly solemn mood neither of them seemed able to help.

'Tell me something, Penelope, did I lose my chance with you?'

'No,' she said, recognising what a serious question it actually was, that she should be as painfully honest with him as she needed to be. 'No, you didn't.'

'I could have tried again, you mean?'

'I mean – there wasn't really a chance.'

'When?'

'Any time.'

'Even the first time, at the beginning?'

'Even then.'

'Ah.'

They walked ten or a dozen steps in silence.

'It was Cambridge?'

'No,' she said. 'But – but we've been through it.'

'Have we, though? Have we *really*?'

'We've talked about it often enough – haven't we?'

'Yes. I suppose we have.'

'Or we've talked our way around it.'

'I see.'

'Do you, Oliver?'

'Not quite hitting the nail on the head? Is that it?'

Now she guessed that he knew she knew, what the true reason had been.

'We've taken our own paths,' he said. 'Tracks through life – '

'Maybe.'

'Haven't we?'

'We found ourselves on the tracks. Both of us, Oliver. But I'm not sure we know how we got on to them. In the first place – '

'Perhaps not.'

'I *thought* I was choosing – '

'And you weren't?' he asked her.

'Not with the writing.'

'That's your character.'

'I suppose it is,' she said.

'But you *can* still choose, make choices.'

'How?'

'Settle down again – '

She anticipated how he was going to continue and interrupted him.

'But not with you, Oliver.'

She remembered the recent lunches, all the small and vital happiness he'd brought her. She reached out and took his hand; it felt awkward, almost lifeless, but also unyielding.

'I care for you very much,' she said. 'But I don't think that would have been – right.'

It was the lamest word.

'You're prettier now,' he told her, 'whatever it's been like for you.'

'Sometimes I feel – statuesque. If I go to a party. I don't feel anything *like* – what you said . . .'

'It's your victory, Penelope.'

'I seem better to you than I am.'

'No. No, that's not why – '

She smiled at him, because *she* knew otherwise. Deny it as he would. She let go his hand: the fingers were like those of a man drawing his last breath.

Some children ran among trees, playing tig. She remembered coming to the park after Guy's death, because they would sometimes walk here as she was doing now; there was a time, lasting several weeks, when she had wanted to systematically repeat every journey she had ever made with him, to revisit every place – in and around London at least – which they had gone to together. But all that she had learned from her excursions was that nothing was the same any more, that change touched everything, never mind that the sun was shining or rain drizzling when the weather had originally been the opposite.

'What are you thinking about?'

'Oh . . .' She nodded at the children.

'Do you wish you had some?'

'Children?'

She would have had Guy's, even without a marriage, but he'd told her he didn't feel ready: she had supposed it was because he was afraid of losing what was between the two of them and she had tried – gently – to persuade him that nothing would be lost. But maybe he had foreseen how it would be if it should ever happen that only she and a child were left, that they would be materially comfortable but that he wouldn't have offered enough about *himself* – or rather, what there was would be too full of contradictions – and that her bafflement and doubt must include the child too, as being half of his. By denying them both parenthood, he was contriving to save the child . . . or so she'd tried to believe on her solitary rambles, following in her own footsteps.

Had he somehow received omens of his own death, coming too soon in the life they shared?

'No,' she said, 'I don't think so.'

'What about?'

'Children.'

'Oh. I see.'

And what about yourself, she might have asked. But she knew better. The line stopped with both of them. (How disappointed her mother would have been to know it.) They had this in common, their uniqueness: two people who wouldn't be reproduced and recreated, who were now united to one another by a single sadness and shame.

- You don't make it a moral point.
- 'Moral'?
- In *Making Do* . . . When Mona Henderson falls for an older man. Fiedler. *She* becomes older too?
- No.
- Wiser?
- She just wants to be happy. Happ*ier*.
- That can be a justification?
- She doesn't think like that. After a while anyway. She recognises something, a spirit between them: they submit to that. Their souls correspond, if you like. That's their good fortune, their 'achievement'. Well, I shouldn't put it like that – I mean, that's *everything*. Isn't it? What else is there left?

Dressed by Jacques Fath, she walked through the wardrobe mirror and into the bedroom. Sunshine through the slats of the shutters striped the carpet, already so faded that its pattern was scarcely visible.

She paused, then took several steps forward. She stopped at the end of the bed. On its cue, a car horn sounded. The woman between the sheets shifted in her afternoon sleep. She stretched out an arm. She delivered her mutter.

The other woman, dressed by Jacques Fath and with an authentically regal bearing, walked around the bottom of the bed towards the far wall, a section of which comprised a screen of blue light. She turned round to consider the woman lying in the bed, very nearly in the dead centre of the space of blue light.

'Cut!'

Queen Astrid's reincarnation standing by the bed relaxed. The actress beneath the sheets rolled on to her back and made a jokey remark. The two women exchanged laughter. Around them the production crew and technicians closed in, the cameraman stepped down from his podium and joined the director who was discussing some point with the floor manager. The lights on their tracks blazed hotter than the Provençal sun *en plein été*.

The actress who'd lain in bed was keen to speak to her, to have her verdict.

'Is this how you see the character?'

'Oh yes,' Penelope replied, and nodded. In fact she felt unable to answer the question, except very literally. She could 'see' what was in front of her, like everyone else: but she was hardly able to judge a good performance from a bad one.

She smiled after she'd spoken, in an inoffensively inattentive way, as if the experience were just a little too much for her. But actually it had failed almost completely to touch her at all. In the end nothing properly matched, except a certain sense of aloneness, which was only an ironic consequence. She was left as she had been left then, without Philip or the queenly Astrid of the Belgians either, occupying her own circle of space, in a reverberating echo pool of silence.

Part Eleven

1

- When did you know that you wanted to write?
- I don't think I ever did. I just started, doodling in a way. I kept lists of things, a bit like a diary – observations on events, on people – but really it was to allow myself to think about them, to consider them.
- You wrote your novels from these?
- I wrote alternative versions of life, about people I'd never met. Mostly in places I'd never been to.
- You grew into the job?
- I wasn't educated to think I had anything to offer in that way.
- Your books are very concerned with mystery.
- Enigma, yes. Of character, events. Time too.
- Future time?
- Time past is just as hypothetical, in its way. It goes in and out of focus. We can make it do whatever we choose –
- *You*'ve remained something of a puzzle too.
- Well, partly that's politic. Not to open yourself up, like a watch. But it's in the nature of writing, so I've found: your own personality becomes less, *im*-personality is more satisfying in the end. I'm not making a romantic myth out of it, but the *watching* aspect becomes important: yourself as a receiver. That old cliché – clichés are very undervalued, don't you think? they're a sort of junk wisdom, off-the-peg – anyway, that hoary old notion of some force moving the pen between your fingers and the page.
- Has that allowed you to take risks? It's said of some writers, they stop distinguishing between their characters and the rest of us, they start playing people off against one another as if they *were* characters.
- I'm not sure I *do* distinguish between the written and the real, but not maybe as you're meaning. It's so complex – At school they'd talk about the 'real' life waiting outside: but where *we* were, *inside*, that was just as 'real'.
- You haven't given up living, though?
- No. No, not yet.
- Could you say what your novels are about?
- About? Well . . . I think I'm trying to trace connections, inside a life. Even if they don't prove to be all they seem to – to show it isn't all adding up to

323

mayhem, there's a sort of internal logic, of character, of 'destiny' if that's how we can understand it and not as God's, as defined by ourselves, our failures and strengths of character –

– Imposed on us?

– Well, some are. But we also have choice. A measure of choice. That's the real dichotomy in every one of the books, I think. How much *do* we control our lives? There's a certain amount that's given to us, which is defined in the womb. But some things we can do. Living in history, public 'general' history, with that as our background, but knowing we can also effect a limited amount of will –

– You don't normally 'explain' your novels, do you?

– It's frustrating when you're asked what a book is 'about', and you have to paraphrase it. The point is, you've spent however many thousand words, arranging each of them in such a way in relation to the others, because they *hold* your meaning. Sometimes it's as delicate and fragile as a web, you know? Sometimes elusiveness is built into it too. Or you give a choice of interpretation to your words, they could be read either this way or that. But that doesn't satisfy certain people, they've got to find the heart, cut it out and drag it from the corpse, bleeding . . . I did once want to write a novel, or try to, where nothing was actually accounted for. My little counterblast to the 'So and so, who looks like this, did such-and-such, and the reason was this, etcetera' type of novel. Because that's not how life operates, is it?

– And you want to get as close to life as you can?

– Yes. Certainly. I think you pull people in by dealing in atmosphere, you lure them, or you try to. Events don't have to be realistic within that, and the atmosphere doesn't have to be familiar: but something or other rings true eventually, and what I hope it is is the difficulty of definition, of even understanding yourself. There has to be some protecting element of doubt about yourself. That way you avoid the awful peril of bigotry and intolerance, when a person thinks they're perfectly in command of themself and they see the whole of another person in their vulnerability. Really of course that's violence, too much assertion, so instead of 'humiliation' I'm offering 'humility' as a virtue –

– You're very aware of what people think about you? Journalists, for instance?

– Oh, some of them think they know me much better than I can know myself. I don't *believe* that's the case. It'd be strange when I write about characters actually able to confront the lacks in themselves, who're actually quite objective about themselves, many of them women – it'd be strange if I lacked objectivity about myself, don't you think? If I couldn't step out of myself and walk a circle round about, and see myself in another dimension? What appears in print of course has to be syphoned through someone else, through their prejudices – often it's written at speed, a tape recorder hasn't worked properly – and what appears is a flat, two-dimensional, rather humourless, rather unironic representation. Yes, sometimes that can be very depressing, dispiriting.

– Do you think you're fairly much in control?

– Not with journalists.

– Do you have periods of doubt? Self-doubt?

– Depressions, for instance?

– Yes.

324

- I've noticed, with myself – it's curious – how often a good, productive spell, a couple of days maybe, is preceded by a couple of days of the opposite: feeling very undernourished mentally, washed out, purposeless. It doesn't happen the other way about. I've always been surprised by that.
- *Your* being puzzled – that's part of the enigma?
- Yes. Yes, I suppose it is. If anything about an enigma can ever be sure . . .

In 1966 Penelope returned to Cornwall.

The lane down to the bay was no wider than it had been, although there were more villas up on the headland. Pebbledash walls had been painted white, and rudimentary electric lighting from lampposts provided. Two of the original large Edwardian houses had been turned into private hotels, and there was a car park and a kiosk where the lane ended, behind the beach. But the atmosphere of the place was little different. The tennis courts survived, and the club-house was only a modernised version of the old one. The same trees still turned the bottom part of the lane into the same tunnel of shade. The little church with the twisted steeple still cowered behind its hawthorn hedge; a few gravestones were new, but the stone had already started to weather.

She had booked accommodation in a modern chalet-style hotel at the top of the hill, on the Pendizzick road, and there she gathered her thoughts. The place wasn't disturbing her with memories as she'd thought that maybe it might: quite the contrary, she felt this was like a homecoming. She enjoyed the ease of the locale – collecting her newspapers from the post office, picking up her lunchtime order from the Tyrolean Bakery in Cove with alpine cowbells still behind the door, lapsing into holiday customs – and she knew memories weren't unrelated to her sense of contentment. She was experiencing the pleasurable shock of the familiar, time was only catching up with itself again, and she was conscious of a strand of continuity in her life she hadn't had for a long time.

She also found that she could work well here, which was certainly more than she had been expecting. In London she would sit for too long looking out into the strip of garden, or into the other rooms on the crescent, or at her fellow readers in the London Library where she sometimes went to share in the simulation of industry. At the Mawgan Lodge Hotel she was less herself than a woman called Prudence Shaw, who had returned to an area very much like this one after a broken affair and was piecing together the case for the defence, why it should be that her private life – as distinct from her professional one as an academic – should prove itself so often unsatisfactory. Her parents had brought her here long ago, to a house they rented every year, and from that family past – fraught and claustrophobic – many complicitous truths were to be extracted . . .

She sat in her room writing and thought of the process of becoming someone other, and she remembered reading or hearing that when a sea anemone has some damage done to it, something plucked off, it will make itself anew, and so the water flower duly became a prime motif in her story. On her walks down the lane to the bay and back again she heard the wood-pigeons in the trees and wondered how she could have forgotten that unvarying rhythm of throaty chortles as the birds puffed themselves up and preened, how it could have slipped her memory when she wasn't devoid of birdsong in Kensington, with owls and jays and even, once, a famous nightingale at Brompton Cross.

Her productivity encouraged her, and as a result she became *more* productive. She settled back into the routine and enthusiasm of writing, having her thoughts run away from her so that she had to set off after them with her pen, scuttling across blank pages in pursuit. Recently she had lost that sense of urgency, and recovering it made her feel paradoxically quieter, much more peaceable in herself. No spa retreat with thalassotherapy and mudpacks and salt floats and hours of staring up at domed ceilings could have done her so much good as to have her confidence in her abilities returned to her. She had a presentiment that this was going to be one of her better books, with a new verve and momentum in her storytelling.

And so it turned out, to complete the mental (and circumstantial) harmonies of that holiday. She couldn't dissociate the end-result from its origins, and she felt she had added another layer of associations to those already provided by memory, that the place now contained more of 'her' than the shadowy teenage girl outdone by the personalities of Oliver and, especially, of Valerie. She believed she now had more of a claim on the spot than she'd had arriving, drawn to it by a compulsive curiosity (and an uncomfortable realisation that long ago she had been humiliated here, by what she had failed at the time to understand).

There was no humiliation on any count the following June, when the book was published. She wanted to go back to Cornwall, but she told herself, not so soon: the year after perhaps, when she would be in less danger of becoming too thick again with Prudence Shaw or finding their existences in any wise confused.

She returned to Polwynn in 1968. She was determined that her customs shouldn't affect her work, and that covering old ground shouldn't involve occupying a bedroom that would remind her of her long stay at the Mawgan Lodge Hotel. She rented a cottage instead, set beside a field about a third of the way down the lane, not far below the post office, and reached by a narrow, very uneven track which threatened to break her car's axles and crack the spine of the chassis.

They met in the Tyrolean Bakery in the small, straggling beach town further along the estuary.

She was being served and had a sense of being watched from behind, but sometimes it happened, someone remembered an image in a photograph. Even wearing a summer panama hat it could happen.

When she turned round to leave, she immediately recognised him. They'd been introduced at a couple of literary parties, and they'd exchanged a few sentences but others with prior claims – his colleagues, his authors – had descended on him.

He was standing with two small children.

'I *thought* so,' he said.

'Hello.'

'I was almost sure it was – '

She smiled. 'And unfortunately it really was?'

'No, no, I'm delighted. I was so sorry we didn't – '

'I tell myself every party's going to be the last one.'

'I wish I could – '

'But *some*one's going to be offended – '

'This is the strangest coincidence, really.'

'I think you're next,' she said and nodded. 'I'll wait outside.'

She took the children with her. They were polite, and said nothing. He came out loaded with paper-bags; he handed them round and she watched, amused at the precision of the routine, who carried what.

He was tall, wiry, with the sort of face her mother would have called 'refined': well-bred, she supposed, inbred in the best way. His fair hair had thinned, he wore rimless glasses. He had fine hands and long fingers. He showed no evidence of too many business lunches.

They walked back to their cars. She discovered he'd been staying on the headland, but it was his last day. He invited her over for a drink in the evening, but she felt it wasn't her place to be there on the last night and so she made up an excuse.

As it was, when she ought to have been wherever she'd told him she would be, he found her on the beach. He was walking a fox-terrier. He didn't ask her why she was here and not being social elsewhere. She realised he didn't squander his words. She sensed some sort of pull between them, and guessed it was reciprocated from the evidence of his attention and his concentration on her. They didn't *have* to smile, or *have* to laugh, or *have* to make clumsy clever-talk. They were (she supposed afterwards) quite natural with each other, undissembling, innocent in a certain sense.

'I'm off to Australia for nine months,' he said.

'Australia?'

'Sydney. We're setting up an office.'

'But you're coming back?'

'In nine months.'

Penelope smiled.

'That sounds interesting.'

'Maybe.'

'You don't sound sure – '

'People take these sensible decisions for you. I do rather feel I'm being sent into orbit.'

She realised he had been looking at her while she'd been confused by the two suns slanting so low in the lenses of his glasses. She took a step or two back. He placed his hand on her arm, on her elbow-bone.

327

'Our walk,' he said. 'Or have you forgotten me so soon?'

She shook her head.

He bent forward and unclipped the leash from the dog's collar. He picked up a small driftwood twig and threw it towards the sea. The dog raced off after it.

'At last,' he said. 'Obligations over for the day.'

He turned her away, so that the headland with its houses, windows lit, was behind them.

'This place,' he said, 'this evening, they've got to see me through the next nine months.'

The following June there was a party at a publishers' in Bedford Square.

She hadn't meant to go. She arrived feeling a little tight-eyed and prim-mouthed, having decided in the taxi that a certain woman of letters who had reviewed her last three novels and slashed them to shreds was bound to be there.

She may or may not have been present, but she ceased to notice. Walking upstairs she heard *his* voice among those nearest the door of the room and the evening changed its character completely.

She ran up the remaining stairs, jealous of whomever he might be speaking to. It wasn't one person but several: they turned out to be his colleagues, and when she walked in he rolled his eyes up to the ceiling, then shook his head with the most careful and grateful of smiles. She edged past him and managed to mumble something, nodding across the room to a long-forgotten face at the same moment he muttered to her: both of them saying the same thing, 'You've saved my life!' She couldn't resist another smile over her shoulder, and saw hers exactly matched by his.

Fate seemed to have a hand in it, just as in Polwynn.

'So, how was Australia?'

He mimed relief. 'It *was.*'

'And now – ?'

'A drink? Somewhere else?'

They took a taxi to the Hilton, to Trader Vic's: for a laugh, they agreed. But she felt they were being quite serious when he told her that they were going back to Polwynn next month. The moments when he imparted the information to her seemed somehow resonant, acute, intense with a significance he wanted her to pick up on.

The next morning she rang the estate agents who arranged holiday lets. Forty-eight hours before they had received a cancellation on the cottage she'd taken last year. Then she knew it was destined to happen.

*

They met again at the Tyrolean Bakery, not altogether by accident.

'You're still a customer?' she asked him.

'Still a customer,' he said. 'And you?'

She nodded, and smiled at the children.

'As before?' he asked her.

'As before, yes.'

2

They decided Veryan was their favourite of the houses they liked in Polwynn. The secluded Edwardian residences behind the beach had grace, but they were too large: although Veryan sat close to the lane, it had intimacy. It looked thoroughly manageable, which would leave all the more time for the things that properly mattered between two people. Creeper-clad, it succeeded in being private too, self-protecting.

They slowed every time they came to it on their evening walk and stopped to look. Ideally Gregor should have been holding her hand, but – unless night had fallen – they didn't take that risk. Their thoughts, she was certain, did duty for actions and for words they couldn't hazard being overheard. They could manage smiles, at least – in the soapy glow of the lamppost mostly hidden in the trees – and these seemed rich with more of that mutual significance.

In Australia Gregor had read twelve of her thirteen books, and bought the one he couldn't find almost immediately on his return, on his first day back on the Bloomsbury beat.

A wind came up one evening as the two of them were climbing the lane, with the dog leading on its leash. Penelope calculatedly loosened her straw hat on her head and, at the most obliging moment just as they reached Veryan, felt it blow off and watched as it wafted over the hedge.

'I'll have to go into the garden now,' she said, not even feigning surprise. 'To fetch it.'

She pushed open the gate and started walking along the path. He followed behind her.

They had the cover of darkness. The rooms were unlit and the curtains undrawn. Their faces almost touched the glass as they peered in through the windows. The geography of the house was tidy, compact, practical. Some toys lay strewn on the floor; perhaps the family had gone away for the night.

'It would be perfect,' she said, looking through from the kitchen to the sitting-room. She felt the heat of his breath on the back of her neck, and didn't turn round.

'For one person?'

'Perhaps. But I think two could be very comfortable as well.'

They walked, quietly, from window to window. The dog seemed to sense the delicacy of the operation.

Standing outside the french windows, on the small covered terrace, his finger tracked the groove on the nape of her neck. She closed her eyes and remained motionless.

His hand spread, the tips parted, and reached on either side of her spine. Then both hands clutched the blade of each shoulder. She let her head roll back, meaning it for what she hoped he would understand, her submission.

They left the garden with few words spoken and walked up the lane; they climbed the stile, then followed the bridle track across the fields to her cottage.

He didn't stay much longer than an hour. But it was enough. She watched him leave, standing by the gate in the hedge. She wondered if the spirit of Valerie was there to see her, in the quiet elation of triumph, poor Penelope become a mistress of life at last.

She woke in the morning, alone again in her bed, thinking of Veryan. He'd told her, 'some day we'll get there.' 'How?' she'd asked. 'If you want something so badly, it will happen.' 'You believe that?' 'Maybe not quite as you imagine it'll happen. But if it means you'll never rest content until it does . . .'

She thought that might be a dangerous philosophy to live your life by: but it made as much sense as any other she had ever heard.

She was just about to dress some time in the middle of the morning and was passing naked through the sunlit rooms of the house when she spotted her yellow sou'wester on a peg. The hat, she remembered, the straw hat, they'd left it unfound in the garden, after she'd let it blow off . . .

She threw on her clothes. When she reached Veryan, having run most of the way, she heard voices in the garden. Children were playing pirates. She stood at the latch gate breathing hard and debating what to do. She chanced to glance up and saw a small girl watching her from a tree-house. She had a patch over one eye; long fair hair hung down beneath the brim of a straw hat, which she was wearing tilted on the back of her head.

The straw hat.

Penelope took her hand off the latch, smiled, and retreated. The girl continued to watch her with her one eye, very seriously and fascinated by her, but too shy or unsure to smile back.

She jumped when she turned round in the General Stores at lunchtime and saw the pirate watching her from behind a swivelling wire bookstand. She still wore the straw hat, jammed on the back of her head.

At the end of the afternoon they had their third sighting of one another. This time the girl was in a group leaving the beach for home. One of the other girls waved, and she recognised her from the Austrian baker's in Cove, it was Gregor's Rebecca. Penelope waved back, cautiously. Her fair-haired friend had lost her black eye-patch but not the straw hat. Two women appeared from the dunes following the children, laden with rugs and towels.

Immediately, without feeling able to study the adults as she wanted to, Penelope turned and walked away. What had she been wearing in Cove, her cotton sun-hat or the straw one? She couldn't remember. Maybe Rebecca wouldn't manage to remember either.

Already the situation was complicating itself: which told Penelope exactly what she'd been hoping to know, that it must be quite real and undeniably true.

They had rented the same house as before, on the headland. She wouldn't let herself be invited. She sometimes met him – by design – with the children, but never with Barbara. She preferred this distance to conceivable embarrassment or suspicion. She took a thief's pleasure in the secrecy; also, she sometimes envied him the routine of his family life, even though he told her he sometimes envied *her* her freedom. It didn't upset her to feel she occasionally had to be accommodated: this was a condition of second-bestness of the most sublime kind, a perverse delight and goad to her, almost – in one of the key sixties words – 'kinky'.

Several times his wife went off with the children for a morning or an afternoon, and several times he set off by himself on a bicycle: those were their opportunities. The dog was a godsend, and it meant they always had an hour in the morning and another at night when they could be together. They would go walking, and he was prepared to offer an excuse if anyone – if Barbara, hearing via a fourth party – should have asked him. But no questions cropped up, and they doubted if any proper sightings – malicious ones anyway – had been made.

She felt completely comfortable with him. He didn't analyse the situation; his heart and soul, she was certain, were truly both in it. Any suspicions she had about herself and her own intentions were rapidly forgotten as she came to plan her days solely for the pleasure of those entr'actes. She knew when she reached the point of not caring about anything else except her time with him that she had overcome her resistance, she had got the better of mediumly-famous Penelope Milne, she was back in the shameless, selfless, witless no-man's-land of love.

Four days after their return to London they met at a too polite soirée. They went off afterwards and had a drink together, in a bar called Tangerine Revolution Seven.

He suggested dinner. Had she any thoughts where?

'Chez moi?' she asked him.

They both must have been in the same quirky mood, because the dinner wasn't eaten and they spent the time in the bedroom instead, until the smell of burning brought her running out and reminded him that this was officially an 'author dinner' and that he'd have to be back in Islington by midnight. 'I *am* an author,' she told him, scraping the sides of the oven. Each looking at the other, naked in the smoking kitchen, they started laughing at the same instant, laughed and laughed and couldn't stop.

'I was looking at your neck in the baker's.'

'My neck?'

From a business trip abroad he had sent her a postcard of Magritte's *The Eternal Evidence*. Portions of a woman's naked body occupied five separate picture frames painted in vertical sequence on Magritte's canvas – head and neck/breasts/lower abdomen and mons pubis/thighs and knees/ankles and feet – and she thought of the gallery of some diabolic collector. *'I look for your neck in other necks, but there's nothing like – '*

She hadn't thought of her neck as special before, or erogenous, nor had anyone ever told her that it was. It was slender, thin; when she wore her hair up, the nape was left bare, except for the strands of hair that escaped. She had received postcards of necks by Titian, Rembrandt and Ingres.

'But before *me*?' she asked him. 'Have there been other necks?'

He hesitated before he shook his head.

'Well, *almost*,' he said, 'once. But it was the year after I got married. So I expect it was – psychological – or psychosomatic, psycho-something – '

'Do you think that's what I am? I'm psycho-something to you?'

'If you were, it would have happened in the seventh year probably. This is the tenth year. This is serious.'

'It is?'

'For me,' he said, 'definitely.'

'Me too,' she told him, without a single second's hesitation.

For a while it suited her to believe she was the beguiling mistress, because it had given her the idea for a character to write about. She didn't ask about Barbara, even though she very much wanted to know. But she saw that he wasn't easy talking about Islington, his life on the hill.

When he wasn't wearing his glasses she didn't quite recognise him. 'And I don't really recognise *you*,' he said, 'you're blurrier.' That was just fine, they agreed, the flat filled again with their laughter, and they were helpless to do a thing about it.

She made no emotional forays to Islington. She hadn't cast eyes on Barbara and she had to make certain deductions, although she realised these might be glib and also largely false. Barbara still held him, after all.

She tried to believe that they each offered him an alternative, and that they were complementary, not incompatible. They were both valid, and she had no cause to especially envy or resent Barbara her share of his life. His wife provided him with something she did not: and Barbara wasn't able to furnish his life with certain qualities which *she* was. So, really, it was as convenient an arrangement as she could have hoped for, selfishly enough. *She* didn't ultimately have the responsibility that Barbara did for the family, and even if their time together had to be measured by the clock a sort of freshness clung to these interludes. In the spaces between them she lived buoyed on hope, and glad in her expectations of the next. The very best she could say of this epoch of her life was that she might have been dreaming it.

For the first time love became the fulcrum of events and destinies in her writing. It shone a light into even the most unlikely and least hopeful circumstances. It shaped lives, it planed them to desirable ends. It was the energy that she felt driving herself, giving her more confidence than she had ever had before.

She was in each of her characters: when she wanted to she was able to feel with them to the tips of their fingers. *He* was there too, in the spirit and soul of him if not in the physical descriptions of her men. It wasn't hard for her to describe thoughts and sensations, she only had to give her own full rein and to record them faithfully. She wasn't giving anything away, it seemed to her; she was only tapping into a ready source of inspiration, making the most of the utilities, turning a situation to the utmost account.

Later it was inevitable that certain savants should 'discover'. It was their discovering rather than her own fictionalising which seemed to intrude on a very private matter. She thought Barbara was unlikely to hear any of the tales; but she became a little more concerned that the motifs in her books would be decoded in too personal terms. Thereafter she and Gregor were both as discreet as they could be, and she kept out of the limelight; she made sure that she covered over her footprints in her work, but even so her mood at that time – being one of all sorts of contentment – beamed out, giving what she wrote a lightness of touch she had never achieved before.

She hadn't ever experienced a feeling so intensely in her life, even with Guy. After only weeks, it seemed, it went a long way beyond reason and common sense.

For the first time in her life she was at the mercy of her body, and she couldn't explain it. Whenever she thought about him her stomach collapsed in on itself and she lost her hunger and thirst; her throat tightened and strained, sometimes she felt stiffness in her arms. But even more startling to her was something quite new, the churning between her legs; she was conscious of her womb as a wasted space, a reserve of all that might be best in her, which she wanted with a terrible urgency to fill, to assuage. It was there that the true lack in herself was to be found: or *not* found, since it was a lack, an unceasing absence. For years she had lived with it unawares, so now it was like waking:

334

she felt she'd been spun round by no devising of her own, turned turtle, the dizziness was constant, her mental compass was haywire.

The attraction had been – almost – immediate. They had never wasted words on it. For him and for her it was the last chance, perhaps. Barbara was his other life and so she knew all that *she* herself must not be.

He occupied her thoughts so much that there were times when she was afraid she'd somehow lose control of her own head, that she would never be able to think calmly or logically again. She tried to apply herself to simple forward-looking tasks – shopping lists, appointments for a plumber or a glazier to call, the laundry's pick-ups and deliveries – but she was soon off the track again, distracted, and *he* was behind it of course, as he always was now. She could sit in a chair for half-an-hour and not stir; one object could hold her eyes for minutes on end and if she closed them she wasn't able to remember what it was she'd just been looking at. She was helpless, and yet she didn't want to be very much different: except that he might rap on the door, she'd go running to it, and there he would be.

She imagined conversations with him in very public places, comprising cryptic words of many meanings interposed with long, intimate silences. They would be standing in a corridor, both leaning against a wall. Time was endless, like the afternoons at Tregarrick when Oliver would recite reams of Homer and Virgil. Her hands would be placed on the wall behind her, she would feel her knees ready to buckle under her. She would always be aware of the same clammy, perspiring heat and, sitting in her chair, she would look down and see, between her legs, the moistness mapping the cotton of the loose cover. A runnel of want would have leaked out of her, and she would be thankful no one could see, that the house was empty and all her own, and there was time and enough – all she needed – to mop the chintz dry with a bathroom towel.

Love was such a dangerous emotion, the more so for reflowering in her late. It was forever ready to betray you, and abandon you, and it came with no sell-by date. She knew that it really was love, as she had once – somehow – known how to breathe and how to begin crawling, then to walk. Here was another vital phase of her existence, for however long it would last at this degree of intensity; this time the impulse welled up from deep down in her gut, and holding out against it might have been a definition of 'impossible'.

'I married her in all good faith,' Gregor told her. 'She's changed since. And *I*'ve changed. But *she*'s changed more, because of the children. I don't suppose I noticed how it started. I was going off to places and didn't have the time. I was doing it *for* her, for the family's sake. But who "she" was, I wasn't really attending to that.'

Penelope nodded. She was listening, very carefully, but she was also thinking of the conversation in her bedroom in Torquay, watching Leopold Kaplan in the dressing-table mirror as he sat on the edge of the bed trying to explain to her.

'I can't leave her,' Gregor said.

335

'No.' She was quite prepared how to reply. 'I know you can't.'

'I mean, you don't *need* it to happen. Do you?'

'You don't have to persuade me,' she said. 'Remember, I'm one of those Strong Women.'

He looked puzzled.

'Who would you *rather* be with?' she asked him. 'Given the chance.'

'You,' he said, without the merest hesitation.

'The thing is not to let nothing happen,' she told him. 'Nothing can happen too easily.'

He nodded.

'I'm with you,' he said. 'I get it.'

'I'm moving. To a house. In Monmouth Square. Between Kensington High Street and Cromwell Road. With no one above or beneath.'

He nodded.

'I suppose I'm becoming a woman of property.'

'Very sensible.'

'"Sensible"? Are you quite sure?'

'Oh yes.'

'It's downhill all the way from Islington, isn't it?'

'I could freewheel it.'

'And a penance climbing all the way back up?'

'The penance becomes part of the pleasure – '

They looked at one another, with no evasions, and smiled with that perfect mutual comprehension of Polwynn.

It was the year that men walked on the moon. It was the year her novel *Luna Caprese* came out.

She was photographed for *Vogue* by Snowdon, against a trompe l'oeil in an Italian restaurant: with a painted green sea and a wide blue sky and a craggy, cypress-silhouetted island behind her, beneath the fishing-net that trailed from the restaurant's ceiling.

She couldn't help smiling, even when she was asked to be more composed. Someone from the magazine had found her a gondolier's boater, and she wore it angled on the back of her head like a schoolgirl's panama. Brightly lit, she perched on a kitchen stool in her own navy-and-white sailor dress, ankles crossed and her hands placed in her lap, smiling into the camera-lens. The stool was a nod to the success of the previous year's collection of short stories, *The Koffee Bar Kind*.

The author was, as the saying went, 'hot'. She was working flat out, at full pelt. With a solid corpus behind her and never flagging, she had the season to herself. This was the flowering of Penelope Milne, her coming into her own.

'I'm forty-nine,' she said, 'do you realise that?'

'Of course I do. And I'm forty-one. What of it?'

'We should know better – '

'Well, that's one thing you *do* learn,' he told her. 'That you don't grow any wiser with time.'

'So – that's that?'

'Yes.'

'I'd sort of guessed it already. I hoped it wasn't a right guess.'

'Afraid so – '

They both crouched in the middle of the mattress, top sheet lost to gravity and the floor long ago.

She said, 'If I were ten years younger – '

' – then you wouldn't be wasting your time with me – '

'And if *you* were ten years younger – '

'Things were different then. A decade ago – '

'Different with Barbara?'

'Yes. But maybe you'd have been looking for something – more *permanent*.'

'Now I know not to. It doesn't *have* to be that.'

'You can accept the situation now? For what – for what it has to be?'

'Oh yes,' she said. 'I can accept it.'

He smiled: but unsurely, she thought.

'I know now,' she said, and tapped her head, 'there's another life going on in there.'

'Your books?'

'No,' she said, 'no, *us*. It's an alternative life, you see. It's indestructible. I think I know how to protect it now.'

' "Now"?'

'I don't think I *did* know. But you learn *some* things, a little wisdom. About what's worth protecting, and preserving.'

'So you don't have to grow stupider after all?'

'You don't remember about your mistakes maybe,' she said, 'and so you make them all over again – '

He ran his middle finger along the line of her shoulder.

'Is this experience talking, by any chance?'

There was no edge in his voice, none. So she could answer him quite truthfully.

'Yes. Experience. Yes.'

He slowly traced the ridge of her spine, from her neck down to a point parallel with the base of her shoulderblades.

'Do you want to know?' she asked him.

'I don't think so.' His voice was even, placid. 'Not really.'

'It was years ago – '

'It doesn't matter – '

'Ten years.'

'Ten years ago Catriona wasn't born.'

'I think it was the most innocent time of my life,' she said. 'With Leopold. Until now.'

His fingers explored her left ear, he was staring at it, fascinated.

'I was very grateful,' she said. 'For what never happened. But I knew what *could* happen, that was the point.'

He was still staring at her ear, intrigued, fondling the concha, the cavity.

'Ten years ago,' he said, 'the odd thing is I *could* have done it – '

She held her breath.

' – left Barbara. It wouldn't have been too late.' His forefinger followed the outside arc of her ear's helix. 'But I expect that's bad faith. "Could have", "might have".'

'I'm not asking you to leave Barbara,' she said.

She heard *his* breath catching in his throat.

'Not that,' she said. 'Really.'

'It's not by choice, not by preference, nothing like that – '

'I know, I know,' she said.

'Or *would* you think better of me if I did? Leave, I mean – '

'I wouldn't think better or worse.'

He sighed.

'Sometimes,' he said, 'I honestly can't believe my good fortune. Having you.'

'Big deal.'

'Famous author – '

She smiled.

'This isn't the sort of job I could ever have hoped to get,' he told her. 'Speaking professionally. Of things literary – '

She turned her head on her neck and looked at him.

'I mean, I reached it by a kind of accident, chiefly because I could sell things. It just happened to be books. That was my introduction, my entrée.'

The backs of his fingers trailed her jaw-line.

'One thing led to another. I got into the editorial side. I had some lucky breaks. Accidents – '

She smiled again.

'No,' he said, 'they were. It was just lucky timing for me: not even hunches. Other people in the place weren't having them, so that was my star on the up. And what goes up . . . At least it'll be a blazing end, quite a performance. But a star burns itself right out of orbit. That's my "experience", seeing it happen to other people. I have to bear it in mind. Not to spend my time in lamentation when it does.'

She nodded, watching his eyes on her chin and then her neck.

'Quite frankly,' he said, 'I've never felt *up* to the job. The flukes made it worse, because everyone imagines I must have a flair. I can get by, just about. But I never had a very literary past. As a child, I mean, as a schoolboy. Doing natural sciences at university: it was down on the c.v., that should have warned them. But it didn't. You pick it up, it's true: what to read, *how* to read, just to skim through, the names to drop. It can be pumped up – you know? – *made* to sound impressive – '

'It's very difficult to bluff an interview,' she told him. 'So I don't really think I can believe you.'

'Hand on heart,' he said.

'You're telling me you're a confidence-trickster?'

She smiled.

His fingers dropped to her left breast, he tried to find the spot under the crease where her heart was beating.

'I'm happy that you told me,' she said.

'Barbara has never had cause to doubt me. She doesn't know. She sees what she wants to see.'

'What you offer to her?'

He nodded.

'I suppose so.'

'But you've gone and told *me*.'

'Yes.'

'Why?'

He raised his shoulders, then let them fall. He breathed out slowly.

'To give you something. Something no one else has. The most private part of me. To let you know – know there are more important things than – than not leaving – '

She was still smiling, but shaking her head.

'It doesn't matter,' she said. 'Please believe me.'

'Maybe too – I wanted to make myself a kind of hostage to you.'

She narrowed her eyes.

'A hostage? Why?'

'Because . . .' he swallowed a mouthful of breath '. . . because – I don't want to extricate myself, I suppose. Because I'm a hostage with Barbara, with the children, and it brings you as close as I *can* bring you to them. Evens stevens. But I want to do the humiliating myself, not to have it forced on me.' He shrugged. 'Because – because love is subjugation, surrender, and I'd turn myself inside out for you if I could.'

Her smile was more hesitant.

'I'm not sure I could allow my characters – my women – ' she said and grimaced ' – to get into such a situation.'

'This is different. We've only got one angle on this. Writing about it, that's different, you can go higher or lower, backwards or forwards.'

He leaned towards the table by the bed and demonstrated, using the hoist of the angle-poise lamp. He switched on the bulb and she screwed up her eyes.

'It's the people who try too hard,' he said, '*not* to let things happen, or to control them, it's *they* who come the croppers.'

'Have I been wasting my time?' she asked him.

'How?'

'Making their lives too neat?'

'"Neat"?'

'Structured. Symmetrical. In that measured prose. The books come to within twenty pages of one another, have you noticed?'

He shook his head.

'So, what do I do?' she asked.

'Do to do what?'

'To get it right.' It mattered to her to know: it was mattering to her very much. 'Mix the chapters up, cut them in half, make montages?'

'Why, though?'

'To get it right.'

'"Right"?'

'To find what isn't there – '

'Pen, I mean it, I'm a fraud. I really don't understand – '

She clasped his arm.

'Of course you do,' she told him.

'No.'

'To get rid of the answers, to get back to the questions. *No* answers, you see!'

Scupper everything.
Delete.
Ruin continuity.
Never seeing further than tomorrow, but only possibly.
The mystery. Of character, motives.
Possibilities, only that.
Walking down a street, turning a corner, she might find the man of her dreams, or she might find the Devil waiting in his guise. (A too smart suit?)
Explain less. Explain the minimum.
Objective: a novel where nothing is to be explained. No intrusions, no judgments, purely external and matter-of-fact description. No help offered. A do-it-yourself novel.
(A murder. The victim is who the murderer believes her to be, but the police can't understand, so the victim turns out not to have been murdered: it's a purely imaginary act. Too difficult to convey?)
As plain as plain can be.
Simplify. Always it can be made simpler.
Short sentences.
A different kind of Penelope Milne Woman. She can't see further back than yesterday or this moment. But not forwards, even to tomorrow.
Mystery, misterioso. A memory, an image, which takes over a life. Making a hostage of yourself, to an impulse, a weakness. Turning yourself inside out.
Pascal: 'Ils veulent trouver la solution la où tout n'est qu'énigme.'
But try for love. 'Don't forget love'. Bring love right out of the shadows.

3

'I've bought the house,' she told him.

'What?'

'Veryan.'

He looked astonished.

'How, though?'

'There was an auction. I bid for it and – '

'You've really bought it? Our house?'

'Veryan, yes.'

He shook his head.

'What – what's it like?'

'"What's it like"?'

'Inside?'

She laughed. 'Just how we thought it would be – '

He handed her a glass of wine. He walked round the table of food, away from her – to the furthest point – and then back again, slowly.

He shook his head as he leaned forward to inspect the vol-au-vents.

'You've really bought it?'

'Oh yes.'

'What would you like?'

'Is that a double-entendre?'

He pointed to the food.

'From all this.'

'Anything – '

'Smoked salmon?'

'Why not?'

He laid two nearly transparent slices on a plate and handed it to her.

'Well, it's there,' she said, looking away among the bowls of salad. 'Veryan. It's waiting.'

She glanced over her shoulder. Unseeing Barbara was deep in conversation with her host. Strands of hair were coming loose from her bluestocking bun and she was vaguely trying to catch them as she talked. Her hands and wrists were scullery red; her neck and what was visible of her chest were both flushed. She had almost spilt the wine from her glass setting it down on a too narrow windowsill.

A good-humoured woman, Penelope guessed, and very little that was sham or petty in her character. She secretly envied her her clumsy involvement in

341

the party situation, not herself having the need to turn and glance over her –
she couldn't help observing – quite amply fleshed shoulder, to spy for hazards.

She showed him photographs of the house, inside and out.
'Some time,' she said, 'we'll both go down. The two of us.'
He nodded.
'I love it,' she told him.
'It – it's charming,' he said.
She watched him frown at his use of the word.
'You won't be disappointed,' she told him.
'No.'
She laid her arm on his shoulder.
'We *could* manage it, couldn't we? You said Barbara wants to visit her
mother with the children – '
'Yes.' He gathered the photographs together. 'I don't know *when* exactly – '
'For a few days. It'd be wonderful.'
He straightened the photographs, setting their ends in exact line.
'I envy you,' he said.
'It's for you too.'
'Yes.'
'I never thought it would happen. But it was worth the wait.'
'It's an investment too.'
She returned the photographs to the packet.
'But *that* wasn't the reason,' she said.
'No, I didn't mean – '
'But you will come soon?'
He nodded, and only now she saw – for the first time – the difficulties there
might be. Maybe the easiest part had been the purchase of the house.
'If we try – ' she said.
'Yes. Yes, of course.'
He smiled. She instantly felt herself relaxing. She could believe again that
Veryan was much more than a matter of bricks and mortar and Cornish
slate, although its solidity wasn't beside the point: after all it was the house
of love given actual form, optimism and hope rendered in a third dimen-
sion.

'I think I've changed my mind,' he said.
'What?'
'About leaving Barbara.'
She repeated him.
'"Leaving Barbara"?'
'I think I can do it.'
'How – how did – '
'I can't stop thinking of *you*, Penelope.'

'Oh. Oh, I see.'
'I don't know what else I *can* do.'

It took her weeks instead of days but she did persuade him in the end, that things were best left as they were. If he walked out on Barbara, it might be great for a couple of months, for novelty's sake: but then he'd find himself thinking about her, more and more, and he'd wonder if he could be fully compensated for giving her up, and he'd start to compare the two of them, and there'd be an endless competition, even though he didn't mean to hurt *either* of them. It could end with the thud of a body falling between two stools – or two beds perhaps – and it was *him* she was thinking about in all this, not herself or Barbara; it might even be that his sanity, nothing less, was at stake.

Sadly he accepted her verdict. He said it with reluctance, but he nodded as he told her – when she asked him – that yes, he saw the wisdom in it. She assured him it was for the best, and she did believe it, even if *he* didn't wholly. She didn't want to have the burden of a shed marriage weighing on them both. The cleverness consisted in knowing when to be content and satisfied, when not to want more. The wisdom was knowing to stop at the line.

'Take the house, Gregor,' she told him.
'What?'
'Stay in Veryan. In August.'
'What about you?'
'I have to get the book finished. *Sugar Shack*. It's quite short but I've said the end of the month, or early September. It's being typed up.' She pointed to the paper piles on her desk. 'You were going to go?'
'Yes. But I think Barbara's fixed up with the agents, the usual let – '
'Oh,' she said. 'Well, it doesn't matter.'
'But *I* want to go. To Veryan.'
She smiled.
'I'll tell her, Barbara, I'll ask her to change it.'
'They can keep the money if they're miffed.'
'We'll pay you fairly – '
'God, absolutely not,' she said. 'It's gratis.'
Barbara was persuaded. They only had to pay a cancellation charge on the house, and their holiday was rearranged. He couldn't get away for longer than a fortnight, but she told him even just two weeks would be two weeks of his presence in the house.
'Mrs Neevey is doing everything. If you want anything, anything at all – '

He sent her postcards from Polwynn. He wrote her three long letters. '*The children mention you every time we go into the baker's.*'

She imagined the two of them lying in the bed in the big bedroom under the roof. She was pained and gladdened at the same time to think it. It drove her on in her new work with a fury.

Someone who worked with him phoned her with the news, guessing that she wouldn't have been told but knowing enough to realise she would have to hear, that she had a perfect right.

There had been an accident on their journey back to London. Near Salisbury a lorry in front of them had slammed on its brakes. Gregor had swerved to avoid ploughing into the back, but as he pulled out a car coming in the opposite direction had . . .

He had died between there and hospital, in the ambulance. Barbara had broken bones. The children were suffering concussion and cuts and bruises, and of course were terribly shocked.

For a moment she thought, I've been here before. She dropped on to a chair. The hall tilted to one side, the floor dipped away to the furthest wedge of corner.

If it hadn't been Veryan, if the house had been half a mile in another direction they would have left sooner, or left later, and they wouldn't have found themselves travelling behind the lorry-driver who stepped on his brakes.

She heard the voice trickling out of the earpiece. It sounded distressed on her account, but also – somehow – irrelevant to her, an effect, like the crackle of interference.

She placed the receiver carefully on the tabletop, then she stood up and walked away. Later she couldn't remember the next few minutes: only finding herself – suddenly – standing at an open window at the back of the house, with the garden expanding and shrinking in turns as she stared down at it.

She panicked briefly. Struggling for breath, she clasped the frame and took a step backwards, then another. She laid her back flat against the wall, then slid slowly, slumping on to the floor.

She felt cold and raw and picked clean. It was the feeling that used to bring the smiling question, 'Has someone walked on your grave?'

She crouched on the floorboards, huddled over her knees. She saw the lorry's brake-lights flashing and the car's front wheels spinning into an alternative death. She heard the collision of metal, thin and tinny as an accident always sounds – the instant silence of the engines – the light after-tinkle of shattered glass falling out – steam hissing, the dripping of mechanical fluids –

She held her head in her hands and howled to bring her fine and fancy house tumbling down.

It was weeks before she had the courage to return to Polwynn.

Mrs Neevey had cleaned the house after their departure, only as instructed. Deciding at last to come down she had telephoned, and when she walked in the door she smelt the pollen from the flowers newly cut and standing in jugs.

A note welcomed her in hesitant script, and repeated how sorry she was to hear about what had happened.

She opened the windows. She tried not to think of *them* filling the spaces of the house, although it was difficult to prevent herself, finding the eggcups stacked on a different shelf of the cupboard and the cutlery placed the other way about in the tray in the drawer. She sat in several chairs, and couldn't settle in any of them. Leaning back she seemed to catch traces of perfume in the fabric of the covers, or shampoo herbs, or – the saddest to take – the fumes of his cigarette tobacco, an American brand, which used to linger in the weave of his clothes and on the pores of his skin when she pressed her nostrils against them. She felt down the sides of the cushions with her fingers, but Mrs Neevey – diligent to a fault – had already vacuumed beneath them.

She sat out on the verandah and wondered which had been their favourite view of the garden. She went to bed eventually, and that was the worst part so far: certain that it was the only bed the two of them could have slept in, but not knowing which side had been his and which hers, who had woken to daylight from the lane and who to light filtered through the pine tree in the back garden. She lay on both sides of the centre where she normally slept, to try to detect hollows worn into the mattress after their fortnight but it wasn't possible; she manoeuvred herself back into the middle, and closed her eyes very tightly to concentrate on sleep.

She couldn't sleep, though. She attempted to put everything out of her mind except a prospect of whiteness, and then blue. She cajoled her body to relax, from her head and neck down, bit by bit by bit. But she forgot somewhere past her midriff, at the top of one leg perhaps, and she was recalling the sensation of his hands distractedly but very effectively massaging the strains and tensions from her body as he lay on his flank, poised over her.

At some point she did drift into sleep at last, until she woke again with a start, her legs and neck twitching. When she opened her eyes all she sensed was her being alone, a terrible desperate flatness, the smothering dark and numbing silence of the house.

She turned over, on to either side, left and right. She switched to her back, her front, her back again. She closed her eyes every time, but not expecting any relief. Eventually, though – somehow or other – she did coast back into sleep. She woke twice more, but only with half her mind and half her power of attention; and so it was that she survived the crossing to the morning.

In fact she didn't stir fully awake until the sounds of a van or a lorry turning redefined her dream, which had her sitting on all the chairs she could find to sit on in the lounge of the Hotel Eden and looking out from the french windows to see a lorry driving past, spreading dust. She reached out to the bedside table and canted the face of the watch towards her, Guy's watch from Geneva – the hands pointed to twenty-past-eight. Immediately she felt ashamed to have slept so long. The sounds of the delivery van grew fainter: it must have turned into the driveway of the private hotel on the other side of the lane.

It struck her for the first time that, after her journey, she hadn't actually been afraid to come into the house. Death in itself held no terrors for her. She had enough experience of it to identify what was to be pitied in it: the person's suffering, and having the stumps drawn when there was more than enough time to go round, when you would only too willingly have offered from your own measure. She had come to think of the slow coasting into death as, probably, a state of ineffable, humiliating boredom. That was why Leopold Kaplan's advice had meant so much, that she should use all her time profitably: but even in her periods of slack too, on her holidays, she always eluded the possibility of tedium by filling what time was given her to the maximum, with the sight of places she would never see again and the company of illuminating strangers. She dreaded to think there might be a hereafter, all that unfillable time – an orgy of time – to kick your heels and twiddle your thumbs doing absolutely nothing at all.

Searching the bookcase for books she meant to take back to London with her, she made a discovery.

A piece of paper, folded, dropped from between two books. She caught it and opened it.

The reverie of love defies all attempts to record it.

She smiled at first, to read his handwriting, and recognised the quote from Stendhal they'd once discussed; then she remembered the circumstances, and burst into tears.

Later she inspected the shelves of books. A second piece of paper dropped out, again quoting Stendhal.

The man whose heart has leapt at the glimpse of his beloved's white satin hat in the distance is surprised at his own indifference to the greatest social beauty.

She leafed through the shelf above and found a third message.

At the salt mines of Salzburg, they throw a leafless wintry bough into one of the abandoned workings. Two or three months later they haul it out covered with a shining deposit of crystals. The smallest twig, no bigger than a tomtit's claw, is studded with a galaxy of scintillating diamonds. The original branch is no longer recognisable.

In the days afterwards she located another five notes in different parts of the house: at the back of the oak corner-cupboard in the sitting-room, in the bureau, behind the sliding panel of mirror in the bathroom cabinet, rolled up inside a vase, and behind the carriage clock in her bedroom.

346

Each discovery profoundly upset her afterwards. She didn't know if she wanted to find another, if she could bear it; but she didn't think she could bear *not* to have the pain in her chest and the hurt of her trapped breath as she spied another folded page. For those restless days and sleepless nights of her visit she walked around the house in a trance, displaced, but simultaneously on perpetual maximum alert, with (it must have been) all her senses primed: unconsciously readied, though, because the images she surprised of herself in the wall mirrors and dimly lit windows betrayed nothing and only showed a woman harassed with tiredness, tested to her furthest point of endurance.

Then she stopped writing. For no special reason, except that the words didn't come easily to her any more. She grew tired of sitting at desks in front of windows, then in armchairs in front of blank walls, and nothing ever happening.

She envied those cool, strong, not very fulfilled women who'd had such a straightforward ingress into the world twenty years before. She forgot how it was that she had managed to suggest the mystery of life in such an orderly, neat way.

She read an interview with a French actress – was it Jeanne Moreau? – who said that the mind and body have to be rested; a furrow can't be tilled without stop, so it should be left to lie fallow for an empty season.

Since Leopold Kaplan's rediscovery of her, she hadn't let up. What she was experiencing now was the obverse side of that creativity, so she tried to persuade herself. It had always happened that she was most productive immediately following a downer, a few days of feeling depressed, inadequate, beached high-and-dry. Maybe this was much the same process but performed on a larger scale: her inertia would pass eventually, if she had the patience to wait.

She went off to Lombardy. When she came back six weeks later she felt no different. She left for Paris; she headed for the Vosges, and ended up in Annecy, well out of season and marooned in fog. In the Old Town one lane was indistinguishable from another, and she had to guess her way by lit shop windows and the touch of her hands on cold, sweating stone, and she endlessly crossed and recrossed the bridges over the canals, pretending to the occasional strangers she encountered that she was bound for this place or that she'd read from the guidebook but hardly caring where.

When she got back to damp and misty London, she felt she already had a headful of fog, tight-packed to a nimbus.

Everything came to a head when *Sugar Shack* appeared – a novella, about dreamers in a roadside café and the things that nearly happen to them. She received the best reviews of her career. She knew it ought to have been the moment of fulfilment, the crowning achievement, the climax of all her previous endeavours.

She read the reviews in the house in Monmouth Square, quite alone. She reread them a number of times. Afterwards she would listen to the silence of the empty rooms. In the stagnancy voices made echoes – Gregor's the most insistent – and she could only think over them, block them out, by turning on the radio and tuning to a talk or a discussion programme. It concerned her how much longer the radio voices might stay effective as a charm against the doubting, denying clamour.

Part Twelve

1

Out of chaos she had composed order.

Well, that was the theory of it. She had at any rate organised the events of her life into what – for the sake of a tidy definition – she might think of as 'harmony'. Using the ungarnished components of the past, or close approximations to them, she had acquired control over what had seemed at the time shapeless and elusive, impenetrable and unstoppable.

- It's your job to tell me why I write.
- But why do *you* think?
- Because life isn't much to be depended on. Events.
- No?
- In a nutshell. That's the 'why'.
- What's it all to prove?
- That even the unsureness has its – rhythms, I suppose. Connections. They come and go.
- Wax and wane, like the moon? In *Luna Caprese*?
- Well, everything you do is to convince yourself that there might be a reason for it. If you let it become a vacuum, then you get sucked in. I know it's not very fine philosophising. But it's the nub of it, for most people.
- What's the antidote? For the women you write about?
- Love, preferably. Love eternal, if it's possible.
- And what happens when that doesn't suffice, or they see through it?
- It's best they have some blind spots. Best for the books that they only know so much about themselves. Leave them trusting.
- Your readers?
- The women in the books.
- Trusting to love?
- Quite often, yes.
- But you're not a romantic writer?
- If I even repeat you, what you've just said, you'll probably quote it in your title for this.
- And if I promise you I won't?
- I try not to make pacts with forces I can't predict –

*

349

She finally noticed that a car, the same car – an ordinary, anonymous Ford Cortina of the Hertz or Avis sort – was making circuits of the square, three evenings in succession. When it stopped, it parked at the kerb a couple of houses' distance away from her, either on the left or the right and every time with the grille and bonnet facing.

It could have been someone with a quite legitimate reason to talk to one of her neighbours. She was uneasy, though. She had never forgotten the loneliness of the time after Guy's dying.

She watched from behind a curtain in the bedroom. It was high summer, darkness never properly came at all these nights, and she made out quite easily that it was a woman's hands holding the wheel.

She could have gone outside and walked past, but maybe it was nothing at all: just a visitor, waiting. She imagined it could be a woman besotted with one of her neighbours; or a mistress waiting to exact her revenge.

She had the idea for a storyline, and she scribbled it down. (Usually it took two or three short stories coming together and knotting to give her the impetus for a new novel . . .)

The car didn't reappear on the fourth evening. She was relieved and decided she could do with some oxygen in her lungs after an afternoon and half an evening spent indoors.

The air in the street was little cooler, and she felt it lapping the house like a bain-marie. The temperature seemed to intensify as she walked past metal, between railings and cars, but not *that* car this evening, the metallic-blue Cortina. Heat rose from the pavement, through her espadrilles, soles slapping as she walked.

She heard the jovial, well-mannered voices of the pub regulars, at the wooden tables under the trees, but she turned left instead of right, and left them to their convivial familiarity.

She took out her keys, found the one for the gardens, and fitted it into the padlock on the gate. The fence's wirework shook, how they used to make it rattle at the Polwynn tennis courts in their teenage indifference as to whether they played a game or not.

Then she was remembering the heat of the vegetation in the churchyard at her mother's funeral, one of the shrubs must have been the same. She forgot to lock the gate behind her, as the instructions read, and only realised when she was twenty or thirty yards further on and heard footsteps on the ground behind her.

She panicked, the breath caught in her throat as she turned round but it wasn't at the sight of a stranger. Walking towards her – distinguishing her from her background, a straggling laburnum bush –

When she could see to focus, all she could do was stare.

It might have been her mother. Older, as she would have become in time. On that first sighting of her, height, colouring and the set of the features all matched: she even held herself with the same imitation of a Queen Mary stoop age had brought. She was dressed smartly, a little *too* smartly and sharply for her mother, but the similarities couldn't be disguised. And the grey eyes beneath their plucked brows

Penelope thought her knees were going to buckle under her. She took deep breaths, as she'd had to do at the funeral, and watched the ground. In the churchyard she hadn't lifted her eyes again until the vicar scattered the red earth and there was a general untensing, a loosening of limbs. Her mother had passed over, and they were left with the day, the clear pure air she had almost forgotten the taste of and all the absurd, feverish twitter of birdsong and the endless rustle of vegetation.

The woman too was looking down at the ground, as if into the grave, then she too lifted her eyes and immediately glanced across at her observer.

In the private gardens of Monmouth Square they both stared at one another for several moments. Penelope was determined not to flinch first. She had her way, and the woman shifted her eyes, to her own feet and to the sleeve of her waisted black Persian lamb jacket that must have been a sapping load for a warm evening in mid-summer.

'I should have recognised you, you know.'

The voice also carried echoes of her mother's.

'You've got your father's eyes.'

'My father?'

'And his mouth.'

'I have?'

'He was a good-looking man, your father.'

'Who – who are – '

'He *was* good-looking – '

'Yes. Yes, I – '

'Do you remember much about him?'

'Who – '

'Yes, you *must* remember – '

'Quite – quite a bit, yes.' Penelope moistened her lips. 'Not everything, not as much . . .'

The woman nodded.

'You start to forget,' Penelope said.

The woman hitched her bag on her arm, preparing herself to say what she had to.

'I died,' she told her, 'on an operating table, I believe. In a hospital.'

Penelope stared at her.

'Nearly forty years ago.'

Penelope was unconscious of everything else except the woman and her words.

'So now you're looking at a freak.' The woman smiled. 'You're talking to a ghost.'

Penelope shook her head, wholly at a loss. Was she a lunatic on the run from somewhere – ?

'I don't quite know what that makes *you*. By implication. Talking to me.'

The woman, still smiling, undid the satin tie of her jacket. Penelope couldn't take her eyes off the face, the resemblance . . .

'Of course I know we're spectres of our own deaths and all that – '

'I don't – I don't see – '

'But I can't really expect you to. When you assume that I'm dead anyway.'

'But – I've just met you – '

'You've assumed for forty years. That I've been in my hereafter.'

'How?'

'With your mother. Only she's not going to have sight or sound of me.'

'You knew my mother?'

'Oh yes. I think you could say that.'

'What you were saying – I don't understand.'

'No?'

'No.'

'Well, why should you?'

'Who – who are you?'

'I've come back from the dead, just as I told you.'

Penelope glanced over her shoulder, across the street, to the heads in discussion over their beer glasses and sherry schooners, under the trees. How quickly could she run there?

'You can't guess?'

'"Guess"?'

'I used to be told I looked so like her. Colouring, complexion – '

'Like my mother?'

'Like Eveline, yes.'

'I thought – when I saw you – '

'Or rather, it was the other way round – for a while.'

'How?'

'Eveline had her looks – how can I put it? – worked upon. She was older, so she had the onus of – well, lots of things. Mother wasn't the easiest person – '

'"Mother"?'

'*Your* grandmother.'

'Then – '

'Probably we should sit down. You *do* look a little pale. Even paler than ghosts are supposed to.'

Penelope felt herself being piloted towards a bench.

'The hereafter is rather dull. Maybe your mother'll be able to get things into some shape. She was a very good organiser, Eveline. Of lots of things. I expect she did a very capable job on yours truly, my "story".'

Penelope watched the feet beneath her making slow and automatic progress on the gravel. She had a demonic urge to open her mouth and laugh out loud.

'I suppose she felt she had to do *some*thing about me. My death was as

352

conclusive as she could get. Anyway, I was probably as good as dead. Do you think, maybe she was saving me, in some odd way?'

Penelope sat down. The woman lowered herself on to the bench more slowly. The low, powerful sunlight through the trees emphasised her age.

'Well, it's rather late for introductions, and you know now anyway, but *I* am your aunt. Louise.'

Penelope shook her head, from side to side to side.

'But – *why*?'

'Why am I your aunt?' The woman smiled.

'No. Why did she tell me that?'

'That I was dead?'

'In hospital – ' Penelope swallowed ' – in the operating theatre.'

'Well, it doesn't come much more final. I don't suppose I was going to make a come-back from *that*, was I?'

It was her mother's face as it would have been: slipping a little, with cracks in the structure, quite heavily dusted with powder. The light caught her again. Her neck was thinner, with a gulch, and the eyes were starting to sink. Yet *she* had been famously striking once while her mother had been, merely, pretty: gold against silver, as it were.

Penelope shook her head again.

'Why did she want . . .'

'Oh, Eveline had her reasons.'

'What reasons?'

'What is it they say on the wireless? "Are you sitting comfortably?" Not on *this* seat, though.' She shifted position on the slats, rearranging her jacket, smoothing its folds. 'It's not really such a simple story either. And not quite innocent. I suppose your mother thought she had no alternative, and I'd given up any right to be treated fairly. But I'll have to begin at the beginning.'

Penelope nodded, trying to recover her breath, her composure. She strained to remember what she was about to be told.

The proper beginning was her grandmother's womb. By some fluke of natural science the first egg fertilised developed into Eveline, and the second – two years later – became a person christened Louise. In a matriarchal family, primogeniture had a particular emphasis – and cruelty – attached to it. From the outset, even in early childhood, Eveline was the one expected to behave sensibly and responsibly, to act her age, while Louise was allowed much more leeway.

'It just became Eveline's lot. She never used to complain about it. She was supposed to be the serious one, while I was – not hell-bent on pleasure – but I had the leisure and disposition to enjoy myself. Getting the most out of life, it used to be called: it still is, I dare say. I'm not sure that I did, actually. But by comparison with Eveline I suppose I must have done. She wasn't out-and-out serious, I mean *solemn*: but she took after our mother too much, your grandmother, I think she knew what was happening to her, and somehow she felt she was powerless to do very much about it. By then – when she was eighteen or twenty or whatever – she'd become a bit of a martyr as well. It gives some people a peculiar sort of pleasure: you know, a frisson?'

Penelope shifted uneasily beneath her aunt's sudden, sympathetic scrutiny of her. She realised she was being pitied.

'It just *happened*. And we sort of drifted into *being* these people. That's the way of it. Well, *almost* being these people, because that's not *quite* how we were. We were also sisters, and we saw into each other's nature a bit, and that was because we each of us recognised something: of ourselves in the other person, I mean.'

The story continued. Penelope had an unsettling sensation as she listened to it that portions were already familiar to her, but they were half-forgotten or perhaps had happened to someone else, whose telling of them she had partially overheard. The next sequence concerned an occasional Sunday afternoon guest at her widowed grandmother's house, a former Fusilier officer trained by her husband, and the impression he made on the two daughters. He was at his ease in the house, but not to the extent that the young women's mother could have complained of his being louche; indeed she considered him with rare good favour, because he reminded her in some ways of her late husband. His presence in the house on Sunday afternoons became one high point of the week for the three of them, and also – no one could really doubt – for him too.

'It went on like that. Quintin actually became quite a favourite with my mother – he knew what to say to her – and then I think she started to regard him in a different way. He seemed to be a man with prospects, some ambition – he'd left the army by then, he was working for a Far Eastern trading company in their London offices. He had a very amiable manner, he could get on with other people. And Mother's friends were always scouting around for young men who might fit the bill for Eveline. My mother married at twenty, so I suppose she thought that was meet for us too. For Eveline at any rate, because she was really the one in my mother's image. So, gradually it was *assumed* that there might be something in it – between them – although nothing was ever said on the subject, in so many words. There was just the assumption. Eveline believed in it, and Quintin was happy to go along with it.

'That was when I went away. Friends of my mother had friends who were sending a daughter to school in Switzerland, but she was nervous and they'd convinced themselves she needed companionship, and somehow she wasn't going to get it with all those foreign girls. Well, however it happened, they got to hear of me, that I had another year ahead of me before I'd be quite "educated" myself, and they suggested to my mother they pay the major whack of the fees if I went over with her. By then I'd met the girl. All that was wrong with her was that she let her parents dominate her; she was quite highly-strung, but we got along not too badly. She was quite plain, and maybe they thought I'd be able to "bring her out", to give her trivial tips, you know?

354

I'd show her how to present herself, since I was supposed to be able to do that for myself.

'So, *I* swanned off to Lausanne and Quintin wrote to me several times, and I wrote back: quite affectionately, I admit, but in a sisterly way. I think – '

'"Think"?' Penelope repeated, since the word and its particular stress seemed to invite repetition.

'Yes. Although . . .'

Her aunt who had returned from the dead was silent briefly.

'It's hard to remember. Exactly. I wasn't quite – well, blameless. I probably knew I could – what shall I say? – I could work an effect. "Come on", as they say. Maybe Eveline could have done too, but it would have been in a more heavy-handed way. I had a lighter touch, you see. I'm not being conceited: it just – maybe it *explains* certain things. They used to say – Mother especially – they said I did things without thinking, but people were so ready to read meanings into the slightest actions. Maybe I allowed them to. I'm sorry, I'm not putting this very well at all . . .'

She pulled at the heel of one shoe and sat rubbing the ball of her ankle.

'I think what I'm trying to say is, Quintin might have thought I meant more than I did. I meant *something* of course. But I knew the way things were going, that really Eveline was becoming pledged to him, gradually. And of course in the end that's what happened. Your mother and father *did* become engaged. And I was truly pleased for them, for their sakes. I was very happy I'd have such a man for my brother-in-law.'

She replaced the shoe on her foot.

'Your mother was happy. They got married and in good time *you* were born. But later – later I think she learned – '

'Yes,' Penelope said. 'She told me. About Nancy.'

'Nancy?'

'The maid we had.'

'Oh.'

'She said it was for the best, really. I suppose it must have hurt her, a bit. But she wanted to let me know she was – she had a broader mind than I might have thought. That's why she told me.'

'What else did she tell you?'

'Nothing really.'

'About later?'

'"Later"? No. Why?'

'I think she always felt she'd been acted against. When Quintin died, for instance.'

'"Acted against"?'

'What – what do you know about that?'

'The accident?'

'Yes. The accident.'

'He – he was on business. At a hotel. He slipped on some ice.'

'He was with *me*.'

Penelope stared at her.

'It was a rendezvous.'

'But – but – '

'We were having an affair.'

'What?'

'He told me he always told Eveline he'd been away "on business", when he got back.'

'Yes. Yes, he – ' Penelope's voice cracked with dryness ' – he did.'

'Of course there *were* business trips, a few, and there were other trips that he didn't tell *me* about. But I was your mother's sister, I knew just as she did that no one was ever going to hold him all to herself.'

Penelope stared and didn't speak.

'He wasn't calculating about it. Quintin. I should think there were a dozen women who each loved him, in their way. I didn't want to know about them particularly. I asked him not to tell me.'

'What? You – and he – ?'

'I was always the – an exotic bloom to him. Ever since I came back from Lausanne. Via Rome, Como, and all the rest of it. I married Robert – solid Robert. He'd just landed his first job. Quintin didn't think he was at all suitable for me, far too dull. Which is just where he was wrong.'

'He was a scientist?'

'Yes. Nuclear engineering eventually.'

Penelope watched her aunt fingering the pile on the collar of her coat: such an absurd coat for the weather, as if to prove she wasn't really here at all.

'At least I console myself – and maybe your mother consoled *her*self – that we were sisters, peas of one pod, and when he was with me it meant he was never able to forget your mother. I mean, there was no *danger*. If he did see her in me. She was "base" to him, a harbour, and the other way about. But I – I don't know.'

The jacket was pulled open.

'Your mother was the cake, the rich and rather dry fruit-cake, and I was the sweet marzipan and icing. Something like that. He never asked me to abandon Robert, or not to have children – '

'Your children?'

'*Your* cousins.'

'I – ' Penelope swallowed, a dehydrated rasp. 'I really don't – '

'That's the story.' Her aunt examined the protruding bones of her ankles.

' – know what to say.'

'I think the obligation to *say* is mine. But – but you're still here sitting beside me – '

'What?'

'You haven't abandoned me?'

'No. No, I – '

They were able to exchange hesitant smiles.

'I knew your mother knew, I could have restrained myself – at the time – I do realise that. I realise it *now*, years afterwards. Years too late. Then, though – it wasn't the same. But I wasn't – I wasn't *threatening* anyone. The marriage withstood me all right. I wanted to think – that I *complemented* your mother somehow. I wasn't a sea-siren. I was landlocked into my life. *I* couldn't be one, a mermaid. Maybe I just made it seem too easy, though. But if I'd eluded your father, I'd have seemed more desirable to him. That's not praising myself. I told you, I was exotic to him: because I'd done things your mother hadn't been allowed to. Because she'd grown up so quickly, because everyone had expectations of her. I felt sorry for her, for that. Maybe I wasn't helping her any, I see that now: but sometimes I used to think, way at the back of my mind, that I actually was. Consolidating the marriage even.'

The two women sat together, side by side, and shared a long silence.

It was Penelope who spoke first.

'After my mother died – '

She paused. Her aunt completed the question.

' – why didn't I do something?'

Penelope nodded.

'We went away. About a year after your father – the accident – Robert had the chance of a job in Holland. I persuaded him to go. We travelled quite a bit after that. We were in America for a while. New York State, Arizona. Then Scandinavia. Germany, Düsseldorf.'

'And now – where – ?'

'Now we're in Majorca. Robert retired. I sort-of-sell antiques in my spare time, but it's just playing at it really. A toy job.'

Penelope nodded again.

'I didn't know about Eveline getting so bad. I'd have tried – If we ever did come to London I'd look up the telephone directory to see her name. Then one year it wasn't in. I thought she might have sold up and gone off somewhere . . .'

'How did you find *me*, though?'

'Well, it wasn't easy. But I saw an article in a magazine. It said you lived in a Kensington Square, and it described the pub where the person went to write it all up afterwards. I suppose it was a long shot but I bought a gazetteer and toured around in the car. I knew you had a yellow front door, that was in the article. It only took me two or three hours. I came back, I watched the house, to catch a sight of you.'

'And – and that's how?'

'That's how.'

Penelope smiled. In spite of herself she suddenly felt she was mellowing, opening to the woman for her honesty, and the loss of someone she had loved, and her clinical murder.

'I don't know what on earth we're doing out here. Please – come back to the house with me.'

Her aunt shook her head.

'Thanks,' she said. 'But – perhaps I shouldn't.'

'Why not? It's only – ' Penelope pointed.

'Your mother – '

'All that's over. Mother's been dead for so long now – '

'I can hear her spinning at the very thought.'

'No.'

Penelope placed her hand on her aunt's arm.

'Come on – '

But the arm resisted, gently enough.

'It's best not,' she said, 'honestly. But thank you.'

'You really won't?'

'I'd rather she *was* spinning, in a way. Otherwise, poor Quintin's death – it just becomes – I don't know, unfortunate. Not a tragedy.'

'What *did* happen?'

'We'd arranged to leave the hotel separately. It was very frosty. He said I should go first: I was driving back, like him. Then – when I'd gone – that stupid thing happened, him falling. It was absurd.'

'When did you find out?'

'The next day. Through someone. Then I phoned Eveline. That's when she put her curse on me. I wasn't even to come to his funeral.'

'She understood?'

'Yes, somehow. I may have left some evidence behind. Or maybe it was our blood: sisterly telepathy. Anyway, it all became very King Lear after that. Or Winter's Tale. I was banished.'

'Did he – did Robert know?'

'I doubt it. Or maybe Eveline told him. He started looking about for other jobs, places for us to go. So maybe he *did* know. It's quite conceivable.'

'Have a drink with me. Or coffee.'

'I've got to go back. I'm packing up tonight. I've a flight tomorrow and I told Robert I'd get in touch with some people for him.'

'Isn't he with you?'

'Majorca was also for his health. He's got arthritis. Those Dutch winters. And we went to Sweden for a while: it's drier, but very cold, and I don't care what doctors say, it isn't just dampness in the air that brings it on.'

Penelope nodded, with a serious expression. Her aunt stood up.

'What if I came out some time?' Penelope said, rising too. 'To Majorca?'

Her aunt's smile was brief, a little tense.

'It's not that I wouldn't *like* you to come,' she said. 'But Eveline – '

Penelope shook her head.

'You have to begin again, though. Not let the past rule – '

'But everyone's past is different,' her aunt said. 'It has to be treated differently. There's a generation between us. It began – you were only one or two, I suppose – '

'But I – I don't mind,' Penelope said. 'Truly. That is all past and done.'

'I'm not sure, Penelope.' Her aunt sighed. 'Maybe I was wrong, I shouldn't have done this. I shouldn't have come today – '

'No, I'm *glad* you did. I'm very glad – '

'They would have been proud of you, Penelope.'

'Do you think so?'

'Don't *you*? Becoming written about and talked about.'

'I don't know. Rollo might have thought I'd done something to prove myself. I think my mother would have thought it was a bit vulgar – '

'Your father *was* very proud of you.'

'But I was a child.'

'He felt he'd done *one* thing right with you,' her aunt said. Then her face fell. 'I shouldn't have said that.'

Penelope leaned forward and planted a kiss on her cheek. Her aunt seemed pleased, but not to have expected it.

They parted there and then, with a long handshake, with real smiles. Penelope debated whether or not to say 'thank you', but it didn't feel comfortable in her throat. She stood watching as the unghosted woman walked off across the gravel. She concentrated on remembering the elegant cut of the Persian lamb jacket, the stylish mode of hair sculpted on her head, the black (lizard?) shoes with black velvet bows. Her mother's eyes might have contracted at the spectacle and she might have pursed her lips, but secretly she would have been – if not prideful in her own way, and certainly not forgiving – at the very least, as was her nature, impressed.

Twenty or thirty yards away her aunt stopped; she looked back, over her shoulder.

'He was so frightened of failing, Quintin,' she called across. 'That's what I meant. If he'd known about you – '

She didn't say any more. As she watched over her shoulder she smiled, but sadly. They had both done their best, that was all, and he couldn't have asked any more of them, of his daughter and his forbidden lover.

'I don't see how there can be a conclusion. That would be false to the rest of the book. The least I could do was try to preserve the right of a person or an event or an object not to yield a final meaning. I've never tied all the loose strings tight at the end of a novel, to end on a wedding or a hand closing a door for the last time. All right, it might be understood that that's what's very likely to happen, but I haven't said so: there should always be room for that margin of doubt, of conceivable alteration. This is reader-liberation! Well actually, it's just a case of treating the reader intelligently and respectfully. I'm saying, don't take my word for it! Supply your own ending, it's *your* story too! Well, why not? The ending is as unclear as our purpose: why we're here, to glorify a God or just to confirm an incontrovertible, desolate scientific fact.'

. . . Anyway, you asked me about your grandmother. It would have been me your mother was talking to on the phone that night – or morning. It was very sad. Mother lived too long, and I think she lost heart in the end. She'd had such a full life, being an army wife suited her very well. It was still rather feudal. Fa died when he was fifty-two, it was quite unexpected, and a terrible shock. She thought the best thing was to try to live as she always had, which meant giving us all certain airs and graces. Eveline saw through everything rather more than me. Mother was very pleased about her going to Borneo, and having Quintin, because he'd been one of Fa's officers when he joined up. On that subject – Mother always made Fa's chosen ones feel very much at home, and Quintin's had been such a peculiar home, with Rollo & Co., the very opposite of ours. It took a lot of courage to do what he did, and maybe he thought *I* understood that better than Eveline.

Anyway, Mother tried, but she rather lost heart after a while. (Oh, I've said that, sorry.) It was odd, I think she started to actually resent Fa for dying when he had and leaving her with two daughters. She wanted to believe Quintin was a reincarnation, although he'd given up his commission after the war and gone straight into a good job in London. I don't think she would have let him get away. Maybe she even guessed about his interest in me from the start, from Day One, but she'd marked him out for Eveline, and nothing was to get in the way of that arrangement. (E. was a bit mopey sometimes, which might have been another reason: to calm her down, I mean, as well as because she was older than me, two years, which seemed more of a difference then.)

It's strange how history repeats itself: Quintin dying young too, like Fa. Probably Eveline really felt some resentment as well. Mother had a flightier side to her, it was maybe bad for her, but Eveline was stronger, stronger-willed, so she seemed to cope longer and better, but again with Eveline something snapped in the end, didn't it? (What you told me in your letter about the war.) It wasn't Mother's *nerves*, though, like Eveline's: she'd always been so much in charge, Mother, suddenly it was as if the very opposite, which was also inside her – the reverse of that control, what had never been allowed to surface for all those years, the other side of the coin – it broke through: something despairing, quite unlike the bustling Mother *we*'d known with every moment in her day accounted for, in command of everything. Men liked her, I'm sure, but she'd preferred to stay a colonel's widow; it wasn't quite 'done' in those times to marry a second time, if you didn't want more children. At any rate, this terrible dark melancholy showed itself, and it was discovered that there had been a son born before Eveline, but he'd died at three weeks old, she kept talking about it, on and on. She realised something was 'happening' between Quintin and me, and she tried so hard to ignore it. And I've always wondered if we knew the whole story: if Mother's baby wasn't premature, if the birth wasn't induced by – I'm guessing – a shock: if there wasn't an aspect of the marriage with Fa we didn't know about. You see, there was a curious time when Eveline and I were very young, when a great silence seemed to descend on the family. We moved house, and the silence left us, but we never really forgot. And I think that somehow came back to Mother at the end. She spent an awful lot of time in front of mirrors making herself up, tiddlying herself. That was while she was still in her own home.

Of course, Fa died in the war. I've sometimes wondered about that. So many people were killed. She lost a brother too. She must have wondered afterwards what it was all *for*: giving up what had been so precious to her. Fa, Uncle Oz, and our baby brother: death had come far too close, far too soon. Maybe she got to see it around her in the house: and Quintin dying, of course. Death and darkness, gathering about the house, as if really it was *her* it had in its sights, just slowly wearing her down, and down, and down, to break her resistance . . .

Poor Mother, and by then it was too late for her to know how to help herself . . .

Penelope still couldn't write, hardly a word.

She gave interviews instead, some; she reviewed, spoke on several radio programmes, replied to letters. But it all seemed peripheral to the real business of her life.

She read about herself, her past achievements, and was too sceptical at first, too incredulous, to know how to despair.

She's good on 'class', perceptive about the details – sometimes minuscule to an unaided eye, but ultimately telling – the ones that serve to distinguish us. But I don't feel she's one of those writers who treats class in a way that actually upholds the system, petrifies it, while they *seem* to be only doing their best to be objective. You feel she's viewing the situation from no point at all, or from very far outside it. I know that can't strictly be true, but nonetheless that's the impression she gives.

In the background of those women's lives, in their past, there's a hysteria of a kind. It has to do with the fear of losing status and trappings, of slipping *between* classes, which means downwards. Usually they've never been very sure about their exact place on the social grid to begin with. It makes the mature women only more determined to be as little defined in such terms as they possibly can be. Again, that isn't strictly possible but they do have a brave stab at resisting definition. And they *are* gutsy, the women, for all their determination to remember simple commonplace 'manners'. They also have a refinement of perception – a subtlety, I should say, refinement in the sense of 'clarification' – and that's able to bypass the clutter of class-thinking, as Penelope Milne very well realises.

For two-and-a-half-years in all she couldn't write properly. Nothing came together. She went back to the reviews of her past work and couldn't believe them. As time went on she didn't even have the heart to *hope* that she would ever write another book. The cogs of her brain wouldn't turn. Thinking exhausted her. She lost the flow of sentences, the rhythm of words. But she wondered what she possibly had to express with them anyway.

2

There are no photographs in evidence, which an interviewer relies on for additional 'background'. The surfaces of the sitting-room are tidy, dustless; nothing has been left lying around, by accident or by design, to allow a scribbled observation or to prompt a question. The paintings show landscapes on the point of becoming abstracts of shape and colour: there's little that's recognisable about the lilac skies and white boulders above the fireplace. The only ornaments are several pieces of Chinese porcelain: celadon green and blue-and-white against the white walls and woodwork. The books are in another room; this couldn't be excused for a working space or a den. Here friends and strangers are entertained.

She's extremely observant. She is also mindful not to disclose what she may be thinking.

Her own appearance accords with the surroundings. She has made herself attractive, in an almost impersonal way. She is svelte and composed, with good posture: her clothes are in the best of taste, youthful – a boxy, Mao-collared jade-coloured suit, jacket and skirt to just below the knee – without risking either good sense or decorum. (And many women, who don't know so well, make that mistake.) Her grey hair is expensively cut, as Delphine Seyrig wears hers in 'The Discreet Charm of the Bourgeoisie'. She is fortunate, her face has grown thinner in the last ten years: it gives certain women a fineness, a look of classical authority, which doesn't allow one to judge on the separate features of the face. Maybe her mouth is a fraction too wide, and her nose a fraction less than the classical length, and her eyes a shade too large to balance the overall proportions of her face. But the final effect of the whole *is* very convincing. It hasn't happened by chance: the very little mauve colouring brushed on her eyelids is exactly the same colour as her lipstick, and the pearl studs in her ears are in pleasing harmony with a pearl and gilt bracelet on one wrist, and in both cases one's eyes move between the two. Her hands are slim, like her ankles and feet; her legs are as trim as the rest of her, and she knows how to sit with her calves neatly angled beneath her knees and thighs. Her voice is soft, but pleasant, and unplaceable.

In the conversation that follows she willingly tells me what I can't otherwise presume to have an inkling of. For instance, that her right eye is very weak, so that she is dependent almost totally on the left one: 'I see the world in mono'. She has had back pains for many years: they come and go, but she can never be certain of their timing, so travel has its hazards. She recently discovered that she has an allergy to certain wheat products and she raises her eyes to the ceiling and says, 'If you want a conversation killer, then that's it!' and manages to laugh at the inconvenience to her and what she claims is an embarrassment to prospective hostesses.

Otherwise, I tell her, she is in the good books of Whoever disposes these things. But she pooh-poohs the judgment. As we talk she mentions forgotten authors, and when I congratulate her on her own indisputable success she is cagey of admitting the term.

362

'That's really not why it's done.'

'Why *do* you do it?'

'For my own benefit probably, my peace of mind – to be candid. It's getting things out of my mind or defending some conviction I may have, that I did such and such a thing correctly. It's to get a measure of things, really for myself, which means it may only be partial. But no doubt it suits *me*.'

'Your books are autobiography-in-code?'

'They're not autobiography, I'm always saying that. But autobiography-in-code . . .? It's a life recomposed, I suppose, imagined afresh – '

'You felt you *could* "recompose" it?'

'Well, let's say some people have a facility for words: the rhythm of words, of course, also the ability to make them sound – somehow – inevitable on the page. You write a short story – trying to make a reader think it's inevitable, it could *only* be written in that way, it couldn't be improved upon. That's just a means of establishing your own selfish order on circumstances, on the world. So "success" in that respect doesn't compare with – what? – the selflessness of a nun in a slum hospice: or, say, a man in a lifeboat ploughing into a storm. I don't "deserve". But interviews – they're the payment exacted by the Devil maybe.'

She smiles elusively.

'I gather from other articles,' I say, 'that you don't enjoy publicity over-much.'

'I don't write for an ego-trip. I would have willingly let myself be published under a pseudonym, but these days that isn't thought of as very sensible. It's too fraught for the ego to stand it, putting yourself in the pillory so rotten fruit can be thrown at you. There are much subtler ways of humiliating yourself. Perhaps it's really an outer ring of Hell – or Purgatory, let's say – yet I've no one to blame for that. *I* have to blame my own nature, because it drove me to it.'

'You always wanted to write novels?'

'After twenty-one or so, I couldn't see myself not doing it. I knew then that I had to, because I wasn't really educated for it, so it must have been an instinct. It was that which convinced me it was quite "necessary", and it wasn't just an idea that had got into my head by mistake. If I'd believed so since the age of twelve I might have thought I was forcing myself to go along with such an idea. But it wasn't like that at all. It served some need.'

'Therapeutic?'

'That makes it too close to autobiography. Wouldn't therapeutic mean making yourself a heroine every time? – or at least virtuous in feeling wronged? It was all much further from "life" – so-called – than that.'

'But you said it served a need.'

'At certain points of your life you're left open to an awful fear you're not somehow proving consistent. Not just your views, your *character*. Maybe some people enjoy that. But you may feel you want something that lets you touch base. Perhaps my life has been bittier than other people's, less complete: smithereened when it shouldn't have been. Just being alone and doing the thing – writing about something, about anything – there seemed to be an essential "you". But it's more involved than that even, because the "you" is imagining yourself into different situations, lots of them. Maybe you do it to convince yourself you have an experience that allows you better to judge the world, even if you've got doubts. I mean, you can be high-minded in writing something, and "acute" and all the rest of it, but still be incredibly naïve and stupid just in the business

363

of doing it: quoting things incorrectly, getting facts wrong, and a critic points them out and makes you look a fool. But . . . I've lost the thread – '

'About *why* you should want to write a novel.'

'Well, practically, it might be you can't do anything in life better. And it's in for a penny, in for a pound, in a way. It also gave a woman something she needed, in the fifties anyway, some sort of choice in making a life for herself, and not having to be dependent on someone else, a man. So that became a sort of a stance, and then the sixties came and everything was scoured to find new faces, and I was forty-something then, too old for the trendies but it's supposed to be an age when you write best, you come to fruition, so it was happy timing in one sense. And by then it was a sort of conveyor belt, and you were made to feel you were in competition with other people – which is ridiculous, it's the very opposite – and you were a "certain type" of writer, and it was thought you had to plough that field all that you could, and trust the publicity people would do the rest. And so it went on – so it *goes* on – '

The question I asked has had a circle walked round about it.

'It just became "what you did"?'

'Having a paid job, you sometimes think, if I stopped doing this tomorrow someone else could just take over, and do the job in much the same way, and quite likely nobody else will notice it's another person: this job isn't "me". And I suppose a wife could get to feel that too, inside a marriage. I wanted to do something that only "*I*" could – do well or badly – but which no one else could do in the same way. You can practise a bit at it, although I feel you can only develop something that's already inside you, in your nature, wherever it came from, a disposition. It's not as if you can switch off from it. Going on holiday, you don't just "forget", you're always in a state of readiness.'

'And what was it that *you* could do? – which made your words so distinguishably your own?'

She smiles. She shakes her head.

'I've interrupted you,' I say, 'I'm very sorry.'

'No. It's just, this is a blind alleyway, I think, this question. I couldn't tell you the answer. A good reviewer or critic has a certain type of ability – a good one, I stress – it's they who have the particular quality of vision that could give you the answer you need. "Long vision" maybe: mine would be too myopic, I'm sorry.'

The declining is effected very pleasantly. She has clearly suffered much from those who put their oblique questions to elicit too vulnerable answers into their tape-recorders and whose approach to the books is too simplistic and condescending. She shows no residual irritation or despondency. She just prefers to give very, very little away, however that free flow of words is intended to persuade you otherwise.

'I'm not sure why anyone should be interested in reading all this,' she says, smiling.

'They will be,' I reply. 'It's our job to make them want to.'

She drops her shoulders, seemingly resigned.

'Would you say,' I ask, 'you were fundamentally a lonely person?'

She ponders for several moments.

'More than some and less than some,' she answers. 'Everyone is, in a certain vital sense.'

'The book-illustrations only ever show a single character on the covers. Or sometimes just a room, with furniture, like a haunted room.'

'I suppose it's how we come to terms with that vital fact which defines us,' she says. 'It's that which makes us interesting. How we confront a terribly simple and

364

painful truth. It destroys some people but others overcome it, they learn and grow, they find contentment, happiness even. It isn't likely to be "either/or", probably you oscillate between two poles.'

'Your central character is always a woman.'

'Men define themselves by status, against other men, they're territorial. Women – because of the social set-up – are much more introspective, more open to attack but also self-dependent, at a certain level. (This is a hapless simplification, of course . . .) I'm not sure I trust groups of women, they can be mischievous and catty and unforgiving, and men *can* be more straightforward, sometimes it's because of their dullness. But I think, for my own purposes, a single woman is manageable, she's cope-able with. I can keep a single woman in check, more or less. Or if I can't,' she adds, smiling, 'I seem to have fooled people for a very long time that I can.'

'Women like yourself?'

'I can get out of answering you, I suppose, by saying people are never quite "like".'

'Approximately – '

'Well, I dare say that's the artful part: how much you muddle any similarity there may be.'

'Independent women, though, with jobs. And the urge to establish one essential relationship.'

She moves her spectacles about the glass top of the side-table as if she's thinking how to outmanoeuvre the subject.

'A woman *with* a job can meet more people in a book than one who doesn't work, that's all. I couldn't make a single woman fill a whole book by herself, and someone who's evidently terribly important to other reviewers said that my men are rather too alike, variations on a theme, so I probably couldn't manage more than one of them in a book either. It's all utterly pragmatic, you see, I just do it to save myself. Nothing nobler, I'm afraid, than the mere gut impulse for self-preservation.'

She could make it sound so easy.

She was always promising her publishers and Kaplan's, something is coming –

Talking about the books she used to write depressed her so much that for days after an interview she was helpless, comatose, too far gone even for tears.

She had been going back to Cornwall on average twice a year. People said to her, shouldn't she think of selling the house and trying somewhere else? She didn't feel she could explain to them why it was so important to her to keep it, because it had been *their* house, hers and Gregor's.

At first it gave her pain to return, but the memories came more easily after the first couple of years. What she was able to remember counted for more in the end than the unwitnessed accident. She tracked down a photograph of him and placed it on top of the bureau, in a frame, but she decided the gesture was somehow too formal, too unsubtle, and she preferred the sitting-room without it, since it then became the room the two of them were sharing equally.

In 1973, three years after his death, she was looking in the corner cupboard when her hand felt a card or a piece of paper on the top shelf, under some glasses and above the level of her eyes. She took down the schooners and slid the card off the shelf.

365

'Please, P, don't forget me. I'm counting on you. Gregor.'

The discovery laid her low for a couple of days. On the third she forced herself to work. She sat down at the bureau in the sitting-room, with the lid flat in front of her and her pen poised over a notepad. At some point in her wholly unproductive trance she spotted a piece of paper sticking out from beneath one of the drawers. She hadn't noticed it before. Perhaps it had been lying there and the motion of the drawer being opened and closed had coaxed it forward, fraction by fraction.

She pulled at the corner. It was flat and unfolded. She recognised the handwriting. *'Some day, P. Much better late than never at all. Just hold on. G.'*

She tugged at the other drawers, she pulled them out of their runners. She rummaged through all the contents again but found nothing new, nothing that she didn't expect to find.

For the next two days she tried to believe that it hadn't happened. She wanted to apply herself to all the jobs in the house she hadn't tackled for years; but she decided it was too risky. On the third day, however, less on her guard, she was checking the towels in the bathroom stool. She couldn't remember if the two at the bottom had been removed since the day she moved in. The few towels she used she kept in the airing-cupboard. She thought washing the pair and hanging them out in the garden might freshen them.

Beneath the pink bathtowel at the bottom of the pile – she'd bought it for the Baker Street flat, in her early naïve anticipation of moving in with Leopold – she found the third message. It was written on a blank white postcard. *'However long it takes . . . A human lifetime is the batting of a god's eyelid in sleep: a few years is less than the reverberation of an eyelash. Gregor.'*

The next morning she packed, shut up the house, and drove back to London. Near Exeter the lorry in front of her on the quiet road slammed on its wet brakes, but she was ready for it and stopped with just a few saving inches between them and thankfully with nothing to be seen behind in her back window. When she lifted her head from her hands on the wheel, the lorry had gone; the country road wound prettily and harmlessly in front of her, like the scene on a calendar or the lid of a biscuit tin.

Next Easter she went back. She pulled Veryan apart, from the stuffy attic to the dusty floorboards beneath the sitting-room rugs. She opened every book, examined inside and under every drawer, emptied the kitchen cupboards. She quizzed Mrs Neevey.

Sitting in an armchair she smelt him, even after four years. That set her off on another search, looking for any single piece of evidence she hadn't been able to find, any confirmation that he had actually been here in the house. But she found nothing more. She stared at the cups and tumblers on their shelves, wondering which of them he had used; she sat on all the chairs at the kitchen table, trying to decide where he would have placed himself. Sometimes she almost forgot he'd had a wife with him and three children. In the ancient days a sacrifice might have brought him back. The postcards he'd sent her of their fortnight were the palest substitutes, and it occurred to her that compared with four years ago the colours were already wearing to a thin wash, only very faint approximations to a time and a place.

'"Frustrated expectations". Could we say that of the women in your novels?'
'I suppose so, yes.'
'When did you discover the world plays its cards so close to its chest?'
'From Day One probably.'
'Frustrated in their plans for love especially?'
'Yes. I think so.'
'They may find it, but not as they plan, not as they expect?'
'Well, some of them fall for the convenient image. The old cliché. Not that clichés haven't a lot of truth about them. But they hope too hard. What "happens" is likely to creep up on you, from behind or the flanks, when you're least expecting it.'
'This has "happened" to you?'
'Well . . .'
'In love too?'
'It falls to everyone, I imagine.'
'First love?'
'Love's not love to begin with. It's too impulsive, too inexperienced. It rushes into things. It's ridiculous, but I can feel sorry for it.'
'And so you wrote *Luna Caprese*?'
'The moon is common to everyone. But the situations are all pretty much different. Developments. Variations. She vows she'll never be made a fool of again. She sees those photographic stills in the cinema window. She thinks she'll be her own woman. She *thinks* so, anyway that's the plan.'
'It takes her a long while, though.'
'You don't learn it all in a day.'
'The moon means a kind of idiocy, doesn't it?'
'"Means"?' I can't explain. The moon is the moon. A different moon to every one of us.'

It was about *The Tennis Club Rules*, five months after a new paperback reissue.
Valerie was steeled to speak her mind.
'I think you took something that we all owned – '
Her victim sat in her chair waiting for the rapier-thrust.
' – and you desecrated it.'
Penelope cleared a frog from her throat. She felt the channel for her breath very tight.
'No, Valerie.'
'Oh yes.'
'I think you're – '
'Please don't tell me, Pen. I think I have a perfect right to complain.'
'But – but why?'
'*What*?' Valerie threw her napkin on to the table. 'You can actually say that to me? You dare to say that?'

Her voice was loud enough for others in the Palm Court to hear.

'Please – you've taken it the wrong way – '

'Well, that was a bloody risk, then, wasn't it? On *your* part?'

'It's not . . . The book isn't about *us* – '

'It isn't?' Valerie laughed for effect, mirthlessly. 'Well, you could have fooled me. Tell that to everyone who's read it.'

'No one – no one could recognise you. Honestly.'

'What does that remark mean? So I *am* in it.'

'No. No, not – '

'Or because I'd be mortified with shame if they did, I suppose? Of course they'll "recognise" it: that place, and us, anyone – '

'No.'

'Anyway – that's bad enough – but it's your thinking you could get away with it, picking on us. It's just beyond me – '

'Bits,' Penelope said, 'bits. And it's not – not straight. It's all muddled up.'

'The important bit. Us. The two of us. And Oliver.'

' "Charles" – '

'Well, it's Oliver, of course it is.'

'*He* didn't think so. Oliver – '

'Oh, *bugger* what he thinks.'

'Please. Do you think – oh, I don't know – it's a conspiracy or something – ?'

'What is?'

'Me and him? Oliver?'

'You said it wasn't him.'

'Conspiring, I mean. Against you.'

'Of course you are.'

'No. Not at – '

'You've discussed it with him?'

'Before it came out – I sent it to him.'

'Oh, you did, did you?'

'We couldn't find you, Valerie. You were on one of your cruises – '

'Did you *try* to find me?'

'Yes. Yes, of course.'

'You know I never read novels anyway.'

'But I thought – '

'You were guilty about it?'

'No. No, it's because I wasn't – '

Valerie closed her eyes with exasperation, then opened them again.

'I might've known he'd side with *you* – '

'It's not siding.'

'Well, he didn't kick up a fuss, did he? And *someone* has to tell you.'

Penelope shook her head. Valerie was unstoppable.

'I think you've taken our trust and you've betrayed it. Just to write a bloody book. You've thought the past – ' Valerie lowered her voice ' – it was yours to take and bugger about with.'

'No. No, that's not it.'

'Don't tell me – '

'I think you're – '

'Shut up a minute, I haven't finished. Of course you'll lie till you're blue in the face, but you've got to be told.'

Penelope stared at the edge of the tablecloth, she crimped it with the tips of her fingers.

'You'll just go on selling it, will you? Flogging it off. You'll go on betraying people – '

' "Betraying"?'

'You know the word – ?'

'I haven't, Valerie. You really don't understand.'

'I *didn't*. I certainly do now. Your background, how you were brought up, you've betrayed that too. Writing books and making yourself the heroine – '

'No.'

' – and it doesn't matter about anyone else, do what you like, screw *them*.'

'No, Valerie.'

'You've got a bloody nerve, even showing up today, I really think you have.'

'Well . . . I wasn't expecting – I mean, that you'd say these things – '

'Oh, you weren't? I suppose you've hardened yourself by now. Your father, your mother, your mother's friend – '

'No.'

' – school, that chap in France you told me about – '

'It wasn't him either.'

'I have *seen* the books, you know, some of them. Even if I haven't read them line by line.'

'But – '

'It's the spirit of him, even if he's got green hair and three arms.'

'This – this is quite ridiculous – '

'Oh, to *you* I'm sure it is.'

Valerie looked down at the hand placed on her arm; she scowled and shook it off.

'You're – ' Penelope hesitated.

'I'm what?'

' – are you – I don't know – are you jealous? Is that it?'

'Of *you*? Christ Almighty – '

Valerie snatched her bag off the chair next to her and stood up.

'Right now,' she said, 'I think I'd like to scratch your face.'

Penelope closed her eyes.

'And tear that bloody smile off it you used to have.'

Penelope sighed.

'It was only the church,' she said. The words were spoken in a desultory tone of voice she hadn't intended.

'"Only"? What the hell do you mean, "only"?'

'The pew. The girl, with the boy.'

'What do you mean, "only"?'

'I mean – it's nothing, it's what happens, it's quite natural – '

'"Only"? "Only" that? That's all – ?'

Penelope stared up at her.

'That wasn't enough, I suppose?'

'Do you remember – ' Penelope began.

'Remember what?'

'Well . . . who he was?'

'I really *could* do you damage – '

She walked away. Penelope got up, left her bag and coat, followed her across the room. Heads were turning.

'In that bloody hat you sit there and say "only"?'

'I just meant . . .'

'What else did you think you'd put in it? Or were you keeping it, saving it up?'

They stood staring. Their faces were only inches apart. Their eyes held one another's. There were several seconds of a terrible tension between them, in which the unspoken and unacknowledged asserted itself.

Valerie dropped her eyes first.

'You bitch, Pen . . .'

Her voice was low, weary. She slipped her hands into her gloves.

'I can't bear this, Valerie.'

'Shouldn't you have thought of that beforehand?'

'I really don't know why you're *so* angry.'

'I think I've a right, a perfect right.'

'I'm sorry, then. Very sorry, Valerie. Please – try not to overreact.'

'Pigs'll fly first.'

'Don't let's fall out.'

'You're a vampire, Penelope Milne. A bloodsucker – '

Valerie paid for them both, and said she was going to find a taxi; she told her she'd be out of the country for a while and as far as she was concerned . . .

Penelope saw the appraising look she gave herself in the mirror as she made for the doors. Even a mink collar and diamond clips and three strings of Asprey pearls couldn't give her face confidence. She looked nervy, staring out of herself at her reflection with alarm: either on account of what she might find – or she did it defensively, for what might be found out by others about her.

Penelope guessed that she'd rehearsed her anger, in the hope of discovering something else: not to know what she remembered of the incident in the church, but to gauge how much else – up in Oliver's bedroom – had *not* been

370

remembered for the book. Only, of course, they couldn't discuss that in words, it had to be transmitted into the ether: because they had once been so close, and because there was still a degree of clairvoyant communication between the two of them, meaning there were certain things they didn't need to say, which had never been discussed and never would be now. The anger was an obligation: impelling Valerie to let her know that *she* hadn't forgotten everything either as she might have given the impression once – a kind of self-induced amnesia – and that there were areas which had to remain as silences between them, stellar black holes among the admissible, to two who had been close enough then for each to be the other's sister.

A yellow front door, I was told.

There's only one in the square. The yellow is very yellow. 'It's just a yellow door,' Penelope Milne says, looking at it. 'Isn't it?'

'But it must mean something.'

'It means I wanted to have a yellow door.'

'You lived in flats before this house?'

'Yes. Yes, I did.'

We continue standing on the top step.

'So a front door was important to you?'

'Well, flats have front doors too.'

'But flats aren't the same,' I persist. 'They're more anonymous, they don't invite you to stamp your personality on them. They could be for hiding in. Bolt-holes.'

She shrugs and looks past me, as if uneasy that someone in the square might be watching.

'A front door,' I continue, 'life's on the level. But it's also announcing something.'

'It is?'

'Surely – '

'Then you'll have to tell me what – '

'Your presence, of course. Thus yellow. And your boldness – the yellow again – and your independence. Of mind, of attitude.'

'Actually I picked it off a colour chart.'

'But you'd made up your mind long before.'

'Had I?'

'What does yellow mean to you?'

'Daffodils and yellow finches,' she replies. 'Now, hadn't you better come inside?'

'Come into my parlour?'

'There are no flies on me.'

'But then that's exactly what you'd expect a spider *would* say to you, isn't it?'

Inside, on the other side of the yellow door, the décor is surprisingly muted. Ivory walls, white woodwork. Good furniture, but unostentatious. Good pictures too, almost abstract: yet you can see what they're *meant* to be. There are no photographs.

'The brightness,' I say, 'is uplifting for the spirits?'

She nods. 'I suppose so.'

We sit upstairs, on the first floor, with a view of the square and nests perched in the bare trees.

'Do you call this your drawing-room?'

371

'We're sitting. So I think a sitting-room.'

'What did you have at home? – when you were young?'

'Well,' she says, 'it was a drawing-room, to start with.'

'Where? In London?'

'Far away. In Borneo.'

'Tell me – '

– about it, please, I'm going to ask her. But she waves her hand.

'No, no,' she says. 'It's so long ago.'

'All the more interesting – '

'No one's interested in a little girl living in the jungle, more or less.'

Change of tack. Back to the décor.

'What would your Women make of all this?' I ask her.

'The house?'

'How you've arranged it.'

'I really don't know. They've never had that problem. Other people's houses, yes, but I rather gloss over their *own* interior decoration, don't I?'

'This is "you", though? This is Penelope Milne?'

'Yes. Well, it has to be mine, I think.'

'How would you describe it?'

'Oh . . . I wanted a neutral background. For myself.'

'Why was that?'

'So I could better picture other backgrounds, maybe.'

'This is like a scientist's lab? An operating theatre?'

'It's so antiseptic, you think?'

'I didn't – '

' – say that. No. But it *is* what you meant – '

Another change of tack.

'What do you remember of the background – the rooms – you grew up in?'

'Rather dark,' she says. 'Rather solid.'

'Solid meaning – weighty? Like sculpture almost?'

'I suppose so. Furniture was bigger, it had to look grander.'

'Solids throw shadows.'

'Yes,' she says, 'of course.'

'Did you believe in it?' I ask.

'In what?'

'The substance – '

'Look – ' Her tone changes, to the very positive and ultra-polite. 'Perhaps I don't need to be here,' she says, uncrossing her legs. 'You could just write this on your own, without me?'

'No, no – '

'And I could try to get on with my work.'

'Maybe if I – '

'I think,' she says, standing up, 'that would be a much better idea, don't you?'

It's made clear to me that she isn't going to resume the conversation, that her mind is made up. I offer my arguments: why our not continuing certainly *would* be time wasted, but her automaton politeness is now quite impenetrable. Her smile is very thin indeed.

She leads the way downstairs, too quickly for strangers' eyes to go wandering. It strikes me there's something very *determined* about this most tasteful, somewhat anaemic neutral décor: that she has chosen to have things so with a dare-all passion, and that this is the last sort of interior that accrues from not thinking and not planning. The past doesn't intrude here, it isn't permitted to. There's so much light and openness, and yet the origin of it may be quite otherwise. Penelope Milne has just denied what she wants you to believe, namely that this is a 'safe house', placid and still with this (negative) harmony of its shade-card hues. What balance there is is probably harder won than she cares to acknowledge: and she only acknowledges what she will, which is why we're now breezing through the hallway.

There are no opportunities for false turnings, lost directions. She doesn't have second thoughts, and she puts a brave, bland face on the situation.

'I'm sorry you've been put to this trouble,' she says, 'but I don't think an interview was a good idea.'

'You do give them sometimes?'

'Well, they're not my favourite occupation.'

'They aren't?'

'I'm not an actress, I can't pitch myself to it, I can't perform.'

'That's what you feel you have to do?'

'It's projection, isn't it?'

She opens the front door and stands back to let me pass through. I can remember the gesture done before, in plays, in films.

'I think it's best if we don't go any further,' she says. It's a statement, not a probe. 'I – I have to be in the mood.'

'Another time?'

'I don't *think* so,' she replies, with the stress placed on the verb, as if there were even remotely the possibility.

'And can we expect another book soon?'

'I – '

'It's been four, five years since the last. Your last *proper*-length book.'

She doesn't reply.

The door's yellow is brighter than a Spanish lemon, almost shrill. But seen from the pavement the white of the exterior walls somehow contains it and tempers it, so I doubt if there have been any complaints from the local preservationists.

Did I pursue the subject beyond my brief? Which of the novels began: 'First impressions are invariably the correct ones, prejudice not yet having acquired its vice-grip'?

The yellowness isn't irrelevant. It has struck a vital nerve.

A sideline of inquiry occurs to me on the taxi-ride back. I'm one of the godless, so what hope is there of me remembering off the top of my head?

The colour yellow may have either of two opposed symbolic meanings, depending on the way in which it is used. A golden yellow is the emblem of the sun, and of divinity . . . St Peter wears a yellow mantle because yellow is the symbol of revealed truth. On the other hand, yellow is sometimes used to suggest infernal light, degradation, jealousy, treason, and deceit. Thus, the traitor Judas is frequently painted in a garment of dingy yellow. In the Middle Ages heretics were obliged to wear yellow. In periods of plague, yellow crosses were used to identify contagious areas, and this use led to the custom of using yellow to indicate contagion.

George Ferguson, *Signs and Symbols in Christian Art*

. . . So, just whenever *you* feel ready, Penelope. For goodness' sake, don't worry about it and not on my account. There aren't many other writers with such a good, solid backlist. Not to mention the business of translation, which is constant – and America too.

Write when and how *you* feel like it. I can't presume to judge, Penelope. My humble job is editing: working on your books has been the highlight of my time here. And it will continue to be so, I know that.

Do let's have dinner, and we don't need to discuss novels – yours or anyone's – at all! Next Wednesday, yes? At Scott's?

Affectionately, as ever

love, Mariel

She telephoned Valerie.

'It's not what I meant, really.'

'Maybe it isn't. But that's how it strikes me.'

'Not Oliver, though – '

'So you said.'

'It *resembles* that time,' Penelope said. 'At Tregarrick. But it isn't quite.'

'Close enough as damn it.'

'No, Valerie – '

'I think it's clear what you think of *me*.'

'I thought – I thought you might *like* it.'

'What? *What* did you say?'

'It's how – how I prefer to remember it.'

'You said it was just like that time.'

'Well – with the edges smoothed.'

'This is going over my head.'

'I only meant it for the best, Valerie.'

'I wish you'd just left it alone, that's all.'

'Why?'

'It's like seeing a ciné film of yourself, it's creepy, it's unnatural, having the past brought up again. You should just live through it.'

'And forget it?'

'Well, time's as dispensable as anything else.'

'That's what you think, Valerie?'

'Yes. Yes, of course it is. For God's sake. What else *should* I think about it?'

Also in 1974, after her return from Polwynn, she saw Topaz sitting in Harrods' top-floor restaurant.

She was standing in the queue when she noticed the woman, and in front of her the débris of an afternoon cream tea.

Her own eyes must have gelled. She had to reach out a hand for the velvet cord that segregated those waiting from the casual drifters-by. It wasn't the floppy bow tie but the gent's felt hat and the copper bracelets she recognised after more than forty years.

The person was an older one, of course, and at first she couldn't credit it as true. Then, when the woman finished dabbing her mouth with a paper napkin, Penelope saw more proof: the elegant wrists, and the beauty spot on her left cheek she would sit watching whenever they were invited to make the journey out to Hazehill and stayed on for tea and more of the talk.

She still couldn't believe it to be true, although she had the evidence of her own eyes and her memory. There *had* been a terrible tragedy in Nice, a fire had rased a hotel and from the destruction bodies had been recovered, but so disfigured and reduced that no one could identify them, even as to say whether they were male or female.

Her grandmother had been wearing her rings, so it must have been her grandfather who'd had a charred arm about her where they still lay in bed, smothered by smoke and fumes. Naturally the presumption had been that Topaz must have perished anonymously.

Instead of which . . .

One of the poles which held the velvet cord started to totter on its base. The people ahead in the queue looked round as a second pole rocked. Voices spoke on both sides of her and Penelope felt herself the centre of their attention.

Someone steadied one of the poles. Another voice, more commanding, told her to let go of the rope, please, madam, would you?

Penelope stared at her own hand in astonishment, as if *it* could have been responsible for any such devilment. She sensed the heads still turning in her direction while, where they weren't looking, the fire still blazed in the Nice hotel, flames leapt like spirits from the windows and curtains blew like ghosts, and burning shutters crashed like muffled thunder into the garden.

The authoritative voice was asking her if she was alone and would she now like to be seated, did she feel up to – She turned and stared at the man. He had a self-important but worthless little moustache, like a caterpillar crawling along his top lip. He exactly resembled the dago manager of some foreign hotel, one where fatal conflagrations started in the middle of the night and left guests roasted to cinders in their beds, those that could be accounted for.

Unless, of course, what had happened to Topaz had been in the way of spontaneous combustion?

When she remembered to look, reconnoitring the room over the man's high, narrow, bony shoulder, she saw that the woman was getting to her feet.

'We shall have a table presently, madam. Perhaps you would like a seat while you're waiting? It *is* a very warm day – '

She moved past the man, who had unhitched the velvet cord rope in some way. She passed between tables, unaware – until days later – that more heads were turning to look at her. At one point she felt a firm handhold on her arm but she shook it off, with just as much firmness, and walked on.

The woman was getting away from her, somehow, even though she wasn't letting her out of her sights and even though she wasn't letting a single second be lost. The woman didn't look back, not once, from under her gent's felt hat she always used to buy (on Rollo's account?) from Lock's in Duke Street. Among the teapots and water jugs and plates on stands Penelope swam after her, undeterred by all the counter-currents in the room. Her quarry had the better of her, though – notwithstanding her age and the fact that she must have been surprised – and at the end she left her standing, or rather sinking, among the dishes of strawberry jam and the pots of clotted cream and the waves of chatter rolling over each other as if to infinity.

She lost her finally among the bodies in the corridor, which all seemed to be conspiring to hold her back.

'Are you all right, madam?'

She spun round. A woman in a camouflaged store uniform was focusing two pinhead pupils on her, which didn't quite tally with her smile.

'I'm sorry – ?'

'I wondered if you were feeling all right, madam?'

Penelope nodded. But not enough, it seemed, to convince the woman.

'It's a hot day,' she said. 'Madam. Sometimes the heat overcomes our customers. Being such a big store. Would you like – '

'I'm feeling quite well,' Penelope heard herself telling the woman. 'Thank you.'

She walked on. She didn't know where she was going, but it didn't matter: she'd lost the scent and now she would never know what had really happened in Nice, on the night of the tragedy. Topaz *must* have seen her – her escape was so fleet of foot; she would never again risk discovery by returning, even to such impersonal, anonymous surroundings as these.

By now she must have been seventy-five years old, at least: perhaps closer to eighty-five. She hadn't looked more than sixty. But she'd had a much younger woman's stamina and concentration of purpose to want to outrun her and finally to do so.

Penelope stood near a window, feeling winded. People and traffic moved down on the street, four storeys beneath her; only the thin skin of glass so cold against her fingers on such a broiling day kept her from shattering the unseen but necessary logic of that unceasing rhythm of life.

Later, back home in Monmouth Square, Penelope remembered how Topaz had always moved about Hazehill with most mysterious ease and in silence, so that even her mother – who'd had eyes in the back of her head – had been startled by her presence sometimes, inhabiting the house like a spectre's. Hers had been a fluid personality, a frequent absence of soul even, which would seem to cause the sudden, otherwise inexplicable changes of expression and voice in her grandparents: the three of them must have been so interdependent latterly that they flowed in and out of each other as if there was no private inner territory to be defined by borders and excluding barriers. After their long, shared life it must have been an instinct as unthinking as drawing breath. Until, that is, that

376

last suffocating panic as the air was crowded out of the bedroom by the weight of acrid black smoke.

Only after that did it occur to her that while *she* might have known who Topaz was, Topaz had not seen her since she was a child. So how could she have suspected her own suspicion after she'd caught sight of her across the room?

But perhaps she lived in the perpetual fear of someone uncovering the alternative story of her past life and death. Her own intense, ashen-faced curiosity would have been sufficient in itself to upset her and trigger the alarm bells. She must have been primed to spot anyone's attention that settled on herself in particular; she had learned to distrust any watching, appraising, recollecting eyes. She was wary like a hunted animal, as if her life depended on the keenest effort of vigilance.

Dependent lives were the nub of it. What had happened in Nice, that *she* had been able to survive death and a granite gravestone while *they* didn't? Why had she not announced the fact of her survival, instead of keeping it to herself and privately celebrating on scones and jam and Devonshire clotted cream in a crowded afternoon tea-room? Had she allowed them to trust her too much, those two persons in her life who had most to lose, namely the breath and spirit in their bodies?

That night Penelope dreamed of the fire in Nice.

At the windows human fists smashed at the glass, then flames raged out, thirty or forty feet high, like uncontrollable frenzied genies. A vine crackled in the blaze; she could hear – beneath the roar of fire in the building – the cracking and popping of seed pods. In a fountain water bubbled and simmered. The lawn was an orange and black carpet of sweeping heat. Vainly birds tried to fly with their wings on fire.

The glare might have been melting the cornea on her eyes and she had to close the lids. The cries of those trapped inside the vanishing shell of building were lost to her, and she felt herself as heavy as concrete with such savage heat. Her brain seemed to be stunned by it. She couldn't move, and her thoughts stuck.

Les Anglais, she remembered, her grandparents, they were still inside, but she had no conception of how they could be got out. Her grandparents! – somehow, in the first terrible, disabling shock of the fire, she'd forgotten about their companion, Topaz. Now, though, she was remembering that she'd forgotten, as if there was more to the situation than her just standing here, in front of the burning hotel on the Rue Richaud at Nice.

There was a diabolical din, a massive wrenching, and a portion of the roof was caving in. She had an instinct to move away but she couldn't, her feet were rooted to the spot. Beams and spars were tumbling down into the bedrooms, and presumably – with the whole structure quaking – the floors were about to give way and the ceilings beneath them would collapse. Anyone still inside didn't

377

stand an earthly chance of escaping. Knotted sheets hung from windows, but only from a few. The crackling vine ripped apart and collapsed, hauling flames like dragon-fire with it.

She felt she must be incriminated in what was happening because she was doing nothing to assist, to remedy human suffering. Lives were in the process of being consumed and she was only standing, clamped to the turf, fixed by the heat, and watching through melting eyes.

When she floundered awake she found there were tears smearing her eyes. She hadn't wept in a dream before, never, she hadn't thought it to be possible.

She lay on the pillow looking up at the ceiling, striped by a streetlight that had found a gap where one curtain didn't touch the wall.

And now, in another room in London, Topaz lay, unconscious in all probability, sleeping the sleep of the unjust and undeserving. Penelope didn't know where the true nightmare was located, in the dreaming or her waking state.

An interview with Penelope Milne, that was the editorial brief: three-and-a-half thousand words, four if it's good.

First it entails a phone call to her publishers, then to her agents, then back to her publishers, who are not at liberty to give me her telephone number but who agree to contact her themselves.

A long wait ensues. At last the publishers contact me. Originally she said 'no', quite definitely. But she left an answerphone message early the next morning; she wanted to know more about what we had in mind. The publishers called her. That afternoon she rang them back and told them 'no' a second time. A call was placed to her on another matter; she mentioned the interview again, and said it might be possible although she would need a couple of days to think about it. But her final verdict when it comes is 'no', she really doesn't think so, thank you very much nevertheless.

By and large she has stopped attending launches, lunches, junkets, publicity confections. Inevitably there are rumours why not. She made herself public once, so what has changed her mind?

Opinions on the matter aren't so easy to come by. Perhaps she has been ill, or she has possibly suffered a deep loss, or it might be that she is jealous of certain of her sister-writers, or she is wrestling with a major block. In any case, social life of the literary sort is now Vanity Fair to her.

The sighting of Topaz knocked the stuffing out of her.

At a certain point she thought she was coping, and was on top of the situation. She could sit down, teacup and saucer in hand, and reason out to herself the possibilities: that the woman had only looked like her, or that she'd been thinking of Topaz beneath the level of her consciousness and she had somehow *willed* the resemblance. She could cope thus far.

But beyond that, with one particular possibility – that it *had* been Topaz after all – she felt the air was being sucked out of the room, how it had in a Nice bedroom, and she fought for breath. Beyond that point there was yet another mental staging post – reached in the course of another long night when

378

she couldn't sleep and outside in the trees the wind was making a sound like a raging fire, like an inferno – another prospect, that she had been able to look through a gash in what had then been present time, to catch the spirit of Topaz, her dematerialised essence, still at large in the world.

She couldn't decide which was worse: the absurdity of seeing the ghost of a person who had died in a fire, or the implications of having cast eyes on the living substance of someone who hadn't died in the fire after all and might well have caused the hotel to be set alight years ago.

She felt she was rendered helpless and impotent between the two potentialities.

And then came 1975:

the sighting of Topaz kno   looking at it.

you've betrayed that too. Writing   'Penelope Miln   ne stuffing

'It's just a yellow   of her sister-

She hadn't wept in a dream before,   e that she v.   having the past brought up again. You should

it's unnatural,   and making yourself   ing.   then flames

The ceiling,   of the unjust and un

When she fi   eeping the   eetl   had for   gap where

Ton   Your background, how you were brought up, you've betrayed that

frenzied   ed   s. A vine crac   she hadn't thought it   ws human hands smashed at   and he could

awake she found there were tears   e.   By and large she had stopped attending launches, lunches, could only be considered an act of God, and

Mass would   ed it

clamped to the turf, fixed by the heat   ust a   here are no flies on me '   lust   uncontr

fla   ed out, thirty   ty feet h.   u've be   T

ken

after her return from Polwynn, she saw – sitting in Harrods'

'I think y

3

. . . Well, it's over now, Penelope, it's behind us, and this new book is going to put you right back with a vengeance. ('A Flame Coat', not 'The', yes?) Whatever the reasons were, the experience has liberated you. The 'thing' has gone. I can't tell you how happy I am to get your letters and phone calls again, and no, you could *never* take up too much of my time. *Please* keep writing, Penelope, and keep that fiction coming!

Show them all the surprises you've got up your sleeve – get them clearing *lots* of space for you on the bookshop shelves. This is Penelope Milne Mark II, newer and even BETTER, and all the good things before were just a foretaste!!

I meant it, anything I can do to help, to make things as easy as poss. for your writing, just say the word. *Please*. Still lunch on Friday, I do hope?

Meantime, much love

Mariel

The Polwynn tennis courts are where they have always been. There are still two; the club-house is much the same size as it used to be, in the 1930s, but the wooden building is of more modern design and has a glassed-in verandah and outside doors that can be locked. Several benches have been placed along the cinder path that runs along two sides of the courts, and anyone is free to watch the activities through the wire-netting. Mostly it's friends or family of the players who come, or the next booking very obviously referring to their watches to remind whoever are on court that it's time for the change-over.

Penelope sits down on a bench. The nearer court is occupied by a pair of teenage girls, the other by two couples in their fifties or sixties playing doubles. Neither the girls nor the couples are embarrassed by the attention of the people who walk by or bothered by the motion of the cars passing behind the gaps between the trees. As she sits watching, a four o'clock booking arrive, a mixed foursome, two of them pushing bicycles. They're in their later teens at least, a pair of young women and two young men. They talk ceaselessly, hardly pausing for breath, as if that's how they affirm they are who they are. She listens to them, she can't help listening, because in fact she has no option. They talk about everything and about nothing, about present time (or so little of the past and future that it hardly matters), charting from the selfish self a complete circle of interests and pleasures and dislikes they feel no need to pass beyond, each circle – it seems to Penelope – overlapping on the others and making links as proof and unbreakable as the entwining Olympic rings.

*

She sits on the bench remembering her mother's account of how the English on the compound in Borneo had elected to build themselves their own tennis facilities after the last house went up, six courts in all.

To a few killjoys the completed pavilion was certainly more imposing than required, but individual notions on requirements varied. For some it was only a quick dash from home to the courts and such a convenience was hardly necessary, but for others it was somewhere else to take visitors: and those who came calling to Borneo were either those who could afford to or who were there on professional business, and so regarded as temporary grandees. The club-house *did* have such 'official' functions therefore (it had to impress guests), as well as permitting the regulars a neutral talking-place/escape. And all this was in addition to the practical advantages of the tennis courts so far as playing was concerned, since they were considered superior to most remembered from England: the economics of Borneo life allowed a court-keeper, a gardener, two ball-boys and two club-house bearers to be permanently employed. This was to be no second-rate, imitation arrangement, it was more bona fide than England itself, Chislehurst or Dorking or Petersfield.

The standards of play similarly weren't of the amateur, soggy-serve weekend variety. A number of the old hands took pride in their skills; for good and bad, that either inspired or shamed the others. The rhythmical returns were audible from the courts most evenings, and most often the little girl fell asleep in her bed hearing them faintly, even though the windows of her room were usually kept closed against insects and birds. Even from so far away in place and time the racquets still sounded taut, the white balls keen, muscles toned, hopes and voices high.

Her mother, she remembers, very seldom played. Her father had greater enjoyment for the game and would sometimes spend a couple of hours there when he felt he could get away from his job, when there was some covering reason for his absence not to be noticed. She had lain in bed some evenings, not knowing which of the serves and returns were her father's and which lobs and volleys were his partner's or his opponent's. It had been a happy confusion for her, lulling her into sleep.

And a little of the happiness comes back to her now in Polwynn, the comfort of being held by a locale and having your own place within that. With an aerial flight of fancy from Cornwall to Borneo she is able to breathe in time with the heaving tropical bushes and trees. The shale has gone to pot and to seed. The mesh netting has pulled away from the posts, the posts tilt askew. Voices carry, though, from the lane of rampant, escaped vegetation: the gay spirits of people who never appear. She disentangles her father's laughter from the others'. It's deeper, even – occasionally – a bellow, 'stomach-laughter' as her mother calls it disapprovingly when she encounters it in others; which is really (of all things) envy's doing, because her mother is starting to lose that simple knack, of being able to forget herself long enough to let the laughter rise, or even to find the haywire logic in events that is the trigger.

382

C.A.: Or revenge?

P.M.: Revenge? I don't think so.

C.A.: Someone – Evelyn Waugh, was it? – gave the surname of his Oxford tutor whenever he created a bastard of a character. It was supposed to have driven the man to suicide.

P.M.: Well, it might be a temptation.

C.A.: But it isn't for you? It hasn't ever been? In more than thirty years?

P.M.: Not consciously so.

C.A.: But these things are always hidden, aren't they? They're in the subconscious.

P.M.: Other people have to tell me about that, I'm afraid. It's pretty much foreign territory to me.

C.A.: You do disclaim knowledge, don't you? Learning, the academic business –

P.M.: Well, I disclaim that I'm educated. In that way.

C.A.: But education as such, that isn't a prerequisite in your own occupation, is it?

P.M.: Maybe not.

C.A.: Are you aware of the lack?

P.M.: Only because some people *make* me aware of the lack.

C.A.: Academics – a clutch of Oxford dons – crop up in *The Continuity Girl*. Have your paths crossed in fact?

P.M.: Well, thirty years ago. Twenty.

C.A.: You remembered them?

P.M.: I didn't quite have a perspective on them, maybe.

C.A.: But there wouldn't have been a book without them, would there?

P.M.: I dare say not. I defer to you.

C.A.: Because you think I've the advantage of an education?

P.M.: Well, haven't you?

C.A.: Perhaps in all the wrong things. The study of the obvious.

P.M.: Fiction enacts the search for what is lost. It's making maps, of places that no longer exist. So, what isn't there is just as important as what is. It's the study of the *un*obvious: the elusive and the disappeared.

She sat down at her desk and closed her eyes, trying to remember Tiktiki. The pencil twitched between her fingers. She started to write.

Paradise Valley. Thunder Point. Yellow Man's Bay. Penepolis, The Capital.

She ran the end of the pencil along the notebook's spiral.

The Silver Mine. The Bee Hives. The Spanish Wreck. The . . .

She tapped the pencil against the wing of her nose.

The . . .

She picked up the telephone receiver and heard call-box pips.

Her caller sounded only distantly familiar to her. She tried very hard to think who he was as the line crackled in her ear.

'Are you very busy, Penelope? Tied up?'

She delayed. Then she knew: but not from his breathlessness.

'Oliver?'

'Just for a little while.'

'You're not in London?'

'Yes. Yes, I was wondering, if you weren't – '

'Oh,' she said, 'but I *am*. Sort of.'

It was unfair, she was doing him a wrong.

'Just this evening, Oliver.'

Anyway, it was a truth in part. She was waiting for a call from an American publisher who was visiting London. If she went out she'd miss it; if she invited Oliver here, it might cramp her telephone style, and there was just the possibility that Stanger would call by in person.

She could hear Oliver's disappointment. His breath was catching in his throat. She made out the sound of traffic in the background: and voices shouting, roughly to her Kensington ear.

'Where are you?' she asked.

'Oh . . . just somewhere. You know?'

She wondered if he was quite sober.

'How *are* you, Oliver?'

'That's a long story.'

'But you're well?'

'I'm in one piece.'

Of course, she thought, Stanger might be trying to get through to her now, at this very moment.

'I'm glad.'

'*Are* you, Penelope? What about?'

'That you're well.'

'I only said I was in one piece.'

'Yes, but . . .'

She heard him pulling the receiver close to his mouth.

'I *would* like to see you, Pen. Please.'

'Another evening,' she said. 'We could arrange it.'

'But I've – '

'It's just not too convenient,' she said, meaning to sound reasonable. 'Tonight.'

'Have you so many friends?'

She hesitated. She couldn't quite fathom the tone.

'No,' she said, 'not *so* many.'

'But enough?'

'Enough,' she said. 'Yes, I think so. For me. But it's about business – '

'You know I *do* appreciate you, Pen.'

She mumbled something, taken aback.

'What was that?'

'I – I'm glad,' she told him.

'You're one person I feel I could let myself talk to. You know?'

She heard an urgency suddenly: although, she considered, it might have been there from the start, only she hadn't detected it earlier.

384

'Of course,' she said, 'you can talk to me.'

'And you'll listen?'

'Yes,' she said. 'Yes, I shall listen.'

'Whatever I have to tell you?'

'Whatever – whatever you have to tell me.'

'Even if not *when*ever – '

'If we could just *plan* it, Oliver.'

'You can't always plan, though.'

'No,' she said. 'No, you can't.'

Who knew that better than herself? And now she was talking like someone to whom order and system were the bedrock of her existence.

'It's just tonight,' she told him. 'I – I'm tied up. As you said. An American publisher, you see – '

He didn't reply for several seconds.

'I thought I'd try,' he said.

'I'm glad you did. Very glad, Oliver.'

'Some other time,' he said.

'Yes. Yes, we shall – '

He hung on. She wondered for what precisely.

'I think you'd let me speak,' he said. 'Talk about it, I mean.'

'Of course I would,' she told him.

If she'd known what 'it' was, that is. Perhaps she *should* have replied 'yes', and taken her chance with Stanger's telephone call? It crossed her mind to go back on all she'd said: but then he would see that it had been a convenient fabrication, and he mightn't have trusted her as he wanted to, as seemed so important to him.

So she thought better of it, and didn't refute herself. She tried to sound bright instead.

'Whenever you like, Oliver. *You* say.'

'It's difficult over the phone. That's what I meant.'

'How long are you up in London?'

'A day or two.'

'Then back to Cambridge?'

'Where else?'

He sounded grudging about the place: while she had supposed it must be the acme of everything an academic might hope for in life.

'I could come down,' she said, 'or you could have supper here. I'm sure we can work something out – '

It sounded to her unfortunately like a brush-off. She was thinking what to do about it when other voices overlaid his. Then the voices, or different ones, started shouting. She couldn't hear the sense of the words.

'Are you near a bar?' she asked him. 'A pub?'

'What was that?' he called down the line to her.

'Are you – '

But she couldn't have made herself heard. There was a sound like knocking, on wood or glass.

Oliver was yelling to her. About it being too difficult to speak, he would – She thought she heard him say 'angel'.

The word embarrassed her. But she was spared having to reply.

A few seconds later the receiver was put down, quite noisily, so that her right ear held the sound for several moments.

This wasn't ending as she'd meant it to. She was left with the fact that he had telephoned her. He'd sounded anxious, and they'd feigned between them that he wasn't, and that she had the busyness of her life to accommodate. The conversation had wandered too far from truth, and yet that was its understood starting-point and also the end they'd been working towards.

Three hours after Stanger had left, the phone rang again, at two o'clock in the morning, in a dream.

She trampled air getting out of bed: cold air. Her feet landed on the rug. She grabbed her dressing-gown and went staggering, blindly, through to the hall.

She picked up the receiver. An unhurried, matter-of-fact voice. Police, Inspector. Apologies for ringing. But her telephone number had been found: among papers carried by a certain Oliver Hutton.

'What's happened to him?' she asked.

'There's been an incident, madam.'

She heard more at the hospital, where he was in intensive care after an operation. He had been stabbed in the chest, in a lane off Leicester Square. A cinema had been emptying at the same time, and there were several witnesses. Apparently there'd been an altercation: and the young man he was in dispute with had produced a weapon, a flick-knife.

'Who? *Who* was the man?'

'It seems they'd met before. So we've got one or two things on him. Just a pick-up by all accounts – '

It was said with such casualness. Thrown away. She was shocked for several seconds, then slowly she ceased to be.

He was on the danger list for days. He had a perforated lung. They operated on him a second time.

Valerie couldn't be found. Mrs Hutton's sister came down from Cumbria. Various dons put in an appearance, among them the two who so long ago had barely tolerated her with such obviousness.

The police pieced together the details of Oliver's other life in London, which seemed to her not relevant and indeed prurient. She asked them not to tell her but they told her nonetheless. She wondered how they could have garnered the information so quickly, unless they had had their eyes on the situation for some time. They spoke about him as if he were already dead.

Apparently he had spent his weekdays in Cambridge but regularly came up to London at the weekends, renting a small three-room flat in a very respectable block just off Edgware Road, the Marble Arch end. Among his London neighbours a consensus of opinion had been arrived at, which was that no one had been in a position to form any true opinions. He had spoken very little to anybody; normally he'd had company with him, which had made conversation yet more stilted. His Bayswater (as distinct from Leicester Square) company had invariably been presentable single men, always younger than himself: some could say positively that it was a different man on each occasion, or on most occasions. 'Clean-looking', 'clean-cut', 'smart-ish' were the impressions of those with sharper memories concerning the appearance of their neighbour's 'friends'. There had been no sociable introductions even when they were encountered walking up or down the staircase. Usually the visitor would be sighted over the interval of a weekend, Friday afternoon through to Monday morning, and those who'd given the matter thought assumed that the two men must have been sharing quarters under the same roof. One elderly woman with a common wall between her flat and the victim's chipped in with her offering too: she used to hear voices and movements until all hours, but they'd probably woken late because few sounds had ever travelled through to her before midday.

Penelope was allowed to visit the flat to pick up some things for him.

She saw for herself that there was only one bedroom, equipped with a double bed, and no provision for a couch-bed, the put-you-up sort.

The surroundings saddened her. They were furnished with the informed good taste she might have expected, remembering the Cambridge rooms, but they also dispirited her with the pervasive intimation of solitude: certainly there was that companionable bed with two conspicuous hollows worn in its mattress, but everything else was insistently cerebral, which made her think (correctly or not) that one mind and only one must have been responsible. The walls were hung with antique maps of English shires, like nothing so much as abstract art. The books were fussily arranged on the shelves in alphabetical order, and very evidently none was out of its proper place. The television set was piously concealed behind an embroidered fire screen. There were no plants or receptacles for flowers or even ornaments, but three outsized mirrors on the sitting-room walls invited personal scrutiny and introspection in their cold glass. The chairs were right-angled cane bergère with petite, under-stuffed cushions. Primly functional gas-fires were set into two neutered fireplaces. A wireless set was tuned on Radio 3.

It was the pied-à-terre of a bachelor, a tidy and disciplined, maybe compulsive, man. It was also a house of secrets. Jars and tubes of jellies and lubricants filled one of the shelves in the bathroom. A small bronze statue of a satyr in lewd, lustful heat occupied pride of place on the bedroom mantelpiece. The Indian carpet around the bed was spotted with a plethora of long-dried white stains. Something stomach-turning – solid but pliable and quite long – was lying

387

wrapped in a brown paper-bag, deliberately so that she wouldn't see, but she did catch a glimpse of its authentic, flesh-pink colouring.

She didn't touch anything. She didn't sit down. She kept moving and wouldn't let herself stand still. She wanted to get away but she also wanted to make the most of these moments of intimate contact with him – a sorry and reduced presence now – while she was suddenly remembering so much about that time they had shared, which hadn't been forgotten but, rather, overlooked by her in the drift of years since.

She sat waiting to speak to the doctor. When the door opened she was elsewhere in her thoughts, in Cambridge, in Oliver's college set. She put on her plucky smile for the woman.

She was being scrutinised with the inquisitiveness a wife or a fiancée would have merited.

'I'm a friend of Mr Hutton's,' she explained.

A coloured doctor; she wondered how Valerie would have taken that.

'You liked cucumber with anchovies.'

'I'm sorry – ?'

'On your sandwiches.'

'On my sandwiches?'

She had quite forgotten.

'And a slice of apple on Bovril. On toast.'

'How – how do you . . .'

The woman spoke a name, which didn't register with her.

'In Lithgow Road.'

'Lithgow Road?'

'Mrs Milne's.'

'The house – ?'

'I had the green room. As your mother called it – '

Penelope stared, first at the wrinkle-lines etched in her neck, then at the alertness in her eyes.

'I – but I didn't recognise you – '

'Well, it's been years, years – '

'I'm so sorry, really.'

'I knew you from your photographs. I'm Shabana.'

'Of course, of course.'

They shook hands. Penelope felt her face must be brick-red. She wouldn't have recognised this dignified mien and frizzy halo of grey hair from any of her memories of 'then'. If her mother had foreseen, she mightn't have felt so obliged to keep the canteen of best silver locked and sacrosanct.

'I've read some of your books. When I get the time!'

'Yes?'

'When you have that house in – I'm useless with titles – *Making Amends*, was it – ?'

'*Making Do and Mending.*'

'Yes, *Making Do and Mending*, that's right. Well, the house in that, with the PGs. I always used to think of Lithgow Road.'

'Oh that was – just a house.' Penelope shifted her weight from one foot to the other. 'You know?'

'But in my mind's eye – it was like going back to the old days.'

'Oh. Was it?' Penelope asked, hearing how hesitant she sounded.

'But I *enjoyed* that, really.'

The doctor smiled. The pale, petal-pink caste-mark on her brow lifted.

'It *is* long ago. But they were good times.'

Penelope wasn't sure how that could have been.

'In our house?'

'Yes. Yes, of course.'

Penelope fastened the buttons on her coat.

'That's how I remember it,' the woman said and smiled. 'Sunny evenings. The bicycles outside, leaning against the railings.'

(The railings. Of course. They had all been appropriated and sawn off the wall for the war effort. Somehow she had failed to remember –)

'Walking along the street, seeing the dust floating in the air and catching the perfume from the gardens. And the smell of the fencing – '

Penelope looked up.

'Creosote,' she said. 'I expect it was – '

'Yes. And the gardens being watered. The evenings were always so busy but still. Always sunny. Before the war.'

Penelope watched the woman. She was being, as far as she could judge, quite sincere.

'I don't know,' she said, without meaning to.

' "Don't know"?' the woman repeated.

'I mean – ' Penelope smiled, feeling embarrassed ' – I'm not sure I remember it so well. I don't think I was trying to remember – '

'But you did remember. In the book. You remembered so much.'

'Not about the evenings. Or the railings. I don't know how I – '

'But about the smells in the house you did. And the cooking, and the polish. How the PGs, each of them, how they changed the feel of a room when they walked into it. It's just, you *make* me remember the evenings. I'd started to forget. You brought the atmosphere back.'

Downstairs they shook hands. Tight grips. Penelope thanked the doctor for all she was doing for Oliver. The woman nodded, almost self-deprecatingly, as if she didn't want to intrude into the privacy of the relationship.

'We're friends,' Penelope said, thinking the point had to be made. 'Oliver – Mr Hutton – and myself.'

Maybe the woman imagined they lived in fashionable sin: or maybe she didn't. She had sharp clever eyes, unmisted by the sentiment of nostalgia. Did she think she wasn't aware of Oliver's other life?

'Just friends,' Penelope repeated, and felt uncomfortable with herself: as if by saying it she was betraying the friendship, afraid it might be conferring some shame on her, for her failing to see –

'Keep on writing,' the woman said. 'Won't you?'

'Oh yes.'

'Well . . .'

'The hospital's waiting for you, I'm sure – '

Further smiles, further firm handshakes.

But back in the car Penelope started to tremble. What if the woman hadn't been so intelligent and understanding? She closed her eyes and visualised the knife being drawn in the alleyway, the cold glint of the blade, the inexorability of steel so sharp its touch can hardly be felt, incising through skin into gut.

She had grasped the wheel and leaned her head on her hands, just as some of her women had done in their past adventures. She always had to cut away from those scenes, to allow herself a graceful, credible exit, lest she became too embroiled. All she needed now was to be able to believe in herself, back in the house in Monmouth Square, in a different London: safe at her desk, too safe, performing her familiar precision surgery on the past and sparing nothing and no one, sipping weak lemon tea from a tall glass and imagining herself invulnerable and uncompassionable in the fastness of her hermitage.

Recovery was a glib term in the circumstances.

Finally he was Oliver again, but not the same one: a sallower, more care-worn version. Physically he was much weaker after several months in hospital. He needed access to a respirator, and one was provided in his rooms in Cambridge, optimistically.

However, he was determined to pick up the threads, and she did what she could to help ease him slowly, tentatively, back into the semblance of the life before, or one of the lives. He let her see his gratitude. Of course he realised that she knew what she now did, about the attack and about his other London existence. Somehow they both accommodated themselves to the knowledge of the knowledge. It was too late, she felt, for anything like prudery, to turn into the fair-weather sort of friend who only deserved disowning: and anyway there was the history of the two proposals and the two rejections to confirm that certain matters could now be 'understood' between the two of them.

As time went on, she occasionally succumbed to the hypothesis, if only I had . . . Maybe she could have saved him from what had happened, and she wouldn't have lived to see on his face this concentration of pain which was more than the drugs could deal with. But she suspected that being his wife would have changed nothing. Visiting the college, and sitting with him in the walled Fellows' garden after the few yards' walk to the bench, and calculating if he had put on a little girth since last time, she felt they might even have looked the parts, husband and wife, and that that would have been the sum of it if they really had been, only playing parts. When she left him for the drive back to London she always felt less than three-dimensional: *appearing* as if she were only herself instead of *being* so.

He bought her a hat for her birthday: not just any hat but one a 'friend' had found for him, in a specialist shop in Paris. It was circa 1956, a Dior-sold accessory, a wide-brimmed dark navy picture hat festooned with life-size, full-blown pink and yellow crêpe rose blooms.

She kept it stored in its cardboard box, wrapped in sheets of clean tissue paper. Sometimes she took it out and wore it, back in Monmouth Square, in the privacy of her bedroom. She speculated on its owner, who and where, and why it had been traded in. Standing in front of the mirror, in a bare-shouldered party dress and jewellery, she felt that wearing such a hat she would have been capable of achieving anything: or at any rate she might have done when the hat had been the height of the fashion and all the rage, back in 1956. One evening she put on Guy's watch and engagement ring, the wrist-rope of pearls Leopold Kaplan had bought her five weeks before he died; she opened a bottle of champagne Gregor had once bought her and she drank from her glass. She remembered the pose of royal Astrid in that first tinted postcard photograph she'd bought in Amsterdam, and she sat in the same manner on the sofa by the window, in a London twilight. She had resisted pity for so long, she who was supposed to be one of fortune's favourites, but she felt now it had been long enough. An old Simon and Garfunkel tune was playing on the radio in the bedroom, 'I am a rock', and she thought bravery was a pyrrhic victory, that an island was a desolate thing to be. She accepted the best reading, that sitting here had been determined by the rolling dice and that, such being so, she had done all anyone might have done.

But . . .

In the mirror she couldn't see herself, because it hung high and she was sitting so close to the ground, and all that was visible to her was the furniture and the space between the objects. She thought it could only be the beautiful hat's fault, that she was feeling the way she was, so low, because the hat must be haunted: but the haunting seemed inverted, the hat remained and it was she who was fading from the elegant, pastel scene – two lives lived, in herself and her books, yet less than one achieved – and her transubstantiation with twilight falling on this mild, gentlest of evenings to a Kensington ghost.

She was staying in Perthshire, at the Gleneagles Hotel, after the publication of *Calypso*. The weather was crisp, clear and healthy, and her mind was very nearly set at rest.

It was the name on that fourth morning which drew her eye to the story on one of *The Scotsman*'s inside pages.

'Jocelyn Frith'. Joss.

A man had been found drowned in an en suite bathroom at the North British Hotel in Edinburgh. Police were treating the matter as suspicious. The dead man had been staying at the hotel for several days, under a different name from that found among his personal belongings. There was no suicide note. An autopsy would be carried out.

She bought the English papers from the hotel shop but couldn't find any reference in them to the business.

She was hugely perplexed.

That night she went to bed troubled. She couldn't sleep.

She got up and stood at the window, pulling the curtain back. The sky was curdled, white stirred into cheesy blue. The hills were pale, and Glen Devon looked lunar. The arc of the fountain on the terrace wavered, as if the little stone cherub was less sure of his strength when there was no one around to see.

The next morning she read *The Scotsman* three times from cover to cover but there was no further mention of the death at the North British Hotel.

She bought all the English papers but they didn't carry any coverage either.

The next day she felt her eyes hurting with the concentration of perusing columns of newsprint. But there was nothing more to be found on the matter.

When a jovial North-of-Englander, a golfer with a white Porsche, started chatting her up either in the bar or the Eagle's Nest restaurant she hardly noticed. She only knew she must have smiled a little too animatedly. She didn't notice at what point it was that he stopped looking out for her and cast his eyes elsewhere, giving up the game as lost.

In 1980, after the paperback publication of a short novel *Soft Clocks*, she went back to Switzerland.

She dutifully inspected the cities – Basle, Berne, Zürich, Lausanne, Lucerne – while saving the important one, the reason for her being here, until last.

Lake Leman was peacock blue and the pale stone of Geneva sparkled in May sunlight. A taxi took her from the station to the Hotel Des Bergues. From her room she could look across to the Jet d'Eau and the Quai Ador; she was able to catch the steamers docking at the Jardin Anglais. The cars glinted on the lakeside road to Collonge-Bellerive.

On the third day, Sunday, she spent the morning and beyond at the Jardin Alpin and decided she was hungry enough to take a late lunch back at the hotel. She changed into youthful khaki American co-ordinates, read the respective menus of the Pavillon and Amphitryon, and presented herself at the former.

At some point during the entrée she might have had her heart in her mouth, not asparagus tips.

She thought she was going to choke and picked up her glass of mineral water and swallowed a mouthful.

Across the room four people were rising from their table, a couple with two teenage children. It was the man she was watching. His dimensions, his posture, how he pulled back the woman's chair and held her arm, a smile and a nod for the waiter –

At first, after he died, she hadn't been able to stop looking for resemblances of Guy in men of a particular age and style. She'd had to believe that he was dead; what she hadn't been allowed was a last opportunity to look at him. Even if he'd been lying in a police morgue, she would have gone to see, because she was sure nothing that might have happened would have made him unrecognisable to her. Instead there had been no funeral ceremony and no rites, and she'd been deprived of her widow's dues.

'Did you see them?' she asked a waiter in a stranger's voice. 'Those people – '

'Madame – ?'

'A family – they just walked out – '

She was immobilised for some time and couldn't co-ordinate her movements. It was insane. Then she stood up, rockily. As she did so, the strap of her bag caught on the arm of the chair. She tugged herself free and hurried off across the room, watching movements in the foyer. She thought it was one of the two children disappearing through the swing doors.

By the time she'd run to the doors and pushed through them a silver-blue Mercedes coupé was driving out into the traffic. The driver's window was down, his arm rested on the ledge of the door and his hand tapped on the roof, how it had as he waited for her to rush up the area steps from the publisher's basement.

She returned to the dining-room, having some difficulty breathing, to ask the maître who they were. While other diners stared at her from their tables, she was given a name, 'Müller'.

Upstairs in her room she skimmed through the telephone directory. There were dozens of 'Müllers'. She slammed the directory shut.

She rang the restaurant and asked the maître if he knew a Christian name or an initial, if he knew anything about them, where they lived. He sounded suspicious but she disregarded that. He told her, unfortunately 'no', he knew nothing more about Monsieur Müller. She believed that he wasn't being reticent, that he really didn't know. She asked if the family often came. 'Occasionally': or the gentleman would come with a business colleague, for lunch. She asked if Monsieur Müller was from Geneva, but the maître told her he was unable to say.

If she hadn't looked up at the exact moment she had, she wouldn't have seen the man, or the closeness of the resemblance to Guy. Guy, that is, after twenty-five years, with grey hair and a widow's peak: Guy otherwise just as she would have remembered him.

She found a motel beside the main road, between Versoix and Coppet, and asked the taxi-driver to stop.

After checking in, she carried her suitcase herself.

The rooms, reached by a steep wooden staircase, stood on stilts. She made her way up on to the top open-air corridor. Through a screen of conifers she caught glimpses of the lake. As she walked along the boards to her room she heard a radio set behind one door and a couple feuding with each other behind another.

The room was small and very plainly furnished. The mattress was comfortable enough – she pushed hard down on the springs – and she was glad to be spared the chilly duvet of Mittel-Europa. She perched on the edge of the bed, and wondered what was happening to her, that it had come to this.

She switched on the wall radio and turned the channel wand. She stopped when she heard a tune she recognised. 'Round, like a circle in a spiral, like a wheel within a wheel . . .'

She leaned back and laid her head on the pillows. This was ridiculous, of course. But she had lost the hold on her life completely.

And now somewhere out there was Guy. If it hadn't been that hotel she'd gone to, if she'd chosen to have lunch out at the Jardin Botanique – It could only have been meant to happen surely, and in that case she was only meant to be here –

The little bathroom was practical in a bleak way, and windowless, lit by a tube of humming striplight. She got up and stared at herself in the mirror above the basin and forgot all about time. Faces floated beneath her own: her mother's, her father's briefly, more vaguely her two grandmothers'. She touched her chin, her cheeks, her temples, as if something so obvious, so immediate and personal, wasn't to be taken on trust any more, as if this lie of 'herself' couldn't possibly hold up for very much longer.

Six French-franc notes and nine Swiss notes.

Two Swiss postage stamps.

A colour postcard of the Jardin Alpin in Geneva.

A black-and-white postcard reproduction of a Corot painting hanging in the Jeu de Paume.

A book, Simenon's *L'Ombre Chinoise*.

A very small, four-inch-long, lethally sharp rapier, unfolding like a penknife and with a steel finger-hold.

A receipt issued by a Bristol post office, acknowledging collection from the counter of a package in the name of 'Mr Miller'.

4

First, she explained, she'd gone to Harley Street for her appointment, then she'd come on for lunch, as arranged.

Mariel was sitting at the bar with a gin-and-tonic.

'I'll get you one, Penelope.'

'A vodka, please.'

'Bloody Mary?'

'No, just a vodka.'

Mariel was nervous as if she already suspected.

'You're looking much better, Penelope.'

It was the beginning, the scratch point from which they started to make the roundabout progression to a disclosure.

Mariel looked shocked as her companion described the consulting-room scene she had been practising en route to the restaurant from Kensington in the taxi. She performed her part in it as any of her stronger Women would have done, taking it straight, right on the chin: only shaking afterwards when the door had been quietly closed behind her and she was making her way downstairs, hand clasping the balustrade.

It was the first time she'd seen Mariel lost for words. She had always resisted telling her that she'd stolen bits and pieces from her over the years to flesh out some of her Women. Now she averted her eyes: first to her nearly depleted glass, then to the traffic in the street outside.

A few seconds later she felt the handhold on her wrist. She smiled with pleasure and sheer relief, that Mariel wasn't going to let her down.

Then she shrugged. She couldn't think what to say in reply to all that concern. Solicited, unnecessary attention.

She picked up the menu.

'I suggest,' she said, 'that we eat now.'

'Penelope – '

'I know, how can I? But it's a longish stretch, walking from Harley Street.'

'No.' Mariel shook her head. 'No, that's not what I meant.' She was smiling and crying at the same time; she leaned her other elbow on the counter of the bar and wiped at her eyes.

'What, then?'

'You're like those women – your women – '

'Oh.' She shrugged again, as if they hadn't been in her thoughts or plans at all this morning. '*Them.*'

'They're *you*, Penelope.'

'Any resemblance to a living person – ' she paused ' – or a dead one – ' she lifted her glass ' – is entirely coincidental – '

They were shown to their table. Their orders were taken and fresh glasses brought and filled.

'It's not a novel I'm writing, Mariel.'

'I know it isn't.'

'It could be. But I remember too much too clearly.'

Mariel nodded.

'Shall I fool everyone else, though?' Penelope asked her.

'Do you really care? – if you do or not?'

'I just want to get it written.'

'Well, *how* it's put down doesn't matter.'

'If I get the time, that is.'

'Do what you can, Penelope. If it's what you – '

'I'm trying.'

'I can't believe I'm being so – *pragmatic* about this.'

'You're helping me, encouraging me. You're being selfless, Mariel.'

'Maybe I'll realise I've been a prime bitch. I'll bet it's what people'll be thinking – '

'When have you ever minded something like that?'

'True enough. What do *you* think, Penelope? That's all that matters to me.'

'I told you, you're encouraging me. You're helping me to write it. My book of books. *Penelope's Story*. That's what a true editor *should* do.'

'I wish I had your confidence in me.'

'Leopold could do it as well. He had presentiments. He told me I wasn't to waste breath, or time, or anything else. He saw his own end too, I'm sure. Sometimes it seems it was a long time, having him here. It's just, I worked very hard, I think. In a burst of activity. Somehow I cottoned on that I had to.'

'Is there anything more I can do for you, Penelope?'

'You've done all you possibly can.'

'But *more* than that?'

'I'm quite comfortable, really. I don't have to type anything, I've hardly to lift a finger. There's a very good woman can read my handwriting, and she can type from a cassette – '

'Tell me, won't you?'

'Of course I shall.'

'What will you call it?'

'*About A Hat* maybe.'

'And it's coming on?'

'More slowly than it should – '

'Don't, if it's pushing yourself too far.'

'But there has to be a – what's it called? – '

'What's what?'

' – a pay-off. That's it. There has to be a pay-off.'

'"*Has* to be"?'

'So we're reliably informed – '

'Who by?'

'Those who know better. Critics, reviewers.'

'Do you need one?'

'Apparently.'

'Have you any ideas?'

'There's the final pay-off of all, of course. That's sort of decided, though, and you just work towards it.'

'Penelope – '

'Suddenly it's all so beautifully simple: clean: clear-cut.'

'Let's change the – '

'Everything will just fall into place, and all the little mysteries will belong to the final one, the enigma. Do you see, Mariel? It could hardly be improved upon, could it now?'

They had been Guy's dimensions, his posture, the profile, how he'd pulled back the woman's chair and held her arm, the way he'd smiled and nodded to the waiter –

Grey hair, worn a little longer, a widow's peak. The silver-blue Mercedes, with the driver's window down. His arm resting on the ledge of the door, as he always used to position himself negotiating slow traffic, and his hand tapping on the roof. But with one vital difference: for 'right' now read 'left'. His left arm resting on the driver's windowsill, his left hand tapping a tattoo on the roof.

'The awful thing is . . .'

For several moments neither of them spoke. Then Mariel strangled a sound suspiciously like a sob. She shook her head, looked down at the table, moved the ashtray closer to the posy of flowers and pushed her cup and saucer towards the condiments.

' . . . this is like the lunch Harriet Ross had. With her friend.'

Penelope stared at her.

'In *The Blue Hour*.'

Penelope was fully conscious she was staring.

'Yes,' she said. 'Of course.'

But she had forgotten. It had only seemed the best idea for today, that she should tell Mariel she had been to see a doctor, that he had confirmed a terminal prognosis. She had suddenly felt so badly in need of sympathy, and she also wanted to warn Mariel that she was in mortal fear of another year like 1975, that there might not be another book, that it could turn out to be less than all it was meant to be and come finally to nothing. She also knew that

397

she'd had enough of London, that if her life had had the grace and aptness of a story in a book it would have finished by now. It should have ended when she was enjoying one of her little triumphs, when she still had luck on her side.

She had stopped being interested in books, and in the other people who wrote them. Mostly they were self-advertisers, or they allowed themselves to be taken up by journalists who patronised them; the interesting minds held themselves back, or they were fated to obscurity because too few of the professional taste-makers with their received opinions were concerned enough or competent enough to discover what might be worth reading in fifty years' time. It was like a horse-fair, and she wasn't offering herself for the trading of flesh and reputation and scruples.

She had one more book in her, only one, the one that would come closest. There was that, but nothing else.

She was starting to believe that she had outlived the real: that she lived only reel to reel, and that already she could feel the slack dragging in what was left to her. She didn't know how she could hope to explain that in cogent words, even to Mariel, who would have told her to take a holiday, a long rest. But that wouldn't have persuaded her any differently, to make her *dis*believe that she was on the point of – mysteriously – living her life over again, starting to lap herself.

'A Mercedes, Penelope, a Merc. One day, that's what we'll get ourselves.'
   'Will we, Guy?'
   'Just right for us, don't you think?'
   'You're the man who knows about cars.'
   'Great engineering. Great take-off.'
   'What would they say at the bank?'
   'What indeed, my lovely?'

Penelope sat at the lunch table smiling at Mariel in a boozy way.

Her Women, in their prime, would have known it was a mark of defeat. In their shame they would have sought to preserve appearances, but maybe the truth was that some of them – Harriet Ross, Prudence Shaw and Camilla Holt came imprecisely to her mind – had been prigs, or prigesses. Perhaps they had been less worthy of readers' admiration than their pity: although pity was the deadliest sin to give in to if it didn't spare the self.

She had no clear pictures left in her head. She felt a frightening lack of control over the elements of her life, except her capacity to tell an old friend an elaborate, clichéd lie. The inventor now suspected that she was an invention of someone else's mind: sitting in Monmouth Square imagining characters and writing out their lives (and in one case writing about a woman writing out other lives in a novel), she had wholly failed to entertain the possibility that the process might not begin with her and that there could be an originator beyond. Maybe some people, calling the deviser 'God', got round the problem that way. But she had been able to get by quite well without Him, and instead she had put her quota of faith into her own achievements, past and future. Now, by a gradual process, past and future were being disputed, even denied, and so faith which might have been her salvation was left clutching at straws, wisps.

There was no Eden Hotel. The building still stood, but it had been converted to a Zen centre. She saw a large circle of shaven monks, plump businessmen and rebellious housewives squatting on the lawn holding hands.

She booked into a hotel in the town, the first one that appeared in the Michelin list, meriting two peaked towers. She was handed the registration form; she hesitated before filling it in, then signing it. A porter was called for 'Mademoiselle Gerrault', and she was shown up to an imposing suite of sitting-room, bedroom and bathroom on the first floor, at the back of the hotel. She telephoned reception and asked if it would be possible to have similar accommodation at the front, on the street, and higher up: voices conferred, and she was told that there was no problem about that, a suite just a little larger was available upstairs, it being out-of-the-season.

'"Out-of-the-season",' she repeated. 'Yes, of course.'

Lying on top of the bed with the shutters closed, she watched the smoke rising from her cigarette and she thought how easy it would be, to cause a building to kindle. She stretched out an arm, over the side of the bed, and let the cigarette dangle. It would be so absurdly easy, it could be done by doing absolutely nothing at all, by just resisting the resistance, by simply letting go the cigarette.

She gazed at the position of her forearm, her wrists, her long fingers, the cigarette like a conductor. If she were to very slightly loosen her fingers, one by one . . .

Knuckles rapped on the door. She twitched upright, pushing on her elbows. '*Entrez!*'

A master-key turned in the lock and the door opened. A woman looked in at her; her face showed extreme bafflement.

Penelope smiled.

The woman fumbled for an explanation. She'd thought Madame Meurice was supposed to be occupying these rooms, it was in her register that . . . *She* was the housekeeper – she rattled the bunches of keys at her waist – and naturally it was her responsibility to make sure . . .

Penelope said, she was sorry but it must be a case of mistaken identity. The other guest would probably now be on the floor beneath.

It was very strange, the housekeeper told her, such things rarely happened: especially this now being '*la morte-saison*'.

'"*La morte-saison*",' Penelope repeated.

The housekeeper's eyes opened wider.

'Mademoiselle – '

The woman pointed.

'*Prenez-garde!*'

'Oh. Yes. Yes, I'm so sorry – '

She immediately jerked round on the mattress and stubbed out the cigarette in the ashtray on the bedside table.

'I'm sorry – I almost – '

The housekeeper advanced and knelt down, brushing at the hot ash that had fallen on to the carpet.

'It's all right,' Penelope said, 'there's no harm done – '

That was her good luck, the woman said, fortune was her friend . . .

Penelope, smiling meekly, held the door open for her as she left. She closed it slowly behind her. Already her mind was on a different tack. She turned away. She repeated the words into the space between her mouth and the wall's wood panelling.

'Mistaken identity . . . *La morte-saison* . . .'

Suddenly she was remembering how Guy's footsteps used to sound – or rather, how they didn't sound – walking up the stairs to the flat: stone steps, and shoes for the bank with steel tips on the heels, but never a clue that he was there until she heard his key already turning in the lock.

'I've altered the names, of course,' she told Mariel.

'To protect the innocent?'

'They're hardly that.'

'*Your* innocence, then?'

'You don't live to be sixty – *just* 'live', that is – and keep everything you had, you know. There's a lot of moral baggage goes missing – '

'It has to go *some*where, though. It gets found. It's just unclaimed – '

'That is, if you *want* it back again. Maybe it's a relief, at last you've got rid of all that – that dead, dragging weight – '

Local police on the French Riviera are continuing their investigations into the disappearance of British novelist Penelope Milne. Her crashed car was found on a stretch of hairpin coastal road, but there was no sign of Miss Milne.

One theory is that she may have been badly injured or severely concussed and wandered from the scene of the accident. The road is a dangerous one, with a two-hundred-feet drop over rocks to the sea below. It has also been suggested that this may have been a suicide attempt which misfired, with the car failing to leave the road and hitting the trunk of a tree instead. However, acquaintances of the novelist in London have dismissed this second theory as extremely unlikely.

Miss Milne's books have been popular with readers and critically acclaimed for the past twenty years, although she first started writing during the war. Several of her novels have been adapted for television, and one – *The Continuity Girl* – was made into a successful cinema

400

film. A French film company recently bought rights on *The Staircase Mystery*, which appeared in 1973.

Possibly.
Scene with French joiner leaving his house to travel along the coast road to his nearest town. Rusty Renault 4. Brilliant sunlight. White rocks below, aquamarine sea.
It's he who discovers her car, a little hidden from sight. It has skidded off the road, into a tree: another metre to the right would have carried it off the clifftop and over the edge.
It's empty. Oil is still dripping from underneath. He shouts, to see where the driver might have got to. But there's no reply. He runs to the cliff edge and looks over and down, to waves – crashing on the rocky foreshore.

French police divers searching for novelist Penelope Milne off the Corniche coastline where the wreck of her car was found have failed to locate her body. A land search has been called off following three days of intense activity, with more than fifty police and army personnel combing surrounding countryside.

Requests have been broadcast on national radio and television asking any motorists who may have witnessed the accident or given help to Miss Milne to inform the police at Villefranche or to contact any local gendarmerie.

The novelist's disappearance has caught hold of the French public's attention. A straw hat of a kind Miss Milne has been photographed wearing was found on a narrow ledge halfway down the hazardous, sometimes nearly vertical two-hundred-feet drop of cliff to boulders and the sea. It has been noted in this style-conscious country that Miss Milne was particularly fond of hats, a fact which has engaged rather less attention in her native Britain even though she has often sported one for photographers. Owing to this novel-like mystery which may yet have tragic consequences, Miss Milne has gained an immense new audience among the French. Her books have been selling 'comme des petits pains' in the cities, and her two publishers here are already reprinting to meet the demand. Informed media gossip has it that a French film of her early novel *Solférino*, about British agents serving in the Resistance, will go into production soon, to be directed by Jean-Claude Rosset.

Part Thirteen

1

There is a growing suspicion that we are not alone. The universe that we see is no more than a flotsam in a vast sea of dark matter, invisible to our present technology. Like H. G. Wells' invisible man, the dark matter gives its presence away by jostling the visible crowd, so we know that it is there.

. . . We are certain that dark matter exists. The question is – what is it made of? Is it conventional stuff – small stars too cool to shine, or exotic, previously unknown material? If the latter, is there an entire universe parallel to our own . . .?

Guardian, 13 February 1987

A street in an Australian suburb. A Volvo sedan pulls into a driveway. The driver gets out; she walks to the back of the car, to the trunk, and lifts the lid. She takes out her groceries, packed in a brown paper carton overprinted 'Shopping at Jack's is a Happiness Experience'.

Inside the house she makes a beaker of instant coffee in the kitchen, then moves through to the sitting-room. She sits down at a desk in front of a window. She looks out at a view, at the lawn's trimness, at the other residences in their gardens, at identically angled television receivers, at a passing gull which has tired of the bay, at a haze of insects above a hedge, at the slow blue light creeping along the avenue of virtuous white pavements.

One afternoon with nothing to do and the thermometer outside the window at 93° she stopped turning over channels at a film. She thought she recognised something, a place or a time.

It was a British film, in black-and-white, with a wartime feel. In the low-ceilinged bedroom of an oversized, *Homes and Gardens* cottage, a man in a three-piece tweed suit was clambering off a bed. He held a hand to his head, to show his puzzlement. A woman was standing watching him, wearing a sharkskin suit and an expression of disbelief. She was pretty and reminded Penelope of Jean Kent. Maybe it was. She didn't recognise the man, but she thought his name might come to her.

403

The actor stopped in front of a mirror on the wall and lowered his head to look into the glass. He took his hand away. He stared in complete ignorance at his reflection.

The camera turned to the Jean Kent woman. She took a step forward, then stopped herself. Her tongue moistened her lips.

The camera returned to the man. He was still looking into the mirror. He noticed the woman over the shoulder of the reflected stranger in front of him. He concentrated on her for several seconds.

'I say, I'm most terribly sorry,' he told her in a clipped, pukka accent. 'This – this is quite ridiculous, you know.'

The Jean Kent woman stood watching him, on her guard. The studio lights were directed on to her face, but flatteringly softened.

The man shook his head.

'I can't think *who* I am, you see.'

The woman spoke. 'You don't?' Her voice was as docked and plummy as his, and Penelope knew definitely from that that they were meant for one another.

The man turned round from the mirror. The puzzlement receded, to show *his* face too in a much more favourable light.

The woman's mouth attempted a smile. She lifted a hand to her brow.

'I'm afraid,' she said, 'I don't understand what's happening at all.'

'That makes two of us.'

The camera angle widened to include them both in the next shot. The man stood stockstill; the woman took a couple of steps backwards.

'I'm sorry,' the man said, 'this must be frightfully inconvenient to you.'

The Jean Kent woman didn't know how to reply.

'A complete stranger. Here in your – '

'It is,' she said, but politely. 'Rath-*er*.'

'I just – don't remember.' He placed a hand to his head again, and the puzzlement returned.

'Nothing?' she asked him.

'I'm afraid – afraid *not*.'

'Not even your name?'

'Not even that.'

'Oh, *try*. Can't you?'

'It may – come back.'

'Do you remember *any*thing?'

'Not – not at the moment.'

'But how did you get here?'

'I don't know.'

'We've been away, you see. My husband's up in Town today.'

'And the house was empty?'

'Yes.'

'But – but I got here somehow? Into the house?'

404

'Yes. I found one of the french windows open.'

'Good Lord! Did I do that?'

'I don't know.'

'That's the maddening thing, you see. *I* don't know either.'

He took his hand away from his head again. He smiled cautiously. The woman lowered her eyes.

'I mean,' he said, 'I'm sure I'm not a villain or anything like that.'

She lifted her eyes again and looked momentarily alarmed.

'I give you my word of honour.'

The appearance of the man seemed to pacify her in some way.

'Oh, I'm sure you *can* remember something. Please, you must try – '

'Yes. Yes, I must.'

'Have you had an accident?'

The word came out as 'eccident'. The voice sounded all too familiar to Penelope, even in another decade and in another continent and climate.

'I'm not hurt,' the man said. 'Just dazed. A bit.'

'You're not injured? Or bruised? Your suit isn't damaged?'

The man looked down at himself.

'Not that I can see.'

'How *very* queer.'

The tone of voice was quite uncynical, and Penelope wondered if that was quite accurate, given the circumstances.

She registered the woman's shoulder-length hair and curled fringe, the wide shoulders on her slim belted jacket and the narrow fit of the skirt, the sturdy heels of her shoes, the liberal application of lipstick. Once it had been the epitome of well-bred modern style. Once it must have seemed to many women that to look like that would be to have their prayers answered: it would be a passport to fulfilment and their better life to come.

One afternoon in Sydney a tune wafted out of a car radio as she was crossing York Street. It was John Lennon's voice, a song that had been around for a couple of years, but which she had never listened to properly: until hearing it that afternoon dodging the city traffic and hurrying for the sidewalk.

Life, the voice told her beaming through hot ether, is what happens to you when you're busy making other plans.

She sits on the terrace of the Harbor Restaurant one lunchtime in the summer of 1982 and opens the *Sydney Morning Herald*.

Her eyes travel the columns of type, this way and that. She starts to read a story about a bomb explosion in an underground car-park in Geneva, and for a few moments she imagines her terror at being in such a situation. Then she thinks of her last visit, to the Hotel Des Bergues, and she catches herself out remembering.

She reads on: that the city police believe an international crime syndicate was behind the attack, that informers have been grassing on dealers trading

405

in illegal arms and supplies on a hitherto unknown scale. Laundered cocaine money is involved in it somehow, and South American diplomats, but she starts to lose the sense of the article at this point. The sentence beyond the next one refers to the use of fine art as currency exchange, smuggled canvases by Monet, Van Gogh, Gauguin, Corot.

It all seems to her one hell of a long way from Sydney Cove, New South Wales. She turns the page and finds a fashion article. Gloves are making a come-back: that's one place she has already been, although it was a long time ago. A model is photographed at the Australian Jockey Club at Randwick, sporting long white gloves and a polka-dot dress and a picture hat with a wide brim. Really she's rather kitsch, but she is also the next season's high fashion, apparently.

Penelope smiles to herself in a sceptical way. She turns to the weather chart because there is nothing else she feels she wants to read. Always her eyes search out London first on the alphabetical list of capital cities and weather centres. No one else can ever see where she is looking, so she does it with impunity, because it hardly requires her actual memories any more and she doesn't need to think she is betraying her life post-1980. This morning she also finds, among the 'G's, 'Geneva': 55F, 13C, Fair. An averagely temperate day without extremes, when the brain should have been working to best effect in that pleasantly bracing crystalline air, where great men gather to think and order the world. Someone must have known very well what they were doing when they targeted that unfortunate man without a name (yet), a kind of stool-pigeon possibly (the police have been reticent on that point), blown to smithereens along with his car the second he turned the key in the ignition lock.

In 1983 she saw Valerie on the television news.

Terrorists had hijacked a cruise-liner in the Caribbean, and the siege became a running headline story over four days. The gunmen were themselves gunned to death in a bloody show-down in the ship's casino. Valerie saw it all and was interviewed by an American NBC reporter. She looked in good form, considering. She explained, in a modern mid-Atlantic accent, that her jewellery had been snatched from her and thrown overboard. 'I guess,' she said, 'it's down there at the bottom of the sea. But I'm alive,' she added, 'and so is my husband, thank God.' The camera panned to include the figure of an elderly, white-haired, but bronzed and upright man wearing an eye-patch. He spoke with something of a Southern States drawl. Valerie held his arm and her eyes shone, as if they had tears in them. Jewel-less she might be for the moment but she had her husband beside her, and they had their affection for one another.

Penelope gawped in her Sydney sitting-room: at the daring and profes-sionalism if not the bravery and good fortune. Such dutifulness would surely be rewarded by other jewels: if, she thought, other jewels weren't already secure in a safe deposit box somewhere. Then the couple were gone from the screen, the reporter was winding up, and Valerie's moments of global glory via the satellite were over.

Afterwards Penelope couldn't settle. She ran a bath. She got in and lay back and let the water cover her. She had been looking at a woman in her sixties with wrinkles and the evidence of a facelift. It might be the last time she would set eyes on Valerie Whatever-She'd-Become. She could close her eyes and now they were young again. She wondered which was the true picture, and who the phantoms were. The more she tried to remember the face on the screen, the less able she was to bring it back into her mind, even a couple of hours afterwards.

At last she pulled the rubber plug on its chain and watched the water being sucked out. In her other life it had drained away anticlockwise: in this second life, where a complementary but converse, antipodal logic applied, the water whirled away with the clock.

In Cambridge Oliver is settling into eccentricity and an ageing bachelor's loneliness, hemmed in further by the inconveniences of so-so health.

The sun goes down slowly behind towers and pinnacles, it blazes in mullioned windows; chapel glass stains ancient flagstones, dribbling jewel colours, ruby and emerald and amethyst. Footsteps run through courts; standard lamps are switched on in panelled rooms, and old men starting awake in leather armchairs fear the very worst, that the barbarians have mustered and are clamouring at the gates.

A wind and a chill seep in from the fens, and leaves on the trees show a little colour, russet and flush. Kettles steam and whistle to the boil: an extra spoonful of tea is added for the pot. It's the slack time of the day, when nothing so much happens, *le temps mort*: the interlude of quietly waiting for whatever will happen next, watching the daylight that remains in courts falter, then – very, very slowly – dim.

The coffee-shop was fitted out as a Viennese café. There were dark panelled walls hung with ovals of mirror inside gilded frames; banquettes of green leather ran along the walls, and the tables were topped with white marble. The only fault she could find with the room was that it was too new. The designers had done what they could, though: wall-lamps with ivory silk shades nicely diffused the light, and made the room more romantic and more secretive. Less subtly perhaps – or perhaps not – there was taped zither music; this made fun of the real thing in one sense, but in another it put all sorts of images from films and stage musicals into her head, so that as she sat on one of the banquettes sipping mocha and cutting into her slice of sachertorte she was remembering herself when she was young, watching and listening and imagining the experience for herself. The experience was now doubly far away from her, from here in Sydney, but it also seemed to her doubly authentic, because a historical past and a personal one crossed in her memory.

She came into The Kaffee Kartner whenever she ventured into the heart of the city. She liked its dimness after the concrete-and-glass glare of the streets; she enjoyed walking to it through the vast glittery atrium of the hotel, thirty storeys of cascading Babylonian greenery dripping from balconies, and the sky visible through a canopy of clear curving glass, and a galaxy of twinkling lights on all levels like crystal stalactites, and see-through glass-sided elevators like gold and silver cages riding to the top and down (the fastest lifts in the subcontinent), pools of waterlilies and one stocked with tame pink flamingoes, a piano bar set on a fragrant tropical island, every camp invention of the modern hotel that was imaginable made confirmably true. But it was the Mittel-Europäischer coffee-house she liked best, because it seemed the most extravagant gesture of all to encounter on downtown Pitt Street, an extra indulgence among all the reflecting chrome and twisted glass and the bronze-flanked towers and pristine terrazzo piazzas. The café made her feel subterfuge. Passing through the hotel's more open public spaces, those lavish acres of common ground, she would hear many more languages than she could recognise: but that was for business, and social talk, while The Kaffee Kartner was custom-built for quiet private introspection.

She usually ordered the same from the costumed waiter, her mocha and her slice of sachertorte. The redesigning of the classic uniform of European waiters in bygone days – black and green with a long, starched, starkly white apron – added to the effect of being elsewhere. She didn't believe she wished to be back *there*, in Europe; but at least imagining so for a short while blunted the sharp corners of Australia, as it were. The mocha – she took it without the froth of cream on top – was strong and, some days, as black and thick as treacle at the bottom of the cup, and she would think of the rejuvenating mud used in mountain spas. (Her mind, glad for the system, ran in the same smooth tracks.) The sachertorte was rich and sticky, as it ought to have been, with a properly bitter taste, even though it probably originated no further from her than the hotel's hi-tech, twenty-first-century, state-of-the-art kitchens, which she'd read about in a Sunday colour supplement.

The effect, though, was everything.

She had been here a dozen times or more – it could have been as many as twenty – when more or less the last thing that she could have expected to happen did happen.

It was a sweltering day outside. As she'd walked she'd felt the heat of the pavements tearing through the soles of her shoes. She'd watched the air dancing ahead of her as it rose in the gulleys between the office towers. A geyser had burst at some arterial point on the street grid and the water was sizzling on the tarmacadam. In other spots the roads were cracking and buckling as she looked. It was a day for manic suicide jumps and holy visions on backstreets. Songs from *West Side Story* had been going through her head, until she touched the grillework of a wire fence and nearly branded herself on the scorching hot metal. On the other side an Alsatian dog barked dementedly at her. It was, in every way, an exceptional day.

She had run for cover and quiet, like a shade-loving desert creature, quite greedy for coolness and solitude. In the hotel's lobby and skyward atrium she had skirted shoals of businessmen in their lightweight suits or shirtsleeves. Chunky gold bracelet watches spread over thick hairy wrists. Hands scratched idly or irritably at half-weight polyester-and-cotton behinds. A man's importance among his peers was measured by the quality but principally the size of his briefcase.

She was glad she hadn't been a part of that world, as one of the wives who are the service-industry to its own concept of grandeur. Such men needed to believe they were believed in. She hadn't the knack of bolstering shaky pride and massaging a precarious ego, but she hadn't felt it to be a lack in her life before. Thankfully their voices were lost in the height and opulence of the building. The falling garden of greenery smothered the commercial chatter like a final judgment.

So she retired to the peace and seclusion of the coffee-shop at the back of the hotel, and it was there – as she sat sipping her mocha and anticipating with placid pleasure the taste of the slice of sachertorte lying on her plate – there and then it was, in this metropolitan temple of a modern, homogeneous, mercantile society, that the past made its final lurching thrust at the heart in her chest.

It was how he was standing, with his left hand in the back left-hand pocket of his trousers, and his shoulders flexing. He had stood exactly like that in the gallery of the French town, instructing her how to read that mysterious, winey painting of the Enchanted Castle. Her attention then had moved between the two: him, it, him, it, how he was standing.

She sat forward on the banquette staring at him. She was suddenly cold, and felt herself shaking. She couldn't have planned for this, it was a final lesson to her, there's nothing you can do to help yourself.

He was talking to someone, a man of his own age. Thirty-five, or forty perhaps. He still ran his hand through the hair on the back of his head, even though time had thinned it. She noticed the gold signet ring, still in place on his little finger. The years between might never have been. It hadn't once occurred to her that she could have come to this particular end, sitting upstairs in an air-conditioned hotel bedroom watching television while her husband did his business downstairs at the counter in a synthetic coffee-house. But it wouldn't have been so very different finally, would it, because here she was with him, sharing the same envelope of space and time.

Not exactly *him*, of course. It must have been his son. But she recognised those proportions, between the mouth (a fraction too small) and the nose (a fraction too long), and the eyes (maybe a shade too close together). A *tight* face. And the pose, left hand in his back trouser-pocket and his other hand combing through his hair. *That* ring.

She thought he might be about to turn round, so she lowered her head, stirring up the grounds from the bottom of her cup. It she had been his wife upstairs, Mrs Kyte, she could have boosted the air-conditioning: here she was becoming quite dizzy and queasy for the lack of cold, reviving fresh air. She felt again the blasting oven-heat of those French afternoons, which she had sensed cooking all the 'self' out of her until she might become someone else. She could have been there now, in the bleached rocky highlands of Provence, instead of where her ailing reason informed her she was – by The Rocks, Sydney, Australia.

Maybe it's the mocha's doing, she considered. I'm not really responsible for what I'm thinking, it's the caffeine again, so I'm let off the hook. At school she had refused to believe that David Copperfield could possibly have caught sight of Mr Micawber for the first time in years, walking along the other side of the street in Canterbury he was walking along himself. But that was tame stuff compared to this, after forty-something years and ten thousand miles and eleven time-zones.

She risked raising her eyes again. The two men were looking the other way and still talking. Henry Kyte or his son was still standing with his left hand tucked into the back left-hand pocket of his trousers; she watched him running his other hand through the hair on the back of his head.

She wondered, and where does it go from here?

They weren't supposed to take over.

Her Aunt Louise had returned from the dead, via any of the furriers mentioned en passant in the novels. Henry Kyte had burst the cocoon of his youth, where she had left him in the novels, eternally promising more to inexperienced, impressionable young women than he could ever provide. Topaz refused to lie down, in the adulterous beds provided for her, where she sacrificed sanity to timeless, supertemporal love.

She felt she was sitting on top of a trunk trying to keep the lid shut simply by the force of her will rather than by what weight her body had, but the trunk shook and the lid was forcing itself against her as it was pushed from beneath.

And worst of all to the balance of her mind, there had been Guy . . .

It was too much for her. She slept only fitfully in the sweltering winter nights of the southern hemisphere. She rose mid-morning with dark circles under her bloodshot eyes. When she did doze off, she encountered familiar dreams, trawling just beneath the surface of consciousness: most often she was in the driving-seat of the car on the French sea road, but even with her hands on the controls she felt herself driving straight for the edge, for the blurring blue of the sea and the sky.

Always there had been the assurance that once this latest novel was finished, she would begin another one. Always. It was understood, within and outwith the story of the book she was writing. She had only written one book in the first person, but even with those cogitating Women at their centres the imputation was there, that because throwaway references were made to the content of earlier books other books would surely follow this one being held in the reader's hands, only their principals would grow a little older and a little

410

more matronly in appearance and become a little more dependent on the past and their recollections.

Seven years had passed, and there were no new heroines.

She told herself that fundamentally the climate was wrong, that it was impossible to think straight here: and thinking crooked didn't have the discipline to it which she knew was needed. Sydney had no associations for her, nor did any of the places outside where she travelled looking for inspiration. She would have had to go back, to England, and she felt she would have been as ghostly there as her Aunt Louise had once seemed to her, manifesting herself from a hire-car in the familiar habitat of Monmouth Square.

On afternoon television she saw another old movie of the 1940s, American film noir, with a girl trailed up a clock-tower and confronted by the man in pursuit. There was a struggle and at some point the clock's mechanism became jammed. Passers-by on the streets looked up and saw the minute hand moving against nature. There but for the grace of a camera team went she, she thought, running time backwards, so serve her right: there she was, but for a script, without which these felt to her like wasted days – stocking up from the Happy Jack hypermarket once a fortnight only to spend her mornings looking out the window at a lawn and a sprinkler and watching old black-and-white films in the afternoon and, if she had the energy left, driving down to the beach for a swim. Hat-wise she had reverted to a common-or-garden white cotton sun-hat with a green lining, confused by the speed of the fashions in the magazines and seeing very few hats being worn and discovering there was a dearth of milliners in the new Sydney. Seen in mirrors, the result – herself wearing a seventeen-dollar beach hat – looked curiously innocuous: as if she could offer a threat to no one, as if this might actually be all there was to her, and nothing more. Living without certainty had kept her thin at any rate: she wasn't carrying any of the surplus she watched fearfully on the beach as it tottered past her, the magazine experts wouldn't have given up hope on her, they would have seen that she had 'possibilities', those open to a women in her sixth age.

In the window of a theatrical prop dealer and costumier, on Queensferry Street – Java shadow puppets standing up on their sticks, wires folded.

Penelope goes driving. After six years she's shutting up the house, she leaves Sydney.

She travels north, with no destination in mind. She checks into a series of motels. She sits on high stools drinking gin-shakes in bars. She has several encounters with strangers, of the verbal sort. They each tell her their 'story', about one incident which seems very much to be the sum of their life: the consciousness of an 'identity'. She wonders why they're on the road, if they've outlived their lives in a sense, if they've hung on too long after the ending of their story.

411

2

She hired a car in Brisbane.

She was driving between Rockhampton and Mackay when she spotted a lone hitch-hiker. She stopped and the woman got in.

'I really don't care where I go, thanks. Anywhere.'

She was in her middle-thirties probably, and spoke with a Sydney accent; she was wearing jeans and a T-shirt, but high-heeled shoes. Her carry-all was travel-stained white canvas manufactured to look like leather.

They chatted for a while, about nothing very much. It was the first time she had ever given a lift to a stranger. But she had dispensed with caution on this one occasion, she wasn't even fearful. If there was a knife hidden in the scuffed white leather-look bag she would discover soon enough.

But the woman only wanted to speak. She asked, 'Do you mind if I tell you a story?'

'"A story"?'

'It's *my* story.'

'No,' Penelope said, 'not at all.'

'You're sure?'

'I'm quite sure.'

The woman collected her breath.

'We were Vanilla, Misti and Kool,' she began. '*I* was Vanilla. Misti was my friend, and Kool was our pimp.'

Penelope nodded.

'For official reasons we really worked the Morisoyando – 'to die dreaming' – it's a club, down in King's Cross. Go-go. D'you know that stretch?'

'Well, I've been. Passed through. But I don't really *know* it – '

'Of course we were on the game.' The woman settled into the seat. 'Sometimes it was at the club and I did the hotels too, because Kool thought I could, and Misti usually cruised the harbour streets in a car. A Holden sedan, although Kool could have bought her something classier, a European make. Anyway – ' the woman moved sideways on the seat, folding her knees beneath her. ' – I was doing the club for a while – we did a strip-tease, and a pretty mild lezzie act – and this same bloke kept coming in lunchtimes. Nice-looking, a bit like Richard Gere, only not quite, and Misti told me one day I'd gone out to the drugstore on the corner that he'd come asking for me. We did meet and he was very – well, pleasant. He took me for a ride in a big maroon Bentley, but that's all it was, a drive, although of course I offered. But he said it was

412

fine, just to have me there with him. He kept looking at my face and fingering it, like he was a sculptor or something. But he had nice hands and he smelt of some expensive eau-de-Cologne.'

Penelope watched the road.

'He didn't stop coming to the club. He bought me presents, perfume or spray mainly, I suppose from where he must have bought his own. We sat upstairs for a while, but usually we drove. He didn't talk much about himself, hardly at all, but it's common enough, so I didn't make anything of it.

'I got kinda used to these afternoons. Once or twice, if he'd said he was coming, he had to cancel right at the last minute. Another time I was with him in the Bentley when the car-phone rang and he picked it up and started saying "yes, sir", "no, sir". I asked him who it was, and he said he worked for someone, very big. I supposed it was an industrialist or someone, a banker even, and Craig worked for him in some important way, and lucrative too, but everyone has a boss in corporations, no matter how high you get.'

Penelope put her movements on cruise-control, just to listen.

'I hardly knew anything about him. It was Misti who told me – she was out motor-servicing one day – she said she'd seen the Bentley going through a gateway, out in Vaucluse. She knew the registration number, and she's very sharp on models of car, so I trusted what she told me. I brought it up the next time we met, in his car, and he sat thinking for a while and then he said I could come over one day, on Sunday. He picked me up and we drove out, and it was very grand, like the set of a TV-soap. Half-timbered, like an English manor house or something. We had tea in a great drawing-room with a balcony – he called it a 'minstrel's gallery'. It was a huge house but all the time there was just ourselves. I asked, weren't there staff, but he told me Sunday was their day off, so I nodded as if that wasn't so surprising to me, I'd seen this life before.

'Just after that Misti told me she'd been in Double Bay hustling – it's how she likes to get a tan, but she's never in the daylight long enough to take one – and she'd seen Craig with a woman. At first she'd thought it was me, we were the same height but the woman's hair was fairer. And she guessed I couldn't afford to be carrying a Nina Ricci carrier-bag.

'Craig started spending more time with me after that and I put the Double Bay sighting out of my mind, or I tried to. Well, I guess I couldn't. One day I put on a light wig and he did a classic double-take. Then he told me I really suited fairer hair, and had I never thought of it? He was in quite a good mood and so was I, and when he stopped the car and said we should go walking I didn't even worry about Kool, who didn't know I was seeing him out of the club. We went to the Castlereagh arcades. I just laughed when he asked the assistant in David Jones' if she had blonde colouring that would suit me. Back at the club Misti bet me for a dare I wouldn't do it – I suppose she was remembering the woman she'd seen with him – but a dare's a dare for me and anyway, I'd had an argument with Kool and felt like doing something –

well, only *quite* reckless. Kool hated change, you see, without saying it to us, and he'd always hit girls – hit them hard – when they changed their look and didn't tell him first.

'I guess he must've thought it was an improvement. Anyhow, he didn't say anything about it, although he perves like crazy. He's got such a sticky beak too, he knew Craig came to see me and he took the money I got from upstairs, so he wasn't complaining. (Although he would have done if he'd known it was going on outside too, if he'd got wind I was down in Vaucluse.)

'Where was I? . . . I'd got my hair coloured . . . I didn't even make a deal of it when Craig just stopped the car – we always met discreetly – in Double Bay this time, at the Nina Ricci place, and I followed him in and he bought me this suit. I did say in the car, I've a friend who thought she saw you with a woman with a carrier-bag from the shop, and he was as easy about it as you like, he just said, his boss's wife shopped there and sometimes she took him with her because her husband wasn't interested. He couldn't really say no, she had a lot of influence, and it had only taken up half an hour or so, so he had obliged.

'Then for a while after that afternoon I didn't hear from him. I didn't have a phone number, I didn't know how to contact him. But another afternoon I went out to Vaucluse, to the house. Not to go in, just to see what was what. I mean, he might have had to go off on some big important business trip. I walked about the garden for a while, under the trees, it was like a park. I was ready to go when the car drove in, the maroon Bentley. I stayed and watched it go up to the house. I saw Craig get out of the front and hold the back door open for a fat man with no hair. Then someone else got out from the other door, on my side, a woman with long legs and a hat, and Craig waited before he followed them both up the steps. He closed the front door behind the three of them and that was the end of that.

'Then he got in touch with me again, after a week or so. That's always how it happens, how it has to be – *they* get in touch with *you*. Anyway, he picked me up on Bourke Street. He was all uptight, I got the feeling. I was wearing my Ricci suit and he seemed relieved I'd put it on. I thought, *this* time it's going to get beyond harmless kisses. I really thought he was frigid or something, that's not uncommon, it's just some guys aren't brave enough to come right out to you with it. Or tell themselves. Anyway, I just had a feeling, that it was going to be different.

'Well, it *was* going to be different, but not how I'd imagined it, no how. We drove out through the quiet streets, the avenues, so I knew we were going to the house. Sure enough. We passed through the gates. Instead of driving up to the house, though, he turned off, the wheels rolled on to this soft track. I saw a lake ahead, the house's own private lake, and a boathouse. He said, he thought we could just "look around" for a while. I thought, maybe he couldn't make it work in the house – the sex business – that the boathouse was his fantasy. Anyway, he gets out and I pull down the visor mirror and see myself, fairer, blonder, in an expensive colour of soft pink you've got to have the confidence of money, years of it, to wear it right. So, we did walk about for a while. Now he looked not so psyched up, but just nervous. Very nervous. He looked back at the house a few times, and sometimes at his watch. And then of course I knew – what I suppose I was trying not to admit – that none of it was really true: that the car wasn't his and the house wasn't either, they belonged to the man he worked for, that he wasn't a city executive after all but a humble chauffeur who didn't have to wear a uniform, that he only took up with me on the time he got off. I started to tell him that it didn't really matter to me, but I didn't look at him, because I didn't want to embarrass him. I mean, the Nina Ricci suit was real enough, and the gifts of perfume, and the time he'd bought, all in clean notes inside envelopes. I just walked on, saying it all just to show that I didn't really mind, it wasn't the first time things hadn't been what they'd seemed to be.

'I can remember . . . I was on the boardwalk, I was looking down, I could see a fish under the surface of the water, something quite big. I was thinking, I'd never really got on with water, even though I was an Australian kid – those stinging blowflies on the beaches – and this didn't win me over any. Fish are a big no-no to me, they're okay served up with a sauce, like at Mischa's, but if Hitchcock had made his film about fish instead of crows I'd have been more scared, not less . . . Also, I was concentrating on not getting my heel caught in the wood, it was soft damp wood, rotten right through, when suddenly everything went from under me. In a flash. I turned head-over-heels, the broken boards were flying everywhere, and the next thing I was in the water. My head went down first, I saw it all with my eyes, the blue sky and my legs somewhere above me and the bubbles blowing up out of my mouth. I forgot that Craig should have been trying to save me. I must've turned over again, and I was seeing William Street again, and Misti's face, and Kool's, and I was down among the weeds, the 'undies', and scattering gravel with my hands. I was thinking I was a fish too or an eel or something. I was thinking this must be how I'm going to live from now on, so you just adapt yourself to it, girl. And somehow I'd still forgotten about Craig not diving in after me. Then I saw the fish I'd been looking down at, and it was watching me in such a hungry way, with its mouth opening and closing and all its razor teeth on show, and then I just panicked, and thrashed about and landed on my back and saw the sky way above me and the scattered planks lying on the surface, which was why I knew where the surface was, and somehow – just as all the breath seemed to be sucked out of me and I could feel my stomach crumpling – I willed myself, with the last effort I knew I had left. And I felt myself rising. It was levitation, and the easiest thing after all even though you had to concentrate so very hard, you had to *make* yourself into the effect, the motion. I held up my arms to reach for it, daylight, and somehow eventually I got there, I broke the surface. I stretched and caught hold of a piece of wood, a great chunk of it, and I floated on it. I thought I felt something in my ankle – a sharp serrating pain, like the edge of a bread-knife – and I kicked out with my feet. Maybe it was the big fish. And that was the extra propulsion I needed, the last effort of all, to be able to touch the post of the boardwalk.

'Somehow I got up, I pulled myself out, although it took me an age. But I knew I couldn't drown now, having come so far, from the bottom of the pond, from death even and back. Truly. I was almost out for the count, but not quite and I went staggering for the boathouse. No Craig, no sign of him anywhere. But I could see the house proper from the boathouse when I got to it, between the planking on the walls. I could hear sounds – a car, a door or a trunk lid banging shut – and that's when I saw them, him first – Craig – running down the steps followed by her, the woman, in a pink suit like the one I was wearing. (Although it was hanging right off me –) Her hair was fair, blonde-ish, just how Misti had told me it was. They got into the car and drove off, I watched them, the two fools. Fools to say they loved each other. Or maybe they did. No, I have to doubt it, how *could* they have done? Maybe *she* did, but why then should he have gone to such lengths for her? But her husband was rich, of course, and perhaps *she* was, in some form or other.'

Penelope shook her head.

'I guess they had to convince her husband it was *her* when they dragged me up from the bottom. He'd know she was lost to him, he'd never think there was a reason to keep on looking for her.'

Penelope shook her head again.

'It's what happened,' the woman told her. 'It's a true story, honest to God.'

'Yes,' Penelope said. 'Yes, I'm sure it is.'

'Really, it's the story of my life. Being dumped on.'

'What are you going to do about it?'

'"Do"?'

'Yes.'

'What d'you mean?'

She might have mentioned the police; a crime was involved, two crimes in all probability.

'Are you just going to continue taking it?'

'I don't know. Probably. Why not?'

'The question ought to be "why", shouldn't it?'

'Should it?'

'Unless you're quite happy that should be your story.'

'No, I'm not.'

'Are you sure?'

'Yes,' the woman said and nodded.

'Then I'm glad for you, Vanilla.'

'But I don't know who *you* are,' she said, 'you haven't told me.'

'I'm called Penelope Milne. I go about dispensing wisdom. Generally being wise for everyone's good except my own. That's my calling.'

'Your calling. That's what you want it to be?'

416

'I don't know. I think I was wise before my time. Too clever on everyone else's behalf. But I should have been taking better care of *myself*, better than I really was.'

'Maybe you're making up an excuse for yourself?'

'I was so frightened of being put down. You know? Taken advantage of. I was determined I wouldn't be. Maybe that's another stance, another extreme. We're extreme people, I think, Vanilla, you and I. You've drowned, almost, and I've lived two lives instead of one.'

She stared ahead though the windscreen. The land appeared to sweep up into the sky and where the horizon should have been there was a dense glow of sun and heat, as if the world was in a state of molten flux.

The limit of her travels is a Queensland town with an airport. She discovers that it's possible to fly-connect to virtually anywhere she might want to go. She consults maps and timetables and sees that she can make the journey – by a circuitous route, via Java, and using several planes – to Banjarmasin, in Borneo.

She flies first to Darwin. There someone has half-told her her story when the next flight is called. She hesitates between them but an urgent tone in the tannoy voice summons her and she runs for the queue.

The plane had been sprayed ice-diamond blue. The girl behind the check-in desk told her it was a something-or-other, a Fokker maybe, as if that information might mean something to her.

'They're little beauts.'

Well yes, Penelope thought, they would be, wouldn't they?

'Baggage?' a man in shirtsleeve uniform asked her.

' "Luggage", it used to be,' she told him.

'Well, lady, nowadays folks travel much lighter.'

'Yes,' she replied. 'I have a holdall. Also a hatbox.'

'Haven't come across one of *those* before.'

'A hat,' she told him, 'is really me.'

'Is that so?' he said, and she knew he was smiling at her age and eccentricity.

'It's very robust.'

'The plane, lady?'

'My *boîte à chapeau*,' she said. 'The hatbox.'

'I'm sure it is. Did you get it in Aussie?'

Now he was patronising her.

'In London.'

The man placed it on top of some other items on a trolley, along with the holdall.

'Won't be long now,' he said, 'if you just want to sit down in embarkation a few minutes.'

417

From her seat she smiled at a mother and child. The woman smiled back. The pair were wearing pastel colours, and the shapeless exercise clothes that were the rage, which restricted none of the body's movements. But it's the mind, she realised, that's the problem area: is it as unrestricted as either of you want it to be? Why are you waiting for a plane? – what is it you're escaping from and to?

She sat beneath a ceiling fan and positioned her face to catch its cool draught. A poster high on the wall showed the first island they were travelling to. It appeared lush, and palmy, with virginally pure beach sand and a blue, blue sea. She hoped the photograph hadn't been retouched.

The child was using coloured felt-tip pens to draw in a pad, and was saying nothing. Penelope remembered Tiktiki. She had used coloured pencils, out of a tin box her father had brought her back from one of his absences that probably hadn't been business trips at all. But that had had nothing to do with Tiktiki, except that it provided her with the pencils to use – and was unconsciously the cause why she wanted to make her escape, to a place that obeyed all her own requirements and edicts, which she created and uncreated on a whim, decreeing there be a volcano here or a silver-mine there. An eraser for coloured pencilmarks allowed her to do whatever she chose to do, to resite a river or a ravine, or to refashion a stretch of the craggy coastline.

The child in the embarkation lounge had the same authority invested in her. Her face was almost fierce with concentration. Penelope wondered if her mother knew, if the mother remembered what a term like 'authority' or 'command' meant. Why else should her mouth, too raspberry-ripe with lipstick, have betrayed that occasional petulant back-pull?

She stood up and walked about.

A woman's sang-froid voice sounded through the speaker on the wall. There would be a brief delay. She expressed apologies on the captain's and the airline's behalf.

Penelope sat down again, elsewhere, near a young woman who smiled at her. She said that her name was 'Lea'.

'Hello. I'm Penelope.'

After the smile the woman's face alternately showed nervousness and a bright optimism.

'I'm going back to be with my boyfriend,' she said.

'He lives on Java?'

'He's an Aussie, like me, but he works for a trading company.'

'Do you – live there too? Or work there?'

'I guess now I'll be living there. If he'll have me back – '

'You've been there before?'

'Really I'll have to tell you,' the woman said. 'May I?'

'Yes. Yes, if you'd like to – '

Penelope settled back in the low chair.

'I moved out with Al last March. I had a job in Sydney before that. It wasn't the best job in the world, but there are many worse ones. I was a secretary, to a major financier.'

'I see.'

'But because Al was going, I didn't see the point in staying. So anyway I flew out after him. We had a flat, the company's, nothing like the Sydney one, but you can make very good money if you're there for two or three years. He said it wouldn't be longer than that but I knew I'd never survive all that time in Sydney without him. So I suppose it must've been love that took me, which made me do it.'

'Yes,' Penelope said. 'Yes, I suppose it must have been.'

'Anyway, it went fine for – I don't know – six or seven months, I guess. Then it got that the flat seemed too small to me, and not what we'd been used to. Nothing like, really. And being at a loose end didn't help. And the climate. I also started to see everything just as it affected *me*, you see. And I think I began to ignore Al quite a bit too.'

'Ah.'

'It went on like that for a while, and not getting any better. Getting worse in fact. I didn't see all the things that were so good about Al, not any more.'

'Something's changed your mind, though?'

'What?'

'You see it differently now. Am I right?'

The woman manoeuvred her chair closer.

'Things got to the stage, I didn't think I could stay there any more. In Tengah. So I booked a flight back, without telling him – connecting flights, because there's nothing direct. I'm sure now it was the worst thing I could have done to him. I sort-of-know that, a girl he worked with found me and told me, how low he got. But I only heard that a lot later.'

'You came back? Here?'

'Yes, to Aussie. I didn't stop so long in Sydney, though. I tried to get a job, but nothing came up like the old one. I hadn't thought it was so brilliant at the time, but you live and learn.'

'They do say so . . .'

'Originally we met in Queensland. On vacation. It's a pretty corny name, I know, the place was called Coral Strand. Summer romance stuff, that's why I started to tell myself it couldn't have been true, just old-fashioned schmaltz. I went back there, on my own. I even found the guest-house we'd moved to, and I checked in again. Seeing the other couples going about, it didn't pacify me. I kept thinking what I'd given up in the first place, a flat, and my independence, and now I didn't have anything. I'd never let myself get so close to a man before.'

'A-ha . . .'

Lea continued. 'There was a woman staying in the guest-house. She was in her forties, I guess, late forties. Quite neat, careful with her appearance.

419

Two of the other people staying there, on two separate occasions they told me they'd presumed we must be related, the woman and me, only – they hinted – only we weren't speaking to one another. When I looked properly, I saw why they might've mistaken us. But it had happened in Sydney too, people saying they thought they'd seen me somewhere I knew I hadn't been, and I had to tell them it was only someone who looked very like me. Our posture too, that matched, I held myself with a very straight back and so did the woman. I once had to have an operation, when I was in my teens, and it left me like that, a bit rigid ("Like a surfboard" I've had said to me more than once).'

Penelope nodded and attempted to smile, *cordialmente*.

'This woman – I discovered her name was "Jones" too, like mine, and I decided that was why people must've thought we were related. I didn't get to know her Christian name, she never told me that and she didn't ask me mine. I don't know, it just got forgotten when we started chatting. She worked in Melbourne, it was promotion for her after Sydney. I asked her why she'd come so far, to Coral Strand, and she just said the place had "associations" for her, and I didn't tell her it had for me too, although she'd probably figured that out.

'I saw she wasn't married, she didn't wear any rings. She didn't talk about anyone special. We went for walks. We didn't talk so much, but that didn't matter. We both liked hot chocolate, and there was a café where we could get it. We sat out in the sun. I couldn't really tell how like me she looked. We window-shopped, our tastes on a lot of things were pretty similar, for colour and so on. We never knew the time, because – like me – she didn't wear a watch when she didn't have to.

'About the third time I started to notice more. We were both left-handed. She got some sand in her left eye and she couldn't really see because her right eye was lazy, like mine. We had blueberries in the hotel one night – we still had our own tables, by the way – and the berries brought me out in a rash and I saw her shake her head at the waitress, meaning she didn't want them, and she told me they had exactly the same effect on her.

'I used to watch her watching the couples on the quay, on the shore. She'd be watching them closely but not really *concentrating*: studying them but thinking of something else at the same time. Once she had to find her dark glasses because her eyes were red, and I pretended I hadn't seen.

'She had a stomach-bug one evening, and didn't appear for dinner. It was odd, I thought, how no one seemed to notice her absence, just because she was a single person. I was offered her table, but I said "no thanks", I wasn't sure why. She recovered, quite quickly. When I *really* listened to what she was saying, I realised everything was being – well, filtered through herself. It must've come through long years and experience. It was like a voice talking in a monotone. She had lots of little habits too, rituals: touching all the cutlery, checking how her collar sat, then her shoulders, then her cuffs, her belt, the pleats on her skirt. I'd presumed she was quite a – a resilient person, and

420

tough for the world. But then I saw that if anything cut through the normal and routine she was startled and knocked a bit out of kilter. When she had to give up her window table to a favoured couple and ended up looking lost in a dark corner. When a whole roadway was taken up for pipes to be laid, which meant she had to find a different route to the quay. Or finding the hot chocolate machine was out of commission and would something else do instead. Even spilling spots of something on to her skirt or trousers, that meant having to change.

'When I got back from swimming one morning, I was told there'd been a call for me. Whoever it was – a man – hadn't left a message but he'd said he would call back. I also heard that the woman – Ms Jones – she'd left very suddenly, with three days of her holiday still to go. She'd asked the owner if I might have her room, on the sea side, for those three days at least. It turned out it was the room *we*'d been in, Al and I, although I'd calculated it was the one next door to it. But I looked into the next one when a girl was cleaning it and I saw it hadn't a fireplace, so I knew definitely that I'd been wrong. When I moved in I found a vase of yellow roses, my favourite, and I thought it must've been *her* doing, the other Ms Jones, until the owner told me my telephone caller had had them delivered.

'That was Al, of course. I felt blasted right off-course. I also found a half-used bottle of perfume in one of the drawers: 'Diorissimo', which was the first present Al ever bought me, and because it brought everything rushing back I couldn't wear it now. But this time I put it on and I also skipped dinner and there was the most incredible sunset that evening and the radio was playing some tune we used to dance to and every cliché seemed to be converging on that room. And of course he phoned again, which was why I was afraid to leave the room in case I missed him, and I felt that seeing the sad and lonely life the other Ms Jones had, it was confirming the answer I knew I was going to give him.'

The young woman crossed her arms; she sighed.

'I'm sorry,' she said. 'I'm sighing because I'm happy. Because I know now.'

'But what about – ?'

'About *her*.'

' – the other Ms Jones?'

'Yes.'

'Ah.'

'What do *you* think – ?' the woman asked.

'I can't – '

' – that it was *me*? She and me . . .?'

She was smiling. Penelope didn't know how to respond.

'It might have been,' Lea said. 'Me. In another twenty years. I think it's quite possible. Al always told me, I should keep an open mind – about spectres, the whole supernatural thing. He says, not everything in this life has an explanation you can put a neat rule-line under. I guess he's right too.'

Penelope stared at her.

'This story – '

'Oh, it happened. It happened like I'm telling it to you now, Penny. But I'm going back to Al, and that's all that matters to me. We'll come back to Aussie eventually. I don't care some people will think it's putting the cause of my sex back – '

'*I* don't think that – '

Lea touched her arm. '*I* know that, Penny. But this is my ending, this is the one for me. I think I want to be loved just once in my life. Deep enough too, so I don't judge the consequences first.'

Penelope nodded.

'Another crazy thing, you know,' the woman said as they stood up, answering the tannoy call to assemble, 'when I was clearing out the drawers in the sea-view bedroom – maybe it was the same drawer the perfume was in, Ms Jones's perfume it must have been – something made me look at the newpaper lining and I read that the financier, the one I'd been working for, his wife had disappeared. She was much younger than him, quite glamorous, and there'd always been stories that the marriage was a bit shaky. Really it was for convenience. I imagined, maybe she too's seen the folly of her ways – you know? – she's gone off to find somebody she can really love: somebody true and deserving who'll cherish her, make her feel loved. Do you think – ?'

Penelope smiled, vaguely, as they walked towards the exit doors.

'I'm not sure,' she said. 'Yes, perhaps.'

'Anyhow, I thought it must be an omen. A good sign.'

'Yes. Yes, I think that's the best way to take it.'

'A – what's it called? – an augury.'

Their tickets were taken from them.

Lea said, 'I know I'm at the front of the plane.'

Penelope looked at the boarding-card in her hand. 'I'm row eleven.'

'Al has to see me coming off first. I gave the check-in girl twenty dollars, I even explained it to her. She looked a bit lost, I thought. You know?'

' "Lost"?'

'Stuck up here behind her desk, in nowhere virtually. Like she's running from something.'

'I read in a book,' Penelope said, 'we're attracted to certain landscapes because they answer to something – certain qualities – in ourselves.'

'And now we're heading out – '

'Yes.'

'Or back to where we were.'

Penelope nodded. She looked over her shoulder, across the tarmac, to Australia dissolving in its gassy heat.

'You're not sorry?' Lea asked her.

'I think I've worked that out for myself,' Penelope said. 'Now I'm not taking the journey – the journey's taking *me*.'

Penelope settles into her seat on the 'Bluebird'.
 The plane takes off, into a clear azurine sky.
 She thinks she hears someone mention that the weather is going to change, but she lays her head back and slowly lets go, drifts into sleep.

It was strange to her that from up here she could see so much.

She was looking down into the mouths of capricious volcanos, tepidly steaming where the dried lava crust covering their lakes had cracked. She could tell trees apart by their colour, distinguish between them and the other vegetation, and even identify some of the species. Villages lay beneath her, huts, tracks, also rivers, streams, a lake, and a spouting geyser. They hovered above beaches of luminescent white sand. She could see the fish swimming in the sea, and the fronds of weed and flanks of pink coral, and the haunted pirate wrecks lying on the sandy ocean floor. More land passed beneath them, rocks, trees. The foliage became thicker and denser. She saw the plane's shadow but she failed to observe that the sky above them was lowering, to the colour of iron. Their shadow was lost in the rampant greenness of trees. More rocks stuck up out of the growth, like fangs. She thought she spotted smoke, but it wasn't; instead she recognised low, stray cloud matter. Water trickled down the outer porthole window. The wisps of cloud became snags, then longer trails, then heavy wads. Before long the ground beneath wasn't visible to her. She thought it was possible that they were losing height, the engine-humming in her ears was louder. She gulped, to unblock the passages. The plane pitched a little, her stomach jumped, they must have hit the cloud. The air about her in the cabin felt colder. They encountered more cloud, and maybe wind was stirred into it; the fuselage rocked, the wing closer to her might have been splitting in its socket. The light through the window darkened to sombre, leaden London grey, how the streets had looked the first time she'd seen them as a child, watching from the taxi-cab that had collected them from the Southampton train at the station. At least on their other island home, on Borneo, there had always been the possibility of spectacular blue forked lightning, of a sort the Englanders had never set eyes on before. In London the greyness seemed to have seeped into the stone of the buildings, into the pavements, into the people's clothes and faces, into their spirits. Now she closed her eyes to hold the sensation of the memory, to remember the little girl and how it had been.

This, I suppose, must be Penelope's death.

A native is climbing a steep track, up a wooded cliffside. He stumbles over something, a length of partly charred blue metal. He looks up, ahead, and sees another larger piece, also smoke-blackened, held in the branches of a tree.

He walks on. In another tree he spots an upholstered chair, turned upside down. In the vicinity of that tree he comes across what he knows to be a suitcase, the form of it anyway but with nothing inside. A smaller suitcase – which he has no experience to recognise is a hatbox – is caught fast between two rocks. A few yards further on he sees the arm of his first body of that day, projecting from under a bush: the skin has also been seared by sudden flame and smoke, it has shrunk like pig's crackling on the bone.

This is the valley which the spirits keep for themselves, where lightning turns night as bright as day. He shouldn't be here at all, it's forbidden to him, as the merest of mortals.

He sees a second body, then a third. He starts to tremble inside the skin of his own body. He has heard of these things from his earliest days, from the time when he was first able to remember. He knows that he does wrong in venturing so far, that the spirits have their own place and that no village man or woman ought to dare question the legends. If anyone does and is discovered, if their nerve fails, the spirits will visit the terrible, primal fury on them, unaccountably savage and which has no reason and no mercy to it: which is absolute.

Part Fourteen

Appendix A
Bibliography

Finnegan Begin Again 1948
The Enchanted Castle 1953
Solférino 1956
A Geneva Watch 1957
Careless Talk 1958
The Blue Hour 1959
Her Mother's Daughter 1961
Making Do and Mending 1962
The Tennis Club Rules 1963
The Year the Avocado Came to London 1965
The Continuity Girl 1966
The Sea Garden 1967
The Koffee Bar Kind (Short Stories) 1968
Luna Caprese 1969
Sugar Shack 1971
The Staircase Mystery 1974
A Flame Coat 1976
Calypso 1977
Soft Clocks 1978
Greenwich Meantime . . . (Incomplete) 1979
Penelope's Hat 1989

Appendix B

This is Penelope Milne's twenty-first book to be published. It is the one she waited longest to write.

Her characters are almost spectral, liquid, sometimes they hardly hold their shape from one page to the next. It occurs to me that her men are like variations on one grand, rhapsodic theme. The sense of 'place' is uncharacteristically tentative. We gain little knowledge of what Penelope looks like – in physical terms – but she takes us on the most intimate journey, from one of her very first memories to her last living moments and beyond.

The dust-jacket's blurb is daunting. Loss, confusion, love, coincidence, enigma, guilt, hope, death, misapprehension, innocence, faith, despair, happiness – and always imagination, for good or bad.

A long list, and a tall order. But it is the book she most wanted to write, and she took all her life to do so.

She is the eye and she is also what she sees, witness and the one witnessed, subject and object, she is inside and outside herself. She is her book's own metacentre.

And by her own reckoning the story she has to tell is not unconcerned with material coverings for the head.

We did meet for that final lunch.

She told me beforehand she was going to see a doctor first: not a psychiatrist, she explained, but a consultant who had already conducted an examination, of her body not her mind. On the telephone from Kensington she allowed me to believe my worst fears. She mentioned, almost as an aside, her pancreas.

I sat waiting for her in the restaurant. I was nervous, of course, and I thought back on other lunches we'd had together over the years. I remembered the first, just after Leopold Kaplan changed her publishers. I had recently moved to the same house he selected for her; one of the directors, whose career had begun elsewhere, had told me about *his* first meeting with Penelope Milne in 1947 – how she had clung to an outsized handbag except when she was eating and pulled at the netting in her hair, how she had dropped her fork into her lap and then missed the rim of her water glass with her bottom lip and spilt some on to the cover. When he asked her if Helen Finnegan's mother in the novel was in any ways like her own, she stared at him and went quite still in her chair: but he laughed, to relax her, and told her it was a marvellous likeness of *his* late mother and was she by any chance clairvoyant?

The woman who walked into the hotel restaurant on our first meeting had learned a lot in the intervening years. She wore a fondant-green straw hat and a well-cut silk dress in a marginally lighter shade of pastel green; she carried her white gloves nonchalantly in both hands and walked with great poise behind the maître d' to the table. She was too polite, and I suppose too well-adjusted, to want to run verbal circles around me, although I was so naïve I probably deserved it. The very opposite was the case, she was extremely attentive and helpful, and I was very soon put at my ease. She told me she was finishing *A Geneva Watch*, about the mysteries of a marriage, and that the book to follow that one would be about a young woman and an older man who meet, and which might be called *The Blue Hour* (she might make him something to do with films, or possibly television: or keep that possibility for later). I had picked up that she and Leopold Kaplan were close, and she had the confidence to neither explain and excuse herself nor to keep her affection for the man from revealing itself in the conversation. I was very impressed by her.

Between then and our last lunch much water had eddied under the proverbial bridge. The good times had come, 'the best of times', and then at their apex things started to come unstuck. Inexplicably (to me) the good turned to bad, how people are turned out of their contentment in folk-tales, and she treated the business with matter-of-fact honesty, as if the down-turn was only inevitable, as the pull of gravity is. But the problems were wholly self-induced, so far as I could judge later. She had a very receptive, appreciative audience in this country and in seven or eight others, and most of the critics were with her, but she lost her nerve. I didn't perceive the causes at the time, but – on the evidence offered in *Penelope's Hat* – now I think I do.

The names have been changed, as she said she would do, except for her own. I suppose she meant it as her grand act of retribution for all those tedious, stolidly uncomprehending questions from interviewers down the years. It was her bid for poetic justice, also for a final and lasting confusion – her own particular version of nemesis.

I wish I could be sure that she hasn't played into their hands, however. The prosecution might claim the point as their own, and the case as won. But why should she have left herself so open? The defence could return: why should she have chosen to affirm what she had always denied, that what happens and what gets written are equivalent values?

The components are in variable measure; there is no one consistent formula. Only *she* knew and she took that same elusive knowledge with her – beyond Sydney, New South Wales, into death.

For a while, in 1975, she was in a small private nursing-home at Gerrards Cross, and I went down to Buckinghamshire at the weekends to see her.

We drove about in the car; we took walks and had long conversations. She let

429

me know she was suffering from what she said was her guilt. I tried to persuade her otherwise, but I didn't have much success. She showed me a short story she was writing, called 'Voodoo Klub', set in a fictional Soho watering-hole. It was about a washed-up woman who once wrote books and stories and now spends her time there; she hasn't been a directly autobiographical writer but she has undeniably 'borrowed', and she sees that leasing from life to have been – truly – robbing certain persons of certain parts of their existence, even a kind of wishing extinction upon them. I believe that at that time Penelope understood it to be *literally* true of herself: by committing a version of 'life' to paper within the subject's own lifetime, she was somehow putting a voodoo curse on them.

We would drive around inside a neat six-mile radius of Gerrards Cross, while she talked about the sticking of pins into wax dolls. I persisted in keeping cheerful notwithstanding, and told myself that Penelope was only getting the matter off her chest. After a while she talked less about 'guilt': but instead she talked more about the past getting its own back, exacting a terrible retribution on her. I couldn't catch on to what she was meaning, and she wasn't usually very coherent about it.

With these pages in front of me however I now begin to see. I still don't know whether or not her fears were valid, but they were certainly *real*, on those Saturday and Sunday afternoons in Buckinghamshire. She thought that by recomposing her life as (sometimes preferential, more often *selective*) stories she had set herself up as an artificer, and – even writing in her very understated English way – she had stolen some of the gods' own fire. She wasn't a conventionally 'religious' person but she retained a fear: she described to me how Ayah Chan used to tell her about the spirits who lived in volcanoes, in springs, in the garden shrubbery, and perhaps she had a fear of that same hollowness the young girl she calls by her own name discovered when the canon was brusquely shown the door of the Belsize house so soon after her father's funeral. She had looked for believable patterns and symmetries in her life, purposes, but the mandala effect of creating so much was only this – that it could all be undone again: *what had lifted her up could drag her back down*, and in the violent process her imagination's strength was turned to weakness. That was the bitter unhappiness of this period in her life, and tragically it never left her after that. Writing came to seem to have been a Faustian deal: something won – an ability to 'cope' with what happened to her, by refashioning it into the formality and stylistic discipline and semantic evasiveness of Prose – but which would have to be paid for later. Now the 'later' had caught up with her.

But not every visit to Gerrards Cross was such heavy going. It would be too easy to give a misleading impression of those regular weekend afternoons. We sometimes sat in tea-shops and she was content to study whoever came in and out. She could make mocking fun of herself, and she laughed us along several village high streets, past bemused locals and trippers like ourselves.

430

A number of times *I* also felt weighted with guilt, driving her back to the nursing home (quite a euphemism, as she realised) and delivering her back into the care of the expensive professionals.

She took their advice as to when she ought to be discharged and offered no contest. At last I collected her and her belongings in the car and we drove back to London, to Monmouth Square. I was rather anxious in my own mind that she wouldn't now associate me too much with those visits, or that mutual embarrassment should drive a wedge between us. But we continued to stay close, thankfully, and the subject of Gerrards Cross was discreetly dropped from our conversation in that later time.

Back home in Kensington she soon got down to work again. In only four and a half years she wrote a couple of novels and novella. Their tone is fairly dispassionate, as if she didn't want to approach too near to the heart of her matter – the very different twin sisters in *A Flame Coat* (the childhood object of envy of one of them), the woman who photographs her lovers and gives them dubious, sanity-destroying eternity in *Calypso*, a daughter discovering a long-dead father alive and well with a second wife and second daughter in *Soft Clocks*. She embarked on a fourth book, to have been called *Greenwich Meantime* . . ., about a pair of lovers who make a pact to keep their love perpetual: they select a particular place of rendezvous and after their deaths, some years apart, they direct their souls (no longer holding with ordinary living-time) to the special prearranged spot.

The last book may have been one too many for her to take on. I was naturally concerned that she shouldn't tire herself out. But I also felt that it did her no good to sit idle, to merely 'tick over'. Certainly I should have insisted on more frequent holidays. I should have held back longer on the contracts (it bothered her to be paid in advance and so to have her inspiration depended on – a common enough superstition), I should have advised more time between the publication of one book and the next, I should have done this or that – but it's very easy to be so practically sensible with the blessed boon of hindsight.

Once, on someone's instigation, a Catholic priest had called at the house in Monmouth Square. He had found her very courteous, and generous with her hospitality, but ultimately he had failed to take them anywhere in their conversation. She had politely reminded him that others must have more pressing demands to make on his time and she wouldn't want to think she had denied any of them the solace and comfort he might . . .

In 1986 Penelope Gerrault – as she called herself – died of a heart attack, in her sleep, in Kirribilli, Sydney.

My precise reactions to the news are not important: anyway, my feelings were of too many sorts to catalogue, from deep sorrow to frustration and even anger, with everything between.

431

She had left instructions as to what was to be done after the event. I was named as her literary executrix.

I flew out to Australia as soon as I could. On the plane I whiled away the hours when I wasn't asleep threading one memory to another to another. I wondered how she could have let me go through the traumas of first, believing she was terminally ill when she wasn't, and then my shock at the supposedly accidental disappearance on the Corniche, followed by the all-time-low depression after the memorial service. Or, on second thoughts, would it have occurred to her in the state of mind she must have been in at the time to consider my feelings when she ran the car so ambiguously off the road, just as she records here?

The taxi dropped me at a clapboard-fronted bungalow. The lawn had been mown recently, the flowerbeds were in neat order. The house was smaller than its neighbours but it was a more substantial version of lesser imitations to be found all over the suburbs of Australia. A stoep ran along the front and one side, and there was an upholstered swing-couch that hung on chains.

Inside the house the rooms were spacious, bright, air-conditioned. The furnishings were tasteful, simple and functional, and new-looking. There was no evidence of a life remembered: no photographs or souvenirs, no inherited gew-gaws. The laying surfaces were mainly left clear, and those that weren't were uncluttered. There seemed to be no places, no questionable corners, where shadows could gather. Daylight circulated easily through and between the rooms.

On a shelf I noticed a copy of every book in its published British hardback form, twenty of them in all. Each one had been read, some – the spines cracked when I opened them – had been reread a number of times maybe. The manuscript of *Penelope's Hat* lay on top of a desk, most of it typed in what was probably a second draft, with elastic bands round the pile of A4 sheets. Some sections were still in note form, as reproduced. The pages were unnumbered but arranged in the order in which they are presented here, epigrams included.

I choose to believe that she foresaw the scene, that one hot and humid afternoon I would sit down over-dressed on the Scandinavian swivel-chair and start reading. And keep on reading. I have no doubts that she knew this would be the final end of *Penelope's Hat*: you, her eventual arbiter, would sit or lie holding it in front of you, the final object, in your hands. She realised that I would do more or less as I have done, and that I should write my concluding words and receive them back in a printer's galley proofs for checking over.

In the still sitting-room of the house I imagined several times that she was looking over my shoulder, and several times I looked round – equably, let me say, and not fearfully, not at all: I wanted nothing better than to see her standing there, alive, alive and well. But the presence was a sleight of my mind. I was surrounded by quiet and composure, too much of it, except that now and then a temperamental lawn-mower in the vicinity would cut whining into the tranquillity, only emphasising those chastening silences on either side, the solidity of emptiness that filled the house.

Betrayal seems to haunt her. It's innocent when the child doesn't tell her mother that Mr Chapman has phoned. It's accidental as she peaches wordlessly on Romilly. When Valerie rounds on her she can't believe that what she has done in the books isn't deliberate – that she has continued to strand people in time: the two Huttons and their parents, her own mother, Margot, Topaz. She has made public, however cryptically, what should have been allowed to be consumed by time. Even if she hasn't disguised her own weaknesses, she has refused other people to outgrow theirs. She convinces herself that she loved her husband but it's clear to anyone who reads her account that she's telling us her heart has won out over her head. She feels she has to dissect the mute silence of the intimacy which is the very kernel of her relationship with Leopold Kaplan. With Gregor she declares a secret – theoretically – to the world, and can't stop herself. She's often asked 'why she writes', but she can never reply. The too frank answer would be, it's self-exposure and it's the exposure of others: she can't help it, and she knows to be ashamed. Her experience and her nature have both made her so, and maybe she would have been happier if Mr Chapman had taken them to South Africa or if Henry Kyte had pounced and the thing – the need to render fictionally – could have been curbed, put an end to, and the poison drawn before it infected her. Or at least she could have given herself to Oliver and just perhaps rescued one person from a fate comparable to her own. But after her life with Guy, what choice did she have but to write, write, write.

I am uncertain how much of the whole to accept.

At least she *is* Penelope Milne in the book. She could have used a fictional allonym for herself, but she chose not to. The books she writes about herself writing all bear their actual titles, and the Prudence Shaws and Camilla Holts are as they are, as they first arrived on my desk. She didn't have to invent the interviews and reviews and radio conversations.

I knew that she had been married (and widowed), and I was aware of her relationship with the man she calls Leopold Kaplan. I cannot be sure about Philip and the postcards; the person I suspect Gregor to have been wasn't involved in publishing as an *editor*, but the events correspond to a chronology that resulted finally in her turning inward, much less open. Polwynn isn't Polwynn, of course, but it isn't hard to locate. I visited the house that is Veryan and can vouchsafe the descriptions. Monmouth Square sits between Kensington High Street and Cromwell Road. There may have been a fire in Nice, or Cannes or Antibes, or maybe not. She may have seen Topaz in Harrods in 1974 but the possibility is the thing, and the terror that this is one of her subjects fighting back. The car may have been meant to roll over the clifftop and crash on to the rocks, or maybe she subconsciously intended to save her skin: either way the hopelessness and fear and guilt that had taken hold of her were as real and confirmable as anything else in her life could have been.

In the bungalow there was a drawerful of newspaper clippings, photocopies, pages with – sometimes – single typed quotations.

Here are two of my findings.

The first comprises three associated reflections of Simone Weil, retyped from a book or article.

All the natural movements of the soul are controlled by laws analogous to those of physical gravity. Grace is the only exception.

Grace fills empty spaces, but it can only enter where there is a void to receive it, and it is grace itself which makes this void.

The imagination is continually at work filling up all the fissures through which grace might pass.

The second is a xerox of a newspaper report which appeared in *The Times* of London on 30 August 1935.

Grief in Belgium
Lucerne, Aug. 29

The Queen of the Belgians was killed and the King injured in a motor accident near Lucerne this morning.

. . . the sun was shining and the roads had dried after last night's rainfall. King Leopold and Queen Astrid decided to motor to a spot where they were to make a climbing excursion, and shortly before 9.30 they left their villa, crossed the town of Lucerne and took – on the right bank of the lake – the road leading to Küssnacht and the Lake of Zug. It is a modern road, very wide, and skirts the lake amid rich orchards. The party was made up of two cars. The first, a two-seater, was driven by the King himself and the Queen was sitting by his side. The chauffeur was in the dickey behind.

The King's car passed the village of Mörlischachen and was running at about 30 miles an hour on a straight stretch. There was no obstacle in view and the road was in a perfect condition. Suddenly, at 10 o'clock, about a mile from Küssnacht, the right wheels of the car mounted the concrete border of the footpath, on which they ran for about 17 yards to a spot where the footpath sank a little to give passage into a field. Here the King apparently lost control of the car, which turned to the right, descended a steep embankment, and about 20 yards further on struck a tree, against which the Queen was thrown with great violence. The car rolled further down for another 12 yards, struck another tree, continued its wild run, passed over a stone wall, and fell into the lake 12 feet below.

The occupants of the second car and some peasants hastened to the spot. The Queen, with her skull fractured, was found still alive, but she died soon after. The King, who was thrown out and dazed when the car struck the second tree, had injuries to his head and one arm and was tended by a doctor at once summoned from Küssnacht. The chauffeur fell with the car into the lake, here only 2 feet deep, but escaped with cuts in the face from glass splinters.

When the King recovered he made enquiries about the Queen and went to her, calling her by name. He then took her in his arms, where she died shortly after the last sacrament had been administered to her by the curé of Küssnacht, who had been called to the spot.

The King left Switzerland tonight by the St Gothard-Basle express, which also took the body of Queen Astrid . . .

The accident has caused general consternation in Switzerland, where the Belgian royal couple were great favourites, and the peasants crowded at the gate of the villa to enquire after the King's condition.

In 1981 they were building a headquarters building for a Japanese bank in the City, sinking the piles. I read in a newspaper that the excavation drills had bored into a storehouse of old Roman gold: also, that several recent skeletons had been found, with remnants of coupon clothing in the wartime-cut clinging to them.

A series of bombs did explode in public places in Switzerland in the early 1980s. One blew apart a concrete riverside walkway in Zürich, another went off in the foyer of an office building on the outskirts of central Geneva, at Le Prieure.

In 1956 Scotland Yard revealed that a dry-cleaner's on Marylebone High Street had been used as a front for illegal armament sales to foreign purchasers: a number of those involved were impeccable English types with distinguished war records and they were referred to by a senior inspector as a modern 'league of gentlemen'.

The dying was accidental.

In a desk drawer was a travel agency wallet containing Singapore Airlines tickets to Bandar Seri via Jakarta. Java had become Jawa and now Borneo was Kalimantan/Sabah/Sarawak/Brunei, but for Penelope it was the starting- and finishing-point after all. The last pages of the book had already been written. She only had to add a little final local 'colour' when she got to her journey's end.

She knew that it had to be a ghostly arrival if she was to let herself come out tops; to show that the betrayals (if they were) were justified, she had to demonstrate that out of the turbulence of living, that farrago, a thin connecting line of sanity can be traced: of *sanctity* even, reposing in the self and memory and imagination. If the woman lived in the child, it would somehow make her existence add up in the last count and deliver her from the perilous vision of chaos without limit.

That is my own theory.

The pages might have been lying on top of the desk in the bungalow's study – as I found them – for weeks, or for months, or even for years. She was waiting for the one thing which this equivocal skill of hers was unable to do for her – namely, to make an ending. If it had been at all possible, I am convinced she would have worked up the inspiration for it from somewhere. But suicide would have been regarded by the world in general as defeat, failure to 'cope'.

Now it was only a matter of time, of waiting, of wise patience. In her imagination she had already reached the other side: she had found a small moment of intense stillness – the woman and the child together – which was able to give purpose even to the prospect of dying.

Appendix C

Dear Mariel,

Penelope's Hat is to be a fable, a parable, about what happens to you when you do too much of what *I* have done.

Read and be warned.

I've forgotten just what is clinically 'true' and what isn't. Does it matter? It's quite 'true' enough, as much as I could make it.

Best love,

PS   I wrote the book. Yes. Agreed.
     But then, didn't the story also write *me*?

PPS Answer the above. Do not take less than 400 pages
     to do so. Cover both sides. Against the clock;
     penalties for late submission.

Appendix D

She started walking towards the house. Under her feet was the pliant firmness of grass, to all intents and purposes looking and feeling like an English lawn.

She made no sound.

It was coolest here, even without direct shade above her head. Where the lawn ran to, behind banks of red-flowering coral-tree and gold mohur, she was aware of true heat massing, as if it was lying in ambush. This time, though, she felt she was ready and prepared for it, not like all the other times. Even so, she pulled down the brim of her sun-hat. She noticed that she carried no shadow with her. She noticed too the absence of daisies in the grass; the green had been bleached out of it, till it looked in places like harvest straw. Proper straw would have rustled, but her feet in their plimsoles were silent as they walked over this dry, packed matter that passed as lawn.

She continued, head down, fumbling with the little raw silk scarf on her head. A shadow intruded into her line of vision, a tropical shadow, bold and razor-sharp and very black. It was only the state of things in such a climate after all, where everything could be absurdly clear-cut, where comparisons were as black-and-white as it was possible to be.

She stepped on to the spiky shadow, like a zigzag hole cut on the turf. But she didn't fall. Above her was the roof of the verandah, and above that the roof of the house itself. The shadow had layers of shadow in it and she found herself walking up a flight of shallow steps. They weren't unfamiliar, their number – seven – came as no surprise to her, although their shallowness seemed to cause her now no effort of movement.

At the top of the steps she stood on planed boards. The temperature here dropped ten or fifteen degrees. Ahead of her was the full run of the verandah.

She hesitated. A series of french windows led into rooms. She recognised the sound, the slow turning of fans, the monotonous mechanical clicking, but she still couldn't hear her own breathing. When she took another few steps forward she listened for the squeaking of her soles, but then forgot, her attention was so taken up by the stuttering of the fans. Ttrrrpp. Ttrrrpp. Ttrrrpp.

Where now, now that she was here?

She turned her head and glanced over her shoulder, the way she had come. From the coolness of the verandah she looked out at the garden broiling in white sunshine. From here the trees were burnished, with shiny metal leaves. The lawn was a trampled stubble-field. Birds chattered regardless, insects rattled.

Although there was no draught, the vegetation heaved, as if it hid a crouching dragon. (Later, back in England, Rollo had taught her how to play snapdragon, seizing the raisins from a silver dish of flaming brandy.)

She was able to recall a mindless Christmas game, and she seriously wondered how she could have forgotten any single part of this, which had been her life.

But the sets of double-doors didn't confuse her as she was afraid they would. Like the gradient of the steps, the sequence of the rooms wasn't any surprise to her, even though she couldn't have told beforehand which followed which. The morning-room, the sitting-room, the dining-room, the guest room . . .

The last would be commandeered whenever there was a party; the two beds would be taken out and chairs brought in, to provide a refuge for those who weren't inclined to the dancing in the sitting-room, where the carpet would have been rolled back and the gramophone would be all but jigging itself as the tunes sizzled through the speaker, behind the gauze screen, which was the bright colour of yellow gold. (How did she know the colour, if it wasn't that she remembered very well for herself?)

She walked past the doors of the guest-room, to the corner. At right angles to the first was a second, shorter length of verandah. She hesitated again and looked over her shoulder, back to the baking lawn, before changing her direction.

A couple of basketwork chairs had been pushed against the wall, as far from the sun as they could be got. It occurred to her, perhaps I ought to rest, but on second thoughts she realised there wasn't enough tiredness in her for that.

She looked down at the two plimsoles, at the hands waving on the ends of her arms. She turned the coral bracelet on her wrist, she'd bought it in the airport shop at Darwin.

The first pair of windows also belonged to the guest-room; she walked past them. She could see that the second pair were open, and she approached carefully: not for fear of making any noise, but because she knew the moment was important, it had been so very long in coming.

She concentrated on the last few steps, she took them stealthily. She might have been playing Grandma's Footsteps, 'What's the time, Mr Wolf?' Slowing, she lost some of her momentum. Suddenly she felt almost leaden, and timorous. She reached out her hand for the doorjamb to steady herself. For several seconds she trained her eyes on the boards, then for several more on the fringe of the rug in the room.

When she lifted them she saw a little girl of five or six years old standing by herself in the middle of the room, preoccupied by her surroundings. She was looking about her with solemn attention; at the bed and the chest-of-drawers and a straight-backed chair with a plump cushion on the seat. None of the furniture was scaled for a child, but it was surely her room: paper and crayons were strewn on a table, a teddy bear and a doll sat propped up legs akimbo on top of the chest beside a pink conch shell, a book lay beneath the bed doing

439

the splits with its covers splayed, a sandal lay against a ball foot of the chest as if it was preparing to scale the height of drawers.

The child's head turned slowly on her neck, even though there had been nothing for her to hear, no give-away. She looked over her left shoulder, to the end of the room where the windows were.

The woman's eyes and the child's held one another's. The child's heart was juddering in her chest, she could hardly breathe; somehow the woman heard and her brow creased. The child didn't look away and the woman's own heart skipped a beat, then another, she had to open her mouth for air; she closed her eyes and when she opened them again the child was still there.

Then the woman, for no reason she could think of, smiled. The little girl watched, but her mouth didn't respond; her eyes had opened wider.

The woman took a step forward. The child didn't understand and moved backwards, two paces for that one; her lips pulled back, and out of her throat rose a long, pained, passionate cry the woman recognised as her own voice.

When she tried to speak herself, to say something that would give comfort, no sound came out. But she could hear the cry of her voice in the room, quite distinctly and no mistaking it.

The louder *it* was, the surer *she* was. But then it faded, and her own confidence waned too; she strained to hear, she could scarcely see.

Now there was the distance of glass in the room, the sigh of the wind, and she heard very close by the french window banging shut.

Suddenly she felt as tenuous as the glass, as cold as Heaven. She was shifting among reflections and resemblances, caught in a pane of the door.

She found for herself first the shape of a long blue shadow from behind, then of a certain eaglewood tree which used to grow in the garden, with feminine hips and a graceful ballerina pose of branches like arms in a dozen stages of imitating flight, and it was the last thing of all she remembered as she turned out of herself into thin air.

440